"The February revolution, in Solzhenitsyn's considered judgment, was a disaster of the first order and not a welcome, democratic eruption in a country ill-prepared for democracy. A reader of *March 1917* (Node III of *The Red Wheel* . . .) would be hard put to quarrel with Solzhenitsyn's judgment. As this great work of history and literature attests, February indeed was the root of all the evils to come and not a brief shining display of Russian democracy."
—*National Review*

"*The Red Wheel* and *The Gulag Archipelago* have been called Solzhenitsyn's two 'cathedrals.' You cannot fully understand the horrors of communism and the history of the 20th century without reading them."
—*New York Journal of Books*

"Aleksandr Solzhenitsyn spent many years in the latter part of his long life working on *The Red Wheel*, a multivolume chronicle of 'the whirlwind of revolution in Russia.' Until now, only two parts of this hugely ambitious work had appeared in English translation, followed by a long hiatus. Now, at last—on the centenary of the Russian Revolution—the first part of another volume has appeared in English, *March 1917*, with translations of the remainder of the work promised. . . . *The Red Wheel*—like Solzhenitsyn's life and work taken whole—is a testament to hope married to determination."
—*The Christian Century*

"The latest Solzhenitsyn book to appear in English, *March 1917*, focuses on the great turning point of Russian, indeed world, history: the Russian Revolution."
—*The New Criterion*

"In *March 1917*, Solzhenitsyn attempts the impossible and succeeds, evoking a fully formed world through episodic narratives that insist on the prosaic integrity of every life, from tsars to peasants. What emerges is a rich history that's truly greater than the sum of its parts."
—*Foreword Reviews* (starred review)

THE RED WHEEL

A Narrative in Discrete Periods of Time

The Center for Ethics and Culture Solzhenitsyn Series

The Center for Ethics and Culture Solzhenitsyn Series showcases the contributions and continuing inspiration of Aleksandr Solzhenitsyn (1918–2008), the Nobel Prize–winning novelist and historian. The series makes available works of Solzhenitsyn, including previously untranslated works, and aims to provide the leading platform for exploring the many facets of his enduring legacy. In his novels, essays, memoirs, and speeches, Solzhenitsyn revealed the devastating core of totalitarianism and warned against political, economic, and cultural dangers to the human spirit. In addition to publishing his work, this new series features thoughtful writers and commentators who draw inspiration from Solzhenitsyn's abiding care for Christianity and the West, and for the best of the Russian tradition. Through contributions in politics, literature, philosophy, and the arts, these writers follow Solzhenitsyn's trail in a world filled with new pitfalls and new possibilities for human freedom and human dignity.

Aleksandr Solzhenitsyn

MARCH 1917

THE RED WHEEL / NODE III
(8 March – 31 March)

BOOK 2

Translated by Marian Schwartz

UNIVERSITY OF NOTRE DAME PRESS

NOTRE DAME, INDIANA

Published by the University of Notre Dame Press
Notre Dame, Indiana 46556
undpress.nd.edu

Translated from book 2 of books 1–4:

"Март Семнадцатого" (1)
© A. I. Solzhenitsyn, 1986, 2008

"Март Семнадцатого" (2)
© A. I. Solzhenitsyn, 1986, 2008

"Март Семнадцатого" (3)
© A. I. Solzhenitsyn, 1987, 2008

"Март Семнадцатого" (4)
© A. I. Solzhenitsyn, 1988, 2008

Published in the United States of America

Paperback edition published in 2022

Library of Congress Cataloging-in-Publication Data

Names: Solzhenitsyn, Aleksandr Isaevich, 1918–2008, author. |
Schwartz, Marian, 1951– translator.
Title: March 1917 : The Red Wheel, node III (8 March/31 March), book 2 /
Aleksandr Solzhenitsyn ; translated by Marian Schwartz.
Other titles: Krasnoe koleso. Mart semnadtsatogo. Kniga 1. English |
Red Wheel, node III (8 March/31 March), book 2
Description: Notre Dame, Indiana : University of Notre Dame Press, 2019. |
Includes index.
Identifiers: LCCN 2019030194 | ISBN 9780268106850 (hardcover : alk. paper) |
ISBN 9780268106867 (paperback : alk. paper)
Subjects: LCSH: Russia—History—February Revolution, 1917—Fiction.
Classification: LCC PG3488.O4 K67613 2017 | DDC 891.73/44—dc23
LC record available at https://lccn.loc.gov/2019030194

Publisher's Note

March 1917 (consisting of books 1–4) is the centerpiece of *The Red Wheel*, Aleksandr Solzhenitsyn's multivolume historical novel on the roots and outbreak of the Russian Revolution, which he divided into four "nodes." *March 1917* is the third node.

The first node, *August 1914*, ends in the disastrous defeat of the Russians by the Germans at the Battle of Tannenberg in World War I. The second node, *November 1916*, offers a panorama of Russia on the eve of revolution. *August 1914* and *November 1916* focus on Russia's crises, revolutionary terrorism and its suppression, the missed opportunity of Pyotr Stolypin's reforms, and the souring of patriotism as Russia suffered in the world war.

March 1917 tells the story of the beginning of the revolution in Petrograd, as riots go unchecked, units of the army mutiny, and both the state and the numerous opposition leaders are incapable of controlling events. The present volume, book 2 of *March 1917*, is set during March 13–15. It will be followed by English translations of the next two books of *March 1917*, describing events through March 31, and the two books of *April 1917*.

The nodes of *The Red Wheel* can be read consecutively or independently. All blend fictional characters with numerous historical personages, usually introduced under their own names and with accurate biographical data. The depiction of historical characters and events is based on the author's extensive research in archives, administrative records, newspapers, memoirs, émigré collections, unpublished correspondence, family records, and other contemporary sources. In many sections the historical novel turns into dramatic history. Plots and subplots abound.

The English translations by H. T. Willetts of *August 1914* and *November 1916*, published by Farrar, Straus and Giroux in 1989 and 1999, respectively, appeared as Knot I and Knot II. The present translation, in accordance with the wishes of the Solzhenitsyn estate, has chosen the term "Node" as more faithful to the author's intent. Both terms refer, as in mathematics, to discrete points on a continuous line.

In a 1983 interview with Bernard Pivot, Aleksandr Solzhenitsyn described his narrative concept as follows: "*The Red Wheel* is the narrative of revolution in Russia, its movement through the whirlwind of revolution. This is an immense scope of material, and . . . it would be impossible to describe this many events and this many characters over such a lengthy stretch of time. That is why I have chosen the method of nodal points, or Nodes. I select short segments of time, of two or three weeks' duration, where the most vivid events unfold, or else where the decisive causes of future events are formed. And I describe in detail only these short segments. These are the Nodes. Through these nodal points I convey the general vector, the overall shape of this complex curve."

Dates in the original Russian text were given in the Old Style, according to the Julian calendar used in Russia until 1918. In the English translations these dates have been changed, in accordance with the author's wishes, to the New Style (Gregorian) calendar, putting them thirteen days ahead of the old dates. The March 1917 revolution thus corresponds to the February Revolution in Russian history (Old Style), just as the revolution that placed the Bolsheviks in power in November of that year is commonly referred to as the October Revolution.

In the "screen" sequences in this book, the different margins represent different instructions for the shooting of a film: sound effects or camera direction, action, and dialogue (in italics). The symbol "=" indicates "cut to." Chapters numbered with a double-prime (") show newspaper headlines of the day.

*   *   *

The English translation was made possible through a generous anonymous donation to the Solzhenitsyn Initiative at the Wilson Center's Kennan Institute, which is gratefully acknowledged.

The maps and the Index of Names have been adapted and revised from the versions in the French translation, *La Roue rouge*, Troisième nœud, *Mars dix-sept*, tomes 1–2, with the kind permission of Fayard and approval of the Solzhenitsyn estate.

Contents

CONTENTS / ix

CONTENTS / xi

CONTENTS / xiii

CONTENTS / xv

CONTENTS / xvii

CONTENTS / xix

[1 7 1]

Shlyapnikov had made decent headway on the Executive Committee. He had been entrusted with the entire Vyborg side and with knocking together a workers' militia. As far as his sleepless, by now dulled head could tell, this was a real and important victory. An armed Vyborg side would weigh more than any vote in the Soviet of Deputies, and certainly more than the entire State Duma. It was, as Lenin liked to say, the *main link*. And now it seemed to Shlyapnikov that he had laid hold of this main link.

But what if it wasn't? What if it wasn't the main one? If matters continued the way they had today, the emigres would come flooding in immediately. Lenin would, too, and in his own meticulous manner he would rebuke Shlyapnikov for every mistake in his quarrelsome, offensive way. Shlyapnikov shrank at the thought of that haranguing.

Nonetheless, events and opportunities had opened up so expansively and so suddenly, just try to guess which one you should saddle.

The muddle-headed EC session had ended just before morning, and as strong as Shlyapnikov was, he was tottering.

He had to set up his own permanent watch here, in the Tauride, so that he would learn each piece of news right away. But there wasn't even anyone to do this; you couldn't find anyone appropriate. Except maybe Stasova. (She had arrived in Petersburg from exile in the autumn, to see her aged parents, and had found a footing here.) At least for the daytime hours: let her treat it as a job and keep an eye out here. And we could call it—the CC Secretariat? She could bring in some other girl, too.

All right, go get some sleep. Shlyapnikov had no need to hoof it; he could take a motorcar.

Right then, though, a student ran over from the telephone. They'd just called to say there'd been a gang attack on Gorky's apartment!

Wouldn't you know it! That was quite a sting! Indeed, things could not be all that good. This was bound to happen: a notable revolutionary figure! Aleksei Maksimych—no harm could be allowed to come to him, he is like our best party member, more ours than the Mensheviks'. He's given us money, too, and in 1905, in his Moscow apartment, during the uprising, he supported thirteen Georgian militiamen, and we made bombs there.

It was the Bolshevik law: you have to rescue your own!

1

He buttoned his coat, pulled his cap down low (neither of which he'd taken off all those hours of the session in the warm palace, there being nowhere to put them)—and stepped outside.

In the open area in front of the palace, men were warming themselves around three bonfires. There were soldiers here and there.

"I am the commissar of the Vyborg side!" Shlyapnikov shouted not all that loudly, having lost his voice, but in a tone that was new for him, a new right to give loud orders. "Is there a motorcar?"

His tone was picked up on and understood immediately (no Duma deputy would dare shout like that), and several soldier volunteers came running; this was better than freezing.

"There are! Where are you going?"

And they led him to one.

"Whose motorcar is this?" Shlyapnikov asked for no particular reason, out of interest.

"Minister of War Belyaev's! We took it from the courtyard."

Now they'd shaken the driver in his sheepskin jacket behind the wheel.

"I am a member of the Executive Committee of the Soviet of Workers' Deputies! Start the engine!" He stepped back and called out: "Hey, men! Who's coming with me to the Petersburg side? I have an assignment!"

A dozen volunteers immediately ran up from the bonfire. He let three with rifles onto the back seat and himself sat up front, slammed the door, and a couple of men immediately lay down on the running boards, their rifles facing forward across the fenders.

They were off!

The streets were nearly deserted, but alive. Occasionally shots were fired somewhere. Or men would stroll by with rifles, in a throng. Trucks would race toward them or pass them and honk, and there would be several men with bayonets poking out in the back. Frightened ordinary citizens made their way on foot.

He urged the driver to drive faster. What was happening to Gorky? Would we be in time to take Maksimych back?

Yesterday, could Shlyapnikov have imagined, as he was hiding out with the Pavlovs, that the next night he would be riding in the motorcar of the Minister of War?

Near the District Court fire—which was still giving off powerful heat and steam from the street snow—men stopped them for questioning and shouted hurrah—and then they jerked nonstop down the French Embankment and onto the deserted Trinity Bridge.

If not for the glow behind them, and the darkness up ahead—no, there was one small fire hard on the left, that must be the Okhrana—and if not for the wild truck with the bayonets oncoming on the bridge, it would be a night like any other: snowy in the Neva's blackness, the dark Peter and Paul

Fortress, the sparse chains of streetlamps here and there—an ordinary Petersburg night. Except for that glow.

Shlyapnikov looked over his left shoulder. The entire swath of palaces was totally dark—including the Winter Palace.

Whereas the sky was clear, starry, frosty.

They made a major detour around the Peter and Paul Fortress, killing their lights so as not to draw gunfire, and drove onto dark Kronverksky.

Here was Gorky's building; Shlyapnikov would recognize it in the dark.

No sign of havoc from the outside. All the windows were dark. The front door was locked.

But he couldn't leave it like this. He knocked loudly.

The doorman didn't come out immediately. Then he didn't want to open up. Seeing the bayonets, though, he did.

"What's going on here? What kind of gang was it? Was there a raid?"

"No, none."

Shlyapnikov didn't believe it. He dashed up the stairs.

And in front of Gorky's door—an untrampled floor, cleanliness, silence, no havoc whatsoever.

Had some jokesters played a trick on him?

But he couldn't leave now, like this! He rang the doorbell anyway.

And rang it again. Fright and commotion inside: "Who is it?"

"It's Shlyapnikov. Forgive me, I need Aleksei Maksimych."

If only to verify his safety. If only to assure him, should anything happen, he can. . . .

Finally, they opened the door. Behind several women stood Aleksei Maksimovich in a terry robe, stooped, displeased, wrinkling his broad-spread, duckish nose, his yellow mustache hanging to his chin, and his voice resentful.

"What on earth is this, Aleksan Gavrilych? Why? Why are you here?"

He didn't invite him in and sent him away without even asking the news.

[1 7 2]

Nikolai couldn't live without Alix the way a man can't live with his chest eaten out or half his head lopped off. He had great military passions, and in the atmosphere of GHQ he seemingly should have flourished in this masculine military life—but no! The very first day he felt distracted, a lack, a longing—and empty and sad was the rare day when a letter from her did not arrive. (Although the following day there were always two.) Whenever one did come, Nikolai would unseal it with a quickened beating of his heart and plunge into it and inhale the fragrance of the perfumed pages (sometimes there were even flowers enclosed)—and how he was drawn to his wife immediately, straight away! As she always repeated, so he, too, was convinced that separation made their love even stronger. He himself failed to write her letters only on days when he had too many papers or audiences, but even over those papers and during those audiences she was constantly on his mind, and even more so during hours of leisure or on outings. Only when he reviewed his lined-up regiments did he forget her for a few brief minutes. Even the heir's presence with his father at GHQ only slightly dissipated and ameliorated this ever-present lack of his clever wife in his existence. Due to the heir's ill health, though, he often couldn't travel with his father, and then a dreary loneliness surrounded Nikolai like a wall, and even one week at GHQ seemed like a year, and three an eternity. Indeed, he almost never lasted three weeks there, or else the Empress herself would come to Mogilev.

How much more torturous were these four days spent this time at GHQ, due to the children's illness and the alarming reports from Petrograd. The Emperor was utterly spent by his nerves and his persistence in refusing concessions to the mounting chorus. He was utterly spent and needed to be reunited quickly with his wife, with whom he had been joined for the past twenty-two years, like two trees branching off a single trunk.

After his late tea, when Voeikov and Frederiks presented him the alarms from Tsarskoye Selo and Nikolai had decided to go there, he had felt immediate relief. When he entered his train car at close to two o'clock in the morning, his relief was even greater (although the train would not be ready until five or six in the morning).

He still had time. He calmed down. But he still wasn't sleepy. What the Emperor did feel obligated to do was to speak with Nikolai Iudovich about the details of his expedition and his intentions. Their cars weren't far apart, so he summoned the general.

The conversation left him quite satisfied, and his soul was even more relieved. What a thorough grounding in the people, what wisdom this old man had, and what devotion to his Emperor! This man could be relied upon, a courageous combat general. (He now regretted that in 1915 he had not agreed with his wife and appointed him Minister of War, considering him too obstinate; if he had, perhaps they would have seen none of the present disturbances.)

His entire mood was anything but troubled now that he himself was on his way there.

Right then Nikolai finally received the evening telegram from Khabalov, who was somehow very much panicked and said he could not restore order in the capital, and most of the units had betrayed their duty, fraternizing with the rebels and even turning their weapons against loyal troops. And now a large part of the capital was in the rebels' hands.

Could such a thing really be? This was unthinkable rubbish.

Nikolai Iudovich thought the same and was not the least bit discouraged.

"I'll drive them all out, clear them out! Your Imperial Majesty, you can have confidence in me as you would in yourself. I will do everything possible and impossible!"

His loyal, shovel-shaped, humble beard seemed to confirm this.

Out of delicacy, the Emperor hesitated to ask the general the precise hour of his departure from Mogilev with the St. George battalion, but obviously it would not be during the night (which would have been good!) but early in the morning.

However, if Ivanov didn't begin his detachment's movement until morning and one of his first objectives was to defend Tsarskoye Selo, then wouldn't the royal trains' urgent departure lose its meaning? No, because lately they had been taking another, more roundabout but also more convenient route, via the Nikolaevsky railroad. While they were making this detour, Ivanov would already be in Tsarskoye. Alix had already been promised that he would depart tonight. He would feel awkward in front of his suite making any change: the order had been given and they had boarded.

As they parted, he made the sign of the cross over the old general. And they exchanged three kisses.

More than anything, the train's movement in itself was a relief. Nikolai now needed to be filled with peace and emotional repose. And to get away from the constant telegrams and dispatches that had simply been pouring into GHQ. Less news meant fewer decisions. To spend nearly twenty-four hours without these upheavals was so much easier! And then to reach Tsarskoye and be convinced that your loved ones are whole and not taken — and feeling firm, to resolve everything as one with Alix. Nikolai didn't know exactly what he would resolve and do, but there he would at least get his bearings after a few hours.

After five in the morning, in the train's initial movement, his car's even rocking yielded a marvelous combination: the illusion of simultaneous movement and peace.

[1 7 3]

He no longer had any hope whatsoever of sleep. This wasted trip to Gorky's had killed the last hour for sleep.

Anyway, he was now the commissar of the Vyborg side, which meant he had to be everywhere at once, and get both there and back to the Tauride in time for all the sessions. They raced to the Vyborg. The cold seat chilled him through his coat. Again two soldiers lay on the running boards, and they raced through the nearly deserted, awakening, liberated city. Liberated! That was remarkable! If anyone was not to be seen, it was a city policeman. All the soldiers had become a force on their side, not the enemy's!

On the Vyborg, on the contrary, armed posts of workers appeared at the intersections—something one of ours had posted. One of these posts in front of the Ericsson Works even stopped him: there was no going any farther. The wheeled units, the wretches, were sitting in their barracks with machine guns and resisting, and the entire further section of Sampsonievsky was deserted and no one was walking or riding there.

What do you think should be done? Here we are gathering forces, machine guns, but we want to bring in artillery, too, to take out the wheeled units' barracks with cannons. Won't persuasion work? No, it hasn't worked at all.

Strike the battalion directly?

Just yesterday they didn't know, and they'd debated how to take the weapons into their own hands. And now the weapons were all ours!

What about the Moscow Regiment's barracks? All ours entirely. The officers were rendered harmless yesterday. And the Interdistrict group assembled a workers' militia here to catch and kill officers one by one.

Well, that was their business, they were moving ahead everywhere.

But Shlyapnikov wasn't used to being constrained on his own Vyborg side even under surveillance, and now, in the liberated city, might he really not get to Serdobolskaya? He knew here not only the streets but all the garden paths, those shortcuts stamped out and maintained by feet even in the winter, because people always took the shortest way. Even in these faceless snowy paths he would never go astray.

He stopped his motorcar full of soldiers and told them to wait for him here for two hours, while he raced down the paths.

Indeed, people were scurrying down them. A couple of times, bullets whistled by so close and low that Shlyapnikov plopped down both times on the trampled snow and lay there and looked at its humps and the footprint patterns.

He lay in a snowy field all alone and thought: Here's your liberated city, Executive Committee member, commissar of the Vyborg side. What a disgrace: in the center you got around everywhere, while here on our Vyborg side . . . ? No, this had to end, truly, even if it took cannons.

He did reach the Pavlovs', of course. Their conspiratorial apartment was unrecognizable. A dozen comrades had gathered openly. They were making a racket, red banners were leaned up at the front door, and they were preparing poles for new ones, and the rooms were heaped to overflowing with the rifles, swords, and bullets they'd acquired.

Maria Georgievna of the golden hands had abandoned her sewing and was feeding them something.

Shlyapnikov was given a bowl of hot cabbage soup.

So. What do you have here? Choosing deputies for the Soviet? Assembling a workers' militia? . . .

Whereas we in the Tauride. . . . It's a tough business, brothers. We can't let the moment slip. This is the time to rip all the ground out from under the Mensheviks.

And the Kadets all the more so.

As for the Tsar—don't even ask.

[1 7 4]

The two Nekrasov brothers, little Greve, and Rybakov, an elderly ensign from the reserves, were spending the night at Staff Captain Stepanov's apartment. At dawn they were awakened by the frantic soldier-doorman from the officers' wing:

"Your honors! You have to leave quickly. A few of the gentlemen officers in the assembly arsenal have changed into soldier's clothes and gone. *Civilians* have come, and they're looking for officers, to kill. I told them nobody was here. They threatened to kill me, too, if I was lying. They're standing right at the front door! Take the service door!"

A combat wakeup call, the usual. They'd slept dressed and now they threw on their greatcoats even before the first shiver and ran down the staircase. They thought—across the parade ground and into the 2nd Company, where they had taken away their swords yesterday and were promised protection. (They never did take their revolvers from the officers' club!) But there were already workers, with and without rifles, walking around the parade ground in the splashing light.

Too late! There was no way to break through.

All of a sudden, a sergeant came up from the porter's room, a vaguely familiar face, and identified himself as the regimental church's sexton. Wouldn't the gentlemen officers come to his place? No one would look for them there. Out the service door it was just a few steps away, quite close. Well, then, let's go.

The Nekrasov brothers knew their regimental yard well, yet had never noticed this place. Right there, quite close, was the regimental storehouse, long and blind—and in it, it turned out, at the butt end, was the sexton's room, separated from the storehouse by a solid brick wall.

They slipped through before it got light.

Their practiced eye examined the room not as a room but sizing it up militarily. Narrow and long, crosswise to the storehouse itself. There was a door in one long wall and a window onto the church in one short wall, and the rest was solid. Through the window, nearly the entire room could be shot at; through the door, only the central part.

Vsevolod's orderly came with them, and inside there was already another soldier. And so they were seven.

They began to sit. Like in prison. They waited for an hour, an hour and a half—for what? It was exhausting. The dawn filtered through the window. And lit it fully. No one came. But they didn't know anything either.

They decided to send the orderly to do some basic reconnoitering and to the 2nd Company to get the sergeant major to send them his men and rescue them.

He was gone a long time, but he brought a lot back: they couldn't go to the 2nd Company, which was filled with workers with red armbands, and the sergeant major couldn't make a peep.

So much for giving that company their swords. . . .

And the officers' club, he related, had been thoroughly routed in the night. They'd ripped down the pictures and portraits and slashed them. Smashed the chandeliers. Broken the unupholstered furniture and chopped up the upholstered furniture with swords.

And yesterday Sergei had been afraid of firing from the club to keep them from touching it. . . .

What had happened in their apartment? He sent to find out. Sergey's orderly was keeping guard there, and it turned out he'd barely lied his way out and avoided being beaten up by the mutineers. They were playing the piano keys with their rifle butts. They'd dragged out the boots, clothing, and linens. They'd divvied up a stack of medals and swaggered around with them hanging off each of them.

Now they sent him to take a look around the barracks. Were there officers anywhere?

The orderly returned: not a one anywhere.

What could they do? Leave the regimental yard? Change clothes?

The lower ranks of the group went and cautiously brought soldiers' greatcoats for all four officers. Ensign Rybakov changed immediately; an unrefined face, no different from a soldier. He left.

But the Nekrasov brothers hesitated. It was humiliating. They kept their own clothing on. So did little Greve.

They sat there another hour, exchanging little conversation. When each conversation only tears at your soul, better your own inner state, even if it is freezing. A mutiny, and in all Petrograd, and in a few hours, and a success— that's a revolution! How did it strike? Who was at the top? What would happen now? There was no revolution at the front; they would come and deal with it; in fact wouldn't even have to deal with anyone here. No one here knew how to hold a rifle. But the regiment was disgraced. As was their own honor. And that meant their lives.

There was no gunfire coming from anywhere. They couldn't believe that their regiment was devastated, that strangers were roaming around looking for blood.

And they were hungry—more and more so. They hadn't eaten anything since yesterday. If only they could get some bread. The sexton said he would. He left.

And came back and called for both soldiers. They returned soon after—with a boiling samovar, trays of food, and a big box of cigarettes, all sent by the regimental priest's wife.

This was their downfall! They hadn't been sufficiently cautious. Three men walking single file across the parade ground, a samovar, a tray—someone had noticed.

Before they could brew tea and take a bite of bread, a woman's voice nearby screamed piercingly:

"There's the officers! They're in here!"

Before they could make up their minds and decide what to do, there were other shouts, the tramping of a running crowd, and without so much as a "Come out!," so quickly, while the sexton was putting on the latch—a shot through the door! And it wounded him. He was knocked off his feet, landed on the floor, and crawled to the side, touching his shoulder and praying out loud.

They kept up their fire at the door, and the shouting got thicker and thicker, and the crowd came running, shouting:

"Beat the bloodsuckers!"

"They drank our blood long enough!"—

and cursing, and cursing, and a savage howl—where had so much hatred come from? Where had it been? How had they lived without knowing it?

And shots, all at the door, and not even low, not competently, but at shoulder height. But no one stayed in the firing zone. Greve managed to squat down and crawl away from the samovar. The sexton crawled as far as the bed, Vsevolod gave him a pillow to stanch the wound and himself lay on the floor under the windowsill. Sergei managed to squeeze into the corner behind the bed. Both soldiers were on the floor.

Outside everyone was hollering and shooting. And again inexperience: all they had to do was run around to the window, where they could fire on almost everything in the room.

But they didn't. It was still the same loud, angry hubbub of voices, common folk, men and women, curses about bloodsuckers and disorderly shooting at the door.

Then a voice broke out:

"Comrades! Maybe there's no one in there. Don't shoot! Wait, don't shoot!"

It got quiet. There, in the room, they got very quiet. It was a mousetrap; there was nowhere to go. And they had no weapons.

But did they need any? Who were they going to kill? Weapons wouldn't save them, there was no breaking out.

They pushed the door. It wasn't closed? Had a bullet knocked off the latch? One soldier looked in, from the Moscow Regiment. A young, intelligent face, like good campaigners sometimes have, a stranger. He gestured: Sit there, don't come out. To Vsevolod's orderly:

"Why on earth aren't you coming out, you fool? They will kill you!" And he dragged him out by the scruff of his neck and pushed him outside.

"Here he is, the sloven! There's no one else there. Disperse!"

The shouts quieted down. They stopped shooting. They talked and talked agitatedly, and it seemed they were dispersing.

Now the officers had no hesitations or doubts, they quickly put on the soldier greatcoats to slip out at the first opportunity. They should have changed clothes immediately that morning. Pride. They would have been gone by now, and the sexton wouldn't have been wounded.

They had no way to help him, he was pressing the cushion to his shoulder.

But before they could button up their greatcoats there was a new roar and firing at the door again, now more confidently. Evidently the orderly had told them. They squeezed into their corners. The brothers shook hands.

They kept it up, and then a voice:

"Hey, maybe they'll come out themselves? Come on, stop shooting!"

But they were afraid to come in themselves: after all, the first few would get cut down. That was why they hadn't broken in all this time.

"Come on out whoever you are!"

There was nothing left to do. And now, where were they to go in greatcoats? They were ashamed. Why had they even put them on? They threw off the soldier greatcoats, didn't have time to pull on their own, and went out in just their tunics, the three of them. Captain, staff captain, and ensign. Vsevolod forgot his stick, so went without it.

Stepping back from the door fifteen paces, the workers stood in a dark, solid semicircle; they all had red armbands on their coat sleeves. They all had their rifles "at the ready," whatever they thought that meant. They were shaking. Some had the cartridge belts they'd looted from the storehouse across a shoulder.

All at once all the faces in a single sweep, not a single one not examined, all remembered forever, for the remaining minutes of life: more of them young, and all of them embittered.

Behind them a large crowd, including women, shaking their fists over the shoulders of those in front and shouting:

"Beat the bloodsuckers!"—and cursing.

"Surrender your weapons!"

"We have no weapons. We surrendered them yesterday."

They didn't believe it. One of the Ericsson men cautiously stepped out in front; the factory was right nearby, and they had all walked and ridden streetcars by it and met each other however many times. And never had the officers noted so much ill will toward themselves.

The man approached and frisked the officers' belts and pockets. He was amazed they had no weapons. They saw all this and the crowd got louder:

"Why bother with them? Shoot the bloodsuckers!"

"Step back and don't get in the way!"

"We're tired of you giving us orders! Now we're giving the orders!"

The leader who'd done the frisking stepped away from the doomed men.

And with new tension—no longer of a dangerous search but of triumph—they stepped aside, making room for others who wished to do this, some making ready, some already taking aim. But no one fired; evidently they were awaiting their leader's order.

How complex life is but how simple all fatal decisions: Here. And now. But more than anything, astonishment: We fought and died for this country. Why does it hate us?

Little Greve, a boy facing a crowd of adults, froze. Vsevolod Nekrasov muttered: "Damn idiots. . . ." But Sergei stood up straight, showed his chest with its St. George Cross, and sighed for the last time; he had not thought to die here, or this way. He had time to feel sorry for his old parents, that they were losing both sons in the same moment—and both at Russian hands. But he couldn't have found anything to say to the murderers out loud—in justification, to make them stop.

Right then, before the order came, a new shout cut through from the side, from the regimental church's porch:

"Stop! Stop! Don't shoot!"

And from the porch steps, where they could see well, ten or so Moscow men ran this way, and pushing the crowd aside, pushing them aside, pushing through energetically—made their way through—and burst into the semicircle between the executioners and the doomed men:

"Stop! Don't touch them! These are good officers!"

"We know them. Don't touch them!"

While the officers themselves didn't have the chance to recognize them.

No, there was no stopping it.

"Step back!" the embittered red armbands shouted. "It's none of your business! Step back or we'll hit you, too!"

But the soldiers put themselves in the way. One shouted:

"You're killing a war cripple, you heroes of the rear!"

That sent a shiver through the circle:

"Where's the cripple?"

"Here!" They pointed to Vsevolod Nekrasov. "Look!" And they looked at his leg.

Handing over his rifle, one of the workers came up and started feeling Vsevolod's leg, through his pants, lower and lower. He shouted as if about a mannequin:

"He's right! A wooden leg!"

And the now still, harsh, laborers' dark semicircle began to diffuse, stir, break up:

"A cripple. . . ."

"Gave his leg. . . ."

"How do you like that? Nearly made a mistake. . . ."

They still had people to execute. There was the tall, open staff captain and a nice young little ensign. No, now they too were spared for that leg. The semicircle broke up—and they approached like guilty men, approached as if already friends:

"Got coats? You'll freeze."

"Go bring them coats."

"We have a wounded man there, a sergeant," Sergei said.

"We'll get him to the infirmary right away!" said the soldier-rescuers. But they were entirely unfamiliar faces; the brothers didn't recognize them.

"Go have a smoke," the crowd now offered.

"And sit down and eat something; your samovar's getting cold."

But the senior worker, iron-hewn, took it back:

"No time to eat or sit around. There's an order to present all prisoners to the State Duma. Collect your things."

[1 7 5]

Maslovsky still hadn't managed to slip away and go home or even get some sleep here. But he was much fortified morally by the fact that the Military Commission had come under the State Duma's responsibility. A responsibility now shared with Rodzyanko.

And what of it! A hereditary aristocrat and however many military men in his line—couldn't he in his youth have become a brilliant officer? But back then he could see the withering away of aristocratic life; no laurels to be won there. Maslovsky went into anthropology, a Central Asian expedition, scientific efforts, not very successful—but then all of society moved off toward revolution, and so did Maslovsky. And nearly singed his wings. For the last few years, on the quiet, he had begun his literary experiments. He would have liked to be a writer.

He had seen correctly all those twenty years before what it would be like to be an officer in these last few days. Like a wolf among men, everyone hunting him.

The *voyenka* (as the *Soviets* had started calling their Military Commission yesterday) was worn out in alarm, ignorance, and helplessness, but by the latter half of the night it was strengthened by a pleasant event, one of the simple human joys: someone brought in a large pot of warm cutlets, browned and juicy, fried with onions—and a round loaf of white bread. Revolution or no—the stomach had its own demands! There weren't any forks so they tore up the loaf with their fingers and then cut it with a penknife, and grabbed the cutlets with their fingers, too, and in this way ate everything clean without ever finding out who had cooked it or where.

Otherwise the military situation was troubled and more dangerous than during the day due to the Tauride Palace's nighttime defenselessness and total lack of any organized military force. At any moment, Khabalov could drive the riffraff from the open area out front with a single volley and take the Tauride Palace with his bare hands.

There weren't even any curious or defenders crowding near the *voyenka*'s doors; everyone had fanned out to sleep.

Fortunately, the disembarkation of the 177th Regiment at the Nikolaevsky Station turned out to have been fabricated. However, other ominous news came in about the disembarkation of some regiment at the Baltic Station. The Kronstadt commandant informed them—probably he'd intended to report to Khabalov but for some reason he had landed through channels at the State Duma—that a major movement of a disorganized crowd of troops had begun from Oranienbaum to Petrograd assembling possibly as many as 15,000. True, by this time, the Semyonovsky Regiment was already considered to have crossed over to the rebellion's side, and the Jäger Regiment, too, so they instructed them to send out a security detachment of 500 Semyonovsky men and 300 Jägers, the right way, with officers and machine guns, to block this vague nighttime deployment. (Officers! Were there any left, and how were they doing? But reinforcing them was the State Duma's instruction.)

Like the evening, though, the night came down to not a single order sent being confirmed or a single picket or patrol sent out ever returned. It all spilled out and was lost, as if it had never been sent in the first place.

Petrograd was threatened along all four rail lines—the Nikolaevsky, Vindava, Warsaw, and Baltic—but it couldn't prevent an attack or put up a defense. Petrograd itself held hidden government forces about whose intentions nothing was known and whose actions might be discovered too late. Also unknown was where the government was. It had not been found in the Mariinsky Palace, so had it obviously moved to the Admiralty? It had been there all this time, undoubtedly with a direct line to GHQ, which was pouring out instructions, and preparing an all-round strangulation of the rebellion. General Ivanov was already leading a nightmarish force.

Engelhardt, having left for the Preobrazhensky battalion—following the general law of disappearance—had not reappeared by morning.

There was a puzzle: Might he, under this convenient pretext, simply have hidden from a dangerous place? While Maslovsky perished here desperately and foolishly!

Indeed, if it weren't for the sailor Filippovsky, he would have slipped away, too. But the hardy Filippovsky sat and wrote as if it weren't night, wrote random orders—on the State Duma Vice President's stationery. Imagine!

Presenting the greatest danger, it seemed to Maslovsky, was the Peter and Paul Fortress, perhaps due to the special feeling any revolutionary had toward it. The fortress had not surrendered. No! Ideally, they plug it up, close all the exits from the outside. But where was he going to find men willing to go there in the night and cold and stand around—getting fired upon from the fortress's loopholes?

Two zealous sergeants and a few soldiers were all the *voyenka* had to handle dispatches and instructions.

The night seemed endless—and menacing to the end. Revolutionary duty nailed him there. (Still, when they attacked, from the main entrance, Maslovsky would have time to leave through the side door onto Tauride Street, and from there it was three steps home, and they wouldn't arrest a civilian.)

How much he had gone through in this sleepless night. More like an entire lifetime!

Just before six in the morning, the telephone informed him that the Petrograd and Izmailovsky battalions had definitely gone over to the side of the people. (In the Izmailovsky, dissenting officers had been beset and some killed, either eight or eighteen.)

There had been no events or battles anywhere else. With the coming of the light, people began calling to demand protection: the Gunpowder Factory, the Okhta explosives factory, the naval and artillery ordnance yards. Military sentries had deserted everywhere. Security was needed above all for the explosives factories, of course. One evildoer with a box of matches . . . But there was absolutely no one anywhere to send.

And yet, what could not have been believed yesterday evening, that now another day had come and revolutionary power was still standing—and it was to that power that everyone was turning.

Outside the doors, willing men were jostling; they could be sent.

With morning well under way, after two hours of light, Engelhardt showed up, evidently having slept and now wearing the uniform and aiguillettes of a General Staffer, and with him as well was Professor Yurevich of the Military Medical Academy, whom Engelhardt immediately, entirely inappropriately, declared commandant of the Tauride Palace—and this man started giving out orders as well, getting mixed up with the others.

Maslovsky was angry at Engelhardt for his nighttime absence, but he was also calmed by his sumptuous arrival now. How entirely respectable everything looked! He should go put on his military dress, too. Damn it, we'll still be fighting this Tsarism for a while!

However, Engelhardt bitterly reported that the Preobrazhensky men, despite his fervent nighttime speech, had not budged or attacked anything. Not only was there no unity between the officers and soldiers, there was none even among the officers. That nighttime telephone call to Shidlovsky had been almost a coincidence—but it had decided so much!

Nonetheless, Engelhardt now did send the Preobrazhensky men an order: occupy the State Bank and telephone exchange and set up posts at the Hermitage and Aleksandr III Museum. There ought to be enough of their nighttime promise for these nonhazardous assignments. At the very least, the Preobrazhensky battalion should post guards around the Tauride Palace and maintain order here.

Through Engelhardt it was now possible to learn things that all their nighttime reconnoitering had failed to. It was a strange situation when they had polite telephone conversations with the General Staff, two supposedly warring sides: The government was not at the Admiralty. It wasn't anywhere at all. It didn't exist. Khabalov had moved to the Winter Palace for the night, but Grand Duke Mikhail had gone there and forced him back to the Admiralty. Khabalov had five squadrons, four companies, and two batteries.

This kind of frankness was astonishing and suspect. Might Engelhardt have been just as frank in these telephone calls in return? Had he admitted that the Tauride had no guard? Maslovsky kept an even more bilious eye on Engelhardt, Yurevich, and Obodovsky. Why was this engineer here, where had he come from, and who had invited him? He'd been sitting here for several hours. Maslovsky whispered to Filippovsky that no one should trust this bourgeois public, that the Soviets had been wrong to let the running of military affairs be snatched away.

Actually, the telephone calls had stopped; there had been a disaster at the telephone exchange: that morning the young ladies had all fled. A note to that effect had come from Rodzyanko saying that to restore the exchange's operations they had to send motorcars to collect the young ladies from their homes. Moreover, they had to collect the dead body lying inside the station.

Occupying the telephone and telegraph was the right thing to do, so as not to repeat the mistakes of 1905.

Was he to understand that Khabalov was no longer defending the telephone exchange? Obodovsky advised otherwise: send a detachment there from the electrotechnical battalion, which could occupy the station and also operate it. Unfortunately, though, on the occasion of the revolution, this battalion had fled as well, and it was no easier to collect them than it was the young ladies.

Now, in the afternoon, more and more officials were gathering. Here was Duma deputy Rzhevsky, and some Prince Chikolini, and some Ivanov—and everyone was giving orders without coordinating with each other, and signing orders, on random Duma forms, haphazardly—either "Military Commission Chairman," or "for the Chairman," or "Tauride Palace Commandant," or "for the Commandant," but Engelhardt also wrote: "Chief of the Petrograd Garrison."

They sent an order to the 2nd Naval Depot to occupy the Winter Palace and arrest any ministers they found there and any agents of the government.

Maslovsky and Filippovsky, separately, had the idea of sending several small groups to arrest the ministers in their apartments, not forgetting to include Stürmer. They had to get going on truly revolutionary matters! We'll be fighting this Tsarism for a while.

And somewhere, entire battalions were floundering without a command, including the heroic first revolutionary Volynian, where all the officers had run off at the very beginning and no one remained. At 8:30, the Tauride simultaneously appointed two ensigns, with equal rights, to assume the provisional command of the Volynian battalion. But before an hour was out, a staff captain appeared from the Volynians laying claim to that command, so they changed their minds and appointed—him.

The main thing now was to convince officers to return to their battalions; without them, the garrison could not be taken in hand.

But after the killing of officers in the Izmailovsky battalion things had gone out of control. A large detail was sent to them with an order to hand over all weapons to the Military Commission. (Fine if they do, but what if they don't?)

*   *   *

Soldiers! The people and all Russia thank you who have risen up for the righteous cause of freedom.

Soldiers! Some of you are still hesitating to join us. Remember your hard life in the village and factories, where the government always oppressed and suppressed you!

Soldiers! Remnants from the police, Black Hundreds, and other scoundrels have taken over rooftops and individual apartments. Try, everywhere, to remove them immediately with a fatal bullet, a correct attack.

Soldiers! Do not let people smash stores or loot apartments. This is not the way!

Soviet of Workers' Deputies

*   *   *

[1 7 6]

The previous evening, after fleeing the Winter Palace, the Pavlovsky men ran no farther and started to fall apart, especially the training detachment. And with it Ensign Andrusov.

Back to their barracks they went. On their way, though, women and young ladies jumped out of the crowd, grabbed the Pavlovsky men by the arm, and foisted and even pinned on them pieces of red fabric.

The officers didn't dare shout: Get away! or Don't take it!

Why should they shout anyway? There had been a huge shift in people's moods, and Andrusov was actually delighted. He was a part of something unique.

But yesterday had ended in an even more unusual way. Standing by the training detachment's barracks on Tsaritsyn Street were workers and students with rifles who would not let the soldiers into their own barracks and told them to keep walking the streets.

So changed were all the rules that the disheartened soldiers didn't dare try to push through, even though they wanted their dinner and bed. Their officer especially didn't dare order them to do this; the very young officer especially sniffed this thrilling new air.

There didn't seem to be anything at all for the officers to do here, with the soldiers. It was much safer to separate.

Such was the mounting sense of unknown danger that it would even be better for them to hide, to go missing.

Right there, on Tsaritsyn Street, there was an officer infirmary, and some of the Pavlovsky officers had managed to change into hospital robes and lie down. Andrusov actually envied them, the dodgers.

Soon after, though, one of the soldiers from the shelterless training detachment wandered into that infirmary and discovered his healthy officers. A disgrace for them.

In his loitering about, Andrusov ran into Kostya Grimm, and they got the idea of asking to spend the night at their quartermaster's apartment—just two buildings down. (It was dangerous for officers to travel all the way across the city because of all the soldiers they didn't know.)

Meanwhile, they learned the soldiers were looking to kill Captain Chistyakov. They learned from the quartermaster that Chistyakov was hiding nearby, with another quartermaster. Grimm called home and told them to send Chistyakov, dressed as a civilian, to Vasilievsky Island, to the home of his father, a well-known liberal member of the State Council; no one would touch him there.

But no matter what clothes you put on Captain Chistyakov, there was no concealing his noticeable bandaged arm or hiding his intransigent eyes. They refused.

Vadim Andrusov called home, too. His father, a Kadet, and his mother were ecstatic over what was happening. The people's long-awaited liberation had begun! We were being given the gift of an ages-old dream coming true. Now life would begin! Now order would begin. No change could make things any worse; it had been impossible to endure any longer.

Vadim complained to them that close up it wasn't all that comfortable or pleasant.

But he himself was reenergized: truly, in the spirit of his family and upbringing, why shouldn't he join the general celebration?

That night he and Kostya discussed what to do. The unusual had entered their life in an unusual way, so why shouldn't they join in the people's victory, so dreamed of and awaited?

These shifts were easy at a young age. They held the continuation of the spectacle that had begun yesterday.

But outside, under the windows, soldiers were still roaming late in the evening, and those armed men were still not letting them into the barracks.

In the morning they woke up and checked on their mood. Yes! They'd arisen revolutionaries!

They pinned red rosettes on their greatcoats.

An extraordinarily lightness filled their feet, chests, and heads, as if they were no longer tethered to the earth. And they were seized with the notion of making mischief. They felt as if they might at any moment accomplish something free and great and even become famous.

But it was awkward to go to their own soldiers in the training detachment like this. They couldn't. So they went to the marching company that the day before yesterday had mutinied before everyone else.

The men there were still asleep.

The two ensigns started walking around the rooms, shouting:

"Why are you sleeping? Get up! Revolution!"

But even this was insufficient, and the men began waking listlessly. Then Andrusov and Grimm started shouting, for some reason, whatever popped into their heads:

"Get up! The Tsar is gone!"

When they heard this, the Pavlovsky men jumped up in a great flurry.

Then they realized that this meant now no one would be punished for the mutiny and the nineteen arrested wouldn't be tried.

They tossed up both ensigns, and both of them felt increasingly merry and unbound.

They went to the assembly for breakfast. A few young officers had red bits, too, while the few senior officers still there gave them a censorious look.

Captain Chistyakov was gone, too.

Right then the former commander of the Guards Corps, the bulky General Bezobrazov, appeared and began telling the officers in the billiards room that in the event of a summons for the battalion to go out, they shouldn't let the crowd near but should stop it first with an order and then fire a salvo.

All this sounded wild, out of some irretrievable past. The young officers didn't even try to argue with him; they just stood up and exited demonstratively.

Then Vadim and Kostya went to the Tauride Palace on foot. Now they could move freely among the unfamiliar soldier mass. People saw their red rosettes, didn't disarm them, greeted them.

They jostled around the Tauride Palace for a while and found the Military Commission, which rejoiced at their arrival and immediately wrote out instructions: Grimm was to command his Pavlovsky platoon, attached to the State Duma. And Andrusov was to assume command of the Pavlovsky detachment posted at the Mikhailovsky manège.

Thus they both found themselves in the thick of things, young officers of the revolution.

Documents – 2

FROM DISPATCHES TO THE MILITARY COMMISSION

(13 March, morning)

—Immediately send 350 reinforcements to Ligovka, the corner of Chubarov Lane. Major siege, 6 (six) machine guns operating.

/Noted in pencil: not borne out/

—Medics from the Winter Palace infirmary ask us to send a detachment of troops in order to arrest individuals hiding there. . . . The Palace is not in anyone's power. The sentries have been removed, but supporters of the old government are still inside.

On the medics' behalf, university student R. *Ize*

—The drunken crowds who looted the Astoria Hotel have been seen in the vicinity of the Senate.

—The corner of Inzhenernaya and Sadovaya is bad. We have no patrols in this district.

—All is calm in the city. The soldiers are complaining of the cold and have decided to head for their barracks. 18 armored vehicles have been seized. On the outskirts, stores are being looted.

—Those freed from the Petrograd Transit Prison are asking that a place be designated for them to go and get a bed, an apartment, food and a weapon, as well as a pass.

Freed Political Prisoner (signature)

—According to reports that have come in, two suspicious subjects are handing out alcoholic beverages to military personnel and spreading knowingly false and alarming rumors.

Member of the Food Supply Comm. (signature)

—An order has been given to organize protection for the Arsenal, where there is apparently an attack under way.

—At the corner of Sadovaya and Inzhenernaya they are asking for immediate assistance in calming drunken soldiers.

—A store of weapons is being emptied out and sent off. The carrying off of shells must cease. They can remove them on horses across Lesnoye. They are awaiting troops from Finland.

Kuzma of the 1st Reserve Regiment

—ORDER. Volunteer Dmitri Tairov and Private Vladimir Mayakovsky shall conduct an election for representatives at the military vehicle school and organize vehicle repair.

B. Engelhardt

[1 7 7]

Having spent the night in an armchair, Shulgin was not rested, and in the morning there was nothing nice and hot to drink, and the looted Duma buffet was idle. But for some reason his soul was filled with the mood of the French Revolution.

This comparison was easily drawn. It had been on the minds of many yesterday evening as well, but today it surged forth with new strength. The distant, cold-blooded reader Shulgin had been taken as a confederate—perhaps even a victim?—of those, indeed frightening, days.

What of yesterday! Yesterday evening's Duma crush was recalled now, perhaps, as a blissful sparseness. Yesterday people had merely been breaking through, whereas today, knowing no restraint, a grayish, brownish, blackish, senseless mass, a sticky human jam, had come thronging and thronging through the front door—and filled the entire palace with senseless joy, for its own senseless sojourn here. Yesterday, lost soldiers had at least been seeking a night's shelter, afraid to return to their barracks, but what about today? All the offices and halls, down to the last corner, and even the rooms, had been occupied and taken over by the crowd, moving and mixing, that dull crowd, simply riffraff suppressing any sensible activity here. Russia had no government, and all spheres of life required direction and intervention, but the Duma Committee members not only couldn't work, they couldn't even find each other or simply move around the building.

Shulgin discovered that this mass had more or less one face, and a rather brutish face it was.

He quickly realized that he had already seen all this, read about this, but had not put his heart into it. After all, this had happened in France 128 years ago! When young people in small groups in the Ekaterininsky Hall attempted to sing the Marseillaise, the Russian version, muddling the tune—

> Forswear the old world,
> Shake its dust from our feet,

Shulgin heard the *other*, the first, the original Marseillaise and its horrifying words:

> To arms, citizens!
> Let us march! Let an impure blood
> Water our furrows!

Whose impure blood did they have in mind? Back then it was shown it doesn't stop at the royal milieu.

And now here we have the Tsar's portrait torn to shreds.

Revolting.

The Emperor's full-length portrait hung for ten years behind the Duma tribune, a patient witness to all the speeches and obstructions, yet nonetheless a symbol of the state's stability. And all of a sudden, this morning, they'd seen that soldiers' bayonets had shredded the portrait, and scraps of it were hanging across the gilt frame.

These few insolent bayonet strikes had suddenly changed the entire picture. Not only had the Petrograd episode not subsided, this might be, might well be a great revolution.

Neither the entire Duma Committee nor Rodzyanko himself could protect the portrait or stop anything.

It occurred to Shulgin that this was how it had been in Kiev, he always remembered, eleven years ago. A crowd had broken into the City Duma, primarily Jews there, as the soldiers had not mutinied—and in the very same way they'd ripped all the portraits of emperors and poked out their eyes. A ginger Jewish student ran his head through the Emperor's portrait and wearing the broken canvas had shouted frenziedly: "Now I'm the Tsar!" They'd broken the Tsar's crown that was attached to the balcony, wrenched it off, and thrown it to the pavement in front of a crowd of ten thousand.

They were sitting out this human stampede in Rodzyanko's large, luxurious office, where they were among their own and could discuss things.

Not that any decision whatsoever could be reached. Understandably, they needed to act and not let anarchy develop, but they didn't know what to do or how to do it. For two full days their brains had failed to digest this enormous something that had come falling down on them—quite a lot more than they had been calling for, expecting, or wanting.

Who were they supposed to act against anyway? And *who* was to do the acting? As Shulgin had correctly warned them, they'd broken their lances, broken them for the glory of the people invested with the people's trust, worthy, honest, and talented people—but where were they now? On the Provisional Committee, seemingly the Duma's summit? But look around and there was nothing but mediocrity; it was just embarrassing. Fair enough, this was just a Committee and not the government, but who was talented and *invested* enough to be taken into the government?

And Rodzyanko's elephantine hulk, what use was it? At times he'd been so stubborn with the Emperor himself, and now he couldn't get that gaggle of pretenders and imposters, that council of so-called deputies who'd seized the building of the very Duma, off the budget commission.

Unlike all of them, conscious he was still young, subtle, agile, he who just eleven years ago had been a Kiev ensign, Shulgin was thirsting to stand out from the present discombobulation and to act.

Right then he heard a conversation about how there'd been a call at dawn from the Peter and Paul Fortress. The commandant had expressed a desire to speak with State Duma deputies—and here they still hadn't sent anyone. He'd heard! And in his romantic soul the entire scene suddenly unfolded and took on a different light. After all, if this resembled the French Revolution, then it resembled it in *this*, too! The Peter and Paul Fortress was the Bastille! And this repulsive crowd was just about to get the notion to take the Peter and Paul Fortress by storm! To liberate the perhaps nonexistent or few prisoners there and execute the commandant's service. He had to hurry to effectively avert this horror!

It had come in handy that he'd spent the night here; he hadn't suffered in that armchair in vain. He started proposing to Rodzyanko and everyone on the Committee that they send him. He hastened to convince them for fear they would send someone else. Everyone was so befuddled, though, that they didn't even appreciate the importance of this step, and they nodded willingly, good thing they had a volunteer.

He dashed into the bracing cold before he'd finished buttoning up.

Before, to drive through the city—he would never have been able to get a motorcar. But now they brought one up at once. A quarter of Petrograd's vehicles seemed to be parked in front of the Tauride, awaiting the honor of taking someone somewhere. (While the other three quarters were racing through the city to gunfire and shouts.)

But they brought him one with a little red flag and bristling bayonets: there wasn't the least room for anyone to latch onto that didn't already have a soldier with a bayonet. The door was opened for Shulgin by a prompt officer with epaulets removed who'd been appointed from the Military Commission.

Shulgin, the famed monarchist, didn't even notice that he'd headed out to take the Peter and Paul Fortress under a red flag.

He wouldn't have gone had it not been for the grandeur of his mission, the analogies. But the entire French Revolution got rolling because of the storming of the Bastille. He had to avert such an unfortunate development, to free the political prisoners in front of the crowd and show it the empty cells.

Shulgin didn't recognize the streets: such unusual figures, with lots of red patches from bows and armbands; unusual traffic. People weren't walking, they were thronging down Shpalernaya toward the Duma. There were simply a lot of armed men, soldiers and civilians, not in any kind of formation, on foot and in trucks.

The District Court was still smoldering—red-hot ruins, ashes, smoke from being doused.

It was clear, frosty and sunny, and the Neva opened up from the French Embankment, sparkling with snow, being traversed here and there by small black figures.

From the Trinity Bridge he could see the long, gray, articulated wall of the Peter and Paul Fortress, the cathedral's cupolas, and the bell tower's soaring, immortal gold spire. And the imperial standard on one tower, a black eagle on a yellow field: the dynasty's resting place.

A great moment. His heart was pounding.

Across the bridge, not far away, the mosque's blue cupola came into view. In an open area, on the way to the fortress, there was a crowded rally, and a student was shouting from a truck about freedom, freedom, freedom—and everyone was listening as if to something long-awaited.

But they weren't crossing the little bridge over the canal to the fortress, where there were paired sentries on the other side.

And alongside them, an awaiting officer. Before Shulgin's companion could wave his handkerchief, the officer was already hurrying toward them.

"How good you've come! We've been waiting for you eagerly! Please, the commandant is expecting you!"

Right then they were overtaken by someone from the crowd, someone wearing an officer's greatcoat but without epaulets. . . . There was no room, but he squeezed onto the running board between the revolutionary soldiers.

The sentries gawked.

They drove through the outside gates. And passed under the St. Peter Gate.

At the cathedral they turned and drove up to the chief commandant's residence.

Inside it was dark and cramped, an antique structure.

Finally, here was the commandant, an adjutant general covered in medals but not very military-looking, rather podgy. And several officers with him. Everyone was uneasy.

Shulgin, narrow of build and slender, presented himself in a pleasant tone, saying he was a State Duma deputy and sent by the State Duma Committee.

Agitated, completely losing the imposing dignity of his service and rank, the old general tried to convince the young deputy with the pointed gaze and pointed mustache:

"Deputy, sir. . . . Please, do not think we are opposed to the State Duma. On the contrary, we are very glad that at such a dangerous time there is at least some kind of authority. . . . We declined to invite General Khabalov's detachment here. . . . But how does the State Duma view this? Shouldn't what is in the Peter and Paul Fortress be protected? We have a precious cathedral. We have the entire dynasty's resting place. A mint. And last, an arsenal. The mob cannot be allowed to break in! And what can they do? No matter what the government, it is going to protect this. The duty of our oath is to protect it, we cannot allow . . ."

Simple and clear notions. But the Committee had been thinking not about this but only about uniting the Peter and Paul Fortress and the people!

Shulgin had quite enough daring and less than enough self-control to answer confidently:

"Your Excellency! Do not trouble yourself trying to prove that which is clear to each and every sane person. Inasmuch as you have recognized the

State Duma's authority, which is the main thing, then, in the name of the State Duma, I confirm to you and even personally insist that the fortress and everything that pertains to it must be protected no matter what!"

The general brightened, took heart, and thanked him:

"Thank you, deputy, sir. Now we are at ease and know what to hew to. But might you not leave us this in the form of a written order? It may be we will have need to show it, to prove it. . . ."

Shulgin's boldness knew no bounds. He immediately sat down at a table and wrote out the following order for the fortress commandant: Secure the fortress using all available forces and do not allow any intrusion by unauthorized persons.

However, he also expressed his impatient thought, the one he had barely kept from opening with upon entering: why the Bastille fell. The political prisoners had to be released publicly and the empty cells shown to representatives of the crowd outside.

The general and one of the officers were amazed. What political prisoners? There are no prisoners here of any kind.

Shulgin expressed relieved surprise. No prisoners at all? But everyone believes there are, everyone assumes there are. This entire ominous fortress in the middle of the city, with its terrible memory, held not a single prisoner?

Other than the nineteen mutinous Pavlovsky soldiers brought in the night before last. The commandant himself was happy to release them, not knowing what to do with them.

"There really is not a single political?"

Not a one! There had been General Sukhomlinov, the Minister of War. But he'd been released in the late autumn.

"You mean to say all the cells are empty?"

"Yes. You can see for yourself."

The general was prepared to release the nineteen Pavlovsky men that very minute. However, he felt it was humiliating and impossible to show the cells to the crowd's delegates, even for his most junior officer.

And Shulgin lacked the perseverance to convince him.

Meanwhile, a senior officer asked him to make a speech to the fortress garrison saying that the State Duma demanded that discipline be maintained.

Certainly, he could do that.

In the expansive courtyard near the bell tower, where the snow had been cleared away, a few hundred soldiers had lined up, in a half-infantry square. That seemed like a lot.

Only then did Shulgin guess that the officers were afraid not of an assault from without but of these, their own soldiers. At a time like this, it really wasn't very comfortable being locked up in a fortress with inscrutable soldiers.

The soldiers squinted at Shulgin in the bright light. And he squinted at them. And right then they didn't seem to him as dull and hopeless as those in the Tauride. It proved not at all difficult to make a speech before this meek formation, without other speakers interrupting. All that could be heard was his solitary, high, not very strong voice.

He reminded them there was a war under way. That the German was just lying in wait to fall upon us. And if we were to weaken in the least, he would sweep away our defenses and instead of the freedom we were all dreaming of we would have the German around our neck. An army is maintained by discipline, and they had to obey their superiors. Your officers are in full agreement with the State Duma, and I have given them an order to defend the fortress at all cost!

(This sounded good: "I have given them an order!" Oh, what a revolution does!)

Someone shouted:

"Hurrah for *Comrade* Shulgin!"

It had already seeped in here.

But no loud, united "hurrah" burst out.

He said goodbye to the officers and got into the motorcar. The fortress was saved!

(Oh, he'd forgotten to grab one other vivid impression: to look at the Trubetskoi Bastion! He had been in such a hurry to get to the Tauride; he felt he needed to be present there.)

Once again that delegate from the crowd, the officer greatcoat without epaulets, hopped onto the running board. Across the little bridge he gave a speech to the crowd from the motorcar's running board, saying that the Peter and Paul Fortress was also for freedom.

And the crowd shouted "hurrah!"

Right then, trucks drove up with lots of bayonets, the men kept cocking their guns. Why hadn't the Peter and Paul Fortress raised a red flag? They threatened to open military actions.

Shulgin's escort jumped over, to their motorcar, and shouted that here the State Duma deputy had already turned the fortress in favor of freedom and the people. They were going to raise the red flag right away, they just hadn't had time!

Shulgin, meanwhile, drove away—back across the Trinity Bridge and down the embankment. And down the same troubled, armed Shpalernaya.

In front of the palace, the crowd was even larger and thicker. The soldier formations were getting in each others' way. What was going on! What was going on!

Somehow he pushed through, pushed through the entrance hall, through the inside crush—to Rodzyanko's office. After all that rubbish, what happiness to be among his own people. Before they had been alien deputies, co-workers, and now they were friends who had once lived with me on a well-ordered planet.

Here they listened to his tale with attention and approval.

But the impenetrable Nekrasov, with his immobile gaze, from under his immobile whiskers, which looked planted, suddenly said:

"Oh, fine. Now they can fire on the Admiralty from the Peter and Paul. Lob over a dozen or so shells maybe."

Shulgin turned around abruptly, as if stung. This he hadn't expected. Not here.

"What? We, the Duma, thank God, are not making the revolution, are we?"

And he turned his eyes to Shidlovsky, Konovalov, Rzhevsky, and Rodzyanko himself.

But no one could support him because no one himself understood anymore.

And Nekrasov, who yesterday at a private meeting had demanded a military dictatorship against the disturbances, now objected implacably, his blue eyes did not flash, and his voice did not jump:

"Then what are we doing? We have seized power."

"Excuse me, gentlemen, I fail to understand you!" Shulgin exclaimed resonantly, emotionally. "We were against the ministers, but when did we turn against the Russian military authorities?"

*   *   *

Retreat is impossible. Freedom or death. The enemy is merciless.

What must a soldier do now? Seize all telegraphs, the telephone network, the train stations, the power stations, the State Bank, and the ministries. Do not disperse to your barracks. Wait for leaflets! Long live the second revolution!

Petersburg Interdistrict Committee of the RSDRP [Russian Social Democratic Workers Party] Petersburg Committee of Socialist Revolutionaries

*   *   *

[178]

Since morning, even though he'd had a few hours' sleep, General Khabalov had understood even less than yesterday; his thinking had grown quite fuzzy.

In these twenty-four hours of revolution, if you didn't count Kutepov's missing detachment, the troops under his command had not carried out a single attack or a single military movement, apparently hadn't even fired a single shot, and had neither been subject to nor fought off a single attack, which was why they didn't have a single wounded man or a single casualty; nonetheless, they had lost all their strength, all their spirit, and had indeed decreased noticeably in numbers. Twenty-four hours ago, this had been the sole military force in the capital and had been considered its master. Today it had withdrawn to a doomed pocket, the Admiralty rectangle, from which nearly every man, including the commander himself, now had but one thought: how to flee.

Ever since his advice to fight their way out of the city was rejected, Tyazhelnikov had been unable to understand or propose anything either.

Since early morning their concern had been to obtain food and forage to feed their combat personnel and horses. They still had too few cartridges. Khabalov had been calling around to various districts of the city, asking the commanders of military units and institutions to send him reinforcements, food, and cartridges—but he had received refusals from everywhere, and more adamantly than yesterday. No one would touch him.

After that, telephone communications in the city suddenly vanished. This meant the telephone exchange had fallen into the rebels' hands. And that was two blocks away.

They happened to get a hold of a little bread, which they passed out to some of the lower ranks.

Not only did the horses have no hay, they had no water, either. It was hard to drink from faucets, there weren't any buckets, and it was too far to carry. The horses stood in the courtyards, heads hanging.

The Cossack squadron was released to the barracks of the Horse Guards Regiment for watering. They did get there safely, but on the way back they were fired upon and two horses were killed.

Stray bullets started to fly, too, from the upper stories of buildings along Admiralty Prospect, and two more horses were killed. The Admiralty did not return fire.

But there was no attack from anywhere, nor was there an advancing foe. Maybe it would have been easier if they could see him. The machine guns took up the corners of the second floor for firing; the weapons were opposite the gates onto Palace Square, they had nothing to do, however.

But although the city was now quiet, mute, and there was no communication with it, the palace telephone line and the telegraph line to GHQ were intact. The main equipment was at the General Staff, cater-corner, but there was an extension in the Admiralty. That morning, using this line, Khabalov had telegraphed Alekseev at GHQ, saying that the situation was difficult in the extreme, and there remained 600 infantry and 500 cavalry loyal to their oath, with 15 machine guns, 12 guns in all and only 80 shells.

By the same telegraph there arrived a very encouraging inquiry from General Ivanov consisting of a number of points. It confirmed Ivanov's presumptive arrival with many troops. Khabalov was delighted to answer all questions, but he didn't dare dream he could last until that blissful hour when he handed over responsibility and then, perhaps, even the command itself over a hostile, hateful, ungraspable, and inhospitable Petrograd. (How he dreamed of leaving again for his Ural Cossack army!)

He only had to last twenty-four hours.

But how could he last if the entire capital had been lost in the previous twenty-four hours?

Elsewhere in this enormous building, in his official apartment, was Minister of the Navy Grigorovich, who had pled illness. But Khabalov could not resort to his assistance or counsel; since yesterday he had not once troubled himself to come, had not made a single good gesture toward Khabalov's troops. Rather he had tried, through subordinates, to crowd them in their rooms, and they were fortunate he had let him use the direct line.

Around Khabalov were a great many senior officers—immeasurably more than was required for these troops. Therefore never once did he have occasion to pass through to the troops, take a look, or address them. The officers saying it outright, but their mournful look, all too few words, and inaction conveyed the lost feeling that had overtaken the last handful of loyal men.

They, the junior officers and soldiers, were loyal, loyal indeed; but they couldn't help but see that their command had absolutely no idea what to do and was only drifting from building to building, driven out of everywhere. As to the government itself, they knew it had scattered. The spirit of pointlessness and inaction was more corrupting than hunger or the lack of cartridges. In these past twenty-four hours the entire city had hurled itself into a triumphant rebellion, and every hour of delay they spent here without bringing protection or use to anyone, threatened each of them here with retribution or punishment from the rebellion.

It had reached the unthinkable: good Izmailovsky officers went to their colonel and requested permission to leave altogether.

Other Guards officers asked General Zankevich whether he might not find it possible to make contact with the Duma Committee, as the officers of the Preobrazhensky Regiment had already done, according to rumors.

Herein lay the particular strangeness and pointlessness of military actions: the enemy was unclear. Where and who was he? Other than the Khabalov detachment, all that was left in the capital was the State Duma, but it couldn't be their enemy, could it? Why not reach an agreement with the Duma? What the officers couldn't understand most of all was why this contradicted their oath.

Zankevich could find no answer. (Privately, he himself had been thinking the same thing regarding himself.)

Only Artillery Colonel Potekhin, the battery commander on crutches, began on the staircase to talk to a small handful of soldiers—but right away more of them gathered, and more, and everyone wanted to listen since no one was explaining anything! Standing on crutches, he gave loud and clear encouragement to the whole murky staircase:

"Don't lose heart, soldiers! Don't mind that the city has been seized by rebellious gangs, and don't weaken! This is a temporary clouding of minds among people at the rear. Russia would perish if this went any further. But

Russia is with us, not them! All Russia is at the front and standing up against the enemy. This rebellion is the best help for the Germans. Don't lose heart. Get through the privations. Because at the front it can be even harder. We will hold out until victory is ours!"

His words seemed to sit very well. No one objected. However, none of the officers added anything more. The soldiers stood there a while and then started dispersing. Holding on to what had been said. Or perhaps already dropping it.

But what was it like in all these circumstances for Minister of War Belyaev, who had fallen into this death trap? How he regretted that yesterday evening, when there was gunfire on the Moika, he had abandoned his official residence. Since then he had called there and been connected over the military line several times and learned that the building had not been looted and no one had come and he might have stayed there quite safely. Now he was between a rock and a hard place. If the rebels were victorious, they wouldn't forgive his presence here, among the Khabalov remnants. (One of the Preobrazhensky men had telephoned to say that in the night they had received an order to advance on Khabalov's detachment. And from the windows they could already see groups of armed civilians and soldiers gathering here and there.) If the Emperor's troops came, the Minister of War would not be forgiven fleeing this place. The question arose, though, why he had to get caught up in this story at all? Take Grigorovich, who had concocted an illness and yet was sitting tight in his own ministry apparently and dealing with naval affairs. The same went for Belyaev and Zankevich (they had exchanged thoughts). They could be sitting in their office at the General Staff, right here, cater-corner, 200 yards away, running their military affairs, and who was fighting whom in Petrograd didn't affect them at all. Was the revolution aimed against military men?

Whenever the telephone was available, Belyaev would call Rodzyanko again, counting very much on their relationship helping him from that direction. But Rodzyanko brought no good news. He could not guarantee what the angered crowd would do with Khabalov's detachment. He strongly advised Belyaev to cease resistance and disperse his troops.

This was not in Belyaev's competence, though.

Having wound up here, he had to make a good impression in front of his superiors, who continued to exist, having sent an expeditionary corps. He decided that as long as the line was working he would send his dispatches there.

But what could he say in a dispatch? He couldn't convey all this horror, this sense of doom. And he could get a reputation as an alarmist. Put it more cautiously this way:

". . . The situation remains alarming. The rebels have taken over the most important institutions, so that any normal flow of life in state establishments has ceased. . . ."

And then directly: ". . . Troops are abandoning their weapons and going over to the rebels' side or adopting neutrality. The speediest arrival of troops is extremely desirable, and until their arrival the rebellion and disturbances will only increase. . . ."

If only they would send them faster. What was taking them so long?

[1 7 9]

Early that morning, at the Pavlovs' apartment, a draft of the Bolshevik Manifesto was thrust into Shlyapnikov's hands. Shlyapnikov liked this. In secret from all the parties, to come out first with a Manifesto "To All Citizens of Russia"—take that! We'll arm ourselves separately! The Interdistrict group and SRs had already managed to print a leaflet—but we've done an entire Manifesto! Lenin should praise us.

Too bad Matveika Ryss had gone over to the Interdistrict group—now that was a pen! Somehow he knew how to write menacingly, a fire in every line—humiliating our enemies and encouraging us.

All right, we'll do without you.

They'd already written on this manifesto and crossed things out, and all sorts of things had been scribbled since yesterday evening. They wrote it all over again. And still it was neither clean nor ready.

Oh, the most frustrating work—writing a public document, especially when you're short on time. Never mind the beauty of the word, just so an important slogan wasn't distorted. It was so easy to make a mistake, and on the most level ground; political formulas crept across like fog, their edge nowhere to be found. You thought you had it, there, in your hands—and again it slipped away.

You had to have some searing slogan here, something that would set everyone on fire down to their toes!

They debated whether to put the Soviet of Workers' Deputies in the Manifesto. Shlyapnikov strained a little and thought: but what was this Soviet of Deputies? It had existed since yesterday, and we didn't have a majority in it, nor will we. We had to bowl them over: at the head of a republican regime—and that means kicking the Tsar out!—to create a revolutionary government! (And with our weapons we'll get a better foothold there.)

The men liked it. Molotov corrected him: Nonetheless, it's a provisional government. Well, all right, "provisional revolutionary."

Right now we had to move words like this into the masses' consciousness so that no one could take them back, to make it hard to turn back. But Molotov, that driveller, would never get it done if you gave him a week to spend on it.

Besides, the men were freezing by the motorcar, and who knew whether the war minister's driver had run off yet.

All right, let's go! There, in the Tauride, we'll finish up before the session.

They were steering well clear of the Wheeled Batallion units. That's fine, people were walking around, there was no gunfire. But the wheeled units weren't surrendering. So stubborn! What was there for them in the Tsarist regime? How people's minds do get befuddled.

Up until the Liteiny Bridge they saw nothing but red on people. But once they'd crossed the bridge they also saw some white armbands. Just who were they? City militia, they were told. Oh no, that's not our force.

Shpalernaya was jam-packed. Soldiers out of formation and armed workers were thronging to and fro. Honking motorcars and snarling trucks.

Shlyapnikov's plan was the following: the Soviet had created its own newspaper, and our man—Bonch-Bruevich—had seized the printing press. Now Shlyapnikov called him on the telephone from the Tauride straightaway—and Bonch-Bruevich promised to run the Bolsheviks' Manifesto this afternoon, as a separate issue of the newspaper. And not a peep to anyone.

That's how we get things done, Vyacheslav! We'll outrun everyone!

Bonch wanted the text in a hurry. They went to find a room.

There were lots of rooms, but none were empty. But no one knew the members of the Bolshevik CC by face; no one was paying attention. A bunch of them squeezed onto the small sofa on the side, used their laps to read and add pencil corrections, and finished their debating.

"The Tsarist gang's well-being . . . is built on the people's bones. . . ." That's good, let that stand. "The revolutionary proletariat must save the country from the utter ruin that the Tsarist government has readied for it. . . ." That's right, too. But not quite right. You have to feel the moment spilling over. The soldiers have been with us since yesterday, and rather than offend them we should be luring them into united ranks. That means we should write: "not only the proletariat, but the revolutionary army as well." Yes. . . . "Having shaken off ages-old slavery. . . ." That doesn't hurt. ". . . The Provisional Revolutionary government at the head of a republican regime . . ."—ah, that's good, kill all the birds with one stone! I'll tell Bonch not to stint on printing ink for that sentence. True, we're not telling them how to create this government. But that's going to take a lot of thinking, and it depends on who does the seizing first. Our cause is this: all rights and liberties, confiscation of all lands, an eight-hour day, and a Constituent Assembly. Did we miss anything?

And also: *confiscate* all food supplies. Very simple! When we confiscate everything, then we can distribute it. Otherwise, what's there to distribute?

"The hydra of reaction . . ."—that's good. ". . . Vanquish anti-popular counterrevolutionary schemes. . . ." That's right.

Now for the war question—we have to take it by the throat. No, that's weak, that's shillyshallying: "the proletariat doesn't approve of the war and doesn't want land seizures." No!

But even a straight "down with the war"—and lots of workers will recoil.

How about this: "The revolutionary government should enter into relations with the proletariats of the warring countries," see? Not with the governments but over their heads—with the proletariats! How the government might do that is not our concern. Our business is to provide a program that takes their breath away!

Something else that has to go in: that the revolutionary government has to be elected immediately. By the factories, plants, and mutinous troops. A slogan!

And add this: **throughout Russia!** "The red banner of insurrection is rising throughout Russia." It doesn't matter that it wasn't anywhere today. Tomorrow it will be. That was why we are writing, so that it happens. "Throughout Russia, take the cause of freedom into your own hands! Overthrow the Tsarist lackeys! Call on the soldiers to fight Tsarist power!" In fact, straight like this even: "Create governments of the revolutionary people across all towns and villages!"

That came out powerfully. That would thunder! Sear them so there's no going back for anyone! That's our way.

A signature, of course: "Central Committee of the Russian Social Democratic Party." Let someone there figure out that there was more than one committee, and more than one social democratic party—but we are the first, and so, the only!

Will Bonch make all this out? If he puts his glasses on, he will.

[1 8 0]

Just as a man at the front gets used to sleeping even to exploding shells, so, too, Kutepov slept through the night soundly in the threatened home, where they could have burst in at any minute and demanded his blood. Only after waking up rather late did he recall the danger and all his efforts of the previous day, and all their futility.

It was a bitter feeling.

He had always had a presentiment, for some reason, that he would end fatefully, not just killed in war but in some fateful way—as, evidently, he could have yesterday and might today. But he didn't have the faintest idea what had happened in a single day with the entire Petrograd government, how it had collapsed.

That the reserve battalions were rubbish and no kind of guard was clear. Following the principle of economy, so as not to transport them so far, they had chosen local workers (who already get leaflets), and Finns from the outskirts, and shop clerks, landlords, and those previously exempt—mama's boys who had slithered out of this so far. They listened open-mouthed to the wounded being treated about the drumfire and the gassing, and the only thing they wanted was not to end up at the front. And the officers were all passing through; they hadn't had a chance to remember the soldiers, let alone know what their heads were stuffed with.

But that the government could find itself without a single buttress and could scatter in a single day having faced no cohesive forces whatsoever? That was beyond his comprehension.

Aleksandr Pavlovich walked over to the window of his small room and looked out cautiously. He saw a stretch of Liteiny Prospect, the garden of the Hall of the Army and Navy, and the corner of Kirochnaya Street. The traffic was unusual: lots of armed and excited men, each one sporting something red. One group was standing perfectly still directly in front of Musin-Pushkin's residence, not taking its eye off the windows and doors. More than likely there was the same across from the back gate.

Nonetheless, he did not regret that he had refused to change into a soldier's uniform yesterday. Death itself must always be dignified; herein lay the officer's calling.

Over tea he was given incontrovertible evidence: the government had dispersed, and Protopopov was hiding at Tsarskoye Selo; policemen were being killed all over or else taken as prisoners to the Duma; no trace remained of the old government, not even the military authority, and no one knew of a single instance of resistance to the revolution other than his detachment's actions yesterday.

This he could not fathom.

In the morning, the infirmary's directors wanted to continue the telephone collection of news, but the telephone fell silent. Kutepov regretted he hadn't managed to call his sisters, but yesterday he had let them know where he was.

They were watching out the windows. The pickets were tense and guarding all exits. The owners of the building were very worried—due to Kutepov's presence, although they tried not to show it.

All of a sudden they saw two armored cars and two trucks turning the corner at Kirochnaya. They were all filled with armed workers. The vehicles stopped in the middle of Liteiny, and the workers jumped down, shouted, and pointed out the windows to each other. They attracted workers ambling down Liteiny as well.

From the armored cars they raised their machine-gun barrels at the building windows—and thronged toward the main entrance.

The owners began rushing about. Not opening up was impossible. The senior nurse ran in and started trying to talk Kutepov into putting on a medic's robe; otherwise they'd kill him.

But even now, Kutepov found this saving masquerade repugnant.

He asked the owners to open up and say they knew nothing about him. And leave him completely alone. (Later he realized it would have been strange, impossible even for them not to know about the presence of an un-wounded colonel in uniform. He had put them in a very awkward position.)

Here there was a small corner parlor with doors in adjoining walls; one door let out on a suite of rooms on the Liteiny side, the other to a transverse suite, and opposite each door was a large mirror, so that coming from far away you saw yourself. This room attracted Kutepov, and he decided to await the new regime here. There was a chair in an obscure corner between the doors, and he sat on that, leaving the two doors wide open.

From there he could see a worker carrying a revolver running through each of the suites in each of the mirrors. They looked so much alike—similar height and build, similar dark workman's clothing, and the red rosette on the left side of their chest—that at first he imagined one was the reflection of the other, and then he realized that couldn't be.

Even later he realized that if he could see them from his corner, then each of them had already seen him in his corner. But he did not rise to meet them.

Instead, something else happened: they didn't see him. Or rather, they were probably entranced by how terrifying they looked; it was unlikely they were used to large mirrors. There was also bright sunshine streaming in the windows. They also happened to stand in the doorway not a second before the other but simultaneously—and turning their heads slightly, they saw each other with their pointing revolver and saw that each had run as far as he could, having reached this empty room. Had one of them appeared before the other, he would have had time to survey the room.

Not losing time, they turned just as simultaneously and quickly retraced their route, now showing in the mirror their equally similar backs, but without any red.

They moved off—and Kutepov crossed himself. This was what was called a simple Divine miracle. God had simply averted their eyes. That meant He still had plans for Kutepov.

The building search continued, and they checked the medics and wounded, but no one else came—except the relieved owners themselves half an hour later. They were not only relieved but proud they had been able to safeguard the colonel.

In the attic, the searchers found the weapons the detachment had laid down yesterday, and it took them a long time to carry them out to their trucks—but they left the wounded alone. And drove away again down Kirochnaya—probably to boast to the State Duma.

And lifted all the patrols across from the building.

After going through this, people came to their senses, and everyone told lively stories about what they'd witnessed and thought. They were astonished at the colonel's salvation.

Kutepov begged the owners' forgiveness for everything, but he hoped he could stay here a little longer.

Meanwhile, martial music burst out from Liteiny. Cautiously, Kutepov walked over to the window and was amazed to see not some alien banner but his own Preobrazhensky banner and the Preobrazhensky uniform on the soldiers.

They, too, turned off Liteiny and onto Kirochnaya—also, more than likely, headed for the Duma.

On top of everything else, he had to experience this punishment, this reproach, this humiliation of his own regiment!

It was hard to watch.

He knew, though, that the genuine Preobrazhensky Regiment, and the genuine army, and the genuine men were all at the front, and soon, very soon, any hour now, they would drive out all this vermin.

What was most remarkable and astounding, though, was that the reserve battalion was marching without a single officer. The battalion was led by four noncommissioned officers, sergeants, one of whom, Umrilov, Kutepov easily recognized. There was actually not a single one of the officers who had been so well disposed toward the Duma. What did that mean?

Actually, he noted, the battalion wasn't moving badly at all. Not at all.

[1 8 1]

Rodzyanko lived two blocks from the Duma. He'd had the night, if not the full night, had slept soundly, and had woken up quite refreshed. Instantly, there arose before him an integral picture of all the events of the preceding day and his own heroic conduct. And once more, he wondered at both those things afresh.

Did he repent of having taken power? No, his top position had given him no choice. In the revolutionary situation, even more so than in peacetime, he had naturally become the top arbiter.

His conscience as a loyal subject was also clean: he had been compelled by circumstances and the insistence of well-known individuals who had not wished to concede in a timely fashion, while they still could. It was they who had created all these ruinous circumstances; Rodzyanko was only trying to save Russia.

True, this new situation was very unusual—power assumed without the Emperor's knowledge. But he had telegraphed the Emperor! Why hadn't the Emperor responded?

Those two telegrams Sunday evening and Monday morning were his justification.

And now that power had been taken, what choice did he have? Only to move forward decisively—and consolidate that power. Stand up for it in the face of both the Emperor and revolutionary anarchy.

But this was a difficult balance. Here, the crowd was raging. While there they were sending eight regiments to Petrograd. He had to balance the two.

The President could still make telegraph and telephone attempts to stop the incoming regiments.

Rodzyanko was by no means a mutineer against the throne! Not only did he not want to shake the monarchy itself, he was working to save it!

Instead, it had come to pass that by his midnight decision he had unwillingly joined the opposition to the Supreme Power, and . . .

This was what he had to do, he realized over breakfast: he had to continue to maintain continuous contact with the commanders-in-chief. How grateful and timely were the replies from Brusilov and Ruzsky. He had to continue that contact! He had to quickly send a telegram directive to all the commanders-in-chief of the army groups and fleets saying that the Provisional Committee of the State Duma had simply been compelled to take governmental power because the entire former Council of Ministers had absented itself from governance. A perfectly natural step, and who could think of anything better? The generals would be concerned that military efforts not be broken off, and in this he had to assure them that the Duma Committee was their most loyal ally.

Thus it would be senseless for them to send troops to Petrograd themselves. Yes, this was the correct path!

Naturally, sending direct telegrams to the commanders-in-chief, circumventing the Supreme Commander, meant ignoring the military chain of command. But at the moment, Rodzyanko was not in military service.

With these clear but alarming thoughts, feeling in excellent bodily health, however, Rodzyanko took a motorcar to the Tauride and wanted them to take him all the way to the entrance. You couldn't say that the welter here recognized in him the master of the house or was awaiting him. The people and motorcars were crowded in crosswise, they were living their own excitement, their own movements, and the driver's cry that this was the motorcar of the State Duma's President did not make much of an impression. They drove on a little farther—but in the end he had to get out and just push through.

Perhaps for Shcheglovitov this was a solution—that he was locked in and thereby protected. Otherwise they would tear him to shreds, but this way he was safely hidden. That's all right. He could sit out a few days—and we'd release him.

Even less did the President recognize the interior of his palace. Piled together by the walls of the entrance and Cupola Hall were sacks, barrels, and cases—and there was the unpleasant feeling that the palace was already under siege. A great many soldiers were scurrying about neither in formation or in harmony, as were all kinds of lively, suspicious civilians and especially nimble young people. All of this was in motion, busy doing something—and once again, none of them broke off or stopped what they were doing or moved back to respectfully let the Duma President pass. Such was the invasion of strangers that the Duma itself was hard to recognize. Rodzyanko didn't even try to delve any farther into the Ekaterininsky Hall and, naturally, did not head for the right wing, which since yesterday had been increasingly occupied by that Soviet of their deputies—but headed, rather, to the left, where Duma deputies still resided, albeit in a congested state, holding onto just a few main rooms. Including the office of the President himself, an oasis of reflection.

Rodzyanko reached his presidential desk—and was immediately beset on all sides by the fact that even at dawn, events and alarms and people's desires had not died down.

The most unpleasant thing of all struck the President keenly: in the White Hall of sessions, unknown persons had shredded the large portrait of the Emperor with their bayonets.

It was as if they'd stabbed Rodzyanko himself in the pit of his stomach! The Emperor's large portrait, which had reigned over the hall, behind Rodzyanko! He felt very uneasy.

He couldn't even bring himself to go see with his own eyes. Everyone would see that the President had come, and what of it? Why no clap of thunder? . . . What could he do against this crazed crowd?

Right then there was news: at dawn the Emperor had left GHQ and was moving in the direction of Petrograd!

It was as if he'd learned about the portrait—and was coming to impose punishment.

And stand at the head of his eight regiments?

Storm clouds.

Right then, a call came in on the palace line, Count Benckendorff telephoning from Tsarskoye to say that the heir's health was in a very serious state and the Empress was requesting safety around the palace in this troubled situation.

How many years had this omnipotent Tsaritsa lorded it over the Duma President, shown him disdain, turned the Emperor away from sensible concessions—but here her scanty feminine powers had been curtailed and, quashing her pride, she was asking for help?

Yes, Rodzyanko was himself worried that something bad might happen to the Tsar's family or the heir. Just yesterday evening he had told Belyaev to convey to the palace, and now repeated the same reply to Benckendorff:

"Count! When a house is on fire, the first thing people do is carry out the sick."

It is so very clear. Has she actually not realized she should leave posthaste, to minimize her problems and cares?

Right then Belyaev—speak of the devil—the only one of the ministers, so obliging, telephoned from the Admiralty, for Khabalov, feeling out the possibility of a safe capitulation.

This was good. War had to be avoided in the capital.

But the Tauride had reinforced its own headquarters with the "military commission" the President had allowed last night. Now Guchkov arrived, overjoyed, suggesting that he head up this "commission." An excellent solution! Rodzyanko rejoiced. He was one of us, an Octobrist, and a strong man. An important addition.

Right then another important reinforcement occurred to the President: they should contact the Allies. The English and French ambassadors. And secure their support for the Provisional Committee. This could go a long way toward strengthening the Committee.

A marvelous idea! Not over the telephone, of course; anyway, all city telephones were out now. His own imposing figure could not go, could not escape notice. Rather, send completely confidentially some respectable person who could be trusted to ask the ambassadors to immediately express their opinion about what was going on. (Not that there could be any doubt that they were ecstatic.) And their wishes.

Even . . . even, farsightedly outstripping events . . . what further move did they find desirous . . . in the sense of constitutional changes . . . ?

The Allies' support was worth those eight regiments.

For now he had to choose and instruct a dignitary as an emissary. And sign a circular telegram to the commanders-in-chief saying that the Committee had taken on the difficult task of forming a new government. Then the Committee members, some of whom had spent the night in the Duma, came up to offer their doubts and suggestions.

Suddenly news was brought that an entire battalion was approaching the State Duma! The first fully assembled battalion in all these days!

An important moment that would decide a great deal in further events! People became excited, restive. What regiment is it?

Someone looked from afar and realized it was the Preobrazhensky men!

The Provisional Committee was unprepared for such a joyous surprise, a program had not been drawn up as to who should speak or what he should say.

A pale, high-strung, and self-confident Kerensky rushed to speak. But no, Rodzyanko could not concede the Preobrazhensky Regiment to him; these he had to greet himself! (In addition, he had begun to realize that Kerensky was shouting the wrong things to the crowd.)

With an imperious gesture such as Duma deputies were used to obeying, Rodzyanko indicated that he himself would speak.

However, while they were fussing and deciding here, the battalion and band not only entered the open area and moved toward the front steps but, it turned out, surged inside—and no one dared detain them. The moment was inopportune for Rodzyanko to go out, so he waited. The Preobrazhensky men fell out of formation and blended in inside the entrance hall and Cupola Hall—and then they spread out and fell apart in the Ekaterininsky.

That hall really was suited for military parades, too, and even an inflated reserve battalion standing in four ranks far from filled the whole infantry square.

Mikhail Vladimirovich found it exceptionally pleasant to go out to greet this battalion specifically, which had supported him in the night at the decisive moment. As he was getting ready to go speak, he thought that after his speech he would ask the gentlemen officers to stop by his office—and have a heartfelt talk with them separately.

But before Rodzyanko could reach the formation, someone dashed up and warned him: The battalion's come—without officers! Brought by sergeants.

What's this? How is that possible? What did this mean? Why without officers?

This turned everything on its head. It was the officers who had telephoned to say they were supporting him and their regiment was joining them—and it was the officers who weren't there?

But there was no time to ponder this now. He entered the Ekaterininsky. The sergeants' command rang out: "Attention!"

The larger the hall and the more numerous the audience, the more Rodzyanko's mighty voice cranked up. His speech was unprepared and there was no time to think it through, but his heart showed him the correct way:

"First and foremost, Orthodox warriors," he started off richly, although reminding them: "allow me as an old soldier to greet you." And with new energy, new strength and precision: "Splendid! Well done!"

"Your health! Hurrah! Yr'xcellency!" the tall Preobrazhensky soldiers responded pretty well.

Good. They'd found an initial rapport immediately. Rodzyanko began paternally:

"Allow me to express my thanks to you for coming here. Coming to help the State Duma deputies institute order!"

He surveyed the ranks. No one was objecting.

"And to secure our glory! And the honor of our homeland! Your brothers are fighting there, in far-off trenches, for Russia's greatness, and I'm proud that since the war's very beginning my son has been in the glorious Preobrazhensky ranks." That was one more connection between them. But now to turn them and give them the bit: "In order for you to help the cause of instituting order that the State Duma has taken up, though, you must not be a mob! You know as well as I that without officers, soldiers cannot exist. And now I'm asking you to obey your officers and trust them as we do. Return calmly to your barracks"—he could already sense that the presence of this support in the Tauride could become very trying—"so that at the first call you can go where you are needed."

Clever man, he had comfortably turned everything around! He had turned rebels into patriots. But he had nothing more specific to say about what should be done, and he did not conclude with any commanding words. Because of this a muddle of soldiers' voices rang out. Some were shouting that they were very glad; others that they agreed; and still others asked him to tell them what to do.

But what could he tell them? Rodzyanko labored to explain more:

"The old regime cannot lead Russia out onto the right path. Our first objective is to set up a new regime that everyone trusts and that can glorify our Mother Russia."

They readily agreed to this, too.

After all, by "old regime" he meant only the government and certainly not the Emperor—but could they take it to mean the Emperor? And he had not interfered.

"And so let us not waste time on long conversations. Right now you need to find your officers. Gather up your comrades who have wandered out into the city. Close ranks. Carry out the requirements of military discipline strictly. And await orders from the Provisional Committee of the State Duma. This is the only way to win."

And more heatedly:

"If we do not do this today, tomorrow may be too late. Only full unity of the army, the people, and the State Duma can ensure our might!"

And he covered it all like a booming metal roof:

"Hur-rah!"

A couple of thousand gullets bawled out a truly thunderous "hurrah"— inappropriate, even, in this hall, enough to make its columns sway!

It had all gone excellently.

But there was still the puzzle of what had happened to the officers.

[1 8 2]

*   *   *

After the nighttime departure of the machine-gun regiments' principal forces from Oranienbaum, looting started there of the wine cellars, stores, and shops, as well as disorderly gunfire—for two full days.

Meanwhile the machine-gun regiments marched through the night toward Petrograd, picking up garrisons along the way.

*   *   *

At night's end and still early in the morning, the ransacking of the Astoria Hotel continued; there was something left to drink there and items to profit by.

In order to leave the besieged hotel to go to their embassy across the square, the Italians clustered together carrying a large Italian flag on a pole.

Staying at the Astoria on his Petrograd leave, too, was Lieutenant General Mannerheim, commander of the 12th Cavalry Division. He put on a civilian coat and a fur cap, removed the spurs from his boots, and left the hotel unimpeded. He went over to the industrialist Nobel, who hid him.

Many windows in the hotel were smashed and the heating was cut off.

* * *

Even before first light, bread lines began huddling near the bakeries.

* * *

There was no one to receive the Tsar's nighttime telegram saying the government's resignation had not been accepted. The ministers had not waited around; they'd scattered. Only in the morning did the telegraph office telephone Pokrovsky at home and tell him.

* * *

The District Court burned all night and into the morning. The ceilings collapsed and columns of sparks whooshed up with a crack. The glow brightly lit the warehouses of the Chief Artillery Administration. Amateur pilferers were on the alert. They dragged out cases and smashed them open with axes. Here was a case of soldiers' gloves, which they grabbed. They wouldn't go on their hands—and got tossed to the sidewalk.

* * *

People had had a good night's sleep and early in the morning were again thronging onto the streets, assembling into armed detachments in search of enemies of the revolution. The criminals released yesterday—some dressing as soldiers, some acquiring rifles—became bolder by the hour. There was no barrier to them whatsoever for the full extent of the city. All authority had been swept away, all communications had been cut, and all laws had lost their force. In all the city, each person could protect only himself and expect an attack from anyone and everyone.

There turned out to be many even among the general population who were eager to rob. After yesterday's pogroms, though, the doors and windows of many stores had been solidly boarded up. And there were radiating bullet holes in plate-glass shop windows here and there.

* * *

On the Neva, the Franco-Russian Company had its cruiser *Aurora* under repair. In the morning, workers broke in and the cruiser *joined* the revolution.

They seized rifles, revolvers, and machine guns. The cruiser's commander, Captain First Rank Nikolsky, and two senior officers were dragged out onshore and killed. First Lieutenant Agranovich was wounded in the neck by a bayonet.

*　　*　　*

The search for policemen was renewed early in the morning. They broke into buildings and apartments and searched with and without denunciations. Those running away forced their way through closed gates. Arrested city and local policemen were being led along, some having changed into civilian clothing—one in a cabbie's belted wool caftan, another in a sheepskin vest—and some not having changed at all and wearing their own black greatcoat with the orange cord. Men usually seen as pompous and stern walked along distraught and frightened, with bruises and scratches, beaten.

Here was an old one with a broad neck whom they hadn't let put on his coat. A woman was shouting: "Piss in his face!"

They were led by an overly joyous convoy, five or so to one, some with their rifle on a belt, some over a shoulder, some at the ready, and the most rabid of them in front, his sword bared, pushing passersby aside. And little boys with sticks.

Hostile shouts from the crowd.

A tied-up policeman was being dragged through the snow by his feet. Someone ran up and shot him dead.

*　　*　　*

Whatever police stations hadn't been burned down yesterday—were burning now. Burning in a bonfire in front of a station were chairs and papers, which the flame was tossing up in the air. More and more papers kept being thrown out through the broken windows, and someone was stirring them in the fire with a long stick. Some in the crowd were gawking, some getting warm, little boys were dancing around, flapping the empty sleeves of their mothers' jackets, a merry romp.

Reluctant refugees were taking their belongings out of buildings near the fire and migrating to other buildings. Only those people felt the misfortune.

*　　*　　*

Bonfires near police officers' apartments were also burning the household goods and furniture that had been thrown out.

On Mokhovaya, a piano was hurled through an officer's window and crashed on the sidewalk, only to be finished off with rifle butts on the spot.

A speaker standing on a box was asking his soldier comrades not to throw cartridges into the bonfire; they would be needed in the fight against the counterrevolution. But once they'd started this entertainment, there was no tearing themselves away and everyone started throwing them. The cartridges exploded with a crack, drowning out the speaker.

*   *   *

What was red: everything from large panels to torn strips. And comical red handkerchiefs with white edging. They were attaching red to caps (then it was a cockade), chests, sleeves, bayonets, sabers, and sticks (then it was a flag), tying it around necks, on shoulders. Bows, rosettes, burrs, and ribbons.

A civilian could still get through without red, though he'd be shamed, but a military man who looked like an officer—no way. It was dangerous for an officer to show his face outside at all.

*   *   *

There was merrymaking everywhere. However many soldiers there were in Petrograd—160,000—apparently they were all here. Ordinary citizens, too! The soldiers were embracing the people, and the public was weeping. And no one was silent. Everyone was talking, or shouting, or raving joyously!

To compensate for the slowness of human bodies, trucks and cars were racing madly in all directions. Trucks overflowing with armed men: workers, soldiers, sailors, a university student in ecstasy, and even a young lady, and even an officer with a big scrap of red. Thirty crammed in together, and bayonets bristling from everyone—over the side and pointing up, and also men standing with rifles on the running boards. Blood-red flags were poking out of the trucks as well, three or four apiece. Some had machine guns, too. Or some fool would be aiming his revolver straight ahead, leaning on the cab.

Gigantic bayonet hedgehogs raced and raced, snorting and wailing, overtaking each other and barely missing each other oncoming, and honking, warning, and turning and gnashing gears—a bacchanalia of great big hedgehogs! Unheard-of motorized forces had broken free of their underground slavery and were frolicking, rampaging, promising to show lots lots more.

*   *   *

There was a lot of shooting everywhere, aimed at nothing in particular, and it was dangerous to go anywhere. People were shooting out of mischief. And to vent their nervous excitement. All one soldier had to do was accidently squeeze the trigger for gunfire to take over an entire block. There were people wounded by stray bullets in the bread lines. Shots were fired in the air as a kind of salute. "Enough, of this fighting!" And shots at the ground, at the feet of passersby. Shooting madness. All you heard was bullets flying everywhere, many ricocheting off walls, and because it was all so unfamiliar, people understood nothing and hid from the bullets behind notice columns. Everyone was keyed up because of these incomprehensible close shots. At any moment the crowd could be cast from ecstasy into fear and hatred.

Everyone assured everyone that it was policemen hiding in attics and moving stealthily from roof to roof, which was why the gunfire came from a new place each time. Everyone gazed up anxiously at the attic windows of each large apartment building. No sooner had someone pointed up than everyone was demanding the building be fired upon and searched.

* * *

An officer was walking along in full uniform without any red. Rabble drove him off the street onto a building staircase—where they shot him, splattering the walls with blood and brains.

And this same crowd had carried these same officers through the streets in July 1914! . . . And that same war was still going on.

In a crowd, a man ceases to be himself, and each man ceases to think soberly. Emotions, shouts, and gestures are picked up on and spread, like fire. Apparently, the crowd obeys no one. But it easily follows a leader. But then the leader does not belong to himself and might not recognize himself as leader, only stays afloat on a single surge for two minutes, then dissolves in its wake, becoming a nobody. Only a criminal, only a natural-born killer, only someone infected with vengeance leads and does not falter. This is his element!

* * *

Trucks had been distributing stacks and stacks of the first issue of *Izvestia of the Soviet of Workers' Deputies* from yesterday throughout the city since ten in the morning, passing them out and tossing them from the top; they must have printed hundreds of thousands. A truck would stop, its body shuddering, hands would reach out, and from up top they would throw down bundles and separate leaflets, and people chased after them, tore them out of each others' hands, and snatched them up from the snow. Afterward, everyone on the streets would read this one and only newspaper. But all it had was: the Soviet of Workers' Deputies proclamation that had been wrung out of the literary commission.

In incomparably fewer numbers was the typewritten text, off a collotype, of the first proclamation of the Provisional Committee of the State Duma, stating that such had been created and was assuming responsibility. University students read it out loud, also from the backs of trucks.

*   *   *

A motorcar was driving down Sadovaya and announcing that coming up behind it were three newly joined battalions. Wild enthusiasm and shouts! People waited at the curb. For some reason, though, no battalions ever came.

*   *   *

Meals were disrupted in many barracks. Soldiers roamed the streets, gloomily now—in search of getting something to eat somewhere.

They'd been going around like that all day, many without rifles even, empty-handed. First they were ready to grab a bit more and then they'd shy away: What have we done? Would they be let back into the barracks or would the *civilians* drive them out again?

*   *   *

Vanya Redchenkov worked up his nerve and went out past the barrack gates. Right away he saw an empty truck and a very drunk sailor loitering next to it. Across his shoulder on a cord he had a sword without its sheath and he was holding a revolver. When he saw Vanya, he rejoiced and started shouting and calling him over:

"Comrade! Rrrrr!" he mimed starting up the engine. "Rrrrr?"

"I'm not a driver," Vanya said meekly. "I'm just a new guy here. I don't know."

The sailor wouldn't hear of it, wouldn't let go of his point, and twitched, angry now:

"Rrrrr!"

But at that moment his cord broke and his saber clattered on the icy pavement. He flung himself after the saber—and Vanya fled through the gates.

*
* *

Hey, people, come on out!
High-and-mighty's met his match!
Now we're free to yell and shout!
And a bottle down the hatch!

[1 8 3]

The navy's Decembrists may have been late to events, but events themselves were working in their favor, events themselves were developing extremely well, magnificently, stunningly: the languid, indecisive Duma deputies had nonetheless formed a provisional government from their number! They'd found the nerve! And weren't afraid to inform GHQ of this fact. Let the Colonel find out about events, how they'd finally made a move without his participation!

GHQ was silent for now, bewildered. And the Navy's General Staff had reported from Petrograd here, to the staff of the Baltic fleet, that the entire capital was in the mutineers' hands. The tone made it clear that even the Minister of the Navy sympathized with them. (Grigorovich was a diplomat; both Tsarskoye Selo and the Tauride Palace were always pleased with him.)

Pointed communiqués arrived in the middle of the night, and Vice Admiral Nepenin called in Prince Cherkassky that very night. His like-mindedness was telling the admiral not to wait for events to develop further, not to play for time, not to hide his own opinions or position, but to occupy his position boldly and openly. Candor suited the frankness of Nepenin's character, but also, given these events—so long-awaited but so sudden—to be equal to them! Most of all he valued his sincere relations with the navy, for which all crews had to love him. He liked to make the grand gesture—and not take it back.

He ordered that the crews be told about the upheavals in Petrograd, about the suspicion of certain previous officeholders of treason—and of the creation of the new government.

Actually, before they could send the decree to the ships for announcement, corrective information came in from Petrograd saying that what the Duma deputies had created was not a new government but merely some vague committee. The text of the announcement to the crews had to be changed.

On the other hand, Nepenin felt a desire to himself make a tour of all the dreadnought and battleship squads and himself read out his decree. He treasured the unity with the sailors that arose from one's presence, one's appearance, one's voice, more precious and influential than abstract lines of a decree on strengthening battle readiness—so that the enemy, having received exaggerated reports of our upheavals, would not try to take advantage of them. Admiral Nepenin knew how to speak to the sailors with a manner of rough simplicity that won them over.

After this momentous tour of the ships, when he himself informed his sailors of the onset of a new era, Nepenin assembled the flag officers on the staff's *Krechet* (both Prince Cherkassky and Rengarten were present in connection with their staff duties) and energetically told them that since he had had no instructions whatsoever from GHQ or the Minister of the Navy, he would act as he deemed necessary. And his point of view was noninterference in the revolution. ("Noninterference" in reality meant helping it out at the critical moment.)

Some of the flag officers were in a celebratory mood because of the revolution being made in the name of the homeland's salvation. Others at least did not object. Nor could those who strongly opposed this bring themselves to object either. Sitting here were men older the Nepenin. However, he had surpassed them strikingly with his knowledge, capabilities, and brilliant decisiveness, and this was recognized.

The flag officers assented.

However, at a closed discussion set up for today, three Decembrists still expressed doubts. Was it all that clear? And was Adrian taking a sure enough step?

Cherkassky asked:

"What if something *starts up on the ships?* What will you do, Fedya?" But why would anything start on the ships if the fleet's leadership openly sympathized with the revolution?

No, still. Hypothetically.

Fedya Dovkont replied ingenuously:

"I'm going to support the new regime."

Cherkassky picked up on this:

"You mean you'd go and join up with the mutineers? That's wrong, Fedya. Joining the crowd is easy, but it would be pretty unproductive to perish there by the bullet of some character 'upholding his oath.' You can't be sure the entire sailor mass is going to immediately understand the revolutionary objectives in full and immediately rid itself of its Black Hundreds. No, we need a better thought-out plan."

It was true, there would always be Black Hundred types among the popular crowd, and they cast a shadow over the whole situation so you didn't know what turn to expect.

No, they had to act so as to bring the greatest benefit to the cause as a whole. A better thought-out plan would mean sure influence at the highest levels. They started formulating a plan.

They had to be prepared for GHQ and the Tsar to order the fleet to support the old regime. Then Adrian would face a dilemma, and their circle's task would be to block this reactionary inclination. Our objective would be to do everything to make sure the admiral's decision worked for Russia's salvation, even if it ran counter to orders from above!

Or another instance: if an order from above to suppress didn't come in, but insurrection nonetheless began spontaneously on the ships or in Helsingfors, or in Reval, and demonstrations of sympathy for the revolution arose—and the admiral once again had to decide unilaterally whether to try to impede the upheavals or even use military force to prevent them from being impeded. We would have to bend him toward the latter.

In both instances, the circle's main task was to influence Nepenin in the right direction: Don't submit to the Tsar's orders! And don't impede revolutionary demonstrations! Moreover, to make sure this decision of the admiral's was openly reported to the ships' commands and openly communicated to GHQ. Actually, Nepenin's direct nature was a guarantee of this.

They decided then and there to go to the Commander one by one, from most junior to most senior, and firmly state all these views. Each should even add personally that they would not carry out even *his* order if it was counter to their own convictions! No matter how the first conversation ended—a second and then a third would follow.

Moreover, Rengarten took on cultivating Captain First Rank Shchastny and Cherkassky Captain First Rank Kedrov; their position was influential and they had to be drawn in.

Documents – 3

TO THE COMMANDERS-IN-CHIEF OF ALL ARMY GROUPS AND OF THE BALTIC AND BLACK SEA FLEETS

13 March 1917

The Provisional Committee of the State Duma, having taken into its hands the creation of normal conditions of life and governance in the capital, invites the Army and Navy to maintain complete calm and nurture full confidence that the common cause of the struggle against the foreign enemy will not be undermined or weakened for a minute. . . .

The Provisional Committee, with the assistance of forces and units in the capital and with the sympathy of the population, will in the near future establish calm in the rear and restore proper activity.

Provisional Committee Chairman

Rodzyanko

[184]

The Empress's mind had always worked at night and even on untroubled days often waited until three to get to sleep or even four in the morning—so when could she have fallen asleep today? She rose early. The doctors' prescriptions to stay in bed in the morning had ceased to be her rule; events called for extraordinary actions and decisions.

Always before, though, when Nicky went to GHQ, she had had tested methods for her actions: learn the correct decision from their Friend, then meet with the ministers and suggest these actions to them and repeat the same work in long letters to the Emperor.

But now events had ensued that exceeded all that had come before in their menace—but their Friend was no longer alive and not a single minister could be summoned, all communications were lost—and there was nowhere to send a letter to the Emperor, and it was still unknown what his arrival might bring this coming night. Through whom would he rule over events?

The Empress was full of the most masculine decisiveness and was pre-pared for the most courageous actions, but now she felt she could not do without a man's arm and support—and she had no such man in her entire suite. All the senior generals and colonels were merely her subordinates and could offer no supporting arm.

No, there was one! Aide-de-Camp Sablin was not merely an aide-de-camp but "wholly ours" (as she and their Friend had once established), "one of two honest friends" (the first being Anya), a part of all of us, almost a member of the imperial family, who had identical views of everything, a warm heart, a noble gaze, and who shared all their joys and sorrows, a companion during the best days of their yacht cruises, the Emperor's companion at GHQ. True, he was young, but the Empress had been guiding him for many years. He himself was unmarried and had no close family or friends, and he always said that no one was closer to him than the Tsar's family.

But now, so nearby in Petrograd, where had he been all day yesterday? Why hadn't he rushed here when he saw the turn of events? The Empress waited for him until late in the evening, but he never appeared. This was cause for astonishment. What so insuperable could have prevented him?

Early this morning she walked into the red drawing room, where Lili Dehn had spent the night and had not yet arisen—and asked her to tele-phone Sablin immediately and find out why he hadn't come.

Lili got through quickly. Sablin turned out to be at home, and Lili told him how the Empress needed his support and was waiting for him, but Sablin replied that his entire building was surrounded by fires and the streets were being vigilantly guarded by mutinous sailors—so there was no possibility of him coming.

In his aide-de-camp uniform? Couldn't he get through in civilian dress, though? His refusal was stunning. The unhealthy flush of the Empress's face intensified. She rested her hand on her expanded heart and held it there. Anyone else could shirk his duty like that! But not her very own Sablin!

Meanwhile, taking advantage of the telephone's continuous operation, Lili was able to call home, speak with the nanny, learn about her son, and also telephone several friends—and gather information, what they knew about events and were seeing around them. All the information was terrible: the city was done for, all the old authorities were gone, no one knew even of any loyal troops—but they did know that in the Duma Rodzyanko had an-nounced the creation of a Provisional Committee to govern events.

This last news the Empress actually liked. This meant that at the last mo-ment the Duma had appreciated the danger it itself had caused and had come to its senses. After all, there already was some committee of socialists and revolutionaries that didn't recognize the Duma. So in these ominous hours of mutiny and chaos even these Duma characters were closer to us, one could still talk to them in some kind of human language. Aide-de-Camp

Linevich, who had been sent to see Rodzyanko, had not yet returned. How would Rodzyanko receive him?

They were hiding everything from their sick children, who didn't know what was going on. Even now the children didn't know that everything had been balancing on a knife's edge since yesterday as to whether or not they would leave. Several times over this sleepless night, the Empress had inclined in one direction and then the other.

She was now pacing from room to room, biting her lips, going to and from her patients.

She liked the responsibility and always liked her own definite opinions, her own unerring decisions, but today this responsibility was too much for her! If only her daughters and Anya had been sick and not her son, she might have summoned the nerve to go. But how could she risk the heir, his skin cracked with rash, with a fever, a cough, and sore eyes—how could she risk the concentrated hope of the dynasty and Russia?

Perhaps this illness of the children's was for the good. Who knew God's will? Perhaps their illness was their salvation, for no one would make an attempt on their lives.

Never had she felt so seriously that one might *not know*, driven minute by minute, which decision was right and which was wrong; here it was slipping through her fingers! At this moment, she would have asked her Emperor and husband and would have proceeded without argument however he ordered, but right now he was en route and their communications had been cut off.

Where was she going to break away and go if he would be arriving himself the next night?

What was strange was something else, that since late yesterday evening, even since yesterday, the entire day, she had been bombarding him with desperate telegrams, and he, so responsive to her every word, had not responded that he had heard her alarm.

Then again, there was the cavalry from Novgorod (on its way? already approaching?)—and that was his best reply.

Not imagining how early the Empress had been awake, only at ten o'clock in the morning did Benckendorff and General Groten request an audience with her.

Their news from the city had been the nighttime call from General Khabalov in the Winter Palace and the difficult position for the loyal troops. Their report was that, according to Voeikov's instructions, they had since yesterday, without reporting to the Empress, been making preparations for her own train—and now all was ready for loading and departure if she so ordered!

Oh! Once again, and so agonizingly, they were demanding this decision from her!

No! Definitely not! This would be ruinous for the children. (And how much more trouble to evacuate the capricious Anya with her full suite of doctors.) They would await the Emperor's arrival here. There was less than twenty-four hours left.

Instead, overcoming her aversion, she instructed Benckendorff to telephone Rodzyanko and remind him of the heir's illness and request protection for the imperial family.

Tsarskoye Selo was no longer calm. There were officers and soldiers who had fled revolutionary Petrograd—both entire detachments and singly—a company of Volynians, a mixed group from the Petrograd Regiment—but they found no shelter in the regiments stationed here and marched on, to Gatchina. The reserve battalions of imperial riflemen—how do you like that!—had been stirred up, too. From their barracks they could hear gunfire and then music and songs. People were saying that there had been clashes between the different men, those wishing to rebel and those not. People were saying that revolutionary vehicles had arrived from Petrograd. (True, the Tsarskoye Selo commandant transmitted reassurance to the palace that the Tsarskoye Selo artillery had no shells. How about that? This was meant as reassurance? *What* were we afraid of?)

Benckendorff returned from the telephone. Rodzyanko hadn't promised anything and had said only this: "When a building is on fire, the first thing people do is carry out the sick."

My God, how pitiless! What a terrible thing to say! The specter of that decision—carrying out the sick—again approached.

Commandant Groten, seeing the Empress's agonized hesitations, proposed strengthening the Convoy and Combined Regiment and bringing the Guards Crew into the palace as well.

The Empress beamed and immediately agreed. Of all the Guards, beloved units under the imperial family's patronage, the Guards Crew was the most beloved of all, in its heart close to the entire family.

The healthy younger daughters, hearing that they were bringing in the Crew, rejoiced: "It will be just like on the yacht! Cozy!"

Right then Count Apraksin, head of the Empress's chancellery, reported. He had made his way from Petrograd dressed as a civilian, without his court regalia. Scenes from the insane capital stood before his eyes, which made it all the more stunning to him that here, in the palace, it was as if nothing had changed. He set about vigorously trying to convince the Empress of the mounting danger that could surge here at any moment. He believed without a doubt that she must leave urgently and go to—Novgorod!

At the word "Novgorod," a bright light passed over the Empress's weary, flushed face, which, due to her many illnesses always looked older than her years, and in the last few days even harsher. This was what Apraksin had been counting on:

"Novgorod, exactly, which has been so devoted to the dynasty, Your Majesty! Somewhere a pure place like that had to be found where loyal people could gather and where the resistance could begin. In any case, the most august children will be in safety there. That is worth the risk of moving even the sick!"

A smile of glorious reminiscence shone on the Empress's hard, elongated face—hard, like all her smiles. But her smile already held a refusal. She shook her head with assurance.

The count couldn't imagine how dangerous it was to transport the sick in this condition. Nor was there any necessity as yet. Ancient Novgorod would itself come here and rescue us.

But how could they hold out until this rescue? Until the Emperor's arrival?

The Empress paced around the room, beset by doubts. She needed a man's support, not subordinate individuals—right now, this minute! She couldn't withstand any greater burden of decisions—not just for her family and palace, after all, but for Petrograd, which had been left in her care!

And why had Pavel, who was sitting right here in Tsarskoye Selo, not come, not shown himself, not made his presence known, not requested orders? The eldest of the grand dukes! The most senior of the adjutant generals! Was he that wounded over the many years of family insult? Had he felt that rejected by the Tsar's ban after their Friend's murder?

This silent contest of self-esteems—the Empress's and Pavel's—had been going on for days. Who would yield first? . . .

After all, though, he was the Inspector of the Guards! He was obligated to, after all! If the Guard would not obey him, let him go to the front and have loyal men brought from there.

She shared this with Lili, who offered a golden thought: Perhaps Grand Duke Pavel Aleksandrovich didn't dare violate etiquette. What if he simply didn't dare be the first to address her?

Could that be? Then this opened up the possibility of the Empress addressing him first and in so doing lift the ban.

"Lili, my sweet, telephone the grand duke in my name and say I have asked him to come here immediately, to the palace."

But this decision did nothing to ease things for her; there had yet to be an answer from Pavel. It was eleven thirty when Commandant Groten came again and reported that they had had word from the railroad that in two hours all lines would be cut and all traffic stopped.

Two hours! So even if she did make up her mind to go, there wouldn't be time to gather up!

The noose was tightening!

So—should she go? What was right?

[1 8 5]

The night had passed in the wheeled battalion, and the scouts sent to District headquarters had not returned. Nor had District headquarters sent anyone else with instructions. And the telephone had been out of service since the previous night.

So Colonel Balkashin had learned nothing about what was happening in the city. What should he do? Everything had collapsed like a sudden landslide. Yesterday morning he had arisen to begin the battalion's usual training day—and had been besieged straightaway by an unexpected and unknown foe. He was unprepared and unequipped and didn't have a single instruction, such as rarely happens even in war.

That night he had had an idea: since the crowds had dispersed, go out in battle formation to the center of the city. There would be no obstacles; all the rebels would be asleep. However, he did not have the right to abandon the battalion's large complex and all its technical equipment, which would be cleaned out; they'd already started in on the garages on Serdobolskaya.

No signs had reached him of battles being waged in the city or of loyal troops resisting. But even harder to imagine was how a garrison of 150,000 men could collapse in a faint, impotent, all at once.

So Balkashin left his wheeled units where they were.

Early in the morning, intense shooting could be heard from their storehouse on Serdobolskaya. But he did not send reinforcements. Everything there, at least, was behind the walls of a stone building, whereas here there were wooden barracks, a wooden fence, and basically no protection.

He ordered trenches dug in the frozen ground along the smaller perimeter. But there weren't enough crowbars and pickaxes.

Meanwhile, on Sampsonievsky Prospect, crowds of armed workers and soldiers had gathered once again—and they were very angry.

Then two armored vehicles drove up—a frightening weapon in street fighting!—and aimed machine guns at the wheeled units' barracks. And stopped there.

If he tried to storm them, there would be losses.

And it wasn't his call to start.

Right then a third armored vehicle came up.

Oh, if only they'd left in the night!

There were shouts to surrender.

The wheeled units were silent.

And then the machine guns started firing.

And there was nowhere to take cover! Helpless targets awaiting a bullet at any point, each barracks had wounded and dead.

Their own six machine guns answered through the windows and cracks, also unshielded, drawing fire. Captain Karamyshev, commander of the machine-gun crew, himself fired and cut down someone.

There was nothing to bandage the wounded with. They had never prepared for battle here, and there was nowhere to evacuate. They just lay there and suffered through to the end.

The battalion still bore through the cross fire. The rebels fell silent. It got quiet.

One of the company commanders tried to persuade Colonel Balkashin to surrender. Balkashin shamed him.

The crowd came closer—and started trying to knock down the fence. A section did fall. And they set fire to the fallen fence in two places.

He felt sorry for the poor soldiers. But it would have been against all military regulations to surrender to a savage crowd. Balkashin made a tour of the barracks and tried to convince the companies to hold out.

Meanwhile, the crowd also set fire to the outermost barracks, which they had to abandon and then gather in the middle ones.

Right then—it was already past noon—two three-inch guns joined the besiegers. They took up battle position—and started smashing the barracks at point-blank range, creating breaches, setting fire to the walls! It was worse than the front, where men sit in the earth. Ceilings came crashing down, along with bunks and soldiers' trunks. The barracks were no longer a safe haven, and those who survived dashed out into the yard and ran behind the mounds of snow, while others threw away their rifles.

Then Colonel Balkashin made one final attempt. He began lining up the training detachment with the band in front in order to surprise and wedge through, so the others could follow behind.

But they were cut off by buckshot and bullets and weren't allowed to prepare a forward rush, and the soldiers began to flee.

Where were they supposed to break through, anyway? A long stretch of Sampsonievsky had been entirely blocked by the crowd, after all.

Then Balkashin raised his arm to indicate to his men in the yard that he would fix everything immediately. And without exchanging words with any of the officers, he went out past the gates alone.

His unexpected appearance provoked a cessation of shooting. The St. George officer, who had been wounded several times before, here, too, raised his arm, calling for attention, and in a thick, commanding voice announced:

"Everyone listen! The soldiers of the wheeled units aren't to blame. Don't fire at them! I was the one who gave them the order to defend the barracks, upholding my oath. But now I am giving . . ."

Suddenly it hit them! A ragged volley burst out, some firing sooner, some later, and the colonel fell down dead.

And they rushed to finish him off with bayonets and knives.

The crowd ran past, through the gates, especially to kill any officers they saw. And to beat soldiers.

Some managed to run through the snow-covered gardens.

Fires were burning in many places and there were clouds of smoke.

The soldiers came out to surrender with raised hands.

And were beaten.

[1 8 6]

It was a miracle: it had come to pass! And so instantaneously that not a single head could fathom it: the oppressive, three-hundred-year regime had fallen so easily, it was as if it had never been! Just last night the full significance of it could not have been appreciated. But this morning they had woken up and learned that the revolution had won out everywhere—of its own accord, without a sound, the way snow can fall at night, regally adorning everything. Of course, all the rest of Russia still lay in darkness and obscurity, but already Admiral Nepenin had telegraphed from Helsingfors to say that the entire Baltic Fleet had joined the revolution.

So bloodless a victory! An incredible celebration! For some reason, the Tsarist regime's resistance had always been envisioned in long, deadly battles. The victory's surprise made Shingarev feel deep down both a joyous luminescence and also an alarming letdown. It was so good as to be alarming, as if this could not possibly be the case. This morning, the Kadet Central Committee had gathered for breakfast at Vinaver's and discussed how to slow the revolution.

Many Duma deputies were in this same state of emotional disarray. They were lounging around the Tauride Palace—no, they were elbowing their way through their usual rooms—in that timidity, distress, and indeterminacy when you don't know how to behave.

How many times in his three-piece suit, starched shirt, and tie had Shingarev crossed this ordinarily deserted Ekaterininsky Hall, occasionally with the addition of a well-dressed public in the gallery, walked through, always devoted heart and soul to the needs of the huge, albeit unseen, amorphous "people," the focus of all his thoughts and all his speeches—and never had he dreamed that this "people" might itself show up in the Tauride Palace— several thousand of them, ten thousand. Infinitely touching was the trust with which soldiers had quit their units and come to the State Duma specifically, having heard of it, trusting it, the temple of free speech, to come under its roof and protection. After all, for many of them, who were not from Petrograd, this city was darker than the forest primeval, and here they had found themselves a reliable light and haven.

How much marvelous naiveté had there been in this coming to the Duma with a marching band to listen to encouraging speeches! The Life Grenadiers had gone straight to the Ekaterininsky Hall and immediately fallen into formation. Rodzyanko stood on a chair that was even heavier and stronger than he himself and bawled out a greeting over their heads.

And the Life Grenadiers barked back "Your health!" with gusto such as was not heard from the combined Potemkin band after the taking of Izmail.

"Thank you!" Rodzyanko thundered. "Thank you for coming to help us restore the order destroyed by the incompetence of the old authorities! The State Duma has formed a Committee to lead our glorious homeland onto the path of victory and ensure its glorious future. . . . Orthodox soldiers! Listen to your officers. They will teach you no ill. The gentlemen officers who brought you here are in full agreement with the State Duma deputies."

Where had he come up with this? Some officers looked like they'd come to their execution—heads hanging, eyes unseeing.

"I beg you to disperse calmly to your barracks. Once again, thank you for coming here! Long live Holy Russia! Hurrah for Mother Russia!"

The "hurrah" was eagerly picked up and rolled out. And Rodzyanko carefully climbed down from the chair.

Climbing onto the chair after him with some difficulty was Milyukov, who was also none too accustomed to such exercises. He began without even a greeting, perhaps not finding one. Even more, his voice was wrong, especially for this kind of crowd. Never in his life had Pavel Nikolaevich spoken before common folk, only in front of academic and parliamentary audiences. However, his mustache bristled decisively and he gazed quite boldly at the soldiers' formation. And in a raspy voice he insisted:

"Since power has fallen from our enemies' hands, we must take it into our own. And we must do so immediately. Today. What do we need to do today?" Milyukov asked rhetorically. "To do this we must first of all be organized, united and subordinate to a single authority."

The unintelligible drift of his words went right by the formation. He just didn't know how to speak at such a moment! Shingarev knew how his own voice sounded, incomparably convincing everyone even before he spoke. Just let him speak and his sincere touch would immediately gather in the sympathy of all Petrograd's soldiers and convince them of everything it should! But he wasn't a member of the Duma Committee, and the Kadet party had a rather strict hierarchy and division of duties.

"The Provisional Committee of the State Duma is just such an authority. We must submit to it and no other authority!" the stern gentleman in the starched collar and spectacles insisted fervently to the soldiers. "For dual power is dangerous and threatens to scatter and disintegrate our forces."

Shingarev got to wondering why he was raising the threat of "dual power"? If he meant the throne, then dual power was the Committee's only possibility for now. But if he meant the disorderly revolutionaries holding rallies here, in the Tauride Palace, then they weren't amounting to much of a power.

Pavel Nikolaevich totally avoided the word "revolution" and did not mention the ongoing war with Germany (so as not to lose his audience at the very first step?). His tedious voice dragged out his tedious line of arguments, and brief flashes of clarity made no inroads:

"Remember, the sole condition of our strength is organization! A disorganized crowd does not embody power. We must get organized today. Anyone who doesn't have one, go find an officer to stand under, an officer under the command of the State Duma. Remember, the enemy does not nod."

Only toward the end did something break through the jumble of repetitions: "The enemy is preparing to wipe us off the face of the earth." To encourage the soldiers or perhaps himself, he asked: "That's not going to happen, is it?"

"It's not!" they shouted separately and uncertainly to him.

Even the soldiers sensed the oddity of this joy, this victory, which seemed boundless but without any fullness whatsoever.

The grenadiers turned and shuffled noisily, starting to free space for some other arriving battalion.

Shingarev walked over to Milyukov. Pavel Nikolaevich blinked, apparently displeased with himself, a sour expression. He was feeling battered. Early this morning he had spoken unsuccessfully before the soldiers at the Okhta. But he'd had enough psychological energy to work through what was unpleasant on his own.

By convention between them, Shingarev, number two in the Kadets' Duma faction, always consulted with Milyukov about what he should do. Now that they'd driven out the blind and insane regime, someone had to sit down and go to work in its place. He was quite prepared when Milyukov said apprehensively:

"Andrei Ivanych, those fast thinkers from the Soviet of Workers' Deputies have already set up their own food supply commission. They could take over all food supplies right now—and that's the feeding conduit. We have to defend our positions there. You know, for now, until the situation becomes clear, why don't you go see them where they're meeting and try to become chairman. After all, you're smarter than all of them. And of all the Kadets, you're the most abreast of the topic."

Shingarev agreed. In the past few months, he had indeed been drawn imperceptibly, even privately, into the discussion about bread. Yes, he should join that commission. Until Kadet power was stronger, and Shingarev could worthily take up his parliamentary specialty, which he had trained in for so many years: finance.

As they had always supposed, Shingarev was to be Minister of Finance.

[1 8 7]

General Nikolai Iudovich Ivanov, the anticipated savior of the homeland and throne, got little sleep that night. Once the worrying starts, there's no sleeping. He woke early, as was his habit. In the morning come the best ideas! How could he start out for Petrograd and lead the troops entrusted to him without properly analyzing this confused Petrograd situation? Clearly, he first had to obtain the fullest possible clarifications. And the best way to do this was by summoning Khabalov to the direct telegraph line and proposing he answer the main questions. Of which, Iudovich calculated as he sat at a little table on his favorite upholstered sofa in the train car, there were ten.

He was already at the general quartermaster's section with these questions by eight in the morning (meanwhile thinking over as well his report to Alekseev concerning the imposed dictatorship and how to avoid it, and his instruction to his adjutant to purchase food here in Mogilev, where there was so much of it, for the general's acquaintances in the capital.)

They requested Petrograd. From the rooms of the General Staff a reply came that General Khabalov was at the Admiralty and, if he left there, revolutionaries could arrest him on the street. But for now there was a spur of the direct line to the Admiralty so you can be connected.

(That was the situation in the capital! So where was he to go? . . .)

Fine, then, let him reply at least through a proxy. They transmitted the ten questions.

Alekseev was already up. And Nikolai Iudovich presented to him on his adjutant general's telegram that the previous night, at about three in the morning, His Imperial Majesty had seen fit to order him to report to the Supreme Commander's chief of staff, who was to report to the prime minister, that all the ministers were to carry out all of Adjutant General Ivanov's demands without question. If the credibility of this authority required verification through communication with the royal train, General Ivanov was prepared to wait.

There could be no such verification right now, yet Alekseev could not confirm such an important instruction based on a verbal communication. But he informed the general that he had given orders to provide him with additional artillery, even heavy artillery, en route.

Ivanov reminded him that given how very few troops he had, Guards from the Southwestern Army Group should be added.

Beyond this, Alekseev did nothing to speed up Ivanov's departure and interfered no more.

But Nikolai Iudovich's mission had two parts: if he did have to defend himself, then he'd want more troops; but if he didn't have to fight (as seemed to be the case based on the Petrograd situation), then they could be fewer and could approach as belatedly as possible because then he would have to answer less to the new government for this whole journey.

He neither insisted to the chief of military transport nor sent a categorical telegram to Ruzsky in the Northern Army Group and Evert in the Western covering specific deadlines for supplying all these infantry and cavalry regiments but merely indicated that he would be waiting not today but early tomorrow morning at the Tsarskoye Selo station. Some of these regiments had not yet set out, some were already on troop trains, still others were preparing to embark at their initial stations. With such a mass of troops, his mission could not end well! In any event, he did not assign a single unit to go directly to Petrograd but told them to stop just shy of it.

Meanwhile, the St. George battalion, light brown epaulets with a ribbon down the center, many with three and four George crosses apiece, and led by General Pozharsky, was already quite prepared to move, although it, too, seemed to lack great zeal. Pozharsky was not at all like the valorous prince on Red Square, not wiry but fat and greatly displeased with this journey, as was evident.

The adjutant general himself, who had his own train car, was not going with them yet. He had to stay back a little longer to look around, think, and await Khabalov's replies.

At twelve o'clock, Khabalov's reply to the ten questions arrived.

And so: Which units were in order and which were misbehaving? The few under Khabalov's command were named; the others had gone over to the revolutionaries or were neutral with them by agreement. Which train stations were being guarded? They were all in the revolutionaries' power.

Not much of a start. . . .

In which parts of the city was order being maintained? The entire city was in the revolutionaries' power, the telephones weren't functioning, and there were no communications with the different parts of the city.

So then from which side could he enter the city?

Were all the ministries functioning properly? Khabalov didn't think any were anymore.

Were there many weapons in the mutineers' hands? Mutineers held all the artillery facilities. Which military authorities were at your command? Just the chief of staff.

Well. Given these answers, the correct decision for Adjutant General Ivanov would have been not to go at all.

But there are times when a general has as much freedom as a soldier.

All he could do was drag his train car behind the St. George battalion.

[188]

All that night, Minister of War Belyaev had been no burden to Khabalov at all. He hadn't interjected a single order or offered a single piece of advice. The line to GHQ was still functioning, and the palace telephone line had been preserved—and he sat there, nearby, receiving communiqués and sending communiqués and compiling reports.

Close to noon, an adjutant showed up from the Minister of the Navy and in the name of his superior demanded the Admiralty be cleared out immediately. Otherwise the rebels promised in twenty minutes to open fire from the Peter and Paul Fortress—over which a red flag had in fact appeared.

So there you had it. Grigorovich hadn't even brought this news himself. He'd wanted to drive them out for a long time, but he couldn't bring himself to do so in his own name, so he was glad at the pretext.

Now that push had come without which they could not extricate themselves from their disastrous ossification. The ultimatum and short deadline compelled the command to make a decision.

But what was there to decide? Move again? There was nowhere to go except perhaps back to the city governor's offices. But there was scarcely any point to that. A meeting was held of the senior officers present, in the room (they'd forgotten about Belyaev), and a rushed one at that, since they only had twenty minutes.

Everyone was of one mind: a continued defense was impossible. But they couldn't leave with weapons, either. If they came out with weapons, the crowd would attack and our men would respond. That meant we had to put down our weapons here, in the Admiralty, store them here for safekeeping and go out unarmed. The crowd wouldn't attack troops like that.

Surrender outright? There wasn't anyone to surrender to, there were no such troops. They would just disperse unarmed, to their barracks, to their apartments.

Commands raced through the Admiralty's long and booming formal halls and courtyards. The artillery dragged their gun-locks into a pile. Machine guns and rifles were thrown into the large room designated by the building superintendent.

Everyone felt relief. It was ending somehow, and ending without a single shot fired. Good.

Except for Colonel Potekhin on crutches, who was furious, and maybe two or three others.

Everyone rushed to disperse, riding or on foot. (The twenty minutes passed several times over, but the Peter and Paul Fortress didn't fire.)

A battery drove through the gates on Palace Square to return to Pavlovsk. Past the gates they were immediately beset by young women and men who tied red scraps of fabric to their weapons, caissons, and horses' harnesses.

A "hurrah" rang out from various clusters on the streets and there was shooting into the air.

The Izmailovsky men came out traveling light and singing: "Soar, falcons, soar like eagles!"

A few riflemen refused to surrender their weapons and left with them. No one bothered them particularly.

City Governor Balk had released the last police earlier that morning; now they could not have left unharmed.

In the confusion, they didn't notice where Generals Belyaev and Zankevich had disappeared.

Of the remaining generals and higher ranks the building superintendent demanded that they vacate all occupied rooms and move to the tea room on the third floor.

There, with windows on Senate Square, they had a large overview.

An overview for contemplation, had anyone been so inclined.

The higher ranks took seats and dulled their hunger with cigarettes.

Later the danger from stray bullets (some were cracking against the walls and on the roof nearby) forced them to move to a room that looked onto the inner courtyard.

Freed from his exorbitant burden, Khabalov now paced and thought.

And this is what he thought: none of the Petrograd figures knew him by face; his photograph had never been printed. If he were detained separately from his staff, he could say he was a Cossack general on leave.

[1 8 9]

With the unswervingness of military habit, once having understood and accepted his orders, General Alekseev honestly pursued them as far as their own logic required. That night, after giving his first instructions about sending troops to Petrograd the previous evening, Alekseev had known no rest. After seeing the Emperor off, he went to bed irritated, but could barely sleep. Mentally he added up all the troops being sent and saw that they were lacking artillery.

At two in the morning he rose and dressed. His aides were all asleep. Fine. He liked it that way. He went to the communications room himself. And dictated a telegram to the Northern Army Group and the Western about each sending additionally one cavalry and one infantry battery apiece, not forgetting to add about sending shells.

Each telegram began as follows: "The Sovereign Emperor has enjoined. . . ." It was a grave moment, and who knew what resistance might arise there to carrying this out, but you don't argue with the Sovereign Emperor. That was why he needed to be here, at GHQ, and it was a pity he had left, though Alekseev had no desire to admit this to the Army Group commanders-in-chief.

Right then Alekseev was handed a telegram from the Minister of War for the palace commandant. This was the protocol for when they wanted it to be brought directly to the Emperor's attention. Telegrams like this usually bypassed Alekseev, but Voeikov was at the train station already, and the telegram had to be read. It was brief but stunning. The rebels had occupied the Mariinsky Palace; some ministers had managed to escape, while about the others there was no information.

So there was no more government at all! While negotiations were under way as to whether or not it should resign, it no longer existed. . . .

Well, well.

But maybe this was for the best. Maybe this was the way to establish a ministry of public trust and no military actions of any kind would be necessary. . . . Even better.

He sent this on to catch up with Voeikov at the train station. Maybe the Emperor would realize his mistake and return.

The long-ailing Alekseev still lay there and dozed but didn't sleep—and for some reason was gripped by concern for Moscow. It was hard to imagine all the consequences if this spread to Moscow as well. Once again he rose and dressed, and once again he went to the telegraph room: once something has been conceived, it's terrible to delay it for even an hour. Shortly before four in the morning he sent a telegram to General Mrozovsky, commander of the Moscow District, inquiring about the moods in Moscow and presenting to him, in the Emperor's name, the authority to declare a state of siege for Moscow at any moment. He especially drew attention to the Moscow rail hub, on which the movement of grain to the army groups and many provinces depended.

This was the last thing for the night. He was tired and fell asleep for a few hours.

Upon awakening after eight in the morning assurance arrived from Evert that the designated regiments were beginning embarkation at noon; and a brief, gloomy message from Khabalov saying that no loyal troops remained and the situation had reached an extreme point. . . .

Right then an admiral from naval headquarters came to see Alekseev and showed him two telegrams from the Admiralty. One had been lying there since the night, but everyone had been asleep, and the second had come this morning. The morning one reported that the rebels had occupied the entire city, Khabalov had settled in the Admiralty as a last redoubt, and this would serve only the useless destruction of precious documents and instruments.

This was very bad. Alekseev began sending more and more telegrams on reinforcing Ivanov. From the Northern Army Group, another battalion from the Vyborg Fortress Artillery. If the troops being sent had to wage a battle against the entire large city, they could not do it without solid artillery.

A great deal had been put together. But Ivanov—Ivanov was no good.

However, the Emperor had so ordered.

And had himself left.

Ivanov had been in no hurry to leave, and the deadlines were now his business.

But the Minister of War was there somewhere, too! Alekseev was obligated to telegraph him the new, oral, supreme order: seek out all means to convey to all the ministers (no matter where they were or whether they comprised a government) that they were obligated to carry out faithfully all requests from Adjutant General Ivanov, commander-in-chief of the Petrograd District.

The Minister of the Navy was there, too! He had to be warned to assist and even obey Ivanov as well. And thinking for Grigorovich, Alekseev gave him a telegram: If Ivanov so demanded, allot him two solid battalions from the Kronstadt Fortress Artillery.

Thus he sent telegrams as they came to mind, nearly every five minutes, as long as the line to the Admiralty was functioning.

Grigorovich did not reply. But Belyaev was in one piece and not dozing and had not abandoned his post! Such a thing could not have been predicted when he was appointed Minister of War merely for his knowledge of foreign languages. And now he was managing to tap out his own telegrams.

Before Alekseev could send one, another would arrive from Belyaev: the troops were abandoning their weapons and going over to the rebels' side, the ministries' normal life had ended, Pokrovsky and Krieger-Voinovsky had barely escaped the Mariinsky Palace in the night. The arrival of a reliable armed force was desirable, otherwise the rebellion could grow. . . .

Yes. The gloomy burden had only increased, along with an awareness of how little had been accomplished. Sullen and hunched, Alekseev walked between the desks—and once Ivanov had left decided on a major addition: to send to Petrograd troops from the Southwestern Army Group as well, as Ivanov had requested. And not just any regiments but three Guards regiments, including the Preobrazhensky itself. He might also have to ready a Guards cavalry division.

He sent this telegram to Brusilov.

Seemingly, this would be more than enough.

The Emperor had acted badly abandoning GHQ and leaving at a time like this. But General Alekseev now felt somewhat freer. He didn't have to run fussily with each telegram and report and try to persuade; he could sit at his desk and take decisions.

On the other hand, no matter how little the Emperor had done as Supreme Commander here, nonetheless, given the stress of events, it would have been easier to feel his protective cover. The way a rifle's gunstock needs a firmly attached shoulder in order not to recoil.

But what was this? It was already nine o'clock, the imperial letter trains were en route, and not a single confirmation had come from them. (Only Voeikov could send anything; station chiefs did not have the right to report.) The Emperor had not simply left, he had left without communications capability! His station could only be estimated. If something were even more urgent, how could Alekseev get in touch?

Meanwhile, worse news was coming in from Petrograd over private lines saying that military and police officers were being killed, many buildings were on fire, and the State Council President had been arrested!

Contradicting this was a telegram sent by the Duma President saying that power had transferred to the Provisional Committee of the State Duma. That wasn't bad at all, and now he could hope for the restoration of order.

Even GHQ hadn't had time to absorb the news, so what could the army group commanders-in-chief know? Alekseev ordered a detailed report compiled for them of all Petrograd events of the past few days and after noon he sent it off, accompanied by the following conclusion:

"We all bear a sacred duty to our Emperor and our homeland to uphold the loyalty to the oath among the troops of the field armies."

So long as the army didn't flinch and the transport lines were maintained, the Petrograd rebellion wouldn't be hard to overpower.

The transport lines. . . . Alekseev inquired by telegram of the foolhardy Belyaev, who was apparently the sole public figure in Petrograd now: where was Krieger-Voinovsky, the Minister of Roads and Railways, who had managed to escape the Mariinsky Palace. Could his ministry run the railroad network?

Belyaev didn't hesitate to find out and in less than an hour replied conscientiously that the Minister of Roads and Railways was hiding in someone's private apartment and could not perform his functions.

For this instance, though, the post of Deputy Minister of Roads and Railways in the theater of military actions that Gurko had created at GHQ might be useful. Authority over the entire railroad network could be transferred to him without delay.

Holding this position at GHQ was General Kislyakov. Up until now his post had had a low profile, and Alekseev had not dealt with him. But now he had become the most central of figures. And Alekseev wrote him an order saying that he was immediately taking over, through him, administration of all the country's railroads.

He was all the more insistent because of the recent upheavals that had led to significant disruptions in the food supply for the Southwestern Front.

This was at twelve-thirty. Apparently, in the middle of the day General Alekseev had taken all possible measures to halt the rebellion—and had run out of ideas.

Also, perhaps, a telegram to all district commanders telling them to take extreme measures to protect railroad workers at hub stations, repair shops, and depots from outside attempts to spread the troubles to them. And to make sure they were all supplied with food.

Right then, though, General Kislyakov, who previously had been seen only in the officers' headquarters dining room—bulky and fat, with a broad pale face, albeit young—brought a report. He went on for a long time, agitated, laying out the various railroad details, in great number, and with the point that up until now he had directed railroads at the front only in the technical respect and not at all in the economic-administrative, and suddenly transferring such administration to GHQ could cause more difficulties in the smooth functioning of the entire rail network. Now, before sufficient signs had appeared that the central railroad administration had been disturbed, such an administrative transfer would be extremely ill-advised and harmful. This was insofar as it concerned railroads at the front. Regarding the Empire's **entire** network, General Kislyakov was even at pains to subject this problem to preliminary discussion, so far was it beyond his scope.

He minced, the redhead, in long complex sentences, but his gaze as he did so was cast down diagonally across his twisted face.

There can be nicknames so justified as to be inevitable: Kislyakov the Sourpuss. A hopeless, sour-musty smell wafted toward Alekseev from this podgy man. All the months he had been in his post—and he'd never been seen.

But without him, Alekseev in particular couldn't immediately take over an administration entirely unfamiliar to him.

What should he do? He would have to delay this measure. And see how the railroads functioned on their own, without a ministry.

He also remembered that a great share of the supplies were in the Zemgor's hands. So that GHQ was not invulnerable.

[1 9 0]

Russia's railroad engineer class was studded with talent, knowledge, and ability. It absorbed the flower of male youth due to the desirability of the work and the high bar for entrance. Idlers and revolutionaries didn't even try. The five years of training involved determined labor, top-notch scientific training, and energetic summer fieldwork. The very nature of the railroad service, given Russia's far-flung expanses, produced effective and bold workers who knew how to solve the most complicated problems, who had a good knowledge of life and people and the value of all labor, and who could pay properly for every job performed by a subordinate. In this system, jobs were to be had only through talent and experience, not through patronage. Since he was not chasing after his daily bread, each railroad engineer could devote all his time and strength to this varied work, always on the verge of new challenges. Their travel for surveys, construction, and railroad meetings and their own travel free of charge gave them a broad overview of their country and Europe as well. Ordinarily, true railroad engineers had no time left for family, let alone public affairs.

Aleksandr Aleksandrovich Bublikov had never fit into the life role of a railroad engineer, though. No work on an active railroad or on the construction of a new one had ever satisfied him. He'd moved into general economics and been asked to work on various commissions under the ministry and to shape general issues—but no, that wasn't it, it wasn't enough! Finally he'd had the good idea of running for the State Duma and in 1912 had been elected to it from Perm Province, where he'd worked in railroad surveys. He had so put his hopes in this! But even here his passion for action languished. The Duma had about twenty main loudmouths, more from the Kadet party than the others, and they took up four-fifths of all the Duma's time. What kind of action was that? The others were supposed to keep quiet and vote, and they could work on commissions. Bublikov recognized an especially rebellious talent, if not genius, in himself, that he had not been able to apply. And here he was forty-two years old.

His name was humorous, too—bringing to mind bagels—and impeded any serious political role.

Bublikov belonged to the Russian intelligentsia, of course—there's no getting away from your origins—but in essence he profoundly differed from its main type. The main type of Russian intellectual drowned in morality, in

discussions about what was good and what was bad, and was capable of sobbing and sacrificing—but shunned economics and had no ability whatsoever to govern. Whereas Bublikov had a distinct sense of his power to govern, though the railroads were too narrow in scope for him and he hadn't
had a chance at all of Russia as a whole.

But yesterday's thunderclap had set his heart to pounding that his moment
had come! He rushed to inspire the deputies to open a thunderous Duma session! But the cowardly deputy crowd didn't dare. Listening to their languid
blather in the Semi-Circular Hall was enough to make you sick when masses
in the thousands were moving through the city and a cloud of reaction was
forming somewhere! Bublikov dashed back and forth through the agitated,
roiling Tauride Palace, scrutinizing everything sharply and nervously rubbing
his hands. The events rolling out were unusual—and a practical solution had
to be found in an unusual, energetic, and timely way. But the simplest decisions are the hardest of all to come by. The key idea, the necessary idea
wouldn't come, and events were rolling along catch as catch can.

So Bublikov spent the night in the Tauride Palace, like everyone else,
and saw more and more manifestly that a guiding individual was not rising
over the revolution, which was defenseless against suppression. So it was!
Early in the morning a rumor started about General Ivanov's expedition
against Petrograd.

The ball was in play! Would they suppress it? What should he do? What
should he do? Meanwhile, the Duma leaders kept nattering on while undertaking nothing serious. The forces of suppression were the entire Field
Army, for which the Petrograd garrison was no match.

All Russia, with its entire liberal intelligentsia and explosive young people as gunpowder, was dozing, snow-swept, and knew nothing of events in
Petrograd.

Right then the brilliantly simple idea Bublikov had been looking for
came to him—as it only could have to a railroad man. Passive, peasant-
bourgeois Russia was irrelevant; active Russia was stretched out all along the
nerves of the railroads; it was a state within a state. All the railroads—to
Vladivostok, to Turkestan—had a unified telegraph network, the most vital
network, and its center was at the Ministry of Roads and Railways. This network, as Bublikov well knew, absolutely did not depend on or merge with
the network of the Ministry of Internal Affairs. It was serviced by freethink-
ing telegraph operators. So here's the thing. Seize this communications hub
and find your voice speaking to all Russia!

He rushed to find—not Kerensky or Chkheidze—but the top man, and
right away: Rodzyanko. He found his hulk roaming, surrounded by various
seekers, and tried to attract his attention and draw him aside confidentially
and even began to speak—but Rodzyanko didn't hear him and swept along
distractedly.

Then Bublikov lay in wait for Rodzyanko upon his return from a speech to a regiment. Rodzyanko's chest was heaving like a blacksmith's. Bublikov tried to wedge into Rodzyanko's mind the idea of seizing the ministry—but the giant actually took fright and his huge shoulders froze. He utterly failed to understand that **he had to seize power**! They couldn't wait passively for the Tsar's troops to advance. Rodzyanko was still breathing obedience to the law. Bublikov stood in front of him, an ordinary bourgeois with a sleek outward appearance, distinguished only by his mercurial agility—which he was unable to convey. And Rodzyanko sailed away.

Damn it! Who else could he obtain permission from to act, though? Should he risk acting without permission? That would be in Bublikov's spirit. But he might not have enough support at the crucial moment.

Meanwhile, lounging around the Tauride Palace among the thickening multitude of idlers, Bublikov took a closer look, realizing that all the agents and assistants he needed had assembled right here, adventurists, you had only to pick them out, call to them, and draw them around you. He started talking with one and then another. Among the first to catch his eye was an attractive and obliging hussar cavalry captain with a luxuriant blond mustache. He was alone, without his hussars, obviously free, obviously seeking out meetings and conversations and smiling readily at everyone.

"Would you like to take part in a revolutionary operation?" Bublikov asked him at one of the gatherings in the crush.

"At your service. Cavalry Captain Sosnovsky!" he responded with cheerful readiness.

Then he found a free young soldier with an intelligent but decisive face, Rulevsky, a former Polish socialist and now a Social Democrat Zimmerwaldist, a bookkeeper in the fees department of the Northwestern Railroad. Excellent! He was ready, too. Bublikov also found the shaggy, curly-headed Eduard Shmuskes, who either was or had been a university student and was also seeking intense revolutionary occupation.

The forces of revolution were taking shape! People were languishing, bursting to do something—one had to know how to steer them!

Ever more resolved, Bublikov got a hold of a piece of paper and a pen, found a spot in some room, and in his distinct handwriting wrote credentials for himself from the Committee of the State Duma for taking over the Ministry of Roads and Railways. He took this paper off to look for Rodzyanko, found him, still in motion, pushing his way through the crowd with someone going somewhere, and also in motion continued trying to convince him that he could not fail to undertake something to defend freedom. Rodzyanko was absent-mindedly surprised: "Well, if it's so necessary, then go take it over." Whether it was because this was the third attempt, or because Rodzyanko in the last few hours had started thinking more boldly, he took Bublikov's credentials, put them up against a column in the Ekaterininsky Hall, and signed them. He signed without great interest, more to get rid of the importunate deputy.

But Bublikov immediately handed him a vigorous proclamation, which he had also written and which he intended to send out over the telegraph. It began, "As of this date, I have taken over the Ministry of Roads and Railways and am announcing the following decree from the State Duma President." Thus, Rodzyanko read his own decree that he himself had known nothing about. "The old regime, which created havoc for all branches of state governance, has fallen!"

At this, Rodzyanko stopped short:

"You can't put it that way. The old regime is still . . ."

What? He didn't realize the regime had fallen? *He* didn't realize that? Who did, then? Go make a revolution with them!

And if it hasn't fallen—then we have to give it a shove.

"But this is exactly what we should write!" Bublikov insisted animatedly, feeling this with his whole revolutionary core. "It's fallen! That makes an immediate impression. And then it will fall!"

"No, no," Rodzyanko mumbled. "Something more circumspect."

Fine: "The old regime has proved impotent?"

Agreed.

He also got Rodzyanko's permission to take two trucks on an expedition; the vehicles and soldiers gathered in front of the Duma were at its disposal.

Sosnovsky and Shmuskes ran to assemble a party and gathered over fifty, and two ensigns even joined them. Bublikov himself, papers in pocket and without a weapon, exited with a happy revolutionary step. An extraordinary moment in his life! A third truck eagerly joined the first two, and Bublikov immediately commandeered an idle motorcar, which required no one's permission. All the soldiers had rifles across their backs, bayonets pointing up, so that when they climbed out of the truck they nearly stabbed each other. Some of them seemed to be drunk.

They drove to the Fontanka and on toward Voznesensky Prospect.

The roiling Tauride Palace they left behind was only a façade. The action was here: Aleksandr Bublikov, someone no one knew, was on his way to take the Empire's nerve center into his own audacious hands!

How dissolute the agitated streets looked! In some places it was deserted and there was gunfire, in others there were crowds, a cluster of soldiers or workers rushing somewhere with rifles pointed forward, a medical truck carrying wounded men and nurses, people looting a shop, arrested officers being led along, and trucks like the ones in the Bublikov column, and they fired salutes on meeting.

When they reached the ministry, the soldiers poured out of the backs of the trucks, Shmuskes and the ensigns posted pairs of guards at the gates, the main entrance, and the emergency exits, while Sosnovsky and Rulevsky to the right and left of the swift Bublikov, who was reckless despite his noble appearance, and at the head of two dozen soldiers more—burst inside. Bublikov had been here more than once, he knew its layout, and he indicated where posts needed to be set—at the intersection of corridors, at the telegraph hub, at the minister's and deputy minister's offices—and ordered them to assemble all senior ranks of the department in the office of the administrative chief of roads and railways.

Indeed, they had already seen, here and there people had run out the doors in fright or peeked out, and the rumor of the new regime's arrival was racing everywhere! Bublikov could sense them fully: of course, they were worn down with fear over what was going to happen to them and were happy to fall under a firm authority, into a fixed position. Any minute now, Bublikov himself would announce to them ominously that they could continue their work and they would be happy. Meanwhile, fluffy-mustached Cavalry Captain Sosnovsky had become the building's commandant and chief of ministry security, while the bare-faced soldier Rulevsky was now chief of telegraph communications, and in half an hour through the web of lines along all the Empire's railroads, telegraph operators in peaceful, remote, and snow-bound stations would begin to receive and send on through their region fiery words only possible in a revolution:

"The Committee of the State Duma, having taken into its hands the creation of a new regime, is addressing you in the name of the fatherland. The country is expecting more of you than the mere performance of your duty. It is expecting great deeds!"

That was fine, but who was going to run the ministry? Political fervor alone wasn't enough; you had to know all the details of leadership. Either the minister himself or his two deputies had to be won over.

Bublikov was informed that Krieger-Voinovsky had not moved to his official apartment attached to the ministry; only the house staff of Trepov, the former minister, was there. Krieger had not been there early that morning and had only just arrived—and was in his office.

But he wasn't trying to break away and give orders? That meant he would surrender.

Bublikov now felt equal to anything, and he set off freely to see the minister. The power was undoubtedly his—the half a hundred bayonets here and all Petrograd. But now, passing through the heavy door and crossing the length of the office, toward the desk where a short, perfectly bald fifty-year-old Krieger-Voinovsky was sitting wearing his railroad frockcoat richly festooned with badges, Bublikov with each step was losing his composure and sinking back to his engineer rank where, alone with serious people, his commissarship looked like charlatanry and Krieger undoubtedly surpassed him in experience and knowledge. To those railroad loops and engineer pin, Bublikov looked like a traitor.

What he came up with was something not loud and commissar-like but polite:

"Eduard Bronislavovich. Here I am . . . appointed by Rodzyanko. Perhaps you could recognize the Committee of the State Duma and leave it at that? And take charge."

Had Krieger-Voinovsky stood up right then with menacing authority and said no one should dare touch the whole railroad business, Bublikov's engineering consciousness might have returned to him and he might have gotten cold feet at least somewhat. In any case, he would have conceded a great deal, simply based on the sense of the matter.

But Krieger—Krieger himself looked up from his desk crushed, taken aback, and his lower eyelids and lower lip hung down on his little face. And apologetically rather than imperiously:

"Aleksan Sanych. . . . You understand, I have given my oath to the Sovereign Emperor, and as long as he is on the throne . . ."

The engineer's fog lifted from Bublikov's head, so painstakingly coiffed by the barber, and his legs filled with the hot lead of commissarship.

"Then forgive me," he said, "I must put you under arrest." But magnanimously: "Where do you prefer? Here? Or in your apartment? Or at the State Duma?"

"I would prefer it here, Aleksan Sanych," Krieger chose without hesitation. "Especially if you leave me a telephone."

"But of course, of course! Then, forgive me, there will be guards at your door. And Trepov's house staff will bring you your meals."

Bublikov made haste. Krieger was a recent and liberal minister, but even so. His deputy, Ustrugov, a very old-fashioned monarchist, would be needed in the work if the railroads were to run as if nothing had happened. Meanwhile, he had to dispatch his fiery telegram!

Under Rodzyanko's signature he added on his own behalf:

"As a member of your family, I firmly believe that you will be able to vindicate the hopes of our homeland. State Duma Commissar Bublikov."

He had thrown at Russia the Beast of Revolution, a revolution that had yet to occur—but in hopes that it would!

Krieger was quite content. Bublikov had found him selecting his own papers, letters, and books that he wanted to save, expecting the worst for himself. What he had experienced since yesterday evening was unimaginable. For a long time after the government's session he had been unable to leave the Mariinsky Palace. It was dangerous, people were shooting, and there was a rumor that men were going around to ministers' apartments conducting searches. But he couldn't stay, either. Revolutionaries had broken into the palace. Krieger and Pokrovsky had hurried across the courtyard and to the gate onto Demidov Lane, but it turned out to be locked, and they were told by people outside that it was dangerous there, too. A trap! They returned, but the crowd was already smashing, toppling, and ransacking the palace. Then both ministers, although both were liberal and might have counted on being spared, went down the back staircase to the corridor of rooms for the couriers, doormen, and guards and sat out the whole night in a dark corner on fire-wood and casks, although men did burst in there, too, looked around, asked questions. At dawn, when the palace had calmed down somewhat, the courier's little boy led them back out through a certain yard and gates. On the square, the crowd was raging, smashing the Astoria, but other streets were deserted, although fully lit, which made it terrifying, and not a single yard-man anywhere. After spending a few hours with an acquaintance, Krieger felt obligated to go to his ministry. No one had released him from his duty. And now Bublikov and his soldiers had descended on him.

Oh well, Krieger had been minister for all of three months. He had left each session of the Council of Ministers with a sense of hopelessness; he had not felt the Emperor's solid support. In the first years of the war, as he had come to see, the Emperor had had a brisk look, had shown interest in everything, and had expressed himself quite intelligently. But at Krieger's ministerial reports this autumn, the Tsar had impressed him as a weary man already less sensitive to failures and adversities. And this January he had been quite broken, indifferent to everything, believing no more in any successes and putting everything to God's will. Where were the ministers to derive their strength?

Why did the Tsar have to be so at odds with the State Duma? Why did he have to appoint as ministers men who did not know Russia? Why did he have to appoint random, uncultivated men as governors and city governors and leave the cities without strong units in time of war? Even before that, why did he have to get mired in this war at all and lay himself out so excessively for the Bulgarians and then the Serbs, neglecting his own domestic disarray?

If everything had been proceeding this way due to the Emperor's lack of will, why should a random Krieger in the Ministry of Roads and Railways do battle now?

[1 9 1]

So they sat, five to seven generals and colonels, drinking plain black cof-fee—waiting to be taken. A foolish end to their official efforts.

They wondered where Belyaev and Zankevich had gone.

Although there were no more guards, no more sentries, anywhere. It had been nearly an hour and they hadn't burst into the Admiralty, evidently fearing an ambush or a defense.

Finally, the noise of a crowd, the tramping of many people over the slop-ing stairs, and the shouts reached them here, in this closed room.

"Keep going! . . . Higher! . . . See, they've hidden, the mother-loving, mother-loving . . ."

That was when it got frightening—frightening to imagine the face of the enraged crowd when it burst in. What might a revolutionary crowd do? Tear them to pieces, that's what.

The moment had come! They pushed the door noisily and not just one came in but several at once, many, squeezed in, rushed in. In a minute, the room was full.

The military and police generals couldn't help but all stand, though no one had told them to.

Among those in the front was an ensign wearing a rifleman's uniform and nice new field gear, drunk, dun, pimply, holding a large Mauser, which he aimed at each man's face in turn.

Another was a very young little soldier, also drunk, wearing an unbuttoned greatcoat with red-piped epaulets, his face a gentle color. He was holding a bared officer's sword with an Order of St. Anna sword-knot—and waving it scarily in front of the generals' heads. His young hand didn't look like it would be able to hold it up and the sword might be lowered on someone at any moment. He was shouting reedily and continuously and cursing more than anyone, apparently feeling he was in charge.

Between them stood a common woman, meek even, and silent, a streak of gray peeking out from her kerchief, but over her long coat she had an officer's sword belted on a broad leather strap.

There were more and more figures, but you couldn't take them all in right away; the eye was drawn to that Mauser and the sword's slashings. The soldier was shouting:

"Where've you got Khabalov there?"

His Mauser was aimed.

"Who's Khabalov?"

But for some reason Khabalov didn't respond. The generals started exchanging glances—but didn't see him. He'd disappeared.

Then the Mauser aimed:

"And who are you?"

"I"—collecting what was left of his sang-froid—"am Petrograd City Governor Balk. Arrest me and take me to the Duma."

Arrest me! So they wouldn't get the idea of shooting him. The State Duma had become a haven, a refuge, a shelter for education and mutual understanding. What was frightening was just these men, from the people. If only he could get to the Duma!

"Well, go on!" they told Balk.

And he left the room first. At first they made way, but then a terrible, overtaking, joyous shout rang out behind him, so that his back was expecting a thrust, and he hunched over—but nothing happened. He looked around and his colleagues, the top police, were following behind him. And an ill, multiply wounded Tyazhelnikov. Yes, and Khabalov, too, apparently, he was part of their group, he'd joined them from somewhere.

The unarmed part of the crowd had spread through the building in search of abandoned weapons. The armed men were leading the captives.

They left through the main entrance on Admiralty Square, past the Atlases supporting the globes. Parked here were two trucks with red flags near the engines. Balk and his deputy got in next to the driver of the first and someone went in the back; Khabalov and Tyazhelnikov got into the second vehicle.

The crowd was shouting, cursing, reviling, and laughing—and it was all covered in "hurrah!"

The driver of the first jack-rabbited off—and immediately crashed into an iron post, dislocating it—and went no farther. Despite all his efforts, the engine wouldn't work.

The second truck caught up to them with a grinding, turned right, and disappeared down Nevsky.

While the first driver tried everything to get going—and cursed.

At first, relief crept through Balk, but then he realized that their journey had only been made more difficult.

All of a sudden, a passenger car jumped out from the direction of the city governor's offices on Gorokhovaya and opened fire with a machine gun.

In a panic, everyone around the truck started throwing themselves on the snow, and the driver jumped down and ran away—while the captives sat and stood where they were.

Nearby, some old man in felt boots dropped to one knee for return fire according to the rules and tried to dispatch a bullet—but evidently the mechanism was unfamiliar to him and nothing came of it.

But someone did return fire.

The gunfire lasted for more than a minute without wounding or killing anyone. All of a sudden that mysterious vehicle stopped shooting, dashed off toward Palace Square—and vanished beyond it.

The driver returned, but still could do nothing with the truck.

Balk had realized that the most dangerous part was this trip, whereas salvation was in the Duma.

"If the vehicle won't run, take us to the Duma on foot," he demanded.

There remained of the principal ones the ensign with the Mauser, who fancifully and slurringly ordered everyone to get out and walk.

They set out surrounded by a dense, motley, volunteer convoy, abandoning the truck.

But in the middle of Palace Square, there was a private open motorcar without a red flag driving across. The ensign fired in the air twice, stopped the motorcar, ejected all the passengers and sat his main captives on the sunken seats, while the armed men clung to the running boards and fenders—and they set off like this, slowly, badly overloaded.

They drove out onto the Palace Embankment. The sun blinded them.

One man on a running board kept raising his rifle high and shaking it, kept raising it and shaking it, and shouting until his throat burst: "Hurrah!"

People were also waving rifles and revolvers in reply from the sidewalks, and they, too, were shouting "hurrah," and a few were firing into the air.

A soldier from the other running board shouted to them:

"Hey, comrades! Don't you go shooting! Save your cartridges. We're going to need 'em!"

Balk would have been recognized by every yardman here, but they were hiding and nowhere to be seen. Near the Winter Palace two English officers were walking toward them, one known to Balk; his unusually tall figure was known by everyone who had ever visited the Astoria. The officer stopped now, turned toward the riders, and keeping both hands in his pockets, his body rocking back and forth, laughed mildly, laughed, guffawed at the sight of their motorcar and the arrested generals, and kept turning so as not to miss out on the comic spectacle. He even pulled his hand out of his pocket, pointing at them as they went.

The overloaded vehicle creaked and clanked its springs on the snowy humps, stopping twice—and Balk went numb at the thought that it had broken down again and they would shoot him before getting him there.

The streets weren't busy until they started getting close to the Duma. There everything was more crowded, and the motorcar honked, scattering people. In one spot there was a lone cannon, unmanned and unloaded—its barrel pointing toward them.

Then they saw a few artillery officers on horses, without greatcoats, all with big red bows on their chests, and the public was shouting greetings and "hurrah" to them—and they were bowing with pleasure.

Starting at the Duma gates, the solid mass of people got even denser, and the motorcar, unable to go on, gave up the ghost right there.

The crowd beset them with curses, ridicule, and threats.

Some drunkard, a yardman to look at him, was bellowing loudly and while dropping to the ground kept trying to get at Balk's eyes with his fingers, which were spread like a bear spear.

The people around were making fun of him and egging him on. In this crush, in these last few steps, anything might happen—he could be hit on the head and killed.

But pushing toward them were several students from the Military Medical Academy—who formed a protective ring around the arrested men.

They entered the Duma.

There, sitting at a table and crowding around were the victorious youth, primarily Jewish. Some young men had terrifying, antiquated revolvers. They recognized Balk immediately and started shouting:

"City Governor! Were you the one who gave the order for your police to fire machine guns at the people?"

Balk had no idea what they were talking about. What machine guns? The police had never had anything of the kind.

One student mockingly objected:

"Comrades, comrades! Now there is complete freedom of speech and action, so don't put pressure on the city governor!"

They led Balk on, diagonally across the filled Ekaterininsky Hall, where other youths were ecstatically marking time with the soldiers—for some reason the soldiers were marching in a large formation here, in the hall, in full battle gear.

It was all like a dream or a madhouse.

Someone shouted:

"To the ministers' pavilion!"

They were led down a well-lit corridor. At the pavilion entrance, in front of the sentries, an exhausted Metropolitan Pitirim was sitting in an armchair in his white vestments—and saying he couldn't get up or walk.

In a room in the pavilion, several silent arrested ministers were already sitting at a large table. They had been forbidden to talk.

But Khabalov wasn't there.

[192]

Since the war began, all three older Krivoshein brothers had been in a rush, as if afraid of being late to die for Russia. Even their father said, What studies when we have to beat the enemy?

When the war began, the two oldest quit university and volunteered for the artillery. Since then, both had received a soldier's St. George Cross and were second lieutenants.

The third son, Igor, having barely graduated from high school the year before, abandoned any thought of university and immediately entered the last accelerated course at the Corps of Pages. Since the previous autumn he had been an ensign in the Life Guards Mounted Artillery, had undergone training in a reserve battery in Pavlovsk, and was happily catching up very quickly to the main events of the war.

But in his few short weeks of proud leave before the front, his fate and heart already there—Igor never did get a chance to take a walk in the capital!—the turmoil began. When yesterday a well-disposed sergeant had warned him on Voskresensky that they were killing officers on Kirochnaya, Igor had experienced dismay, unease, and insult—new emotions and in a new situation he had never known before. A year before, he'd been a carefree high school boy, nothing for any crowd to envy, but this past year they'd bred in him an officer's dignity—and all of a sudden it had set him against his own Russian crowd?

Now, as he was returning home, he heard from Rittikh how the next rank of his fellow pages were all worked up and thirsting for battle, a domestic one now.

What should he do? Confusion, unreadiness. All the rest of yesterday and half the day today, Igor sat home, humiliated, only glancing onto Sergievskaya from the fourth floor to see who was passing down the street, what kind of strange public in what combinations. Yesterday a maddened crowd of the first mutinous Volynians had rolled through there, and then lots of various groups and individuals, and vehicles, with and without gunfire, with red flags and red tokens, giving a definite impression of what was happening on the main streets.

It was humiliating to hide away. Not that Igor was afraid. He would definitely have gone through the streets, maybe even intervened somewhere; he did not have a keen sense of the situation's novelty. But his father sternly besieged him, saying there was nothing he could do and he would only be setting himself up to be spat upon. (To say nothing of his mother!) Go in civilian dress? But he hadn't earned an officer's uniform just to avoid it now and hide.

His soul filled with revulsion at the infamy playing out in Petrograd, when all the best men, the entire army, was fighting a holy war.

Igor went from the formal rooms to his own, on the courtyard side, where he couldn't see the irritating street flickerings and he could have imagined that nothing was going on in Petrograd if only a burning smell weren't still wafting in from the District Court.

All of a sudden he heard the doors slam in a non-family way and heavy steps, and entirely strange voices, and in reply to them his mother's insulted and rising voice. Then Igor dashed out as he was, in his tunic, a pistol at his waist, hurried there—and before he could take in the entire scene and the several armed soldiers, some with greatcoats half-buttoned, and his mother behind a chair facing them—they noticed him and cried out:

"There he is!"

Blood rushed to Igor's face. They'd come for him? They'd been looking for him?

For some reason his father hadn't come out. His aunt whispered that he'd gone to see Rittikh home.

But his mother was intoning:

"I have two sons at the front! And this one's on his way! How dare you? There's a war going on! And you're rebelling! What do you call this?"

And his aunt looked stern.

But they weren't the least bit ashamed, and they weren't about to argue. They'd come here by right of force, and they meant to do something. Igor scanned their faces—and suddenly did not feel his usual admiration for the Russian soldier. Instead of daring, quick service, patience, or humor, there was something dull and incoherent, animal-like, and repulsive in these faces. One said:

"There was shooting from this building. We were told you have an officer. And here he is."

(Someone in the building had actually pointed them out! Someone who smiled every day when they passed.)

"Surrender your pistol, your honor!"

A gun is an officer's honor. Not yet used a single time in battle! Surrender his honor!

Otherwise he would have to shoot his way out. Right now. They stood there menacingly, already twirling their bayonets.

Tall, slender, skinny Igor leaned his head back, pale.

"Surrender it, Igor," his mother asked him.

He was being suffocated by despair and grief, and he himself didn't even remember how he'd done this, in a daze.

But they were walking over the carpets in their muddy boots, and one had wandered into his mother's boudoir and his father's study, his aunt behind him. Another, a civilian, was pacing here, around the parlor, between the armchairs that stood in twos and threes around the knickknack-covered end tables, looked at the bas relief of the "Ascension of the Lord," and said archly:

"This apartment of yours is a palace!"

A third grabbed a decanter of water, took out the stopper, and sniffed to make sure it wasn't vodka.

Although Igor surrendered his pistol, that didn't make things better. They started saying they were going to take him with them.

"No!" his mother shouted, and she barred the way with her arms. "You'll kill him."

The civilian said with a crooked smile:

"Don't worry, madam, we won't kill him."

The civilian was a half-educated, venomous breed. He assured her they were just taking him away for questioning. Igor put on his greatcoat, without his sword, and reassuring his mother, followed them down the stairs.

On the sunny street, the entire detail abandoned him immediately, though. The civilian told one soldier, a rather simple fellow, to take the prisoner to the Duma and hand him over to the commandant. While he himself and the rest of his band headed on down Sergievskaya. This entire foray into the building, the confiscation of the pistol, and the arrest had obviously been a passing episode for them.

Take him away and hand him over to the commandant! That meant arrest, not questioning.

How instantaneously Igor's fate had changed! From a proud officer on his way to the front, he had turned into a prisoner walking in humiliation down the sidewalk two paces in front of his convoy's bayonet, under the public's curious looks.

He tried with his bearing, tossed-back head, and proud face to show everyone that he was no criminal and scorned this arrest.

How wild this must have looked: an arrested officer being led down the sidewalk!

All the passersby stopped and looked. With astonishment and fear—but no one cursed him. Rather, they were sympathetic:

"He must have fired from the attic."

"He must have a German name."

Here was a situation! Igor couldn't defend himself even from these sympathetic surmises, he couldn't vindicate himself or tell these people, man to man, how randomly and unfortunately this had come to pass. The invisible barrier of arrest had already torn him away from simple human conversation.

How was his mama managing there? And what would his father say when he returned? But he would say something calming.

It was good that Rittikh had left and hadn't been taken.

In front of the Duma, especially in the open space, there was a terrible crush. They nearly pushed through, and ended up going around the trucks and motorcycles. Here no one was at all surprised at the arrested officer, but he himself couldn't help but see the crowd.

This was hardly the first crowd in his life, but he'd never noticed anything like this: the cruelty evident in so many faces, and not in a particular moment of arousal, but in their ordinary, half-cheerful standing on a sunny day outside the Tauride Palace. As if they had ripped the outer film off a well-known anthropological, psychological, national, and class type—and their ruthlessness had shown through right away.

It was awful, as if he'd landed not among his own people but on another planet, where anything might happen.

In the palace itself, the muddled crush was even worse, and the convoy soldier became quite distraught: where was he and what commandant was he looking for? The prisoner himself started asking, guiding him.

Finally they got through—not to the commandant but to an overfilled room where all kinds of people were standing and sitting, waiting, also having been brought here, obviously, still with their convoys or without—while at the table, walled or hemmed in, sat some commission, a few civilian Duma deputies, questioning and recording—on scraps of paper that were piled up in disorderly fashion and falling off the table.

All these people had human faces, attentive and smiling, only tired.

One such pleasant man asked Igor:

"What did they arrest you for?"

Now, though, Igor himself didn't soften, so much insult had he accumulated on his prisoner's journey, and all that insult was squeezing his throat. In a dry thin voice, he replied:

"Probably because my name is German. And for shooting from the attic."

"And what is your name exactly?"

"Krivoshein."

"Excuse me, why is that German?" the other man smiled.

"It's as German as my shooting from the attic."

"Are you related to Aleksandr Vasilievich?"

"His son."

"My God!"

He immediately wrote out on a scrap of paper that he had been questioned at the State Duma and could not be arrested.

Now without his convoy (who had gone missing at the threshold), Igor once again pushed through the human chaos—and went outside.

His brief arrest had given him new insight, though. On so many faces he had seen this bared, newborn cruelty—and couldn't stop seeing it.

Something new had come into our world.

[1 9 3]

The members of the Executive Committee who had left the palace for the night, to say nothing of those who had spent it there—had no sensation of there even having been a night: one unbroken fever had gripped them yesterday as the day drew to a close and had continued in the darkness and since the late dawning as well. But by eleven o'clock in the morning it had drawn them all back to Room no. 13 (and it was good they had this room, separate from their ragtag Soviet; they must hold onto it with their own bodies and not let anyone in). As soon as they assembled here, they were shaken even more powerfully by their amazement at all that had happened—and fear of the oncoming retribution—and the explosive overload of political tasks that could not be put off. Just the day before yesterday, Sunday, they had each been living their own small, mundane life, not preparing for anything quick, given the faded and forgotten revolutionary plans, and now there'd been an earthquake, an eruption that had carried them to the top— but General Ivanov had eight, if not sixteen regiments marching, rolling in—and the EC members had just these hours to decide everything for the workers, for the soldiers, for the ordinary citizens, for Petrograd, for the Army, for all Russia, to decide a hundred questions at once, and each of them was paramount and urgent, and taken together they could be called the Fate of the Revolution!

Even sorting through and dividing up these questions and establishing an order for them—even that would take more than a single day, let alone resolving them. And there might be just a single day left until the run-up of Ivanov's ominous punitive force, and that looming threat was a terrible hindrance to practical discussion. But the EC members had perhaps one single hour until the opening of the general meeting of the Soviet of Workers' Deputies in the next room, no. 12, where many more people would probably show up than yesterday. Yesterday people had come at random, not chosen by anyone, but today the factories might elect as many as a few hundred people—and that room at capacity could hold two hundred. So what now? Break off the EC session in an hour and all crowd into the meeting of the Soviet of which they were the EC? But that made absolutely no sense! The Soviet had done what it needed to yesterday when it approved the Executive Committee, and now it had nothing more worthwhile to do.

"But what should we do about the soldiers, comrades? Are we also including the soldiers in the Soviet of Workers' Deputies?"

"By no means, comrades! Petty bourgeois elements should not join a proletarian organ!"

"Otherwise, comrades, we risk isolating ourselves from the masses."

It was clear that soldier deputies were also being elected by company, and it was clear they'd been and would continue making their way to the Tauride Palace. Blast it!

Send a few to the Soviet's meeting and leave it at that. And it was clear who: Chkheidze. He was suited for the task because he was the Soviet's chairman, and also because he'd become lethargic from what was going on, as if he'd been drinking a lot, warmed up, melted away. Here, in the EC, he was utterly useless in practical discussion.

But who else? They turned their gazes to one another as to whom to send, each thinking only not me, a distasteful task. Yes, actually, the EC members, who had only now for the first time sat around the desk of the Duma Budget Commission chairman—only now for the first time had they looked around them, and even now not thoroughly. They would have liked to see here, apart from themselves personally, more illustrious and established individuals—but in all Petrograd now, there were none more illustrious to be scraped together. Some of them, apparently, had been voted on yesterday in the next room, some had been coopted as "authoritative left-leaning individuals," and some had apparently just taken a seat here; in any case, they all now had to be considered reliable members of the Executive Committee. (The name, "Executive Committee," had to sound terrible to the public, like *that* secret Executive Committee that killed Aleksandr II and then wrote an ultimatum to Aleksandr III. Now it had resurfaced and was in charge!) But although everyone present occupied exactly one chair and the chairs could be counted—you still couldn't count the members of the EC. Some were sitting, others kept jumping up with or without some urgent call, and still others, one recalled, had been brought onto the EC but for some reason weren't present, and others still, like Kantorovich and Zaslavsky, outstanding pens, they would have liked very much to have a part in this and be present, but no opportunity had been found to coopt them, so that they would have to move to the next room and run the Soviet of Workers' Deputies. Thus, the EC members could not be definitively counted: there were either still fifteen, or now twenty-five, either prominent, party-affiliated figures had already been coopted or else this had only begun, but in any case, Shlyapnikov had already brought in Bolsheviks no one had elected: Molotov, a certain Shutko with an idiotic face, and Bramson from the Trudoviks had confidently taken a seat, and the clever Krotovsky from the Interdistrict group, who yesterday had been late when the seats were being divvied up.

Somehow there were a lot of clever and smart but nonetheless weak and unrepresentative people here, so whom could they send to the Soviet? Many gazed hopefully at the burly, broad-shouldered Nakhamkes. Would he push through a vote in the Soviet for the resolutions the EC had already approved?

Room no. 13 had two doors: one through no. 12 and another directly onto the corridor. There was also a door curtain dividing no. 13 itself in half. Behind the curtain, the EC had already taken seats around the table; in front of the curtain, gatekeepers of a kind, access barrers, had gathered, even one burly Life Grenadier, to stop the press coming from the corridor. And the first secretaries appeared—from among the families of the EC members.

Even besieged, though, even vague in number, even in constant movement, the EC was called upon right now to decide the revolution's defense! And this included everything at once, in a tangled clump. They called on the population not to waste cartridges. And to surrender their weapons to the district commissariats (instead of the former police stations). To create a new militia to replace the former police—which meant, on the contrary, handing out weapons. (While not losing sight of the fact that this militia might have to fight the Duma Committee's armed forces.) And what was to be done about the Army as a whole? Who was going to defend them and how from Ivanov's punitive forces, which were advancing relentlessly? What about rail service to Moscow? It had to be restored; this was a vulnerable point for the capital. And what about streetcar service in Petrograd? On the contrary, don't restore it, so as not to provoke the strikers' dissatisfaction. And the post and telegraph office? They had to be watched and taken into our hands! (Who would the Tsar communicate with? And the Tsaritsa? And GHQ? What about the Duma Committee itself? It would do no harm for us to know that as well.)

"Comrades! Comrades! Any activity requires money, though! Who is going to finance us?"

They had barely eaten since the day before, hadn't required a change of clothes yet, had taken the rooms without paying, and had not yet demanded a salary for themselves, so that they had no need of any financing. But here they had brought and set out around the table mugs of sweet strong tea and cheese and butter sandwiches. That made discussion easier.

Financing? Let the Duma Committee finance the Soviet's activities!

A magnificent idea! The economics-trained minds immediately developed it further: all means of state financing must be immediately taken out of the old regime's hands! This required that revolutionary watches immediately be engaged for the purpose of protecting the State Bank! The treasury! The mint! The dispatch of state securities! Seize all monetary funds! (Parvus's tremendous idea in 1905, the Financial Manifesto.)

"No, comrades, that is beyond us for now. How about this. Let the Soviet *instruct* the Duma Committee to carry all this out!"

"No, comrades, it has to be milder," Peshekhonov, who had wandered in, objected. "Let credit and monetary operations proceed as usual, and the Soviet and Duma Committee can select a financial oversight committee. . . ."

"Not enough! Not enough! That's not the language to be using with Duma deputies! They're over there issuing proclamations without asking us."

"Tell Chkheidze and Kerensky to demand that the proclamation texts be cleared with us!"

Clarify the formal relationship with the Duma Committee in general! And limit it!

Yes, but the soldiers. The soldiers! If they elected one per company, they would immediately overwhelm the workers. But if a separate soldiers' Soviet were created, that would be competition! And should the army be drawn into the political struggle anyway?

Do we have any choice? They've probably done their electing already, right?

Nakhamkes went to the Soviet and said that the workers and soldiers were still very few; the best forces were absent: they were going around shooting and conducting searches. While those present had just now voted in favor of all the EC's decisions.

The moral-political fact that the Soviet had convened was in itself significant.

But it had become more and more impossible for the EC itself to function! As it was, issues kept producing splits between the members seated at the table. And then every five to ten minutes someone burst through the door, past the barriers, and sometimes past the curtain: couriers and petitioners, delegates from institutions and public groups, or simply God knows who. And each burst in with a special statement! An urgent report! A matter of exceptional importance! That could not suffer delay! Linked with the Fate of the Revolution!

And each time it would be dangerous not to hear them out, since the Fate of the Revolution rested on precisely this report! And each time it turned out to be nonsense or a minor episode. (There were reports about robberies, fires, and pogroms—and the Executive Committee gave instructions, not expecting them to be implemented, sent protective detachments without any confidence that they would even form.)

Separately, one, another, or a third EC member was asked to come outside by representatives of various organizations or public groups—lawyers, doctors, pharmacists, salesclerks, the Union of Zemstvos and Towns, teachers, postal and telegraph officials, stage artists—demanding seats on the Soviet of Workers' Deputies. There was only one possibility: concede.

With all this commotion, jerking around, and running out and in—what kind of work could they do? Who understood that the most important, unseen work was being fought out at a higher level: the party alignment in the EC. This was the key to all future politics. Who would seize the majority here? The rightists? The leftists? At each coopting, or entrance, or exit, the majority changed abruptly. And several eyes were following this balance above all.

Actually, when everyone took a good look around, the only hopeless rightist here was Gvozdev, although until yesterday he had been in prison for being leftist and most of the leftists hadn't. Also, probably, Bogdanov was too much a defensist, as was Erlich, although inconsistently. All the remaining Mensheviks were at least in some way leftists—either internationalists or Initiativists, or both. As for Aleksandrovich, who among the SRs was more leftist than he?

Nonetheless, Shlyapnikov believed that only the Bolsheviks were properly leftist. He had already come up with five of these here, and he could add a sixth, the Interdistrict man Krotovsky, but that did not outbalance the rafts of Mensheviks. Now, pinching himself to stay awake, he tried to follow the combinations vigilantly as they arose. Herein lay the meaning of all the discussions. At each question, which decision was for *us* and which for *them?* Soldiers? Let them into the same Soviet as the workers (they will be for us and outweigh the sensible Mensheviks)! Ultimately they finished their debate: include the soldiers in the general Soviet, but as a separate section. (And this was a success.)

Gvozdev languished at the session, feeling isolated, finding no direct work, and with no hope of being in charge of anything. Whereas Himmer, although he kept running out more than anyone, was simply eating his heart out due to his fortunate or unfortunate ability to always see a hundred steps ahead. Oh, what they were discussing here wasn't what was important! Other than the threat from General Ivanov, there was no more important question now than coming up with an overall political formula: how could they *construct a regime* that corresponded to democracy's interests? And facilitated the revolution's correct development? And the international socialist movement's success? And at the same time not get burned and come falling down from the height they'd reached. Before a regime itself could be constructed, this process had to be taken actively in hand! And that meant actively building a relationship with the Duma Committee while simultaneously forcing it to move against Tsarism, and simultaneously limiting it in every way. The key question here was taking over the army. Naturally, the Duma Committee would want to take the army into its sticky, plutocratic paws—which would mean stealing the real strength from the people. So they had to maneuver in such a way that the soldiers didn't fall into former officers' iron cuffs; rather they had to create entirely new, revolutionary relations inside the army. Milyukov and Rodzyanko could not be believed for a minute. The army had to be torn decisively from their hands. But how was this to be done?

Oh, it was his misfortune to be so smart! His misfortune that he always figured out before everyone else, more precisely than anyone else—but they didn't listen to him. Here, too, on the EC, they didn't listen to him, although they had assembled a fairly good Zimmerwaldist nucleus. Plus the three of them who were unaffiliated—Himmer himself, Nakhamkes, and Sokolov. This was a foundation for a leftist majority if they could somehow bring the morass along with them. And if Shlyapnikov hadn't been pushing his own stupid, unreasonable people onto the EC . . . what political combinations could have been created!

But today, there was no reaching an agreement on anything, not even naming the editorial board of *Izvestia of the Soviet of Workers' Deputies.* The Bolsheviks were demanding 100% Bolsheviks! Then the Mensheviks demanded 100% Mensheviks! Just try to work with them, you smart, independent socialist!

Right then Himmer was summoned again, and in fact about the *Izvestia* business. Summoning him was Bonch-Bruevich, from behind the curtain.

[1 9 4]

Peshekhonov didn't mind and had no fear of walking to the Petersburg side and back, and got a good night's sleep as a result. Now, as it was getting on toward twelve, he strode back to the Tauride Palace fresh.

He retained from yesterday evening a lingering sensation of great chaos and the wrong thing being done, their agonizing, hours-long literary commission being just one example. Nothing could make him repeat yesterday's blunders and he was alarmed by the necessity of correcting something in the general course of things. Matters could not go on so uncontrollably and blindly given the great external threat.

But it was no longer so easy to get into the palace. A full Grenadiers Life Guards battalion had arrived to declare that it was going over to the side of the revolution—the same Grenadiers battalion, from the Petersburg side, past which Peshekhonov yesterday had broken through so boldly by himself. Was that really only last evening? How everything had changed! Here they had come to swear an oath to the revolution! Now they were coming out of the palace and filling the entire space in front of the Tauride Palace. They wouldn't have left and would have willingly listened here; their route hadn't taken them close by and listening to speeches was a novelty for them—and then there was the sun, the light frost, a celebration! But the sounds of a new band came down Shpalernaya. The Grenadiers weren't the only ones who'd had the good idea of coming here.

As the Grenadiers reluctantly flowed out of the open space, Peshekhonov was able to move toward the doors and would have gone inside if they hadn't explained to him that the Mikhailovsky Artillery School had arrived!

That was where his son was studying! And although, due to myopia, Aleksei Vasilich had no hope of picking out his son in the formation, he could at least listen to the ceremony in order later to exchange thoughts with his son. So he lingered on the front steps.

Now, next to him, loud, bulky Rodzyanko spoke, although he seemed to have lost some of his self-confidence. And Kerensky, wrought up, in his new role.

There was a noticeable disparity between their speeches. Rodzyanko spoke about loyalty to Russia, military discipline, and victory over their enemies. Kerensky said nothing about that, as if there were no war, but rather spoke about the triumph of the revolutionary people and the coming, long-awaited freedom. No one noticed these contradictions, though, or they imagined that they weren't contradicting each other—and the cadets shouted "hurrah" with equal delight at both.

All the remaining free space in the open area was packed with the curious public. Also having to squeeze through it were the convoys leading prisoners. You could see the Metropolitan's headdress moving through slowly, white in the crowd; he, too, had been arrested and was being led along. What was the point of this excess? Outrageous.

Inside, though, the palace could not be compared with yesterday. Yesterday the people had merely been guests, and today there was an inundation. Inside the Cupola Hall and in the corridors there wasn't the same joyous, outside sunlight, which made it dark and uncomfortable.

He turned right, into the room where the Soviet had met yesterday. Today, its session should have been opening right now; but today they were verifying mandates—documents with clumsy notations—and the work was proceeding slowly.

He squeezed into Room no. 13 for the EC session. Right then the Menshevik Sokolovsky ran up to Peshekhonov and told him that at the night session of the Executive Committee he had been appointed commissar of the Petersburg side, that is, its absolute master and governor—and he was supposed to head there and take power.

Peshekhonov hesitated. The position of the former local police chief? The EC resolution was in no way binding on him, although if everyone was going to reject its resolutions, what would come of that? He also understood that here, in the Tauride Palace, he had to represent the interests and viewpoints of his own Populist Socialist party. On the other hand, though, no good would come of this if each party was going to place its own party interests above the common interests. That dreamed-of time had come when everyone had to demonstrate unanimity and selflessness.

So he decided to go! A vital business! In the thick of the people! (Which he had always striven for.)

But to do this he needed to take along a staff of colleagues. First, a few workers from the Petersburg side, which he easily found near the mandates commission. All the factories had sent more than they were supposed to, one man per thousand, and now the extras, having had a taste of political action, didn't want to leave. These were the ones Peshekhonov picked up.

Then he needed a few intellectuals—but these were very easily found.

After that somehow he had to legally distinguish himself from or cooperate with the district authorities placed there by the Committee of the State Duma, so Peshekhonov headed for the Duma half. Right then he saw Milyukov in the office next to Rodzyanko's. Milyukov's eyes flashed firmly behind his spectacles, eyes Peshekhonov had always found a little scary, though others didn't see that.

He met Peshekhonov's question about local power with a grave raising of the eyebrows, like at some untimely nonsense.

"Well," he said, almost with contempt, "if you find that this suits you, proceed."

Peshekhonov realized that the Duma Committee hadn't even given any thought to the fact that it needed its own local authorities, which meant it was living in the clouds and had yet to get a grip on anything. He couldn't help but notice how far ahead the Soviet was. After all, it was yesterday at midnight when the Duma Committee was only discussing whether or not to accept power, whereas the Soviet was already issuing commands and had commissions. During the night the Soviet had managed to connect with factories and plants and to summon delegates. Since yesterday the Soviet's proclamations had been passed out and read on the streets. The populace was starting to see the Tauride Palace as the site of the elected Soviet—but did everyone know about the Duma Committee yet? Peshekhonov liked this practicality of the Soviet, which was to the revolution's undoubted good.

Peshekhonov pinned on a huge red bow so that everyone could see it from a long way off.

Right then someone suggested to him that he should start by creating his own military force. He could collect as many soldiers as he wanted in front of the palace on Shpalernaya, but where was he to get a good officer who would agree to go and whom the soldiers would obey? Peshekhonov headed for the Military Commission's room.

They didn't let him in that easily; the guard was numerous, and everyone took great satisfaction in verifying him. He had to identify himself as the Petersburg side commissar. Inside there were several colonels, and it felt like a headquarters. Peshekhonov could not share the soldiers' mistrust for officers, of course, but for some reason it even rankled him, due to his mistrust and apprehension, that high-ranking Tsarist officers were here taking responsibility for safeguarding the revolution from the Tsar. But right then he noticed the SR Maslovsky in a military uniform and without epaulets and told him about his need. Maslovsky left with him immediately, led him to the next room, where several officers were sitting, and immediately introduced a charming young ensign, with a frank and bold gaze: Lenartovich.

Apparently he had been expecting another appointment, and a shadow ran across his forehead, but he gave his head a shake and agreed. This shake of the head was very attractive and established a simplicity with the ensign straight off.

He also still had to get two vehicles, which were found ready. Instantly the ensign called together ten or so soldiers—either ones he knew or entirely new ones.

They were off.

However, before they'd gone down the embankment as far as the Trinity Bridge, they were stopped by some self-appointed marshals distinguished not by armbands but only by red rosettes, like everyone else had. It turned out they couldn't drive onto the bridge because it was being fired upon from somewhere. From the other side? No, the Engineers Castle, apparently.

Lenartovich jumped out of the second vehicle and was right there, by Peshekhonov's side, and without even consulting, with an excess of military decisiveness, immediately ordered his soldiers to get out, led them past the cover of the last building, spread them out, ordered them to hold their rifles at the ready—and went on the attack against the Engineers Castle across the entire Field of Mars! He himself, on the flank, grabbed a sword, and slender and tall, carried it picturesquely over his head. Peshekhonov admired him—and got flustered and made no objection.

They kept going.

However, it was rather a long way to go, attacking across the entire Field of Mars and across the Moika! What could ten soldiers do against an entire castle? And also—was that where they were shooting from? The Engineers Castle could not still be against the revolution; otherwise it would have been attacked already. What should the Petersburg side commissar do? Stay with the vehicles by the bridge? Or take up his place without the armed force he'd lost?

Contemplating all this, Peshekhonov himself jumped out of his vehicle and hobbled along like a civilian after his armed forces. They'd already advanced quite a ways, and the soldiers were expressing no hesitation. Actually, they'd heard no bullets, either.

On the left flank, just as picturesquely and handsomely, his sword over his head, Ensign Lenartovich was stepping lightly.

Peshekhonov called out to him, but he didn't turn around. Then he caught up with Lenartovich, who turned around with a shudder.

Peshekhonov told him he shouldn't attack; they should go to their assigned place.

But Lenartovich was all aflame with the cause and couldn't lower himself to petty considerations.

"You have to understand. This looks silly," Peshekhonov argued. "What am I supposed to do here, stand by the bridge for half an hour or an hour?"

He didn't relent but strode on farther so as not to lag behind his soldiers.

Peshekhonov was right behind him.

"My dear fellow, you agreed to stay with me, and I'm the commissar of the Petersburg side. The Engineers Castle is not a part of that, someone else will—"

Without stopping entirely, Lenartovich turned his stunned face toward him:

"How can you think like that!" he exclaimed reproachfully. "As if the Revolution could really be divided up into ours and theirs! Now it's all ours."

And he went on.

Peshekhonov, angry, shouted to him:

"Young man! Be so kind as to obey! I am the commissar!"

A wounded moan, like an a-a-ah, tore from Lenartovich's breast. He slowed his pace and slowly, slowly began lowering his sword into its scabbard. And in a wounded voice he shouted to the soldiers bitterly and disappointedly:

"Stand fast! . . . Halt attack. . . ."

[1 9 5]

The Nekrasov brothers and little Greve wound up at the State Duma in anything but a simple way. The red armbands from the Ericsson had led the three of them down Sampsonievsky in their officer greatcoats—and from the sidewalks and even the window vents, worker women shouted: "Beat the bloodsuckers!"

They were led by only about seven men, but they knew what they were doing and drew around them and were accompanied by a new crowd, and everyone was ablaze with hatred.

"Why bother with them?" they shouted. "Finish 'em the hell off here!"

The crowd closed around them, and the Ericsson men could go no farther. They argued with the crowd, but the crowd wouldn't listen. Some bearded, drunken soldier straight from the barracks latched onto them and kept thrusting his bayonet, trying to jab one of the officers. Whether it was his or some other bayonet, Sergei felt a stab from behind. And then he had a glimpse of a raised rifle butt that didn't reach his head. The fact that the escorting workers wouldn't surrender their prisoners and were trying to explain something only fueled the crowd's fury—their shouts and curses, their waving of arms. What kind of hatred was this? And why toward officers?

They could reach out and attack them at any minute. Once again everything grew dark, and once again this insult—from their own people! Once again they thought it was all over! For the second time in a brief hour. The escorting workers couldn't move or defend them.

And suddenly, in pursuit, several Moscow Regiment men cut in—the very ones who had already saved them once! Oh, men! They shoved back the rifle butts and fists, turned away the bayonets, and shouted immediately and loudly that these were loyal officers, they'd fought together, and one of them was a war cripple.

This didn't touch the crowd or get heard by everyone here as it had by the sexton's door, but the attackers did cool down.

Right then a canvas-covered truck drove up, and the Moscow soldiers and Ericsson men pushed the officers through the crowd—toward the truck. They pushed them in and five of the workers climbed on as a convoy.

They never did get to thank the Moscow men or even find out what company they were from.

If it hadn't been for the vehicle, it would have been quite a task to get through to the Duma, and they would have been stopped and torn to pieces ten times over. Even the truck was stopped more than once in the crowd, so jammed were the streets by the people and their excited, fair-like mood. Sometimes the convoy would shout through the back or from the driver's cab:

"We're transporting arrested officers!"
and there would be a joyous roar and shouts of "hurrah" with raised arms.

While under the canvas the escorting workers chatted peacefully and curiously with the officers:

"How is it, gentlemen officers, here your soldiers say you're good, so why don't you join the people?"

All in a single hour—they were to live, they were to die, and now they'd have to find it in them to debate. The officers explained:

"Starting a revolution during time of war is a crime and Russia's ruin. You simply don't know what you're doing."

They drove off the Liteiny Bridge—and there was a three-inch cannon, its barrel pointed down the embankment, and several soldiers with red bows hovering around it—but it didn't look as though they knew how to fire it.

Closer to the Tauride Palace the crowd was just as thick but had fewer common folk and more intellectuals. From makeshift platforms, from parapets and steps—in different places orators were speaking heatedly to a tight circle. There were a great many soldiers—freed from their formation, from the most various units, like the free civilian public. The street and open area in front of the palace were already so solidly packed that the truck couldn't move at all. They took the prisoners out and, squeezing through, led them along. Here there were shouts, even half-friendly ones:

"Gentlemen officers! Why are you against the people?"

The palace entrance and halls turned out to be not less but even more cramped, and the prisoners and their escorts were pressed into a small cluster, and no one was paying any attention to them at all. The escorts kept trying to find out where and to whom they were supposed to deliver their prisoners. Together they made their way down the wing's corridor.

In a large room, a line worse than a bread line snaked around in several segments: prisoners waiting to be searched. It was all police—officers, district policemen, gendarmes. In front, by little tables, were several university students, high school pupils, and workers with armbands asking questions, making notes, and then, in the corner, separated off by benches, undressing them to their drawers. Several soldiers and workers, learning the prison trade, frisked them and felt the removed uniforms, trousers, and footwear. Many spectators had collected there, near the benches, and everyone waited with interest to see what they would find. The Ericsson men, having now abandoned their convoy concerns, also went to watch.

The officers stood in the line waiting their turn for disgrace. Of course, even for the police this procedure was unbearably humiliating, but for the combat officers, their pride was seriously hurt: Oh, why hadn't they resisted all the way? Just yesterday they could have died straightaway.

Right then a quick, thin young civilian gentleman with a crewcut appeared wearing a frock coat and starched collar with his tie awry—and behind him an aged nurse with a tray. They pushed through to the registering men, and the nurse began serving them—and only them, not the prisoners—bread and meat, while the gentleman was saying something and gesticulating. All of a sudden they put a stop to the searches, and those already undressed and waiting began to dress again.

The officers heaved a sigh of relief. The nurse was going back and they asked her who that was. She replied:

"Duma Deputy Kerensky."

Then he himself made his way back. His face was exhausted—but also unusually animated, with a quick gaze and a boyishness even.

Vsevolod Nekrasov, stepping with his stick, moved toward him and grabbed his sleeve:

"Gentlemen Deputy! The three of us here are officers of the Moscow Life Guards Regiment. Among the prisoners, as we see, we are the only three combat officers. We would like to know whether they're going to undress us as well. What awaits us in general?"

With quick attention the young deputy examined them and saw Vsevolod's stick:

"You were wounded?"

"Yes. My leg's been amputated."

"And you're a St. George officer?" This to Sergei, having noticed the cross under his unbuttoned greatcoat.

The deputy was no taller than those around him; however, taking advantage of the small space around himself, he confidently spoke to the entire, droning room, as if he'd been preparing this speech the whole time. The buzzing died down and everyone listened.

"Comrades! What disgrace is this?" he hurled out in a light voice that carried well. "A revolutionary people—and you're arresting invalided officers and St. George officers? Officers are essential to the army! There's a war going on. There can be no excesses against officers!"

He waited a moment for objections—but none were forthcoming. The convoy that had brought them had disappeared the moment they slipped out of the crowd. In the rocking sea of rebellion, one confident, resonant voice had immediately replaced the entire law.

"Let's go!" Kerensky, no longer in doubt, said imperiously to the officers and led all three of them away.

Once they were out in the corridor, with a shade of even royal benevolence:

"You are perfectly free, gentlemen! Go get safe conducts. But I don't advise you to leave the palace today."

And for a while he walked alongside them through the crush and jumble of clothing and faces, explaining which room they needed:

"Gentlemen! You do love our homeland, after all! Join the popular movement."

Great was the temptation to assent to the man who had saved them from a cell and disgrace. But Sergei replied:

"It is precisely because we do love our homeland, deputy, sir, that we cannot make revolution in time of war."

[196]

What happened? What had befallen him was precisely that terrible something that he had been endeavoring to avoid by a coup d'état, the most terrible and elemental something: a mob uprising.

The Guchkov plot had not succeeded, and now that a revolution had burst out anyway and everything had been swept aside by a giant hand—now for the second day it seemed to Guchkov that the plot's difficulties had been wholly insignificant, and in March they would have been likely to—had to—succeed.

Yesterday it had begun, and Guchkov had been flustered as to what he should do. It had begun in his presence, he was here, in Petrograd—and what was he to do? He needed, simultaneously, both to somehow halt the popular movement and instantaneously wrench concessions from the Tsar. Guchkov (feeling himself to be a military man) rushed to the General Staff and—not that he had that right—tried to get Zankevich to put it down! (He felt a strange ambivalence: clearly it had to be crushed, yet he wished the movement success.) Then he rushed to his dozing and terrified State Council. A few of the members were loitering around the Mariinsky, incapable of anything—and Guchkov started pulling them together and calling people on the telephone, and jointly they sent the Tsar a telegram. Guchkov observed with malicious joy the ministers' final helpless castings about.

And that was all he'd managed to accomplish yesterday.

This morning he headed for the Duma. (Even if he'd wanted to stay home he couldn't have. Maria Ilinichna had outdone herself and this morning had made quite a scene—the astonishing inability of women to have any feeling whatsoever for the general situation or to see anything beyond the crests of their own feelings—thereby driving him out of the house today as well. He had hastened to the Duma with all the more enthusiasm.)

He already knew from a morning telephone call both that the State Duma Committee had been formed and that the Soviet of Workers' Deputies, in imitation of '05 (and devised, just as in '05, by revolutionary quasi-intellectuals), had made itself a nest right there in the Tauride Palace and started smoking. He had to hurry to join in events and actively intervene! (Still not knowing exactly how.)

He had only two blocks to go from Voskresensky.

Although Guchkov hadn't belonged to the Duma for four years, his place was undoubtedly there. He retained a tacit, unofficial right to be in the first row with the Duma's leaders. He hurried there not drawn by curiosity but because of this tacit right. He was one of the most deserving in the process of renewal and the royal couple's chief foe, and now that everything had been tossed in the air, it was natural for him to take the helm, without hypocrisy or antics. He had his sights set not on being prime minister (although he would have handled that excellently)—a line consisting of Rodzyanko, Milyukov, and Lvov had already formed for that seat—but on the number two or three spot in the government in any case. Due to his continuous proximity to military affairs, he appointed himself Minister of War.

But what a stupid crowd! He had to defend his right to every next step. Guchkov was used to believing that all Russia knew him, all Russia had sent telegrams during his illness—but here, in front of the Tauride Palace grating and in the open space, absolutely no one recognized his face except for a couple of university students. He was let through, but simply because of his respectable fur collar, serious appearance, and gold pince-nez, on the surmise that this gentleman had important business in the Duma. However, why were they themselves crowding here in such excessive, foolish numbers? Who could have foreseen this, that the revolution would send everyone running to the Duma and crowding there, like sheep, even in a considerable frost?

But what was this in comparison with what was inside? People were squeezed in doorways, and in the Cupola Hall there was an eddy spinning right at the entrance so that he had to elbow his way through. There was the bust of Aleksandr II put there by the peasant deputies in honor of the fiftieth anniversary of emancipation—now decked out with a red bow. Red bows, ribbons, and pins bristled on nearly everyone who had come. The Ekaterininsky was thick with crowds, and in a few places he caught glimpses of rallies.

Nonetheless, Guchkov quickly found the principal Duma deputies and learned about the Military Commission and understood his task: to take it into his firm hands, make it a regular headquarters, and wholly attach it to the Duma Committee. To do that he had to quickly place here if not generals then efficient colonels. Given Guchkov's acquaintances and military authority, this didn't take long.

He found some suspicious socialists—a bilious Academy librarian and a nervous lieutenant—and fixing them with contempt, moved them aside. He himself pressed on Engelhardt, who was anything but swift. He suddenly found the irreplaceable Obodovsky, rejoiced, and made him basically senior until his colonels arrived. Then he sat down and effortlessly wrote an order to the commanders of all units of the Petrograd garrison to report to him daily about their available personnel. And to present a list of officers who had returned to perform their duties. (That is, if we have anyone left?) Under no circumstances were they to allow the confiscation from officers of the weapons they needed to perform their service. As of 15 March, they were to restore proper activities in all military institutions and schools. (It would be unrealistic to restore them by tomorrow.)

When afterward Guchkov went and pushed through to see Rodzyanko, he saw over the crowd Rodzyanko's elevated, capless, semi-cupola of a head moving toward the exit. He pushed through to him on the diagonal, in pursuit.

Once again they made it through the eddy and accumulation of the Cupola Hall and onto the front steps.

And saw before them a genuine miracle: a strict formation of cadets from the Mikhailovsky School in four ranks stretched out in the open area facing the palace, while the others were pushed aside.

Their pure cadet faces shone with readiness and devotion, not that dissolute, fearful, and wanton expression on the soldiers'. Here was who would be their buttress in the coming days!

Not only were all their officers in place (it was glorious to see a genuine formation), but so was the general, the head of the school, who gave a booming order in front of the Duma President:

"Attention! Present arms! Officers!"

And in a dashing movement of several hundred hands, the rifles were shifted from "order arms" to "shoulder arms," and the muffled handling of gunstocks merged into a single expressive sound.

Rodzyanko, recalling his youth, himself stood up straighter, his head bare, listened to the report, gave the necessary "at ease," and the rifles were lowered to order arms—and in a voice created for reviews, he sent this out to meet the cadets' loyalty:

". . . I welcome you who have come here and thereby proven your desire to help the efforts of the State Duma! I welcome you as well because you, our youth, are great Russia's foundation and future happiness. I firmly believe that we will reach the goal that will give our homeland happiness."

He spoke as if nothing had happened, in any case not like a rebel at all, but as if no revolution had taken place as far as he knew. He could even give a speech like this in the presence of the Sovereign Emperor, and he spoke quite naturally, from the heart:

"I firmly believe that there burns in your heart a fervent love for your homeland and that you will lead our glorious troops to great military deeds! Long live the Mikhailovsky Artillery School!"

All of it so assuredly, the final slogan all the more so. A noisy "hurrah!"

Suddenly someone's shout, but not from the cadet formation, pierced through the air to remind him:

"Be the people's friend, Rodzyanko!"

But the President would not stoop to that kind of confirmation and pursued his own line:

"Remember the homeland and its happiness! Await orders from the Provisional Committee of the State Duma! This is the only way to be victorious!"

(Over whom? Wilhelm, naturally.)

Promising young exclamations rang out.

True though this may have been, Rodzyanko had not set his foot on the revolutionary field, nothing going on suggested that at all; that was a false path, too.

Stamping impatiently and moving forward was a very excited Vladimir Lvov, his eyes glittering—and he stepped up to make a speech:

"Long live unity, fraternity, equality, and freedom among us!"

It would have been proper for Guchkov to speak, and he would have said something intelligent and appropriate. He already had an approximate idea of what he would say and was a little nervous.

But before he could move away from the foolish Lvov and take a step forward, Kerensky, on Lvov's other side, suddenly stepped forward—erect, his arm held out easily, like an artist greeting his public, but not the way one talks to the troops:

"Comrade workers, soldiers, officers, and citizens!" he exclaimed explosively, passing over the cadets altogether and apparently addressing the crowd more than the formation. "The fact that you have come here on this great and momentous day gives me faith that the old, barbaric system has perished irrevocably."

And in this way he stepped straight across everything gradual, transitional, and contentious—the fact that the entire state system had perished was for him undeniable. Not a stone left standing!

A buzz of approval passed through—again not the formation of cadets and not any louder than they had shouted "hurrah" to Rodzyanko. Apparently, the crowd was willing to approve of it all equally, just so the words keep coming.

What a dangerous man! What was he going on about? This would have its consequences. People's ears were getting used to hearing this sort of thing. And he couldn't be cut off or shut up in front of everyone. Meanwhile, Kerensky plunged on:

"Comrades! We are living through a moment when we have to ask ourselves whether Russia can live if the old regime continues to exist. Do you feel this?" he exclaimed, himself shaking hard.

Something was conveyed, and someone shouted from somewhere:

"Yes!"

Receiving this response, he continued:

"We have gathered here to give our solemn vow that Russia will be free!"

Where had this fidgeter come up with all this? From his own flatly squeezed head, it would seem. Was that really why they had gathered? In fact, the objective was for those soldiers who, having left their barracks and made the revolution, now somehow to return to them and surrender their weapons.

"Let us swear!" Kerensky was speaking as one would to children.

Someone readily raised his arms, apparently one of the cadets:

"We swear!"

"Comrades!" The leftist lawyer was not satisfied. "Our very first task right now is organization. In the next few days we have to create total calm in the city and total order in our ranks. We have to achieve total unity between soldiers and officers!" Finally he had woken up. "Officers have to be the soldiers' senior comrades!" (Even this he was twisting around.) "Right now the entire nation has made a single solid alliance against our most terrible enemy, more terrible than our foreign enemy! Against the old regime!"

What had he done? What had he done! The madman had hacked through all the restraining ropes—and Guchkov had lost all desire to speak. He didn't know how to fix this. Inside him everything seemed to be collapsing.

But Kerensky carried on:

"Long live the free citizen of free Russia! Hurrah!"—in a delicate voice.

But it was covered by an amiable and long "hurra-a-ah!"

Guchkov returned from that rally with his feelings in knots. Events had not only leapt ahead of everything imaginable, but they continued to unravel dangerously—and he couldn't see any way to secure them.

[197]

What kind of fate was this? In principle not a military man, even despising the army, Obodovsky kept ending up in military posts, either dealing with equipment or, as now, directly—practically organizing the military authority.

He hadn't come to the Tauride Palace to get bogged down in the political prattle. And other than politics there was just one practical matter, here, in the Military Commission. In a few evening hours yesterday, having personally defended the Chief Artillery Administration, the GAU (by shouting at the soldier-looters and driving them out), Obodovsky in the night had come here to get a sentry for the GAU and had sent one such, but they'd then asked him how to maintain the armored cars, which were breaking down, what should be requested from the Mikhailovsky manège, and he sat down to write—a magneto, tools—and then the next and the next, to procure lubricants and gaskets, then cannon Garfords, then to examine the cannon that had arrived, and so he stayed. And then he signed audacious military instructions such as people in this room were beginning to do: "on behalf of the Chairman of the Military Commission."

He'd spent the night here.

Today, in the early morning hours, the main issue had been negotiations with the Peter and Paul Fortress commandant, who had shown great readiness to surrender, which was the key to taking the entire capital. They didn't have the forces to storm the Admiralty, so they decided to starve them and let them fall apart. After restoring telephone station operations, Obodovsky's next concern was to gradually occupy and guard all of the city's power stations. An electrical outage would harm the revolution and bolster the hostile troops outside. Then, through great persistence and long arguing, Obodovsky got a solid guard sent to the Chemical Committee's building and the military's chemical laboratory; otherwise, there could be accidents involving gases and, moreover, the loss of secret information if German spies managed to infiltrate.

While he was dealing with all this, though, he missed the fact that right here, at one of the neighboring tables, they had written instructions to some rider, maybe even a circus rider, to take fifty men and go arrest the counter-intelligence section at Military District Headquarters without grasping that they were fighting spies, not revolutionaries. Apparently this had come of the indiscriminate hatred felt by the frowning Maslovsky, who was stalking about, exuding malice.

As in many places—at mines, on geological committees, in front of high-ranking bureaucrats—Obodovsky had to shout nervously, strain his voice and heart, and demand the instructions be canceled. So at this point he insisted on sending a guard to the secret department at Military District headquarters.

The telegraph office had to be occupied and order there maintained. Vehicle repair also had to be organized at the military automotive school.

But much more important was that Obodovsky sketched out what kind of public appeal should be issued to officers, telling them where to go to get warrants for universal access and win the soldiers' trust. The Military Commission could not order officers to do this, but for their own good the commission had to convince them, appealing to their prestige as officers and citing the military threat.

Meanwhile, some as yet ungathered forces had to stop the looting, pogroms, and shooting from attics that was going on in the city. Complaints about this shooting were so common and unanimous that at first Obodovsky and everyone there believed them and sent reconnaissance groups out to find the machine guns being fired, which had been precisely pointed out, and take them off the roofs. But the hours passed, and not a single group discovered a single machine gun on an indicated roof or any other.

Since there were so many idle civilians and university students, they came up with another measure: give them white armbands and rifles and send them on patrols and as pickets to specific points. Vehicles under the white flag would make the rounds of those points. Maybe that way the looting, drunkenness, and shooting would stop.

A tentative explanation reached the Duma walls that the regiments from Oranienbaum and Strelna were moving this way not against the revolution but approvingly, to support it.

And supposedly the Tsarskoye Selo garrison was also coming over to the revolution's side!

From far away, Ivanov's troops were moving ominously on Petrograd.

The arrow of revolution was swinging tremulously, just as it was supposed to tremble and swing.

At first it seemed as though there were no defense forces at all and nothing was being pulled in or assembled.

Then it seemed as though the foe had even less than that, nothing at all, and everything was falling apart.

Suddenly, at eleven o'clock in the morning, a dispatch arrived saying that Ivanov's troops were already disembarking at the Nikolaevsky Station!

That was fast! Already! But there was absolutely no one to send to block them.

All they could do was rely on the first revolutionary battalion, the Volynian, especially since their barracks were right on the way. An order was sent to the Volynians: two companies with machine guns were to head out to meet them.

The night's tenseness was rekindled, everyone was moving around the room in fits and starts, and anyone who smoked was smoking.

Right then, at an unfortunate moment for him, a slender, precise naval officer showed up from one of the naval crews with a dagger and revolver, having given up nothing on the way, in the gleam of his uniform and covered in crosses and medals. He had been delegated by his officers' assembly to clarify the purposes and intentions of the coup before carrying out the Tauride Palace's instructions. The coup's political goals remained vague, and the officers of the crew wanted formal guarantees that events were not directed against the monarch.

He stood at attention.

At the tensest moment! When a battle was anticipated between the Nikolaevsky Station and the Volynian barracks, and in half an hour they themselves might need to slip away from here!

Under the indignant gazes of the Soviet's Maslovsky and Filippovsky, Engelhardt's entire face and neck turned red, as if they suspected him of treason!—and he ordered the naval officer arrested: "held until clarification of his authority."

The sergeant on duty and a few cocky soldiers jumped right up and now took away the officer's weapon and led him to the palace galleries where the prisoner rooms were.

Meanwhile Obodovsky, inconsistent as he was, admired this sailor as he once had admired the Irkutsk commandant Lastochkin. It is always inspiring to see loyalty to duty, even if that duty is to the contrary! In any case, this sailor elicited more respect than Captains Ivanov and Chikolini from the imperial service, who had just been hanging around.

The goals of the coup were clear to Obodovsky but not at all to Engelhardt, which is why he had turned red. Rodzyanko himself still didn't understand what was going to happen to the Tsar. These thoughts don't enter our minds so easily; and if it takes us decades to get used to them, then what of the naval officers?

But what was happening outside the Nikolaevsky Station? You could thrash about and still not find out anything about that; there weren't any direct dispatches coming in. At twelve-thirty they learned for certain that the Volynians had no intention of acting in defense of the revolution and hadn't budged. There was cursing at the Military Commission: in an hour and a half, if that disembarked regiment didn't lose its nerve, it could reach the Tauride Palace in marching order or join up with and rescue Khabalov.

But this was the peculiarity of revolution, that the regiments of reaction were supposed to lose their nerve and fall apart!

They ordered the Volynians a second time: act immediately!

But they didn't go this time, either.

Had no one disembarked at the Nikolaevsky? Apparently not.

Meanwhile, billeting officers had been sent out for the troops approaching from Oranienbaum—to establish contact with them.

And were they to think about protecting defense factories?

In the meantime, what should they do about the military schools? Yesterday they'd been neutral, but the schools couldn't remain in an indeterminate state; they had to hold training classes for war, even during days of revolution. Who was supposed to order them to continue their classes? The Military Commission, evidently; there simply was no one else. (Actually, what about the General Staff? The huge General Staff with its hundreds of officers, its wings spread on the expansive Palace Square, had remained neutrally silent.)

They also wrote instructions to the heads of the Mikhailovsky and Vladimirsky schools. But it was worse with the Pavlovsky. Had there been internal clashes there and had counterrevolutionary moods revealed themselves? No one knew for certain. But if the schools came out against the revolution, that was a terrible force. They all had officers and were armed and united—it was the sole force in the city. They had to be neutralized!

Their experience with the crew officer raised a question about the Guards Crew in its barracks on the Kryukov Canal as well. After all, they were under the command of Grand Duke Kirill—and to what good could he command them?

The revolution fed on and was strengthened only by audacity. Thus had it been since time immemorial. Lieutenant Filippovsky shook his forelock and signed and handed a document to Lieutenant Grekov: by order of the Provisional Government (which did not exist), take charge of the Guards Crew and at the same time the 2nd Baltic Naval Depot—that is, two general's posts simultaneously. (How would Grand Duke Kirill take this insult?)

Then Guchkov showed up, and Obodovsky was very glad to see him, and vice versa, since they seemed to have been in constant collaboration since their work on the War Industry Committee.

Guchkov possessed an invariably dignified restraint; he always remembered that he was known by all Russia, that everyone saw him and appearances were important. But right now, despite this, it was clear that he was distraught, that he hadn't thought circumstances would be so messy.

Not having been brought here by anyone, Guchkov nonetheless assumed he would become the center here by virtue of having shown up. Engelhardt couldn't help but be drawn to him, and after a brief conversation between them, they then went to see Rodzyanko, and it was announced to the whole room that Engelhardt would now be the deputy and Aleksandr Ivanych the chairman of the Military Commission.

The Soviet part of the commission started hissing, but under their breath; they were used to the idea of being perpetually put off here. Guchkov ignored the librarian Maslovsky, no matter how he tried to interject comments, on principle.

Guchkov sat down, and in the general conversation he was presented with the instructions of the last few hours. He laughed at some and was stunned by others. Actually, there was little to laugh about.

Under Guchkov, a few more dispatches came through and instructions were approved: occupy the Anichkov Palace; occupy the Hall of the Army and Navy—which the soldiery might also ransack; appoint a commandant for the looted Hotel Astoria—for which there was no one more suitable than a professor from the Military Medical Academy sitting right there. Someone else had to be appointed to command the 9th Cavalry Reserve Regiment. They appointed and sent off a captain, but exactly fifteen minutes later the regiment's indignant commander appeared and they had to issue another order—so that this captain came under the regiment's commander. (All the better; he would have his own colonel.)

An order was brought from Rodzyanko, and now it had only to be confirmed in writing, that a certain Eduard Shmuskes, who was not an officer but a university student, apparently, should take a party of fifty men and occupy the Ministry of Roads and Railways.

Guchkov was sitting not facing the desk but sideways, leaning on an elbow, and could only watch how, in the hubbub of the Military Commission, these orders were born, written up, and skedaddled off every five minutes.

Right then the following stunning dispatch was brought:

"The sentry standing at the corner of Kirochnaya and Shpalernaya has reported that according to information provided by private individuals, about three hundred officers armed with machine guns have assembled at the General Staff Academy for the purpose of attacking the Tauride Palace."

Maslovsky immediately interjected that it was quite likely that the Academy's officers were inclined very much toward reaction, only the teachers were too frail to pick up machine guns, though some of the students well might, although they did not number three hundred or even two hundred. . . . And that some of them should be arrested.

But Obodovsky laughed nervously and nearly shouted that there was no such *corner* of Kirochnaya and Shpalernaya. They were parallel and not even neighboring, so there could be no block between them. And also, "provided by private individuals" . . .

After this dispatch, Guchkov had apparently made up his mind and so sat in the corner with Obodovsky and told him quietly:

"Pyotr Akimovich! I'm glad you're here, and in the next few hours I will be counting on you alone. What we have here isn't a military headquarters, it's a . . ."—and he used an obscene word. "There is one military man here, and that's you. It's not Engelhardt's fault that such a thing has befallen him. . . . We can push this Soviet gang out altogether. Hold on for just a few hours, I beg of you, until evening. By evening I'll bring genuine officers here from the General Staff, and we'll set up a military chancellery. By evening there will be a headquarters here."

Obodovsky accepted all this as proper. But he hastened to show Guchkov his draft of an appeal to the officers.

"Aleksandr Ivanych, a headquarters alone isn't going to save anything. Your general order isn't enough. We won't accomplish anything if we don't restore the officers' status and people's trust in them."

Guchkov's eyes were yellow and unhealthy. He read the draft, making changes here and there—and took it to show Rodzyanko.

[198]

Baron Raden, commander of the Dagestan Regiment, on his way back to the front from leave in Estland, arrived at the Baltic Train Station on the morning of 13 March. Rumors had already forewarned him of the disturbances in Petrograd. But on the platform, having barely left the train car, he was surrounded by a mixed crowd of soldiers and civilians armed with revolvers, swords, and rifles. There were similar clusters all along the platform awaiting the train's approach and rushing to all the doors.

Colonel Raden turned pale, straightened up, and said he was on his way to the front and would not surrender his weapon. (He had no idea how he might resist, but he was thinking of hand-to-hand combat.)

The crowd burst into a cacophony of voices. Some started shouting: "To the front? Let him have his sword, he needs it!" Others demanded he surrender it. They started asking when he was going and how. The colonel replied that he was transferring to the Vindava Station and had no intention of spending an extra moment in Petrograd. Meanwhile, they were moving toward the train station building, where those surrounding him agreed that he had to deposit his weapon along with his things at the left-luggage office, otherwise they couldn't vouch for his life.

But who was he to give it to in left-luggage? The usual station services were absent, and the entire station was a transient, agitated, motley throng. They agreed to the colonel placing his suitcase far under the table and putting his sword and revolver on his suitcase.

That crowd dispersed.

After leaving his things, the colonel started walking through the station. He came across a few officers, all of whom had had their weapons taken away by force. On the square in front of the station there was machine gun and rifle fire, and a dead policeman lay there. It wasn't clear how they were to get to the Vindava Station.

Right then, a large new crowd of armed, dissolute, and in part drunken soldiers arrived at the Baltic Station led by what looked to be an ensign who had changed clothes. They, too, demanded Colonel Raden's weapon, and one of the station porters showed them that it was lying on the suitcase under the table. They seized the weapon and seized the colonel himself, twisting his arms behind his back, pointing their revolvers at his head, and shouting that he was against the people.

When several barrels are pointing at your head at once, it's hard to talk to living people as a still living person. But the baron answered them in a still loud voice that he was on his way to the front. Again the crowd's opinions diverged, and again some stood up for him—and the rest demanded he be killed. Ultimately, they let Colonel Raden go much the worse for wear.

But during that time both his sword and his revolver were carried off. Though the suitcase remained.

What could he do? There was no hope of a cabby. No matter how twisted daily life in the city was, the colonel could not violate regulations and carry his own large suitcase; he had to find someone to do that. This was where any officer's independence stopped. Someone calling himself a porter agreed to carry it.

They started out on foot, through the Izmailovsky companies. Along the way, some but not all the soldiers saluted him, and the rabble shouted threats and abuse and shot over the colonel's head, into the air, to scare him. Around the Izmailovsky Regiment's barracks, the entire street was filled with Izmailovsky soldiers, but without their weapons and in great turmoil. Something incomprehensible had happened to them.

It was the same once again around the Semyonovsky Regiment's barracks.

There was shooting everywhere—an ordinary street phenomenon by now. Motorcars were driving around with red flags, machine guns, and armed soldiers or sailors from naval crews. Riding around on horses, too, were soldiers who had woven red ribbons into their horses' manes. They were storming entryways where they thought police had holed up.

There weren't any guards or railroad gendarmes at the Vindava Station, either. In the same way, still bound by the impossibility of carrying his own things, Colonel Raden was pushed away from them by a new onrushing crowd. When the crowd thinned out, his belongings had vanished, and he was left with the greatcoat and tall fur hat he was wearing.

Thus he was finally independent and free.

Given this anarchy, there was no point trying to find his stolen things.

A few unarmed officers came up to the colonel and suggested they all go together to the State Duma, where the new government was in session. The colonel replied that there could only be usurpers there, and he had no wish to have anything to do with them and advised them against it, saying it was vile.

While he was waiting for the train to Mogilev, he saw lots of officers heading for the Duma.

The colonel tried fervently to convince one of them not to go—and soldiers heard this and he nearly got killed again.

[199]

Train journeys have a poetry all their own: the special lulling relaxation, the inaccessibility to reports, ministers, and generals, the changing views out the window, the pleasant reading. To avoid any jolts, the top speed of the imperial trains was set at a mere twenty-five miles an hour. Sleep was peaceful then.

Journeys fell into two groups: sad (moving away from Alix) and joyous (moving toward Alix). This would have been the latter now if it weren't for his alarm over his dear ones and their illness.

He slept for a long time. And woke up at around noon. What a bright, cheerful sun was shining! Wasn't that a good sign? He looked out the window with pleasure. Beneath the snowdrifts, beneath the ridges buried in snow was Russia—intact and not at all rebellious. Landscapes dear to his heart: hills and copses under deep blankets, awaiting spring. There was utter calm and order at the stations. In front of the station buildings stood strapping duty gendarmes.

In this blinding, snowy tranquility, all the city's disturbances seemed, if not invented, then minor and surmountable. What if there were disturbances on a few streets against a great state?

A string of undisturbed thoughts, and in part memories, passed unhurriedly through his mind.

No matter how many days Nikolai was away from his family, each time he returned to them with such renewed and total joy, it was as if the separation had lasted a year. Above all—joy for Alix. Only when he had pressed her to his heart, told her everything, and learned everything about their days of separation did he become entirely himself. But only a little less was the joy of his son, in whom Nikolai sensed an enigmatic physical repetition of himself, only broken by a terrible disease, while the father enjoyed enviable health—hence his even more insistent paternal duty and connection with his son. And four daughters. Four! Three of them were already of marriageable age with a hazy destiny—as if in a dungeon due to their father's royal status. Once the war ended, they would marry. At the same time, he loved Anastasia no less, his sixteen-year-old *Shvybzik*. Nikolai longed for them all and knew no greater happiness than to live with them always and see them every day.

But there was one other female being, organically included among them all: Anya Taneeva. Always there, always nearby, always making a threesome, she had inevitably bonded tenderly with everyone, including Nikolai. Her relationship with Nikolai had no name, no place in human classifications. Not an ecstatic subject of her Emperor (although that is exactly what was said in letters), not like an older daughter toward her father, of course (although there was an age difference of sixteen years), and not a beloved, because there was no room in Nikolai's heart for a second love, given his ardor for Alix. At the same time, though, there was something tender and inalienable that belonged to the two of them alone and was expressed in full only when they met alone.

There had been a dangerous moment when this might have crossed all kinds of lines—in the spring of 1914, in the Crimea. As always, Alix's many illnesses had her chained either to her bed, or to her comfortable chair, and there were all the concerns about the heir, while Nikolai, as always, had a great need for movement, for tennis, and this heavenly-eyed woman inevitably accompanied him on his long outings—by motorcar or horse or on foot. They got carried away, but Alix firmly intervened in time. It ended (after stormy scenes between the women) with Anya being driven out of Livadia and the family. Even Alix felt that this was cruel and intolerable for her herself, though, and Anya was restored to the intimacy of family and friends, though Alix herself now kept track of Anya's relations with Nikolai.

All three accepted these conditions. Anya's little house was hung with enlarged photographs of the Emperor. She brought her voluminous letters to Alix and offered to burn them if the Empress felt the letters would anger the Emperor. Alix passed them all on, naturally, and he, reading them, on a promise to his wife, destroyed them. And if there was a direct telegram from Anya, he told Alix.

Within these well-defined limits—within any others it would have been improper—something tender persisted and something tender echoed between them. Added to this was the entire horrible story of the railroad disaster, when Anya lay ill for months and had special need for kindness, and Nikolai would visit her, and later she began walking, though with a crutch (but even the crutch couldn't spoil her blue and white charm). Occasionally they did meet briefly and alone. (She wanted to more often!) All this was cloaked in a soundless sound, an unrelenting, touching tone, an invisible flower in continuous bloom. All this made his return to Tsarskoye that much more tender and precious. Today this motif blended with the others as well and ran and ran like the telegraph lines alongside the train—never broken and never overtaken.

The lines stretched on and on, sagging in the middle and swooping up toward the poles; there was sun shining and half-shadows over the snowdrifts. What Divine beauty, and how fine it would be for our country and all humanity to live if there wasn't so much evil intent and impatience!

And these lines—fine—had brought nothing today, no news.

Maybe everything in the capital had calmed down? God willing.

But no, Voeikov had simply overslept and all the telegrams always went through him. Now he came—and shattered this reassuring, caressing solitude.

First, it turned out that last night, while they were waiting in Mogilev, Alekseev had forwarded to the train Belyaev's telegram, which consisted of a few sentences. But the sentences were horrible: rebels had occupied the Mariinsky Palace, some of the ministers had fled, and some may have been arrested.

Oh ho! This was serious.

With a gentle reproach—faint, barely a reproach—the Emperor looked at the palace commandant. How was it he hadn't handed this over last night, when they were still in Mogilev?

But the man didn't even turn red. His chiseled face never did.

Anything else?

Yes, this. A telegram to the Emperor from fifteen members of the State Council had been forwarded from GHQ and caught up to him.

The Emperor read it and was at a loss. These men repeated over and over that the popular masses had been brought to the point of despair. That deep in the popular soul (which they knew!) there had sunk a hatred for the government and suspicions against the regime.

Nikolai read all this as the ravings of madmen. He encountered here not a single correlation to reality, not a single sober word. It was simply impossible to understand how serious, educated men could write and sign such nonsense. Though look who'd signed—Guchkov, and Grimm, and Krym, and Shmurlo, and Veinstein—almost all from the same Progressive Bloc.

Somehow, imperceptibly, they had taken the State Council's place. Selected to the State Council from society were the government's bitter enemies, while from the Emperor they had appointed all kinds of honorable and helpless wrecks—the kind who had to be consoled upon retirement. The leftists easily had the upper hand there over the rightists.

These fifteen were directly demanding that His Imperial Majesty decisively change the course of domestic policy, dismiss the current government, and order the formation of a new one, to be governed in accord with the people's representatives. That is, the Duma.

Who could the pertinacious, ambitious Guchkov have had in mind if not himself? With cautious hatred he had not let a single movement by the Emperor out of his sight. And he had once seemed so amiable.

Nikolai was brought to despair by the fact that in one and the same country and in one and the same language it was so impossible to be understood.

Never, nowhere, had Nikolai seen this hatred or these suspicions in the people's soul.

Once again there was the continuous movement between sun and snows. Only now alarm was gnawing at him. The Mariinsky Palace? What was going on there? Going to have breakfast with his suite, the Emperor sensed their gloom and alarm. Indeed, he had told them nothing yesterday at evening tea about his decision to go that very night, and it was not his way to explain his motivations to the suite. Even now, at breakfast, the Emperor could not allay the disbelief on their brows; that would have been shockingly unusual and improper. They discussed the weather, the journey, and various minor events.

At the stations, as before, there was neither disarray nor disorder of any kind but rather the same neat railroad personnel and appointed authorities. In Smolensk, the governor came out to greet him. Everyone along the line knew the imperial trains were passing, and everyone had been prepared for their uninterrupted passage.

At a small station an infantry train going the other way waited, and they, too, knew. A unit had already been lined up on the platform, their band out front, and the rest leaped out of the heated cars and formed up—and everyone gazed passionately into the windows, following the train with their eyes, and no one knew in which of the two dark blue trains, in which of the ten train cars, at which window the Tsar might be found—but the band played continuously, "God Save the Tsar" to continuous shouts of "hurrah." Nikolai took pity on them and went up to the window—and they saw him!—and a "hurrah" of incredible strength soared! All the soldiers' faces were inspired, ecstatic. The sight of the Tsar had swooped them up in joy and self-sacrifice.

What could the Petrograd disturbances, the Duma's insanity, and the insanity of the State Council members amount to?

Nikolai stood immobile and gazing brightly at the wide window until he came to the end of the platform, until the exultant regiment was lost from view.

From Vyazma he sent an affectionate telegram to Tsarskoye:
"Thoughts always together. Glorious weather. Hope are feeling well and quiet. Many troops sent from front. Fondest love. Nicky."

[2 0 0]

Actually, it was extremely offensive. There could be no justification for not including Vladimir Bonch-Bruevich on the Executive Committee of the Soviet of Workers' Deputies. If he wasn't the representative of any workers, then neither was whoever was convening there. Perhaps he was less of a "prominent leftist figure" than Sukhanov or Steklov, but definitely not less than Kapelinsky. How was a publisher worse than a journalist for a revolutionary administration? Very much to blame here was Shlyapnikov, who could have nominated the prominent Bolshevik. Lately, though, Bonch's relations with the Bolsheviks' Central Committee had not been very good, which was why this had happened.

He found it insulting given that he, having declared himself a Marxist fifteen years ago (while his brother Mikhail had gone off to kowtow in service to the Tsar), had since then made so many revolutionary contributions, including the Rasputin investigation, how he had concealed his sectarianism, and even in the last few days this contribution: he had convinced the Cossack sectarians not to shoot and had had them pass this along to the other Cossacks— and now, on the day of triumph, to find himself out of the picture?

Yesterday Bonch had strapped an army belt around his paunch, fastened on his huge revolver, and walked here among them, jostled among them— but had not been chosen for the Executive Committee. Fine, he would be commissar for the printing presses. He went to seize the *Kopeika* printing press on Ligovka. This turned out to be very simple because no one resisted— and that night he put out the first issue of the Soviet's *Izvestia*.

The beginning was simple, but then a number of complications arose, as did a number of dangers due to which Bonch had already sent the Tauride Palace two very decisive notes and finally showed up there himself and called Himmer out of the EC session.

In fact, Himmer had not been assigned to oversee *Izvestia*, and he had no obligation in this regard. But as the farthest-seeing member of the EC, he could not decline. When Bonch began attacking him rudely, saying that their entire session here and all their discussions were worthless if *Izvestia* didn't come out, that only what was printed in a newspaper existed in reality, Himmer couldn't help but admit the great truth in this.

Bonch complained of the following difficulties he had uncovered: the owners weren't resisting the seizure, but the press workers, despite the revolution, wanted to be paid for their labor, which meant he needed money. Then, in view of the ongoing nature of the work, he couldn't let workers leave the press, which meant he had to feed them something. Then, since the entire city now knew where *Izvestia* was being printed, there was a great danger of the Black Hundreds attacking. Therefore, he needed a guard, at least forty men, with machine guns, posted down the entire block. Simultaneously, this would be an iron dictatorship over the printers. But a guard also had to be continuously supported, which meant feeding them. So now Bonch was asking the Soviet of Deputies to provide for all this—enough for 100 men.

An epigram going around about Bonch flashed through Himmer's mind:

His hungry she-Bonch by his side,
Bonch went roaming far and wide.

It had yet to be verified whether he had sixty workers. Inevitably, though, one way or another, the problem had to be resolved.

Himmer also felt he represented the revolutionary government. And as someone with authority, he replied decisively:

"Fine, Vladimir Dmitrich. The Soviet doesn't have any money yet either, but you don't need to pay them this minute. Promise the workers any terms, just so they print. As for food, we'll supply that; I'll take care of that right away. And a guard—we'll try to get you that as well."

But Bonch-Bruevich loomed up over clever little Himmer like a paunchy barrel:

"Don't just try! Send a guard immediately! It will be getting dark soon, and we can't stay there like that when it's dark. The Black Hundreds will crush us."

Fine. He gave Bonch his promise. They parted.

Something really did have to be done. But what? The difficulty of acting when no one knows you by name or face. Lots of people knew Gvozdev, but no one knew you.

Somewhere in a far corner of the Tauride Palace the revolution's food storeroom was being created. But just signing and sending a requisition wouldn't help. They wouldn't read it there and wouldn't know the signatures of the EC members. And what form could he use? To whom exactly would he write? That meant he had to go to the storeroom himself.

But walking in the Tauride Palace now meant elbowing his way through. What kind of mad, senseless crowd was this? Why had they all been driven here? What did they want? What were they expecting? You couldn't help but become exasperated trying to get through on business while these stupid backs and ugly faces kept barring your way. Through the drafts, over the slippery muck that had collected on the floors, searching for that door, searching for that room.

Himmer lost a lot of time just getting to the storeroom, where some unknown person was distributing food at his own discretion and everyone was tugging at him. He also had to attract the man's attention and then admonish him. Finally the man wrote out the order. But there was nothing in which to deliver the food. Now he had to find a vehicle and someone to escort it. And a guard for the vehicle so it didn't get looted en route. And get it to the storeroom quickly.

Separately, he had to take care of the main guard. For this he had to make his way to the Military Commission. So Himmer headed that way.

Every member of the commission (each one also a deputy chairman) was acting, doing as much as he could, each surrounded by a dozen claimants and complainants, accepting denunciations, sending instructions, ordering that details be formed, and could not be certain of anything.

Himmer caught the attention of Filippovsky, the SR, the man closest to the Soviet. But even the energetic Filippovsky was worn out and drawn. He agreed that *Izvestia* had to be protected, but not only did he not have forty men with machine guns, he couldn't even appoint anyone to command such a party. There were some officers crowding about, as if just asking for an appointment, but when Filippovsky tried to propose they command the printing press detail, none obeyed, citing other more important missions or the lack of men.

Himmer despaired and himself went to mill among the idle officers, searching for a volunteer. A Cossack ensign of mature years agreed, but only if he was given a party; he didn't have anyone. The ensign's appointment was signed by the engineer Obodovsky—but there still wasn't a detachment.

What, was Himmer himself supposed to find a detachment as well? Go out now to the soldiers and agitate? This was something he was not prepared to do. He could not go out and speak before the crowd; he knew in advance it would be a failure and had a presentiment that the tentativeness of his figure and his far from military manner would immediately undermine his speech.

But there was someone who seemed created for this: Kerensky! Here was the solution: seek out Kerensky among the Tauride Palace's many thousands now and convince him to assemble a detachment. Perhaps no one else could be found in this mass—but Kerensky could because he was the most garish and popular, and all paths led to him.

He was found deep in the Duma wing, in a room where at least twenty people were simultaneously demanding, besieging, and trying to reach him, and Kerensky, pivoting quickly, changing subjects and breaking off his own sentences, was trying not only to understand and satisfy these twenty but also to understand and embrace, satisfy, and serve the entire vast Great Revolution that was tearing his chest asunder! He alone was capable of this! He felt that. He held himself erect and steady! An ill-wisher on the sidelines might think that his thin, inspired, burning face looked rather harried, but in fact he was experiencing an inexhaustible surge and had the strength to do this a thousand times over.

Himmer appreciated this and regretted that in this state Kerensky was scarcely going to be able to grasp all the main springs of the strategic and political situation, but Himmer rushed to push his specific question through, tightly grasping the button of Kerensky's frock coat and not letting him go.

Not only the risk of losing a visible button at a bad time but also Kerensky's willingness to hear out each of the twenty and grasp their problem helped Himmer. He also took advantage of the ominous words about the Fate of the Revolution—and a keen awareness cut through Kerensky's inflamed eyes.

The moment he heard what Himmer had to say, he immediately agreed and broke away from all the other nineteen—and raced off so that Himmer could barely keep up. Strangely, Kerensky didn't have to push the crowds aside as everyone else did. Like a meteor, he burned himself a path—and Himmer sat on his fiery tail and grabbed his ensign along the way.

Kerensky flew into the overfilled Ekaterininsky Hall and up, not subject to the force of gravity, onto some table or platform—and over the sea of heads turned in different directions, without any preparation, his fiery speech soared, saying that the entire fate of the revolution was on a razor's edge and depended on forty volunteers agreeing to do sentry duty whom he had to line up here, right now, this minute!

Whether such was the force of his eloquence or the comparative safety of sentry duty, but even before the far ends of the hall could hear him and turn this way, volunteers were surging forward from different sides and the elderly ensign was starting to line them up.

[2 0 1]

"So, are you starving?"

"No, you with the pocks, wait a minute, you listen here! However long we've been wearing the gray coat, and even before—when've we ever had an honor like this, to gather here, in the chamber—and now we're . . . ? We've been like this for more than a day, we're a little short on praise, forget going to training. . . . Just so they fix us for meals. There haven't been any meals. These people here, instead of giving speeches, they should set up feeding for all the soldiers!"

"Aren't you clever. Feeding! Where are workers going to get feeding for you?"

"They can take it where it is!"

"It's in storehouses. The rich have it. There are supplies somewhere. Where could it have gone? They're hiding it from us."

"That's what I'm saying. Take it! Pick a Commission and it can go clean them out."

"What Commission? What are we, armless or something? 'Stead of hanging around this here Soviet for nothing, we should spread out through the streets. Comb them with bayonets. And take it!"

All those hours, people had been pressing in and pressing in to the large room where they'd declared the *Soviet of Deputies*. Very few were coming out of the cold; no, they were nice and dry and warm—to look at, they'd spent the night. They were scared to go to their barracks, and here young ladies gave them tea and bread with a slice of sausage—and now they'd see whatever was going to happen. Men held them back at the doors and asked for some kind of paper or at least to prove in words what unit they were from or what factory. Some were able to prove something and others pressed and went through in a body, lots of soldiers, some with rifles, the way they'd left the barracks yesterday, and what could you do about them?

But in the middle at first there was plenty of room, and they even put their behinds on the chairs and benches, while the big shots among the educated ones from the box room next door, whoever was holding a pass—they were sitting at a table. But more and more new ones pushed through, and so many people piled in standing that sitting was unbearable. You couldn't see anything, or hear half, more and more came in, and people's backs pressed into your face—so people started half-standing. When it got even more crowded so that everyone's knees were being pressed against the chairs—why didn't they just break them, damn it, or throw them out! Or like this, the smarter ones: climb onto the chair—now that was good! To see from there, forward, backward, even spew out a speech, or just goggle at this wild assemblage!

They kept pressing and pressing on the big shots—who were already squeezed to the wall. They couldn't see anything and had also climbed and stood on their table. Now there was no towering over them from any chair.

Below, in the crush, you couldn't remove a fur hat anywhere, and holding it was awkward, so your head was just going to bake. On the other hand, it was a golden opportunity for discussing, for sure! A soldier's place is with his mates. Over the last evening and day, soldiers had met other soldiers from different battalions as they moved around. And here, if someone was nearby, that also meant a conversation. Talking to a neighbor warms the heart.

"The pegs on those girls, scraped, sanded, polished—the works. . . ."

"Yeah, you think the Petersburg girls are even gonna look at the filthy likes of us?"

And from a table, waving his arms, someone in a leather jacket, from the motor detachment:

"Comrade soldiers! Your frivolous discussions are blocking the revolution's bright horizon! However much we've fought bloody Tsarism—we have to talk about that! In 1905 and 1906. Today, too, that hangman, General Ivanov, he's on his way here like a storm cloud to strangle our freedom. And we need to mobilize and organize. But what are we doing? Shooting in the air and that's it."

"That's not us, that's the kids."

"And who brings them, the cartridges? Who feeds them into the fires?"

"You'll have enough cartridges! We have a whole arsenal of those cartridges. They used to count 'em out, but now it's take all you want."

Then a redbeard climbed on the table, hale and hardy as a butcher. And he read out from a paper or recited from memory what had to be voted on. Voting meant raising an empty hand—raising, lowering, it's not hard, that we can do. Sort of like an oath. Do away with the police—good. Seize everywhere they make or keep money—fine. Don't let the streetcars out—no need, we walk anyway. They voted and voted—and then they were done.

It made you think. What, were those scholars smarter than us or something? It's just they have their grammar, they're used to this. But what we do is beside them. And the words they have, they're no kindness to our ear.

"Hey, brothers, if only we could stuff our bellies—we're free now, after all, and we're going to start living, right?"

Service caps, shaggy fur hats, black seaman's caps trimmed in yellow, and exposed shaved heads without anything, some with a languid look, some a buttoned-up one, and here were civilians in black clothes, more what we're used to, and there they went getting together and tittle-tattling, and they outtalked us:

"Comrade soldiers! We don't need to explain to you that the people's victory has to be safeguarded! The revolution's enemies are preparing a horrible bloodletting for us, but we aren't seeing your fine revolutionary ranks."

"Leftolutionaries. . . . How come they keep harping about the left side?"

"We have to crush the hydra of reaction—but what are we doing for that?"

Tongues had already been loosened, though, and the response was immediate:

"Hold on, I'll tell you. So, in our barracks . . ."

As to who had what in our barracks—there were enthusiasts on all sides, to give a good listen. It was like being in all the battalions at once. Five voices right off.

Some just wanted to figure out what had lightened everyone's hearts and loosened their tongues. Too hard to clear out of here. Your belly let you down, though.

To that civilian:

"Hey, listen up! Defend freedom with our lives—that we can. You could feed us some more, though."

Right then everyone, the shouters and the silent ones, heard: a machine-gun round! And close! Nearby!

And another round!

Right here, nearby, somewhere close to the palace!

And—striking at the people! a machine gun! That's no joke! A machine gun talks like it means it!

And the people here, crowded in, they could all be mowed down, by a single machine gun. People started churning, hollering. Either they're shooting at us, or we at them, but it doesn't matter—it's a battle!

And our rifles—some of them don't have cartridges. And some of us stacked ours in the corridor.

People were jerking toward the exit, squeezing through—

"Hey, easy with that bayonet. Damn! Don't stab me!" when someone goes and shouts through the wide-open door:

"Cossacks!"

"Oh, my poor miserable heart, I'm under the chopper, they're going to hack off all our heads this minute!"

What happened then, no one was sure except for what was right in front of him: some were looking at the door, some at the wall, some at the floor, and they were all squeezed in, and there was tromping overhead, and some at the windows: the windows on the garden. The Cossacks wouldn't be galloping from the street into the garden, would they?

Windows started breaking! They're striking here already? Yow!

Hey, that's us, we broke the glass with our rifle butts—but you can't jump out, it'd cut—so more of the butt? Jump out on the snow, and then make a run for it?

The first few minutes it was the heaviest, then it spaced out. But those who dashed into the hall—people were pressing on all sides there, too, so where were you supposed to jump?

And sure enough, everyone was shouting but not hearing anyone's voices. Maybe someone was trying to persuade them that this was nothing—but after that shout: *Cossacks!*

A few more machine-gun rounds.

While apparently no one was firing ours in reply.

This way, little by little, things quieted down.

Quieted down, and people looked around: no galloping Cossacks, no machine guns cutting them down.

People started returning—some coming inside from out, through the broken windows, some even back to the Soviet: where can we talk?

The big shots had run off, too. Gathering again.

[2 0 2]

After Guchkov's arrival, Maslovsky realized that his time on the Military Commission was coming to an end and this hypocritical Obodovsky, having forgotten his revolutionary past, was prepared to cater to the franchised circles. It had been a big mistake for the Soviet to forfeit its positions at the revolution's headquarters, the principal bridgehead for governance and authority. Sokolov had been right the night before in not wanting to let Engelhardt in, but the Soviet didn't have enough of its own military personnel and was too busy organizing itself.

Now, for what might be their last unsupervised hours here, they had to carry out as many important instructions as possible. Filippovsky, who hadn't slept for the last twenty-four hours, was signing instruction after instruction written on the letterhead of the State Duma Vice President (he should take a small pad like this, too), one nearly every five minutes.

It turned out that the rifles taken to the State Duma had run out and they needed to bring at least another five hundred from somewhere, so quickly were they being distributed. As detachments were being formed, many volunteers offered to go without rifles. They had to bring more revolver cartridges to the Duma building, too. (And somehow they had to form a separate special reserve for the Soviet.) They had to lance the counterrevolutionary boil at the Pavlovsky School. Lieutenant Filippovsky, writing out the letters painstakingly, especially the capitals, which here were almost in a row, which was the whole point, had written an instruction to General Valberg on the same grandiose Duma letterhead:

"To the Head of the Pavlovsky School. In the name of the Provisional Committee of the State Duma, I order you to surrender the school entrusted to you to the Military Commission of the Provisional Committee of the State Duma. . . ."

And he sent it on two motorcycles.

He continued to concentrate over the pages of letterhead, where to seize or guard something else, where to suppress something. In the Military Commission's room, despite the guard in the corridor, there was the usual crush, always unmanageable people who had come for some unknown reason—and Kerensky, also to demand, take, or send someone somewhere.

At that moment, quite close to the palace, but on the other side of the building, they heard a distinct, booming machine-gun round! And another! And another!

The machine-gun sound requires no explanation, especially to military men! Someone had broken through, and a battle was being waged near the Duma's very walls!

Everyone dashed out! Everyone suddenly found themselves not in the stronghold of headquarters but without a weapon and in a trap that was not so easy to escape.

The Military Commission's windows looked out on the open area in front, and there, in the confusion of motorcars, motorcycles, cannons, horses, and people, chaos arose, everything started eddying, trying to back up or leave, motorcars were starting up and not, people were pushing and shoving each other and shouting—only there was no obvious shooting, and you could tell from the open area that they themselves didn't see their foe.

You couldn't even get out of that open area or make your way to it via the corridor and entrance hall! In some five minutes, retribution might burst through, weapons at the ready—and they'd be caught, arrested, and then the noose!

Maslovsky despaired and rushed about madly. After all, he was forty years old and not a military man at all. . . . It was quite clear! Protopopov's machine-gunners had come down from the roofs and gone on the attack. Certain death was now here! Or else they'd be taken prisoner—and sent to hard labor. Oh, how little he'd felt like coming here yesterday! Even his wife had tried to dissuade him, but Kapelinsky had caught him unawares! How he'd longed at dawn to slip away to his own apartment—but he'd been held back by a false sense of revolutionary shame.

Some of the unnamed officers who'd been crowding here tried to push out of the room.

But a machine-gun round—again! And another, again! Incredibly close, simply right here, right under the palace's very walls!

No one knew how all this might have ended here, at the Military Commission, had Kerensky not been among them.

But he was! And all the same worries, all the same thoughts, only with even greater speed, decisiveness, and accountability for the revolution's entire fate—and not just for himself—raced around in his head, and he immediately reached a decision, or rather, carried it out, because for him execution had always come faster than the decision itself. Kerensky flew up from the floor, as if on invisible wings, and was already standing on the windowsill, one hand holding onto the upright bolt, the other opening the window pane wide, sunk into the frame's edge and sticking his narrow, rectangular head out, through the small window itself; it fit through quite easily.

Looking at the eddying insanity out front, he shouted through the window, in his own voice, so gloriously ringing and sharp on the tribune, though now a little hoarse:

"Everyone to his position! Everyone to his battle post! . . . Defend the State Duma! . . . This is Kerensky speaking! They're firing on the State Duma!"

This terrible historical fate, a tragic end to the new revolution, had appeared like a nightmare before the pale-faced Military Commission. The Tauride Palace was already drowning in blood!

"They're firing on the State Duma! This is I, Kerensky, speaking to you! . . . Defend your young freedom! Defend the revolution! Everyone to their place! Bear arms for action! . . ."

But in front of the palace, not everyone knew his place, and not everyone had a weapon, and not everyone knew how to use one. In that tumultuous panic, in the shouts, swearing, snorting, and roar, basically no one heard or noticed that someone was shouting from some small window.

But here in the room everyone heard—and Kerensky's bravery made a poor impression on the military men. Someone remarked tactlessly that this command through the window could have an effect the reverse of mobilization. Kerensky, who had already fluttered down from the window-sill to the middle of the room, folding his wings back into his shoulder blades, glanced at that insolent man with radiant anger, still not having quite returned from his flight to simple ambulation, and shouted with piercing notes:

"I would ask that you not admonish me! . . . I would ask everyone see to his own obligations—and not interfere with my instructions!"

Had this been a real attack on the Tauride—by a machine-gun detachment, an infantry half-company, or a quarter-company of Cossacks—we don't know how global events would have proceeded or whether many would have been rescued from the revolutionary ruins. But there was no more machine-gun fire, or any other, no Cossack whooping either—and gradually calm fell out front, and in the Ekaterininsky Hall, and in the corridors, and in the Military Commission's room itself—and Aleksandr Fyodorovich was given an unimpeded opportunity to betake himself away on his own affairs.

The reason for the shooting was soon clarified. A revolutionary detachment in the Tauride Garden had been checking to see how well the machine guns it had inherited fired. As to Cossacks—there'd never been any.

Although soon it would be nearly twenty-four hours since the Military Commission had been continuously seeing to only the most essential matters and instructions—now they had to admit that all the measures they'd taken were utterly unsatisfactory, and as they saw, the Tauride Palace was in no way prepared for a defense.

Nor was the capital as a whole. All these regiments filtering in from outlying areas to congratulate Petrograd to the glory of the revolution—immediately after their congratulations had slipped away, vanished, they all had nothing to do but get fed and sleep, and this stream hadn't added a single platoon to the revolution's defense.

Filippovsky latched onto this and wrote an order:

"To the Commander of the 9th Reserve Cavalry Regiment.

"*Immediately* bring in as many squadrons as possible in full battle gear, plus a machine-gun crew, to guard the Tauride Palace, along with the appropriate number of officers.

"Chairman of the Military Commission."

That general had asked to take command—now let him go to work.

Even if he brought an entire cavalry regiment, in no way would that be too much for the Tauride's defense.

The Soviet and bourgeois part of the Military Commission jointly sought out more reserves. And what had happened to the Preobrazhensky Battalion that had sworn loyalty to the Duma? Not long ago, that morning, they'd come with congratulations. . . .

Actually, this entire panic at the Tauride Palace had demonstrated something else: just how bereft of forces the Tsarist government was.

[2 0 3]

*   *   *

A red flag was raised on the main spire of the Peter and Paul Fortress. Everyone watched, rejoiced, and told those who hadn't seen it. Enthusiasm! Tsarism's principal stronghold!

The sprawling stone fortress polyhedron over the Neva had raised questions about just how many doomed political prisoners were languishing there. The crowd in front of the gates was agitated, demanding the prisoners be handed over. At last, deputy-witnesses were let in to examine the cells— and they learned that all the bastion-ravelins were empty. They came out to the crowd, which shouted "hurrah" and began to disperse.

*   *   *

After the government troops left the Admiralty, it was gradually inundated by riffraff, who started looting the Naval General Staff and workshops. A new worry for Minister of the Navy Grigorovich, who asked Rodzyanko for a sentry for protection.

*   *   *

On the gates and gratings of the Winter Palace, pieces of red fabric hung here and there over the eagles and monograms.

And a new activity was picked up throughout the city: tearing up tricolor flags.

*   *   *

Count Frederiks's home on Pochtamtskaya was stormed. The crowd went on a rampage and threw furniture and appointments out the windows and off the balcony from the second and third floors. A large piano crashed to the pavement with a heavy clank. Then they set fire to it, and the large crowd wouldn't let the firefighters put it out, only to contain it so the neighboring buildings wouldn't catch fire. (Next door was the post office, with new telegraph equipment.)

Countess Frederiks suffered a stroke and they wanted to put her in the English hospital, but she was refused. Evidently British Ambassador Buchanan didn't want to take a demonstrative step in favor of the old regime.

*　　*　　*

Two ugly mugs were dragging a small sled across Theater Square; lashed to it was a policeman's dead body on its back. Some they met stopped and asked, laughing, how the copper had been killed. Two boys, each fourteen, ran up from behind and tried to stick a cigarette in the dead man's mouth.

Sometimes the bodies of murdered policemen were tossed into garbage pits.

*　　*　　*

At the Nikolaevsky Station, the soldiery was pressing, pressing into the lunchroom, demanding snacks. Then they broke in, drove the cooks out, ate up all they could, broke every last plate, and absconded with the dining room silver and linens. They said they were taking it to the Duma.

Trains arrived—and the soldiers wouldn't let the porters on the platform work and instead of them hauled the passengers' luggage and earned some money.

*　　*　　*

The Oranienbaum machine-gun regiments entered the city through the Narva gate over the course of several hours, for half a day, so far did they stretch. To keep the machine guns from freezing, they carried them wound round with felt. Their cartridge belts hung crosswise, crosswise over their greatcoats. Their greatcoat collars and their mustaches and beards had turned white from their journey's breathing.

*　　*　　*

Educated Petersburg dwellers were as if in a waking dream, full of doubts, fears, and joyous decisiveness. For an entire day, someone would sit by the telephone collecting telephone rumors.

But the domestic, if she wasn't old, had a lot of running to do: out through the streets to look out for something, learn something, run back to her employers and tell them, and run off again. There were club-like clusters at nearly all the gates.

In apartments, the samovar was kept going surrounded by food to eat—for the friends and acquaintances who came. The conversations were sweet:

an overthrow, the most respectable kind, the State Duma had given it its name. Now, evidently, we would have a monarchy on the English model. Since the Duma had taken power, everything would proceed smoothly and the war would soon end.

Actually, though, where was he, the Tsar? And weren't his troops on their way to Petrograd?

Against the Duma? They wouldn't dare.

But if the Tsar were removed, would the money in the banks be lost?

* * *

A sharp long honking, to make everyone scatter. A luxurious long blue motorcar with gold imperial eagles on the doors, a red flag at the wheel, completely filled with armed sailors. Shouting and waving.

A unit, marching harmoniously to a drumbeat—suddenly disintegrated at a random shot fired from behind.

Soldiers without officers! . . .

Revolutionary soldiers—many without belts, in unfastened greatcoats. Joyous but distraught bewildered faces. Cartridge belts removed from machine guns and now worn like decoration on many: across a shoulder, around the waist, or simply carried.

* * *

A crowd thronged down Ligovka toward Znamenskaya Square—lots of soldiers, civilians in black, and boys—escorting a tall uniformed gendarme they'd seized. Again and again people intruded on the crowd from all sides, stopping them. Shouts.

A rifle, butt up, rose behind the gendarme and was brought down hard on his head. The gendarme's cap flew off. And the same rifle took a second swing—and came down a second time, on his bare head. Drawing blood. The gendarme looked around, said something, and crossed himself. He was beaten by several more hands and fell.

* * *

A handful of armed men burst into the Putilov Factory's head office: "Hand over the cash box!" Refusal. They grabbed the factory's military director, Major General Dubnitsky: "We're taking you to the Duma!" His aide, General Bordelius: "I won't leave you. We served together. . . ." The generals were taken out at the Narva gate: "No point driving bloodsuckers around!" They drove them with bayonets as far as the Baltic Station, beating them—and drowned them under the ice of the Obvodny Canal.

*   *   *

It was called *picking off coppers*. At a suspected building, they would fire pistols, rifles, and machine guns, aiming them at the walls, too, and breaking the windows. Eagerly, merrily, they would fire a hundred rifles at once. (And eagerly pose afterward for the photographer: soldiers in tall fur hats, soldiers in service caps, a motorist with goggles raised to his visor, and a civilian in a soft hat.)

Who was the skirmish with there? They climbed the stairs to do a search, checking all the apartments on the way to see whether officers were hiding or there might be weapons. (Or a watch, or a cigar case.) They scrambled onto roofs, waving their arms, walking along the eaves—only no one ever once found or picked off a *copper* anywhere. That's how uncatchable they were.

People said that if they found a machine gun in a building, they'd burn it down.

*   *   *

Minister Bark was arrested by his own servant, who mocked him.

*   *   *

A street gathering at a feeding station for soldiers. A table covered with a white tablecloth, a box for coins, and two female students shivering with the cold, their hands in muffs.

A woman galloped down Nevsky hatless, her face mad with joy. Her hair fanned out behind her.

*   *   *

Military motorcyclists! They seemed like men from the future, a new kind of man. Their special clothing, the long leather gloves on their hands and the leather strap of their service cap under their chin. They were confident, mighty!

Could you ever guess what was hidden behind their whirlwind? One aviator raced around and around on a motorcycle: his father's home was on Zhukovskaya, and he'd taken a room at the Astoria for his lover.

*   *   *

The crowd was remarkable for who **wasn't** in it. Both yesterday and today there'd been absolutely no priests to be seen. As soon as they finished their services in church, they went straight home.

*   *   *

Drink and get drunk! If only they could find where. Drunks—there were more and more of them in the crowd.

Drunken sailors from the naval crew at Kolomna were breaking into apartments and looting.

Gangs of adolescents with revolvers and rifles and soldier's caps. Firing a lot.

*   *   *

A yardman in a yellow vest and a clean apron was shoveling clumps of bloody snow with a wooden shovel. A light steam rose from the snow.

[2 0 4]

Nelidov's host was Agafangel Diomidovich, and for some reason this name suggested safety.

He'd come to invite him to breakfast—after a stroll through the streets, fresh from the frost, sturdy, and already with a large bald spot, and dark from his years and metal dust. He expressed no joy the way those yesterday with the red rags had. His cheeks were deeply sunken, his chin and gaze firm. From behind his long black mustache, he said:

"No, your honor, you mustn't even think of going. Today'll boil up worse than yesterday. And don't you be shy. It's just a little close in here, but don't judge it too hard. Rest."

They had their breakfast—boiled potato with sunflower oil, cabbage and pickles, Lenten. A mug of tea, no sugar.

And again his host left, but not for the factory—work had come to a halt everywhere.

Captain Nelidov remained in his tiny little room with the one window. When the host removed the shutter in the morning, a narrow nook opened up in front of another building's brick wall covered in dirty snow and factory soot. That was it. In the city crowd waves might be roiling, moving from place to place and shouting, but here two icicles were hanging under the eave, also dirty, not dripping, no wind stirring, no sparrow flying. Nothing.

Nelidov had awoken early, when it was still dark—and was immediately wide awake, and his rested mind was seething, seething: What was going on? Why wasn't he himself acting? What was his status? Prisoner? Internee? Casualty? Deserter? No category fit, it was unlike anything.

Over and over what had happened yesterday burned through him. The danger not of perishing—but of perishing at the hands of Russian soldiers! And after that scene—how could he remain an officer? What did his epaulets mean? What did the whole army mean? An army falls apart if just one order isn't carried out; so what do you call it when soldiers are killing officers?

Had he been well, of course, he wouldn't have been lying here. He would have been racing to his battalion in the dead of night, when the crowds were gone, breaking or shooting his way through where he had to. Instead he was nailed down by his numb leg; he wasn't even a quarter of a warrior.

The day was apparently sunny, but in this nook you couldn't tell by looking out the window. The crampedness of this poor and strange apartment, seemingly not two versts from his barracks but in some other city, with no one to talk to, nothing of his own, and idleness—and Nelidov was overcome with such melancholy, he couldn't imagine getting through the day.

There was no furniture other than the bed, the bureau, a roughly upholstered armchair, and an ordinary chair; it wouldn't have fit. There was a potted geranium on the sill of the small window, which was divided into four by the sash but had no venting pane. A small, dark icon of the Mother of God under a cheap, simple casing hung in the corner. And on the bureau, pinned above the white lace runner, was a two-panel calendar, a 1917 calendar placed onto calendar plates from the House of Romanov's tricentennial: depicted on the left panel was Mikhail Fyodorovich, and on the right the present Emperor.

That was all there was in the little room, and not a single book. Not that he felt like reading.

Nelidov had never been in prison, but that day he had a prison experience: almost no room to turn around and nothing to look at. Lying down was nauseating and so was sitting up. His soul burned. Perhaps, then, prison was especially hard when you've imprisoned yourself.

It wasn't even the silence of the grave making him melancholy. No, it was that on the other side of the thin wall his hosts' tenant, a pretty young seamstress, sang the whole time. When she worked on her machine, she fell silent and all you could hear was its tapping. But when her work was without the machine, that's when she sang. Sometimes simple songs, which was fine. But from time to time she started up something revolutionary. Nelidov didn't know those songs, but he couldn't help but guess what they were.

> Down the dusty road the wagon speeds,
> Two gendarmes seated on either side.
> > Smash these shackles,
> > Give me liberty,
> I'll teach you to love freedom!

How attached she'd become to this tune. And she sang cheerfully, with spirit. At this small window in the brick nook—this one day, evidently, was a bright spot for her, and if not for this urgent work, she would have flown outside, so she settled for singing.

This cheerful voice and these mutinous words through the wall only added to his melancholy.

She didn't leave it at this, though. She ran out and around to see the captain in his little room.

"Well, how about it, captain," she addressed him saucily. "The old days are over, aren't they?"

And a flaxen tress fell onto her silly little unpretentious face.

At first Nelidov thought she was mocking him and that she might run off at any moment and bring a crowd here for retribution. (He wasn't afraid. Somehow he just didn't care.) But no, she wished him no ill and wasn't mocking him at all. She wanted to share the general joy and was amazed at his torpor. Her eyes goggled and she studied how wonderfully and strangely his gold epaulets looked in this poor little apartment.

"What's that you have?" She touched the oblique blue cross on his chest, the St. Andrew Guards Cross. "What are these here little letters, not ours?"

At the tips of the cross were: SAPR, that is, Sanctus Andreas Patronus Russiae. But who even knew Latin? Who was it written for, indeed?

"Saint Andrew, Russia's protector."

"And who's that on the horse?"

"St. George the Dragonslayer."

"But why?"

"It's Moscow's coat of arms."

"But why Moscow?"

"Because our regiment was renamed the Moscow Regiment for the Battle of Borodino. Right before the Napoleonic war, Emperor Aleksandr Pavlovich formed our regiment out of the Preobrazhensky Battalion, but at first it was called the Lithuanian."

The seamstress squealed with joy, having realized something, ran off— and returned immediately with a large bow fashioned of bright red calico:

"This is for you. Let me pin it on."

He sat in the armchair perfectly still while she pushed forward to pin the bow next to the St. Andrew cross and giggled.

Nelidov moved her arm aside, moved it, and did everything he could to explain that he couldn't.

The red bow was like a toad to him.

The seamstress was offended and ran behind her wall—and once again sang merrily:

> And what they took away by force—
> By force we shall take back!

Once again, as if nothing had happened, she flitted in and tried to pin the bow on the captain, silly thing.

Who had put all this into her head?

She tore at his melancholy and sawed away at his nerves. He tried not to listen to her singing.

When she finished sewing and went away, that made things easier.

He stood by the bureau and looked at the calendar. He examined the Emperor's darkened, troubled face.

Michael Fyodorovich did have his cares, of course, but all this took a back seat in the picture to his historical boyar costume. Whereas Nikolai Aleksandrovich stepped out of the calendar as if perfectly alive.

Nelidov thought that he, just a captain, had by a miracle descended into this room and his epaulets shone oddly here. Whereas the Emperor could enter any poor home naturally and simply. Even this old worker felt him as his own.

For some reason he'd given an officer safe haven. A worker in a workers' district had provided him a safe haven!

And so? Workers were serious men. Nelidov remembered how at the beginning of the war, before embarking from the Warsaw Station, he'd given his mobilized Petersburg workers leave to say goodbye to their families again—and every last one of them had returned on time. "You think we don't understand? We're going to defend our brother Serbs from the German." And they had fought excellently. They were loyal men, but we'd let them get stirred up.

The hours dragged, the hours dragged, such melancholy, as if he'd lost himself, lost his whole life, and would never get anything back. He was ready for anything bad if only he could put an end to this inaction and captivity. Captain Nelidov couldn't be so passive! In the battalion he could have at least helped maintain order by explaining things.

Toward the end of the day, Agafangel Diomidovich returned—and went immediately to see his guest. Just yesterday in the porter's room he'd seemed so alien, from another world, and now here he sat down on the bed, wearing his rough, dark, traditional shirt, his artless haircut, his coarse hair, his large bald spots and inherent firmness, which had not succumbed to his age and years of labor. Nelidov looked at him with respect, now sharing a common lot with him. How fenced off and divided were the sons of the one and the same people. Why?

Agafangel Diomidovich had walked all over the city—Liteiny, Nevsky, and beyond—and had seen everything. People were on a rampage. There were no authorities left in all Petersburg. Go rob anyone you like. Fires, retribution, disorderly and foolish gunfire, people killed by stray bullets, too.

And there was no sign of joy from what he'd seen.

"Oh, it'll be bad." And a pause: "Oh, there'll be suffering aplenty for the people." And a pause: "No one is thinking about what they're doing."

How, where did it start? Nelidov wanted to understand.

"Just you try and not go striking," the host said. "They'll poke your eyes out with a screw, even we're afraid of 'em. There's just a handful, but they're at the top of everything. The cheeky one gets the upper hand, that's how it always is. Hey, what they came up with — drove out all the authorities. As if you could live without 'em."

How was Nelidov going to get out of here?

His host: Don't even think about it. They'll rip you to shreds. Today the people have even more fervor than yesterday, they've tasted blood. The Moscow barracks surrendered anyway. Now the other barracks, at the end of Sampsonievsky, they're firing back. (The Wheeled Battalion, Nelidov realized.)

But their battalion couldn't have ceased to exist, and that meant there couldn't not be officers there. And Nelidov needed to go there.

All right, that night after dinner his host sent the neighbor boy to find Nelidov's superior at the Moscow Battalion and whisper in his ear.

The boy came back late: Captain Yakovlev ordered Captain Nelidov to be at the barracks early in the morning.

"All right," Agafangel Diomidovich got it. "There's a carter here I know. He'll harness up and take you early morning in the dark. And I'll wrap you in my winter coat as far as the barracks."

[205]

Still on his way to the Petersburg side, still riding, Peshekhonov contemplated where he should set up his commissariat. It had to be a large space, with easy entrance and exit (he was already envisaging an accumulation like in the Tauride Palace) — and right in the middle of the Petersburg side. He chose the Elite, a movie house next to his own apartment, on the same square — where Kamennoostrovsky crossed Bolshoi Prospect and Arkhiereiskaya Street — where last night, in the novelty of the excitement, in the crowd, he had greeted the first revolutionary vehicles.

But today these vehicles were already so many and had raced down so many streets of the capital that following the raptures they started to baffle and even irritate residents. When the new commissar's vehicles rode up to the Elite (it was locked, so they had to find the yardman and send for the owner), they saw that Kamennoostrovsky up ahead toward the islands was jammed with the same kind of vehicles, which were bumping into one another and so were stopped there along with their whole jubilant revolutionary audience. Passersby told Peshekhonov that up ahead someone wasn't letting them through and was checking them.

Aleksei Vasilich liked this. Here was a first use for his military detachment as long as there was nothing else to do. He called Ensign Lenartovich over and told him:

"My good man, take your detachment up ahead there and help this glorious cause. After all, since yesterday any party could come up to any owner, demand the key to his garage and his driver, purportedly for revolutionary needs—and take a joy ride through the city. They were even taking young ladies along, a very pleasant activity. And now look where they are all headed, everyone to the islands—what was there to do there? So go help with your force. Every pass has to be checked, and anyone who doesn't have a genuine right—remove them immediately and confiscate the vehicle. In the name of the Petersburg side's commissar. Meanwhile, that will give us extra vehicles."

This entire assignment could not equal yesterday's assignment to seize the Mariinsky Palace or today's opportunity to attack the Engineers Castle; nonetheless, it too had major revolutionary significance, which Sasha liked. Immediately he loudly summoned his ten soldiers, formed them up in two columns single file, rifles on belts—and led them, sometimes loudly commanding the men, sometimes ordering those in front to make way. After all his years of disdain for military commands and formation, he was taking sweet revenge right now—when everyone around him started disdaining formation and walking every which way, even unbuttoned, and dragging rifles like useless sticks.

Sasha noted with astonishment the power military discipline had against laxity: there were hundreds of soldiers here, on Kamennoostrovsky, in this congestion and on the sidewalks, and Lenartovich was leading only ten men—but people made way and looked at them with respect. And when they reached the front, their appearance immediately altered the entire situation. There had been some persistent civilian with a red armband (later he turned out to have a warrant from the Military Commission to stop and confiscate idle vehicles), and there was some push by the public irritated at the vehicles, including individual soldiers, maybe out of envy; but the numbers of motorists were more and their throats stronger and they had something to lose, so they were cursing harder, and waving their fists and bayonets, and something would probably have exploded very soon if it hadn't been for Lenartovich's detachment. Quickly sizing up the situation, he led his detachment into the very thick of it, to the line in front of the first detained vehicle, loudly commanded his second column to go out in continuation of the first (he didn't remember the exact command, but the soldiers understood him), turn around, have their rifles at the ready—and thus form a chain from snowdrift to snowdrift.

Although there were only eleven of them, the officer's decisiveness and the unconditional obedience of the nonmutinous soldiers immediately had an effect. Fists were retracted, bayonets were set aside, and the squabblers lowered their voices and started to step back, first themselves, then joined by the vehicles, and to yell at each other, but it wasn't so easy for this noisy and cowardly band to remaneuver and disperse. Meanwhile, Lenartovich and that civilian rushed to check documents, unseat joyriders, and hand other drivers slips of paper: "at the disposal of the Military Commission," "at the disposal of the Petersburg Side Commissar."

Meanwhile, Peshekhonov waited for the movie house's owner. This was a Belgian Jew. Having seen plenty of the Petrograd situation for the second day, he fully realized there wasn't much point in arguing, and here they were acting in the name of the Soviet of Workers' Deputies—so without prompting, the Belgian agreed to offer his movie house to the commissar free of charge, for an arbitrary number of days, adding that he, as a citizen of a free and friendly country, was happy to serve the cause of Russian freedom in any way he could.

And so, the commissar's group entered the empty building and at the very first table called a meeting on how to proceed. In essence, everything was in collapse and ferment, and they were the sole authority here; there was none other between here and the Tauride Palace. The movie house had a telephone, which was good.

Evidently, they needed to identify lines of work and each head up a section. The episode on Kamennoostrovsky suggested that they create a vehicle section; the shortage of food, a food section. Someone would be making announcements to the populace—which meant a publications section. (This was grabbed by a Social Democrat once he realized he could wage propaganda.) And so, all the section heads would be called deputy commissars and wear a red fabric cockade on their caps.

Where to get writing instruments? All the shops were closed. However, seeing vehicles near the movie house, the curious were already dropping by—and soon they were supplied with inkwells, pens, pencils, and paper. Some ladies made cockades out of red ribbon and pinned one on Peshekhonov's Astrakhan hat. One lady ran home, brought back a sheet, and dipping a stick into ink, began outlining in large letters: **Commissariat.**

Peshekhonov sat down to write an announcement that he, the Commissar of the Petersburg Side, had been assigned the mission of instituting freedom and popular rule here, and arrests and searches could be carried out only on his written instruction.

Right then, out of nowhere, an armored car drove up to ask the motorists for gasoline. The armored car was declared mobilized for the revolution and they designated it to be sent out against robberies.

[2 0 6]

Grand Duke Pavel Aleksandrovich, Aleksandr II's youngest son, who had two children by a Greek princess, had been widowed early—and ten years later had expressed the desire to marry the already married Olga Pistohlkors, as a result of which, at the time, the Emperor removed him from the command of the Guards Corps and even stripped him of his personal property (this was very strict, in order to deter his nephew Kirill from an unworthy marriage), and he had been compelled to go abroad. His children, Dmitri and Maria, were taken under the royal couple's wing. He was allowed to return to Russia only with the war and was eager to join the Guards, but the Emperor delayed his appointment, and when Pavel once again was given the Guards Corps he fell ill—and was transferred to the position of inspector general of the Guards, no longer connected with its disposition at the front. He lived at Tsarskoye Selo, where he and his spouse, now raised to "Princess Paley," furnished their own palace with rich collections of art.

Empress Aleksandra Fyodorovna, after becoming reacquainted, having gone through and gradually rejected the entire multitudinous dynastic family except for the Emperor's brother Misha, whom she favored (not without hope of restoring relations with her mother-in-law), and her weak-willed ward Dmitri, who was now mixed up in the murder of the Man of God—in her heart had always made an exception for Pavel and held him apart from the rest of the dynasty. His brothers were dead, making him the eldest in the family. His neutrality in family conflicts had evoked respect from the entire dynastic family, which was also why the family council would send him to the Emperor with petitions about changing policy, about concessions to the Duma gang, and about the dismissal of Stürmer and Protopopov. Through all this, though, Pavel himself had never engaged in intrigue, was sincere, did not hold a grudge, did not take offense at his familial inequality, was loyal to the Emperor, sought nothing for himself, and honestly wanted only to serve Russia. If in part he occasionally intervened in favor of two-faced Ruzsky or directly against the influence of the imperial couple's Friend, this was balanced out by his steady resistance to Nikolasha and always in favor of the Emperor, nor did he show any direct ill will toward the Friend, and his silver-tongued spouse, who had pestered the Emperor with her expressions of devotion in perfumed letters, begged his forgiveness also in part via their Friend. Among the grand dukes there was even an accusation against Pavel for belonging to Grigori's party. When a year ago Pavel had been seriously ill, had suffered from jaundice and loss of weight, and was threatened by a deadly operation, the Empress took pity on him and even crossed the less than proper threshold of Princess Paley's home to visit the patient.

After the first outburst of anger, it was now clear that Pavel was in no way responsible for the actions of his son Dmitri—no more than the royal couple themselves were responsible for him as their ward. It had been unfair to ascribe responsibility to Pavel for another accomplice as well—his stepdaughter Marianna, who despised the Friend. (Marianna had also spread a rumor around Petrograd that the Empress was making a drunkard of the Emperor. There was no limit to the slander uttered in the two capitals.)

In the face of today's circumstances, minor insults receded.

Sixty-year-old Pavel entered the sitting room with his innate dignity. He was slender, tall, imposing, even charming—a handsome young old man with gray hair, wearing stylish tall English boots that made his long slim legs look even slenderer.

The Tsaritsa forbade herself to hold a grudge over the past. But for what had happened today, she could not greet him otherwise than sternly. Inspector General of the Guards, a military man—had he been paying attention when his Guards battalions mutinied in Petrograd and even his men here, at Tsarskoye Selo, were in disarray? How many days had this rebellion been going on—and what had he undertaken? Had he gone out to see the troops?

They sat down at a small round table in her pale lilac study. A vase held completely withered flowers.

Pavel's face expressed the Romanov breeding, and his own decency, and even a courageous readiness, and he was anxious in front of the Empress, although he tried to hide that fact. But he had nothing sensible to reply.

That, unfortunately, General Chebykin, commander of the Petrograd Guard, was in Kislovodsk. That what was now in Petrograd wasn't really the Guard.

This was clear, that it wasn't the Guard. In early February, the Emperor had ordered moved to Petrograd from the Special Army two cavalry divisions—but the District Commander had refused to find room for them in Petrograd or even in the outlying areas. And the Emperor hadn't insisted, sensitive to the army not taking offense at the Guard. That was when they transferred the Guards Crew to Tsarskoye Selo.

But it was obvious that Pavel had a poor understanding of what was going on in the city and where. The Empress questioned him about the details, but he couldn't answer—he had sat out these past few days with his wife in their palace! (While Princess Paley had managed by persistent request to get her two sons transferred from the front to the rear. . . .)

Oh, how many times had the Tsaritsa herself watched the Guards parades! What an indestructible bulwark all these heroes had seemed! And where had they all absconded to in this ominous moment?

"So why don't we have real regiments?" she exclaimed in despair.

"The Emperor left no instructions. . . ."

It was inexplicable. Due to some coincidence, some reticence, among five hundred important state situations, they had neglected, had failed to resolve this five hundred first one? She herself had neglected to insist.

"So why isn't the Guard being called up now?"

"Your Majesty, that is not within my rights. As Inspector General, I am in charge only of the Guard's supplies."

Here he was, wearing a magnificent Guards uniform, he belonged to the service, and he had been a military man from birth—and how many days had he remained calmly at Tsarskoye Selo?

"Then go to the front! Tell them and bring back loyal regiments!" the Empress exclaimed imperiously. She was expecting masculine support—

but Pavel sat there nobly saddened, and the masculine aspect was again left up to her.

Pavel replied that it would be unforgivable willfulness for him to go to the front for troops; there was GHQ for that.

But his face expressed shame—and impotence, and a failure to understand events, and maybe even the weakness of age.

And the Empress, who had summoned him on an impulse of forgiveness, now once again felt the sting of resentment. She said majestically:

"If the royal family had supported the Emperor instead of giving him bad advice, **this** would not have happened!"

Pavel straightened up as he sat and the breeding of his noble face showed through more distinctly:

"Neither the Emperor nor you have any basis for doubting my devotion and honesty. And is this the time to be bringing up old quarrels? Right now we must secure the Emperor's speediest return."

"The Emperor is returning tomorrow morning," Aleksandra Fyodorovna replied coldly.

"Then I shall meet him at the station!" Pavel exclaimed with fervent readiness.

It was true, he worshipped the Emperor. It was true, he was loyal.

But nothing more.

He also had a fussiness to him.

She might not have summoned him at all.

She let him go.

But who could she depend upon?

Everyone had abandoned her, and no one was even telephoning.

The mood at the palace had sunk. The suite was agitated, the house staff were agitated.

How could she hold out until tomorrow morning?

Dr. Derevenko came from the infirmary and told her that disheveled soldiers not in formation were roaming through Tsarskoye, service caps pushed back on their heads, hands in pockets—and laughing. (A few Cossacks could easily disperse them!) But the officers were vacillating or hiding. And revolutionaries had seized all the railroads.

It was unclear how the Emperor would get through.

But right then a telegram came from him.

From Vyazma.

". . . Hope are feeling well and quiet. Many troops sent from front. . . ."

Well, thank God, rescue was on its way! A few hours to wait.

The palace was well protected by posts and patrols.

And the weather at Tsarskoye was exquisite: resplendent sun, blue sky, undisturbed snow.

In weather like this, no evil deed could take place. God would not allow it.

[2 0 7]

The Interdistrict group had proved to be the most militant, practical, and assertive of all the socialist parties. It had arisen as a protest against the ambitious leaders who had split several times and brought down the underground Social Democratic Party. It had arisen as the "third faction," the "uniter," to unite the party from below, to accept willing Bolsheviks and Mensheviks who recognized illegal forms of operation, to sweep away only Liquidators, those unwilling to accept the risk of underground work. The Interdistrict group hadn't sought a resonant name or ranks of thousands (there were only 150 of them, although their plan called for becoming a Russia-wide organization) and didn't even have their own Central Committee, but on the other hand they did have grand objectives. Accomplishing great deeds required an energetic party, not a numerous one. They were much strengthened when Karakhan joined the party, and with his help they sought contacts with émigré leaders. Trotsky was particularly sympathetic.

Since the war's very beginning, their slogan had been "Down with the war," and then, in addition, "Let us turn the imperial war into a civil war." So that there weren't even any particular contradictions between their slogans and the Bolsheviks', but they didn't want to submit to their weakened Petersburg committee and the spectral Swiss Central Committee.

So that autumn, when Matvei Ryss switched from the Bolsheviks to the Interdistrict group, he hadn't felt any betrayal of his slogans. True, Krotovsky, at the party's head, was no luminary, he was even quite a weak mind, and fussy, but what was good was the Interdistrict group's general enthusiasm, the well set-up printing press, and the many leaflets, and they knew how to organize strikes and find the money for them. In fact, it was during just those days that a large group of psychoneurology students thronged to the Interdistrict group, friends of Matvei: "Let us instill the neurological spirit!" They all worshipped the working class.

The Interdistrict group's slogan was: "Keep shaking it until one day it shakes loose." They considered one of their chief objectives to be waging propaganda in the army. They had infiltrated various units quartered in Petrograd and had a good permanent connection with Kronstadt.

Like his friends, Matvei wasn't often seen at lectures at the institute, but the institute was private, the administration liberal, and it turned a blind eye to what its students were actually doing. From month to month that winter, Matvei was overcome more and more by an impatience to act. This inner passion, this impatience, was burning him up inside, and had there been an even more militant party in Petrograd, he would have jumped over to them. That winter, Matvei had come to such a state that he hated any ordinary life and perceived any piece of ordinary life as appeasing the thrice-cursed regime. He had reached such an extreme of fury that if a popular movement didn't arise, he would have to do something himself or with his closest friends. Such heavy, shared clouds of disappointment and animosity hung over the capital, and such universal joy, for example, at Rasputin's murder—all this could not pass without a trace. He was hoping for something major!

Meanwhile he wrote, he wrote leaflets, investing them with all his passion: "They are feasting during a plague of popular calamity!" "The Tsaritsa herself is trading in the people's blood and is selling Russia off piece by piece." "Down with the criminal government and its entire gang of thieves and murderers!"

Throughout these March upheavals, Matvei Ryss had raced around—not so much at the behest of Krotovsky, who had very cold feet, did not believe in the movement's success, and suggested moderating the workers' ardor, as at his own initiative. He would take workers out for a strike, or cobble together a demonstration, or stand among the crowd on the sidewalk and hurl anonymous insults and rocks at the police, and once he himself fired a handgun. He took turns with other young Interdistrict men giving speeches (and spoke nearly as easily as he wrote) from the Aleksandr III pedestal on Znamenskaya and from the parapet at Kazan Cathedral, and when they were driven off, he ran in the crowd, and it was fun. He kept shouting out the same slogans: Give us bread! Give us peace! Down with the war! Down with the Tsar! Nonetheless, up until Sunday evening he had had no idea things would develop this far. He'd just understood it as a buildup for the future. When he learned of the Pavlovsky upheaval, though, he rushed to infiltrate their barracks, but troops had already cordoned them off.

They had also sent leaflets to the Volynians in their barracks, and a few Volynian sergeants had come a couple of times for propaganda classes, but no one, apparently, had paid them much attention. The fact that they had acted and drawn others along was simply a gift of fate.

Matvei had so exhausted himself over all these days that on the morning of the 12th he slept in at his father's apartment on Staro-Nevsky. No one woke him so he slept nearly half the day until the shooting got very loud and very close. He woke up, washed, and barely having breakfasted, ran off to the events. And oh how events had taken off! He was one of the first to espy the bourgeois messengers calling on the revolutionary crowd to turn around and bring greetings to the State Duma. Not on your life! Without any connection whatsoever at that hour to his party, Matvei Ryss understood perfectly well the full perfidy of this device. No! We're going to sweep away both the Tsarist autocracy and the State Duma in one fell swoop!

He shouted until he was hoarse, and he argued—and dissuaded two large groups, turning them away from the Duma.

Right then the cross fire with a government detachment on Liteiny intensified, and Matvei hurried there, in the middle of a failed motorcar attack by revolutionaries. The government detachment held on for several hours under the command of a tall colonel with a black beard, whom they fired at many times but kept missing. On that side the colonel was in command, but on this side no one individual was, and everything depended on who thought of what in what section. Matvei understood that the military advantage was with the detachment anyway inasmuch as it had a unified command. Whereas we had the advantage in propaganda and it was through propaganda that we'd break each and every one standing against us with a rifle, and that would take shouting and agitating. He didn't spare his voice and called on others to do the same, and there were other university students—and each argument and each joke weakened the soldier hearts in the rank.

A few hours later, in the darkness, they overpowered the detachment on Liteiny; it broke up and took cover in the Red Cross building. Now they had to follow up on their victory and drive them out of there, and most of all capture and in front of everyone on the street execute that hardliner colonel. The insurrectionists had no one commanding them. Everyone was in command who wanted to be and only obeyed if he wanted to, thus the disarray. Still, they besieged that building on several sides all night after the soldiers left, setting up posts and shifts—and Matvei explained to new arrivals exactly what animal was sitting there who had to be caught. He himself left for a few hours to sleep and returned as morning came. Whoever had been on duty during the night assured him that he couldn't possibly have slipped away. But when in the morning they gathered their forces and entered the building to search, they found lots of weapons but no colonel. That meant he'd changed clothing and slipped away. Too bad.

So it was that Matvei spent nearly the entire revolution at this one siege on Liteiny.

How infuriating that they'd let him get away!

After that he headed today to the secret address on Svechnoi Lane—clandestine no more—to ask Krotovsky what he should do. He heard that university students were forming a city police force, but he realized that this was nonsense and in bourgeois hands. Krotovsky said:

"Comrade Ryss! Your conduct was correct. Our main objective has been mapped out: the struggle with the officer class and especially the active officer class. We can intensify and continue the revolution only if we undermine the officer class. Otherwise we'll have no soldier mass left because it will subordinate itself to the officers again. Therefore we must quickly issue a persuasive leaflet against the officer class so that they get their teeth knocked out and get stabbed with bayonets. A leaflet like that is more important than anything now. Take care of that. You write better than anyone else."

This was both flattering and the truth. And although he was sorry to be torn away even for a few hours from the living whirlwind of revolution, if it was to become even more fiery, he had to sit down over this leaflet.

Matvei went home, to Staro-Nevsky. His father was a lawyer, their apartment had many rooms, and his parents had long grown used to their son's independent life and did not meddle or interfere.

On his way he could already feel himself composing, could sense that vital feeling needed for a leaflet rising up in him.

Especially for its opening section. Every leaflet had to have an opening section that flayed readers' nerves—after which they were more receptive to a slogan. His main talent was writing this perfect opening section. It was the rare person who knew how to do that, whereas any party committee could add the slogan itself.

Start like this: "Comrade Soldiers! (Soldiers with a capital "S"). It has come to pass! While under the yoke, you rose up. . . ." Even he himself shuddered at this marvelous phrase, "under the yoke." The enslaved, the peasants and workers, have risen up! And the autocratic government has come crashing down in disgrace!

Good! Like a shell exploding! He stopped to jot this down in his notebook; otherwise he'd forget before he got there. He adjusted his scarf—the cold was creeping up his neck—and walked on.

Well, naturally, the tsarist autocracy's gang of servants—he couldn't leave that out. But since the soldiers were for the most part peasants, he needed to develop the peasant theme. And everyone knew the peasant dream: to have somewhere to graze a cow and keep a chicken. And so: while the treasury and monasteries (the anticlerical vein always had to be present) had seized land, while the gentlemen-noblemen had gone mad on their wealth, sucking the people's blood, millions and millions of peasants were swelling up from starvation. The landless peasant had nowhere to put a chicken!

This chicken, straight out of Tolstoy, fit very well here: it sounded so strident, so plaintive.

He jotted it down. A long sentence; his fingers were freezing, too.

He walked along, caught up, not noticing the street. Something more important was happening inside him.

Soldiers! Be on your guard. Make sure the gentlemen and noblemen don't trick the people! A fox tail scares us more than a wolf's fang. . . .

Oh, that's good: the tail and the fang!

In the entry hall, the maid told Matvei that the telephone was back in service and since then Veronika had telephoned him twice.

"All right," he replied. He told her to serve him dinner in his room and went to work.

[2 0 8]

The troika of young Wheeled unit officers taken in the battle on Serdo-bolskaya, separately from their battalion, were paralyzed by incomprehension. They had heard shouts about them being executed, and they had no doubt they would be, given the circumstances under which they'd been taken and the crowd's audible fury. For the first few minutes they rode in the truck scarcely looking out or comprehending what was going on around them. Whether or not there was a revolution no longer concerned their life; this was another, residuary world.

Their savior, an Amur Cossack, did not accompany them; rather they were taken by sailors and university students. The sailors argued there was no point listening to that Cossack, no point taking them to the State Duma, they should shoot them here, in the wastelands of the Vyborg side. But the students objected that there should be a fair revolutionary trial.

The thought of running away never did occur to them. They were tired and their ears were still ringing from the morning gunfire. Anyway, they were surrounded by nothing but crowds with flags and bayonets.

The Tauride Palace itself was utter pandemonium. There were weapons and vehicles, fires were burning, bands were playing, soldiers were crowding around, speeches were being given.

How this alien joy failed to gladden. All the more bitter to die amid general exultation.

For a long time they couldn't be brought into the palace itself. Two trucks were being unloaded, one with sides of meat, another with fireproof cash boxes, and all this was being hauled into the palace by civilians and soldiers.

Right then, the crowd, seeing the arrested officers, shouted menacingly and might easily have crushed the convoy. By now the men were already wishing they could be taken inside as soon as possible.

They were. They pushed through the crowd, past stacked cases, evidently with weapons, past tables where young ladies sat handing out brochures.

Farther on, under the strong guard of red-armband workers, stood a group of their own Wheeled unit officers, from the Sampsonievsky barracks. Some had been badly beaten and others were wearing soldier greatcoats, evidently having changed in hopes of getting away.

While they were jostling, squeezed by the human currents, they exchanged a few sentences. They learned that Balkashin had been killed, as had another eight officers and lots of the men. They also said there was an order from Rodzyanko to shoot them.

Their hearts fell: it wasn't an empty threat. My God, how sad!

They squeezed on farther. They entered an enormous hall with lots of columns, and the students got flustered about where to take them from there.

Suddenly they both—the men under convoy and their convoy—saw and immediately recognized from newspaper portraits: Milyukov! He was walking past, also pushing through. They rejoiced at his firm and round face, mustache, and spectacles as if he were family. The two second lieutenants called out in unison:

"Pavel Nikolaevich!"

He stopped.

"Is it true they're executing us?"

He looked wisely through his spectacles:

"What for? Who are you?"

"Officers from a Wheeled battalion. . . ."

He shook his head with its grayish hair combed back to the side and shook it some more:

"Gentlemen. Gentlemen! How can this be? Why did you resist the new authority so doggedly? All the garrison's units recognized the new authority immediately, whereas you . . ."

"But Pavel Nikolaevich!" The Wheeled officers objected with hope and joy, having simply come to love him in that minute. "We didn't know what was going on here—in the center, in the Duma. How could we know? All communications had been cut. And we're military men, we're in service. . . . How could we surrender to unknown persons?"

"In any case, no one is planning to execute you. Who told you that?"

"Our comrades are also here under convoy, and they say it's Rodzyanko's order."

"Well, that's just nonsense. Where are they?"

"Over there! What should we do now, Pavel Nikolaevich?"

"If you give your word you won't take up arms against the new regime, then, gentlemen, you are free to go."

"Of course, we won't! Of course we give our word! . . . Thank you, Pavel Nikolaevich! . . . Then let our comrades go, too."

"Fine, I'll look into it now. But go get passes from the palace commandant."

They and the now more friendly students went to find the commandant. They searched for a long time. He turned out to be the dashing, arrogant-looking Duma deputy Karaulov wearing a Terek Cossack uniform. He signed their passes.

Where were they supposed to go, though? The barracks were all smashed. They couldn't show up there; they'd be shot anyway.

But now the students invited them to the Polytechnic Institute:

"You can train us in military service."

[209]

Olda had slept poorly, her sleep constantly disturbed by nightmares and jutting corners. Early in the morning, Ninochka Kaul came running to see her—and with shining eyes, in an excited, feverish state, complained that her mama wouldn't let her go to GHQ, to see the Emperor!

"Why do that, Ninochka?"

"No one's defending him! He needs help!"

"But he has his Convoy there, and all those troops! What do you mean!"

"No! He needs help! I can tell!"

"But how are you going to help him?"

"I don't know. I'll see there! I can tell he's in a terrible state! And no one is defending him! He should ride in on a white horse, like his great-grandfather!"

"And where did you come up with that? He's in the middle of his armed forces! He'll ride in all right!"

"Oh, no!" Nina rushed about, the locks of her unruly hair escaping helplessly from her knot of hair in a maidenly way and her cuff rolled up. "No, I'm certain he knows nothing!"

"How could he not know? There's the telegraph for that now."

"Oh no, he surely doesn't know! The horror here! Why isn't anything . . . Surely, they're not reporting to him properly!"

She was carried away, practically through the air. He needed her there! She would go! She would rush off to see the Tsar! And persuade him! But to do that she first had to convince her mama! And only Olda Orestovna could do that!

Nineteen-year-old Nina had graduated from the Smolny Aleksandr Institute for the Children of Middle Officers, no kind of nobility. Presently she was studying medicine. Olda Orestovna knew the entire family well. Nina's father, a lieutenant colonel, had been killed the previous year in the war, her brother was at the front, and Nina was left alone with her mother.

It was as if something had taken root in her, giving her extraordinary strength. Right now, here, in anticipation, she was pouring out how she would tell the Emperor that it was only the rabble rebelling and he had to exercise his stern authority quickly! Nina would have left this very morning and by evening would have been in Mogilev. Classes had been called off and everyone was summoning her to help the revolution—as if she would! But her mama . . .

Olda Orestovna was responsive and touched by Nina's reproach. What's this? Ah . . . yes? Wasn't this exactly what she had preached? Congenitally weak? Bolster him with our loyalty? . . . She took Nina's hands, though, and did not let go, sat her down at the table and poured tea. The young woman was flying so high, a simple no could not bring her down to earth. She had to be shown, step by step, all the difficulties and impossibilities.

Hadn't she seen the dissolute soldiers? They were doubtless at the train stations and on the trains. How could a solitary young lady travel? They would insult her! And various patrols would detain her. In Mogilev itself as well. Even if she did get that far safely, who was going to let her into GHQ? And to see the Emperor himself? No one! What hope could she have that he would hear her out? Such things didn't happen.

Nina felt something almost personal for the Emperor. Once upon a time, her father, upon graduating from the Peterhof Riflery School, was introduced to the Tsar. They were a hundred officers there, and over the years thousands such men had been introduced. But now during the war Nina's brother, still a cadet then, was unloading the wounded at the Pskov train station, and the royal train pulled up, and the Emperor asked his name and immediately: "Your father graduated from the Peterhof school in such and such a year, didn't he? Be like your father." And the boy wept. So the sister now believed he would recognize her, too.

Olda Orestovna kept placing mountains of obstacles around the young woman—who quieted down, lost heart, and began to weep. Her head dropped to the table.

She wandered off broken, dead.

Olda felt sorry for Nina—but was contemptuously sorry for herself as well. That she herself, for all her strength and intelligence, couldn't do a thing, either. What about these three days? She'd only spoken with friends over the telephone and felt distress. Inspire students along the way to Nina's feelings, too? It was not only impossible but also disgraceful to say, but Olda Orestovna was almost as afraid of those young women, put together, en masse, as she was of those dissolute street soldiers. She was as helpless to do anything in her university job as she was anywhere. Anyway, the Bestuzhev courses had fallen apart yesterday.

Today she'd been trying to call Maklakov. At the very center of the whirl-wind and with his perceptive gaze, he ought to have understood the situation more accurately than anyone. On the fourth try she reached him—not at home or in the Duma but at the Ministry of Justice. He was tired and rushed and she felt bad about detaining him.

"Vasili Alekseevich, is there hope, though, that you will keep the movement in check?"

"We're trying. Hoping. Guarantee anything, though—that I cannot do."

If even *they* can't hold them back . . .

What kind of cursed situation was this when no one—neither those who understood nor the strong—could do anything to avert the fateful course? Here it was, the elemental force, the most unstudied thing in history.

The forces of order outside Petrograd were tremendous, incomparable with the mutinous city. Respecting the enigma of the elemental force, though, remembering the instantaneous paralysis of 1905, however—one could realistically worry that the forces of order would be unable to do anything. The sixth day of disturbances, the second day of true revolution—and what of the Emperor?

And this in time of war! In time of war!

On the Petersburg side yesterday, nothing happened; only in the evening did it break through here. And today it spilled out. Andozerskaya went out down Kamennoostrovsky and turned onto Bolshoi.

Most often, great events, far too large for the individual human consciousness to take in, must seem repugnant.

What was stunning was not even the soldiers' instantaneous dissipation but—with the thousands of red scraps—their universal and unbroken joyous look. This suddenly achieved universality had an air of irrevocability.

Although, how could irrevocability have come to pass? Where could the entire strength of a great power have gone in two days?

She was standing at the curb, gazing at the madness of the unbridled vehicles. Beside her, a tall, withered lady with a squirrel muff said quietly, as if to herself, but also for her neighbor:

"Russia is dying. . . ."

Her tearful grief was reflected in her eyes.

Andozerskaya held her up firmly by the elbow:

"*Dum spiro, spero*. While I live, I hope."

But she was brought low by those words. Moving away from these streets where her judgmental look, and lack of a red bow, were especially noticeable, thoughts rolled around heatedly in her mind: that was putting it harshly. And it was untrue! But also very true.

One always had to act up to the last moment. But they also should have acted patiently and persistently much much sooner, during peaceful times.

We'd been given three hundred years.

And we'd been given the past twelve. That meant we'd let them slip.

Our dignitaries, too. Our writers. Our bishops.

And today—none of them were anywhere to be found.

So what could Olda Orestovna do in this madness? It was humiliating to sit at home and learn the news over the telephone.

By evening, though, the revolution itself had come to Andozerskaya's apartment. She heard a sharp doorbell and sharp knock simultaneously, which meant several hands. Scarcely had the maid opened when, without asking, or rather pushing the door, several men barged in: two soldiers, an armed worker—and also an ensign with an anything but bestial, open face and even quite good-looking.

They came in—and kept going—and Olda Orestovna had to hurry to bar the way to her rooms. Everyone was wearing red bows, naturally, including the ensign. And they didn't remove their caps.

"To what do I owe this visit?" Andozerskaya asked icily. She was dressed properly, not for being at home. "Why have you entered without permission?"

They were all taller than she was. Who wasn't! And so much stronger, in a crude way, and already in motion. It was actually odd that she was able to slow them down. The ensign asked with his head slightly tilted back:

"Wasn't it your apartment they were shooting from? We have to search."

"You have no right," Andozerskaya said quite softly with cold indignation.

"The revolution doesn't ask for the right!" the ensign replied loudly, intoxicated with himself, his duties, and the sound of his voice. "It takes it. Seems there was shooting from this building, and we have to find the perpetrator. Do you have someone hiding here?"

Her chill and anger made no impression, and they didn't catch the nuances in her expressions. They were already flowing around her or crowding her back, and they went into the parlor and the dining room. It was twilight already, and they themselves turned the switches, those who knew how.

Andozerskaya didn't exclaim the empty "How dare you?" She could already see that they had the power, but she felt like striking this overbearing ensign somehow. He was the sole one still standing in front of her, and she asked him, looking up, with contempt:

"How is it that you, an officer, went over to the side of the rebels?"

This did not strike him in the least. He even replied with triumphant gaiety:

"Not the rebels, madam, the people! My status as an officer is precisely what obliges me to help the people and not be their oppressor."

But his face was intelligent, and it was worth saying to him as well:

"Oppressors, suppressors—in history that has been thrown around too much. Don't be too sure that one day you might not come to regret these days."

Needless to say, his young ears heard none of this.

She went through the study with him. The ensign apparently was searching seriously for something big among the displayed toys and bric-a-brac and paintings—a hidden person or a rifle. And when she blocked the door to her bedroom, he said unbendingly:

"Permit me. I must."

Disgusted, she let him in.

Here he was also searching for a person or a rifle, but he didn't open the cupboard or look under the bed. He did see on the wall the photographic portrait of Georgi in uniform that Olda had had enlarged that winter from a picture card, however.

"Oh! I know this colonel!" he said.

"You can't know him!" Andozerskaya silenced him.

"No, I do!" the ensign insisted quite cheerfully. He was very carefree, as if he hadn't broken into her home and had been invited as a guest. "Isn't his name Vorotyntsev?"

Andozerskaya was stunned. And felt herself blushing. She despised this ensign, but it was as if he had caught her here with Georgi—and oddly, she found this pleasant in a way.

"Is this your husband? What an encounter!"

An impudent foe, but his connection to Georgi made him like an acquaintance. And she herself hadn't anticipated how happy she would feel at him calling him her husband.

"How do you . . ." she asked in a new tone of voice. "Did you serve with him?"

"He led us, our group, out of an encirclement in East Prussia. Where is he now?"

"You want to know a lot," she stiffened.

"Oh no, I just . . ." he lightly gave that up. "I just: if he's going to oppose the revolution and he and I ever meet again . . ."

They returned to the living room, where the searchers were crowded together.

"Nothing?"

"Nothing."

"Let's go to the next. Goodbye, madam, forgive me."

They left.

The maid rushed to check again. Much as she had kept her eyes on them, in the dining room they'd tried to slip the silver into their pockets. Olda Orestovna started looking, too, and discovered in the study, on an end table, an empty sloping wooden box: the watch had vanished from it.

Probably something else as well.

Nyura ran to chase them down in the next apartment.

But where is he now?

He'd left so hastily, so precipitously. How badly this visit had ended.

[2 1 0]

It had been inevitable since morning that Protopopov would have to free up his haven, to leave the State Control office. The doorman brought him tea and black bread and droned on about him not being found here. The staff assembled and then Feodosiev, the head of State Control himself, his savior, arrived with his intense, intelligent face. He told him that there was total chaos in the city, one could scarcely tell if it was war or not, but surely there was no government. Late in the evening the rebels had burst into the Mariinsky Palace and stormed it unimpeded. And toward the end of the day yesterday Shcheglovitov had been arrested—Aleksandr Dmitrich didn't know?—and still hadn't been released but had been placed under lock and key in the Tauride Palace.

My God, better he hadn't told him! So much had everything died away, he didn't have the strength to move and think, let alone save himself, and Aleksan Dmitrich was prepared to stretch out and die then and there, which would be easier—but then this striking news: they were making arrests! And who were they arresting? Those the public hated most, and there were two of them, Shcheglovitov and Protopopov, and one had already been taken. And of course they were searching for *him* all over the city—and he would be compelled to walk through that city now!

But to remain . . . another twenty-four hours here—was that not possible? . . .

God, how the entire world edifice was capable of collapsing in just a few hours! Yesterday he'd started his morning as the all-powerful Minister of the

Interior, and today he was a criminal who could be caught, who was huddling in his coat, his collar raised. (And it wasn't that cold; they'd notice him raising it.)

The Empress had put such hopes in her minister! Ah, Your Majesty, forgive me. Forgive me! I let it slip away! . . .

Where he might go—he could think of only one place: his brother's. Hide out there with him or move on to somewhere else. But his brother lived on the Kalashnikov Embankment, which meant passing through the center of the city laterally—and there was no avoiding crossing Nevsky.

But crossing Nevsky was absolutely unthinkable: he was sure to be recognized! That's where they'd catch him. And once they caught him, they were unlikely to let him live.

Only now did he realize that he had made a mistake yesterday, in a moment of weakness. It was yesterday, in the darkness, that he should have made his way to his brother's. By now he would be safely hidden, or they would have come up with a way to escape the city altogether. Now, in the light of day, he was walking all alone and certain to be ripped to pieces.

His every nerve was tensed. Every minute he was expecting—not even for them to shout "Protopopov!" but for them to grab him straightaway and clutch at his side, like dogs. In the warmth of his coat he trembled with a faint, continuous shudder. And perspired.

After all, his extinguishing consciousness notwithstanding, he did have the ability to think things through. In no instance could he cross Nevsky! Take the way far past the Moscow Station and somehow, somewhere, continue along the railroad lines and in that way stumble into the Aleksandr Nevsky section. There were fences there, and he might find a gate, and he would attract attention—but of ordinary people. They wouldn't recognize him, and there was no revolutionary crowd there.

This was true terror, this was the most terrible thing in the world—an enraged crowd trying to grab you!

He would choose only small, quiet streets—but there was still no avoiding crossing major ones, and that was the most dangerous, where there were thousands of pairs of eyes.

The first he had to cross was Gorokhovaya. A little farther from the city governor's offices, he crossed it near the canal and then immediately the canal itself.

Right then, on the canal's embankment, he saw coming toward him another strange gentleman in a fur coat, not very tall, his collar raised too high. Squinting, he recognized Shakhovskoy, the Minister of Trade and Industry.

Their eyes didn't meet directly. Had he recognized Protopopov? Perhaps he'd noticed him earlier? But they passed each other without looking.

Oh my! Tsarist ministers walking through the streets and darting past each other without noticing. What was this? Revolution?

Not that he had any desire to talk with any of the ministers. They were traitors, and he had no wish to know them. He would ask the Emperor and Empress for other colleagues henceforth.

He chose the most common street, where not just a minister but even an official of a proper rank wouldn't stray—past the Flour Market, then crossing Sadovaya, and then past Apraksin. Of course, his fur coat stood out here very much.

A menacing armored vehicle drove down Sadovaya.

When you're praying to heaven that they not recognize you, then somehow you try not to look yourself, as if it were all about eyes meeting. Therefore Protopopov saw very little and didn't turn around or look carefully. But at the markets, apparently, they were trading, bringing in and hauling food the same as usual, and there were lines for bread, apparently, and there was a strange, lively racket—someone looting a shop, perhaps, or carrying off various goods and hastily, and talking excitedly.

But, oh! As if this was what Aleksan Dmitrich needed to be figuring out! He was just in a hurry to bring his defenseless body through unharmed. Here and there, on certain streets, but not nearby, there was occasional shooting. But it wasn't gunfire that was making Protopopov tremble so. If a bullet hit him, so be it. That didn't frighten him. What frightened him was being caught. So far everything was going well, no one had touched him, but he couldn't make any mistakes. He was thinking of going left, but he realized that would bring him to Chernyshev Lane and Chernyshev Bridge—and right past his own ministry! That's where he'd get it! That's where they'd tear him to pieces.

He crossed the Fontanka onto Leshtukov Lane, again successfully. Thank God. So far he hadn't encountered any revolutionary gangs, but something stormy and noisy was rushing toward him from Zagorodny Prospect—which he had to cross! He slowed his pace as he went down calm Leshtukov, raised his eyes, and took a good look, stopping before the corner.

Zagorodny Prospect was overflowing. On the sidewalks, even in the street, thronging in great numbers, people were standing and watching a celebratory procession—several open trucks making their way toward the center, red flags poking out on each and people holding them in their hands and waving them at the crowd. Each truck was full to bursting with soldiers and civilians, and the soldiers were shaking their rifles and bowing to the crowd—and the crowd was shouting "hurrah" continuously, many taking off their caps.

Not only did everyone have their collars turned down and their arms thrown up, but they were also removing their caps. A ruffled, reticent gentleman was sure to stand out! It was a very dangerous moment. What saved him was that he was standing in the lane, behind everyone. Once the trucks passed and the entire street was thronged with all those people celebrating,

Protopopov turned down his collar and moved decisively into the crowd, also trying to smile gaily.

That was probably what saved him, his smile, which was full of charm, winning over one and all. People saw him and smiled at him, too, and someone shouted something encouragingly, and then Protopopov touched his cap welcomingly, as if conveying his joy, nearly removing his cap himself. Taut as a string, but smiling, he passed through this horrible sea of gaiety, and when he'd crossed to the other side and moved into a quiet street, he felt himself break out in a sweat and go completely limp. He had already entered the train station district, he'd already gotten through a lot, but even more lay ahead, and he didn't know how many dangers—but his strength had given out. No, he had to rest somewhere, recover from the tension.

Right then he happily remembered something. His mind didn't let him down: nearby, on Yamskaya Street, lived a tailor who had sewn for him several times when he was still just a Duma deputy. Why shouldn't he stop by the tailor's? The tailor didn't know he was the accursed Minister of the Interior, but he did know he was a rich and faultless customer.

Yes! To rest! He didn't remember the address, but he visually remembered both the building and the entrance and how to go from there. As he ascended the dismal Petersburg staircase, he even remembered his name: Ivan Fyodorovich.

There was a bell. A pull of the thick cord and a bell rang inside. Ivan Fyodorovich himself opened, unchanged, wearing a house jacket, a measuring tape around his neck, chalk behind his ear, and his lips damaged, which made his smile uneven.

He immediately recognized Protopopov—he had a good memory—and even his patronymic—Aleksan Dmitrich—and rushed to help him remove his coat. It must have seemed like he had come to make an order. Protopopov had the brief idea of ordering something. But he didn't have the emotional strength for acting, and he nearly collapsed. And he honestly told the tailor, hopefully, holding his shoulders:

"Dear Ivan Fyodorovich! I'm in a bad way. I need to sit a moment and rest. Shelter me for just an hour."

Something flashed across that asymmetrical face, but Ivan Fyodorovich didn't betray anything and led him just as readily and showed him to a seat. Guessing what was happening, he railed against the idlers and rebels shooting guns and robbing shops and bringing life to a standstill.

He had to answer, and he did answer, for that was a good man, not a shadow of shyness at his visitor, a great soul in the body of a common man! How much closer was he to God and the truth than we were. His fat wife came up: Will you drink something? Eat something? Oh, selfless hospitality, oh, the warmth of common folk, but although Protopopov had eaten nothing today—he couldn't eat anything, everything had been taken away, and most of all he felt like not talking and wished they wouldn't look, and felt like dropping his head in his hands, sagging on his own bones, and somehow resting and gathering his strength.

But they thought they needed to distract him with conversation and kept talking about this and that, and now something impossible about the police: supposedly the police had machine guns and were shooting from the roofs; supposedly they'd dressed as soldiers; supposedly policemen had been besieged in the Astoria. . . . They had no idea how correctly they were talking to him. After all, educated people were all against the police. He heard some more disjointed talk, and his depression mounted from this nonsense, but he didn't stir to object.

He couldn't say "Don't talk to me," but evidently he looked quite unwell, and the wife had a good idea. Wouldn't he like to have a lie-down in the bedroom? Shouldn't we call the doctor? He gestured a no to the doctor but a lie-down—if you would allow me. And if . . . ?

He decided to open up to them. Here, and he gave them his brother's address. Could they send someone to find out how things were there, at his brother's? Was it safe?

They led him into the bedroom. Two nickel-plated beds under white coverlets, the entire window filled with flowers, two icons in the corner, and a woodland scene. A large gray tomcat was sleeping here, and they rousted it. Removing only his boots, in anguished exhaustion, Aleksan Dmitrich lay down on top of the coverlet, his head on the plumped stack of pillows.

Everything was burning so inside him that he lost his hearing: apparently there were occasional gunshots and his hosts were saying something to each other, but Aleksan Dmitrich didn't hear, and it was as if none of it had happened. Not only had he lost his hearing, but his hands and feet were numb, and he couldn't rest, and his yesterday evening's joy at being safe had evaporated. He was close to dying.

He fell asleep straight off, very soundly, paralyzed. Then he surfaced from his oblivion, but it was as if he'd been flung up, his mind immediately lit up—with despair. He pictured his own ruin, and the ministers, and Shcheglovitov's arrest, and mutinous Petrograd, the soldiers, the armored vehicles—all this might be fixed by healthy units from the front, of course, but how many days could they hold out until that? Actually, he should get up and go now, but couldn't he now spend the night with the tailor and stay here until the grand deliverance? (That would be good. . . .) Salvation would be to get out of Petrograd altogether, but could he really show up at some train station? He could only imagine the revolutionary hell that must be going on there now.

The tailor shuffled in, leading his nephew. He had run to see Aleksandr Dmitrich's brother, and there was an answer: He couldn't go there. They themselves were expecting a search.

Even more exhausted and feeble, Protopopov leaned back on the pillows.

Yes, he was wholly in *their* hands. The Duma big shots. His former friends. Wasn't he a Duma big shot? What had he done? How could he have abandoned them? For the sake of what? The allure of a ministerial post, and now one major blow and in twenty-four hours it was gone. But the Duma was standing, the victor! Wasn't he from there? Hadn't he been a member for ten years? He had been there ten years—and a minister just five months. Didn't the former outweigh the latter? He had been such an esteemed and prominent Duma deputy, the face of the public, that he had been allowed into secret sessions of the Krivoshein circle on Aptekarsky Island. He had known all the intrigues! In the Progressive Bloc—hadn't he been one of the leaders? Forget that, how much earlier—hadn't he been a participant in the Liberation Movement? How could he have disdained this glorious past— and for the sake of what pathetic illusion? Who might he have been right now in the Tauride Palace! It would have been to him that they brought prisoners, this one or that one. Oh what a cruel and irreparable mistake! Now he was in their hands, and they would be more pitiless with him than with anyone!

He was becoming more and more feverish. He wrapped the coverlet around himself to warm up, warmed up between the shoulder blades with one pillow—oh, if they would bring his coat, but it was hanging in the vestibule and he was embarrassed to go out and get it. You could pile ten fur coats on him, he was so cold inside—oh, how he'd been caught, oh, what could be crueler—and how excessive the retribution would be! Had he spent his whole life in governmental circles, that would be one thing and not at all offensive, but to trip up so irredeemably!

What had induced him, why had he provoked the Duma so disrespectfully and intentionally as well? He'd enraged them, himself spreading rumors that everything would be done without the Duma—land distributed to peasants without the Duma, Jewish civil rights without the Duma—and he himself had boasted that it was he who had arrested the Workers' Group, boasted that he would crush any revolution pitilessly. Why had he boasted? Because they'd enraged him. Why had they hounded him so? Couldn't they have taken his appointment well? After all, initially they'd even congratulated him.

Yes, I made mistake after mistake! But you, my comrades, you made mistakes with respect to me! You didn't have to finish off my forgiving heart right away—that was what gave rise to the bad feelings in it! Didn't I protect Aleksandr Ivanych during the arrest of the Workers' Group and not let him be arrested also? Doesn't that stand in my favor? And the fact that Aleksandr Ivanych's portrait with his touching inscription hung in my office until the day I was appointed minister—won't you give me credit for that? Now, of course, no one remembers about that. Now, of course, everyone is going to be right and I alone am more to blame than anyone. But gentlemen, but friends, but comrades! I simply got lost in this labyrinth! Certainly, I didn't

implement the policy I should have! I made a tremendous mistake, and believe me, believe me, Pavel Nikolaich, this has caused me to suffer deeply!
I chose a course that didn't suit the country's mood. Oh, how I repent of that
right now. If only you knew! Yes, I behaved exceptionally nastily. I kept evolv-
ing in the wrong direction, not the way I should have—but I am *yours!* I am
yours, flesh of your flesh! After all, Mikhail Vladimirovich publicly refused
to shake my hand on the New Year—and how did I respond? With a joke
and by forgetting! Oh no, I can see, you don't treat me with complete trust,
and that distresses me! Yes, yes, you correctly noted that I keep trying to wiggle out of things. Even I myself have felt that, but you should keep me honest. The fact that I joined the ministry was more than a mistake. It was a disaster! The biggest disaster in my life, I now see! But at that moment my
ambition played up in me, it ran and jumped—and I kept acting rashly, irre-
sponsibly! My fatal mistake was to believe that the regime had to be preserved until the war's end. After all, I'm not of firm character. You know I
yield strongly to circumstance. I landed in this milieu—and that was my disaster. At first I found Rasputin distasteful, but then I got used to him. Well, I
saw him about fifteen times, but I couldn't be friendly with him. Yes, it's
hard to deny it, during my ministry I did support the rightists, but believe me,
always without pleasure. For me it was a devil's bargain! Being extremely
rightist is utterly uncharacteristic of me, it contradicts my whole being. Yes,
in my heart I was always a radical. Didn't you sense that? . . . Yes, I did flatter Markov the Second. Oh, what baseness, how it pains me to remember!
Yes, I did seek favor with Prince Andronikov, but I had to disarm any harmful
influence. . . . Dissolve the Duma? I won't hide the fact that I hesitated inwardly, but I never did arrive at that final conviction. The moment I became
minister, people started abusing me so, started trying to destroy me so, but
I'm a human being, too! I was crushed! Or were you told that I promised at
various gatherings that I would save Orthodox Russia and make quick work
of any revolution? But I did that for the sake of eloquence. I assure you! Did
I boast? Well, if you like—yes. But don't attach any importance to that. Ah,
Fyodor Izmailovich, but you always could talk rings around me, and did I
ever try to argue against you? You know, I'm not capable of coherent explication. I fall down in the area of suppositions that change the meaning of
everything that's happening. Gentlemen, I sincerely beg you to show me
what I should say. I fear my delay will arouse your displeasure. . . . Yes, I feel
the terrible weight of the cause I took on. Financial intrigues? None whatsoever. Am I more sinful than anyone else? Where is my sin? I have not
sinned against the law; but against my whole life I have sinned, for I didn't
understand myself, and I wasn't understood. My salvation lay in the Duma!
The worker for the homeland and the happy man would have been preserved. But now I'm ill and exhausted. I've become a kind of monster. Oh,
you are holding all of it against me, all of it. . . . Pavel Nikolaich, what a bad
person you are, Anna Sergeevna is kinder than you and she never would

have. . . . I compared myself to Stolypin? Well, I don't remember that, but that's entirely possible. Ah, my friends, I'm afraid for myself, but that sometimes happens with me, that I *slip*. . . . I sometimes have strange sentences. You noticed that a little during our parliamentary trip. . . . But then you treated me amicably. You must believe that I am devoted to our shared former ideals! Yes, the Duma's true objectives are to win rights from the monarchy, and I had no right to flout this broad interpretation. In this I am guilty, guilty. Oh, I feel your favorable attitude toward me with my whole soul. . . . Oh, allow me to go into the trenches as a private! Oh, send me to quarantined barracks as a medic, and if I survive, then judge me after the war! . . .

What awaits me? Surely not eternal imprisonment?

God Almighty, save me!

My documents? I gave all my documents to that gendarme, Pavel Saveliev, you can easily find him. . . . Because he was my most trusted man. . . . The keys to the fireproof safe? They're in the desk, and here, please, is the key to the desk. . . . Yes, I can sign everything I've said. Yes, willingly, if that's what you wish. . . . But why the 13th? Is today really the 13th? Isn't today the twenty-something? Ah, the new calendar? . . .

This stabbed him and got him up. He sat on the bed, off his head. The new calendar! How hadn't he guessed? The astrologist was speaking according to the new calendar, of course. And his most dangerous days—the 14th, 15th, and 16th—only began tomorrow! . . .

That meant struggle was futile. There was no way out. He had to throw himself on their mercy. Surrender his body—but unburden his tormented soul.

Shcheglovitov had been arrested—and now he would go. Himself. . . .

But he would ask the tailor, and his wife, and his nephew to escort him. So he wouldn't be torn to pieces on the way.

[2 1 1]

Prince Lvov was not the first to name himself head of the future Russian government. He had been named, nominated, and crowned by the public, most of all the Moscow public but also the entire zemstvo public, which had been amazed by the magical activity of the Union of Zemstvos during the war. The yoke of Russia-wide popularity had been placed on his shoulders by unanimous public admiration, and whether or not Prince Georgi Evgenievich wanted it, he had become the hope of the Russian people. Just as the Russian people themselves had been the prince's guiding hope.

The Japanese war had been a rout, but Prince Lvov had returned from it with fame acquired as an organizer of the zemstvos nationwide. Famine came to some provinces—only adding further glory to Prince Lvov's organization. During the years of reaction, he'd been pushed out of the zemstvo or accused of not presenting reports about the expenditure of official and private sums for many years (just go collect them from every office! Indeed, the two did get mixed up, and reports were late and not perfectly balanced) — but the wind of public approval supported the prince, and anyway, everyone admitted that no one else could attract as many funds for philanthropy and use them so productively. His supreme gift was getting money from the government, getting it through visits to the *spheres*, his skill at quiet private conversations when he would cast a spell over any interlocutor and obtain donations or concessions. The prince would have liked to remain in this practical sphere, but along the way he was drawn involuntarily by a political lot, albeit a modest one. Whether the prince was in the reactionary role of a zemstvo official or in the progressive role of deputy in the stormy zemstvo congresses of 1904–05, or even a deputy in the First State Duma, at not one session did he give a single public speech, or even a campaign one (others gave them for him). When in 1905 a zemstvo delegation was appointed to see the Emperor, the same invariable Prince Lvov was proposed as its head. And when by the will of events he was drawn to the scandalous Vyborg, the entire situation gave the prince a nervous shock, and his hand simply physically would not rise to sign the Vyborg appeal, and they led him to his train car, ill. (A Kadet party trial against him was even contemplated.) The prince was elected to the Moscow City Duma on the basis of a fictitious franchise (never having been a Muscovite) and he didn't know how the city worked, but the Kadets forgave him and elected him mayor, though the government did not approve his election. Simultaneously, it cannot be said that Prince Lvov was in disgrace with the Emperor. Both at the beginning of the Japanese war and at the beginning of this one he had been given an audience, and this time he had been kissed. (Also: he had secretly declined an imperial medal so as not to spoil his public image.) Since 1914, his affairs in the Union of Zemstvos had cut a broad, stormy swath, and he had tens of thousands of people working for him, but Prince Lvov only went to his Petersburg offices to get the necessary billion—which he paid out for expenses. These past few years, public momentum had made the prince feel at ease and successful. The prince felt as if the entire industrious Russian people were working under his leadership and he himself had been elevated to being the people's undoubted leader.

An avid desire arose in society to draw Prince Lvov into the political sphere for good. For more than a year, all the drawing room groupings of the future responsible Russian government had been happy to write down the prince for the number one seat of prime minister instead of Rodzyanko. This honorable doom—to become Russia's head—had already changed the prince himself from an irreplaceable operator and hardhead, as he considered himself, into a giant of the political opposition. (There was a little-known justice here: Georgi Evgenievich was descended in the thirty-first generation from Rurik.)

Since last autumn, this pressure of public selection had compelled him finally to take drastic political steps. Yes, the imperial government's unfit behavior—who wouldn't it drive crazy! In November, Prince Lvov had directly demanded that the Progressive Bloc take measures toward the decisive reconstruction of governmental authority. In this state of red-hot impatience among those around him, he agreed to give instructions to the Tiflis mayor to feel out Grand Duke Nikolai Nikolaevich: How did he view the possibility of a coup d'état? This winter he had visited General Alekseev in the Crimea with the same question. How could the prince agree to this? But how could he not agree if everyone saw in him the fatherland's savior? What patriot could stand for open, brazen preparations for a separate peace? Not that there was any particular secret here. All Moscow and Petrograd were gossiping about a coup. Everyone was certain that a coup was imminent, and everyone was calling Prince Lvov the future prime minister. Chairmen of provincial zemstvo boards were openly calling for Prince Lvov. The prince could not fail to recognize and yield to the popular decision. He had been compelled to violate his usual modesty. He called an unsanctioned congress of the Union of Zemstvos for 22 December. And he wrote the first public speech in his life—and what a speech! Nothing like it for fury and harshness had been given even in the Duma, even by Milyukov. (Rivalry with the Duma had fed the flame of the Union of Zemstvos.) From muteness, Georgi Evgenievich had gone straight to an intense high note! This was a gush of indignation, contempt, and hatred! The fatherland was in danger! The fatal hour of its existence! The government had already detached itself from the life of the country, the life of the people, and was entirely caught up in a struggle against the people for the sole purpose of preserving its own personal well-being. They were Russia's wickedest enemies, and this was why they were preparing a peace with Germany. When the government becomes an utter stranger to the people's interests, the time has come to take responsibility for Russia's destiny upon oneself! The country was on the brink of a coup d'état!

All these words had been written down, and the prince may even have written them in a trance. So commandingly had society forced him to take this step that he hadn't even had time to take stock of the scale of his audacity or to be amazed at his own daring. He had been drawn along so triumphantly in the public momentum that he had lost the sense of corporeal cohesion and the resistance of objects characteristic of every man. He was moving toward a heroic speech! It had to pass through his soft throat, which was unaccustomed to shouting—and he was ready!

The people had to take their future into their own hands, and an inevitable line ran through the prince.

True, the congress never did assemble, and instead of his speech the prince took up composing a report with a police officer, and the assembly drifted away to where others were giving their speeches; nonetheless, the prince was undoubtedly prepared to deliver this speech in public. The speech was passed from hand to hand to be read, as if it had been delivered.

Today, however, for the first time, Prince Lvov had been genuinely amazed at his own behavior. Yesterday he had been summoned—no, *drafted*—to his sacred post by telephone call from Petrograd to Moscow. And from still calm Moscow he, feeling altogether light, was able to board a train quickly and travel normally to Petrograd, still wondering and rejoicing the entire ride at how the great people had responded to a great appeal, thereby demonstrating the majestic image of their spiritual integrity. But at the station in Petrograd, first of all, instead of porters or cabbies there were waves of dissolute soldiers, occasional gunfire, various gangs running around, someone's corpse lying on the ground, and officers being insulted—and the prince was rescued only by the people meeting him with a motorcar. Only in this way was the prince able to dive through the tumultuous, roiling streets overflowing with unchecked people, and uncontrolled soldier crowds without officers; there were drunks, weapons firing of their own accord, and several times the motorcar was stopped and there could have been deadly retribution. But they avoided that, reached their destination, and slipped into the tranquil apartment of Baron Meller-Zakomelsky on the Moika, near the Mariinsky Palace.

Here, in the apartment, the ordinary life familiar to us all went on, with a bedroom for the guest and the ritual of breakfast and dinner, but even this calm was deceptive and armed men could have burst in for a search, although, of course, they could be conciliated by human explanation.

The man did not exist on earth whom the meek prince could not disarm and win over in a private conversation, eye to eye. But how could he now step foot among the thousands in the swarming, maddened Tauride Palace, about which such horrors had been recounted? How could he give speeches to the irregular assemblage there—buzzing, overexcited, and waving rifles?

This was so unlike a sacred, industrious people who had gained their sacred freedom!

What the prince had seen from the motorcar on his way to the baron's apartment (they had wanted to take him straight to the Tauride Palace, but he was able to sensibly divert them), even these street impressions were too much for him to digest. The street's unruliness had lashed him in the face—and the prince had felt so singed, he had to collect his emotional forces.

But right then a motorcar arrived from the Tauride Palace for the prince! They had been informed of his arrival.

No, the prince was too shaken to go. He asked them to convey to his Duma well-wishers that today he was quite tired and simply couldn't, but he would definitely come tomorrow.

"No!" The messenger was adamant. "Everyone is waiting! It can't be put off. You have to go now."

"No!" the prince implored. "Give me at least until evening. This evening."

The prince felt so beaten that it was even hard to talk to the baron and his family and to maintain a cheerful expression and a cheerful voice. He gladly went to the room set aside for him, sat down in the peaceful chair—and drooped, caved.

So beleaguered was Prince Lvov. Deep down, he sincerely felt that managing this seething multitude was far beyond his abilities. The prince's entire civil career had been so brilliant, but now he saw that he had been drawn beyond his emotional powers, that he didn't have the might for an ascent like this.

But he couldn't admit this to anyone. It was too late. His triumphant career irrevocably obligated him as well, and he couldn't admit to any of those who had summoned him, elected him, named him, that he felt his weakness, that he couldn't heft this burden.

He lay prostrate in the armchair, having lost all his soaring of the past few years. And it came back to him—the once familiar, now forgotten, unbearable resistance of life in which little Georgi had spent his entire childhood, adolescence, and young adulthood. The ruined estate, the black bread and sauerkraut on the princely table. At his detested high school he was called "chicklet," and studying was like dragging a cart, slow and irritating, and he was held back to repeat a year, and more than once. He chose law school because it was the easiest. And he and his brother had eked out a business in clover seeds and apples, and Moscow in those years had known not Lvov himself but "Prince Lvov's apple pastille" (made from windfall fruit).

He'd lived like this for decades and gotten used to life being hard, to eking out his living. He'd even consulted with the Optina elders as to whether he should become a monk; his modest nature and good manners inclined toward this.

But when he began in government service, combining it with his leftist sympathies (for which he was called the "red prince"), he learned how devastating public contempt could be. In 1892, as an indispensable member of the provincial office, he was forced to accompany the governor on a journey with a military detachment. The peasants had not recognized the courts' decision and had not allowed the forest to be cut down where they were. At a station outside Tula, provincial authorities had greeted Lev Tolstoy, and subsequently the great writer had written a hundred angry pages about the accomplices of evil, having in mind Prince Georgi Evgenievich, although not mentioning him by name, thank God. And if he had? . . . His entire career would have been over for good.

Now, though, Prince Lvov had been named and recognized and he had nowhere to hide or go. Inevitably, he would have to go to the Tauride and take power over Russia.

[2 1 2]

During the second half of the day, telephone service was restored in the Musin-Pushkin home—and Colonel Kutepov was asked to come to the phone.

This was astonishing. Who had found out and where? Was this their enemies checking on him? But he picked up.

It turned out that the same indefatigable Lieutenant Maksheev who yesterday morning had involved the colonel in this entire operation had found out from Kutepov's sisters. Now he was calling from the same place, from the officers' club on Millionnaya, saying they had experienced unusual events and profound moral tribulations and would like to get together and confer with the colonel.

"Getting together is not that easy. Tell me over the telephone."

He hesitated. In vague sentences he made it clear that he was talking about recognizing the new authority.

There could be no doubt. Kutepov replied into the receiver as if dictating:

"Do not disgrace the name of the Preobrazhensky Regiment! You do not have the right to use it, and every step you take is ascribed to the Preobrazhensky account. Enough of the kind of disgrace I have seen today out the window, when I saw your reserve battalion, which means Preobrazhensky soldiers, on their way to the Duma. Thank God, I did not see officers there."

"Oh, this calls for a separate story. . . ."

Maksheev mumbled something, his briskness having disappeared. His mumbling was apparently about the fact that the State Duma was the parliament.

Kutepov cut him off:

"You have turned out to be irresponsible mutineers, even worse than common laborers."

"Aleksandr Palych! Come see us at the officers' club right now and we'll talk! We very much want to see you."

Go to the club? He wanted to. Not hide somewhere but simply go to his own regimental club. That's right. Why in fact should he keep sitting in this building if enemy posts seemed to have been removed and the city had no front line?

He discussed it with his hosts. What if he tried to leave in an ambulance? But without changing clothes or lying on a stretcher!

He had to wait for darkness, another couple of hours. It was getting murkier, snow was falling harder—and darkness was approaching.

A certificate was written up, and a seal affixed, by the Northern Front Administration of the Red Cross saying that the colonel was an official in the medic column. With darkness, the ambulance drove into the courtyard and Kutepov sat between the driver and the doctor. They drove out quickly and sped down Liteiny Prospect.

It wasn't all that simple. They were stopped at nearly every block, and it was on Liteiny that the stops were dangerous for identification. But each time the doctor said briskly:

"Comrades! We've been summoned to pick up wounded men at the Pavlovsky School. There was just a battle there! Don't hold us up, I beg of you!"

And they let them through. (There hadn't been a battle, just a rumor.)

They turned onto the French Embankment, were stopped a couple more times just before the Trinity Bridge—all the idle, volunteer patrols looking menacing—and now they'd dived onto Millionnaya and driven up to the brick barracks. Kutepov entered the officers' club.

Nearly all the officers were there, except for Prince Argutinsky-Dolgoruky, who had fallen quite ill. Everyone looked extremely upset and depressed. They wanted to begin the discussion, but they didn't even feel like telling their stories. Kutepov listened as their senior officer and was accepted as such, and he was in fact that—as the aide to the commander of the Preobrazhensky Regiment. (In fact, Kutepov was a dyed-in-the-wool army man. But in the Japanese war he had distinguished himself to such an extent in the 85th Vyborg Regiment that the Emperor had transferred him to the Guards, a rare instance. Here, too, in 1914, he had been merely a company commander, a staff captain, but over the course of the war he was promoted to colonel. Naturally, Second Lieutenant Rausch von Traubenberg, who had been determined for the Guards since cadet age, and other legacy darlings could despise Kutepov as not a true Guardsman.) Three days, two days before, right here, in free-flowing conversations over breakfast, these young officers had been stunned by Kutepov's lack of freedom-loving thoughts, his bond to duty, no matter what the government. But today they were seeing their hopes routed, and it was actually embarrassing and hard for them to say this, it had to be pulled out little by little from one and then another. They had gone to sleep inspired by their support of the State Duma, and they had woken up prepared for new steps. But something unthinkable had happened. The soldiers had locked them all in, more or less arrested them in the club, and had gone without them to the State Duma!

Although the officers' hearts were longing to go exactly there! Although yesterday only a string of failures had prevented them from supporting the Duma's authority!

Not that this was a true arrest: they'd retained their weapons, and they could have broken down the doors or jumped through the windows—but did they really need that kind of liberation? The wound was too deep, the humiliation inflicted on them by the soldiers. Thus they had spent several hours here, with only themselves, in this awkward state, and the telephone was their only consolation, but it was right during those hours that it had gone out of service. (When service was restored, the thought had already matured of finding Kutepov so that he could rescue them.)

However, upon entering, Kutepov didn't notice any signs of their arrest.

Indeed, after Maksheev had found the colonel at the medic administration, two motorcars had suddenly arrived from the Duma led by their ensign with a written order: all Preobrazhensky battalion officers were to come to the Duma in these vehicles. Only under this order had their detention at the soldiers' hands been lifted—and so they had gone there.

But there was no particular meeting there, the deputies were already worn out from meetings, and none of the main ones came out, but a secondary one explained to them that the entire summons had been concocted for their liberation—and he asked how they had ended up so alienated from their soldiers.

This was indeed what was most agonizing and unclear for them. How had this happened given their progressive views and given the fact that they had always been whole-heartedly for the people? They wanted to be with the soldiers! But the soldiers didn't want to be with them.

Now it was fully revealed to Kutepov what a disaster it had been that he'd been sent to Liteiny with a detachment. Had he been with the main Preobrazhensky and Pavlovsky forces yesterday, he would have put an end to this whole Petrograd commotion yesterday, and in any case he wouldn't have been stomping around on Palace Square for three or four hours for no reason. He would just have marched off and seized the Tauride Palace.

(They also didn't tell him how yesterday they had telephoned the Duma declaring their support. Or how then, in the night, Duma deputies Shidlovsky and Engelhardt had come from the Duma to see the officers, who had not dispersed, and to thank the Preobrazhensky men. They had enrolled them in the Duma force and had ordered them to attack the Admiralty early in the morning—but after sending out reconnaissance, they'd considered the Admiralty too strongly fortified. And after that glorious night they had woken up detained. . . .)

But what the officers did not try to hide was that they were in disarray and confused—and afraid to go join the soldiers in their own barracks. They had remained in their unlocked club as in voluntary captivity and were now asking Kutepov to help them put things right in the battalion. How could they live with the soldiers now? It was an awkward, incredible position. In other regiments yesterday, officers had even been killed.

If they were to understand anything, they had to go straight to the barracks. Kutepov called on them to come along: Captain Priklonsky! Captain Kholodovsky! Captain Skripitsyn!

Yes, they were very much asking him to go through the barracks, talk with the soldiers, and instill order there and the performance of duty. But they themselves . . . they themselves would prefer . . . simply, it had become so awkward, it was such an upside-down situation. . . .

Kutepov looked with amazement at what sort of educated, reflective breed of Guardsmen they all were: they were fearful of joining their own soldiers in the barracks?

He himself had been in battle yesterday, had just been a hunted prey, but here he had raced through the line of fire and on *this* side had felt at home in his regiment's barracks. An instantaneous change of positions such as is typical for a front-line environment: first *they* outflank, then we do.

So no one was going? Fine. Kutepov went himself, freely and willingly, suffering no confusion whatsoever.

He entered the first company—and the duty officer appeared before him and reported clearly and appropriately and answered all the colonel's questions, and everyone who had heard the command stood at attention.

In the second building, the same thing. And in the third. It was all right. Discipline had been maintained.

In a few places they were arguing loudly about something, but upon the colonel's appearance they stopped and stood at attention, like everyone.

He discovered only two soldiers from the Emperor's company inebriated. But he made no attempt to punish them, as if he hadn't noticed.

And no one tried to insult Kutepov anywhere.

He simply hadn't expected such good conditions in the battalion when now all over Petrograd . . . Although, of course, the tension could be felt. But they didn't let on to him in any way.

No, he had to wonder how the battalion was still holding on.

Returning to the club, Kutepov shared his impressions with his officers, who swarmed him, and encouraged them (hopelessly sliding over Skripitsyn's evasive face). He advised them, tomorrow morning, to go to the barracks as if nothing had happened—and keep the soldiers busy until the midday meal, increase the number of orderlies, and after the meal let those who wished go to town, provided they observed all the rules.

Meanwhile a motorcar was arranged for Kutepov and a pass with the sprawling signature of the President of the rebellious State Duma (the Preobrazhensky officers had been given a supply of them).

Two regular sergeants who knew the colonel well accompanied him in the motorcar to Vasilievsky—again through all this brutal red raving, which had by now reached Vasilievsky Island.

They asked:

"What's going to happen, your honor?"

What was going to happen? Kutepov couldn't take it all in, he didn't know. He replied:

"We will remain Preobrazhensky men to the last!"

[213]

Retired Admiral Tipolt was dining with Karpov, a liberal member of the State Council who lived on the Palace Embankment. Although the revolution had been raging in Petrograd for more than a day, Karpov's apartment was untouched, thank God, and dinner was like dinner, weighed down only by the news, in part gloomy, in part altogether mind-boggling. The State Council's President had even been arrested, although that was understandable as he was a well-known reactionary. And so even had one of the deputies—Shirinsky-Shikhmatov, which was also understandable, he being known for his rightist convictions. This horror did not threaten those present here, but they could not be indifferent to the fatherland's fate, and they discussed various rumors and reports concerning the events in Petrograd and the possibility of government troops arriving from the front.

They also discussed the fact that if electricity and water were cut off and the W. C. clogged up—then no one could do anything about it.

All of a sudden there was a very harsh ring at the door, the way decent people don't ring. They exchanged glances, not without fear. What could they do but open up, though? Everyone remained seated at the table, and the maid went to open the door.

Behind the door she saw a small, unprepossessing electrician who had checked this very doorbell of theirs yesterday—holding a gun. Without asking, he stepped into the front hall, and a whole crowd of dissolute soldiers, women, and some very suspicious street types surged in behind him. The maid was so distraught she couldn't utter a word.

Meanwhile, the little electrician walked through to the dining room, also holding his gun out front, and told the host:

"Your Excellency, you are under arrest!"

They were struck dumb, and it took a moment for his wife and daughter to recover. Terrible surmises raced through Karpov's head as to why they were taking him specifically. The admiral had thought no one knew about his presence here and so could not arrest him—and he rose from the table and started making his way toward the door behind the soldiers' backs. However, the electrician noticed this maneuver and aimed his gun at the admiral:

"You are under arrest, too."

Then the admiral protested with all his pomposity and hauteur. The electrician was not about to listen and commanded them both sharply:

"Surrender your medals and cartridges!"

The admiral didn't have his revolver. But he began unfastening his medals. Karpov, on the contrary, did have a revolver and cartridges, and fearing an accusation of concealment, he told his wife to bring and surrender them.

Meanwhile, one of the soldiers approached the table with a bared sword and sliced off a fat pink slice of ham, which he picked up with the other hand and began to eat.

This gesture made a shocking impression on those at the table. His sword could have snagged anything on the table!

The others, stepping around the table, also started reaching and picking up what struck their fancy.

The electrician didn't take anything, but still training the revolver, told the arrested men to collect themselves quickly and leave.

The women began bustling about and asked them to wait. They brought Karpov his fur-trimmed coat and high galoshes and the admiral his greatcoat. Right there, in the dining room, they dressed, since the front hall was packed.

They started down the staircase.

The admiral asked:

"Where are you taking us?"

The electrician replied smartly:

"To the Duma, Your Excellency!"

"On foot?" The admiral was horrified. This was three versts. He had never walked that far.

"How else?"

Karpov's daughter, who had run down with them, thought her father could never make it that far and had an idea:

"Wait! Today they arrested Minister Stürmer right nearby here, and his wonderful motorcar is still in his garage. Take it to the Duma?"

The revolutionaries liked this:

"Well, where is it? Take us!"

She led them to the Stürmers'. They rang just as loudly, demanding the motorcar and driver immediately—and no one dared object.

A little while later they were getting into this wonderful motorcar: the prisoners in back and the electrician in front, but turned around pointing his gun at them.

The daughter shouted asking whether she could come along.

"If you hold on."

But it was too late. Volunteers were clinging all around the motorcar, standing with their bayonets on the running boards and rear end.

They were off. The revolver was kept pointed at the prisoners' chests, and concerned that the gun would fire accidentally from the shaking, the admiral asked:

"Listen, dear man, we aren't running away anywhere. Put your revolver away. It might go off."

"Don't worry, Your Excellency!" the electrician assured him merrily and smartly. "It's not loaded. It's just for show!"

Meanwhile, Karpov's wife rushed to call Rodzyanko from the apartment. Karpov had been his neighbor in their home district, an acquaintance, and had even written several speeches for him.

Rodzyanko met them in the entrance hall, thanked the electrician and entire convoy very much, and let them go when they had led the prisoners to his office.

There, about twenty similarly rescued men were sitting, and senators among them, too. All were waiting for their tormentors to sweep out so they could return to their homes.

FROM THE PAPERS OF THE MILITARY COMMISSION

(13 March)

—At 8 in the evening, a guard was issued for the cellars, Jaegers called in, 17 men, posts occupied in the Department of Appanages. 40 Mokhovaya, complete order. Outsiders in the courtyard with a party of 62 men, looking around. They'd passed through the watchmen's quarters. During their removal, a clash. Another clash with 5 soldiers expected. Relief essential.

—Ensign Tafarov has been assigned to stop any robbery of stores on Kronverksky Prosp. and nearby locations.

Chairman of the Mil. Comm. Prov. Comm. B. Engelhardt

—Corner of Simeonovskaya and Liteiny, Schitt's cellar smashed. Voskresensky, corner of Kirochnaya, Baskov's store looted, men drinking.

Volunteer Sergiev

—27 Kolomenskaya. Crowd looting building.

—Just at Warsaw Station we learned from reliable sources: 35 troop trains coming from front for Tsarskoye Selo and will arrive 4–5 in morning. Mood unknown. Then, at 6 in morning, two letter trains to arrive, the suite's and the Tsar's. Attention must be paid.

A. Konovalenko, member of student circle

—12 looting private apartment on Kirochnaya. Scout sent.

G. A. S.

*   *   *

THE RAGS ARE ON THE BOTTLE,
THE SCRAPS ARE ON A SPREE!

*   *   *

[2 1 4]

The tense daytime hours flowed on, the most important hours for that secret preparation when the troops still had not appeared in reality but were invisibly and inaudibly converging and moving around: some being removed from battle positions; others moving toward the stations; still others embarking; and yet others already on their way. If only these hours could pass unimpeded and the commander could provide for all the finer points—then as his reward all the troops would be in place at the appointed hour, united and prepared to strike.

A dispatch came as expected from the conscientious Belyaev saying that, to spare the Admiralty, the last detachments had been led out of it and, due to their spotty reliability, had been released to their barracks. In Petrograd itself, resistance had ceased, then, but that had been clear even before.

No reply had been forthcoming from Mrozovsky in Moscow, and he had not declared a state of siege — but that might not even be necessary. In the middle of the day, they had verified by telegraph the condition of the Moscow rail hub: no excesses or delays in the trains of any kind. Favorable.

General Alekseev was troubled by a sense of something overlooked. Which was this: given the current situation, they could not rely on the telegraph and telephone, and Ivanov should have a radio set with him. They ordered one sent to him from the Western Army Group, so that it would catch up to him en route. And even this: send one more intermediate one to Nevel, so that it could link three sides: Ivanov's forces, Pskov, and GHQ.

The marvelous preservation of the Minister of War in Petrograd (which demonstrated the fantastic nature of the situation and the fact that all was not lost in the capital) obliged Alekseev to report to him about the measures taken and the troops sent, since he could not send such a report to the Tsar. (The Tsar's trains seemed to have vanished; the stations had not reported on their passing.) Late in the day, Alekseev sent a detailed telegram to Belyaev at the General Staff in Petrograd listing all the units sent, their commanders and scheduled arrivals in the capital (the leading Tarutinsky regiment should begin arriving tomorrow at dawn), even about the removal of the Guard from the Southwestern Army Group, even his own assumptions about further troop additions.

The information from Petrograd was so meager and fragmentary that he had to use even the reports from the Italian and French agents in the capital to their senior representatives at GHQ. Culled from them again were the facts that the prisons had been opened wide and civilians were armed, while officers were being disarmed and arrested, the Astoria had been destroyed by fire, and Protopopov had fled.

On the other hand, there was no confirmation of the existence of any Jacobin government in the Mariinsky Palace such as Belyaev had overheard on the telephone; however, in the Tauride Palace a Provisional Committee of the State Duma had formed and declared itself now in a second telegram saying it had as its goal taken the anarchic events in hand and was temporarily performing, in essense, governmental functions.

But these were sensible men, and they could not sanctify chaos. Moderate men in full mastery of the situation; nothing terrible had happened, only the useless ministers had left. It wasn't the hydra of revolution consuming Petrograd; rather, a group of liberal, enlightened men had taken it into their hands. Given that both the old government and Khabalov's command had vanished, the appearance of the Duma Committee was a positive fact. These were all Duma deputies and for the most part neither socialists nor bloody rogues of any kind, and at their head was the monarchist Rodzyanko.

Alekseev began thinking like this: if the rebellion was calming down, against whom was he gathering and sending troops? Not against Rodzyanko and Milyukov, surely? What foolishness was that? If Petrograd was calming down on its own, against whom were the troops?

But to what extent did this Duma Committee control the capital? Obviously, it didn't. And to what extent had the danger passed of the contagion of rebellion spreading along the railroads?

Actually, it was good he'd listened to Kislyakov and not tried to seize onerous power over the railroads. The telegrams from State Duma Commissar Bublikov that had been sent along the rail lines, evidently on behalf of the Minister of Roads and Railways, were in no way disorganizing but rather called on railroad personnel to facilitate train traffic with redoubled, selfless energy, in the awareness of the importance of transport for the war and the well-being of the rear.

Since the very beginning, this entire pacification operation had not sat well with Alekseev. The troops were needed at the front, their place was there, not moving against their own capital.

All this would be good to report to the Emperor, and perhaps the Emperor would cancel the troops. But in a few hours he himself would be in Tsarskoye Selo and there he would see everything. Alekseev did not have the right to cancel an imperial order.

And despite his new doubts, he not only did not stop or change a single instruction but even filled in their fine points. He even telegraphed a warning to the Northern and Western Army Groups that they might still have to add cavalry regiments and mounted batteries.

In this entire rapid Petrograd mutiny, most puzzling of all was why it had happened at all.

After eight that evening, Alekseev shared this thought with the commanders-in-chief: that in the preparation for this mutiny, the enemy may have taken a fairly active part, and now, naturally, it knew that the revolutionaries had become Petrograd's temporary masters—and the enemy would try to exploit this with vigorous activity at the front. So they had to prepare for spot attacks.

[2 1 5]

Vorotyntsev had been recuperating. Simply recuperating—all day today.

Yesterday he had spent all day moving around in utter incomprehension and agony. He was so beaten, so spent—he couldn't remember ever feeling so devastated.

He could only wonder at where this misfortune had come from. How had he not noticed it?

It was almost morning when they fell asleep, and they didn't awake until midday. It was sunny outside, evidently, but there was a dark blind on the window, and the sun being on the other side meant there was only a half-light in the room. So they didn't get up.

No, no other woman's body, no maternal lap so serene, so broad, could allay his alarms, all this inner suffering—yesterday's and the day before yesterday's. Or from even much longer ago? This body naturally spread out, naturally merged with everything that holds and carries us. It itself was the dear, saving earth, only softer, warmer, and more expansive than the ordinary earth. Only having pressed, clung to her, to this earth, could he drive out his suffering and bring his health back—from her.

But for that he had to lie here a long time, a very long time, and almost without stirring—and even not saying anything for a long time. Then palpably, in his many cells, all through his body's skin, his health was restored to him.

As once in the Grünfliess forest he had lain on the ground and hadn't had the strength to get up and away. His entire salvation had been in not getting away.

Only through an extended, unbroken, immobile length of time was he able to calm down and get well. The secret of this calming was in the length of time: not one hour, not two, not three.

And now—now he might be able to talk about what exactly had happened and with what pain he had arrived yesterday. But would he be able to? Only that he and his wife had not been getting along—and he himself had not known that. And now, there was no reason to stir all this up. Kalisa was already healing him anyway.

And with gratitude and tenderness he kissed her lovely, full forearms.

In the afternoon, she began baring her heart to him. How, you see, she had been married off not at her own choice but by her parents' will. But then she had grown used to her husband. And grown to love him.

And various incidents. Various words spoken to the deceased. Georgi had never heard anything like it. And now he went between listening intently and just giving himself over to this murmuring like a log lying in a rushing brook, being restored in these streams.

He had never listened closely, and how unexpectedly she had led him to where he had always thought there was nothing. But now an entire world was flowing, streaming around him. Did each woman have her own separate world around her?

What had become of yesterday's laceration that made him not want to live?

He was hungry, but she wouldn't let him get up and brought him everything herself and set it out there on a low table. Only when he was sick as a child had he been fed like this, but it didn't seem shamefully lordly.

At one point he grappled with the day's date. What was it? The thirteenth. So he should be going back to the army!

But the light was undoubtedly fading in the window—half the slept-through day was already over, and Georgi never did get dressed the whole day. He'd thought about making that effort, but Kalisa was right. Where could he go now? It was nearly evening. Better in the morning as early as he liked. Rise earlier, go farther.

And so that day floated by—without a single knock at the door or a single foray—and happily there was no telephone in the apartment.

They barely turned on the electricity that evening, so full, so close was it in the darkness.

[2 1 6]

Demosthenes, a lawyer, had saved Hellas. Cicero, a lawyer, had saved Rome. But for the most part, lawyers had always been the estate of revolution. Who else had there been in the Convention?

An artist utters other people's words; a lawyer, words he himself has unearthed in his heart and put together. Herein lay his superiority. But in Russia, only in criminal and especially political cases did a lawyer have room to expand on his eloquence, to shake the judges' emotions and wrest the needed decision from them. In the civil courts, where Korzner worked, in addition to providing legal counsel for a bank, there was such a stack of cases and such a dry atmosphere that oratorical effects and sentences of a general nature were actually considered indecent; a lawyer's speech was prized for its concision and rich legal argumentation.

But the new revolutionary atmosphere had suddenly opened up unlimited space for eloquence. Yesterday evening, Korzner had spoken heatedly in the Duma hall, and wasn't his the decisive, forceful speech that had led them to venture to create the Moscow Provisional Revolutionary Committee?

After that, things had gotten rolling, and that meant writing a proclamation, too! (Korzner became one of its composers.) That meant distributing it through the city!

The dull merchant Chelnokov grasped the sweep of events—and did not resist. And Deputy Mayor Bryansky was called upon to offer the city's printing press for the proclamation.

But then also to arrange for Committee members to attend the City Duma!

This morning, Korzner had postponed all his appointments and canceled his business meetings scheduled for today. Who cared about those now? And in the first half of the day he headed back to the City Duma.

The general atmosphere in Moscow could not have been more invigorating. The newspapers had not come out: a printers' strike. Someone had issued a collotype *Bulletin of the Revolution*—reports and rumors from Petrograd, what the telephones had reported, whether true or not—and the leaflets were passed from hand to hand. Over the course of the day the streetcars had stopped running. News was passed on about factory strikes. In some parts of the city the water mains had stopped, but not in the center. On the streets there were reinforced detachments of mounted policemen and Cossacks in various places, especially at the intersections around the Duma, and on Red Square past Iverskaya—but there wasn't a single instance of them dispersing crowds or impeding their movement. Evidently the government had come to a standstill, waiting neutrally for what was coming. At first not even crowds but, out of timidity, groups, handfuls, penetrated the Duma—however speakers came out to them from the Duma building with brief speeches. Once the crowd started getting denser, they displayed a red flag from the Duma balcony and repeated the main slogans of the proclamation in their speeches: that in Petrograd the revolutionary people had joined with the troops to inflict a decisive blow against the Tsarist government. But the struggle had only begun! Moscow's people must also call upon revolutionary soldiers to join them and seize the arsenal and weapons depots!

After these speeches, some groups did head for the barracks, to turn the soldiers. And more and more new ones kept approaching the Duma, including with revolutionary songs, and merged into the crowd, which was getting thicker. After midday it was already drowning all of Resurrection Square, spilling onto Teatralnaya as well, and in it red flags were being raised, and speakers—and the whole thing was transformed into one solid rally that the police now especially didn't dare touch.

In the Duma itself, people were gathering one by one—revolutionaries. Yes! No one in Moscow had seen, heard, or known of them for a long time, and they themselves had been hiding behind innocent guises—and now they had come at the ready and were declaring themselves more loudly the masters, and demanding that the Revolutionary Committee hand over the authority they had not yet seized into the hands of the not yet created Soviet of Workers' Deputies! They elected their own Executive Committee! Quite insolent!

But it did include decent people, Mensheviks, who were well known: Halperin, Nikitin, Khinchuk, Isuv. And an agreement was reached with them about limiting their functions so that everyone could exist in the Duma.

But events were unfolding in the city. There were stories about individual policemen being disarmed, peacefully, without killings. Police posts started to disappear of their own accord. The large details were wavering. Then a crowd of university students, about four hundred of them, thronged toward the Duma. They were laughing and telling stories about how on Bolshaya Nikitskaya they'd sent away the university attendants, removed the big iron gates, and carried them inside the yard. While other departments continued working.

Then a rumor came that workers and soldiers had seized the Arsenal. Had troops really joined the people? No one had seen them yet. But here on Resurrection Square, groups of soldiers had started showing up, mostly unarmed. They reported that one revolutionary crowd had been about to break into the Spassky barracks but had been pushed out. The movement's fate had to be decided by the troops, but they still hadn't come to the revolution's aid.

Since the previous night, telegraph communications with Petrograd had been cut, and the encouraging reports had stopped for a few hours. They caught arrivals off the trains to find out.

But even the Moscow authorities were behaving vaguely. If at all.

Meanwhile, in the Duma itself, masses of people had crammed in, including many figures with known and little-known names—from the Zemgor, from the merchants' society, from stock exchange committees, from war industry committees, and from cooperatives. Did the Revolutionary Committee created yesterday in such a heroic burst seem to be filling up with all these representatives? No, in fact it was being watered down, spread thin, turning into God knows what. It was no longer being called Revolutionary, or Public Salvation, but rather, Provisional, and now they'd started calling it the Committee of Public Organizations.

Korzner was indignant. These common, unreliable blunderers had made them lose their banner, their sound, their impulse! What if anything could be carried through with them?

The accursed indeterminacy stretched on, as did the troops' failure to join them, and the lack of news from Petrograd.

Indignant, Korzner went home to eat.

When an hour and a half later he came back to the Duma, he found the Committee even more diffuse but having been in continuous session. Among them voices rang out that no one had elected them and it made more sense to yield the floor first to the City Duma itself, which was about to assemble late in the afternoon, evidently without its right wing.

In some rooms of the same building, the Soviet of Workers' Deputies was already meeting—and people also came from there to speak to the crowd.

But Korzner, at the time not a Duma councilor, had become, what? A passive observer? Vexation! How ominously things had glimmered yesterday evening—and here they had thinned into a kind of general flea market. On the other hand, in the past twenty-four hours Korzner had learned something about himself, just how much he needed an outlet for his energy, how much of it had built up inside his lawyer and legal counsel box!

Resurrection Square was buzzing and not dispersing! All of a sudden he heard the special sound of joy, a "hurrah," caps in the air. From the Duma balcony, a formation of several hundred soldiers with arms shouldered appeared from Neglinny Passage, visible now in the darkness, with the streetlamps on. And apparently under their junior officers!

They passed through an opening in the crowd and halted—and the ensign loudly announced that the company had come to serve the revolution and was putting itself at the people's disposal!

"Hurrah!"

The City Duma now had its first protection!

This had an effect on the Duma. Its session became bolder, and late that evening, in an appeal to the Moscow populace, it sent fervent greetings to the State Duma and expressed confidence that those who were pursuing the shameful cause of treason, the old, ruinous regime, would be removed from power, and nothing would dim the dawn breaking over the country.

But Korzner found that, in these flowers of declamation, the distinct *fist* that needed to be thrust under the old regime's nose was lost. In the past twenty-four hours, the revolution in Moscow had not noticeably picked up steam.

The next few hours passed more cheerfully. Military motor shops seized wirelesses. The crowd spilled away from the Duma toward the Sukharev Tower and the Spassky barracks and broke into them after all! Enthusiasts dragged into the Duma building whatever might be of use to repulse the counterrevolution.

And all of a sudden, almost at midnight, loud soldier singing rang out suddenly from Red Square—the words unintelligible, or something about prophetic Oleg, but the chorus repeated was choppy and menacing, in several hundred voices:

> And for our Tsar, our land, our faith,
> A loud hurrah we thunder!

Their own soldiers, their own protection, had run off during that time. And the crowd was no defense; it could scatter at any moment. While those—here they were, past Iverskaya, they were turning toward the Duma, planting their young step, their bayonets in the air perfectly matched!

A flurry went up in the Duma. Others had already run away. But it was too late now. Sent to meet them was Reserves Lieutenant Colonel Gruzinov, who had proudly announced himself immediately prior. Agitated, he came out on the steps:

"Gentlemen? What can I do for you?"

It turned out to be a company from the 4th Ensign School. They'd come "to take a look at what was going on here."

"Perhaps you're hungry, gentlemen?" Gruzinov coaxed them.

No, they wanted to take a look at what was going on. And they started walking around the Duma.

But then it was too late to return to barracks and they demanded a night's lodging!

Chelnokov came up with the idea of putting them in the Metropol—giving them the sitting rooms and billiards room.

[2 1 7]

Unfortunately, the soothing rocking of this train ride had to stop some-where. Just before six in the evening, in Rzhev, the indefatigable Alekseev finally reached his patron with difficult news, forwarding Belyaev's encoded af-ternoon telegram, which said that the last loyal troops had been removed from the Admiralty—in order to prevent an attack on the building—and disbanded.

Did that mean General Khabalov had surrendered and Petrograd had no loyal troops or government left?

Petrograd had seceded from Russia. . . .

But Tsarskoye Selo remained! No alarming news had come in from Tsarskoye Selo, and he estimated General Ivanov should already have oc-cupied it and concentrated his troops there. His family was there! His entire life! He had to hurry there.

The suite received other news. Right then, at the station, a gendarme general announced himself, having come yesterday from Petrograd, and re-counted to the suite horrible, even implausible things: that as of yesterday the entire Petrograd garrison was on the State Duma's side and the city was awaiting the declaration of a new government. The Okhrana had been routed, as had all the police stations, Gostiny Dvor, and the stores on Sen-naya; gendarmes were being killed, officers disarmed, others also killed; there were crowds everywhere and revolutionary shouts and disrespectful things being said about the Empress.

The suite was terribly disturbed. What was this going on? Something had to be undertaken! Wasn't it time to enter into talks with the rebels? Finally, it was the last possible hour to create a responsible ministry! After all, they had Rodzyanko there, and he would be the real leader. They had to get in touch with him!

The mutiny was so widespread that the suite feared for their families and themselves. There wasn't a minute to lose. They had to act! But who dared suggest this to the unconcerned Emperor? Everyone feared provoking his irritation or impatience at hearing them out.

And the Emperor was not asking them any questions. Outwardly he was perfectly calm, as usual. (Always: the more alarmed he was, the less he spoke or let it show.)

Only one person by virtue of his position could and was obligated to re-port: Frederiks, Minister of the Court. But the Emperor had been dragging him around for a long time like an old scarecrow he was sorry to throw out and didn't want to offend. Due to his advanced age, Frederiks had not only weakened but now manifested his dotage. He had been known to think the Russian emperor was Wilhelm and disgrace himself in front of the troops.

Also close to him was his son-in-law, Palace Commandant Voeikov, a very practical mind, but not close to anyone in the suite, and stubborn. He would report to the Emperor only what he himself deemed necessary.

And so it grew dark. Dinner passed in strained, forced conversation, without a word about the Petrograd mutiny.

Then again, they believed in General Ivanov's success.

They rode on. The royal train was traveling even without the Personal Convoy: of the entire Convoy, there were two orderlies. And about ten officers from the railroad battalion. The train rocked steadily, lulling, dark blue, with the royal monogram. And rode into the unguarded, impenetrable, unknowable darkness.

The train was making its way toward insurrectionist Petrograd by an odd, distant, circuitous route.

At nine in the evening, at Likhoslavl, a badly delayed telegram from GHQ caught up with the Emperor. It was a copy of a telegram again from Belyaev to Alekseev, but the news was not new. It reported that loyal troops, under the influence of exhaustion and propaganda, were abandoning their weapons and in part going over to the rebels' side. Officers were being disarmed. The ministries had ceased to function. And also this strange sentence: The ministers of foreign affairs and of railways had yesterday betaken themselves from the Mariinsky Palace and were "at their place." (Their home?) This was like a rebus, it was missing a piece: where were the other ministers, the main government itself? About the Emperor's brother Misha, Belyaev reported that he had not been able to leave for Gatchina and was in the Winter Palace. Belyaev also requested the troops' speediest arrival.

Well, they were getting closer. Old man Ivanov was assembling them around Tsarskoye Selo.

Also in Likhoslavl it was learned from the locals that a new government led by Rodzyanko had been formed in Petrograd. And that in charge of all the railroad telegraphs was a Duma deputy no one had heard of, a certain Bublikov, moreover he was referring to the Emperor's government as "old" and "former."

Leaving out this very last thing, Voeikov reported the rest to the Emperor.

Simply astonishing imposture and effrontery. What Bublikov? Why Bublikov? Even the name was a joke. . . . This was all farcical.

Maybe he should turn around? Change his plan?

What was his decision as Emperor and commander?

Voeikov insisted that there was no serious movement in Petrograd, simply a local uprising.

Right then, fortunately, a telegram was delivered from Alix, a well-timed one. Thank God! What a relief! All day yesterday there had been nothing from her. What alarm!

He immediately telegraphed a reply: "Am glad all is well with you. Hope to be home tomorrow morning. Embrace you and the children. God bless you. Nicky."

Now—all the more, all the more confidently, all the more necessarily—to Tsarskoye!

Likhoslavl was already on the smooth, two-track Nikolaevsky line. There could be only one decision: full speed ahead!

[2 1 8]

For the State Duma deputies who had not disappeared, there was business to attend to, and the most unusual kind. Some joined the Committee itself, and hour after hour, interspersed with time away, they participated in its continuous session and discussion. Others (because of the forced competition with the Soviet of Workers' Deputies) had to accept the ominous title *commissar*. The problem was that with the government's self-flight, nearly all the ministries had been beheaded—so the Committee had decided to send two or three Duma deputies to each to observe, exert influence, clarify, and help guide. True, those sent had a poor notion of what should be done and what was urgent (Maklakov alone in the Ministry of Justice knew precisely). They were even shy about their vague new title of commissar. On top of that, it wasn't easy to get through the streets to all the ministries.

A third group was assigned to speak to the arriving troops—either from the front steps or already in the hall. A fourth was to go to unfamiliar barracks and give speeches in an atmosphere and before an audience they had never prepared for in any way. No subtleties were called for here, only persuading soldiers with heart-rending force not to be in a hurry to celebrate, not to drink, and not to rush into anarchy, but to obey their officers.

So, too, Rodichev, despite being over sixty, traveled around to speak with youthful eagerness. He did have the gift of setting even cold hearts on fire and tugging at his listeners' nerves. Suddenly an opportunity had opened up to speak directly to the people—how could this tire us out, gentlemen? His pince-nez gleamed and sparkled on its long cord, and the sharp triangle of his little beard jutted out. The entire people was openly thronging behind the State Duma! What else could one expect? This gave them the opportunity to master the situation and stand at the head of the movement!

But no matter whether the speeches were successful or sadly unsuccessful—the deputies rushed back to their Duma with relief. True, it was badly spoiled and no longer theirs. In the open area in front of the palace, motorcars or the crush of people had toppled a section of the iron grating and one granite column. Sacks were piled up in the Cupola Hall. And farther inside was a soldiers' camp and senseless jostling, where current collided with current not in the political sense but in the most primitive physical one—who could overpower whom and pass through first. Drafts. In the past twenty-four hours, columns had been scratched up and furniture damaged, and there were grease spots. It had become revolting to use the lavatories, so despoiled by the soldiery, and there was also a line. The coatroom had ceased to exist, and in the room where the deputies had their personal boxes, cartridge belts and even explosives were piled up.

So that one had to make one's way through all this crush, where radical young ladies were still passing out sandwiches and tea to the lingering soldiers, and even fearfully listening to the conversations of the crowd, push into those last few rooms where the spirit of the Duma had been preserved and where the people were mainly our own, and breathe the familiar atmosphere: talk about one's visit to the regiment and hear the others' stories. And if one could, like a forgotten happiness—join in on the discussion of issues of a general nature.

Converging here as well were people who weren't Duma deputies but simply their Petersburg friends, the Kadet public.

What had been heard about the movement of Ivanov's troops? Would they really come here and exact punishment? After all, we aren't revolutionaries, gentlemen! Which is why we have been trying to persuade the soldiers to return to barracks, why we were so happy to see the officers we found. It is we who are putting an end to the revolutionary situation and restoring the order necessary for the conduct of the war. (If the Tsar recognized their Committee, how much it would all be immediately legitimized!) It wasn't we who led to this whole crisis but the spineless monarch and the rotten regime. My God, how could we live under that regime? We had already grown so accustomed to the sufferings it inflicted on us that we could live seemingly happily. To all appearances.

Had the hour of retribution come for them?

It's all right, the soldiers will calm down quickly. On the other hand, there will now be a patriotic surge in the army, and the war will end victoriously and quickly!

The stream of new prisoners—often totally random people—that kept coming in was depressing and excessive, and gratitude had to be expressed to all the volunteer convoys, which had to be dismissed, the detained kept for a few hours until the danger for them had passed—and all this again in these few remaining rooms.

Finally, a public declaration appeared over Rodzyanko's signature stating that the Duma Committee had up until this time issued no instructions concerning any arrests (this was the truth; the epidemic of arrests had had its own momentum), and henceforth arrests could be made only at the Committee's express instruction.

But even to print this declaration—no one knew where to find a press, and they might have to ask the Soviet of Workers' Deputies.

Even more, the Committee lacked the courage to call on the population not to obey that second, paralyzing authority.

It was a terribly vexing situation! All these masses had been flowing into the Tauride Palace out of sympathy for the State Duma, but there was no way to harness these sympathies. The masses had spread through the rooms and only got in the way, and now the second authority had infiltrated and was capturing them. Without that second force, apparently, there could be no restoring order or assembling soldiers in their barracks.

They had to get along somehow. In some mutually amicable way.

Right then Rodichev returned from his however-many trip, this one an evening trip. In the course of one day he had become unrecognizable, so had he lost his morning vivacity. He was hoarse, he had aged, he had put away his pince-nez.

Just now he had been at the Semyonovsky Regiment—and had returned badly upset and shocked. Due to the evening hour, the soldiers gathered for his speech in the big barracks in just their underwear and felt boots. They listened and frowned—and didn't shout "hurrah" at all.

And so they dispersed in their underwear, as though they hadn't listened to him. This was the first time in his life a speech of his had so failed to produce any effect, to say nothing of delight.

It turned out a proclamation had been circulating among them which said that the 1905 revolution had been stolen by the officers, and they would steal today's if the soldiers didn't teach them a lesson.

Someone somewhere was printing up these proclamations; for them, the presses were still operating.

[2 1 9]

For the President, the entire day had been like a swamp about to combust, where he kept trying to feel out at least some firm spots and establish supporting ties.

The stream of prisoners kept pouring in, from policemen to ministers, and all to the Tauride Palace, as if it were Rodzyanko in charge of arrests, and many dignitaries and generals were brought straight to his office. All the mutinous troops had thronged where? To the Tauride Palace. And who had greeted them? Rodzyanko again. Even ordinary soldiers kept rushing to the President's office for some reason. Someone had occupied the Petrograd Telegraph Agency—and here telegrams had been sent to all the provincial newspapers about the fall of the old government—and all in the name of the Provisional Committee—so Rodzyanko again? And now if an investigation were initiated, had he done anything illegal?

Meanwhile, Rodzyanko had remained maximally loyal and patriotic—and had spoken only like that in front of the troops. True, he hadn't said a word about the Emperor, creating a certain vagueness, but he had simply trumpeted to the glory of the homeland! (Forcing himself not to notice this outrage—this formation, its appearance, and the disgraceful absence of officers. He had called for restoring the patriotic conscience, while aware that with an army like *this* they could not survive a day of wartime.)

After all, the government **itself** had fallen out of the hands of its legitimate bearers; the Provisional Committee had merely picked it up and safeguarded it. It was prepared to merge legitimately into a new legitimate government. The Committee, in essence, was already the beginning of that constitutional government for which society and their allies had longed so. And how easily and fortuitously this government had formed! But they lacked the Emperor's sanction to distribute ministerial portfolios.

They also lacked unity and subordination within the Committee itself. Kerensky had impudently made a mockery of obedience by not accounting for where he was or what he was doing, speaking indignantly and in a mutinous spirit before the cadets and the battalions—and he could not be removed and kept in check in public view. In the Committee he anarchically declared that he was indebted to the Soviet of Deputies. Chkheidze had failed to show up at all for twenty-four hours. Meanwhile, both had been brought onto the Committee as a gift to the leftists, in hopes of making them happy and drawing them in—but they had not appreciated this gift. In the same way, Nekrasov, the Duma vice president, was slipping away from Rodzyanko. Milyukov was behaving so stubbornly, independently, and reservedly that Rodzyanko sensed no subordination in him whatsoever. He had always felt a total alienness in him, to the point that he doubted whether Russia existed for Milyukov as a living whole, even though he was concerned with expanding its borders and winning this war.

With pain and insult, Rodzyanko learned, was whispered to in secret, that this morning Prince Lvov had arrived in Petrograd! No doubt summoned by that intriguer Milyukov! In order to begin to push out the President! But he said nothing. . . .

Did you ever! Had Milyukov been in secret contact with the Allies as well?

But right then Rodzyanko had a success. His secret emissary returned after being with Buchanan and Paléologue. He had guessed correctly! The Allied ambassadors, who all these years had been sympathetic to Russian society's struggle against the Russian government, couldn't help but support them! Not on paper, orally for now, out of caution, both ambassadors replied to the President that they recognized the Provisional Committee to be Russia's sole legitimate government and the expresser of the people's will! (Oh, thank you!) They also expressed the following unwritten opinion: that the autocratic order could be successfully replaced by a constitutional one, as long as order was quickly established and the Russian army was able to carry out its duty to the Allies. The revolution had gone far enough and now it had to be reined in.

Which was precisely what Rodzyanko wanted. Very good. After this answer he began to feel more confident.

Rodzyanko spent more than a day in earnest deliberation. For some reason this process could not proceed on its own or quickly. Hours had to pass, various news had to come in, various people, Duma deputies or not, had to consult him, on business or not—and all this was not without benefit in the process of deliberation. And so, over the course of a day, thoughts arose, on their own or by force of circumstances, subjects were illuminated and decisions taken—whether it was people convincing the President or he himself coming to his conclusions.

Nonetheless, the President felt constrained with respect to the Emperor. No matter how bad their relationship of late, no matter how impertinent Rodzyanko had been to the Emperor, he had never considered himself a rebel and would not allow himself to be one. He had simply been trying to save Russia from the wretched, rotten former government. But here was the Emperor's portrait in the Duma hall shredded by bayonets. Here, too, were these arrested ministers, as if the Duma President had imprisoned them. However wretched these ministers were, they should not have been put under lock and key. . . . However, the President did not have the authority to release them. . . . And then there were these speeches of his to the troops: no matter how patriotic, he could never repeat them aloud in the Emperor's presence.

But the Emperor! Why had he been silent? Why had he so arrogantly not answered Rodzyanko's telegrams?

And now he himself was on his way—for retribution?

This movement of his was obscure, alarming, and dangerous. Why was he coming? As though to burst into Petrograd, stamp his foot, and yell at the disobedient? . . . That wasn't like him, but that was why it was so terrifying, because it wasn't.

The efficient Bublikov was reporting on the movement of the royal trains—and asking what should be done.

But what could they devise?

The Emperor was approaching, and the inevitability of meeting and reporting was mounting.

But was Rodzyanko in such a guilty position before him?

Mikhail Vladimirovich had been brought a warm dinner in a basket from home. He could no longer dine calmly in his own office, so he went to a secluded little room and spread a napkin over his exhausted chest, as if things had calmed down a little. What he hadn't understood when he was hungry, he understood better now, full; the food had gone straight to nourish his mind.

After all, it was he who had wanted a proper constitution, and nothing more! Right now he was the most peace-loving man in Petrograd, perhaps in all of Russia. Why should there be any more military actions? Why had they sent eight regiments to Petrograd? Against whom?

The obliging Belyaev informed him over the telephone of the rundown of regiments: Tarutinsky, Borodinsky, Uhlan Tatar, Ural Cossack . . . Eight.

Also possible were the Preobrazhensky and two Guards Riflery. . . . Perhaps that was even more than eight? An advance regiment might arrive in Petrograd at dawn on 14 March.

How dare they? What did they think they were doing?

All the Emperor had to do now was recognize Rodzyanko's cabinet and reconcile everyone—and work amicably for victory over the most evil Germany. And the Emperor? . . .

Rodzyanko had an idea! He realized how he should act against these regiments.

He could not fail to act for he had to stand fast against both Milyukov's intrigue and Lvov's arrival.

It was the same thought, but each time it came as if new: the surest support for the President, support accessible to no one else, was the support of the commanders-in-chief. The thought's special significance was reinforced by responses like those yesterday from Brusilov and Ruzsky. Today he had already sent all the commanders telegrams about the creation of the Provisional Committee, which would bring about normal conditions in the capital so that the Army and Navy could continue their defense of the homeland.

But the subject about which Rodzyanko had thought to be in contact now was inappropriate for a telegram and necessarily more confidential in nature. He had to be in contact with Alekseev and no one else. And right now, when the Emperor was not at GHQ.

Alekseev might be the best intermediary between Rodzyanko and the Emperor. A great deal depended on Alekseev himself since it was he who was sending the troops.

That was what needed to be done. Set up a direct telegraph conversation with Alekseev for late this evening, without telling anyone, not even his own Committee. To do this, go to the General Staff after the many superfluous eyes dwindled.

Of course, Alekseev was intellectually limited and did not have any breadth of even military, let alone governmental, vision. But he should understand if the most essential things were explained to him. That here, in the capital, the hydra of revolution could rise up and sweep everything away. Only the Duma Committee, and only Rodzyanko himself, were a true bulwark against it—and they had to be supported in every way. That the Duma Committee was that long-desired public government, and it had already been formed. That Rodzyanko right now was the sole real power in Petrograd, he alone was master of the situation, and under his leadership full order was being instituted.

Therefore the sending of any troops against Petrograd not only meant the start of malicious, unnecessary, and damaging internecine strife but would also undermine the President's salutary efforts to restrain the revolutionary movement and heal Petrograd. Such an arrival of troops would be ruinous for the order that was already being instituted.

On the contrary, the President's monarchical loyalty had to be appreciated and his present full power in the capital supported.

The ungrateful Soviet of Workers' Deputies was doing what it wanted—but when it came to danger, facing Ivanov's troops, the Soviet was leaving it up to the Duma Committee to act. His own ungrateful Duma Committee obeyed poorly. Ungrateful Petrograd was exulting, rushing about, shooting, and engaging in dissolute behavior. Only Rodzyanko himself could shield them all, the foolish, from Ivanov's punitive troops. And he had to do so selflessly and nobly.

He was sacrificing himself for everyone.

Right then the President's committee men came to him: What about Moscow? We have to topple Moscow, too! Progressive Moscow, the first capital, can't be left in the camp of reaction, can it?

Without Moscow, we are not Russia.

Correct. Also correct. He must apply his weighty hand here, too.

What, again? A telegram! First, to Mayor Chelnokov, for support. Second, to District Commander Mrozovsky, by way of deterrence:

"The old government in Petrograd is no more. Governmental power has been taken by the Duma's Committee under my presidency. I suggest that Your Excellency fall in line immediately. You will answer with your head for allowing bloodshed. Rodzyanko."

Right then, merry voices ran up:

"Protopopov has been seized!"

"Are you certain?" The Duma deputies rejoiced, and Rodzyanko more than anyone, at the traitor's fall. And he added to his telegrams:

"The Minister of the Interior has been arrested."

[2 2 0]

*   *   *

After receiving the telegram from Bublikov, the self-proclaimed railroads commissar, Valuyev, the head of the northwestern railroads, realized that it made sense for him to leave Petrograd and run his network from outside of the city, especially when the royal trains were moving toward the capital and might not find a line for themselves. He went to his Warsaw Station, which had been inundated by an agitated crowd and was barely under control, as had been reported to him. Valuyev gave instructions to prepare a locomotive and train car for him.

But his railroad general's uniform, his sleek, gentlemanly appearance, and his soft beard set him very much apart, and there was no chance of him leaving unnoticed. All it took was a few random throats, and afterward the crowd would take to the idea not to let this person go, though no one knew why. Twice he was taken off the train and dragged off to be torn to pieces. He'd already been dealt several mob-law blows. The priest from the railroad hospital came out with a cross and persuaded the workers to take Valuyev as a prisoner to the State Duma. They put him in a motorcar, surrounded him with security, and set off. But on the Izmailovsky Bridge, the convoy thought someone was firing on the motorcar—perhaps with the purpose of freeing the prisoner? They stopped right there, past the bridge, took Valuyev out—and up against the wall. A firing squad was formed of willing soldiers. Valuyev removed his cap, crossed himself, and said he was dying for his Tsar. One ragged volley and it was all over. They rummaged through the dead man's pockets and took what was there.

✳   ✳   ✳

A party from the 4th Guards Riflery battalion of the Imperial Family reserves, quartered at Tsarskoye Selo, came under its own steam to the Tauride Palace in a sign that the battalion had joined the people.

The Tsar's Guard! Exultation.

The Military Medical Academy joined as well, in full.

✳   ✳   ✳

On Haymarket Square, armored vehicles were smashing up grocers' stores. They tied a policeman to two vehicles and tore him asunder.

✳   ✳   ✳

There was talk in the crowd that someone had fired from the bell tower of St. Sergius Cathedral. An armed patrol went to check. They ascended the bell tower—and found no trace. Suspecting two church watchmen of being policemen who had changed their clothing, they searched them—nothing.

Also, late that night, they came a second time and vigilantly examined the church. And again found nothing.

✳   ✳   ✳

The streetcar lines had been cut. A streetlamp had been toppled. Papers, cigarette butts, and bottles lay scattered. Someone's lost red bow. Passersby.

An open motorcar dashed down the street. In it, an agitator: soot-black beard, fanatical eyes, breaking falsetto. A fist thrown up, his back arched. Shouting something about the hydra not yet finished off, the snake.

Shouting—and waving the driver on, racing onward.

* * *

Alcohol was offered, not denatured.

"From the anatomical museum maybe? Infused on someone's innards? . . ."

* * *

Toward evening, more and more private apartments were raided. A knock and what seemed like the entire street burst in. With rifles and cartridge belts across the shoulder: "There was shooting from here! Are you hiding officers?" A rush to search. (God forbid anyone had an officer's uniform.) The young mistress standing in nervous trembling. Nothing found: "We'll be back!" A Longines clock vanishes from its nail.

While those soldiers who were polite and didn't steal, as they left, they would ask the owners for a tip for their revolutionary labor.

One lady in Lidvall's building underwent ten searches that night, each time a new party of soldiers who demanded wine and food. Once they'd taken it, they'd leave—but soon the next ones would knock. The soldiers were sent by her former servant, who took the trouble to stand guard all night outside. A few days before she'd been sacked and had promised to "remember" the lady.

* * *

Vehicles kept droning, honking, speeding across the bridges. There were shouts of "Hurrah! Hurrah!"

Vehicles came from both sides of the Neva, crossing their shafts of light, revealing sinister crowds moving hurriedly.

* * *

In the evening, in the City Duma in the large Aleksandrovsky Hall, registration was held for university students wishing to join the city's militia. Show up with matriculation documents for confirmation—but it's all right if you don't have them. In the mayor's office, ladies old and young were cutting pieces of white canvas into strips, sewing them on as armbands, and using brushes and red paint to draw the letters "C. M."—City Militia. And affixing the Municipal Board's stamp.

*   *   *

In the evening, snow fell in big soft clumps, turning everything white.

The streets were poorly lit. Many streetlamps had been smashed or had their wires damaged. All the buildings' windows had been carefully curtained. Here and there—rifle fire. Machine guns chattering.

By night, the open space in front of the Tauride was completely deserted again. There were a few dead vehicles. The protective cannons were abandoned, too, covered in snow with no one nearby them.

*   *   *

A rumor started that front-line units were disembarking at the Warsaw Station! Everything and everyone started fleeing at once. Armed men abandoned their rifles and adjacent blocks emptied out.

While nearby, at the Baltic Station, people really were starting to disembark: it was the ensign school from Oranienbaum and a few more of the machine-gunners. A rumor went flying, and at the Tauride Palace people spread it: a bloody battle near the Baltic Station.

*   *   *

Once it had been verified that units supporting the revolution were arriving, the Duma Committee sent deputies to greet the troops with speeches. A motorcar was provided for the trip by Grand Duke Kirill Vladimirovich.

Then the deputies went to Kirill's palace. He met them at the entrance and addressed them, the accompanying soldiers and a handful of gawkers:

"We are all Russians, we are all as one. We all desire the creation of a genuine Russian government."

*   *   *

In Moscow, in the early evening, a mutinous crowd burst into the Spassky barracks, which asked for a hundred mounted men from the artillery barracks on Khodynka as reinforcements, in order to clear out the crowd.

Late in the evening, though, urban agitators infiltrated the artillery barracks, too—and a mutiny began there as well. Unknown men would run into the barracks and shout for everyone to get out. Soldiers gone to bed heard the howling—and never took off their boots. The crowd looted the artillery brigade's stores—and now, armed, firing into the air, drove the sleeping men from the barracks more harshly. The old soldiers, the graybeards, tried to keep the young ones from running out; the officers couldn't have managed this. Soldiers jammed under cots, but the liberators drove them out. The ominous gunfire picked up, though, and the gunners started coming out of one, another, and a third barrack. Zyablov, the duty ensign, hid his revolver and went to persuade the crowd with just a sword. His men: "We don't know why we were driven out," "We'd be happy to be sleeping, but they're driving us out." Evidently, the ringleaders themselves didn't know what to do next. Gradually, the cracking frost quieted everyone down, and by two in the morning they had dispersed.

The brigade commander ordered the officer group to pull the locks off their weapons.

[2 2 1]

Professor Lomonosov joked to his wife that these Petrograd disturbances had begun at a most inopportune time. First, they prevented him from getting his teeth fixed (at the appointed hour it had become impossible to get to his dentist on Pushkinskaya); and second, although it was long since time to end that prolonged general calamity known as the Tsarist regime, perhaps wartime wasn't the best moment.

His teeth had been neglected because he'd only just returned to Petrograd from the Romanian front, where for several months he'd been trying to restore the railroads and get them running. Since autumn, the main troop transports and deliveries of equipment had flowed into Romania, but it was in just that sector that the roads were most decrepit, as no doctrine ever had us fighting there. The railroads were in a state of near collapse (and it was worse for the Romanians), but the worst was the locomotives—so Lomonosov, as one of the leading locomotive engineers, and a railroad general, moreover, was sent.

As a young man, soon after graduating from the institute, almost simultaneously, he began his experiments with locomotives, which had brought him two dozen books and fame. But wherever he served, he did not refuse his assistance to the revolutionarily tarnished, which was natural for any honest educated person in Russia. Sometimes he even had to choose his place of service not only out of consideration for the railroads and personal successes but also so as to be further away from the Okhrana's eye. He had spent time as the traction official for the very distant and neglected Tashkent Railroad, which he quickly turned to profit and prosperity. Soon after, though, his career rocketed him up and took him to Petersburg and the very highest posts, and he took up residence in Tsarskoye Selo.

Generally speaking, the events now in Petrograd could have been expected. The Duma storms of the past few months had been paving the way for major events. But today Lomonosov had lectures. Although his students were hardly going to assemble, and even if they did, was there any point in going on such a day? An actual state councilor could land in a tricky situation. Lomonosov telephoned to postpone his lectures until tomorrow, and today he himself didn't go to town at all, not even to his office, but remained in the tranquility of Tsarskoye Selo.

Most likely, all those street clashes were reckless and hopeless, but something joyful fluttered in his chest. Some of the soldiers had nonetheless stood with the people!

He and his wife devised a small outing before dinner. They took a cab and drove around the Aleksandr Palace, to verify their suspicion that the royal family was fleeing. There had been a hint of this, and a very plausible one, because the disturbances had moved on to Tsarskoye—and it had become dangerous for the palace.

And so, apparently, it was. There were very few sentries posted, and the plainclothes detectives who usually darted around the palace were nowhere to be seen. You got the impression that there was nobody inside the palace at all, like in the summer when the royal family was in Peterhof. It would have been astonishing if they hadn't gotten out already.

Returning home, they came across some Volynians—some of the battalion and nearly all the officers. It turned out that some of the battalion in town had gone over to the rebels, and these men, loyal, had come here from Petrograd on foot.

Oh, what slaves!

They had barely finished their meal when his wife was summoned to the infirmary. According to rumors, that night the palace police administration, directly opposite the infirmary, was to be bombed—and all doctors had to be in place because of likely casualties.

It was a strange time, as if a lot were going on, every hour something somewhere, but all of it scattered in different places and hard to find out about. Had they not come across the Volynians, they might have thought the entire battalion had gone over to the people's side.

But no matter how many of them had, even if it was the entire Petrograd garrison, that decided nothing. All it would take was two divisions with artillery from the front—and the entire uprising would be mincemeat. The uprising's growth would only lead to its death, yielding nothing but victims.

Meanwhile, the impotence of our educated class was shameful and offensive. Everyone despised the regime, but they couldn't push it out. It was very hard to sit at home in inaction. Lomonosov decided to telephone several resourceful Petrograd families, where, of course, they were in close touch with affairs.

But the telephone to Petrograd was out by now.

So he sat at home, in the sticks, all evening. It was late, nearly nine o'clock, when his wife returned. She told him many interesting things. These Volynians had not been accepted at the riflery regiment's barracks where they had been headed. A few officers showed up at the infirmary—to bandage themselves up so they could hide there. His wife asked them categorically to leave.

Then the wife of Gerardi, the palace police chief, showed up with her children and asked for shelter, fearing a bomb at their administration—and hurled abuse at Empress Aleksandra Fyodorovna, saying that because of her so many good people would have to die.

How far things had gone if even this woman was cursing! The situation really was grave. Nerves were taut, and you expected something any minute.

They sat down to tea and there was a ring at the front door. The kitchen maid, shuffling her bare feet over the wooden floor, brought them an official telegram from the ministry.

"War Office. To engineer Lomonosov. Request you come urgently to Petrograd Ministry of Roads and Railways, where you will tell them at the entrance to inform me. By order of the State Duma Committee, Duma Deputy Bublikov."

Shivers ran over Lomonosov's head, which was smoothly cropped from nape to forehead. What new thing was this? He knew Bublikov well. But had the State Duma really dared—and why?—to seize the Ministry of Roads and Railways? The Duma had decided to head up the revolution?

This was either a great page in Russian history or else a farce.

Lomonosov signed for the telegram with a trembling hand and handed the telegram to his wife.

What should he do? It was a dodgy scheme—until the first troops. They would arrive from the front in a couple of days and put an end to it.

Should he go? Straight to his execution. Or to a cell in the Peter and Paul Fortress. It was already late in the evening. It was cozy and calm at home, and his children were here. Snowy Tsarskoye Selo was calm. Not a shot fired. Going was madness.

But anyone who has been a revolutionary in one ill-fated revolution cannot forget, and the defeat burns. And revolutionary loyalty calls. There is the concept of social conscience as well. When everyone must stand united. But afterward you'll be reproached for running scared. For ten years you've been in the reserve; no one has touched or summoned you.

And now they had!

Forty years old, at the height of his powers, who should go if not he? Everything began shaking violently in his chest—danger, joy, and faith.

He could just go to look. That wasn't dangerous.

He stood up:

"Pack my bag for prison conditions. I'm going!"

And he took his revolver from his desk.

[222]

Guchkov had kept his word. That evening officers from the General Staff began showing up at the Military Commission: Colonels Tumanov, Yakubovich, and Tugan-Baranovsky. Obodovsky didn't know any of them, but then someone he did know came, Colonel Pyotr Polovtsov, chief of staff of the Caucasus Native Division—straight from the front, wearing a tall, shaggy fur hat and a brand-new Circassian coat, carrying a dagger and revolver, tall and trim, with an emphatic bearing and a lively, keen-witted face.

Obodovsky had known Polovtsov a long time ago. Back then, at the Mining Institute, sixteen or so years ago, Polovtsov had handed off the student mutual aid fund treasurer position when he quit the institute for the military academy. It can't be said that he endeared himself, quite the opposite. He had the cold ability to switch sides and a calculating mind, but they were considered acquaintances, they had had occasion to see each other before the war began, and he was an interesting companion—both witty and intelligent. From the front? No, not quite directly. He'd gone by GHQ to see to division affairs. What a paradox. Two days ago he'd had an audience with the Tsar and had ridden through Petrograd, and now . . . And here . . .

The General Staffers brought the Military Commission a true military chord, a tone, a cheerful tone even. They began talking among themselves in special intonations, a special jargon. Right then it was also clarified that they were all *Young Turks*—who else might Guchkov have sent?—that group of officers who had worked for military reforms to the point of replacing nearly half the command staff. Therefore they had their shared nicknames, shared jokes, shared ways.

Obodovsky especially had always been in favor of decisive reforms. With the arrival of the General Staffers, he was much relieved, the intolerable tension diminished that if you missed something everything might fall apart. The last thing he signed independently was security for the Putilov Works, but now he could rely on the Staff officers.

Inside, though, a strange hint of objection to them arose. Why would that be? In coming here, Obodovsky had not violated his duty in any way; his place was on this side. But they had all crossed over too easily somehow. What was this? To look into the Tsar's eyes two days ago and now be here, as if nothing had happened? That steadfast naval officer who had been arrested this afternoon had impressed Pyotr Akimovich more.

Maslovsky had lost all heart at their arrival and was clenched in envy and hostility.

But how easily the General Staffers had entered right into the matter as if by routine: which departments to establish, how to classify documents, and who to have do what. Especially since the Preobrazhensky battalion office had appeared with them immediately with First Lieutenant Maksheev, regimental clerks and their typewriters, and the Preobrazhensky musical chorus— for communications. All this, and they themselves, were moved to the second floor, where they could spread out, although the ceilings were low.

Perhaps most valuable was the fact that the General Staffers were in possession of seemingly invisible antennae set up over the city and could guess at and hear things that others could not have imagined. In a single hour the enigmatic, hostile hulk of the General Staff had apparently become a collaborator with the Military Commission. Somehow it had become instantly self-evident that General Zankevich, although yesterday he had commanded Khabalov's troops, was, of course, no enemy and might well stay on to head up the General Staff. (No wonder that today, after noon, Zankevich had sent a certain negligible packet in the name of the Military Commission Chairman, giving a sign that he recognized the new authority.) The same was true for the General Naval Staff. Telephone negotiations began as if they had never stopped, and the Duma's Military Commission was always these staffs' best friend.

In this way information was received immediately that otherwise no one would know where to obtain. First, that Moscow was joining the movement: there had been no serious instructions or resistance from Mrozovsky, nor were any anticipated; the military patrols were not hostile to crowds with red flags; and the police posts had been removed altogether.

Magnificent! Exquisite! Petrograd was not alone!

Second, that Kronstadt as well was joining the revolution. (One might rather have wondered why it hadn't joined earlier, when Oranienbaum did.) There, military units were marching through the streets with music—and the commandant didn't have the power to suppress them.

More and more, Petrograd was not alone!

Even more important, though, the General Staffers by a single effort of mind, here, in bare rooms, had already begun to figure out how they could upset General Ivanov's ominous force. With the same feeling of army unity they could sense this force as one of their own departments. Their memory retained all their army good turns and mutual acquaintances. Someone immediately realized that on the General Staff was a certain Lieutenant Colonel Tilly, who had served directly under Ivanov in the Southwestern Army Group. So now they could take this lieutenant colonel and send him to meet Ivanov as a liaison, to explain the situation in the city and the fact that there was absolutely no one here to fight—and in this way to neutralize Ivanov. No, even better, simply brilliant, was what caustic Polovtsov came up with: let the General Staff, adding to this clarifying lieutenant colonel, assign a full colonel—*to assist* General Ivanov for the better organization of his staff! (Or even as his chief of staff?)

Truly brilliant! They had a good laugh. After all, Ivanov was still part of the overall system of the Russian army—and here the General Staff was collaborating with him, and he should collaborate with the General Staff!

They began telephoning Zankevich.

And from this anecdote—how Academy students had planned to attack the Tauride today—it was decided very simply that tomorrow as many of these students as they liked would be taken on at the Military Commission, and they would not refuse.

But no matter how brilliantly all this was devised, nonetheless, due to their staff's insularity, they did not understand some things as well as Obodovsky. All their connections and all their strategy and maps would save nothing if the revolutionary spirit in the barracks wasn't corrected in such a way that the mass of ordinary officers could return to their places—and be met by the soldiers' trust.

He tried to persuade the General Staffers to think about this, which was unfamiliar for them. They thought that junior officers were provided for as a matter of course, but that was not the case.

Right then, a beaming Engelhardt arrived from Rodzyanko (it cost Engelhardt some effort to hold himself above these undoubted military men): Obodovsky's draft appeal to officers had been signed by Mikhail Vladimirovich. They were assembling them in the Hall of the Army and Navy and would be registering them and in our name passing out unit assignments.

"Good!" Obodovsky rejoiced. But with his permanently unsatisfied attention:

"Gentlemen! Might we begin this work right now, in the Tauride Palace? After all, we have quite a few officers here, from various regiments, and they're feeling at loose ends. Why don't we assemble them for a meeting now, right here, with us?"

[2 2 3]

In a room filled with jostling and commotion, passes were typed out on half-sheets of paper for the Nekrasov brothers and little Greve. "The bearer of this, so-and-so, rank, surname, has been verified by the State Duma and must be allowed unimpeded passage throughout the city. Duma Deputy Karaulov." A dashing older officer wearing a Terek Cossack uniform affixed his large, energetic, and bold signature, which turned into a blot, and sent each man on his way with a handshake.

Our Moscow men already knew full well that they couldn't even poke their noses out of the Duma with these papers, though. They'd already experienced *how* it can be when there is no glimmer of rescue. Having seen plenty, they could no longer believe that these passes would rescue them the next time a crowd closed in to shoot them and tear them to pieces.

That's how far things had gone in twenty-four hours: officers had been *verified,* like suspected thieves, and now were permitted to move freely about the city!

There could be nowhere safer for them today than in the Tauride Palace, no thought of returning to the battalion.

So they were left quasi-free captives of the expansive, multitudinous, droning palace, heretofore unknown to them, which it would never have occurred to them to even try to enter before. Here they were walking around, walking around, or rather jostling around, yielding to wherever the currents took them. Given the free time they had, they could now see and hear a lot.

In a large circular hall under an unlit cupola out of man's reach and so still finely detailed over its entire surface—below was so wet and tracked by muddy feet that the floor's large parquet squares could barely be discerned. And for some reason people were putting out their cigarettes on the lacquered wood case of the large standing clock—which was now smudged with ashes and here and there had butts stuck to it. As did the walls at shoulder level, actually.

Disorderly heaps had been piled up by the walls, and men were still bringing in and unloading food, and military equipment, and whole stacks of lead cartridge cases. Two officers and their sergeants were breaking open the cases right there and squatting to assemble machine guns from the parts.

Sergei and Vsevolod could well have helped them in this work—but who was all this for? And against?

In another grand hall, also with a glass cupola, a white hall for sessions, all the raised semicircles of benches were crammed with soldiers cramped together in Duma seats, and on aisle steps, smoking and gaping mindlessly. Several wore a new kind of soldier expression such as the brothers had never observed in all their career: stupidly pleased, though not delighted, and totally lacking in any hint of readiness, and their gaze didn't distinguish the officers. It was striking to see so many soldiers without any formation, or detail, or organization—just roaming, free. A bizarre impression.

From a high oaken frame behind the president's seat hung the Emperor's full-length portrait, about twelve feet high, in tatters. Above the frame, the carved garland with the crown hadn't been touched—out of reach. It was awful to look at this and feel you were an accomplice to sacrilege.

Meanwhile, in another hall—yet another magnificent long hall, probably a hundred paces in length, with four rows of white columns and enormous chandeliers—there was some kind of speechifying simmering all the time, someone was pontificating, either standing on something or not, in various places at once. Here, in the Duma, there was no suspicion toward the officer uniform, all the officers here seemed to have joined the revolution and could squeeze into these gatherings without hindrance, even speak themselves.

People were talking themselves hoarse. Here they were cursing the scandals of Tsarism; there they were recalling 1905. Entirely unfamiliar, unprecedented speeches; they'd never heard the like uttered. Nor had they seen such ecstatic female students, raptly listening to a speaker—a totally unknown world. Had all this really existed in Russia before, too?

One speaker, a local young civilian, shouted that here was the Tsar forgetting about the foreign enemy and pulling forces back for a campaign against the people.

"Scoundrels," one-legged Vsevolod growled. "Weren't they the ones who forgot about the foreign enemy when they mutinied?"

But he had to growl quietly. It was dangerous. There reigned among the masses this intolerant unanimity of opinion that doesn't happen even in the army: it was enough to speak out half-openly in opposition for that impudent person to be besieged with cursing.

Safety was one thing, but this was abominable. Where did this impressive unanimity come from so quickly? From the first dead bodies. Probably not everyone here thought that way, but everyone was afraid to object.

Occasionally a convoy of unfortunate arrested policemen—in their uniforms or changed into civilian clothing, sometimes accompanied by wives and children—would push through the crowd, and there was no telling whether they'd been seized together or they'd chosen to come along.

Our Moscow men jostled around here long enough to notice that the prisoners were being taken to the palace galleries, where there were rooms being used as cells—where the three of them would have been sitting had they not come across Kerensky.

Some prominent figures were taken not there but to the first floor and the corridor that skirted the hall of sessions. Right then they were leading a tall, imposing gentlemen dressed unofficially and with an estimable gray beard. He was trying to justify himself to the ensign present:

"I'm not guilty of anything! I was just performing my duty, but believe me, I did not sympathize in the least with these orders. There was absolutely no reason to bring me here."

It was offensive to hear justifications from a high-ranking official such as he could not have contemplated yesterday.

In their heads, their own stupor circled, repeating the circling of the Tauride Palace—because they'd had little sleep, and because of the two shootings, and because they hadn't eaten since yesterday—and it was irritating that today they hadn't eaten the breakfast brought to them in the deacon's room.

Some in certain places of the palace were being fed—by female and male students. Primarily soldiers, this multitude of isolated men from disintegrated units were living a new and unified life. People were carrying food in canisters somewhere. But the officers couldn't go ask to eat. It was impossible to feed this entire human sea. There would be shouts: "They brought bread!" And everyone would rush to the door, smothering one another.

Eventually some quick Boy Scouts came to our officers' rescue and offered them each a large sausage sandwich and a mug of tea from their trays.

Still, their safety was more important. All they could do was circle around here, all day, all evening, and even all night—and before dawn, at the most desolate time, when the revolutionary exultation went to bed—leave for relatives' apartments. It would have been even more sensible to change into soldier or civilian clothes—but change where and into what?

For now, they kept walking, and looking, and jostling, and getting their bearings in the vast Duma building. They'd already discovered and been in the left wing, where relative order had been maintained, there was room in the corridors, and there were Duma attendants in livery and rooms guarded from outsiders. Here they could sit, rest, and lie down on the floor if they liked; the Moscow men were so depleted, they were ready to—but it was here that this was improper. They could imagine the Duma's former life in part from this corridor, in part by looking up at the high ceilings, cornices, figured capitals, ornaments, sculpted two-headed eagles, candelabras, chandeliers, and everything that had not yet been soiled by the shuffling of snowy boots—the Duma's former life had more or less been turned upside down in this now quiet scene. Drawn into and rising in this beauty as well was tobacco smoke, thick human steam, and the smell of boots, cloth, and sweat.

At about four o'clock in the afternoon, machine-gun fire boomed close by—and panic ensued in the palace. Indeed, this crowd could easily be mown down like sheep. Our Moscow men rejoiced: Is that our men? We need to get through to them through the back windows on the garden. But they couldn't get through, either. Then everything died down and it was explained as a mistake.

It was evening and they were sleepy. Their heads were drooping, but they couldn't imagine where an officer could lie down to sleep in this churning. The palace was not promising to empty out for the night. Hundreds of electric lamps were still burning, and thousands of people were jostling and jostling.

It turned out that people had already started to note their distinctive threesome as a permanent feature of the present teeming. Who was here and why was something no one could know. All of a sudden a lieutenant stopped them:

"What's the matter, Moscow sirs? Why aren't you going to the session?"

"What session?"

It turned out that a session assembled by the Duma's Military Commission in Room 41 on the second floor was starting for representatives of Petrograd garrison units to familiarize them with the situation in the units.

The three of them had been assumed to have arrived as representatives.

They exchanged glances. Why not go? They fully saw themselves as representatives of their regiment, and far from the worst.

They were led down a passage they hadn't noticed before. There was a narrow staircase going up and ordinary low ceilings and modest rooms.

In Room 41, two dozen officers had already assembled, having hung up their greatcoats. They were sitting on benches and chairs as if nothing were happening, as if officers weren't being torn apart anywhere in the city. Only they hadn't come from all the battalions.

Our three also removed their coats. And signed in.

Seated facing those gathered were three colonels from the General Staff, fresh and unscarred, as confident men ought to be. And also one other, elderly, obviously not a combatant, a Colonel Engelhardt acted as chairman. He suggested that the representatives report on what was happening in their battalions.

The Preobrazhensky and Jägers assured them that everything was going smoothly. Officers had been murdered in the Izmailovsky. Arrests in the Semyonovsky. Staff Captain Sergei Nekrasov recounted without difficulty what had happened in the Moscow: a rout of the watches, a rout of the officers assembly, an inundation of the barracks by workers. (It would have been immodest to recount their own reckoning with the firing squad.)

The colonels nodded, saying they knew this. The Moscow battalion more than others had been taken over by workers, and it was total anarchy there.

Nonetheless, Engelhardt said heatedly, we cannot imagine a situation in which officers could not return to their soldiers. That would be the end of the army, the end of everything! On the contrary, revolutionary enthusiasm would provide a new basis for relations between officer and soldier such as there could not have been before, relations based on total trust and civil unity. On the contrary, they should anticipate unprecedented militant enthusiasm from the soldiers, which will bring us a speedy and easy victory over the Germans. Especially in these conditions of external struggle with Russia's most evil enemy, the Provisional Committee of the State Duma intended to place the officer's rank high. The Military Commission was accepting all officers with arms wide open—and immediately equipping them with the authority for their former or new posts.

Sergei glanced at his brother.

They remembered all too well easing up yesterday, when they surrendered their weapons to the soldiers—and today's two morning encounters with the firing squad. What did they know about the officers who had remained in the battalion, especially the senior ones—Captains Yakovlev, Nelidov, Yakubovich, and Fergen? Were they still alive?

Oh, something worse had happened, something worse and incompatible with Engelhardt's smiles and the Provisional Committee's brisk appeals.

Staff Captain Nekrasov rose and said in the silence:

"Colonel sir! Gentlemen! You have heard that officers in the battalions are being killed. I told you that yesterday afternoon we fired at these soldiers and could not have helped but fire, out of duty. What kind of deputation to them can we be tomorrow? As a whole, all of us—can we really return to what we had before the mutiny?"

[2 2 4]

Today Himmer managed not to miss a good dinner; his comrades had, after all, thought of these very simple needs and took care of each other as well. The revolution was an enchanting spectacle, it was remarkable, but a meal with an appetizer and three courses was the material foundation for further revolutionary initiative. The main thing was that it was convenient— very close to the Tauride Palace, at the head of Fuhrstadtskaya, so an entire throng had set out. A well-known doctor lived there, Manukhin, who had once treated Gorky for tuberculosis on Capri, and Gorky himself, having made a small excursion through the city, was also at this dinner.

True, he also spoiled it. Everything the great writer had seen had put him out of sorts. He grumbled at the universal chaos and excesses, the manifestations of backwardness, even the young ladies riding around the city with soldiers in vehicles—and in all this he saw signs of our execrable Asiatic-Russian savagery. They would drive nails into Jews' skulls, and this would lead to the failure of the remarkably successful revolution, whereas Europeans would have had everything organized long ago. Himmer found these politically myopic conclusions simply ridiculous, and he dared argue (independent of all factions, he tried to remain independent of Gorky as well), saying that, on the contrary, matters had been going brilliantly: not even two full days had passed, and there was no longer a Tsarist government, or an Okhrana, or a Peter and Paul Fortress, and that was simply a miracle. All the excesses, brutalities, and foolishness—no revolution had ever managed to avoid this. To do so was theoretically inconceivable. (In essence, Gorky was a small-minded man and judged from a small-minded standpoint, as he had demonstrated here.) But others echoed Gorky, saying that Russia had always been short on heroes—and Himmer had to keep quiet.

All in all, the dinner took up a lot of time. Agreeing who would spend the night with Dr. Manukhin and who with other acquaintances nearby, they separated—Himmer to the Tauride Palace to spend another couple of hours. He had been restored to fine shape and didn't want to miss another share of observation or share of participation in events.

It was after nine o'clock. The palace had emptied out significantly compared with the daytime; in fact, people were sitting on the floor of the Ekaterininsky, and hundreds of soldiers were already lying down and getting ready to sleep. The palace lighting might have been normal for ordinary times, but given the abundance of people it now seemed insufficient.

The Soviet of Deputies had finally broken up, having been meeting since noon, but still sitting in its spacious room were small groups of however many gawking soldiers and however many civilians who couldn't stop talking about freedom and calm down.

In Room no. 13 there were also still a few EC members who hadn't eaten—Gvozdev, Krasikov, and Kapelinsky—and Himmer energetically entered into a discussion with them on the issues that had come up.

It turned out that over these past few hours, newspaper and printing press owners had been drawn here with their complaints of ruin, sensing that this was the new government. Why weren't they allowing them to publish?

They demagogically appealed to the principles of a free press, that there couldn't be less freedom after the revolution than before.

What could they say? A purely theoretical discussion could be taken quite far. Himmer actively intervened and went off to explain to the discontented men that there had already been a resolution from the Executive Committee. That what was needed here was circumspection; they could not misstep in the counterrevolutionary swamp.

But the printing press issue was acute, and all the parties had already latched on to presses they would have liked to confiscate for themselves, and all that was required was an EC decision that hadn't happened yet today.

The last EC members dispersed, and Himmer promised now to stay on duty until midnight.

They couldn't get along without someone on duty because people were constantly bursting in. For instance, certain self-constituted groups aimed to arrest one of the noxious servants of the old regime, but some had decided to deal with this themselves (and were meeting with no resistance), whereas others still came to the Soviet for oral or written permission.

This was a new feeling for Himmer, and he was astonished. An illegal just the day before yesterday, essentially, without permission to live in his own apartment—and here he was sitting in a comfortable armchair at a massive table deciding the question of freedom or prison for some vice admiral—or Senator Krashennikov, president of the Petersburg High Court, who, one remembered, had sentenced Duma deputies to three months for the Vyborg appeal. That was what revolution was! Retribution! Retribution first and foremost!

The sense of omnipotence filled him with revolutionary pride. How everything had turned around! And what was the authority of the Soviet of Workers' Deputies now if the signature of one unknown member of its EC was now the highest power in Petrograd!

Not to be deluded, though, Himmer did not have that fullness of power. What this demonstrated was the acceleration of the revolutionary element, and although Himmer could easily *allow* the arrest of some victim named for some reason, it was almost pointless for him to *refuse*. Regardless, they would go through with it or get permission from someone else.

What grounds did he have for refusing an arrest anyway? This kind of arrest of a conscientious servant of the Tsarist regime was *a priori* just—and especially so the more intelligent and talented this person was—as a possible engine of Tsarist reaction or architect of a monarchist plot.

Several dozen of these high-level dignitaries were already sitting in the Duma's ministerial pavilion under strict guard, and there was still room for more of the darlings to come. For those further down the ladder, rooms had been set aside along the gallery of the Duma's hall of sessions, where there were already several hundred locked up, probably.

Matters were proceeding excellently!

Himmer would sign, the groups would run off, and others would come.

All of a sudden, with great drama and shouts, a group of eight or ten soldiers burst in, some with bayonets, others without. Himmer thought they, too, were here about the arrest of some general. No. They were simply seething at Rodzyanko's order, which they had just learned about, to return to barracks, everyone, put their weapons back in the arsenals, accept their officers, and perform their service. Having sussed out where they might find justice and protection, the soldiers had burst into the Soviet in hopes of getting the opposite order.

With his exceptional intellectual power, Himmer in an instant assessed—no, *recognized*—the moment that was bound to have come! Oh, how the bourgeoisie had miscalculated! They couldn't wait to put the army back in the officers' hands—and they had moved too quickly, miscalculated, and they would achieve the opposite effect! A fateful moment awaiting an equally thunderous decision by the Soviet, now personally by him, Himmer!

Short, he jumped up to meet the large soldiers, shook all their hands, some of them even twice, thanked them for coming, thanked them for their proletarian trust, invited them all to sit down—and only when they had all sat down did he drop back into his chair.

Meanwhile, he himself was thinking, like a whirlwind, in the thick of the political tangle. He seemed to have started a conversation with the soldiers and to constantly be saying something encouraging to them; in fact, despite the full clarity of the question, he did not have the right to express his decision out loud right now, but he made some tentative probes so that he could present it to his comrades on the EC.

How could he fail to understand the soldiers' condition! The fear of losing the flickering specter of freedom and a new life. Naturally, they had turned to him with mistrust and enflamed indignation against the officer class. One had to know how to exploit this condition for the furtherance of the revolution! But how? How? . . . Here was where he lacked a practical political grasp.

For now Himmer could promise the soldiers only one thing: to investigate everything carefully and raise this question at the Executive Committee session.

Soon after their departure, Sokolov burst in—he always burst rather than walked in. He'd been detained at dinner but was noisy and cheerful all the more.

Himmer buttonholed Sokolov and started discussing with him the general statement of the army question as it had now arisen before the Soviet. Not that Himmer was hoping to get a decision from this blockhead Sokolov, but he thought he could hone his own by talking with him. Here was what was enflaming the soldiers: they didn't want to go back to obeying their officers! This mood had to be correctly channeled. This was a unique moment! Marx and Engels said that disorganizing the army was the condition for a victorious revolution and also its result. And Zimmerwald's directive was to pull the army out from under bourgeois hegemony. Have you heard about this order of Rodzyanko's? . . .

Since it was in the air—of course Sokolov had heard. What could escape him? Then again, no one had laid eyes on the order itself.

It would be good if there were no such order. Maybe there wasn't. But it had been enough this afternoon to listen to Rodzyanko's and Milyukov's disgraceful speeches before the arriving troops, because they said it all: "Return to your barracks and obey your officers!" This was a cunning attack on all the achievements of soldierly freedom, though. Franchised circles were openly and shamelessly calling for order, subordination, and obedience; they were trying again to drive the revolutionary soldiers into the officers' iron handcuffs. "Restore order!" That was the very thing General Ivanov was on the move to do!

Here was the tactic Himmer proposed. Naturally, don't send out openly antiwar slogans. We've kept them tacitly concealed so far, and that is absolutely correct. Until Tsarism is vanquished for good, until the revolutionary government has settled in and strengthened its position. But at the same time we cannot allow the mass of revolutionary soldiers to fall captive to the officer class again. The escape to freedom they accomplished cannot be repeated—and we cannot allow a simple return to barracks. We, the Soviet, must immediately, tomorrow, take some revolutionary step that will renew all the relationships *inside* the army and create in the army an atmosphere of political freedom and civil equality!

Sokolov liked this very much; he agreed to it all.

Something had to be done. Otherwise, what kind of Zimmerwaldists were we?

[2 2 5]

That morning, Milyukov went to the 1st Infantry Regiment in Okhta—and vowed never to visit the regiments again; that wasn't his job. On the large parade ground he'd had to climb a tall tower and from there, in the frosty air, shout, straining his throat—trying to make the mysterious soldier crowd understand the most elementary things: that the public victory had to be reinforced, and for this, unity had to be maintained with the officers, otherwise their regiment would disintegrate into dust. He called on the officers (they were by now ready and willing) to work hand in hand with the State Duma and help organize the authority that had fallen from the hands of the old government, which had choked on its own crimes.

Not only did he find it physically difficult and unpleasant to give this speech, and not only did he not sense any real effect from it, but it was senseless to the point of outrage for him to be doing this. There were plenty of tin-plated gullets around. Pavel Nikolaevich's element was the university public or even a Western one. What did he have in common with the army? Only the fact that, after high school, his unreasonable son had rushed off to volunteer and had perished in Galicia.

Why should Milyukov now go make these low-level speeches when it was his mind that held so many thoughts, complexities, and plans and he should be using the full power of his intellect and vision to mercilessly penetrate the swiftly changing situation?

What everyone had seen and readily understood was that anarchy threatened to undermine the officer class. That the forces of reaction had not been smashed and General Ivanov's punitive expedition was closing in. Behind these outward events they were losing sight of the building blocks: *just how* should they now organize the government? Apparently no one yet had realized what tense and dangerous ambiguities had arisen even in these few rooms that concealed the last remnant of the Duma.

The first ambiguity was the Duma itself. Although it was thanks to its noisy sessions, on the wings of its authority, that everyone here had soared up over Russia, although just yesterday they had sworn on the Duma and just today troops had come to greet the Duma specifically, and the Committee was the Duma Committee, and Milyukov himself had in the Duma's name greeted the 1st Infantry Regiment, and everyone had been fanning specifically the Duma's aura (excessively, as could now be seen), and even today no one among the Duma deputies had come up with or could express a dubious opinion about the Duma—the leader of the Duma majority and the leader of the Kadet Party distinctly, coldly realized that the State Duma was dying. Or even had died, sometime between yesterday and today. The Duma was no more. It was a fiction that it was time to disavow; a genuine politician ought to note these kinds of facts without sentimental regret.

History is rich with such paradoxes: most of all, the Duma had been working to achieve the fall of the Tsarist government, but the moment it did so, it itself became superfluous. The Duma had played out everything useful it might have offered, and in the present hours the entire essence was shifting toward a new governmental authority that had yet to be organized and taken in hand. In this precarious moment, the Duma could not be authoritative.

In addition, the Duma's authority, which at one time had rightly elevated its best leaders and speakers, had contributed a harmful legacy as well: it had disproportionately elevated the authority of its president in the eyes of the public but also, even more irreparably, in Rodzyanko's own eyes. Now he was incapable—and was not even trying—to understand the true correlation of forces and his own false role. His head had swelled so much, he thought that the Provisional Committee had been created at his sanction, and the new government would be created at his sanction, and that he himself would head it. Everything had to be disclosed and named as quickly as possible, but so far it hadn't been made to happen: last night Rodzyanko had been compelled to seize power for the Committee; without that there was no path. And once Rodzyanko had overcome his cowardice and decided to do so, he immediately, with primitive simplicity, had demanded total obedience from all the deputies—an unprecedented feudalism unknown even in the Tsarist governments. All the Duma deputies and Milyukov were simply dumbfounded. For this reason, they had tagged Rodzyanko with a Russian take on Tasso:

The Bouillon came aboil and flowed into the temple.

They were dumbfounded at his aspirations. Quite something! But at that moment it was still too soon to object. Right after, the news about the punitive forces came crashing in, and Rodzyanko became especially necessary for halting the troops. Thus, the unlanced boil had persisted all day and had to be tolerated.

Meanwhile, at Milyukov's summons, Prince Georgi Lvov had arrived from Moscow today. Lvov had to be received at the Tauride Palace and kept from coming face to face with Rodzyanko, so more diplomacy. Lvov had complained of exhaustion over the telephone and had begged to postpone their meeting until tomorrow. This made an unpleasant impression on Milyukov. How could someone fail to sense the pace of events to that extent!

Lvov came. They sat down to talk in one of the rooms. Milyukov looked searchingly—never before had he looked so closely and carefully—at this very neatly combed, every hair in place, very clean, very polite, very gentle prince—perhaps so distinct from all of them here in the Tauride Palace because he hadn't spent a sleepless night there but had slept well on the train and after the train had also put himself in order in a private apartment. Or perhaps because he was from Moscow? Perhaps because he was of the Zemgor and had never engaged in political affairs, if you thought about it, except for the last few months of general excitement? Yes, it was paradoxical! Milyukov looked steadily at the prince and was amazed. It was as if he were made of different stuff, *not one of us*, not from the common stream of society, was not excited or worried about what was exciting and worrying them all. It was as if he didn't sense the searing events around him or, at the least, was hesitant to intervene.

Lvov spoke cautiously, in a vague, mellow way, and when he could get away without speaking at all and could listen—he preferred listening.

Pavel Nikolaevich's chest was engulfed by the saddest sadness there could ever be: the sadness of his own mistake. As if he were engaged to the wrong woman and the wedding was imminent—and there was no breaking it off or fixing it. Milyukov had proposed this candidacy over the pressing, insistent Rodzyanko, and he had promoted him, trusting the prince's Zemgor fame, not having the time to verify him himself. And now everyone believed and accepted it, and Lvov had come, and it was too late to do it over.

Yes, indeed, he, Lvov, was inevitable. The leftists would agree only to a neutral public figure like this. And they could not have a government without leftists; the lost front with them had to be restored.

Pavel Nikolaevich had actually guessed earlier at a certain weakness in Prince Lvov, but he'd thought that this would make it easier to remove him later. He hadn't counted on power having to be transferred during days as stormy as right now. No one could have predicted this instantaneous and decisive catastrophe.

He was engulfed by the fact that all could be lost with this candidate and that he might not even last temporarily.

Several deputies had already taken a seat and were talking. It looked like a vapid salon discussion, not the arrival of a leader. To his neighbor's quiet question:

"Well, how is it?"

Pavel Nikolaevich replied quietly:

"A milksop!"

And this was the very basic *face of trust* to which all Russia was now supposed to calm down!

Prince Lvov sat around as if he were a guest. It hadn't even occurred to him to spend the night at the Tauride Palace, discuss the makeup of his government, be at the ready for breaking circumstances. He sat a while, bade them farewell, and left for his apartment to take to his bed.

Milyukov didn't even try to change his mind. He thought it would be simpler if he himself did the horse trading about the government. Today at the Kadet central committee and at breakfast with Vinaver he had avoided a discussion of the new complement of ministers; there'd been no need.

Generally speaking, Milyukov found no one truly necessary or close. Even with his closest comrades in the party he had avoided personal relations. He found it exhausting to extend his sympathy to the private aspects of life and no less exhausting to meet with such sympathy toward himself. It was more natural and pleasant to spend that limited quantity of tenderness granted us from birth on ladies or for once in one's life to resolve even to change wives.

But right now Milyukov had landed in an isolation greater than even he was used to or desired. Shingarev was his shadow—a worker, but not a leader. He could barely restrain himself with the dimwit Rodzyanko. He had always felt a distance from and distaste for Maklakov. There was a rivalry with Vinaver, although right now he wasn't even in play. Clashes with Nekrasov. And a dull, longstanding hostility toward Guchkov. Of those circulating around here now, Milyukov almost would have preferred Kerensky. But!

But! *Punctum saliens!* Milyukov had long suspected and remarked, and he had been warned, but in these critical hours he had even managed to convince himself that between men as different as the Kadets Nekrasov and Konovalov and the quasi-SR Kerensky, who were seemingly inconceivable in combination, there existed and now had manifested itself some hidden connection, some unexpected agreement on the most paradoxical issues. It was as if they had taken special pains to reach an agreement on every question, in secret from Milyukov.

Undoubtedly, this secret connection could be nothing other than their known but also secret and successfully concealed Masonry. Masonry was an insult to Milyukov. They had suggested that he join, more than once even, and he had always declined. Not only was it alien to his rational nature—any kind of mysticism grated—but it seemed like a childish game, even. And a dishonest game at that, for Masonry disaffirmed all personal talents and merits, replacing them with the conspiracy of membership. This would be suppression of the individual.

Like spreading dough, though, Masonry could not be struck, pointed out, or criticized firmly. Fleeting emptiness and fleeting perplexity.

So too was it now with the selection of candidates for minister. What else could explain this unnatural unanimity: bring Tereshchenko into the government, an idle millionaire who didn't know how to do anything, was suited to nothing, and was known to no one. Simply scandalous. How could this be presented to the public? The fact that he was supported by Guchkov and Konovalov was understandable; they had become friendly together on the War Industry Committee. But why were they joined by Nekrasov, who had jerked the Kadet faction around so much with his leftist opposition? Why, too, was Kerensky, despite all his own party positions, also in favor of Tereshchenko? It could only be collusion.

Milyukov had tried as hard as he could to split them, playing specifically on Kerensky, but nothing had come of it.

Kerensky, who these past few days had been a fetching universal hero, had shown an exceptional lack of constraint. He was constantly running in and out, concerned to play his part in both wings of the palace, but most of all in the middle, among the masses, first receiving prisoners, then bringing documents someone had muddle-headedly brought to the Tauride Palace—and painting himself the savior in it all. Then he would collapse next to you on the sofa, prepared to discuss the government's makeup until morning. Then, five minutes later, he would leap up and run off again.

It remained undecided in principle whether socialists would join the government—and they could demand many seats if they did. Formal talks with them had yet to be held, but Kerensky and Chkheidze personally had been invited for now, and neither one wanted to agree without the Soviet of Deputies. But Kerensky's happily intoxicated eyes gave him away. Here, on the sofa, the discussion about the government's makeup of course comprised his happiest moments. It could not have been otherwise. Milyukov had always been sure of Kerensky's political realism. No socialist games could compare with a hefty ministerial portfolio. Which exactly? For a third-rate lawyer it was hard to beat the Ministry of Justice.

But that would decisively push out Maklakov, the Kadet candidate. Not that that would be so bad. Maklakov had always been a rather unconvincing Kadet.

But where to stick Tereshchenko? It was an utter rebus.

Right then people ran in with sensational news. Protopopov had shown up at the Duma!

Himself? Stunning! Ravishing! What retribution! Now nothing could remain as it was! Kerensky broke off midsentence and ran off to wield power. Many curious people rushed after him. It was a most piquant spectacle, of course.

Milyukov didn't go, though. First of all, his position was too dignified for him to go out as an idle spectator. Secondly, a political opponent has significance only as long as he holds his position. And *personally*—personally Pavel Nikolaevich had never hated, nor had he ever loved, anyone.

[226]

Here's what happened. Protopopov, wearing an expensive fur coat, arrived at the Tauride Palace and entered without anyone recognizing him. Perhaps he might have walked on farther that way, even to the Duma Committee, but he became distraught in the palace's new atmosphere and his nerves couldn't take it. He picked someone out and addressed him:

"Tell me, are you a student?"

"Yes."

"Please, take me to the State Duma deputies. I am former Minister of the Interior Protopopov."

For the first time he had called himself *former*. And right then, his expressive eyes darting neurasthenically, he added that he wished for the common good and so had appeared voluntarily.

This came about so informally, he went so unrecognized—indeed, did anyone even know him? the soldiers didn't know him and hadn't heard his name—but the student calmly jostled with him together to the room where the Duma deputies were sitting in discussion.

They were astonished (even more than they were indignant). Protopopov kneaded his fur cap and with neurasthenic apology smiled and attempted to utter pleasantries.

Right then, there was no iron individual among the Duma deputies who might give orders, but naturally, no one invited him to sit down. So he stood and hesitated by the doorway.

However, someone did instantly rush off with the news—and now in the flung-open door appeared tightly strung, angry, implacable Kerensky. He was as erect as his bones would allow, stern, pale, and even wonderful.

Protopopov turned around and with full remorse, truckling, and hope, said something almost impossible, something no one had yet put this way:

"Your Excellency! I put myself at your disposal."

Never in all his born days had he heard such a thing! His ears weren't prepared for it! But it was this, in part, that softened his heart. Nevertheless he then announced, so dramatically that everyone outside the door and in the crowded corridor could hear:

"Former! minister! of the interior! In the name! of the Executive! Committee!"—it was unclear whether the Duma's or the Soviet's—"I declare! you! under arrest!"

His shout brought people crowding outside the door and even coming in. No one had noticed this mangy gentleman, and he'd turned out to be their main enemy, had he?

Under arrest? Protopopov, happily relieved, as if he had expected, and desired, only this!—had the tactlessness, however, to step toward Kerensky and try to say something to him in confidence.

But the immaculately aloof Kerensky deflected the unworthy man with an imperious gesture of his narrow hand—and with it also gestured to the convoy, which had simply shown up, indicating that he be taken away.

Moving forward, tragically waving the same hand, he exclaimed to the crowd:

"Do not lay a hand on this man!"

Had he not shouted this, no one would have dreamed of touching this gentleman, but now they stretched their arms out to get him; times were such—show us who to tear to pieces. A hand or rifle butt could have descended upon the top of his head at any moment.

Protopopov cast desperate glances, imploring for rescue from somewhere.

Maybe people felt sorry for him.

They led this man hunched over in his fur coat like a leper, like a man being led to execution or something even worse, rifles atilt—and the crowd parted, handing him over to certain punishment.

So they went, across the Ekaterininsky on the diagonal, and then down the corridor to the ministerial pavilion and past a couple of Preobrazhensky sentries.

Only behind the last door did Kerensky, no longer so shrill, in a diminished voice, but still incorruptibly sternly, tell Ensign Znamensky:

"Watch officer! The former Minister of the Interior wishes to make a confidential report to me. Be so kind as to lead him into a separate room."

And he himself graciously proceeded there as well.

Having experienced salvation from the crowd, with fervently grateful eyes for the smallest hint of protection, Protopopov repeated what he had come with:

"Here, Your Excellency. . . . Here. . . ."

And he thrust a key at Kerensky.

His nerves were so shattered, he could not get his words out clearly, and Kerensky did not immediately realize that this was the key to the desk drawer in the ministerial residence on the Fontanka. In that drawer would be found another key, to a fireproof safe. And wrapped in newspaper in that safe were 50,000 rubles belonging to Count Tatishchev.

"Why is his money there?"

Protopopov's shoulders were actually squirming, so ashamed was he. His gift of speech returned, he spoke quickly and haltingly.

In fact, this money no longer belonged to the count but to the Ministry of the Interior. It had been brought to reward a certain indulgence. Naturally, though, Protopopov had not taken a kopeck for himself. So it had been decided that this money would go to help the family of the murdered Rasputin.

But now Protopopov was donating it to the new government.

[2 2 7]

Quick-witted Preobrazhensky Sergeant Fyodor Kruglov, the self-appointed head of sentries for the Tauride Palace, quickly figured out that not one of its posts, often crushed by the crowd, had the significance of this one, at the entrance to the temporary prison for former ministers.

Kruglov had never served as a prison guard and was unlikely to have ever done time himself, but by his inclination he quickly took in what he may have heard in snatches, and this morning, when highly placed prisoners began arriving, he forthwith applied prison rules: all prisoners had to be searched and everything removed from their pockets; all prisoners had to sit on chairs and armchairs around the clock and not lie on a sofa (which they could not have enough of for everyone). And none of them could get up and stretch their legs until the general command for this was given, once or twice a day. They were not to go near the windows, otherwise the sentry would fire. To signal a need for the lavatory, the prisoner had to raise his hand and hold it like that silently.

Kerensky came here several times as the main person in charge of the detention facility. He also announced the general rule of complete silence: prisoners were not to talk among themselves or even exchange the most trivial words but only answer questions from the sentry and officials.

Armed soldiers were posted by the walls of the different rooms to ensure all this was followed. (Volunteers could always be found for these posts, perfect for gawkers.) Sergeant Kruglov himself, tearing himself away from other posts, came here more and more often and paced around, around the seated men, wondering at the destiny that had raised him above all these grand dignitaries.

Kerensky was so pleased with him that he imperiously touched his epaulet:

"Sew on a fourth stripe. I'm awarding it to you!"

And although nothing of the kind had ever happened in the entire Russian army—a fourth shoulder stripe for a noncommissioned officer—Kruglov realized this seriously elevated him—and by nightfall it had been cut out and sewn on, astonishing the generals sitting there.

Kruglov had deep-set eyes and a barking voice, and he broke off any attempts to speak or ask anything. When one of the serving staff addressed the seated men as "sirs," he shouted: "Prisoners, not sirs!"

The harder they pressed their advantage, the stronger the new government would be.

And here, in this single-story pavilion alongside the palace, intended for the ministers' use during breaks in Duma sessions, they were now assembled—some ministers from recent governments, some dignitaries or prominent figures (sometimes here due to the whim of circumstances or the vengefulness of their enemies). For the most part they arrived here carefully dressed, starched and pressed—not that they ever dressed otherwise. Some of them, the most important ones, ended up at the oval table in the hall of ministerial sessions—as if for an important meeting.

They had it all in their heads, they needed no documents, for this kind of discussion. There were three prime ministers, and many long-serving ministers, all of them had written many highly judicious reports to their Emperor and ministerial memoranda, and they had a significant understanding of government problems, much more so than they were accused of in the State Duma. They all kept in memory a string of governmental affairs, of opportunities realized and missed over many years—and so could appreciate better than many Duma deputies all that was happening, consoling or irritating one another. Together they all held in their heads as well an integral image and sense of governmental Russia—but they were fated not to pass this on to anyone; they were forbidden the very exchange of opinions.

Behind the connecting corridor droned a soldier sea of many thousands, and a sea of diverse individuals; here, men of the same class and tone were each seated in a kind of invisible one-man cell—to torment himself with his own miserable lot. In this immobile numbness and silence around the large common table, the governmental considerations in their heads were blocked, crowded out, by their own personal misfortune. They could only wait for whether they would be fed, whether they would be permitted to lie down rather than sit that night, even if in this clothing, even if not changing clothes for the night was torture.

At first, the bright sunny day poured through the windows, then it shifted to overcast; it even snowed. Once there was heavy shooting near the palace, giving rise to a flurry of hope of being freed. But it ended in nothing. And now they faced a long evening under lamplight.

The very last detested government, which had just been overthrown, was actually hardly there: neither Belyaev; nor Protopopov, for whom the entire capital was searching with might and main but who was believed to be at Tsarskoye; nor Rittikh, nor Raev; nor Pokrovsky, nor Krieger-Voinovsky, nor Grigorovich. Public opinion was kindly disposed toward the last three, and the main people looking to make arrests were university students. The only one sitting here was Prince Golitsyn, who was just as bewilderingly out of place here as he had recently been at the head of the government, and also the aging Epicurean Dobrovolsky, who had been taken prisoner the most comfortably. He himself had called from the Italian Embassy to surrender, and Rodzyanko had sent a motorcar for him. Guiltiest of all was Rein, the would-be Minister of Health, but for the Duma's ban on creating that ministry; and they had also brought Shakhovskoy, Bark, and Kulchitsky.

On the other hand, there were the two previous prime ministers: seventy-seven-year-old, cold-blooded Goremykin, with his low, parted side-whiskers, who hadn't failed to bring along a box of cigars, which helped him while away the time here. (Before bringing him in they had hung the chain from his Saint Andrew's Cross over his fur coat by way of ridicule.) And seventy-year-old Stürmer with his limp, rumpled beard and trembling jaw. And then, there were several deputy ministers—occasionally random, occasionally known for their firm convictions. Public opinion, which had a good memory, had snatched here, in addition to Shcheglovitov, Doctor Dubrovin, president of the Union of the Russian People, and a few prominent rightists from the State Council—Shirinsky-Shikhmatov and Stishinsky. (But they never did get Metropolitan Pitirim here; he'd become so weak and ill right at the door that they'd released him.) Khabalov's deception didn't work; they arrested him as well. A few officials from the city governor's office, led by Balk. Weiss, the ill-fated grain plenipotentiary. They also caught Kurlov, who had in no way been expecting arrest and who had been found at home that morning—sitting there, short as he was, with one eye squinting and a cigar in the corner of his mouth. A few generals, the head of the Military Medical Academy, the head of the Army's educational institutions and also the head of the Sea Cadet Corps, Vice Admiral Kartsev, and also Admiral Giers, and the head of the railroad administration. The rest were more minor and unimportant, and instead of being taken into this pavilion, they'd been led upstairs.

Thus, other than a few strong individuals of strong convictions, the makeup of the prisoners gathered was stunning for its incompleteness. Had the arrests been badly carried out? Or had there been no one in imperial Russia to arrest?

The new prisoners sat in their transparent one-room cells in several connecting rooms. Occasionally a view opened from door to door and one could look in and try to guess who had and hadn't been caught. The captive dignitaries examined each other jealously, pleased to find acquaintances ("I'm not alone") and envious at not finding well-known odious individuals such as Nikolai Maklakov and Protopopov. They were offended to see that the main perpetrator of the last few months had had the cunning to slip away! But the sum total of the prisoners' freedom was to turn a silent head and complain to themselves.

The sum total of the freedom remaining to them was whether to pick their feet up under the table or let them down. They were allowed to go to the lavatory one at a time, accompanied, not often and not right away, which can be hard for old men. Only now did they appreciate the degree of their former freedom, even in their resentful retirement: to move about, to stretch their legs, or to give their spine a rest in bed.

Occasionally a few female students would bring them something to eat: sandwiches and tea, which they set on the tables in front of them. This was the full variety to their day-long sitting.

Kerensky would enter pompously and circle the rooms, his figure tautly triumphant:

"Ah, Stishinsky! Actually, you might stand when you're being spoken to by a member of the State Duma Committee."

Kerensky also brought Ensign Znamensky, his friend, whom no one knew, having declared him head of the pavilion guard, over Kruglov. Znamensky told the female students that he was a pedagogue, but his innate grasp also turned out to be suited to a prison, as was his strong voice for shouting, although he spoke more softly than Kruglov. The cruel regime that had been appointed did not ease up under him. They roused the dignitaries' spectral world with the same stentorianness:

"Walk time! Attention, sentries! In the event of disobedience—use your weapon! Everyone up. Everyone!"

But they didn't have to put on their topcoats or fur coats (not that there was anywhere to put them; the dignitaries were just sitting there in them or keeping them underneath themselves in their chairs)—they stood up as they were, some tottering, and obeying Znamensky's pedagogical hand, walked single file around their table, behind the chairs, behind their colleagues' armchairs, once each time around getting to pass by their own chair.

So they trailed in this strange, strung-out file, only elderly and old men, alternating civilians in white starch and military men with heavy twisted epaulets, all portly, all stately, many having attended court ceremonies, and now here they were, with cramped legs, some with spinning heads, without the right to turn them, only to glance sideways—closed in an oval line, such as normal people don't do, and some not knowing whether it wouldn't be better to collapse back into their armchair shortly—until they heard an order in the same thick voice:

"Take your seats."

Also by the walls were half a dozen short velvet sofas, and Ensign Znamensky determined by eye who to allow to lie down for the night.

Deathly silence. Only fretful Admiral Kartsev cried out loudly a few times in the night:

"Some air! . . . I'm suffocating. We need air! . . ."

[2 2 8]

Events were seething somewhere, but they reached the Aleksandr Palace at Tsarskoye Selo only as rumors and mostly through the servants, not officials. There was a rumor that Chamberlain Valuyev had been killed in Petrograd. There was a rumor that General Globachev, head of the Petrograd Okhrana, had made his way to Tsarskoye Selo and his department had been looted of all its secret documents—but he told the head of the palace police this and himself made no attempt to report to the Empress. A horrible rumor came that Count Frederiks's home had been set on fire and the countess taken off to the hospital. Apparently everything standing in Petrograd had been smashed, everything that was the government, while Rodzyanko's new Duma Committee was not master of the situation. And a rumor even reached them, ricocheting off the capital, that Protopopov himself was in Tsarskoye Selo and was actually hiding here, in the palace, or with Vyrubova—and because of this they were going to attack the palace. (The fact that Vyrubova brought misfortune with her—all the domestic staff for some reason had always believed this to be so.)

Ah, Aleksandr Dmitrievich, the hope of the royal family! Why had he not saved anything? . . .

In Tsarskoye Selo itself, the unrest had intensified. People said that armored vehicles had approached the riflemen in the Sofia Regiment's barracks and raised them to go somewhere. That soldiers and officers had assembled at the Tsarskoye Selo town hall. From time to time shots reached them from far away—as if someone were loudly splitting firewood. By evening, there was a coalescing sense of oncoming danger.

But nothing truly bad had happened nearby, and no rebels had come into view. Passage remained free to the Cathedral of Our Lady of St. Theodore, where prayers for the Tsarevich's health were appointed for seven o'clock. The Empress went with her sole healthy daughter Maria as well as several officers from the Convoy and Combined Regiment.

The service was marvelous but did not ease her soul. They returned to the palace just as unimpeded, only there—first from Baroness Buxhoeveden, then from the Benckendorff couple, Madam Schneider, and Lili Dehn—the Empress learned the terrible news, which had already depressed the palace: in Tsarskoye Selo, soldiers had smashed several wine shops and cellars—and these were imperial riflemen? Even with the windows closed, disorderly shooting could be heard, and with the window vents open they could hear military bands, like the drone of breaking waves or the way the noise of a crowd is portrayed in operas. They were told that the prisoners had been released from the prison. But the most terrible rumor—no one knew how it had come, but it was already being asserted all around—was that a huge crowd was thronging from Kolpino to Tsarskoye Selo—some cited thirty thousand, some said three hundred thousand—workers from there and all kind of mutinous rabble. They were coming here to storm the palaces!

True, there was a not inconsiderable force defending the palace. Assembled directly inside the palace, in its extensive cellars and attached barracks, were two companies of the Convoy—the Terek and the Kuban—one company of the railroad regiment, and two battalions of the Combined Guards, and now two companies of their dear Guards Crew had arrived from Aleksandrovka; and there was also an anti-aircraft battery in the palace whose cannons were now tilted back and aimed at the gates. There were a few palace generals at the head and also General Groten, who had fought and had front-line experience. The men had been positioned in a chain along the palace wall, all the way around. Outside the wall, the Convoy's Cossacks were patrolling on horseback.

Their force was not inconsiderable, and they were all devoted, all loyal and prepared to defend—and against them the disjointed crowds of soldiers out of formation should not have any strength, nor had they even attempted to get close.

All of a sudden, though, the military heads realized that their units, maintained for so long for the personal protection of Their Imperial Majesties—how could they be used? If they engaged in battle and defended the palace, then in the cross fire, members of the most august family might suffer harm, and what about the palace itself?

They turned to Her Majesty for clarification.

Aleksandra Fyodorovna maintained all her courage and composure. It was as if she had completely ceased to experience her own constant, tortuous illnesses these past few days. She was now rather the senior of the generals, the first commandant of her own palace fortress, the undisputed head of this motley garrison. Power had been given her for perhaps the first time in her life unmediated, not through her influence on her royal spouse, not through orders to obedient ministers, not to influence through persuasion—but direct power to use force and open fire.

Having languished her entire forty-five-year life due to her imposed female limitedness, due to the fact that direct power over events was not available to her—on this great day of events and given all her assembled decisiveness, bolder and more authoritative than all these court men and generals, the Empress felt the confidence of her decisions betraying her. All objects suddenly doubled and tripled—and she ceased to see singly and correctly: how should she act?

Do battle? . . .

Sole power was proving to be not at all as straightforward as Aleksandra Fyodorovna had viewed it her whole life.

The threat of the palace being attacked, of stray bullets flying through the windows, maybe even at her children (maybe even at the Heir!), and the possible injuries to and deaths of her marvelous, beloved Convoy, whom she knew by face and name, and their families, and the Guards sailors (how many companions on their yacht outings!), and also the Guards from the Combined Regiment—and not even just them, but also those advancing, unknown by name, but also ours, Imperial Guards regiments—robbed her of the strength to give orders to fight.

And those Kolpino workers who were only thirsting to loot and take revenge, and who might roll up here in an hour, surely she could not have pity for them?

How much had she been slandered and cursed for being a German, for being a foreigner, for not considering the people's deaths and pitying only the German prisoners of war—because of this hanging accusation, if not simply as a Christian who had just returned from church service—she could not give the order to fire!

Firing on this Kolpino crowd would be a terrible repetition of the terrible 22 January, that collapse of the mind when, while having all the weapons, you're helpless to do anything.

How many times in her husband's hesitations and dismay had the Empress trembled from her own thirst for action! And now, the generals were turning directly to her for orders, and she could not enjoin anything but weakness.

Her eyebrows relaxed and her lips unpursed.

The threshold of decision.

And also for some reason, something that added to the awfulness of it, was that suddenly the electric lights went out all over Tsarskoye Selo, except for at the palace, and in this gloom, the nighttime mutiny seemed especially secret and menacing.

Right then, Baroness Buxhoeveden called her to the window. There, on the small square in front of the palace, lit by streetlamps and the palace windows, General Resin had led out and positioned two companies of the Combined Regiment—evidently preparing for imminent battle.

Indeed, the rifle shots seemed to be getting closer. Someone said a policeman had been killed at his post five hundred paces away. Shooting was just about to start here as well, and blood would be spilled before her very eyes! And also—how many undefended posts were set out around the park wall! No! This could not be allowed! Blood must not be spilled, especially right before her eyes!

"For God's sake! For God's sake! Let there be no blood for our sake!"

But how?

The Empress gave orders to bring all troops inside the palace perimeter. And remove the posts outside the park wall.

But if they weren't going to wage war, were negotiations inevitable?

Yes, evidently they were. Yes. Reconcile somehow, reach an agreement. Send truce envoys.

Who? Where? To whom?

They thought it over: send Prince Putyatin, chief of palace administration—where? To the town hall, where the rebels were assembling, and suggest neutrality. The palace troops would not fire if there was no attack from
without.

A blurred line wended its way between the gloom of the city and the
bright light of the palace. Anticipation. Occasionally people would move in
with shouts or songs. And move back.

But the strict barring of entry was violated. Certain unknown individuals
infiltrated and in the half-dark whispered with the palace men. A demoral-
izing rumor seeped into the palace and spread that if they even thought of
defending themselves, the artillery would open devastating fire on the
palace. And although Tsarskoye Selo's commandant had warned just this
afternoon that their artillery did not have shells, right now it wasn't easy to
convince rank-and-file defenders that this was indeed the case.

Agitation rose to the highest levels. Many court officials who lived elsewhere, like the Benckendorffs and Apraksin, had assembled at the palace—
and now they had to remain here and find a place for themselves in servants' rooms practically.

Mastering and developing the peace-loving attitude that had been
adopted, Count Apraksin requested the Empress's permission to move the
ill Vyrubova and all four of her sick-nurses and three doctors somewhere
outside the palace in order to lessen the tension and danger for the others.

The Empress was astonished. She had said a peace-loving attitude, but
did that really mean betraying friends?

Oh! How much her relationship with Anya had been through, survived,
and been stifled over the past fourteen years! The Empress had no more
trusting, capricious, and infuriating female soul or even such a subject of
fretful envy—but it would never have occurred to her to sacrifice Anya for
the well-being of others. To move Anya with measles when she couldn't
bring herself to move the children.

Rather, she now saw she would have to part with this count.

Prince Putyatin returned from the town hall. The cease-fire has been approved, but the palace patrols would wear white armbands as a sign of their
peaceableness.

Fine. (Two tablecloths were ripped into armbands.)

The palace garrison must send its representatives to the revolutionary
commandant's office. Fine.

And send truce envoys to the State Duma as a sign of their recognition of it.

Nothing else remained. Fine. (Imperceptibly and without a battle, the
palace garrison had joined the insurgents.)

The triumph, however, was that bloodshed had been avoided.

Right then a message arrived from the post office by telephone, bringing
the Empress unspeakable joy: a new telegram from the Emperor, who was

already in Likhoslavl. He confirmed that he hoped to be home tomorrow morning.

Well, thank God. Thank God! Tomorrow he would be here himself and this uncertainty would end. (For nearly the first time in her life she saw her husband as a firm sovereign.)

She had only to bear the burden of imperial authority until morning.

But right then they began to report that the palace units were confused; the news and threats from without had begun to affect them. There were even vague hints about them leaving the palace.

The officers went around to all the companies and encouraged them that the moment had come to prove their devotion to the Emperor in deed.

Oh no, that was wrong! Right then, the Empress knew a way. How many times, what fervor and delight had all the regiments felt when the Emperor had reviewed them, especially with the Heir. One had to understand this uncomplicated popular soul: they adored the royal family and were prepared for everything when it came to the Tsar.

Right now Marie Antoinette would have gone to make the rounds of her Swiss guards.

The Empress decided to visit her troops' front in the palace yard herself. She was warned that it was very cold. But she seemed to have forgotten her own countless illnesses; never before had she moved so confidently as during these past few days.

Now they would get a look at her, those loyal souls, and they would take heart, and straighten up, and be prepared for any mortal deed!

The large palace yard was illuminated by strong electric light—and several companies were formed up there in an infantry square. The temperature had dropped to nine below zero, and through all the electric glow the sky was awash in stars. Gunfire and songs were heard in dark Tsarskoye Selo, so the men lined up were warned not to respond to her greetings loudly.

The broad doors on the high porch opened wide. Two smart footmen came out and stood on either side, holding overhead silver candelabras with lit candles, which, however, did not add light to the yard.

The tall, calm, sternly majestic Empress emerged wearing a fur coat and fluffy white shawl, and held her head high, as if wearing an invisible crown.

Next to her, wearing a short fur coat, was sweet, plump eighteen-year-old Maria, lacking all majesty.

The troops were given a quiet but distinct command.

The snow creaked under their feet.

The Tsaritsa and Tsarevna reviewed the ranks, nodding and smiling—since they could not salute or issue commands themselves.

And the Tsaritsa found nothing distinct and loud to say to the soldiers—and she was worried about her accent.

She could have said something quietly to the officers. It was even essential that she speak, but she had nothing at all. She felt uncomfortable and could not come up with so many sentences.

Except:

"How cold it is! What a freeze."

Whether it was from the cold or something else, but many of the soldiers' faces were sullen; no universal delight radiated from their faces or broke through in the company's half-strength responses—and it hurt the Empress herself to see this.

Reviewing also turned out to be a difficult royal affair.

The most august personages made their round and left. They should also have gone downstairs to those units that had remained in the cellars, but the Empress's legs refused. She was already drooping.

Soldiers from the yard were being allowed to go into the first-floor hallway in groups and there were given tea.

The sentries standing by the guns jumped up and down to get warm.

In the dark, glow-dotted distance, they heard drunken voices and infrequent gunshots.

[2 2 9]

The train carrying the suite, the B train, was half an hour ahead of the imperial train, the A. Just before ten o'clock in the evening, in Vyshni Volochok, they learned from a gendarme lieutenant colonel that the Nikolaevsky Station in Petrograd was on fire, the station's new commandant, a mere lieutenant, Grekov, had ordered all stationmasters to inform him of all military trains without exception, their makeup, number of people, and type of weapons—if they had Petrograd as their destination. And not to allow those trains to leave the station without the permission of the Provisional Committee of the State Duma.

This, obviously, affected General Ivanov's expedition, word of which had already reached Petrograd. Actually, they were too late. General Ivanov was probably already in Tsarskoye Selo, where loyal regiments were converging.

But if they were following military trains this way, then how much the worse for the Emperor's? Each move of theirs from station to station was noted in mutinous Petrograd; was something being readied against them?

If that were the case, though, they had to undertake something. They could not travel so recklessly!

What did the Emperor think?

However, there had been no instructions to the suite's train to stop and wait. The only thing they could do was leave a messenger for Voeikov at the station to lay out the circumstances.

Half an hour after the B train, the imperial A pulled into Vyshni Volochok. All the suite's concerns were conveyed to Voeikov.

Voeikov was able to strike a proud and independent pose, as if not only the decision to allow such news to reach the Emperor or not belonged to him alone but also the very decision regarding this news.

Making no reply to the suite's messenger and expressing nothing on his haughty face, he moved down the platform and climbed aboard the Emperor's train car.

A few minutes later, the imperial train was allowed to move on.

The bright, calm mood of the sunny day, especially after the exultant soldier greetings, was extinguished in the Emperor with the twilight, the darkness, and the alarming news. He smoked half a cigarette at a time and put them out in an ashtray.

It was humiliating, but the administrator of the expanses and railroads of his country was not even Rodzyanko or Guchkov but some Bublikov, some Grekov. . . . That alone filled his soul with a tedious loathing.

He didn't understand how this could be happening—especially during time of war.

Only the calm, orderly, and obedient look of the stations they passed reassured him that everything else was a touch of raving of some kind.

If all this were taken seriously—that opposition to the Emperor had arisen over the expanses of his state—then perhaps he should apply even more decisive measures? Bring the main forces into action?

(But then, perhaps return to GHQ? . . .)

He had no one, not one person, to consult with, though! Least of all Voeikov, about whom Alix had always told the truth, that he was a poor advisor, that he should be reined in, and even that he was a fair-weather friend.

How could he suddenly return to GHQ? And leave Alix and their sick children to the will of fate?

What must she be experiencing, his poor beloved, in such proximity to the violent uprising? And he had promised her he would arrive tomorrow morning.

How would such a turnaround look to Voeikov and all his courtiers? And later to Alekseev?

A monarch can be more shackled in his movements than any subject.

He couldn't take a final decision until he had reached Alix.

They rolled on. The train moved smoothly down the well-tended Nikolaevsky line.

The Emperor could find nothing to do before his late evening tea. He didn't feel like reading. He smoked a lot.

He recalled his groundless chest pain at mass the day before yesterday, pain that had never been explained—pain despite the healthiest of hearts and entire body. Was this not some sign or presentiment, some long-distance divination?

At Bologoye he was expecting a courier to meet him from Tsarskoye Selo with news from Alix. But when they arrived in Bologoye at close to eleven o'clock, there was no courier. Instead, his suite got hold of a leaflet circulating at the station over Rodzyanko's signature concerning the creation of a provisional committee of the State Duma, which had taken all power from the dismissed Council of Ministers for the purpose of restoring order.

Given the rabble's raging, this might actually be a good thing—but his mistrust for the Duma, which was always intriguing against the Emperor, was too longstanding. Rare was the person the Emperor disliked as resolutely as Rodzyanko. And there was an insolent imposture in taking power away from the Council of Ministers.

But Bologoye itself was perfectly calm. Insofar as they had information, there was protection everywhere as far as Tosno and no disturbances whatsoever.

He had such a short way to go to Alix—and by morning he could be with her! How could he not continue?

Onward!

As Nikolai liked to repeat to himself: the Tsar's heart is in God's hands.

[2 3 0]

The men of His Majesty's Convoy held a special, lofty position, and in their home villages people lifted their eyes to heaven: he's protecting the Tsar himself! It was true. Once a Cossack had been enlisted in the Convoy (based on his appearance, face, or patronage), he became if not a member of the royal family, then its companion. He had seen both the Tsar and the Tsaritsa many times in simple surroundings and various moods, he had accompanied them on journeys, he had guarded the parks where they went on outings, he had been posted near rooms where they spoke, frequently in Russian, and was known to them by name, was used to their nondivinity and to his own, on the contrary, everlasting and assured position above the ordinary Cossack. He did not have to worry about a new uniform, or a raise in pay, or holiday gifts—all this came about invariably, just like the Convoy's Christmas tree and the indispensable visit from the Tsar, the Tsaritsa, and their daughters. His duties were to look dashing in his frightening attire, his tall, shaggy black fur hat above his red or blue Circassian coat with the white undertunic and his heelless boots, to stand imposingly at his post, to respond gaily and clearly to greetings, and when he was free from duty and had completed the morning grooming of the horses, he could play a bouncy game of leapfrog with his equally restive comrades.

His Majesty's Personal Convoy had served with glory under imperial personages for 106 years (never once having gone into battle for them), and herein lay its proud, enduring tradition.

In early 1917, its five hundreds were distributed as follows: one Kuban and one Terek hundred each in Mogilev, at GHQ; and one each in Tsarskoye

Selo, at the palace; a fifth hundred partly in Kiev, with the Dowager Empress, and partly—37 men, 2 officers, a cash box, the Convoy's property, and reserve horses—in Petrograd, in a coach house between Shpalernaya Street, onto which its gates opened, and the Voskresenskaya Embankment, which several officer apartments faced.

Hello, disaster! The gates opened onto Shpalernaya! And so this half-hundred had landed right in the swirling grip of the revolution—it could not have been worse. Had the coach house been on more far-flung streets, they might have waited things out behind locked gates longer since they had food and forage.

They safely sat out the first day, Monday; all this insanity scurried past down Shpalernaya without looking to either side. Even when the soldiers seemed to be strolling, hands in pockets, cigarettes in teeth, an unprecedented spectacle—or when it seemed they were constantly hurrying somewhere. But ever since the previous night, they'd started banging hard and drunkenly at the gates. And now, as of early morning, the jig was up: the crowd, which was banging its rifle butts and shooting all down Shpalernaya, tried to break through all the locked gates one after another, trying to get what was behind them. They weren't after the Convoy in particular, which didn't have a sign, but they asked everyone they came across: What were they hiding there?

The Convoy didn't have a sign, but their Circassian coats and provocative soft hats—here, in the middle of Petrograd, on a day like this—couldn't help but attract the panting crowd: this was something special, not like everyone had.

There was no avoiding opening the gates.

So they feigned poverty, and so did the officers. The Convoy men had "Cossack coats," a kind of lightweight, unlined short coat that had no military markers on it at all and was usually worn under the Circassian coat when it was cold—and now they were all wearing those coats. They opened the gates.

Passersby, runners-by, slipped in and out all day long. They'd see these Cossacks and their horses and not touch anyone. At first it worked.

But then they started asking where their officers were. They weren't here without officers, were they? Kill off yours the way we did ours!

The Cossacks tried to laugh this off. So people started getting ideas about them:

"Just wait, oprichniks! Until tonight!"

Soon all Shpalernaya knew that the *Tsar's oprichniks* had settled there.

This was bad. The Convoy's situation had become intolerable. People might attack that night after all! And carry everything off! Or set a fire.

The Cossacks came up with an idea and, with the officers' permission, began dealing with these roaming soldiers as if they were rebels, too, and responding with all kinds of impudent and foul words. Two or three went to jostle along in the marches and even give speeches. But if they were going to hold out in this manner, then it was only for the day, until the night, and what about tomorrow?

Support from Tsarskoye Selo was not on the way. They hadn't rescued them from this hell, hadn't taken them to the palace along with all the administrative property and cash box, which also had to be protected from sacking. And the telephone to Tsarskoye Selo had stopped working.

Then Captain Makukho, the treasurer, put on more nondescript clothes and that evening went to the State Duma. It wasn't far, after all, his feet weren't going to fall off, but he went there to *find out*.

And he did. The people there were all right, not mean, not killing anyone, but they were very busy, cramped, jostling. They wanted to live, too, and were putting in large reserves. Officers were wandering around, too, and quite a few. Our man, Mikhail Aleksanych Karaulov, a captain in the Terek Cossack forces, kept turning to everyone, and must be he knew some of our officers from previous service. Makukho saw him from a distance—but couldn't elbow his way to him, and without a uniform he wouldn't take him for one of his own, and how could you approach him? What would the conversation be about?

The Cossacks reasoned that they could send their representatives to him, in full Cossack uniform. Down Shpalernaya right now, in the night, a handful would get through somehow—and there, at Karaulov's, ask all their questions about what to do and how to deal with the new situation.

They agreed. Seven Convoy men led by their sergeant put on full Convoy uniform. They also figured that they couldn't go without red bows now. They attached a big red bow to each chest—and off they went down Shpalernaya at a measured pace, laughing at themselves: Look what we've come to! Going to the Duma with red bows. If the need is sufficiently pressing, you'd go see the devil. We're not going to the Duma, we're going to see our fine countryman.

By night, the hostile soldiery on Shpalernaya were so reduced in number, no one bothered them. Even in front of the Tauride Palace the crowd wasn't that thick, and yes, they could enter.

In the midst of it all, through the packed palace, finding Karaulov wasn't all that hard. He was rushing around hung with cartridge pouches, quick and dashing, and he was none other than the Tauride Palace *commandant*.

They approached—and he saw them. His merry eyes felt out the Convoy men:

"Well, what is it, old-timers?" Although most were young. "What do you say?"

They stood where they'd met and then stepped aside. Karaulov kept joking, while the Convoy men shifted from foot to foot. They informed him about the tight spot they were in, no way out, simply, and how could they protect their officers? And there was no help coming from Tsarskoye Selo whatsoever.

"And there won't be!" Karaulov said. "You have to think for yourselves."

But they said they hadn't come up with anything. Their heads weren't suited for that.

Karaulov squinted and advised:

"Here's what you should do, countrymen. Go arrest your officers. Or rather, have them let themselves be arrested voluntarily. That'll mean less harm for them. No one's going to touch them under arrest, and there'll be no reproach against you. You can say you did what you could, you're in favor of the new regime."

The Convoy men liked this advice. Why not? Settle things among themselves, in a good way.

Only couldn't they get some kind of safe conduct—just in case someone tried to put pressure on them?

Karaulov laughed again, led them to the third floor, to the kinds of rooms where the officers were, colonels, and civilians, and someone called Aleksandr Ivanych, and everyone gaped at them and smiled, amazed.

And they were given two whole passes.

One from Karaulov, saying the Convoy half-company was reporting to him.

And a second, Aleksandr Ivanych's order that the State Duma was prescribing that their leaders safeguard the individuals and property now under their protection.

Was that supposed to mean they were to continue protecting Their Majesties? A proper document, then.

[231]

Even up until midnight, the dacha trains kept to their strict schedule, although almost no one was going anywhere—and Lomonosov found himself alone in the first-class car. The conductor passed through as if nothing were wrong. And told Lomonosov that the entire Petrograd garrison had gone over to the Duma's side and there was no more fighting in Petrograd.

Astonishing! Utterly gripping!

On the square next to the Vindava Train Station and on the Semyonovsky parade ground there were still a few streetlamps and people, but it all ended abruptly nearby. He had to walk along the Obukhov Channel in total darkness and desertedness—while nearby he heard shots, either rifles or machine guns.

He gripped the revolver in his pocket. And in the event of authorities showing up—well, he had a perfectly valid, official telegram.

The Fontanka was lit. Cater-corner from the Ministry of Roads and Railways, soldiers could be seen on guard.

An ensign stepped out and Lomonosov showed him the Bublikov telegram. In the entrance hall, several soldiers were sleeping on benches, some on the floor as well. A concerned doorman hurried over to the familiar railroad general and, removing his coat with the green general's lining, complained:

"Look what we've come to, Your Excellency."

"But where's Bublikov?"

"In the office of the administration chief. Only you can't see him without a pass."

A soldier led Lomonosov down familiar staircases and corridors. A hussar cavalry captain with a fluffy, luxuriant blond mustache came out of the reception room and with a certain playful sternness questioned him, went away, and had him wait in the corridor standing—and the soldier wouldn't let him go either. At last, an administrator he knew walked by—and informed Bublikov. They let him in.

The office was brightly lit. But so that it wouldn't shine onto the street, a guard had nailed curtains made of soldier's cloth to the windows. Bublikov was sitting at the administration chief's desk, and there were two other civilians and a railroad man he knew. Bublikov threw his hands up in delight and stepped out from behind his desk. His eyes were darting faster and more keenly than usual, and his hands were moving more than normal, as if he'd had a quick drink, which was odd given his well-kempt hair, mustache, and collar.

"Ah, Yuri Vladimirovich, how pleased I am to see you! I've been expecting you! So, does this mean you're joining us? . . ."

This was incautious and tactless, and Lomonosov in no way wanted to conduct this kind of explanation aloud, in the presence of outsiders. After all, he had come, for now, merely to look. But Bublikov, understanding none of this, declared in high-strung delight:

"All the former ministers have been arrested! All power is held by the Duma Committee! Do you wish to put yourself at the disposal of the new government?"

He was positively aboil. He looked at Lomonosov recklessly. Average height, with the average appearance of a conscientious official—where did this revolutionary sweep come from?

Lomonosov was nearly the same height but stouter, with a round belly and a bare head as round as a kettle, but with a curly beard and eyes that were also quick, sharp, and prickly.

He looked. At Bublikov. At them. He shook hands—and just in case said nothing definite in reply.

Bublikov impulsively sat back down in the administrator's chair and pointed to another one close to him and said just as recklessly:

"And I have taken charge of this ministry and all the country's railroads! I sent a telegram through all Russia! And here's what I instructed: for 250 versts around Petrograd, I'm forbidding the movement of any military trains! And that's it! No suppressing troops can advance! Eh? Brilliant! The railroads in Russia—that's everything!"

It was true. A deafeningly simple solution. Lomonosov liked it. So was it true the new government had tipped the scales? So quickly and decisively? And Bublikov was in essence the new minister?

And this new minister explained that he was sending a few loyal men to various rail lines in order to assert the new authority and to speed up traffic; including Lomonosov to the Moscow-Kiev-Voronezh rail lines.

Ah, no, Lomonosov couldn't agree to that. Who was Moscow for? And what was happening in Kiev? They were divvying up the bearskin when it was still roaming the forest. Ah, no. And where was the Tsar? What was he doing?

Bublikov had seen the refusal on Lomonosov's keen and smart face but had not had time to reply when a wormy-looking soldier with a half-educated face entered from the next office and reported:

"The imperial train has passed through Bologoye and is continuing on to Vishera."

"There's your first answer!" And he changed his plan. "Why don't you follow the imperial train, then?"

This was even more intense, like being set on a knife's edge. But Lomonosov understood and even liked these trawl lines; he'd done them more than once in life: he'd studied at the Cadet Corps—and then decided on divinity school—but had matriculated at the railroads institute. He had toyed with revolution—but himself had advanced to scholar and general. He loved adventures, oh, he did! Right now, the balance was being tipped, but apparently to the good side. If you let the moment slip, a few hours and you'd miss out completely.

"What do you propose doing with the royal train?"

"It hasn't been decided yet!" Bublikov quickly stepped out to the next office. "I'm going to telephone Rodzyanko about this right now."

Lomonosov asked those who remained:

"But why this soldier? Who is this?"

"State Duma Deputy Rulevsky," he was told. "Aleksan Sanych's aide."

Lomonosov was ready to wager that there was no such Duma deputy. He realized there should be a directory in the cupboard here. He went to that corner, looked, and confirmed it: there had never been such a Duma deputy, not in the First, not in the Second, not down to the present day.

Bublikov returned, came over to the corner, and Lomonosov quietly asked:

"Aleksan Sanych, where did this Duma deputy come from?"

"Just let him, for respectability, he has to give orders."

"Do you know him well?"

"He just attached himself at the Tauride Palace."

"How on earth is that possible?"

"What of it? He's helping, and that's fine!" Bublikov was riding the same reckless wave. "He appropriated all the telegraph operators, and that's good! The Russian people possess such a reserve of public-spirited energy, old man! Anyone who steps up should be put to use. We're living through an exceptional moment!"

Who the hell knew. Maybe. This whirlwind had spun Lomonosov around, too! He wasn't going to ask who the Semyonovsky soldiers were guarding the ministry. Who had picked them? What if their mood shifted and they came up here and arrested us all? He'd brought a gun in his pocket, but he'd never actually fired it.

Even more amazing was the fact that distant, even Siberian rail lines, hubs, and stations were obeying Bublikov, whom no one had ever heard of as of this morning. And army trains had been halted for 250 versts.

Give it a try? Join in?

Evidently the Tsar was on his way to Tsarskoye Selo? Well, not to Petrograd, that was for sure.

Meanwhile the self-appointed commandant of the Nikolaevsky Train Station had himself already commanded that the train be taken to Petrograd!

Taken captive!

The Tsar!

While we? . . .

Bublikov had phoned Rodzyanko several times, and all they answered was:

"We're discussing it now. . . . It's still not decided. . . . For now, follow the train."

Could you really concoct a genuine, resounding revolution with Duma deputies?

[232]

General of the Infantry and Adjutant General Aleksei Yermolaevich Evert was a tall, blocky figure, with big hands, a big head and large features, and a direct steely gaze under jutting eyebrows—and even if someone didn't know that this general commanded the Western Army Group, from his entire appearance and bearing he would have to assume such was the case. With his every unfussy step he asserted: I am commander-in-chief!

Even his signature on resolutions was like this—not the usual human handwriting, a ligature of letters—but huge letters, almost nothing but sticks that thickened like clubs. What he valued most in himself was his sound mind, and through this sound mind he filtered army regulations and transposed broad orders for the troops, teaching what a good infantry should be like and what a good cavalry should be like, the kind that, fearing no enemy, knew neither flank nor rear. At the same time, although he was of distant

Swedish origin, he was an Orthodox general and never forgot that a strategy could only be successful when it was blessed by God. At the same time, though, he was an obedient general and liked receiving the most categorical orders from his superiors. When he did not receive them, he would contact GHQ over the wire and ask every way he could for advice. From the top down—there should always be clarity.

Therefore, General Evert was especially disheartened Monday morning when he received, apart from various dispositional instructions, a telegram from the president of the State Duma such as no regulation could allow to be sent to an army group's commander-in-chief. And why to Evert specifically? (He might have guessed that it had gone to the other commanders-in-chief as well, but he felt uncomfortable asking and had no one to ask.) The tone of the telegram itself was impermissible; it spoke impudently about the government and urged him to give the Emperor unseemly advice. This tone and this advice were quite enough to put this scoundrel Rodzyanko in prison.

But the hours were passing, and GHQ knew that Evert had received the telegram—and yet it had given no instructions whatsoever. The hours were passing, and Evert began to think that this was right and proper according to some new instruction and given the troubled Petrograd events. Or otherwise: GHQ had missed the fact that Evert had received this, but then he himself should not conceal it. That meant, according to his duty as a loyal subject, he should report it to GHQ, that is, repeat its full content to GHQ. And once it was transmitted, then, without going into the telegram's impudent meaning, he himself could confirm what was correct in the telegram. Evert also added these direct words of his own: I am a soldier. I neither have interfered nor will interfere in politics. I cannot judge how correct the telegram's contents are. But I cannot help but see the extreme disarray in transport and the significant shortages in delivery of provisions, which could put the army in a desperate position. This means, military action had to be taken against any possible strikes.

Thus Evert emerged from the situation well. He had not remained silent and like a good leader had defended his army group's interests. And had suggested firm measures.

A few more hours passed. And he received from GHQ an order to send four regiments against mutinous Petrograd. So his surmise had been correct: take firm measures! That's what he'd thought.

Swiftly, Evert began carrying out this sensible order. He was counting on being able to report on its full implementation in twenty-four hours, on the night of 14 March.

He couldn't just send these regiments without a paternal sendoff, but he himself couldn't get to the points of embarkation in order to stand before the soldiers with his mighty appearance and word. He decided to inspire them with an extensive written sendoff, through the division chiefs accompanying them to Tsarskoye Selo. That they, the valiant men of the Sevsky, Orlovsky, Pavlograd, and Don Cossacks distinguished by the commander's selection, during a difficult moment for the state, had taken up the Emperor's cause, to restore order inside Russia, without which victory was impossible over our cruel and persistent enemy, who had seized part of our native land and was torturing our brothers in bondage. Without this immediate pacification, supplies for our brave troops would be disrupted and every such day would work to the benefit of our foe. Without this immediate pacification, a glorious peace and the free and expansive flourishing of our homeland would be impossible. The pledge of success for the regiments who had taken up this mission was the strictest order and discipline and serving as a living example of loyal servants of our Tsar and homeland.

Also, immediately afterward, he sent telegrams to his three army commanders saying no agitation could be permitted among the troops of the Western Army Group facing off with Russia's most evil enemy.

And also, working through GHQ's rail warnings, Evert provided for an efficient guard for all front-line railroads. He readied mobile reserves with machine guns under the leadership of firm commanders.

Thus, everything was accomplished in which he could show his firm character with respect to the uprising. His army group, like the entire active front, was a fortress against rebellious Petrograd. All he had left to do was wait for the next news brought to him by his chief of staff, General Kvetsinsky.

Evert kept General Kvetsinsky because he was precise and consistent. But his appearance was not military—bald, flaccid, baggy, with something Oriental to his looks, he seemed as though he'd put on general's clothing and was having a hard time standing up straight in his uniform.

Now, before Evert could get a good sense of his full iron standing under the will of the sovereign Supreme leader, Kvetsinsky brought in a very long and informative telegram from GHQ that reported in detail about all the telegrams that had arrived from Petrograd in the last two days and what news, joyless and inaccurate, they had brought, some of which they had known themselves in Minsk—and then suddenly, in the middle, there was this matter-of-fact mention: "On the night of 12–13 March, the Tsar saw fit to depart for Tsarskoye Selo."

What? What was this? The Supreme leader was not standing at the head of his invincible army? And had instead headed straight into the mutiny's jaws?

Evert crossed himself. It was as if his main bulwark had ceased to back him up.

How could the Emperor risk going?

Not that it was for us to judge, of course.

But now that what was left at the head of GHQ was Alekseev, Evert could no longer be as confident and equanimous.

Terrible news kept trickling in, hour after hour, over the railroad's lines from Petrograd, and some impudent unknown by the name of Bublikov was issuing instructions—while GHQ maintained a silence that now felt alarming rather than confident and reliable.

Only a brief telegram arrived with the convincing assumption that the entire Petrograd mutiny may have been prepared by their foe—who now might start taking action as well.

Correct! This should have been expected. The entire front had to be on its guard. But GHQ's inaction was all the more unsettling.

Evert bore it, he bore it—and finally, after one in the morning of 14 March, he ordered Kvetsinsky to speak with GHQ and find out what was being undertaken there.

Kvetsinsky spoke over the line while Evert sat beside him but did not make his presence known; he didn't want to lose his standing.

At the other end of the line was Lukomsky.

Kvetsinsky complained that insolent telegrams were coming through all the railroad stations from someone named Bublikov and after that Lieutenant Grekov as well (the telegrams had been stopped within the confines of the army group), saying that no military train with Petrograd as its destination could move without the permission of the revolutionary authorities! Such an instruction, were it carried out, would halt traffic of all the regiments sent to Petrograd, including those the Western Army Group had sent and so informed the Minister of War in Petrograd—and by the way, was this the right thing to do? Where was the Minister of War there, was he in power? The commander-in-chief of the Western Army Group wondered whether GHQ deemed it essential to isolate the fighting armies from penetration by these insurrectionist telegrams. This could not be done within the limits of the Western Army Group alone. Be so kind as to inform us of the Supreme Command's view. The Western Army Group does not have timely information. What can GHQ report about the current situation in Petrograd?

Lukomsky began reassuring him that Bublikov's telegram was not in the least revolutionary because it was calling for order and even redoubled work. GHQ did not know Grekov's telegram, but such a thing should have been expected. Generally speaking, it was impossible to cut off telegraph and postal communication with Petrograd because that would raise panic and general confusion. It was essential merely to give instructions that by our oath of duty we must obey only the legitimate authorities. Of course, military trains must proceed without impediment.

A strange interpretation of their oath: let the revolutionaries send out whatever they liked. . . .

Look, Lukomsky reassured him, tomorrow all the railroads in the theater of military operations were likely to be subordinated to GHQ through Kislyakov. And Petrograd? It was calm now. A provisional government comprised from the Duma had taken up administration. The former Minister of

War was sitting in his apartment and yes, evidently, was not well informed about everything.

When he reached the end of the tape, Evert just spat and cursed.

[2 3 3]

Not long before midnight, when the driven flywheel of the military expedition was completing its strokes along two fronts and several railways, and tomorrow results were supposed to come through, General Alekseev was summoned to a direct line by the indefatigable Rodzyanko.

Ordinary telegrams did not suffice for him anymore. He wished to speak personally with the military authorities based on some unknown subordination. Relations between them were strained. And yet here came his summons.

Rodzyanko's mighty voice did not come through over the telegraph, but his exceptional calmness was manifested in the full flow of his sentences. Rodzyanko explained that under the Provisional Government he led, everything in Petrograd was obediently returning to its banks.

(What's that? A government now and no longer a committee? And come to think of it, Bublikov was issuing orders as a minister, as well.)

But what state was the garrison in? Weren't the troops disorganized, disobedient, rebelling?

On the contrary, all the troops in an unbroken chain had ecstatically greeted the Provisional Government. The garrison has in full joined the Provisional Government.

But hadn't officers been arrested, disarmed, hunted?

Nothing of the kind. These were exceptions. The officers were with their units, leading them and awaiting instructions from the Provisional Government. In fact, all life in the capital was quickly returning to normal. For instance, in view of the onset of calm among the populace, the banks and private credit institutions had decided to revive their operations tomorrow.

(But this was a most telling sign. The banks! The general picture was diametrically different. Ultimately, where was GHQ getting all its information? From the overwhelmed, distraught Khabalov, from the tightly wound Belyaev, from random private individuals, and from frightened foreign officers in Petrograd. No matter how you felt about Rodzyanko and his unrelenting know-it-all stance and aplomb, nonetheless he was a figure, the Duma President, and a chamberlain, and a page—and he must have weighed what he said.)

"But, Mikhail Vladimirovich, all this differs too greatly from the other information we have."

"Mikhail Vasilievich, you can rely more on me than on anyone else. My position allows me to see and know more than others. All information flows to me specifically. If you could hear my voice, you would be able to tell that I'm actually hoarse. This is because I've spent half a day welcoming the regiments who have come to the State Duma in well-formed ranks. And this is why I hasten to explain to you that the troops which you, as I've heard, are sending to Petrograd are exceptionally deleterious and might once again topple the normalizing situation into anarchy, to say nothing of provoking a clash, a terrible mutual bloodletting, which everyone, absolutely everyone wants to avoid."

(This did indeed look terrifying: everything was calming, settling down — and Alekseev was sending troops to a bloodbath. . . .)

The Provisional Government was only waiting for His Majesty's arrival in order to present to him the people's wishes. Under these conditions, the sending of troops and the opening of military operations . . .

(Once again, this was sensible. Rodzyanko's information altered the whole picture and was very encouraging, and his arguments simply swung the soul around.)

Was there official confirmation that the government had been replaced? Rodzyanko had sent confirmation today, twice already. Had GHQ really not received it?

Send it again, please.

Fine, happy to.

After the conversation, Alekseev went back to his quarters and thought hard.

Uprising or no, whatever it was — it had passed — and in what light would GHQ appear before society by sending punitive troops? Truly, why incite anarchy now all over again?

In the Emperor's absence, Alekseev personally had sent troops? Not very seemly. In society's view, all the responsibility rested with him.

He had wanted to avert violence against the officers and administration? It turned out nothing of the kind had been going on in Petrograd.

In essence, that famous government of confidence or responsible ministry had formed, which the Emperor had never wanted to allow — and now it had sailed in on a revolutionary wave. What moral right did GHQ now have to send troops against Petrograd?

If only the Emperor were at GHQ now! Alekseev would have reported to him and awaited his orders.

But the Emperor wasn't there, and there was no communication with him, so everything, be it easy or hard, fell to Alekseev alone.

It had been Gurko who had put Lukomsky and Klembovsky there. Actually, Lukomsky was also in favor of a government of popular trust. But Klembovsky was expressing no opinion.

The impossibility of fighting Russian society and its legitimate desires was becoming increasingly clear! Especially during a foreign war.

Besides, would this be such a walk in the park for the army? What could a clash with its own rear lead to? The railroads would be disrupted, and the army would cease to receive food. And it lived only on transports, having no stocks of its own.

The army could not fight effectively if there was a revolution going on in the rear.

All this pulling in of troops to suppress was deeply contrary to Mikhail Vasilievich's convictions.

But he couldn't disobey the Emperor's order, either.

What ill fortune that the Emperor had left! At such a moment. If he were in place right now—how much more convincing would it be to speak up, right here, rather than sending Morse code chasing after him—and where?

Well, if he was gone, he was gone. He knew what he was doing. So be it.

In a few hours the Emperor should be at Tsarskoye Selo. Send it there?

It had been a long time since General Alekseev had agonized over a choice.

He would never agree to serve an illegitimate coup d'état! That was why he had avoided Guchkov and Prince Lvov. But if this had come about anyway and the new government had safely established itself, then did he need to intervene?

Finally, Alekseev decided on this half-measure: not to halt the troops in any way, which would mean the Emperor's decree being strictly carried out. But send a telegram stopping and warning Ivanov, as the most forward general, to delay the leading edge so that it wouldn't have time to engage in battle. To convey his main impressions from his conversation with Rodzyanko, but without naming Rodzyanko, out of tact.

He and Lukomsky cautiously composed a telegram together. Don't give any order to stop, don't give any orders at all, but *advise*. However—ask to report all this to the Emperor upon his arrival (which meant letting him absorb it and take heed).

This had been well devised. They had devised this very well.

Just after one in the morning, this telegram, no. 1833, went to Ivanov over the Tsarskoye Selo palace's special line. And no sooner had it gone—and arrived!—than the line was cut. (Had Petrograd cut it?)

At last Alekseev could breathe after this most difficult of telegrams and go to bed.

But he did not drop off right away, as always digesting and laying it all to rest—and before he could fall asleep, they brought to his bed a strange and unexpected telegram from Brusilov.

Brusilov reported that he could begin the units' embarkation on the trains as of the morning of 15 March (not very soon) or even 16 March (evidently, due to drifting snow, since storms were raging in the southwest). However:

"Be so kind as to inform whether these units are subject to dispatch now or upon receipt of special notification."

The inappropriateness of this question struck Alekseev. What other confirmation and notification, if an order had been sent?

Even more striking, though, was the *timeliness* of this question. How could Brusilov have sensed this without any hint whatsoever?

Or had Rodzyanko also informed him somehow? . . .

The question would give Alekseev no peace. He got up. His cot was behind a railing, not far from his desk, and he went wearing just his linen, lit a small lamp, and found his daily telegram to Brusilov. Was that so? It said:

"As soon as the opportunity arises, depending upon rail transport conditions. . . . Do not fail to inform when circumstances allow you to dispatch these troops."

Not a word here about any second notification from Alekseev. But . . . did this mean it sounded that way? What had Brusilov sensed here?

This was odd. Alekseev had had nothing of the kind in mind and had included nothing of the kind in his orders to the commanders-in-chief, but here apparently *this* had been written—this was undoubtedly his handwriting— and fourteen hours ago?

This had written itself, between thoughts.

Those troops never had set out from the Southwestern Army Group.

Documents – 5

TELEGRAM no. 1833

TO GENERAL IVANOV, TSARSKOYE SELO

GHQ, 14 March, 01:15

Private communications say that total calm fell over Petrograd on 13 March. The troops, which have joined the Provisional Government in full, are being brought to order. The Provisional Government, under Rodzyanko's presidency, meeting in the State Duma, summoned military unit commanders to receive instructions on maintaining order. The appeal to the populace issued by the Provisional Government speaks about Russia's sacrosanct monarchical principle and about the need for new foundations for selecting and appointing a government. They are waiting impatiently for His Majesty's arrival in order to present him with the aforesaid and with the request to accept this wish of the people. If this information is accurate, then the means of your actions will change, and talks will lead to pacification, in order to avoid the disgraceful internecine strife so desired by our enemy and to preserve our institutions and factories and put them back into operation. The appeal from Bublikov, the new Minister of Roads and Railways, to railroad workers, which I received by a circuitous route, calls for intensified work by everyone in order to set disrupted transport to rights. Report all this to His Majesty, as well as the conviction that the matter can be led peacefully to a good conclusion that will strengthen Russia. Alekseev

[2 3 4]

Rodzyanko was thoroughly imbued with his nighttime conversation! It had been a successful idea to speak to GHQ.

Based on Alekseev's brief and at first reluctant replies, Rodzyanko had guessed that unconditional success was coming. Alekseev obviously had no firm information of his own about Petrograd, and so no firm objections, and he had no arguments of his own to advance. The tape was still rolling—but Rodzyanko could already tell that his words were being instilled in Alekseev. Ultimately, albeit the most ordinary general, he was an honest man. In this nighttime conversation, Rodzyanko felt that he had powerfully disrupted the sending of troops to Petrograd. (At the same time, he had felt out that they were still not even on the approach; evidently no regiment was close yet.) If he applied pressure in this direction as well, then the troops might be halted altogether.

Thus have all heroes' great deeds been accomplished ever since Heracles! Alone and not even in view of the crowd. In the dead of night, on his own, at the telegraph, Rodzyanko shielded Petrograd with his broad chest and saved it while the city slept totally unaware! Only his colleagues on the Duma Committee could appreciate it, but even then only those who wished him well. Not Milyukov. Not Nekrasov. Not Kerensky.

A heroic night!

How tactfully and even easily Rodzyanko had achieved this! Simply by force of his own wish. He did not wish the troops to come—and so they weren't. Apparently, he hadn't acted against his conscience in any way. Well, he may have slightly overstated the well-ordered troop ranks—to an old officer's eye this was not so—but he was redeemed by these troops' unprecedented impulse to go to the State Duma! In this their loyalty may have been said to have been manifested, so that here he had not exaggerated. These troops really were awaiting orders from the Duma. Could anyone say they had disobeyed? There had been none of that. Well, he might have put it a little strongly that officers were not being hunted, but that, too, would calm down today. Rodzyanko had spoken from his big, fervent heart, wishing, no matter what, to halt the troops and avert internecine strife, which would undermine a Russia at war.

Rodzyanko had achieved something else as well with this nighttime conversation. He had called his Committee the Provisional Government and himself the head of the new government, and Alekseev had digested this and asked for clarification in an additional telegram. And so Rodzyanko left the General Staff not for home but once again for the Tauride Palace. He felt like conveying his success to his colleagues.

But they were all sound asleep. He ordered a telegram sent to GHQ saying that governmental authority had transferred . . . to the Provisional Committee of the State Duma after all.

After this night, Rodzyanko in his own eyes was all the more the head of the government. To GHQ and the commanders-in-chief he was already prime minister. And in the eyes of the populace, by signing proclamations—who else could he be? Before his colleagues he was virtually the head of government, and now he felt a resistance to Lvov's contrived candidacy. It was only—only with respect to the Emperor that he had in no way yet been appointed.

What he needed right now was to obtain the Emperor's approval for the Duma Committee as the government. Moreover, a *responsible*, parliamentarian government. This would complete its final transformation. And the entire revolution would end well. And everything would return to its sacrosanct places.

But for now the Emperor was in motion, and a telegraph conversation with him was impossible. Even if there had been a telegraph, a conversation like that was impossible. The Emperor was not General Alekseev. You couldn't tap out your demand to him. You could ask to be approved as head of government only in a personal audience.

Not simply "an individual enjoying the entire country's trust" but Rodzyanko specifically! The deaf and obstinate Emperor did not want to hear that!

Of course, there was a hesitation here, an interfering emotion. The President had already frankly circumvented the Emperor several times—in his telegrams to the commanders-in-chief and now in his conversation with Alekseev. Nor had he kept his direct telegram to the Emperor secret but rather had read it out from the front steps, and given it to correspondents, and could not deny the marvelous phrase, which he had been wrong to delete: "I pray to God that in this hour responsibility not fall on the monarch." In all his speeches to the troops, no matter how patriotic Rodzyanko was, he was constantly exceeding the strictly legal limit. He felt this, but he couldn't not do it, and he himself even liked this rebellious sweep, which, it turned out, had always been in his nature—and had now manifested itself here.

In the past two days, Rodzyanko had grown accustomed to freedom—and had no great desire to bend himself to his former obedience.

They had to, the two leading men of state had to meet.

It was already very late, nearly morning. Rodzyanko went home quickly and to bed.

He slept a hero's sleep.

[2 3 5]

At two in the morning, at the Malaya Vishera train station, there was a deep, undisturbed silence. Sleep, a frosty night, the station deserted but brightly lit. Nothing dangerous going on anywhere.

At His Majesty's instructions, given before going to bed, they were to continue steadily onward—to Chudovo, Lyuban, and Tosno.

But a lieutenant from His Majesty's Personal Railroad Battalion ran down the empty platform toward the approaching train, the suite's B train.

The lieutenant himself had only just raced here by hand car, had barely escaped the rebels! There were already two companies of them in Lyuban, and they were obviously moving this way. A Lieutenant Grekov sent a telegram down the line: the commandants of the A and B letter trains were to head for Petrograd's Nikolaevsky Train Station!

The suite was agitated, those who weren't asleep. How deceptive this emptiness and silence was. It might seem that they were moving in the dark night invisible and unknown. But the stationmasters were reporting to the new leaders; Petrograd's rebels, and agitated Moscow, and telegraph operators at small stations—everyone could see, through the night and distance, the two dark blue trains racing into the gaping jaws.

There was no military force whatsoever with the Emperor. One might say there wasn't even any ordinary guard.

Fifteen minutes after the B train, the Tsar's A train pulled up quietly and softly. They stood side by side. Unwilling to subject the trains to danger on his responsibility, the B train commandant decided to awaken Palace Commandant Voeikov in the A train. Voeikov was sound asleep and awoke angrily, with rumpled hair. However, coming to, he quickly grasped the situation and decided to go awaken His Majesty and request instructions. Gradually the entire suite began waking up in alarm as well.

Only in sleep can one get away from these absurdities, incongruities, and disturbances—but a deferential summons pulls, pulls you out, out of that gentle immersion. There was no shelter even in the train's well-loved tranquility.

At first, like anyone asleep, the Emperor was irritated. Justifiably so. What for? Then, taking it more seriously, he arose from his bed and put on his robe. Obviously this was very serious. He and Voeikov looked at the map. They might not get to Tsarskoye via the shortest route through Tosno. Could they skip ahead as far as Chudovo and then turn toward Novgorod? Oh, the route was lengthening and his reunion with his family was receding. However, Voeikov tried to show that even moving as far as Chudovo was dangerous, that they had to turn around from where they were and go back.

Go back *altogether?* . . .

. . . Back! Oh, of course! Oh sleep bewitched, flee my eyes' lids! At the last moment of decision as a man and Tsar—to leap up! Feet in boots, finish putting on his tunic afterward. Yes, go back! To GHQ, of course! How long will it take us to race there? How much have we lost? Twenty-two hours coming here from Mogilev and eighteen hours back—forty hours? We can still make it! Stops only for taking on coal and water. Order Alekseev to ensure the line's safety. Don't even send the troops to Petrograd—just post obstructing detachments on horseback, on all the lines. To the commander of the Moscow District: Do not allow the contagion into Moscow! Dismantle the rails between Moscow and Petrograd! Do not allow so much as a single grain train into Petrograd! General Ivanov must hold the defense of Tsarskoye

Selo. Compose an ultimatum and announce it from Mogilev: the entire Provisional Committee and all the instigators must surrender to the Supreme Commander's Headquarters! All idle, mutinous units are to join marching companies! Whoever they have in charge there now is going to catch it!

... Back? Through Bologoye and Dno and only then to Tsarskoye? But after all, the Tsarskoye Selo garrison is scant, and what if the rebels captured the Empress? ...

Voeikov: They would never dare!

Actually, Ivanov was there, too.

Oh well then, back. We'll go around, through Dno. Once again into the warm, under-the-blanket gentleness, into salutary sleep. Tomorrow in Tsarskoye it will become clear and we'll decide there. For now—sleep. ...

While the locomotives were on the turning table another half-hour passed and a rumor came in, whether true or not, that the rebels were already two versts from Malaya Vishera.

The agitated suite buzzed openly, their shoulders and throats sensing the rebels' terrible grasp. They had to reach an agreement with the State Duma! Concede! Allow a responsible ministry! What was the Emperor still thinking, why was he persisting? We were all going to perish like this.

But no one dared go say such a thing to the Emperor.

And in any case, he was asleep.

On the platform it was frosty, very frosty even, and everyone dispersed.

At half past three in the morning, they first sent the Tsar's train south. The B train twenty minutes later.

Once again the dark blue trains slipped through the darkness, and once again they were watched by all the telegraph operators and the hundred-eyed revolution.

[236]

They had refused to go to their battalion, but how did they imagine what would come next? On the Petersburg side, with the 2nd Cadet Corps, lived the father of their good friend and regiment mate; and they could spend the next day with him. Well, and a second day as well. But after that? They had nowhere to go, after all, but to their own Moscow Battalion.

This is what the one-day revolution had done to them: thrown them out of the army, transformed them from useful officers into nothing, into dangerous and hunted nobodies.

Was this frenzied circle really here to stay? The Petrograd garrison, the entire army, all of Russia could not last a week like this!

Oh, how they regretted, after the false panic, that it wasn't actually an army unit coming to send the rabble to their proper places! If they could have one thing now, it would be the chance to help disperse the mutinous gang. Where was the general that needed them? They hadn't been summoned.

After the meeting at the Military Commission, the Nekrasov brothers and little Greve had begun—what? To search for somewhere to spend the night in the Duma. They were rather irritated that they'd gone to this meeting at all. They would have been able to grab a better place for themselves; soldiers were now lying side by side in the halls. Then again, officers were supposed to be the last to lie down, when everyone was asleep. Anything else was disgraceful.

For some reason, everyone wanted to spend the night in the State Duma, not only those trying to save themselves but also those who were making revolution.

Our officers had to check the rooms—peek into all the rooms, one after the other, as others were doing. They decided to go to the Duma's genteel left wing. There, too, in all the rooms, men had stretched out on the tables, sofas, chairs put together, and the floor. Soldiers, too.

Finally they found a room less crammed: "Secretary to the President of the State Duma." There was only room on the floor, next to the soldiers. Nothing to be done for it. They learned from them: each took three logs from the stove and placed them under his head. All three lay down in a row, without removing their greatcoats, just unbuttoning them. It was warm. The brothers on either side; Greve in between.

One small light had been left on for the room.

During the day, at times they'd been so sleepy, but now you couldn't fall right to sleep. Inside you everything was still in a flurry, and hunger was gnawing, and the logs' ribs cut into your head, and the new unfamiliar and humiliating position.

They kept talking in a half-whisper. They just couldn't settle down.

Vsevolod lay on his side, his wooden leg below, his face toward his friends, and quietly spoke to them both:

"Look, there's this elder who lives in Uglich, Evsei Makarych. He's read the Holy Scriptures a lot and last autumn he predicted that bitter times and burdens would soon come for all Russia. Men would save themselves by putting on rags and going where no one knew them. There would be famine for many years. People would be destroyed and laid waste by the many thousands. At first it would be bad only for some, and then bad for others, and then bad for everyone. Only the seventh generation would live well again."

Yes. . . .

Now they should go to sleep, but not for too long, they mustn't miss the predawn hour, they must leave quietly and in time, otherwise they'd be stuck here another day.

But in their keen sleep they awoke still earlier from Greve's powerful start.

He was sitting up, his eyes were wandering, and he was breathing hard.

"What's the matter, Pavlik?"

He was holding his side and there was suffering on his face: "I dreamed they planted a bayonet in me. Right here."

[2 3 7]

From its difficult, ill-starred positions all near the same Stokhod where last summer and last autumn so many Guards forces had been felled and laid to rest in its riverside swamps, this morning the Preobrazhensky Regiment received an order to come off duty: to leave the trenches for the reserve of its 1st Guards Division.

The soldiers cheered up. The officers cheered up. They were hoping for a few weeks now to rest up, to walk upright, and over land, and not via communications trenches, to know nothing about reconnaissance or guard duty, to sleep lying down, like human beings, and many even in houses.

But before they could stretch out to sleep for their first night, before it had grown dark, the regiment's commander and aide-de-camp in His Majesty's suite, Major General Drenteln, was passed a secret telegram from army group headquarters relaying General Alekseev's secret telegram from GHQ saying that it would do well for the Emperor to summon the Preobrazhensky and the 3rd and 4th Guards Riflery Regiments to Petrograd, to put down the disorders.

So! Drenteln forgot his trench rheumatism.

The order was to embark at the nearest large station: Lutsk. In darkness, the regiment was awakened and raised—and proceeded in marching order to Lutsk in the pitch dark and slush.

They waded through that mud for thirty versts.

No matter what kind of bold and daring fellows they were, by morning they were dead on their feet—and the three battalions had to be given a halt, to sleep a few hours, in the village of Polonnaya Gorka, eight versts from Lutsk. Drenteln himself went ahead, to the station, where the 1st Battalion had already arrived and was preparing to embark.

At the train station, Drenteln found dismay among the station and railroad officials—and in the hall near the cashier hung, pasted on the wall, a handwritten leaflet, a telegram received from some railroad commissar, some unknown Bublikov, who had relayed Rodzyanko's order: the old government had proven impotent and the State Duma had taken into its own hands the forming of a new government.

What raving was this? How was this to be understood? Who had hung it up?

A telegram actually received from Petrograd.

Right then Drenteln was sought out by the communications officer from army headquarters, who passed on instructions from Special Army Commander Gurko to temporarily postpone the regiment's embarkation.

A chill ran through Drenteln. The combination of these two orders was now quite alarming. If something was happening with the government in Petrograd, then that was exactly where the Guard needed to be! **Who** had postponed the transfer? The Emperor himself? Wasn't there some misunderstanding here?

Or even treason? . . .

The particularity of the moment and the particularity of the situation of the Preobrazhensky Regiment gave Drenteln the nerve not to clear this up through the division and corps but to go straight to General Gurko. Army headquarters were right here, not far outside Lutsk, in a Catholic monastery.

He took a motorcar through the empty, nighttime, poorly lit streets, seeing in the streetlamps only splattering slush. Then down a suburban road.

They were checked at the gates—and drove into the courtyard.

Drenteln asked the duty officer to report to the Commander, even though it was four o'clock in the morning. But the duty officer was not surprised, and General Gurko received General Drenteln at his desk in full uniform—either not yet having gone to bed or having already arisen. Always serious, decisive, and keen-witted, he now looked even more avid— pursed mouth, focused, mustache on the alert, narrowed eyes on the alert, focused, and his small head turned quickly.

He did not reprove him for this appeal made without a summons.

An order? An order, general, relayed by Brusilov from Alekseev himself. What basis do we have to doubt this? The Emperor's will has always been conveyed through General Alekseev. None of the army commanders, not even of the army groups, are allowed to communicate directly with the Emperor. We are required to execute. We do not have the right to question.

This was not in reproach of Drenteln, though. General Gurko's lively, darkened eyes were watching very uneasily, and his eyes seemed to express the very same doubt.

But he didn't dare send the Preobrazhensky soldiers to Petrograd himself.

Drenteln felt like a paralytic whose mind works but who can't move a muscle.

And so, pending further events, the regiment would remain in Polonnaya Gorka, and the 1st Battalion would be quartered in the barracks at the station.

At the same station, again walking past and glancing at Bublikov's vile telegram, Drenteln sat down to wait as well.

It wasn't simply that he had been the regiment's—and no ordinary regiment's—commander for more than a year. The Emperor himself had served in this regiment, and Drenteln had served with him then, and been treated kindly, and been close to him, and there were his years in the Emperor's suite, as aide to the head of the traveling chancery until the Empress removed him over his hostility toward Rasputin. (She had even wanted to take the Preobrazhensky away from him.) However, although he had no official right, Drenteln had to and could appeal directly to the Emperor.

From the 1st Battalion he summoned a trusted officer, Lieutenant Travin, and told him to prepare to take a secret letter to the Emperor.

He went to the stationmaster, obtained a good piece of paper and ink, and sat down and began writing at a desk under a bright lamp.

"Your Imperial Majesty, our dear Emperor!

"At the first sign from you, the men of the Preobrazhensky will be brought to the foot of your throne, regardless of the obstacles awaiting them. . . ."

He remembered one thing with relief: there were Preobrazhensky soldiers in Petrograd itself, after all, even if it was a reserve battalion. They were there! And they would not stand for it and would not remain indifferent!

* * *

THEIR STEW BARELY COOKED, THEY LET IT GO COLD.

* * *

[2 3 8]

It was all officers in the train car. About forty were on their way from Tomsk to Oranienbaum for a machine-gunner course at the officer riflery school. In Tikhvin, the commandant entered the car and announced:

"Gentlemen officers! There is a rebellion in Petrograd. I advise against you going there."

Bewilderment. What rebellion? What sort of rebellion? The commandant himself didn't know exactly. Political upheavals? Even if it was a revolution, which people have been expecting, that doesn't affect us. We're military men. We belong to the front. What's the threat to us? That's all right, we'll go take a look.

Aksyonov, a former university student and son of a metalworker father and a Cossack mother, thought to himself: If this is revolution, then we are not its enemies. It's interesting actually.

The layover in Tikhvin was just fifteen minutes; they had to decide. Fewer than half quickly gathered their things and left the train car; more than half remained.

And the train was late. It should have arrived in Petrograd late that evening, but it was already night and they were dozing, exhausted. Someone proposed hiding revolvers in their suitcases. And so they did.

They pulled into the Nikolaevsky Station after two in the morning; the platform was dark. But there was movement on it, and soldiers with red bows immediately burst into the train car. To the light of the train's candle lamps they put their bayonets to the chests of the first men:

"Gennelmen ofvitzers! Put down your guns!"

Then and there, in the train car, to the flickering of candles, not having seen Petrograd or learned anything—and they had to decide? and surrender? Because they'd been dozing, because the hour was inopportune, somehow there was no resistance—so they started surrendering their swords.

It was a strange feeling, like being stripped or spat upon. They went off with their suitcases—where? To the lunchroom.

What lighting there was around the station was meager. Soldiers were roaming, searching. The officers kept to a tight little group, seeking safety in numbers.

The first-class lunchroom was wide open, but looted and smashed, with shards of glass on the floor, no servers, no food, no dishes, some of the chairs broken, some carried off—and sitting right on the little tables were soldiers smoking, talking noisily, ignoring the officers.

One more savage than the next. They passed through the station, which offered neither shelter nor a way to leave. They clustered in a group, all their suitcases together. They stood like that, lost, for an hour or more. A foolish, hopeless situation. The trains to Oranienbaum would not be before morning anyway, and they weren't about to drag themselves now to the Baltic Station on foot.

All of a sudden, four male and two female students entered the hall with cheerful, ringing conversation. They were talking loudly, confidently, like the masters here and as if nothing special was happening. They glanced at the officers, but they wouldn't have paid any attention and would have passed by if Aksyonov, happy to see his own people, hadn't stepped out to them himself. He started talking and introduced himself as a recent student, and the officers were as well. (Some had been university students, but in any case they were young and looked the part.)

Suddenly everything changed.

"Hah! Comrades! Let's go then. At least let us treat you to hot chocolate!"

"Where's that?"

"Right here, on Razyezzhaya. It's not far."

"But we have our suitcases."

There was no checkroom at the station, of course; people had ransacked or stolen it all.

"Oh, leave it here. We'll ask these soldiers." And with confidence of their favorable disposition and obedience, he said to the soldiers sitting nearby: "Comrade soldiers! Are you going to be here a while? Please look after these suitcases."

Confidently spoken—and the soldiers, now altered, promised.

They took the risk and left. A private joke: our revolvers are there.

Along the way they learned from the students that the mutiny in Oranienbaum was even more one-sided, and there was no reason to go there. Both machine-gun regiments had mutinied and had already arrived in Petrograd.

So that's how things were.

On Razyezzhaya, in the courtyard, there was an entire cafeteria, a feeding station for revolutionaries. Lots of these feeding stations had now opened up all over Petrograd, they explained. Where was the food from? They'd started by clubbing together, and now it came from requisitions of private warehouses.

How tortuously the same life during the same moments and right nearby dragged on for some, posing dangers, stirred up and incomprehensible, while for others it was perfectly gay and easy!

Lamps burned brightly, although the tablecloths had been badly smeared by visitors. They made the officers wonderful hot chocolate and served it hot with sandwiches and even yeast buns.

People ate excellently. And talked gaily. Not everyone. There was a kind of intoxication, though you don't get drunk from hot chocolate. In the space of a few hours—the languor of the train car, the surrender of their swords, their dismay, and this hot chocolate. What was happening there with their suitcases?

They didn't feel like leaving and could have stayed on until morning. Where were they to go now if not to Oranienbaum? Who had the power to change an officer's assignment?

They returned through the empty street without the students—defenseless, in a way. Look at how things had turned around: a student was an officer's defense!

But there was no one on Ligovka; it was the most deserted hour.

And their suitcases were all there! The same soldiers reported good-naturedly. One of them, a little more educated, asked:

"Where do you want to go?" (He didn't add "your honor" or "officer sir.")

"To some institution or other." They themselves didn't know in this lost world.

"You should go to the Tauride Palace. They're sure to show you what to do there."

"But we don't know the way. We're not from here. Won't the streetcars start in the morning?"

"Streetcars?" He laughed. "There won't be any. We'll show you the way. Times are such now, and you're officers, and you're going as a group together, people might think anything. We'll show you the way."

So they were going to leave their things again? They left them again.

And headed off. Meanwhile, it was getting light.

Near the monument to Aleksandr III lay a man killed, a civilian, thick red snow underneath him.

The streets were deserted but were starting to liven up. Lines were forming at bread shops.

It was still empty in front of the Tauride Palace. The guard let them in without difficulty.

At a small table a sergeant who had volunteered, not a conscript, was very pleased:

"How good you've come, gentlemen officers! You can help us restore order!"

How pleasant. We were returning to normalcy.

He suggested that some of them assist a lieutenant writing out passes for all the officers who showed up. Others . . . But to Aksyonov:

"Be so kind, gentleman ensign! A platoon of soldiers from a Volynian Guards regiment is about to report. Take them and go to St. Isaac's Square, where people are looting a wine cellar. Restore order and post a sentry."

Aksyonov reached to feel the empty place on his left side, like an amputated limb.

"Your sword?" the ensign guessed. "Gentlemen, that we have. Let's go choose."

In the next room he showed them a pile of discarded swords.

They each chose one and put it on. It wasn't their own, and it wasn't quite right, but it was immediately better, and they felt like human beings.

Meanwhile, the platoon had arrived and was waiting near the front steps. The sergeant approached with his report, although there was no "your honor," but "ensign sir."

It turned out they had far to go, and Aksyonov decided five minutes at a walk, five minutes at a run, constantly counting off, checking discipline. And so? They held up beautifully, as if there'd been no revolution.

That meant things weren't so terrible.

The looters fled as they approached, having caught sight of them across the square.

They boarded up the storehouse. And posted a sentry for an hour.

[2 3 9]

"You, Yuri Vladimirovich, are a brave man. How is it you came to see me like this, immediately? An actual state councilor! You must have realized this looks like shady business."

Bublikov felt good in this office, and in a day or two he would move to Minister Krieger's office. He woke up, exceedingly content with his actions yesterday.

A single lamp burned all the time on the table. It had been a ragged night, taking calls and jumping up.

But now it was morning, seven soon.

From the other sofa, Lomonosov's bass banter:

"I weighed it, naturally.

"After all, the revolution did what it could: toppled the government and seized Petrograd. It has no more strength for anything. Do you see what's going on with the garrison? The garrison melted away, leaving a rabble. There's no detachment to send anywhere. What we're going to repulse Ivanov with, I can't imagine. The Duma, you see, is in total disarray—no leadership and no decisiveness."

Bublikov didn't really think this, but he was checking.

Lomonosov, just as crumpled from lying down fully dressed as Bublikov was, examined the molding on the ceiling:

"Well, Alesan Sanych, the entire freedom-loving tradition in which three Russian generations were raised is worth something. It will deliver us somehow. Even in my general's uniform, I was always a reserve private for the revolution. Every educated man we have has to count; we don't have the right to ignore the call. May I ask what you were expecting when you came here and when you summoned me?"

"You see," Bublikov mused out loud, "it was an impulse! In the Duma I simply felt disgrace over the idleness, how everyone there had lost heart. And I thought, well, how can we not use the Ministry of Roads and Railways, if we're like fish in water here, and no one else understands anything? . . . Generally speaking, there are only three stimuli for human activity. Curiosity. The thirst for glory. And the thirst for comfort. At least I had the first two."

"What about the liberationist tradition?"

"I'm not sure. Look how easy it turned out to be. Just high-handedly start giving orders to all of Russia—and they obey. Russia is used to obeying; our people are good for nothing."

"But so far we haven't ordered them to do anything serious."

"I wouldn't say that! My telegram went all over Russia without resistance. In any case, I guarantee you you'll be my deputy minister. The two current ones will have to be removed. But just in case, just in case . . . You and I can flee via Finland, we'll make it."

Lomonosov, glumly:

"Who hasn't fled via Finland. We won't be the first."

Once again, he was very much shaken.

"I'd like to know how serious these troops of Ivanov's are. If he has four good regiments, they'll crush us in half a day."

Bublikov shouted from his sofa arm:

"But I want to know which way the Tsar turned. Where is he going?"

Lomonosov rolled his head over his bolster and squinted his tenacious eyes:

"Maybe to Moscow? To dig in there?"

"No," Bublikov exulted. "My diagnosis is that he's panicked!"

Lomonosov lowered his feet and sat up, bowing his bare-shaven head with its mighty stretched nape.

"We have to keep him from returning to the troops."

"That's right! Why the hell doesn't this Rodzyanko get off the pot?"

They had been calling him ever since the Tsar had turned around in Vishera—and either they couldn't find him, or they couldn't wake him, and finally Rodzyanko ordered a train from the Nikolaevsky Station—he would go to the Tsar himself—and now they were calling and saying the train was ready but Rodzyanko still hadn't come, he was still half an hour away—while the royal train had passed through Aleshinka and Berezaika. . . .

They jumped up in unison and went next door to the office of Ustrugov, head of the transport service, where they could send communications along the rail lines. They hadn't let Ustrugov go home, he was still sleeping somewhere, and sitting at the telephones was the wide-awake, bony Rulevsky.

Rulevsky had just learned from Bologoye that both royal trains had arrived there.

"Already?" Lomonosov exclaimed. "Then we're holding them ourselves, we're not asking anyone!" He grabbed the receiver.

Bublikov picked up the city line:

"No no, we still have to ask Rodzyanko. I'm his commissar."

And wait again, and again, while they searched for Rodzyanko in the Duma, summoned him, and conferred. Bublikov's hand was already growing numb from holding the receiver when they replied: Yes, hold the royal train in Bologoye and make sure the President's telegram is handed to him.

How afraid they were, they were insuring themselves—hold him up and immediately the justificatory telegram. No, revolutionaries would not come of them!

And when would this Deadwood finally move and start for the station?

On the other hand, Bublikov and Lomonosov felt as if they were in flight, a flight such as they'd never known in their lives. Either all was won or all was lost! No washing up, no drinking tea—they paced, rubbing their hands nervously, four eyes burning: an unprecedented hunt! We're detaining the Tsar!

For some reason, Bologoye wasn't responding. Instead, the Vindava-Rybinsk line, the most loyal of all that night, reported that a demand had come from the imperial train to give the Dno station as its destination.

Lightning fast: Nikolai wants to reach the army?

"Do not allow him under any circumstance!"

"Yes sir, it will be done."

Very good! They rubbed their hands and paced some more and studied the map like a chessboard. That meant not to Moscow at least. The Tsar's movement toward Moscow was dangerous, although even there *it was starting.*

Suddenly, a telegram was delivered from Bologoye:

"The A train has headed with its previous locomotive for Dno, not having received its destination."

Bublikov was furious! He shouted! He cursed! He stamped his feet! And into the receiver: "You let him go, you idiots!"

And also: Traitors! We'll rip your heads off! We'll shoot you!

But what could they do? They had to do something!

Lomonosov stabbed all ten fingers into the wall map. He muttered as he pondered:

"Detain him before Staraya Russa . . ."

But who will detain him? With what?

Blow up a bridge? Dismantle the lines? . . . We can try, but the Duma will get very scared.

And who is going to do this, how can this be controlled at a distance?

"Here's what. We'll block a waypoint with freight trains. Where there are two lines, put two trains. That will do it."

They summoned Ustrugov. He came, that sound transport man, languid from sleep.

Bublikov gave his order.

Ustrugov shuddered and woke up. And his bureaucratic soul gazed forthrightly at the audacious revolutionaries and stammered:

"No, gentlemen. That I cannot do. . . . That order . . . is impossible."

"What?"

"How is that? You're refusing?"

All of a sudden, tall, skinny Rulevsky came running from the corner holding a revolver—which he pointed directly at the bridge of Ustrugov's nose.

"You're refusing?"

Lomonosov gave a chuckle:

"My dear man, you're going to have to obey."

Documents – 6

TELEGRAM

VINDAVA R.R. STA. DNO

14 March (about 08:00)

Be so kind as to immediately send from the Dno station in the direction of Bologoye two freight trains, which should occupy the siding and physically block the movement of any trains whatsoever. For failure to carry this out or for insufficiently swift implementation of the present instruction you will answer as for treason against the fatherland. State Duma Commissar Bublikov.

[2 4 0]

Apparently, they'd never had such a hard time rousing him—after all, he wasn't a young officer anymore. At first, Rodzyanko couldn't figure out or understand anything: he looked at the clock—not yet six? And he went to bed at three? Whose idea was it to ask for him, and why? Oh, that unrelenting Bublikov.

Yesterday evening that Bublikov for no purpose at all, simply out of revolutionary mischief, had suggested stopping the royal train. Rodzyanko had cooled his ardor, saying there was no such goal.

And now he was reporting that *the Tsar had given them the slip*—word for word, *given them the slip*. He'd turned back from Malaya Vishera!

So that's how it was! Rodzyanko was barely awake. What could this mean? Had the Emperor's intentions changed?

But it's very hard for someone wrested from sleep to make sense of anything and even harder to decide anything.

Yes, he'd wanted to see him. Where was he going?

He had to say something.

"Here's what. Send a telegram down the line to the Emperor saying that I'm requesting an audience with him in Bologoye. Get a train ready for me at the Nikolaevsky Station and I'll go soon."

Saying this was all well and good, only he couldn't make himself get up—and how could he go without permission? His colleagues would berate him. Why was he going? To ask for what? Insist on what? And if the Emperor wouldn't agree to anything, then what? He had to confer with his colleagues. But they were asleep—and even if it was right at the Tauride Palace, you still couldn't wake them up or find out anything.

He went back to bed for another half an hour.

His wife woke him two hours later. They kept calling from Bublikov. The train was ready!

Well, this was a human hour now. His head had cleared—and it hit him: Was he going to Moscow? Was the Tsar headed for Moscow?

Of course! He was going to declare his capital there! And from there he would put down the uprising.

But we haven't had time to take over Moscow.

This is bad!

We have to catch him! We have to restrain the Emperor from this madness!

Oh, I missed the moment!

Get washed quickly! A motorcar quickly!

He rode off to the Tauride Palace.

Water doesn't flow under a lying stone. They had to overtake the Emperor! And stop him from doing something irreparable. And seize government power, a responsible ministry, definitively.

Rodzyanko swelled with growing firmness and confidence. Finally the time had come to speak with the Emperor not only in the form of a loyal subject's request. The moment had come to demand.

He sketched out a dignified, independent, essentially equal conversation, even weighted toward the President. A conversation that would open a new era in Russia's history.

In essence, he wanted to take power from the Emperor's weak hands into his own strong ones—for the good of the homeland.

At his February report for some reason he had had a feeling and told the Emperor: This is the last time I'll be with you. We won't see each other again.

But now they would.

In the Tauride Palace, though, before he could convene anyone, Bublikov telephoned to say the royal train had been missed! It had slipped away from Bologoye for Valdai without authorization!

Valdai? Staraya Russa? Where is that? Well, fine, it's not Moscow. And even better that it's not GHQ.

All right, hold my train under steam. I'll be leaving soon!

Where was he headed? If for Petrograd, then he had already been very close, so why go around?

Right then a vigilant secretary—despite all the commotion in the Tauride Palace, the President still had his secretaries—brought him a copy of a note from Grand Duke Kirill to the heads of the Tsarskoye Selo military units. Inasmuch as Kirill's Guards Crew had been assigned to Tsarskoye Selo, then he himself as one such head was informing the others that he, Rear Admiral Kirill, of His Majesty's suite, and his crew had fully endorsed the new government—and he was sure that all the other Tsarskoye Selo units would endorse it as well.

Wonderful! Here was unexpected support! He had amazed and astonished them! Even cheered them up. If prominent members of the dynasty were themselves joining . . . and even calling on others! Our victory!

Rodzyanko was greatly emboldened, a completely different feeling. Our victory! (But why was it that he himself, darling Kirill, hadn't reported directly?)

How was the witch of Tsarskoye Selo doing now?

Speak of the devil. The commandant of the Tsarskoye Selo palace conveyed a request from the Empress to take measures to institute order in Tsarskoye Selo and the vicinity of the palace. And also this request from the Empress: Might Mr. Rodzyanko not come see her this morning to talk things over?

Well, a proper fool who had no idea of life! How could she imagine that the President would go pay her a visit now? How that would look in the eyes of revolutionary Petrograd! Previously, she hadn't even invited him to lunch when he came with his formal reports. And now she was asking him to come? How she humbled herself! But why had she wasted yesterday, and last evening, and last night, and disdained Rodzyanko's advice to get away as quickly as she could? Was she waiting for her spouse? And here he had turned away.

Well, he could send two Duma deputies to calm Tsarskoye down.

Apparently, the day was off to a pretty good start. Dawn was breaking. Soon, once again, probably, military units wishing to salute the Duma would start approaching the Tauride Palace with music and in bad formation. And in general, these marches were better than the soldiers' mutiny. Today, let someone else put his throat at the service of the fatherland while the President went to negotiate with the Tsar.

It was time to inform the Committee of his trip, agree on his authority, and go to the station.

Right then, though, a pale Engelhardt ran in.

Again the situation was such, outsiders around, you couldn't say everything out loud. They stepped aside.

"Mikhail Vladimirovich, something terrible has happened!" said Engelhardt, who was wearing his military uniform but who had a nonmilitary look of extreme fright. "A rumor out of somewhere has started going around the soldiers about some 'Rodzyanko order' that you didn't issue, right? Your supposed order tells everyone to return to barracks, surrender their weapons, and obey their officers."

Rodzyanko's eyebrows and forehead rolled back. He had not issued a direct order to that effect, but he had expressed exactly that. How else? If the soldiers didn't return to barracks and didn't obey their officers . . . ? How long could they behave like hooligans?

"This is a terrible, terrible misunderstanding!" Engelhardt was distressed. "You can't imagine what's brewing! New outbursts in the barracks! They're driving out the returned officers and threatening to kill them! They say there's going to be a massacre of them! And they're threatening to kill you! . . . It's not entirely safe for you to meet with delegations now. . . ."

Rodzyanko felt the blood drain from his head, which was filled with an evil chill.

This was the gratitude he got for having saved them all last night!

Documents – 7

ORDER

(14 March)

Gentlemen officers of the Petrograd garrison and all gentlemen officers now in Petrograd!

The Military Commission of the State Duma invites all gentlemen officers who do not have specific assignments from the Commission to appear on 14 and 15 March in the Hall of the Army and Navy to receive warrants for universal access as well as precise registration and to carry out Commission assignments for the organization of soldiers. . . .

Delay in gentlemen officers reporting to their units will inevitably undermine the prestige of the officer rank. . . . At the present moment, in the face of the enemy standing near the heart of our homeland and prepared to take advantage of its momentary weakness, it is extremely essential that we make every effort to restore the organization of military units. . . .

Do not waste time, gentlemen officers, not a minute of precious time!

[2 4 1]

Georgi was awakened not in the dark by his alarm clock, as had been readied, but when a distant, indirect light fell through the open door. And Kalisa was standing by the bed, waking him.

A hot breakfast was already waiting.

Now, as if in an emergency, he jumped up and dressed; his boots had been polished since yesterday morning. Here he was sitting at the table. Kalisa fed and served him with all devotion and anticipated what else he might want.

Like a wife. No, not like a wife. No, exactly like a wife! He just hadn't seen it before.

He looked at her sunflower-scattered housecoat, looked at her good smile, and was astonished and couldn't believe it: the day before yesterday still a stranger, she had become his. It was as if she had rubbed his heart with a soothing oil.

A couple of times he caught her hand and gratefully buried his face in her palm.

These predawn preparations cut through him with a reminder of other preparations: how he had left for this war. It had been dark then, too, and he'd been awakened by his alarm clock. And Georgi had told Alina: "Don't you get up. Why should you?" Why should she lose the bed warmth (though he himself did want her to see him off). But Alina had easily agreed and stayed in bed, pulling the blanket up—either to sleep away or to luxuriate in the bitter hours. He swallowed something cold in the kitchen and, already in his greatcoat, in full gear, went over to her in bed one more time to kiss her. This was how he'd gone to war, and he himself saw nothing bad in this, although in those days all over Russia womenfolk were running after wagons and trains and wailing.

Only now, when Kalisa hugged him desperately around the neck, burying her face in the lapels of his prickly greatcoat fabric, went out into the court-yard with him and would have gone to the street if it had been decent—only now did he take offense at Alina for that sendoff.

He walked quickly down the deserted Kadashevskaya Embankment. He couldn't avoid stopping at home before the train station. But right now he could easily go home.

The dawn was foggy. The embankment could be seen everywhere, but across the river, separated by an island as well, the fog thickened so that the Kremlin could not be seen, and only a practiced eye could guess it was there.

At the Maly Kamenny Bridge he began waiting for the streetcar, insofar as the fog let him because he couldn't really see. In either direction.

Vorotyntsev stood there like that, lost in thought, distractedly observing where the yardmen were scouring the sidewalk and where the milk and bread deliverers were. He didn't notice that no matter how long since the last streetcar, no one else came to the stop.

Who knows how long he would have stood there, clueless, if a woman with a basket of bubliks hadn't come up and in her luscious dialect, her pity-ing voice, said to him:

"Your honor! Th' streetcars aren't goin'. Fer the second day."

"How's that?" Vorotyntsev turned around. "Why?"

"Uh—don't know. They've uprised."

"What's that now?"—as if this woman might know.

She might:

"They're sayin' there's a big mutiny in Peter. These ones here took it up, too."

"So that's it. . . . Thank you."

That meant Petersburg hadn't quieted down.

Take a cab? But now Georgi realized that in this whole time not a single cab had gone by, and now he couldn't see one either.

Why bother with transport? A foolish city habit. At the front they ticked off distances much greater than this on foot. With a quick light step, he crossed the Maly Kamenny Bridge and continued on to Bolshoi Kamenny.

Now, although the freezing fog hadn't let up, it was definitely daytime, and he himself was closer—and the Kremlin's brick wall began to appear, as did the cathedrals' cupolas and the candle shape of the Ivan the Great Bell Tower.

What was wrong with him that on this visit he hadn't even noticed Mos-cow itself, not a single beloved place? His inner gloom had driven it all out.

Whereas now, crossing toward the Prechistensky Gate, he gazed intently freely, at the bulk of Christ the Savior Cathedral.

There it was! There they were! Everything in its place, Moscow in its place, the world in its place. He mustn't let himself slacken so.

Indeed, not a single streetcar to be heard or seen anywhere. One or two sleigh-cabs rushed by in haste, keeping to one side. And there were very few people.

A little bit later—he wanted to buy a newspaper and find out what was happening where—but the kiosks were shut and no newspaper boys were running around.

At the corner of Lopukhinsky, the bread store was already selling bread and people could be seen inside, but there was no line outside. Chuev's bread store at Yeropkinsky was still shut.

But his joyous sensation—of healing—was preserved. Healing from Alina's torments and complaints. He was free to go to his place at the front. He ascended the stairs without any depression at all, and only when he was opening the door—although he now knew she was away, that she couldn't be here, that she couldn't return this quickly—nonetheless he tensed for a moment. What if she jumped out right now with a heart-rending scream.

But she didn't. Nonetheless, he immediately surveyed the rooms and checked. He looked at the scissors in all the places to see whether they weren't spread like forked tongues again.

But Alina wasn't there, and all the scissors lay calmly closed, as he had left them—when was that? Only the day before yesterday? . . .

He went to check the mailbox—again nothing.

Most important, there wasn't that unified pain of all the apartment—and all his skin—and all his consciousness, the sharp pain from every glance at every object. He looked around and was amazed at how everything had torn at him here the day before yesterday. How could he have tormented himself like that? Now he wasn't irritated, now he could cheerfully shave, collect his things, and all the rest, before Alina descended.

But was he leaving here forever? A month from now was the great offensive, and wouldn't 1917, with its exhaustion and losses, wouldn't it eclipse the three preceding years?

While he was walking around and shaving, he was thinking about whether to write her a letter. Did he need to leave her something, something very brief and simple?

But his feeling of guilt had evaporated. And no other repellant feeling toward Alina had arisen either. This unfortunate ability of hers to turn everything into raging thunder. Even while you were under the missiles.

More than an hour may have passed this way. The fog lifted and the day promised to be clear. Vorotyntsev heard from the street—despite the caulked window frames—the noise of many voices and snatches of singing.

He walked over to the street-side windows and couldn't stick his head out; he couldn't see down well. He walked over to the window facing along

Ostozhenka—and saw the backs of a crowd of about two hundred men, probably young men, workers, not students, They were walking out of step but merrily toward the Prechistensky Gate—carrying something like a red flag on a pole. Someone started singing, and though no one picked it up, everyone's voices were booming.

One man skipped out of the march, ran toward the grating of the Commercial Training School—and there poked through and tore down slantwise a pasted-up notice that Vorotyntsev hadn't seen that morning at dusk. But the notice remained with the skewed ripped piece hanging.

Something was going on! A march like this so early in the morning? He had to get a newspaper. And go read that notice.

He ran downstairs. The portress told him there hadn't been any newspapers since the day before yesterday and people were "going wild" in the city.

He quickly crossed Ostozhenka, walked up to the defaced notice—there were no readers there—and holding up the torn strip—which probably looked funny—he read:

"I declare the city of Moscow to be under a state of siege as of 14 March. Any kind of meeting or gathering is prohibited, as are all types of street demonstrations. The authorities' demands must be implemented immediately. It is forbidden to go out before 7 in the morning or after 8 in the evening except in instances . . .

"Troop Commander of the Moscow Military District Artillery General Mrozovsky."

[2 4 2]

How much sleep had the Empress had today, and how had she held on without it, especially given the distension of her heart, which was overly exacting in digesting all the events? Anticipating the Emperor's arrival, she was up and dressed at five in the morning. It was as if all of it had agreed to leave her in peace—all the illnesses and pains that had shackled her to her bed, to her couch, to her sedan chair, for so many months and years, barely allowing her to appear in society or in Petersburg. Nor did her legs fail her. It even became entirely within her powers—with the elevator broken for the first time—to go up the stairs to visit the children on the second floor.

These past few days, all the justificatory obstacles had fallen away, leaving her with no dodges whatsoever and no choice but to manifest her will and authority in full. Now, though, it turned out there was no one to manifest them through: her lines of authority all ended at the court and continued no further.

They were supposed to telephone the palace the moment the Emperor's train arrived at the station. But at five o'clock he still wasn't there. Nor was he at half past. At nearly six, her lady's maid reported what had been relayed from the station: the Emperor's train was detained, but where, by whom, and why was unknown.

Detained? The Emperor had been **detained** in his own fatherland?

Perhaps by circumstances? Perhaps by a breakdown? A storm? Otherwise, what had the railroad security guards been doing? The authorities? GHQ and General Alekseev?

General Alekseev—how could he allow such a thing, he and the commanders-in-chief? Oh, she had told the Emperor more than once that he was a filthy peasant, that he was listening to Guchkov and to bad letters and had lost his way. The Lord had sent this illness, had pointed with his finger—move him away. But the Emperor had brought him back.

However, all she could do was walk, her body straightened, recovered, down the palace passageways, leaning on the arm of the Combined Regiment's duty officer, Sergei Apukhtin, throwing her ricocheting questions at the walls, and looking out the mute, dark windows.

She angrily asked the walls but inwardly was already preparing herself for anything.

Tsarskoye Selo was dark and still.

She did not conceal her alarm from the early-rising Lili Dehn (who slept near the Empress's bedroom in order not to leave her alone on that floor), who made the rounds of the children with her. Anastasia had a fever; the two older girls were doing poorly. But the Heir, on the contrary, felt better. They were all protected from the outside news, though, left in their fine vale—to lie in the half-dark with a temperature, rash, and cough and not know anything at all, not picture the events going on.

Long and tortuous were these early morning hours before dawn, which brought no resolution or answers of any kind.

In memory of them, the Empress gave Apukhtin her tear-stained hanky and an ashtray from the Imperial Porcelain Factory.

A rumor arrived from the officers of the railroad regiment at the station: yes, mutineers had stopped the royal train somewhere!

At eight o'clock in the morning, when it was already getting light, General Groten came to report that the imperial trains had been stopped in the night at Malaya Vishera and now would not make it before noon. But he did not know the reasons for the halt, either.

How many hours left, though? How could they remain safe for these few hours? Yesterday evening the Tsarskoye Selo garrison had mutinied, and yesterday evening a rebellious crowd from Kolpino had come to storm the palace but thank God did not get that far, perhaps because of the cold. But today?

How she dreaded demeaning herself in front of these Duma beasts! And before that dreadful Rodzyanko, that cow Rodzyanko! However, she had already sent an aide-de-camp to him for an order to protect the palace, and now the next step would be easier. Should she ask Groten to call Rodzyanko immediately and ask him who had dared detain the Emperor and why? And perhaps Mr. Rodzyanko himself could come here to explain?

The noisiest of the mutineers had become her sole legitimate support.

And there was no explanatory telegram whatsoever from the Emperor! To be at her children's sickbed and not know anything about their father!

Should she now send telegrams on the off chance to various stations along his route?

Yes, but where were the grand dukes? A pack of nonentities! The only time their voices were heard was when the income was being divided up from the appanage department or when they were chorusing their defense of dynastic murderers. Right now they were not only not in any rush to come to the Empress's aid, to telephone her or come—they were all gloating in hiding and awaiting the denouement. What had Kirill done? An insignificant, shallow braggart, she had always seen him as such (he had sent his wife to reprimand the Empress!)—and now he had hidden away as such. His Guards Crew was right here—and where was he? And dear, weak-willed Misha, entirely in the hands of his imperious wife, who even in this war had not become a man? And the scapegrace and debauchee, the degenerate Boris, who only held the seat of a Cossack field ataman, after all, he wasn't at GHQ now but was rattling around here somewhere—where was he? Running through their numerous male ranks, the Empress could not conceive of or name a man who might have offered protection. They were all milksops and cowards. Aging Pavel alone at least resembled a man.

But what had he done—and not done?—with the Guard? What had he come up with and done since yesterday?

They also reported that the railroad regiment company that had left the palace for the night had not returned in the morning as it was supposed to.

Her guard was melting away.

That boor Rodzyanko had relayed that there could be no question of him coming—and he knew nothing about the reason for the Emperor's detainment.

He had to know; he was always lying.

But he promised to send someone to Tsarskoye Selo to calm things down—Duma deputies.

The Duma that should have been disbanded entirely long ago, and some beheaded! Those deputies were now showing up like guardian angels for the royal family. God, how far everything had fallen! God, how twisted would all this get!

Meanwhile, the deputation from the palace guard that had been sent yesterday, according to plan, had returned from Petrograd. They had been promised that the palace would not be touched.

They just had to wear white armbands. Armbands signifying what? That this guard was not hostile to the mutinous Tsarskoye Selo troops! . . .

Well, maybe this was all for the best and would turn out peacefully. But where was the Emperor? How could the reason and the place he was detained be ascertained?

The Empress ordered an inquiry made to GHQ, by the direct line.

The most august couple had been separated for an unknown length of time—and here she was left as the sole and single superior. She knew that both her height and appearance were regal, all the manners of a natural-born sovereign. And the sullen gathering of her eyebrows expressed her full inevitable forty-six years. One ability failed her, though: to figure out and pronounce correct decisions.

They reported that the direct line between the palace and GHQ had been cut by order of the State Duma. Henceforth, such communication could go only through the Tauride Palace.

That is, through Duma eavesdroppers. Imagine! Damn them if they thought she was going to lower herself to their eavesdropping!

What did she need GHQ for now anyway, if no one knew where the Emperor was? . . .

[2 4 3]

The news that came in from Petrograd to Baltic Fleet headquarters that night and morning could not have been better: The revolution was in full swing. The Duma's presidium, led by none other than Rodzyanko, was in charge of everything, sort of like a Committee of Public Salvation. All the police precincts had been attacked! All the political prisoners had been released! Order was gradually being restored. One very sad episode on the *Aurora*, where three officers were killed, had briefly caught their attention. But the Minister of the Navy made an agreement with the Duma about guarding the Admiralty, and Rodzyanko was ordering the same for the Naval General Staff.

Alarming news had arrived in the night from Kronstadt, though, about disturbances there—although that was in the garrison's land unit.

Vice Admiral Nepenin had not slept. True to his now accepted rule—to announce everything openly to the crews—he decided that the crews should learn about the Kronstadt disturbances here in Helsingfors from the admiral himself.

At four o'clock in the morning, he ordered Cherkassky and Rengarten woken up and summoned to him. They composed the text of a brisk order for the navy to reinforce battle readiness and at the same time reported on the Petrograd news and the Kronstadt disturbances. By nine o'clock, the order had been sent.

Nepenin was very firm. Yesterday's three evening visits by Decembrists to the Commander of the Fleet had had the very best result. Nepenin had told the senior of them, Prince Cherkassky, that he would be unbending on the position he had adopted. And if the Emperor agreed to something as insane as an order removing Nepenin, for example, the admiral simply would not obey the decree!

In the present astonishing situation, it would be strange to act otherwise!

There was another reason Nepenin was so bold and audacious: at age forty-five he had experienced a second youth. Only this February, just recently, he had married the young widow of his adjutant, who had died when his cruiser blew up.

That morning Rodzyanko's two telegrams from yesterday had arrived with a delay, telegrams appealing to the troops and fleet for calm while the Committee of the State Duma restored order in the rear.

Once again Nepenin called in Cherkassky and Rengarten to read them his reply: he considered the Committee's intentions worthy and correct.

But did it sound not simply like a polite confirmation but an open statement that the Baltic Fleet had essentially endorsed the new authorities?

All the better!

At nine in the morning, the Commander assembled all the flag officers and captains in his state room on the *Krechet*. He read them the intelligence from Petrograd and Rodzyanko's telegrams. And his reply.

Then—his own telegram to the Emperor saying that he was announcing all the facts to his crews and only by such direct and truthful means did he hope to preserve the fleet's obedience and battle readiness. Moreover, he would convey to His Majesty his conviction that it was essential to meet the State Duma halfway.

Indeed, was this not sensible advice? Indeed, what other solution was there?

Cherkassky and Rengarten, standing by the wall, gazed keenly at the faces of the flag officers and captains. Their expressions were varied, but mostly impenetrable. It was impossible to tell clearly who truly accepted this and to what extent, rather than simply being forced to obey.

But the battered, thickset Nepenin was not asking for their consent. He cast a heavy gaze over them all (sensing this resistance) and pressed firmly, quietly, and very imposingly:

"I demand full obedience from you! That is all, gentlemen officers."

And not a word more. He was not suggesting they take a decision. He had taken and brought about the entire decision personally!

But the Decembrists felt that each of their nerves was living an exacerbated, separate life.

Rengarten revealed their plan to Captain First Rank Shchastny—and met with his sympathy.

Only a few hours after this meeting, details reached them from Kronstadt—terrible ones: total anarchy had been unleashed there, and Admiral Viren had been killed and thrown into the ravine near the Naval Cathedral. Also killed was Admiral Butakov. And many officers had been arrested!

What a nightmare! What a false direction for the people's uninstructed rage! What did the admirals have to do with this? Or the officers?

A curse on you, all you Protopopovs and you Hessian princesses! This is all because of you! You've brought us to this! Over the centuries.

Nepenin sent a telegraph to Rodzyanko asking that he restore order in Kronstadt. It was close to him, but inaccessible from here across the icy expanses.

Documents – 8

FROM THE PAPERS OF THE MILITARY COMMISSION

(14 March)

—They are looting Raoul's cellar on St. Isaac's Square.

—Fonarny—a pogrom. 8 in the morning.

—A reliable source tells us that several motorcars have been sent to the Win. Pal. in order to flee the latter. We request appropriate measures be taken to detain them.

Second Lieut. Pashkevich

—Corner of Zhukovskaya and Ligovskaya—attack on Soloviev's cellars. One cellar was defended, but one was smashed. Drunken soldiers going around in threes, one to stand watch—everyone drinking.

—At the corner of Kirochnaya and Voskresensky patrols asked support be sent since soldiers were looting a store.

Red Cross Detachment of the Life Jägers

—To the superintendent of the garage and storehouses of the Guards Economic Society. Drain the wine there is from the barrels in the cellars.

Chairman of the Military Commission

—Military protection needed for the Winter Palace and Hermitage. No government troops there, I myself walked through the entire palace accompanied by the commandant. The commandant himself asks for protection.

[244]

Himmer slept soundly and for a long time at a private apartment, breakfasted to last the day, and with an excellent head walked to the Tauride Palace, squinting at the diverse, red and pink—whatever people had found— bows, armbands, and ribbons on people walking separately or already lined up for a demonstration, and where were they all going? To the Tauride Palace as well.

Everything seemed marvelous, only where was General Ivanov? He could still bring down fire and destroy them.

And so, two full days of revolution had passed, the third was beginning, and no one was worried about forming a government. Imagine! In any event, Soviet circles were busy spinning vainly around current disruptive issues. But Himmer was not about to lose sight of the issue of a government or elucidate it insufficiently for his comrades. The issue of a government was one of his hobby horses, well studied beforehand, and right now his mind had a magnificent grasp of it, better than his eyes did of the city's revolutionary morning streets, still hazy at ten o'clock.

And so, over and over: it was absolutely clear that democracy, even after finding itself master of the situation in the capital, even after heading up the vanguard of the Zimmerwald-minded proletariat (Himmer felt like the concentrate of that proletariat), must not take power in this situation but rather — for the successful routing of Tsarism and the establishment of broad political freedom — it must hand over power to the franchised bourgeoisie. However, did this mean handing it over to class enemies? It had to be handed on specific terms, in order to render their enemies harmless. They had to set conditions for the bourgeoisie that would make it tame, so that it could not use its power to prevent the further unfolding and advancement of the revolution. That is, briefly, they had to *exploit* their enemies for their own purposes.

This soldier fury that would this morning probably play out even more, this reluctance to return weapons — this elemental force would come in very handy. It would weaken the bourgeoisie more surely than anything.

Meanwhile, after pushing through the Tauride Palace crush to the Soviet wing, Himmer saw Kapelinsky, who with his quick, clever, and sympathetic look informed him:

"Have you heard? The royal train was detained by railroaders at Bologoye."

"Ah, is that so? Our little tsar was caught?"

The news was superb, but Himmer did not attach too much significance to it. The question of the fading dynasty should not overshadow the question of a vital government. They had to think about who would form a government and on what terms.

Right then, next to the Soviet, the EC members' household staffs were now gathering and helping to create a recordkeeping office and bringing typewriters from other rooms of the Duma as well. Distracting Himmer from important thoughts, they wanted to slip him some papers to sort through, but right then, distracting him again, they relayed that Kerensky had been looking for him and very much wanted to see him.

In the past two days, Kerensky had become such an important figure that he couldn't make him wait, he had to go. Once again Himmer dove into the crowd, pushing through to see Kerensky in the Duma half.

Everything there was somewhat roomier and quieter. First-year cadets were standing at some of the room doors and barring access. Kerensky turned out to be in one of these defended rooms, although there were plenty of people in it anyway.

Kerensky was sitting — no, he was submerged in, no, he had fallen into — an upholstered armchair with thick armrests — had fallen so that his legs were not drawn under but rather his whole body formed a line, from his polished but worn-down high-laced shoes to the crewcut on his head, which was leaning against the back. One arm had gone missing, but the other was dangling across the armrest, showing its owner's full exhaustion, which actually his face expressed, too.

Kerensky didn't even attempt to change his pose for Sokolov, who had pushed toward him on a chair to make it easier to talk, or now for Himmer when he approached. He sensed that he would now be forgiven any pose. They would hear out his softly spoken words and lean toward him as far as required. Look, he told Himmer, as he had already told Sokolov, they're suggesting that I join the franchised cabinet being formed. A paradox! What should I do? I'd like to know your opinion, and that of the EC core in general.

This was very important! This was very serious! This truly was not an idle question; it touched on the most important thing! Himmer went and found a chair, which he freed from someone, brought it over and sat down, as Sokolov had, closer to Kerensky, as to a sick patient. Kerensky was still stretched out like a fallen stick, and his motionless arm was still dangling.

There, you see! Just three or four days ago at Sokolov's apartment, Kerensky had not found time to listen to Himmer's best theoretical insights—but he hadn't galloped off anywhere, he himself was now asking anyway. Himmer liked it very much when he was asked about a question of principle.

So here's the thing. Himmer himself was a decisive opponent of Soviet democracy taking power, and of it joining a coalition with bourgeois circles. What would the official representative of Soviet democracy be in a bourgeois-imperialist cabinet? He would be a *hostage* and would only tie revolutionary democracy's hands in carrying out its truly grandiose and essentially international objectives.

Kerensky's brow clouded even more, his gaze dulled, and he lost interest. Neither his lips nor his fingers moved. Someone who had just met him wouldn't be able to tell whether he was still hearing. But Himmer knew him well and knew he was.

He had turned elegantly now, however. Believing Kerensky could not join Milyukov's cabinet as the representative of revolutionary democracy, he found the notion of Kerensky joining it as an individual objectively of some use. As a free individual. As someone not connected formally to a single socialist faction. (Actually, Himmer, too, might have joined the cabinet with the same success, but he hadn't been asked.) In that way, Soviet circles would have an admitted leftist in the government. Kerensky wouldn't let the government go too far in its reactionary-imperialist policy. . . .

If Kerensky's languidly contemplative gaze did liven up, then only a little, only a small light nearly extinguished, in order now to have the strength to search for and call out to some other advisor, not necessarily from the EC core, and anyway, who was going to draw that line at where the core stopped?

Himmer grinned bitterly (more inwardly, to himself): Naturally, that wasn't the answer Kerensky was looking for. Naturally, Kerensky wanted to be a *minister*. But at the same time, he ambitiously (and also deliberately) wanted to retain his role as democracy's envoy in the revolution's first government.

But according to all theoretical foundations, this was totally impossible!

Himmer and Sokolov left for the Executive Committee session. They invited Kerensky along—but he didn't budge. He already considered that role unworthy for himself.

He remained immersed—languidly, elegantly, dully. Reflecting. Conjecturing.

[2 4 5 '']

(FROM THE BULLETIN OF PETROGRAD JOURNALISTS)

THE FALL OF THE ADMIRALTY

ALL political prisoners who were languishing in the Peter and Paul Fortress casemates, including nineteen soldiers, have been released.

The **PREOBRAZHENSKY REGIMENT** has gone over to the revolutionary camp, led by its entire officer complement.

. . . Yesterday there were very few officers in the revolutionary army. Today there are many. An insistent demand has been felt to organize the fighting masses, who are filled with the best aspirations. The officers have been invited to render every possible assistance in this difficult work. . . .

Citizens, organize yourselves! That is the main slogan of the moment.

IN THE EKATERININSKY HALL military ranks from different units have been formed into battalions and given arms and are taking up positions in sections of the city according to the disposition established.

THE ARREST OF A.D. PROTOPOPOV . . . A conversation between him and Kerensky took place in a separate room. We will report on its content tomorrow.

SIBERIAN REGIMENTS. Deputies from two Siberian regiments arrived at the Nikolaevsky Train Station on their way to the front, appeared at the Tauride Palace, and offered their services to the Provisional Committee. Their offer was accepted with elation.

. . . The list of old-regime underlings arrested is growing by the hour. . . . It is thought that among those arrested in the past few days there may be individuals in whose arrest the Provisional Committee of the State Duma saw no need.

An APPEAL by a group of CONSCIENTIOUS SOLDIERS . . . states that to their sorrow, certain individuals have attacked shops and destroyed premises. The group of conscientious soldiers believes that these excesses discredit the great movement for the liberation of the people. The appeal asks soldiers not to take part in attacks on stores and wine cellars and, on the contrary, to help dissuade the looters. . . .

HIS MAJESTY'S PERSONAL CONVOY HAS GONE OVER TO THE SIDE OF THE REVOLUTION! — Today a party from His Majesty's Personal Convoy appeared in the Tauride Palace. The convoy members were greeted by M. A. Karaulov, who delivered a speech of welcome to them, calling on them to join the people who had risen up to defend their interests. The Convoy members met Karaulov's speech with a thunderous "hurrah." At Deputy Karaulov's suggestion, the party headed immediately to the barracks to arrest officers who had remained loyal to the bloody regime.

THE DUBROVIN ARCHIVE. A search was conducted in the apartment of Dr. Dubrovin, the quite well-known chairman of the Union of the Russian People. All his archives and a great many files were delivered to the Tauride Palace premises.

WHERE TO DELIVER POLICEMEN

. . . There is no foundation to rumors being spread for provocative purposes that the apartments of private individuals are being searched in buildings from which no one had been shooting. . . .

MOSCOW JOINING

COSSACK REGIMENTS JOINING . . . they are prepared at any moment to stand on the side of the Provisional Committee. . . .

AT THE LAST MOMENT—OFFICIAL RECOGNITION OF THE PROVISIONAL GOVERNMENT BY ENGLAND AND FRANCE . . . The French and English ambassadors have established a working relationship with the Provisional Committee of the State Duma, which expresses the true will of the people and is Russia's sole legitimate provisional government.

[2 4 6]

GHQ had not cut the connection between rebellious Petrograd and the field army—and in the Western Army Group all night and morning hundreds of telegraph operators, railroad workers, and soldiers had been catching the stream of insurrectionist communiqués and proclamations and passing them on officially and unofficially—and the rebel incendiarism had overflowed and spilled out.

But in addition to the anonymous upstarts, the famous Rodzyanko, who had cast off all restraint regarding all of Russia, kept sending his own telegrams as well—into the ether, basically, to no one or to the inhabitants, and then again directly to the army group commanders-in-chief, as if he were an office standing over them—and informed them of the seizure of power by his committee and was already beginning to instruct the army in what to do.

How could all this be? How dare he absent the Emperor's will? And why wasn't GHQ pulling Rodzyanko up sharp? Fine, they could ignore Bublikov, and they could ignore Grekov—but Rodzyanko? After all, he did hold a governmental post!

But GHQ—all morning it had remained silent, as if it knew nothing about the self-appointed government in the capital.

Between ten and eleven in the morning, General Evert himself sat down to the telegraph, identified himself, and summoned Lukomsky. Given his position and their equal rights and because they were the same age, both sixty, he might have summoned Alekseev as well, but he didn't, inasmuch as Alekseev right now was acting for the Supreme Commander. Evert thought that Alekseev might come himself anyway.

However, not only did Alekseev not come, even Lukomsky forced him to wait. Evert's patience snapped, and he sent Kvetsinsky in his place. Later he himself showed up. He cited the numbers of Rodzyanko's two telegrams. GHQ must have received them, too, right?

"At first I thought I wouldn't answer at all. But that might make it seem as though I had accepted them for the record or, even worse, for implementation. Therefore, I think, it is better to reply: The army has sworn an oath to its Emperor and homeland. Its duty is to carry out the wishes of its Supreme leader and to defend the homeland. I would like to know the opinion of Mikhail Vasilievich. Difficult moments require our complete and shared solidarity."

With his large, heavy body, and his decisiveness, and his heavy words, he seemed, from his end of the line, to outweigh all of GHQ, including little Alekseev and Lukomsky. He could not have asked more clearly, directly, and even rudely: Does the Supreme Commander's chief of staff deem it essential to keep the *oath* he gave to the Emperor?

Lukomsky did not go to ask Alekseev but rather decided to answer extensively himself:

"Yes, Adjutant General Alekseev"—he did not say Mikhail Vasilievich!—"today did receive one telegram from Rodzyanko, and its intent was for the army not to get mixed up in the matter for now. General Alekseev wanted to answer that such telegrams bore an absolutely inadmissible attitude toward the army and that it was essential that the sending of such telegrams cease."

Well, good, at least Alekseev had done well and not lost his reason. A rather dense, squinty little man, but he was not going to give in.

"However," Lukomsky continued, "Alekseev has not yet sent this telegram."
And why was that?

". . . He first wanted to clarify whether the Emperor and General Ivanov
had arrived at Tsarskoye Selo."

What did one have to do with the other? He was mixing apples and oranges.

". . . And we haven't been able to get this information up until the present time because by Duma instruction we cannot get a direct line to Tsarskoye Selo."

What? That was out and out mutiny! From civvies? Evert's huge fists
clenched. How could Alekseev put up with this?

Evidently, there was something else. Something else they were not explaining. Or was it the Emperor's vulnerability so close to Petrograd? He
wondered.

". . . Yesterday General Alekseev sent a telegram to Adjutant General
Ivanov about the calm that had descended at that moment in Petrograd,
and he asked him to report to the Emperor that it would be desirable to
avoid the use of open force."

Calm? . . . What about Bublikov and Grekov? Had it cost them their
heads? What about the detaining of military trains? And Rodzyanko's illegal
regime replacing the legitimate government? There was something here
that Evert either didn't know or didn't understand.

Meanwhile, Lukomsky added that disturbances had begun in Moscow
and Kronstadt.

Then all the more necessary to act! What was there to discuss? Your oath!

But Lukomsky further added that General Alekseev had signed a
telegram to His Majesty requesting that he issue an act on pacifying the
population. For now, though, in the absence of communication . . .

Well, perhaps. . . . There was something Evert hadn't grasped.

". . . I will now report your suggestion about Rodzyanko's reply to General Alekseev, who, unfortunately, is feeling unwell."

Well now, he'd remained alone at GHQ—and had broken down.

Pacifying? . . . Doubtless correct.

Evert explained that his proposed reply to Rodzyanko also bore in mind
the need for rapid pacification.

It would be desirable to receive this telegram as well·about the calm that
had been achieved in Petrograd.

He wished Alekseev a speedy recovery.

He stepped away from the telegraph, not very bright, dismayed, understanding less than he'd known before the conversation.

The main thing, of course, was to maintain order.

But what was he to do with this stream of Petrograd telegrams? Hide
them from the population of Minsk? Or, again, for purposes of pacification,
publish them?

He hadn't thought to ask.

Only after two hours was Evert relayed Alekseev's telegram to Ivanov, no. 1833, which had been sent at one o'clock that morning.

Evert began reading—and was even more astounded. It spoke of *total calm*, which had set in in Petrograd, where there had just been anarchic hell (in the past few hours it had been confirmed by officers returned to Minsk from leave). It also referred to some other appeal by the Rodzyanko committee about the inviolable monarchic principle in Russia. But no matter how much Evert looked through the dispatches received and ordered Kvetsinsky to search—nowhere did they find even the shadow of such an appeal. Might it have bypassed Minsk?

Had Alekseev been misled?

Or maybe it was better not to argue with the State Duma?

No, there was something here the discouraged Evert definitely did not understand. And he had no clear instructions from his superiors.

Correctly had it always been said: politics is not the army's business.

A soldier-general cannot implement his own policy.

[2 4 7]

Palace Commandant Voeikov felt he was a very complete individual, sufficient unto himself: filled with his own personal successes, structure, buildings, millions (recently he had profitably sold the Kuvaka mineral spring in Penza Province), and always exceptionally sure of his own opinion. Due to the elderly infirmity of his father-in-law, Count Frederiks, Voeikov had become the principal figure in the suite, and he did not let a minute pass without making sure all the others felt that. Now even the most intimate members of the suite traveling on the A letter train, awakening and seeing through the incoming sun the train's odd direction, were asking Voeikov as he passed through the corridor and getting an enigmatic and irritated reply: "Don't ask questions."

The locale passing by outside was quite unknown; they had not seen the like on any of their regular journeys. This novelty now alarmed the suite even more. Right then they learned from Grabbe that they were taking a roundabout route to Dno, in order to go from there to Tsarskoye Selo on the direct Mogilev line. They also learned from the railroaders accompanying them that the locomotive brigade had refused to be replaced at Bologoye, in order not to detain the Tsar, but had undertaken to get him as far as Dno. They were traveling along a line that was not prepared to let imperial trains through, even more slowly than usual, and the stations themselves learned of them practically on the final stretch. This kind of uncoordinated movement threatened delays even more. The suite whispered about the inevitability of concessions. Would the Emperor really not agree to a responsible ministry? What would that cost him? "Otherwise," Admiral Nilov said, "we are all going to be hanging from the lampposts."

Voeikov, wearing his greatcoat, jumped down at every station, an imposing, decisive figure. At Valdai he was brought a telegram from Rodzyanko
and made to sign for a telegraph reply.

After reading the telegram, Voeikov hopped onto the train, and once
again, telling no one in the suite, he went to awaken the Emperor.

But the Emperor, who had not slept for a long time after Malaya Vishera,
had dozed heavily through the next few hours and slept through the turn at
Bologoye.

It took him a few moments to recall everything.

He came out to see Voeikov wearing his robe.

Nor could he immediately clarify for himself the meaning of the telegram he was handed. From Rodzyanko? Requesting an audience?

Somehow his thoughts had not been about the possibility of a direct and
imminent conversation with Rodzyanko. After his last, hostile, February
audience, when the fatman had arrogantly attempted to school his own
Emperor—and now he was to meet with him again?

But the Duma had been dispersed the day before yesterday. There was
no Duma.

There was no Duma, but there was Rodzyanko. His very solid, imposing
figure naturally towered over a Petrograd engulfed in rebellions. Not only
that, had he created a self-appointed committee there, a virtual government? Had he practically taken over governmental authority? But the situation had changed so that—why not? Yes, perhaps best to receive him.

It's even good that he was asking. This was even a solution.

Yes, we must set things aright somehow. All but the most important ministries—war, interior, and foreign affairs—can be conceded to them, if they
like. Indeed, why be so unyielding? When everyone on all sides decidedly
wants the same thing, it begins to weigh.

The imperial government did not now exist materially, so this was the
natural moment to replace it.

"Fine, summon Rodzyanko."—Where? "To Dno. I agree to receive him
there."

And Voeikov sent off the consent.

They rode on, toward Staraya Russa.

And at that moment doubt began to fill the Emperor, doubt that he had
agreed too readily—right off the mark, immediately upon waking. He had
so easily agreed—and now in a few hours he was going to meet with
Rodzyanko before he saw Alix? What would she say? How would she view
him making this kind of concession without her advice?

But there was a solution: speak with him firmly.

Oh, Lord, on days like these—to be separated from Alix!

How could he keep from making a mistake now?

Nikolai anxiously fingered the chain around his neck—the small icon
chain hung by his wife.

Here he was suffering so, but was she not suffering as well? What was it like for her there now, so near to the raging capital?

On his confused route, Alix had not been able to find him with any telegram.

My God, how badly his heart ached, how his heart was breaking after this unfortunate turn at Vishera, which had lengthened the journey.

Although no, the Lord would not permit this. Ivanov was already there and she was under his protection.

But the train was chugging far from quickly down this quiet, little-traveled line. All the officials—the gendarmes and guard—were in place and once again he was beginning to find it hard to believe in the danger. His hopes deepened that everything would work out and by nightfall today he would reach the peaceful circle of his beloved family.

Because the route had gone wrong, the Emperor had not received any telegrams whatsoever today from GHQ. Even yesterday, there had not been many of them. He realized that there was a revolt in Petrograd but nothing about its essence, in detail.

What had seemed to Nikolai a benefaction at the beginning of their journey—the absence of communications with headquarters bringing ominous dispatches—now was a wrenching lack. His family was in acute danger, and he had no right to learn all this so late and uselessly.

He did not stretch his legs at the stops. He looked out the train car window. As they were moving he attempted to read but couldn't get in the mood.

The time had come for the shared breakfast. They tossed the most insignificant comments back and forth and tried to make jokes about Mordvinov. But even the most restrained faces could not conceal their alarm, and an entreaty to the Emperor emanated mutely from everyone: concede. He could sense their entreaty.

Soon after breakfast they arrived in Staraya Russa. There was a crowd on the platform, including many nuns. The people removed their caps in the freezing cold and bowed to the dark blue train cars with the eagles.

Here Voeikov received and immediately brought three telegrams—all of them via GHQ, but not a single one directly from Alekseev. For some reason the chief of staff himself had nothing to report to his Supreme Commander. All three telegrams were not about the main thing, not about Petrograd directly, as if their vision had been disturbed and the main patch had blurred.

Ruzsky reported to GHQ about the interruption in any communication between Petrograd and Finland, as a result of which he had authorized the corps commander there to take charge of all land troops from the Finnish isthmus.

Minister of the Navy Grigorovich, having no direct connection with His Majesty, had reported to GHQ that he had received a telegram from the Kronstadt commandant about the onset of disturbances yesterday evening.

And finally, the head of the Supreme Commander's naval headquarters had relayed a telegram from the commander of the Baltic Fleet saying that as of four o'clock this morning all communication had been cut off with Kronstadt, where the port commander had been killed and officers arrested.

The main section evaded the eye, but even what there was along its edges turned the heart cold.

The Emperor was receiving so much confused information, and by such a circuitous route!

The more of it he received, the less he understood what was happening. And Alekseev, for some reason, had not provided a clear summary.

[2 4 8]

General Alekseev was not feeling at all well, worse than yesterday. But he had had no rest tonight, either. It was these cares that were making him ill.

In his sleepless nighttime tossing and turning, he had come to see even more clearly how salutary it would be if the Emperor were to recognize the Rodzyanko committee as a responsible ministry. Everything would calm down immediately, without conflict, and the army would prepare patiently and without obstacles for the offensive. All that remained was to convince the Emperor.

And the morning's telegrams added even more. A telegram came from Mrozovsky in Moscow saying that as of yesterday the factories were on strike, the workers were demonstrating and disarming policemen, and crowds were gathering—and they couldn't remain silent about the Petrograd events.

They should hasten to explain about them all the more since Petrograd was calming down! The night reports from the Naval General Staff confirmed that order was gradually being restored in Petrograd and the troops were obeying the Duma more and more; however, decisive actions by the government were essential in order to satisfy public opinion and in this way counter the revolutionaries' propaganda.

Admiral Grigorovich, who was just as ill as Alekseev, having no communication with Tsarskoye Selo, in order to report directly to the arriving Emperor, relayed via Alekseev the telegram from the Kronstadt commandant about how since yesterday evening the Kronstadt garrison had been agitated and there was no one to pacify it and there wasn't a single reliable unit.

It had all come together! Both because calm was beginning to show in Petrograd, and because disturbances were arising in Moscow and Kronstadt, society needed the Emperor's concession! Alekseev increasingly felt the burden of convincing him, all the more so because on his journey the Emperor hadn't had a great deal of information.

Without even drinking his tea, Alekseev began his early morning by composing a persuasive telegram to the Emperor so that it would arrive soon after his arrival in Tsarskoye Selo and immediately provide the correct orientation. He quoted Mrozovsky's alarming telegram in full. He warned that the disturbances would undoubtedly spread from Moscow to other centers of Russia. Then the railroads would be completely disrupted, the army would be ruinously left without supplies, and then disturbances were possible in the army itself.

Thus link after link was connecting inexorably, and Alekseev could clearly see — and wrote — that revolution would be inevitable in Russia, and this would mean a disgraceful conclusion to the war, with all its onerous consequences. The army cannot be asked to fight calmly when a revolution is under way in the rear, especially given the young officer component, with its large percentage of university students. Would they lead their units in such a clash? Before that — wouldn't the army itself be drawn to the upheavals?

This is what Alekseev wrote in his extensive telegram: "My most loyal duty and the duty of my oath obligate me to report all this to Your Imperial Majesty." Before it's too late, take measures to pacify the population. Putting down the disturbances by force would lead both Russia and the army to ruin. You must hasten to support the Duma against radical elements. For the sake of the salvation of Russia and the dynasty, put an individual whom Russia can trust at the head of the government. Herein lies the sole possible salvation. Other advice you have been given will lead Russia to ruin and disgrace and create a danger for the dynasty.

It had been a long time since Alekseev had composed a single letter so persuasively. He experienced great emotional relief once he had written it.

Now to send it immediately. There was no direct connection to Tsarskoye Selo, but he could relay it through the General Staff; no one in Petrograd would detain a telegram like *this*.

It was relayed. And General Alekseev drank his tea and felt restored. Right then a wild, random telegram arrived, for some reason from Novosokolniki, saying that the imperial letter trains had turned from Bologoye toward Dno and had just passed through Valdai.

What was this? Why was this?

Nothing made sense. And the Emperor had sent no reports either from Bologoye or from Valdai. Where was he going? To what end? . . .

But before an hour had passed, an intercepted telegram was brought to GHQ from that same famous Bublikov, a telegram sent to all the stations on the Vindava rail line, saying that two freight trains were to block the siding to the east of the Dno station and make movement impossible for any trains — that is, the imperial trains, undoubtedly.

It was signed: Commissar of the State Duma Committee, State Duma Deputy . . .

The State Duma was mutinously stopping imperial trains? . . .

Rodzyanko? . . .

Oh, had he been wrong to listen to Kislyakov yesterday?

Just then, to heated doubt, Evert summoned GHQ to a direct line. Due to his illness, Alekseev was not coming to the telegraph, and did not go now, as he expected nothing important from Evert — but there was something important. Lukomsky brought an unpleasant tape. Within the limits of generals' permissible etiquette, he—what was this?—he doubted Alekseev's loyalty to his oath?

Outrageous! It was specifically moved by the duty of his oath that Alekseev had given the Emperor his best advice.

Why should he pay any attention to Evert anyway? Evert would have done better not to have backed down from leading the offensive in 1916. As someone who had received insufficient general education and in the crude directness of the military milieu, Evert thought that the simplest thing would be to put down the disturbances by military force. And here he had hastily insulted Rodzyanko.

Just an hour before, Alekseev would have paid no attention to Evert. But now he had to, after this horribly impudent attempt by Bublikov to stop the Tsar—and all in the name of the State Duma?

Both that which turned out to have been vaguely maturing in Alekseev during the night and had kept him from sleeping—had he not given way to Rodzyanko yesterday excessively? had he yielded too much?—and those drafts of a telegram to him that Alekseev had been planning with a hesitant pencil since early morning now were given a nudge by Evert's reproach.

Although Alekseev did not suspect this extremity of mood in his four other commanders-in-chief, Evert's lashing out had exposed GHQ's back and deprived it of its buttress to speak for the whole army.

Yes! Yes! It was becoming clear. Rodzyanko had to be taken down a peg. Without openly damaging the still fragile Duma Committee. But rather Rodzyanko personally, who had gotten carried away.

Alekseev began to put his draft into a telegram, driving on in his tiny, energetic handwriting.

The highest military ranks and the entire army were carrying out their sacred duty to the Tsar and homeland in accordance with their *oath*, he reminded the Samovar. The army had to be walled off from any influence alien to that oath—thus he repeated the sensitive word. Meanwhile, your telegrams to me and the commanders-in-chief and the instructions issued for the railroads in the theater of military operations . . . The Duma Committee has not reckoned with the primer for administering military forces—and could lead to irreparable consequences. . . . The disruption in communication between GHQ and Tsarskoye Selo . . . And the central organs of military administration . . . The imperial letter trains are not being allowed through to Dno. . . . I request immediate instruction to allow the letter trains. . . . No one other than GHQ may have any communications with officers of the armed forces in the field. . . . And GHQ's communications may not be controlled by your lower ranks. . . . Otherwise I will be compelled . . .

The stream of rebukes came easily; it was true. But where was the convincing military argument, the argument that would decisively establish the proper balance? Alekseev could not threaten the newborn popular freedom and beginnings of calm by applying crude military force. He could be personally angry at Rodzyanko, but not so as to undermine his authority, which alone was saving the capital right now.

All he could do was end on a weak note, saying that this would lead to the destruction of the army's food supply and its starvation. Let Rodzyanko himself judge the consequences of the army starving.

He had nothing to threaten him with, it turned out. The army starving.

It wasn't a druggist's weights he described, but rather the iron platforms on which shipments of rye are weighed—an irrevocable and irresistible power.

He sent this telegram. More to cleanse his soul and to let Rodzyanko's pride settle. But his decision—to seek universal reconciliation, the only sensible solution—could not change.

The question of the troops that had been sent hung more and more implacably, though. What should be done with them? As Alekseev sensibly saw, he didn't dare stop them by his own decision. But he couldn't put off a decision either because the troops were converging, advancing, and there could be an irremediable clash at any moment. But no outside event had come to his rescue. The Emperor was traveling on farther, and he was increasingly elusive when it came to giving advice, including for the very persuasive morning telegram Alekseev had sent.

Alekseev ordered a call to Pskov to inquire about the imperial trains; they were closer there. But Pskov reported that order had not been restored in Petrograd and the garrisons of Oranienbaum, Strelna, and Peterhof had joined the rebels. The arrests were continuing. A mass of roaming lower ranks was loitering around Petrograd, many officers had been killed on the streets, and epaulets had been ripped off officers' shoulders. There were many smashed stores.

Things were taking another new turn . . . What a contradiction to Rodzyanko! Who was he to believe? The *total calm* was starting to look spectral. Alekseev had a splitting headache and was not happy he had found this out.

Meanwhile, yesterday's reassuring no. 1833 to Ivanov had been promised to Evert and he couldn't not send it now, even though doing so seemed clumsy. (Ivanov himself had not caught up to this telegram yet!)

But how was all this to be reconciled?

Now that he had chosen an action, though, he had to follow through on it. Send no. 1833 to all army groups.

From the Caucasus they reported that all was calm.

From Evert, that they were continuing to send troops.

And what from the Southwest? . . . This might be the simplest of all. Insofar as they had not yet begun to send troops, then perhaps they shouldn't move yet?

That wouldn't be a halting of troops.

[2 4 9]

*   *   *

Since early morning—Petersburg haze. Foggy and damp. And cold, nine below zero.

Notices to citizens pasted up around town: Surrender your weapons! But no punishment for not surrendering them.

*   *   *

The incinerated District Court: a high plinth topped by two tall stories, long and fronting on both Shpalernaya and Liteiny. All its windows empty, and scorch marks where the fire broke through. And inside, on the white walls, streaks of smoky soot. Only on the curve had the window not fallen out—it was trompe l'oeuil. In many places the noble Bazhenov relief was preserved.

*   *   *

Disorderly gunfire began throughout the city again early. Mostly people were firing at the roofs. "Copper-spotting"—everyone was looking at the roofs and pointing. There the bullets were raising plaster dust, and the ricocheting bullets looked like gunfire from the attics.

"Look for that window! The one they're shooting from."

People crowded around and leaned their heads back.

"How can you tell if the windows're on the seventh floor?"

"I guessed and so can you."

"How's that?"

"Just look: the glass is whole in all the windows, but there's no shine in that one, so you know it's been taken out."

Or broken out already.

A rumor that policemen were shooting from St. Isaac's Cathedral.

*   *   *

A crowd of adolescents and a few adults with them were leading an arrested policeman in uniform down the street, a giant of a man, a bloody mask where his face had been. Little boys were pulling, pushing, pinching, and spitting at him as he went. He was walking without swaying.

They led him into a yard and a few gunshots rang out.

*   *   *

An assistant police officer who'd been arrested yesterday lived in a particular building. Even today from time to time people would come up and shoot at his windows. But there were other apartments in the building, too.

"That's what freedom's for. I shoot wherever I want."

*　　*　　*

Crowds were gathering in solid, greedy bunches—common folk, girls in kerchiefs, and peaked caps, and bowlers, and a lady in a ship-shaped hat. Read something pasted on the wall—no, listen to the loud reader up front.

"Aha!" The public was extremely glad at Protopopov's arrest.

When it was read out that the Minister of Justice had at first hidden at the Italian Embassy:

"Ah! He wanted some macaroni!"

About the appearance of His Majesty's Convoy:

"They got fat on roast goose and piglets at the Tsar's expense, and now . . ."

*　　*　　*

The day was brightening, turning white, and a white sky. And warming up. Over the Winter Palace, instead of the imperial standard—a red flag.

*　　*　　*

Going down the Fontanka: a platform truck and badly beaten police officers sitting and standing on it, surrounded by civilians with red armbands.

Angry shouts from the crowd:

"Where are you taking them? Crush the vipers right where they are! Line 'em up and one bullet from a nasty rifle!"

*　　*　　*

A servant: "Oh, why do they keep shouting Down with the monkary? Does that mean they want to drive out all the monks?"

*　　*　　*

On Nevsky, fewer vehicles than yesterday, but more and more pedestrians and cheeky soldiers flocking down the middle of the street, festively. Again everyone wearing red: bows, ribbons fitted tightly around cockades, on epaulets, around greatcoat buttons, on St. George Crosses, on medals, on bayonet tips, and on young ladies' muffs or chests, sewn on flirtatiously. Not all out of red bunting; some out of silk.

University-student militia appeared at intersections, confiscated officer swords strapped on, with white armbands and the initials CM ("City Militia").

Indignant voices:

"What's this, we've come around to police again? There's freedom for you!"

But red armbands were more effective than white. Red ones were obeyed.

*　　*　　*

More crowding near the Tauride Palace. On Shpalernaya, lots of curious intellectuals. And again some troops on their way to the Duma, others leaving the Duma, everything getting mixed up. Pandemonium. People were saying that the Petrograd gendarme division had arrived to the Marseillaise. Vehicles were honking and sputtering—they had no way through. One truck drove onto the sidewalk and did get through.

*　　*　　*

Coming from Vladimirsky Prospect and crossing Nevsky was the Izmailovsky Battalion. Red ribbons attached to the old battle flag with the regalia of the last century. A band. The crowd flowing toward them, beside themselves with delight:

"Thank you, Izmailovsky men! Long live freedom!"

And the officers, with their red bows, proceeding concentrated and pensive. Saluting back at the crowd.

*　　*　　*

Noncombatant members of His Majesty's Convoy, wearing their short undercoats, without epaulets, so you couldn't tell the unit, left their barracks on Shpalernaya and roamed through the city. One of them was picked up and driven around in a motorcar for a long time in the first row and greeted everywhere as a Cossack. At the corner of Nevsky and Vladimirsky they made him give a speech. All he could think to say was: "Long live the Terek and Kuban host! Hurrah!" And everyone shouted "hurrah" and waved their caps. They drove him farther and fed him at a feeding station.

*　　*　　*

Sailors were marching in a column and with music. Suddenly—gunfire off to the side, where from they couldn't tell. They immediately began falling down, running around the corner, and hopping fences, leaving only their rifles and sailor caps in the snow.

*　　*　　*

At Spaso-Preobrazhenskaya Square, State Duma Deputy Rodichev was holding forth to Semyonovsky soldiers from the top of an oats bin. All of a sudden—machine-gun fire, where from they couldn't tell! Everyone dropped to the ground. No one was hit.

But the thought occurred among the soldiers that they'd been purposely led into this fire.

*　　*　　*

In the crowd, along the sidewalks, many joyous, trusting faces gazing at the troops. A wealthy gentleman at the edge of the pavement kept ripping off his cap, a gray Kamchatka beaver, and twirling it in the air, shouting greetings to the passing demonstrations.

* * *

People also fled the insane asylum.

* * *

A day of wholesale searches was blazing throughout Petrograd. They would break into a building and go to all the apartments in order.
Looting began at the Imperial Porcelain Factory as well.

* * *

A red flag had been attached to the monument to Aleksandr III. It held on.

* * *

Yevgeni Tsezarevich Cavos, approaching Petrograd on the Moscow train, laughed hard at his companion's story, imagining the scenes of the ministers' arrest. But the train halted well before reaching the station. And Cavos agonized over how he was going to drag his several suitcases, and with his unaccustomed hands. You couldn't lift them, you see.—"No, I don't like this. I'm ready to start shouting, Long live Nikolai II!" It was true, it took him and all his things two full days to make it home through the city.

* * *

There were already many ruined and even overturned vehicles on the Petrograd streets. But quite a few people were riding around, on platform trucks—dangling their legs like from a wagon. They were also riding in rich motorcars: there were rifles and tall fur hats behind the fringe of luxurious curtains.
Horsemen were prancing through the streets, and on performing horses, too. The horses were from the Ciniselli Circus. The circus stables had been looted.

* * *

A stray bullet from the Field of Mars killed the artist Ivan Dolmatov—who nine years ago had received honors for his painting, "The Triumph of Destruction"—in his apartment.

[2 5 0]

Petersburg side commissar Peshekhonov had posted not only leaflets throughout the Petersburg side but also a notice in *Izvestia of the Soviet of Workers' Deputies* about the creation of his commissariat at the Elite movie house and had asked the population (without adding "most humbly") to observe calm during the unfolding events in the name of the great cause. Trust the commissars appointed by the new government. Carry out their instructions as well as the duties essential for the population. And send representatives from the plants and factories, one man for every five hundred.

The Romanov empire had stood for three hundred years, and its official-dom had ready-made, developed organizational forms and methods. Here he had to begin, in one day, on a blank slate, in as yet unknown forms, with as yet unfound methods, and with as yet unformulated objectives. Neither Peshe-khonov himself nor his colleagues in the commissariat—that is, the former police unit—could imagine and propose what exactly their activities would be.

By crossing the Neva, he had left the Tauride Palace for what seemed like another country, where he was left to decide governmental issues—and he himself was lost from the Tauride Palace's view as if into a dark abyss. They appointed him and thought of him no more.

Peshekhonov's life dream had been the *people's will*, in both meanings of that great phrase: the people's freedom and the people's rule. And he was brimming with happiness that not only had he lived to see this freedom and this rule embodied in Russia, but now he would personally be participating in instituting this freedom, if only in a small corner.

To his summons the people's response was a hundredfold what the commissariat could handle. One peep from this bridgehead—and in fifteen minutes people were thronging to it. Entire crowds had been clustering around it today since early morning.

Some had shown up to give support and aid. The commissariat's randomly designated sections were immediately overflowing with volunteer colleagues, and at first glance wholly unselfish ones. Intellectuals predominated, but there were other callings as well: there was a Georgian wearing the uniform of a military medic, while a detachment of Boy Scouts, for example, had volunteered for driver duty.

There were even more helpers of another inclination, who had not signed up as colleagues but without warning and at their own initiative had carried out searches, requisitions, and arrests everywhere—and then triumphantly carried and driven their seized trophies and led their prisoners to the commissariat.

Fortunately, Peshekhonov, having noticed back at the Tauride Palace how many prisoners they were bringing in, had foreseen this phenomenon and immediately appointed a "judicial commission" as part of the commissariat. Sometimes a whole crowd would bring the prisoners—but then the crowd would immediately disperse and five minutes later there was no one to find out from or ask on what basis this individual had been detained. They might include the most dangerous criminals but also the most innocent people. What were they to do with them now? The judicial commission had to free some, write up others, and list witnesses.

But no commission was ever formed. By the time the first notice about the commissariat had been affixed to the wall, they had already brought in three prisoners, and Peshekhonov himself had to sort them out. Two turned out to be policemen who had removed their uniforms but been identified. Peshekhonov considered it absolutely pointless to arrest former policemen — and decided to free them after getting their signature that they would not under any circumstance carry out their former superiors' orders and would immediately surrender whatever weapons they still had. The third prisoner was accused by the crowd of expressing his condemnation of the revolution. They ascribed some phrase to him, and he himself, pale, denied having said it. Inwardly, Peshekhonov was filled with trembling and indignation. Rejecting the revolution was the right of every person, otherwise, what kind of freedom would it be? *This man* had to be released immediately!

But it wasn't all that simple! The crowd was pressing in and waiting for the commissar to impose a harsh sentence. "Not guilty" decisions would produce the most unfavorable impression. And so, in order to free them, all three in a row, Peshekhonov had to take an intentionally harsh tone with the accused, and harshly curse the old regime, and express the cruelest threats to those who dared oppose the revolution! — and only in this way maintain his authority with the crowd as a revolutionary figure; otherwise he himself could be suspected of counterrevolution.

Commissar Peshekhonov had declared his authority, and no one seemed to dispute it. But quickly, in an hour or two, he realized, even more distinctly than he had at the Tauride Palace, that no one was an authority in Petrograd right now — not a commissar, not the Soviet of Deputies, and especially not the Duma Committee. The fullness of authority belonged to the crowd. Its authority was taking the law into its own hands, and the crowd itself and everyone understood that this was genuine popular rule.

Peshekhonov could not accept this, though! On the contrary, from the very first hour of the very first day he had had to exert himself over how to mitigate this taking the law into their own hands and how to defend individuals from manifestations of popular rule!

But they kept bringing in prisoners — so to relieve the commissariat, the entire judicial commission had to be moved to another building, nearby on Arkhiereiskaya, where they also created their own lockup in one big room. Five lawyers were assembled there to work, then ten, then twenty in two shifts — and nonetheless, they could barely cope.

An epidemic or bacchanalia of arrests had befallen them — and today of all days! The revolution seemed to be rolling toward its ruin. It would end with all the citizens arresting one another! And Rodzyanko stood at the center of the commotion. His name was heard everywhere, he was signing decrees, he was appointing commissars to ministries, he was telling troops to return to barracks and obey their officers. Strife roiled in people's minds around Rodzyanko's name; strife and arguments ignited on the streets—to the point of fights and arrests—and whichever side proved the stronger dragged the weaker in for arrest. They kept dragging in prisoners to the judicial commission, and when asked "what for?" they replied:

"He's against Rodzyanko!"—

and the next:

"He's for Rodzyanko!"

Right then people ran in to tell them about the apartment of a well-known Black Hundreds supporter, a woman by the name of Poluboyarinova, on Pesochnaya Street, saying that Black Hundreds were thronging there!

A detail was assembled and sent to arrest them—but the couple had gone into hiding and the apartment was empty.

The commissariat had relieved itself of new prisoners, but its rooms were anything but spacious. The Petersburg side and islands had 300,000 inhabitants, and it seemed like a third of them were trying to find their way to the commissariat.

Thanks to an alert ensign, a guard was posted at the commissariat's doors, and entry was to be only by pass. A pass was issued to anyone who declared his need to enter, but this was meant to avert an invasion by entire crowds and especially vagrants. They got it wrong, though, and didn't notice that the table for issuing passes suddenly was such that you couldn't get to it without a pass. They didn't notice right away because somehow people had all managed to get passes and everyone was coming with passes. Then they posted two armed sentries: one in front of the tables where they were issuing passes, so the crowd wouldn't overturn them; and the second sentry right at the entrance itself. (It would have been good to put up railings, but first they had to be found, and they were bound to get broken.)

His comrades wanted to set up a corner for Peshekhonov in the very farthest upper part of the movie house, behind a series of barriers—but the crowd still pushed in there, and by his nature, Peshekhonov couldn't sit there like that anyway. He longed for the crowd, the crush. How could he be there and supervise the activities of the section and what they were doing? If anything? Peshekhonov was now surrounded all day until the evening and squeezed by a demanding crowd. His look wasn't revolutionarily menacing, or lordly, or educated, and he was of absolutely average height and appearance, like a petty bourgeois or a scrawny merchant, his head cropped by clippers, his mustache drooping and tangled with his beard, and obliging to all. So all day he listened, swiveling in every direction, several people talking to him at once, while others tugged at his jacket to draw his attention, and others tugged him to where he needed to go and give orders. Over the course of the day he never once sat down and had a glass of tea.

Perhaps this all could have been set up better, but Peshekhonov had never been an organizer and had not trained to become an administrator, and he knew his own lack of resourcefulness, which he was especially sensible of in this situation. Had they let him think and consider, he would have set it all up better. But everything had flooded in at once, and he had had to act immediately. And whether he himself had decided everything and given orders or everything had been decided and given orders itself could not be ascertained. But apparently things were decided in a way he agreed with, and together with the people.

Fervent volunteer informers pestered him on all sides, some out of vindictiveness and some out of malice, settling scores. One dragged him aside and whispered that some priest had given a counterrevolutionary sermon. Another slipped him a denunciation saying that at some institution someone had assembled a few employees in a room, closed the door, and had what was surely a counterrevolutionary meeting with them. Everyone who hadn't managed to participate in the revolution at the beginning wanted to find a place in it at least now and capture at least one enemy. This is what it sounded like:

"First it was *their* will, and they put us in the lockup, but now it's our will and we're putting them in . . ."

They were prepared to attack practically anyone as a spy. They imagined a hidden machine gun in practically every apartment building.

Peshekhonov stuck the denunciations in his pocket. (In the evening he threw them out; he had a whole stack.)

But most of all they reported about stores of food in apartment buildings and apartments (all stores were labeled speculator's, based on the most fantastic features), they foisted on him lists of the apartments and individuals who had the stores, or they offered to ask the servant, who would know and show them. Anything having to do with food was cause for special aggravation, and now they were rectifying the past in whatever way they understood, but many evidently were counting on—and often succeeding at—profiting off the requisition themselves. The remainder they brought to the commissariat—and then they had to figure out where and how to keep, protect, and distribute it. They started dumping the stores in the commissariat itself, and this included alcoholic beverages (the crowd was especially eager to seek out and requisition wine specifically)—and in such an accessible place! He could not rely on the public or the soldiers themselves who had been posted as guards. Peshekhonov immediately sent several deliveries of wine to the neighboring Peter and Paul Hospital, counting on people not trying to storm that. They had to create a food section, to which they appointed some random activist (who later turned out to be a scoundrel).

Armed men zigged and zagged through the streets, having obtained rifles no one knew where.

People ran to the commissariat to complain about the illegal searches and the destruction of apartments that had begun: "Come defend us! Protect us!"

And they would send someone.

Their own soldiers were melting away. They had to find assistance some-where. Peshekhonov's assistants headed off for the feeding stations to seek help among the soldiers fed there.

Then a wandering, unarmed soldier pushed in and asked for a rifle or gun.

His look was suspicious, and they told him they didn't have any.

"But maybe after all?" he begged peacefully. "What's a soldier supposed to do without a rifle?"

"There aren't any rifles."

"But go off empty-handed, and a copper'll shoot from the roof. Maybe just a gun then."

"There's no gun either."

"Well, there's three of us here," the soldier hesitated, trying to be clever. "Maybe one for three. They could kill you at any corner. Or"—he wa-vered—"if you have to do a search, how can you without a weapon?"

"Comrade, don't hold things up. There aren't any."

Yes! But what about the Okhrana? Yesterday they'd told Peshekhonov that it had burned down, and that calmed him. But it was in his district and he had to check. Some ensign showed up and reported that there were docu-ments left in the Okhrana and the public was carrying them off piece by piece. Peshekhonov immediately appointed this ensign commandant of the Okhrana and told him to post a guard, in case papers had survived. The en-sign went there, posted the guard, and brought back sample documents with lists of secret collaborators. This was astonishing! And a treasure like that had nearly been lost! (The ensign had had the smart idea of entering into rela-tions with Gorky, who would then set about sorting through the archive.)

Right then there was another attack on the commissariat. A high school pupil about sixteen years old, red as fire, bug eyes, and a crazed face, and with him a few civilians, not all of them older than he, and such a press that they immediately broke through the first guards and were already breaking through the next. Peshekhonov came out to meet them. What was this?

Some scoundrel—he gave his name—lived on the same stairwell as this high school pupil. He was a well-known Black Hundreds member—and he subscribed to *New Times*! Apparently he'd opened fire from his windows! We have to arm ourselves against him.

"No, no, we don't have any extra weapons!" Peshekhonov blocked him, stopped him, with both hands.

Behind him, on the staircase going up, on the second floor, lay more than a hundred fine rifles, antique flintlocks, two yatagans, several daggers, a bear-spear, and an Austrian lance. But it would be a disaster if these fell into the hands of such men. (And the rumor had obviously reached them.)

Peshekhonov blocked him with his hands, not relying too much on his own sentries, quite random soldiers he'd led in off the street by the sleeve. They could leave at any moment as well.

The red-headed schoolboy expressed demonic astonishment and con-tempt:

"What? What?" He didn't want to believe it, and a spasm squeezed his throat. "Well, you know, comrades. . . . Well, you know, comrades. . . . I think all of you here are provocateurs!"

*   *   *

ONCE THE MASH SPILLS OVER, YOU CAN'T PUT IT BACK

*   *   *

Documents – 9

On this 14 March, a rumor spread among the soldiers of the Petrograd garrison, that the officers in the regiments were confiscating soldiers' weapons. . . . As Chairman of the Military Commission of the Provisional Committee of the State Duma, I declare that the most decisive measures will be taken to prevent such actions on the part of officers, up to and including execution of the guilty parties by firing squad.

State Duma Deputy B. Engelhardt

[2 5 1]

Man plays a song, but destiny calls the tune. Destiny called it for Colonel Polovtsov as well. On 5 March he was in Gatchina at an audience with Grand Duke Mikhail Aleksandrovich and had not yet been in Petrograd; on 10 March he had an audience with the Emperor at GHQ; on the 12th he was back in the thick of it in Petrograd; and on the evening of the 13th he joined the revolution.

That was how it happened. Chief of staff of the Caucasus Native Division and a great cavalry enthusiast in general, Polovtsov . . . By the way, there was this instance. No one knows about it, it's top secret, but if they did, there would be amazement and laughter. Last year, GHQ's intention to sharply curtail cavalry units became known. They were little used in battles, they incurred major losses, and they ate a lot of fodder. So Polovtsov brilliantly wrote in German and anonymously sent out over the radio one night on the Romanian front a telegram supposedly from von Schmettow congratulating his German general colleagues on the curtailment of the Russian cavalry, which meant the Russians' rejection of offensive operations. Later he learned that this telegram, intercepted, had been reported to the Emperor—and thus the cuts in Cossack regiments were cancelled.

Pyotr Polovtsov was generally considered a patent genius, having graduated first in his class from the General Staff Academy.

In spite of this and the prominent position of his deceased papa, his career advancement had not met expectations, was not what was merited. Indeed, in the past few days, when he had been expecting his promotion to major general, he had received merely "supreme benevolence." He'd missed out again.

So then, as a cavalry enthusiast he had gone in February to try to expedite through top circles his division's reorganization as a Native Corps. Judging from letters from the Caucasus, there was confidence that there would be enough mountain men volunteering for a corps as soon as enlistment was called; they were eager (yet not subject to mobilization). Grand Duke Mikhail supported this, of course, but at GHQ there was opposition, and nothing definite had been managed yet—so Polovtsov had had to return to his division, and he'd decided to go via Petrograd to refresh himself.

In Mogilev he stayed with Aide-de-Camp Adam Zamoisky, and it was with him that he went to Petrograd, but right then . . . Zamoisky tossed back his proud, Polish gentry head and declared that at that moment he, as aide-de-camp, was duty bound to offer his services and sword to the abandoned and threatened Empress. Polovtsov restrained a smile and stayed in the capital to look around, at an acquaintance's apartment. His adventurous heart began to pound at the idea that events and moments like these do not happen even once a century. For a full day he followed what was going on by telephone and telegraphed his division at the same time that he was here, stranded in Petrograd—and yesterday evening he'd received an invitation from Engelhardt to join the Military Commission. He rushed there immediately.

Since he had previously left his sword for safekeeping at General Staff headquarters, he now appeared at the Tauride Palace with a dagger and revolver, wearing a tall shaggy fur hat and a magnificent Circassian coat with silver cartridge pouches. Tall and slim and, as always, striking for his bearing—a degree of bearing and even English perfection of manners that allows for free gestures—an exceedingly powerful even, rather frightening phenomenon for such a comic organization as this Military Commission.

Just then the General Staff officers had assembled here, and everyone knew everyone, all *Young Turks*, assembled by the same Guchkov, making knowing jokes. They'd been the ones expected to make a coup, and now it had made itself, without their help.

He had to keep his eye on the ball, though. The silly officers were just that, all these Tumanovs and Tugan-Baranovskys, and Engelhardt was a nonentity. They were all just chattering, but if anyone was created for directing a headquarters, then it was Polovtsov and, it's funny, the engineer Obodovsky.

The entire day unknown officers had come thronging on their own initiative, offering to serve the people. Lots of them. . . .

But given how ill-defined the complement, duties, and most of all, general military status was, it was also too soon for Polovtsov to unleash all his abilities. For the time being he was holding back, making jokes, chattering on windowsills with one, another, and yet another—and taking a closer look at it all.

They discussed the picante story of His Majesty's Convoy showing up at the Duma. They recalled how the Swiss Guard had remained loyal to Louis XVI. They were all slain on the Tuileries steps, but they didn't surrender.

The Military Commission had moved to the second floor, to calmer, more removed rooms, the former State Duma commandant's apartment, and appropriated his seal, having nothing better. They organized a headquarters and established sections—motor, radio-telegraph, technical assistance, and medical—and set out several tables and typewriters. The Preobrazhensky clerks took their seats, two young women with bold hairstyles were found, passes were stamped, outgoing communications entered, the statements of all those wishing to report something recorded in a notebook, and nice fresh case covers laid out, and adjutants strutted from table to table with them.

During the course of the day, they sent guards to unprotected ministries and departments.

Most amusing was this Military Commission, which was rather out of its league. Communications between the Tsar and Tsarskoye Selo had been switched over to the Tauride Palace, and the Military Commission was brought copies of all telegrams between the Tsar and Tsaritsa—about the children's health and about the Tsar's movements. They could follow them like an entertaining game, and they did not order him constrained if he was on his way to Tsarskoye Selo—but sad to say, he had taken a unilateral decision to turn at Vishera, and moved away. The Military Commission was considered subordinate to the provisional Duma Committee, which couldn't make up its mind about anything and kept bowing to the Soviet of Workers' Deputies—and to please it had by a special resolution included on the Military Commission as well the Soviet's entire Executive Committee. This was nonsense—it was good they'd had the intelligence and sense of humor not to show their faces here; only their sour Academy librarian Maslovsky was hanging around. If someone did show up from there, though, or excessively revolutionary soldiers in the constant deputations expressing their loyalty to the revolution, then the colonels had to shower them with ironic courtesy. There was a lot of fuss in general with these deputations and with the alarms as well. A fresh-faced army doctor showed up and stated that the Senate and Synod had set out machine guns and had a counterrevolutionary press going. And although it was immediately clear that this was a load of rubbish, such was the atmosphere of revolutionary persistence and mistrust that one could not laugh, could not refuse, so Polovtsov was obliged with the most serious look to take this doctor and several Kexholmers and make a long search through the Senate and Synod, find nothing, and write up a report about it.

Here, the impetuously enterprising Duma Cossack Karaulov made him laugh a lot and mixed things up. Either he himself or someone else had thought to appoint him to the fast-turnover post of Petrograd commandant as of the evening of the 13th. And by the morning of the 14th he had published and already posted here and there "Order No. 1 for the City of Petrograd," the reckoning having begun with Karaulov. The order said to mercilessly arrest drunkards, robbers, and arsonists—and all ranks of the gendarmes corps, that is, the last remaining guardians of the order. They sought out the forelocked Cossack and shook him—what was he doing? Without a moment's doubt, he immediately went for a grand gesture, wrote, and managed to print somewhere, and have pasted up—an addition to "Order No. 1," which said that ranks of the Corps of Gendarmes were not subject to arrest, and immediately thereafter "Order No. 2," which ordered yardmen to search and check for attics and roofs occupied by supporters of the old order.

In the Tauride Palace itself, total anarchy was afoot.

If only it were just in the palace! Since the previous night, the barracks had been raging anew here and there at the rumor that "officers were confiscating weapons" seized in the revolutionary turmoil. They burst through here as well: "What? They're luring us to our punishment? Let's muzzle Rodzyanko, too! We could even arrest him!" Deathly afraid, Engelhardt, without conferring with the officers on the commission, not even with Guchkov, to whom he now reported, but he was out—with panicked speed wrote and immediately submitted for printing a horrifying order saying he would take the most decisive measures to prevent the disarming of soldiers, **up to and including the execution of officers.** By the time the members of the Military Commission learned of this it was too late to stop the decree, and it was distributed to the exulting soldiers! Thus, it was the Military Commission itself that had incited panic among the soldiers.

Shoot officers because they held their unit's weapons!

So that the opportunities to soar offered by the revolution were tempting, but he might well come crashing straight to earth. Polovtsov grinned, paced, and refrained from showing his worth. Man plays a song, but destiny calls the tune. . . .

With every passing hour, the Duma Committee was demonstrating its utter helplessness. There was total anarchy in the reserve battalions, especially the Moscow, where workers were in charge and they were killing officers. The regimental barracks were blocked off, and government representatives had no access there. Officers from other battalions were relaying in horror the impossibility of maintaining order. The Soviet's *Izvestia* came out directly opposed to the restoration of order. There wasn't a single battleworthy unit for Petrograd's defense. Meanwhile, the excellent combat Tarutinsky Regiment had disembarked at the Aleksandrovskaya train station, next to Tsarskoye Selo, for actions against Petrograd. But they were hoping to dupe Ivanov, take his foolish general's head into the arms of the Military Commission, and so sent officers to see him.

Kronstadt, too, was growing stormy and by no means to the benefit of the revolution, as had seemed the previous night, when they had rejoiced. Early that morning they had killed Admirals Viren and Butakov, and other officers as well. What was going on there was a black storm, there was no way of knowing for sure, a Pugachevian abyss had gaped open. This was no longer a game. Those wearing colonel's epaulets received this news with a chill, even under the Tauride Palace's sheltering roof.

Everything now depended on what Admiral Nepenin did. Today from Helsingfors he had ordered the Duma Committee's appeals read to the details. That meant Nepenin had joined the revolution. So.

Yes, the revolution promised great possibilities, but it would be better to rein in those possibilities.

But who would do that?

Guchkov's hands, Polovtsov understood, were weak and by no means sufficient for this.

Perhaps he'd been wrong to rush to this Military Commission. Perhaps he'd been wrong to stop off in Petrograd. Should he have sat quietly with his division?

[2 5 2 '']

(FROM *IZVESTIA OF THE SOVIET OF WORKERS' DEPUTIES*)

. . . Opinions have been expressed to the effect that the entire task is merely to "restore order." Such opinions can sow confusion in men's minds. . . . We intentionally are not yet dotting all our i's. But we will do so the next time. **There is no going back to the old regime**—and anyone who tries to reach a compromise with it is committing a crime against the people.

CALL FOR DONATIONS. The people's precious blood is being shed for the cause of freedom. Consequently, no material sacrifices should stop you.

RUSSIAN SOCIAL DEMOCRATIC WORKERS PARTY

PROLETARIATS OF ALL COUNTRIES, UNITE!

Comrades! Petrograd is in the hands of the free people. A few more blows and the old regime will retreat into eternity for good. The enemy, surrounded by hatred and contempt, is hiding like a coward in its cellars in order to assemble its black hosts. Half the sky has already been captured by the red glow of freedom, but the sun has yet to rise, and there are more cruel skirmishes between the people and the old government yet to come. We must set about with feverish haste creating workers organizations. Wrap the unorganized masses in a dense net of organized cells!

Organizing Committee of the Russian Social
Democratic Workers' Party (Mensheviks)

ENEMIES OF THE PEOPLE ARRESTED . . .

SPREAD THE NEWS OF PETROGRAD'S INSURRECTION!

Citizens! So that we are not lonely. . . . Our struggle will be won only if the entire country is with us. The old regime will make every effort to wall off Petrograd from the country.

The next session of the Soviet of Workers' Deputies has been scheduled for 14 March.

BEWARE OF DRUNKENNESS! Drunkenness is a dangerous enemy of the revolution's dignity. Cellars hold large stores of wine and vodka, and the revolutionary people are finding them. The revolutionary people do not need all that. At the historic moment of revolution we must be sober and pure. Swear to this, comrades, to one another! **DESTROY THE VODKA!**

. . . Armed residents of every building should clear their buildings of the murderers who have survived. . . .

AIMLESS SHOOTING AND RIDING AROUND IN MOTOR VEHICLES

Comrades! Let us not waste a single extra bullet. We need them all for the coming struggle against the counterrevolution and the bloodthirsty criminal government. Don't forget that the government is assembling its oprichniks under cover of night in order to drown the cause of revolution in the people's blood. We need the bullets for them. Avoid unnecessary shooting. It only frightens the civilian population and can even kill our comrade revolutionaries. Comrades, do not turn the militias' patrols into pleasure outings with unnecessary gunfire.

The next session of the State Duma Committee has been scheduled for midnight.

STOP THE CRUELTY. The people are settling scores at the present time with the most hated representatives of the old regime. . . . Actual criminals who have executed our brothers, if they resist, must be destroyed. . . . However, we should not treat cruelly those who surrender to the mercy of the revolutionary people. Do not curse and mock them. In the majority, they are harmless, base little men whose blood is not worth staining yourself with.

A gold watch from an unknown soldier has come into the possession of the Soviet of Workers' Deputies.

TO THE WORKERS. The Soviet of Workers' Deputies asks all comrade workers who have weapons to surrender them to the Soviet.

SD, SR, and Bund student groups are calling on their university comrades to energetically enlist in the city militia. Remember, comrades, that the Soviet of Workers' Deputies is your Supreme command.

RETURN TO WORK? Rumors have appeared in the city that metalworkers are supposed to go to work. No, the strike can be ended only by a sovereign resolution of the Soviet of Workers' Deputies. All isolated steps can lead only to demoralization in the great cause of the revolutionary people.

PAY ATTENTION! The State Bank must be occupied, but remember that **they apparently have machine guns.** Gostiny Dvor and the Apraksin Market must be protected from hooligans.

[2 5 3]

Familiar and unfamiliar officers were converging in groups of three, five, and ten on the straight formal marble staircase under the glass cap of the Hall of the Army and Navy, the capital's principal officers' club, and later on the curved, railed galleries of the second and third floors with their many pilasters, mirrors, and doors—blue, gold, and oak—and in the ring of sitting rooms—the dark pink "ladies" room, the coffee room, the greenish "men's" room, the buffet, the gloomy, formal dining room with stained glass windows (there was nothing to eat today)—and in the concert hall itself by the aisle seats—in hopes of getting what from each other? An explanation? Support?

The officers were of every rank and regiment—all without weapons but also without ladies and in the middle of a weekday. No matter how long they had served, be it a year, or a quarter-century, they could never have imagined that such a thing would come to pass in their lifetime or to any officers of any army. In a single day they had all been disarmed, for all intents and purposes stripped of rank, and dismissed from their posts, and some had also been sentenced to death.

And despite all this they had to go on living, walk with an officer's bearing, and depict the look of an officer.

All doomed, they had been driven together now, into a single building at the corner of Liteiny and Kirochnaya, a building that had known their sparkle, success, and pleasures, with its former polish and its former bronze groupings and candelabras, seemingly the last building in Petrograd that for some reason the insolent, all-powerful soldiers had not yet invaded. The officers had been driven together in anticipation of a beginning—but of what or at what hour they didn't know. However sad and frightening this destroyed world was, though, an officer could not let on.

In one group in the pink sitting room, where the pendants from the two fancy chandeliers were tinkling melodically from people walking over the parquet, a lieutenant colonel with a shiny gold front tooth had found the ability to jest:

"Now, gentlemen, a pale of settlement is being set up, only backwards. Officers are forbidden to live in the capitals, and for the right to reside in the form of an exception, short-term passes will be written out, such as this staff captain has. Hurry to the State Duma while they're still writing them."

His expressive, impudent lip with its white-blond mustache curled.

For Raitsev-Yartsev, this was no role or bravado but a way of life. If men in the trenches make jokes about Wilhelm, and about aviators, and about the enemy missiles striking around them, then why change their style and stop making jokes now? After all, every life event is always funny to someone, and that's the truth. And when the officers fled the Petrograd barracks, they themselves didn't notice the funny details, but many soldiers actually pictured it as merry.

When yesterday on Gogol Street a cluster of soldiers turned sharply toward him and one crude one with a heavy jaw shouted at him to surrender his weapon—at a certain second everything flew up and started spinning as if not even in Raitsev-Yartsev's head but somewhere higher, higher, where you had a good view of everything and where it had already come dropping down toward him. He had not been spared after all; though he had hoped he would be. The only solution was to bare his saber and kill one of them with a masterful cavalry thrust, this heavy-hanging jaw here. But then he himself would be torn to pieces immediately. The utter absurdity of dying on a Petersburg street while killing a Russian soldier. The utter absurdity of dying without living to forty, with all the color that filled his chest.

So he wouldn't kill him.

And he wouldn't be killed. So surrender it with an easy, crooked grin, seeing how undoubtedly amusing this was. Lieutenant Colonel Raitsev-Yartsev, a hereditary nobleman and cavalryman, who drew the full force of his courage into his saber's elongated body in its ascent—was now surrendering this soul-saber as an unneeded pendant.

Surrender it with a crooked grin—and then walk on down the street—and seeing coming toward him another similarly disencumbered, greet him with a salute of his right hand and jokingly slap the empty scabbard on his hip with his left.

Previously, he himself would not have believed how ironically he would bear it when he was dishonored.

He told that same story to everyone, though not in all its details.

Right here, in the Hall of the Army and Navy, for a few short hours, by some misunderstanding, they had all been quite safe. Perhaps they could get to their apartments and remain there. But another day or two, and then what? Shouldn't they return to barracks?

But now this was—now this was impossible!

The later they returned, the worse, though, because it would reinforce the soldiers' suspicions.

How could they return if the soldiers held the unit's weapons, to which the officers had no access?

The world had turned upside down.

The new experiment was so unknown, to such an extent was there no one to confer with—they were unforgivably handing out red bows to adorn their chest, even a second for their tall fur hats, and so they joined the soldier formation going to the Duma (and by the way, here, right now, almost no one had anything red attached. Had they removed all their red in the cloakroom? Hidden it in a pocket?)—they were going to the State Duma, after all! Such was Rodzyanko's summons, and he was a legitimate person.

But there was no trust established with the soldiers, who looked at them like wolves anyway.

Who was there left in Petrograd, after all, other than the Duma? And the Duma was calling on them to restore order in their units.

How could they restore what had been knocked out of their hands, though? And what if they couldn't forget? Those minutes of fear. Those minutes of insult.

Certainly, the return to barracks was inevitable. But also incomprehensible. Going back meant demanding that the soldiers not run amok through the city at will but start asking permission for every absence. Was that really still possible? That they surrender their weapons and cartridges from the looted arsenals? Was that, too, possible?

No, the old ways could *not* be restored.

Or should we fall in with the tone that's been adopted there without us over the past few days? Adopt even harsher, undeniably revolutionary notes?

Apathy gripped them. Extreme weariness to the point of being unable to resist, to the point of dull indifference to everything.

A tall, gloomy colonel, his face made of nothing but simple large features, seemingly ten times fewer features than people usually have—faces like that look good in front of a regimental formation—spoke in the teeth of the evidence:

"No, gentlemen, this is all our fault. We are the ones who let the moment slip."

Actually, he wasn't a Guard and evidently not even from a Petrograd garrison.

And Raitsev-Yartsev didn't have to return to barracks. He was in Petrograd on leave; his regiment was at the front. All he faced was an ignominious return without his saber, as far as the first regimental storehouse. He had come here for a safe conduct, so he would not be subjected to new insults.

Meanwhile, an electric bell rang loudly through the building. They were being summoned to the great hall. Right then, a wrought Izamilovsky man walked up to a fellow Izmailovsky officer who was standing in their group and assured him that an hour ago Colonel Engelhardt from the Duma's Military Commission had issued a public order to **execute** officers who tried to force soldiers to return their weapons!

What? What? That can't be!

What nonsense! It was the State Duma, after all, that had called on . . .

They went to the hall and took their seats.

This was unusual for officers: a public meeting. But people were already sitting at the table on stage, and all had something red on their chest—not the provocative bows, of course, but modest boutonnieres. They took seats arbitrarily. They heard the names of the chairman, the secretary, Colonel Peretz, Colonel Zashchuk, and Colonel Drutskoy-Sokolinsky announced. The fumes of revolution had carried them up there.

They began speaking, one after the other. And what they went on about!—

". . . The best of you walked at the head of soldiers to storm the regime. . . ."

Who was it who did that?

". . . Barriers have fallen, and an intrinsic connection is being created between the officer and the soldier. The spirit of serfdom will vanish forever from the military sphere!"

The drone of conversations passed through the hall; they weren't really listening.

". . . Citizen officers! . . ."

That's the way, the new way.

". . . quickly return to your places in the ranks, enlightened and reborn—and restore your spiritual tie with the soldier on the principles of equality and brotherhood. And with the support of that collective ensign who emerged from the ranks of the people. . . ."

Sitting beside Raitsev was a young sailor with an intelligent face:

"A gathering of suicides. Are you really going to sweet-talk *them*? Never. I know them."

"How?"

"I rubbed shoulders with them at the university."

From the stage they were putting forth a plan: either everyone march from here to the Duma right now, and even demonstratively across Nevsky ("Gentlemen! Why everyone? Can't we just send a delegation?"), or else as a delegation, but it must bring a resolution from the entire assembly, a salute to the State Duma in its noble cause of leading the popular movement toward freedom and an act of solidarity, saying that the officers now in Petrograd were all also walking arm in arm with the people. (This arm-in-arm business was very hard to picture right now.) Saying that they had gathered here and (for some reason they insisted it be unanimously, as if the splintering off of a single voice could spoil everything) had resolved unanimously to recognize the authority of the Provisional Committee of the State Duma from now until the convocation of a Constituent Assembly.

Indignant voices droned that this was too monstrous! Weren't they asking too high a price from them for their return to barracks and for their right to walk freely through the Petrograd streets? An Emperor reigned in Russia to whom they had all sworn an oath. How could they now *recognize the authority* of some provisional committee of public figures? What about His Imperial Majesty?

Well, they could also be recognized until the Emperor arrived in the capital city (if only those military trains would go faster; where had they gotten stuck?), or until the formation of a permanent government—but why did they need to be recognized until a Constituent Assembly was convened? Did Russia really not exist, so that it had to be constituted all over again?

Quite a few didn't even understand what the expression "Constituent Assembly" meant.

But they also saw shining young faces—both among the speakers and in the hall.

His neighbor, the marine engineer:

"Are our officers really prepared to oppose them? To know them you first have to bathe in their dragon blood. These explosions in the navy—the *Maria*, and a few outside Arkhangelsk, and the fires at storehouses, and here in January the icebreaker *Chelyuskin* blew up—whose work was that do you think?"

He himself was now a flagship engineer in the White Sea Fleet.

A very small handful were speaking from the stage—there was some Colonel Khomenko, too—but the terrible turn of events had lent strength to their words. Here they were already appealing candidly—not to the heart but to self-preservation. No matter what your convictions, if you are to leave this building, take a step down the street, and wear your epaulets for the next twenty-four hours—you must join them, and *unanimously*! Then you will get your registration and a general pass.

That strapping colonel with the simple features on his valiant face was sitting cater-corner from Raitsev, on the aisle. In a bass voice for his neighbors:

"What baseness! What truckling to the new rulers! What has become of us, gentlemen officers? Was it not we who led regiments all through the war? How quickly they shook us! How many of us are there here?"—looking around at the hall. "A good fifteen hundred. If we count just forty soldiers apiece, we represent 60,000 troops."

"Get used to not counting the soldiers," a response came to him from a row up ahead.

"Fine. We're fifteen hundred."

"Now unarmed."

"Fine. Nearly unarmed. But on the other hand, what experienced men. Why don't we accept this idiotic proposal now—and march unarmed supposedly to congratulate the Duma? But once we get there or even inside—seize the soldiers there by the rifles, take them away, twist them out of their arms—and shoot. And send their drunken assemblage to hell; they won't have a second. There's basically nothing more to it. This is certain success! If we just get up right now, declare our own, reach an agreement—and we're off! But we're already demoralized, and they'll run to report this immediately. We're no longer officers of one common army. What have they done to us, eh?"

Large and decisive, he stood up, those two Izmailovsky men followed him, and they walked down the aisle and out.

The young sailor, Gardenin, looked at Raitsev:

"Shall we go? You aren't going?"

He stood up abruptly—and also left, following them.

No, Raitsev-Yartsev stayed. If only to assess this all from the standpoint of humor.

Engelhardt himself appeared on the stage, very decorous. He read a draft proclamation from a prepared document:

". . . To our greatest sorrow, both among the soldiers and among the officers, there have been traitors to the people's cause, and at their treacherous hand many victims have fallen among honest fighters for freedom. . . ."

Hmm. Wasn't this already close to a call to *execute* them? . . .

[2 5 4]

In the town of Luga, 120 versts from Petrograd along the rail line to Pskov, a garrison was stationed as follows. An artillery brigade intended to be sent to France—still without a single cannon or a single rifle and with an untrained complement. A reserve artillery division made up of new recruits, inexperienced and worried, and also unarmed. A motor company, like any motor company, selected largely from the workers, and unreliable. And an assembly point for Guards cavalry units from several brigades. At the head of the point was General Mengden, a count and the garrison's senior officer, extremely equable, albeit quick-tempered; his cavalrymen loved him and called him "our old man."

The point's senior adjutant was Cavalry Captain Voronovich, who had joined them here a few months ago after recovering from a wound. This cavalry captain was one of the young guns. Before he graduated from the Corps of Pages, he managed to make off for the Japanese war as a volunteer and there earn a St. George Cross, albeit in an easy business. The Corps of Pages didn't want to take him back to complete his course, and so Voronovich would have been stranded for a long time as an army ensign, but the Emperor ordered him accepted. The runaway spent a month in a punishment cell and then, together with Page Maksheev, managed to graduate

from the Corps near the top, so that in their final year they were both promoted to the Empress's court pages and stood guard more than once in her
quarters. In addition, with the St. George Cross, Voronovich was the sole
such one among the cadets, so that they were obliged to salute him—and
later, in the Guards, in the Horse Grenadier Regiment, his St. George was a
rarity because the Guard had not been in the Japanese war. In addition,
due to his quickness, he had also managed to acquire progressive views. But
he also came away with a heavy impression from 1905, when, upon his return from the Far East, he drowned in the spontaneous sea of soldier crowds
and concluded for himself that soldiers could not be left to their own devices. It was from here that he adopted a most confiding style in his relations
with soldiers, especially those who had revolutionary ties. So too here in
Luga, at the point, he had a trusted man, Private Vsyakikh, recently an electrical engineering student, with ties to the SRs.

On 12 March, given the troubling news about Petrograd events, Voronovich summoned Vsyakikh and secretly ordered him to go to Petrograd
and find out properly what was going on there. Then he told his cavalry sergeant to summon his detachment, three hundred old-timers, and addressed
them as follows:

"Men! There are disturbances in Petrograd. We don't know how they will
end, but we need to be prepared *for anything*. I promise I will tell you the
whole truth about what goes on in Petersburg."

Count Mengden alone above them all remained perfectly calm that
everything in Petrograd would end to the good and that the cavalry detachments entrusted to him would remain devoted to the Emperor no matter
what the circumstances. With their help he would at any moment crush
any disturbances in Luga. The detachment leaders suggested measures to
him for separating the cavalrymen from unreliable units. But General
Mengden canceled all such measures:

"Gentlemen, I am certain that we in Luga have nothing to worry about."

On the 13th, a perfectly calm day in Luga, when the rumor came about
General Ivanov's movement, Count Mengden remained even calmer. Now
Ivanov would uncover the scoundrels who had led Petrograd to the point of
insurrection. Now the reforms that should have been made long ago would
be approved. (He was indignant about certain outrages at the highest levels.)

On the morning of the 14th, Vsyakikh was already sitting in the chancellery with an expressive face. The cavalry captain saw the cavalry sergeant
and clerks out in order to be alone with him. Vsyakikh pulled out from
under his greatcoat lapel a tattered copy of the newspaper of the Soviet of
Workers' Deputies and a bulletin by Petrograd journalists with Rodzyanko's
appeal about the Duma Committee taking power.

Voronovich realized that the revolution was a fait accompli. Barely hearing out Vsyakikh's stories, he rushed to the point administration to see Mengden. Every morning, as part of his duties as senior adjutant, he handed

Mengden a file of documents for his signature. Now on top of these documents he included the Petrograd papers, brought them to the general—and waited in the adjutants' room.

A few minutes later, the door of the general's office opened wide and old Mengden, pale with indignation, held out the crumpled papers:

"Take this filth away. And be so kind as to ask the garrison chief to immediately assemble all the commanders of the individual units here."

Half an hour later, everyone had gathered at the administration, agitated. The commander of the motor company reported that there had been disturbances there the entire previous day. At evening roll call, the soldiers had refused to sing the anthem, and today at noon they intended to hold a rally.

A police inspector brought an entire stack of the very leaflets Vsyakikh had been so secretly sent for. They had filtered into Luga themselves.

This time the general was forced to read them. And he did, rustling them in silence. Voronovich watched the count. His open, well-bred, noble face displayed an entire struggle of doubts.

"Gentlemen. . . . I see events in Petrograd have taken such a turn that the troops arriving from the front will have to sustain a genuine battle with the traitors. I do not doubt that the front will remain loyal to His Majesty. And this will resolve everything. Our objective here is to make sure the Luga garrison does not end up on the side of rebellious Petrograd. The garrison's main core, the cavalry units entrusted to me, will of course join the loyal front." Had he decided to suppress? No, based on his own love of peace and magnanimity: "But if any motor company wishes to join the rebels, we will not prevent them! If a reserve artillery division wants to follow its example, good riddance! They are no reinforcement for the rebels because they have no weapons. And also, I have no doubt, the Cossacks will be joining us from the front. And so, I am taking a decision to do everything possible to prevent bloodshed among the garrison's units."

The police inspector was horrified. Did this mean the town would remain prey to rebellious units?

"Your Excellency, are you saying the motor units' rally is not to be stopped?"

"Do not stop it!" The old count held his head majestically.

Soon after, the cavalry point administration had a telephone call from the police saying that the motor units, before their scheduled rally, had joined with their reserve division, put out a red flag, and were coming to town "to raise the cavalry."

For the first time in these past few days, General Mengden became distraught.

"So what are we to do?" he asked Voronovich, his reddened old eyes darting. "Are we really to fire at these scoundrels? I very much want to keep from shedding blood."

Voronovich was glad to be in place with advice and hastened to state it, tipping the general in the direction he was already starting to lean.

"Your Excellency! That a revolution has occurred in Petrograd is an undoubted fact. How it will be expressed at the front is as yet unclear. Why should you rush to adopt a harsh position? Your love of peace is not misleading you. What can our detachments do? We still don't know whether all the soldiers will agree to act against the rest of the garrison. But if they do, that will mean pointless bloodshed for which our officers will pay cruelly afterward. No, you're right. We have to avoid blood, no matter what! Let the motor and artillery units come to us. What can they do? Other than swords, they have no weapons. They'll come, have their say, and go back. It's important that our cavalrymen know that their officers will be with them, and then everything will work out favorably for us internally. Don't speak out! Take pity on your own officers! I will undertake to keep my own detachment from any protest. Order the leaders of the other detachments . . ."

The general sat there in astonishment and dismay. He was becoming enfeebled right before everyone's eyes, a year every minute.

"But I, who have served three Emperors in faith and truth, I cannot betray my duty and oath! Of course, I am opposed to bloodshed. But . . . What do you advise I do? I'm prepared to sacrifice my own life, let them kill me, if only that will help us emerge with honor . . ."

Voronovich implored him only not to speak to the agitated crowd but to go to his quarters and wait calmly.

While he himself rushed to his detachment.

Meanwhile, outside, he could already hear the crowd's muffled approach. From the window, Voronovich saw a mounted gunner with a red armband gallop up to the detachment's front steps. He shouted out:

"Everyone out of the barracks!"

And he galloped to the next detachment.

Voronovich walked through his detachment and found his soldiers in utter confusion. They didn't know what to do. Some were already walking toward the street doors, but they noticed the cavalry captain and stopped.

Now was when he had to bring his leadership to bear. The time had come to guide the masses! He stepped to the middle of the barracks and loudly exclaimed:

"Anyone who wants to, leave; the rest, gather around me!"

The barracks began to hum—and everyone surrounded the cavalry captain.

Then he loudly informed them that there had been a revolution in Petrograd, and he read from the proclamations and leaflets.

They shouted a ragged "hurrah" and asked what they should do.

Voronovich suggested sending one man from each platoon to find out what the gunners wanted.

He himself immediately summoned Vsyakikh to his chancellery and conferred with him. Vsyakikh informed him that the motor company had elected a "military committee" to direct the garrison insurrection. Voronovich

immediately sent Vsyakikh to establish communications with the committee and begin negotiations.

Meanwhile, the gunners took their red flag as far as the cavalry point administration and summoned the cavalrymen "to join the people" and go to
the demonstration. But the cavalrymen wavered, and the men sent from the
platoons returned dissatisfied:

"They're jabbering away, but what exactly they're saying—you can't tell."

This even exceeded Voronovich's expectations. The cavalrymen hadn't
yielded! (Might they have even been willing to fight, then?)

But an hour passed (Vsyakikh hadn't returned; it was taking him forever), and they learned that the gunners were disarming the neighboring
mounted detachment and had entered their barracks.

This was too much. This wouldn't do. They had to hold on. Voronovich
lined up his men and said that the older soldiers should be ashamed to let
new recruits disarm them.

They replied that they would not permit such a disgrace.

They strengthened the guard at the weapon depot and placed a duty platoon at the barracks exit, and stern, slender, tall Voronovich and the duty
sergeant went out on the front steps.

Now the gunners came up, a hundred men or so, all new recruits, aged
eighteen or nineteen, and also a few local high school boys and two or three
suspicious civilians. The crowd could be seen to be holding about forty
rifles, which they had easily taken from the neighboring detachment.

A volunteer stepped out from the crowd, saluted, and suggested to the
cavalry captain that he immediately surrender all the weapons the detachment had.

The cavalry captain asked: "On whose orders?" The volunteer replied
that they had information about the cavalry's insubordination to the State
Duma, and therefore it had been decided to disarm them.

This had been decided by that same "military committee" from which
the cavalry captain had been awaiting news and clarifications. It was a
difficult position, like legs gone sprawling.

Meanwhile, shouts rang out from the crowd, which was intoxicated by its
success in the neighboring detachment:

"What's the point of talking to Mr. Gold Epaulets! Box his ears and go on
into the barracks!"

Right then, the cavalry duty platoon spilled out onto the front steps with
rifles.

The crowd froze.

The sergeant, a re-enlisted man, asked the volunteer why they were making this visit.

The volunteer repeated what he'd said.

"Oh you lop-eared pup!" the sergeant shouted at him. "Who do you
think you're talking to? You were still running around bare-assed when they

were calling me uncle! And you're demanding my rifle? I'll give you a rifle the likes of which you'll be rolling all the way to the firing range! Men"—he turned around to face his men on the front steps—"go on, show these snivelers the way to the firing range."

And about twenty cavalrymen, leaving their rifles with their own men, cut into the crowd, laughing and joking, and quickly relieved the snivelers of all the weapons from the neighboring detachment.

The civilians ran away, and the new recruits and high school pupils looked at their marshal in dismay.

This was not a solution to the problem, though. The cavalry captain walked up to the volunteer and started trying to persuade him.

"You have to understand. If we'd wanted to act against you, then a few hundred well-armed old-timers would make quick work of your whole cannon-less division." Which was perfectly true. "But we don't want any unnecessary or senseless bloodshed. This is good, that it ended peacefully. Go back to your division and explain this to them there. . . ."

That is, to the "military committee." Voronovich would have liked to understand their intent and purpose.

The Petrograd revolution had already triumphed anyway, and it was senseless and pointless to argue with it. Better they repeat it in Luga in the least painful way.

Meanwhile, his cavalrymen were savoring how they were now going to put the neighboring detachment to shame for surrendering its weapons.

[2 5 5]

Although the Soviet of Workers' Deputies' stomping had already collected in the next room, the Executive Committee had no intention of coming out to join them, being busy with actual work. Inevitably, though, they did have to send one man to preside over the meeting. The lively, irrepressible Sokolov went to direct the crowd, while the rest sat around their table behind a curtain, having set the sturdiest possible barrier at the doors so that at least today they would not be bothered.

Not immediately, but suddenly they remembered that perhaps they needed to write minutes. The majority shouted that they didn't, for fear of ending up a secretary. But Kapelinsky was so inclined and was prevailed upon.

Chkheidze began presiding here. But everyone saw that he wasn't fit for this either; having grown old before his time. He was just a little over fifty, and in the Duma he had kept to the extreme left flank dashingly, cockily, but in the past few days he had grown hoarse and been sapped of strength, speaking to the soldiers lounging around in the Duma. Most of all, though, he was exhausted from the surge of happiness. The entire Duma had been wrong, and the handful of the Social Democratic faction alone had been right! Here the people's revolution they had predicted had come to pass, and he wanted, dreamed of nothing more and could not guide it. This fulfillment of desires, this total, overwhelming happiness, had, in the end, made him soft. He couldn't keep up with recognizing who had the floor and had no inclination or even power to take it away from anyone. He nodded blissfully at contradictory opinions, and looked as if he were dozing off. (They also kept bringing him things to sign—a pass, other scraps.)

His neighbors attempted to run the meeting for him, and then everything became confused, they didn't listen to the stutterer Skobelev, and Kerensky of course wasn't present, he hadn't even run in for appearances' sake, already openly despising this EC—and the session simply moved on to shouting matches and arguments, whoever could seize the floor.

There were enough urgent issues today to last a whole day of sessions, but in the end they could not avoid the issue of a government. Who would set up the revolutionary government and how? The Bolsheviks insisted with one voice that the Executive Committee immediately seize power Russia-wide. But restless Himmer, in his penetrating voice, had announced previously that, as he had learned, franchised circles were preparing to create a government at top speed—he didn't try to conceal his approval—and that meant the Executive Committee would have to work out and adopt its own position.

If they had to they had to. They began speaking up.

Himmer hastened to seize their general attention, revealing that he had been studying just this issue and had come to the following conclusions. Naturally, the goal of the imperialist bourgeoisie, those Guchkovs and Milyukovs, was clear: to eliminate tyranny only over themselves and reinforce the dictatorship of capital and rents. Of course, to do this they would have to create a semi-free, so-called liberal political regime and a fully empowered parliament. But they would halt the revolution at this imitation of "the West's great democracies"—in fact, the dictatorship of capital—in addition having also harnessed the revolution for the purposes of national imperialism and "loyalty to our valiant allies." To any thinking Marxist, this tactic was thoroughly and compellingly clear.

Himmer's speech dragged on like a lecture, but he spoke so importunately and bitingly, and such undoubtedly Marxist theory shone through here, that they listened to him.

The rightist Mensheviks here, the Organizing Committee—did they realize where Himmer was leading them? Hardly. And certainly not Gvozdev, who was sitting with a lost expression, as if he wasn't listening. But the leftists were deceived as well. The only SR here, but a fiery one, Aleksandrovich, and the only Interdistrict man here, but an unbending one, Krotovsky, and Shlyapnikov and the loyal Bolsheviks kept beaming more and more because Himmer, the representative of the *swamp*, was playing right into their hands. A wonderful speech! If their left wing would unite with the swamp, then they could immediately push through a resolution about the seizure of all revolutionary power by the Soviet of Deputies!

However, the swamp was viscously turning further in such a way that the democratic masses at the present time did not have the real forces for the country's immediate socialist transformation.

Krotovsky had a fat-eared, fat-cheeked, fat-lipped face, which expressed his laughter: Who was going to give orders everywhere—on the streets, at the train stations, in the barracks? The Duma Committee? It was agents of the Soviet or its volunteer associates who were giving orders everywhere. Who else today had authority among the masses? They heeded the Soviet's proclamations as they would decrees.

(This might well have been true, but at the same time, this step was frightening: taking power themselves, having never been prepared to do so. How? What? At what moment? When the old government was by no means destroyed and might come charging in again.)

No and no! Himmer insisted. At the present moment democracy is in no condition to achieve its goals with only its own forces. Without the franchised elements we cannot cope with the machinery of governance. This means we have to exploit the imperialist bourgeoisie as a factor in our hands! In essence, we must, under a bourgeois administration, establish the dictatorship of the democratic classes!

This was a gripping idea of which Himmer was proud. Not all the leaders of the world proletariat could have come up with such a one. He drilled his fingers by turns in the direction of his interlocutors. Herein lay the peculiarity of the situation, and herein lay what had to be the venomous gift of the Greeks: offer power to the bourgeoisie on terms such that they would *ensure total freedom for us to struggle against the bourgeoisie itself!* It might also well be that they would see through this and not choose to seize power on these terms. But the proletariat must *force* them to seize power!

That might be too smart for its own good. It was funny! The impetuous Aleksandrovich was shouting, and Shlyapnikov's bass came in: We find your concerns that the bourgeoisie will end up in power simply ridiculous! No class has ever voluntarily refused power! What has been pushing our bourgeoisie into opposing the Tsar all these years if not a thirst for power?

But although they kept pouncing like this, they didn't have genuine persistence. The leftists had a certain lack of confidence. (Of course, it would be calmer if Milyukov took power; let them wrack their brains.)

Evidently, Shlyapnikov felt very much out of place here and was often distracted by his own people coming in, and then he would disappear from the session. The Bolsheviks, you see, saw the main thing not in the Soviet but in the fact that meanwhile they had seized the Vyborg side and the Narva side, too, apparently. But here, at the session, they only knew to vote as one. According to their primitive notion, the insurrection in Petrograd was already the beginning of a world socialist revolution, therefore there could be no talk of any franchised government—rather they themselves had to seize the fullness of power! (Indeed, they had already printed their manifesto in *Izvestia* as an expression of the Soviet's general program. What effrontery!)

But Himmer led them along subtly and complexly: find a way to keep your own hands free and direct the government from behind its back.

Kapelinsky listened enchantedly to the speakers, once in a while forgetting to take minutes—and who needed them anyway? What were they against the living act!

Shekhter grasped and supported the main point, that in no instance could socialists participate in a bourgeois government. That would be a betrayal of revolutionary social democracy. If the socialists did join a coalition, workers would get the illusion that socialism was on its way—and then murderous disenchantment would ensue.

Everything was coalescing more and more against the defensists, whose voices were very timid, saying that the war was a national war and they could not decline responsibility for it.

That rallied all the Zimmerwaldists even more so against them. Participation in a coalition was a betrayal of Zimmerwald!

Himmer had perceptively foreseen the paradox that the Bolsheviks, the Interdistrict group, and the SRs would have to vote for his program; there was no getting out of it. Without even appreciating its beauties and profundities, they would vote for it anyway.

True, the Bundists Erlich and Rafes defended the coalition subtly and intelligently one after the other. They proceeded out of caution. They proffered the well-known theory that revolution here was bourgeois and had to go through a free bourgeois development, and that was an entire era.

The other strong defenders of the coalition—Peshekhonov and the Menshevik Bogdanov—were not in attendance.

Right then, to everyone's surprise, the heretofore content and happy Chkheidze started bellowing. Perhaps because he had met longer than anyone with this franchised bourgeoisie in the Duma, but he started shouting angrily and even incoherently that he would definitely not permit any coalition! He would vote against it, and not only that, he would break it!

So long had he spent on the edge of the parliamentary opposition, he had become used to fearing the slightest complicity in government—for himself and for his friends. He believed we would do better nudging a franchised government from without.

And he dropped his weary head to his chest.

Skobelev, of course, was at one with him.

A few wavered and exchanged opinions.

It was interesting that none of the twenty present demanded preventing the creation of a bourgeois government, although they knew that every hour it was moving closer toward formation. Herein lay the inexorability of the events Himmer had foreseen.

Right then Nakhamkes spoke. He could speak in various ways: he could thunder, and very well, and he knew very well how to be cautious. (The rumor had reached him that General Ivanov was leading twenty-six troop trains to Petrograd to suppress and that five regiments were on their way from the Karelian isthmus. What forces were defending the Tauride Palace, everyone could see: none whatsoever. In this situation, seizing power simply meant slipping one's head in the noose.) Nakhamkes was now arguing that at the present time revolutionary democracy could not possibly bear the burdens of authority. Nor were there now in its midst prominent names that could create an authoritative government. Not only that, they were utterly unfamiliar with the machinery of government administration. Let the franchised Duma deputies take power and finish bringing down Tsarism. One had to be content with the revolution triumphing in a moderate bourgeois form for now; later, we would give it a shove and topple it. For now the Duma Committee's decision to take upon itself the responsible role must be welcomed. The Committee would cope best with the Tsarist counterrevolution.

And so, three possible decisions were put forth. The far leftists'—a wholly socialist government. The defensists and Bundists—sharing power with the bourgeoisie and joining a coalition. And the center's, call it a swamp, but herein lay its entire brilliance: don't take power for ourselves, and don't share it with the bourgeoisie, but leave our hands free—and give it a shove!

They seemed to be heading for a vote—but they never got there. It was tough going. It was also amazing that they could talk for so long on a single topic. Time and again people would rush into Room no. 13 on "emergency and urgent matters." They reported on excesses, on the shooting, on the pogroms, some complained about the attackers, others about the defenders. A rumor was brought from Kronstadt that two admirals had been killed and some officers had been beaten, so apparently someone should be sent there, too. Some EC members dashed out to see those who had summoned them, others returned, and still others went to nudge the Soviet's plenum along in the next room.

Right then, a considerable noise came from behind the curtain, even louder than the session itself—and firmly pulling the curtain aside, an imposing colonel accompanied by a young naval cadet with a martial look presented himself to the EC session.

Not that long ago, many here, illegal and quasi-legal, would have staggered back in fright at such a colonel's appearance among them. Not that long ago the colonel, too, might have just shouted at them to disperse or unleashed the cavalry on them. But now he stood tall, as before a session of generals, and reported.

That the Executive Committee of the Soviet of Workers' Deputies possessed the fullness of power, everyone was to obey it alone, and he, a colonel, had been sent to apply for their assistance.

"What happened? Why have you burst in?"

Many were standing, the session was broken up, and rather than omnipotence, the EC members felt their helplessness.

[2 5 6]

"Forgive me, though, but what kind of military cheek is this! What does this colonel want of the Executive Committee, and how dare he disrupt our session?"

All was confusion, so many were talking, they couldn't immediately understand.

The colonel, too, was not explaining himself in military fashion but disjointedly, adding long, supplementary phrases. They could not immediately understand the essence of things from his polite expressions: President Rodzyanko of the State Duma intended to leave for a meeting with the Tsar and for this he had ordered for himself a special train at the Vindava Station. The train was ready, but now information had come in that the railroaders were refusing to send it off because they obeyed only the Soviet of Deputies. Therefore, it was the Duma Committee's most humble request to the Soviet that it allow the train to leave.

What was this? Why must the EC . . . (Aha! That meant the authority was ours!) Why were they interrupting without permission? And who were these railroaders? We haven't heard anything about this!

But just as everything was already topsy-turvy, so now this subordinate naval cadet, instead of acting the mute adjutant, came forward and in an angry, trembling voice, with angry eyes, declared to the entire Executive Committee:

"I will permit myself to ask, in the name of the sailors and officers, what your attitude is toward the war and the defense of the homeland. In order to recognize your authority, we have to know. . . . If at this moment the President of the State . . ."

A mere boy! On top of everything else! He wants to know! The very question everyone had been purposely avoiding for over two days!

"No, this is too much! Be so kind as to remove yourselves, gentlemen, and we will discuss this without you!"

"But what railroaders? . . ."

Skobelev hinted that he could say—after these men had left.

They were seen out and told there would be a reply.

Skobelev explained that there was one reliable man, Rulevsky, a bookkeeper for the collections service of the Northwestern railroads. In the revolution's movement, he had abandoned his bookkeeping and joined Bublikov's headquarters in the Ministry of Roads and Railways. From time to time, he reported on what was going on there and checked up on them. He had telephoned to say that preparations were being made for Rodzyanko's trip to consult with the Tsar and that they'd tried different stations. Skobelev let the Vindava Station know to stop the readied train, but he hadn't had time to tell the EC.

What do you have the time to do? . . . (People were constantly after him with documents and files—permissions, passes, directives . . .)

Now they were so overwrought, they were all on their feet, as if they had to flee a fire.

And in fact, why was Rodzyanko going? Tell us, State Duma! He wants to latch on to the revolution! What could his purpose be? Can we really trust him? Or the entire Duma Committee? After all, they're still not connected with the revolution in any way, and now they've decided to parlay with the Tsar. At our expense! And then they're going to turn the whole army against the revolution? That means ruin! There can be no doubt here! Don't give any permission whatsoever! Skobelev was right for detaining it! The Tsar cannot cope with Petrograd himself, so the Duma will help him! (But then how can they be entrusted with authority? Does this mean they shouldn't be given authority?) The revolution's entire fate might depend on this trip! Do not allow it under any circumstance! Thank the railroaders for their correct understanding of their duty to the revolution!

Apparently, other opinions were not voiced. No, there was this: should Chkheidze accompany Rodzyanko to provide oversight? By a majority they decided to *refuse* anyway!

They started sitting down. And took their seats.

But this episode shook them into wondering whether they had all been wrong to ignore the issue of the dynasty's fate, which they had thought was far off and almost swept away already. But no! Obviously, the Soviet had to issue a clear statement saying that the Romanov dynasty had to go!

But then there was another question. What about Kerensky? After all, he was there, on the Duma Committee, and had not been showing up here. So did he know about the preparations for this treacherous journey? Why didn't he prevent it? Why didn't he inform us? Summon Kerensky here!

Invite him.

We must go back to the question of taking power!

The session was splitting up into individual units, each going somewhere, scurrying off. (They did have to eat and drink at some point. Comrades! We'll organize something here right away!)

Comrades! We have to move on to a vote on the question of taking power. Comrades! (this was Himmer) the vote isn't all there is either. We also have to discuss and work out the *conditions* under which we agree to allow the bourgeoisie to take temporary power, in or without a coalition! After all, we are allowing it *conditionally*! . . .

But right then people ran in to report that somewhere officers were being beaten and torn to pieces. Even in Kronstadt . . . (Although this was a historical inevitability.) Something had to be published that would decisively and irrevocably force the officer mass to join the revolution! (Nakhamkes started writing.)

Right then, in walked Kerensky.

He didn't walk in, he burst in, pale, half out of his mind, frazzled, his tie awry, though his short crewcut was rigid, otherwise . . . There was despair on his face. Did he know something terrible? . . .

(Were Ivanov's troops approaching? Were we all done for? . . .)

"What are you doing? How can you!" Kerensky exclaimed before he could get to more intelligible sentences. But how upset he was! "You here, knowing nothing, are preventing Rodzyanko from going. Do you really not understand that I'm there, and if it were necessary, I would stop him myself?" He swayed and they pushed up a chair for him. He collapsed and leaned his chest sideways to the table and his head dropped.

They rushed to help him. Someone held his head, and someone loosened his tie and unfastened his collar. They brought water and splashed him.

Coming around, he found the strength to speak. In a tragic whisper, nonetheless everyone could hear:

"Am I really in that wing, in hostile encirclement, for anything other than to defend democracy's interests? If danger arises for us, I'll be the first to see it! I'll be the first to render it harmless! You can count on me! I am thoroughly cognizant of my duty to the revolution, as must each of us be! . . . But under these conditions, the lack of trust you're expressing for the Duma Committee is a lack of trust in me personally! This lack of trust is inappropriate! It's dangerous! Criminal! . . . It may well be that it won't be Rodzyanko going at all. This is about the trip, not Rodzyanko. He might even obtain an abdication! You don't understand anything, and you're getting in the way!"

They listened to him in a way they hadn't listened to each other the entire day.

Abdication? Well, if . . . Well, that's another matter. . . .

Kerensky demanded, now in a firm voice, that they permit Rodzyanko's trip, for the final assertion of the new government!

Voices appeared in his support—first from the supporters of coalition, then from others.

And new debates began, anything but brief ones, and the matter proceeded as if it was no longer about the train but about the relationship between the palace's two wings. Yes, that was how it was shaping up!

A vote was taken to allow the trip. With the qualification that Chkheidze or someone else must accompany Rodzyanko.

[2 5 7]

Kutepov awoke in anguish and spent the morning in anguish at his sisters'. There could be no leave for him, no private life, if something like this was going on.

However, full of strength and military considerations, he also could not intervene in events without his unit, without his incomparable Preobrazhensky Regiment, which was sitting in the trenches far away in Galicia.

There was nothing he could do; however, even in isolation he couldn't languish. And although his sisters were still fainting from the danger he had survived on Liteiny, and although they kept talking incessantly about how savagely officers were being dealt with on the streets, Kutepov felt the humiliation of hiding at home and the impossibility of staying there. He should give up his leave and depart for the front.

But he could not abandon this misbegotten reserve battalion either.

The telephone was working again. He called the officers' club, and Maksheev rejoiced and begged him to come, but he couldn't send a motorcar because there were almost none left in the battalion and the officers didn't have them at their disposal. Such a strange situation.

Kutepov said:

"Fine, I'll walk."

"But how will you get here?"

It was scarcely as dangerous as was being drawn for easily frightened people, scarcely more dangerous than to go on the attack under a hail of bullets or for an infantryman to meet a cavalryman's attack. Here the bullets were flying almost randomly, mostly in the air, and the unmounted men you encountered doubtless wielded a sword worse than you.

He still had to cross Bolshoi Prospect, go down Kadetskaya Line, then down the University Embankment, over the Palace Bridge, past the Winter Palace—and that was it. Holding his armed pistol in his greatcoat pocket, without a holster, and with his sword clearly visible at his left side, Kutepov walked in great tension, prepared for battle every second and with everyone he met. He did not look everyone in the face especially challengingly, but he did not look down, either, but rather ahead, at eye level, at his straight, narrow path, seeing beyond any oncoming face.

At the same time, though, he couldn't help but notice the abominable red scraps on everyone, an unusual, farcical revelry that had overtaken everyone like a kind of insanity. And there were silly smiles stuck to or floating on most faces. The crowd was delighted without knowing why—the collapse of order and the onset of anarchy, which would mean everyone is in trouble.

A few other proclamations had been pasted on the walls, but Kutepov's peripheral vision didn't pick up even their large headings, and he certainly didn't go up to read them.

There were many stray individual soldiers, not part of any detachment—and some, struck by the colonel's menacing and weary look, by the confidence of his step, saluted him, and rather snappily. Then the colonel responded to them immediately. But many were utterly dissolute, in clusters, with weapons, and giving no greetings whatsoever—and these Kutepov passed by as if not noticing but in fact very much tensed. Any such cluster could include men who remembered him from Liteiny, who had guarded the building and been out for his blood. His chances of being attacked were greater than for any other officer walking down the street. There were very few of them, almost none, mostly restless ensigns who had already joined the revolution, with the same red bows and crowded together with university students.

There was an especially dense convergence of students and soldiers directly in front of the university; the crowd took up half the embankment, speeches were being made in some clusters, and from the snatches that reached Kutepov he realized that they were feeding everyone who came, which was why they'd collected here.

But it was as if the rays of his tension shot forward, a mute resolute order to "stand aside!"—and the colonel cleared the way for himself. He passed like a missile through a cloud of smoke—and not a single close hand made any attempt on him from behind. They looked at the tall, short-bearded, steely colonel—and stepped aside, let him through, did not shout insults, did not cavil that he wasn't wearing red.

Of course, this was random, depending on who he encountered; he might have clashed with someone and simply gone to his death. Instead, he passed through.

Right before him, a couple of armored cars rumbled across the Palace Bridge and past the Stock Exchange. He had time to think that armored cars, which had been removed from the cause for the two years of positional war, were no good without roads and over torn-up ground—but here they came in handy, through city streets, carrying the revolution's soldiers and scaring unarmed residents to death.

Traffic on the Palace Bridge was heavy and free-flowing, and no one barred the way. Here for the first time he noticed the weather. Nothing remarkable. The morning fog had dissipated, but in the space over the snowy Neva, beyond the Trinity Bridge, one sensed a shroud. The sun peeked through but not all the way out.

Had it been twenty below zero, there wouldn't have been any of these crowds.

There might not even have been a revolution.

It felt as though all this general dissoluteness had smeared his soul with something dirty.

In view of the stern, taciturn, semicircular General Staff, it was especially repulsive to feel what the capital had become.

Kutepov arrived at the Preobrazhensky club just in time for breakfast. All the officers were happy to see him. They had the following news. This morning, a large detachment of Preobrazhensky men from the 3rd Company, from Kirochnaya, rebels, arrived without officers in three trucks—and presented the 1st Company duty officer with an order from the Military Commission of the State Duma to inspect the buildings and remove any machine guns. There were just two such training machine guns present, and those were taken away. But besides the company buildings, the armed rebels insultingly went through the officers' club as well, pretending they were in fact searching for machine guns, or something else, or just as a threat.

"And you didn't drive them out?"

They hadn't dared. One reckless step and all could be lost.

And yet there were genuine combat officers there. Here was Boris Skripitsyn with his St. George sword, whom Kutepov remembered well in battle last September.

And they were certain they had acted correctly! This was confirmed by the fact that the rebels left without a conflict, and afterward they brought a confidential instruction from the Military Commission to send their battalion chancellery to the Tauride Palace to help. And to send sentries to guard the nearby palaces. So Maksheev sent a half-company to guard the Winter Palace, a quarter of a company to the palace of Grand Duchess Maria Pavlovna, a quarter to the palace of Mikhail Nikolaevich, and a quarter to the palace of the Prince of Oldenburg. The Preobrazhensky men saw in this business with sentries the good sense of the new authorities and the as yet concealed onset of pacification. And this kept the soldiers busy. They had also sent details to the telephone station and the Ministry of Foreign Affairs and had sent out patrols down Millionnaya, the Moika, and the embankments from the Summer Garden to Senate Square.

"And what are these patrols supposed to do?"

"The Military Commission charged them with dispersing gatherings."

"That would be good. But they won't disperse anyone. Forces and decisiveness like that aren't enough. The first such gathering is the Tauride Palace. That's where to begin."

The officers looked at the colonel respectfully—and with mistrust.

Here is what they saw and liked: that the Preobrazhensky officers had become a legitimate service—and were released from the bitter necessity of dragging themselves to the Hall of the Army and Navy for an officer's rally to obtain protective permission for themselves.

But what was happening at the Hall of the Army and Navy? Kutepov knew nothing.

They showed him the appeal.

"My God! My God!" was all Kutepov could say. He pictured this mass humiliation of officers.

By the way, it was cater-corner from Musin-Pushkin's house. At the very same spot on Liteiny where the day before yesterday he had led his unsuccessful containment—and even then none of those hundreds of officers had come to his aid. If they had, it all might have ended differently.

How quickly and without a fight had the capital's entire officer class been broken!

What could now be done?

Here's what. Captains Skripitsyn and Kholodovsky had an idea and went up to the colonel. Officers from the General Staff were now being appointed to the Military Commission. So here was an idea: the colonel should go directly to them now and explain that things could not go on this way. The situation had to be saved immediately and energetically.

"Nonsense," Kutepov said. "They see all this perfectly well. Each officer of the imperial army must accept responsibility for understanding everything independently."

But he paced back and forth, back and forth—and kept coming back to the fact of his own humiliating self-incarceration, even here, at the club.

"But what if, in fact?" Kutepov said to Kholodovsky. "Let's try our luck. You never know what might happen."

There was a motorcar for their trip. With a little red flag. Otherwise you couldn't get anywhere near the palace.

[2 5 8]

That's what happens when you don't get the deed done right away. Rodzyanko didn't make a decisive departure before dawn to catch up with him in Bologoye—and after that the trip just wouldn't come together.

Milyukov was instantly on his guard and said they had to think this over properly. And he kept the Committee from assembling to decide, saying that each person had to think and also consult. There were pluses and there were minuses; it was a very demonstrative step.

Yes, of course, the step was exceptionally important. But also in the President's character. At such a moment only a step like this could save something.

But they had to wait for the Emperor's answer as well. It was polite, after all, to wait for consent and not rush in on one's own initiative.

There were telephone negotiations with Bublikov at the Ministry of Roads and Railways, who, they gradually understood, turned out to have taken an audacious and mutinous step, ordering the Emperor's train detained before it reached Staraya Russa! The President would never have agreed to such a thing himself.

No! It was ignoble. We'll meet anyway. Rodzyanko ordered any detainment of the royal train canceled. But he wasn't at all certain those knaves would carry out his order.

The President's special train had long been ready at the Nikolaevsky Station. Then it was detained practically by the station commandant! Then people arrived at the station from Bublikov and the train was again ready. The road was even cleared for it, passenger trains had been detained, and Mikhail Vladimirovich was already on his way home to change clothes and go to the station when he got to thinking. Why should he chase through Bologoye after the departed royal train now? It would be quicker to meet him on the Vindava line at Dno. He ordered the train at the Nikolaevsky Station canceled and one readied at the Vindava Station.

Meanwhile, he himself was living and moving under mortal threat. After all, he was the one the soldiers had threatened to kill! And right then, in the palace, in the crush or in direct contact, and all with rifles—it would have cost them nothing to kill him! But the old Horse Guard would have despised himself if he'd let such base threats frighten him.

Actually, Engelhardt had hastily issued a pacifying order about not disarming soldiers. Although to what mess this might lead was beyond imagining.

Meanwhile, the soldiers—greeting, not threatening—kept dribbling into the Tauride Palace in formations, units, streams, some only as far as the front steps, some getting into the Ekaterininsky Hall. As they arrived, they all invariably wanted to hear a welcoming speech.

However, there were getting to be fewer and fewer among the Duma deputies and the Provisional Committee willing to go to the crowd and shout themselves hoarse, and many deputies were hiding in their apartments altogether and not showing their faces at the Tauride Palace. From the sinister and brigandish Soviet of Deputies, Chkheidze and Skobelev were always willing to speak to the delegations, as were some active but unknown Jews—and what might they do or say? In order to prevent the garrison's complete disintegration, the President had no choice but to keep taking on these speeches, practically single-handed, until he left.

Again single-handed! As so many times in his life. As he had represented the Duma to the Emperor during the months of their ominous confrontation and misunderstanding. As he had tonight stopped troop movement against Petrograd. As he had carried the entire Provisional Committee on his shoulders. And in these speeches of greeting—again! It was the lot of heroically inclined natures, and Rodzyanko was not complaining. To whom much has been given, much is asked.

And God had sent him a voice! And his appearance was majestic, menacingly distinguished, and if there were dissolute murderers in the crowd, then not a single threat was made out loud. Rodzyanko drew out entire thousands of soldiers with his trumpeting voice—to an awareness of their duty, to an awareness of the danger the fatherland was in and that Germany, their ferocious enemy, had to be vanquished. And although he had said the same thing ten, even twenty times in the past few days, scarcely altering a word, such was the love for Russia that burned in him that he had enough fervor to say it even for the eightieth time. He now realized that the hall of the Duma sessions had been too small and confining for him. Here was an audience that befitted his Zaporozhian Cossack bass, his vast chest!

Naturally, he would have liked to express himself more pointedly and carve up those instigators, those scoundrels from the Soviet of Deputies who had woven their predatory nest in the Duma and were no kind of patriots but rather rascals, if not brigands—here they had already taken over the Tauride

Palace and all Petrograd as well. Yes, all Petrograd! Mikhail Vladimirovich wanted to go home to change for his journey—but he was brought a report of something incredible. Some railroaders at the Vindava Station were refusing to prepare a train for him! They were demanding an order for it from the Soviet of Deputies! Was that so!

That meant the President, who had taken up power in the entire country, was not master of a single locomotive and train? Outrageous! The President possessed the entire fullness of power—and he couldn't give instructions for such a trifle? The trip, on which Russia's fate depended, was being decided by some roguish *deputies*! He would have to send someone to those self-appointed scoundrels and stoop to negotiations! The humiliation was supremely insulting to Rodzyanko's proud soul.

Nonetheless, he had the presence of mind not to utter fateful words. The word "freedom" in the sense of "don't obey anyone" was being heard everywhere—and Rodzyanko silently circumvented this freedom of theirs but called on them to subordinate themselves to the homeland's defense. He shouted that we would not hand Mother Russia over to the cursed German to be torn to shreds—and they shouted back a thunderous "hurrah!"

But it was as if the capital were drunk. Not only military delegations but even high school pupils, even clerks of some kind, were coming to the palace—and someone was supposed to speak to them as well? Now the President was insulted. He should be sitting at his desk, sorting all this out, and pondering what was important enough that it couldn't wait an hour or a minute. (Although, even in his office so many extraneous people had accumulated that perhaps he could go to some small room?)

And now there was another novelty. Not only did all Petrograd know and extol Rodzyanko, but the entire country, from provincial towns and various distant places, railroad workers and officials, city dumas, zemstvo assemblies, and public organizations, was sending in the President's name greetings and assurances of their support for the Provisional Committee and for him personally, that he stood at the head of a popular movement.

Reading these telegrams was music to his ears. To the point of tears.

However, in addition to pleasant telegrams they also brought urgent and quite unpleasant ones, too. Two from Admiral Nepenin saying, first, that he considered the Committee's intentions worthy and correct. This was excellent. But soon after followed one saying that he was requesting assistance in establishing order in Kronstadt, where Admirals Viren and Butakov and officers had been killed.

These Kronstadt killings ran like a knife over his nerves. They clouded these bright days with bloodstains, and something had to be done—but what? Who could you send there? . . . There really wasn't anyone. . . .

Then, from General Ruzsky. With a patent complaint. By his accustomed right to observe Petrograd from the Northern Army Group, a right taken from him by Supreme decision just this winter, or by his right as an aide and accomplice in the recent telegram, Ruzsky was now asking what kind of order there was in the capital. And could the Chairman of the Duma Committee rein in the shooting and the roving soldier element and provide guarantees that there would be no interruption in rail service or the delivery of supplies to the Northern Army Group.

The very fact that the question was posed implied doubt.

And what could Rodzyanko say about order in the capital? To say there was none would be a humiliating admission of his own impotence. To say there was would be a lie.

Rodzyanko wired Ruzsky saying that all measures to preserve order in the capital had been taken and calm was being restored, albeit with great difficulty. But what could he say about rail service, since he himself had been deprived of a train? As God sees fit. . . .

Nonetheless, there was something positive in this exchange of telegrams that reinforced direct contact with the closest commander-in-chief (some of whose troops were still on their way to Petrograd?). This could come in very handy in the next few hours.

There was a very unpleasant telegram from Alekseev, unexpected after their good conversation in the night, a telegram of rebuke that did not try to conceal its tone of rebuke, as of a senior to a junior. Alekseev reproached Rodzyanko for his telegrams to him and the commanders-in-chief, saying they violated the most basic primer on military administration.

That might well be the case, Rodzyanko agreed. However, these were exceptional circumstances! But what had changed since the night? Why had he issued no such rebukes last night? All of a sudden all the mutual understanding achieved during their nighttime conversation seemed to have been lost. Things were getting obscured and were changing at GHQ far away; hence they were impossible to understand and difficult to correct remotely.

Alekseev also reproached him for his instructions over the telegraph lines and rails, for the interruption in communications between GHQ and Tsarskoye Selo, and for the attempt to prevent the special trains from getting to the Dno station—all the outrages that Bublikov himself had committed, without asking, and now it had gone as far as GHQ. This was an outrage, of course, but it would not be helpful to explain to Alekseev, undermining himself, that Rodzyanko had not coped and he did not have the authority to run everything.

What was totally missing in the telegram was anything about the troops sent against Petrograd. Were they still on their way? Or not? Held back?

Although, if Alekseev was silent about this, then that wasn't bad. In any case, he hadn't made any threat.

This telegram upset Mikhail Vladimirovich.

But right then they came with a good piece of news: the Soviet of Workers' Deputies had lifted all their objections to the trip. On condition that Chkheidze go as well.

This spoiled everything! What good was Chkheidze? What was the point of Chkheidze?

Although, he could go! And for balance he would also take Shidlovsky.

Consent for the meeting had also come from the Emperor en route. Wonderful! He could go!

Now, one more telegram, which they could send on the Vindava line:

To His Imperial Majesty. I am now leaving by special train for the Dno station to report to you, Sire, on the state of affairs and on essential measures for Russia's salvation. I earnestly beg you to wait for my arrival, for every minute is precious. Rodzyanko.

Every moment was precious, and no more speeches to delegations. No more telegrams, documents, or questions. Mikhail Vladimirovich was leaving! He had to bring to the confused Emperor, from all Russia, from the entire people, a simple and clear solution: a responsible ministry. With Rodzyanko at its head. Well, and a few amendments to the Constitution.

Although . . . although the sweep of events was such that people had now quietly begun to talk about passing the throne on to Aleksei.

What of it? Perhaps. Perhaps it was inevitable.

Although Chkheidze had come and said he would not allow any transfer to Aleksei—only abdication.

Look who he was saddled with now. Abandoning the throne to the tyranny of fate? Such a thing I will not allow!

Here, in the few remaining rooms of the Duma wing, his Committee's own members were obviously avoiding the President's eyes and exchanging whispers. They could only be whispering against him—in order to make Georgi Lvov prime minister. If this was so, then the President would not bother with these intriguers or even confer with them. Rather, in his own spirit, he would take a big step. He would go to this meeting with the Emperor and obtain his irrevocable confirmation as prime minister.

The final instructions had been given and the key to his desk given to his secretary, but right then people gathered—Milyukov, Nekrasov, Konovalov, and Vladimir Lvov—as if the President had summoned them to a meeting.

"Permit us, Mikhail Vladimirovich!" Milyukov said, his mustache poking up and his pitiless eyes tensed. "We here, members of the Committee, have conferred and find that your trip right now is untimely and ambiguous."

And he fixed his obstructing, freezing gaze on him.

Nekrasov flaunted his grasping wolfishness, not even trying to pretend to be good-natured, as usual.

Somber Lvov wrinkled his nose so that it looked pitted.

Pudgy-nosed, thick-lipped Konovalov, wearing his gold pince-nez as usual, expressed little but occupied space by his girth.

It was as if you were fleeing and they'd stuck out a stick to trip you.

"What's that? Why? Who finds?" Rodzyanko asked incoherently.

"We do," Nekrasov rapped out. (A mere boy! They had let him at thirty-five be Vice President of the Duma!)

"And . . . what do you find?"

"We find, Mikhail Vladimirovich," Milyukov dictated, "that your trip is not backed up by ideas. Not only have the purpose, task, and limits of your authority not been discussed, but the very necessity of such a trip is dubious."

His own people? Weren't letting him go?

[2 5 9]

So has our freedom ended at this? Is this it? Stack your rifle in a pyramid, don't touch it, go back to depending completely on officers? Yesterday and the day before it was as if the wind had blown them out, out of the barracks and the streets, and they were nowhere to be found. But here they were coming back. They arrived warily—and now they were going to give our brothers lip. What was going to happen now? Trip up—and pay with your head. For one, we've had a taste of freedom and aren't much for giving it up, and for another, we don't want to pay with our heads. No, we don't agree! We have to stand shoulder to shoulder, brothers! Here, they say, here's some order from Rodzyanko, the main general, to clean the soldiers out of rifles and make them obey the officers. No, brothers, we've got to find a defense. But where's a defense for us? But that defense exists, and anyone who's been there has seen it for himself: The **Soviet**! That's not our brother there, either, it's gentlemen, too—but another kind that's against it all. We're up to our knees in revolt, but they're up to their waists. So if anyone's going to give us advice, it's them. Go to them now, men!

Others thronged, too, from different barracks, not knowing what the palace was called or the room—but from memory of the streets and from what they'd heard, they forged their way.

Just forged ahead, and that a meeting of the Soviet of Workers' Deputies had been scheduled there in Room no. 12 for noon—hardly anyone knew about that. People blocked them at the doorway and asked for their *mandates*—hell, get your own dates! Step aside! Don't go stopping us! And if it's a soldier stopping you, then just say I'm from such-and-such a company and they elected me!

While inside, the workers in their black clothes were just smatterings, and it was gray greatcoats all around. They crammed into the room, and crammed some more—but there were places to sit only by the walls, on the makeshift benches, boards laid across—otherwise everyone was upright. But then the ones sitting behind the ones standing couldn't see anything, so rather than sit they climbed on those benches. And another table up ahead was all trampled, and a few people were climbing onto it, and shouting, and shaking their fists, and some rogue from the Finland Regiment said:

"Comrades! While we're chatting so fondly here, the counterrevolution isn't dozing, it's gathering terrible forces! That franchised bigwig Rodzyanko issued an order for all soldiers to return and obey!"

And they shouted to him, from over there and over here:

"Burn the order!"

"Arrest Rodzyanko!"

"Barely shook them off—and they're back? We didn't really break the blueblood?"

"We didn't beat 'em enough, didn't stab 'em enough, we should've more!"

"Now they say we shouldn't. They're putting us in our place."

"But who's saying that? It's their crowd saying that. And you're no part of it."

But that rogue kept fanning the flames:

"Comrades, don't trust those fake officer smiles! They were handlers and executioners before, and they still are."

It was getting more and more crammed, the doors wouldn't shut anymore, and so many people were crowding in the doorway that there wasn't room to spit. Fevers were rising, and arms were shaking, and not enough room to roll a cig: that was their idea from the start—make us bend worse than before.

A quaking discussion, talk from every corner, napes turned in every direction—and right then one of those leaders from the next room went and climbed on the table—his arms branching, so nimble, bald but with a black spade of a beard. He climbed up and yelled out that they were opening the session of the Soviet of Workers' Deputies now.

They shouted at him:

"What about the soldiers? Who do you think we are? There's more of us."

The workers shouted:

"You weren't elected."

"But we have elected ones, from the companies!"

Through the doors they shouted again, all fired up:

"Heard of that Rodzyanko order? To lock us up in barracks?"

Lock us up in barracks? Unbridled heads spun around, eyeballs popping:

"What? Where?"

"Maybe they're locking our barracks right now! While we're here giving ourselves sore throats! That's where our kitchen is, at the barracks!"

The bald black-beard on the table, his jacket unbuttoned, was just dancing, so gleeful at the soldiers' ire. And he shouted in a high voice:

"Comrades! We're hereby opening the session of the Soviet of Workers' and Soldiers' Deputies. We have to discuss the most important questions right away. First, what do we think about those officers who didn't participate in the uprising with us and are returning to their units now? Not whether we should be giving the officers our weapons—but should we let the officers themselves carry weapons?"

"Yeah!" the soldier crush hooted. "They understand what's what here, and they won't betray us."

"Who should the soldiers obey now anyway? Clearly not the officers. Clearly the Soviet of Workers' and Soldiers' Deputies. And what are we supposed to think about the Military Commission? At the crucial moment we didn't see officers and representatives of the bourgeoisie there. But now it's all colonels, no soldiers, and without them there's no deciding anything."

"Drive 'em out!" they shouted. "Only you can't get out of this crowd here, or else we'd run right over and crush that nest of theirs."

Then that bald one, Comrade Sokolov, tugged at the other rein:

"But at the head of it is Colonel Engelhardt, who fought in the Japanese war. He's the greatest expert on military matters."

"Well, let him stay, then," the soldiers immediately relented.

"The only way to decide all this is by an authoritative vote by our assembly. If a conflict does arise, we'll have to declare that the Military Commission is being handed over to the Soviet. Give your blessing to strengthening the authority of democratic forces. But until we've broken the enemy for good, we have to hold back on clashing with the bourgeoisie. And now Comrade Maksim has the floor!"

Maksim was already right there, also nimble and knowledgeable:

"Since the Committee of the State Duma is acting menacingly toward the revolutionary army, I propose that the comrade soldiers not surrender their weapons to a single officer! The only place we need an officer is at the front. Let the officer command just his formation. But once the formation is over—the officer is a citizen enjoying the same rights as everyone else. Don't issue them any weapons, though."

A man of robust voice and height trumpeted from his seat:

"Right! We can't line up in formation or turn around without them. That would be no detachment. But march back from the front—and that's it, equals."

Others had their doubts, though:

"You can't do without officers altogether. We'd be lost, brothers."

"And it's no officer without a weapon. And, too, we'd be a useless herd."

"But salute? Or not salute?"

"Not!" one shouted raggedly. "Now they should salute us first!"

Soldier company committees had to be elected, they instructed from the table, and all the weapons put under their control. No matter who tried—

"Comrades! . . ."

That was the new way, everyone a "comrade."

And again that Finland rogue they called Lindya, who was some kind of madman, waved his arms and bawled out at the top of his lungs:

"Guchkov the merchant is calling on soldiers to 'forget old scores.' Anyone who forgets old scores is an ass!"

"Right!"

"Any officer who didn't take part in the revolution shouldn't be accepted or let into barracks at all! Choose others instead of them! There can be no question of officers keeping all their former authority!"

People clapped. This, too, was the new way—clapping. Right then a Semyonovsky man climbed on the table:

"Comrades! While we're squeezing each other's ribs here, not far away, in another room, that very same Military Commission is meeting. And cooking up a plot against us. How to seize and disarm us here and now."

The crowd started pounding the floor: "It's true, we need to get ourselves over there!" But Sokolov waved his arms to calm them down, as if to say, don't:

"Comrades, we've already resolved that no military unit is to obey the Military Commission if its order diverges from the resolution of the Soviet of Workers' Deputies. And we'll bring soldiers onto the Military Commission."

But one countryman standing on the windowsill:

"No! The officer now should be whoever the company says. And whoever it doesn't say can go stand on the left flank."

"We like that!" they shouted.

What about epaulets?

Once freedom starts spreading, there's no stopping it. They shouted:

"Make the epaulets equal, too!"

"Then without Your Honors!"

"And if officers live in private apartments—is that something equal? We aren't going to get equality that way. Let 'em live in barracks, with us."

"Where'll we find cots like that?"

"In the bunks!"

"No, brothers! You still have to give an officer a break. He's got a soft upbringing, and a soft body, too."

"How can we get along without officers? What about the war?"

"What about the war? They drive our forces into position so the German can thin us out."

"No, why, we're not against going into position."

"But they might end the war by then."

"Who's doing that?" . . .

Our heads were so muddled, how could we agree on anything? Some were shouting one thing, others something completely different.

Only Sokolov, on the table, not hoarse, wasn't discouraged.

"Comrades! Let's instruct the Executive Committee to elaborate and write down all these suggestions of yours about officers."

"But you don't have any of our soldiers there either!"

"Come on, brothers, let's push our soldiers in there!"

The head man did not agree:

"No, comrades, that's awkward. Since soldier deputies haven't been delegated from the companies yet. And not everyone here is authorized. . . ."

"The hell we aren't! When we have to drag munitions we're authorized!"

Swivel right, swivel left, a look back at the back door—no help.

"Fine, then, comrades. Let's elect them, provisionally, for three days. Three men."

People started hollering:

"Five!"

"Ten!"

They immediately started raising hands. Who to choose? This wasn't their own company. No one knew anyone. Whoever they'd heard and seen, whoever'd hollered loudest—those. Look—that Lindya. And a sailor. And get that Maksim in there? But he's not ours, he's no soldier.

Anyway, they were choosing not by a count of hands, which were like branches in a forest, but also by shouting.

It took a long time.

Meanwhile, Comrade Maksim read from a prepared paper:

"Here, comrades, is a draft proclamation to the garrison. . . . Don't give your weapons up to the officers. Hand them over to the battalion committees instead. Delegate soldier deputies to the Military Commission. . . . Let the Executive Committee, in accordance with the opinions expressed, issue an appeal and send it out to the garrison units. . . ."

Sokolov gathered up ten or so deputies and they went into the back room.

That didn't make it any roomier here, it was still jam-packed. But it wasn't time to disperse, either. Not everyone had said his piece, or about everything. This discussion filled them up better than porridge.

[260]

In the morning, they brought Captain Nelidov in a carting sleigh and bundled up in a watchman's ordinary sheepskin coat as far as the gates of the Moscow Battalion, where he climbed out, shed the coat, and was again in his officer's greatcoat with his sword. They had ridden down Lesnoi, and the first thing he'd seen had pained him: the gate battered and ripped off.

They'd thought to arrive in darkness, but the cabby got held up and now not only was everyone long since up and about but from the parade ground you could see what almost looked like a battalion in formation.

Nelidov expected to be detained at the gate. But there weren't any sentries and he limped along freely.

Yes, the battalion seemed to have been or was being lined up by company, but at the same time lots of soldiers were lounging around the parade ground in every direction—either they hadn't lined up yet or had already left it. The dark figures of workers flashed by, as if this was shelter for them here, too. But Captain Yakovlev, on horseback, was trying to line up the battalion or anticipating doing so. There were few officers with the formation to be seen—just a few young ensigns.

Leaning on his stick, Nelidov began crossing the parade ground toward Yakovlev, who noticed, rode toward him, and leaning over from his horse, explained that an election had been held here for commanders. He, Yakovlev, had been elected battalion commander, the 1st Company had chosen just a warrant officer, and the 2nd and 4th had confirmed Nelidov and Fergen. An hour before, some unknown ensign had come with a document from the State Duma authorizing him to lead our battalion straight to the Duma, which it had to salute for some reason. The battalion was completely ravaged and disrupted and in no mood for joyous marches, and not all the soldiers wanted to go. But there was this order and they would have to obey. Yakovlev couldn't hand the battalion over to a newcomer, though, and had decided to lead it himself.

In Nelidov's chest, it was all reeling: Salute whom? On what occasion? And what kind of procedure was this? He was already the commander of the 2nd Company, so why did he need to be elected as well?

Nelidov strode toward his company. Right then several soldiers left the formation and came toward him, without asking permission to step out or address him, and declared that the company had elected him their new commander. This was stated amiably rather than insultingly, as if it were an award. Among them he saw the guilty sergeants who had been at the clinic the day before yesterday.

The company was sloppily lined up and making a racket—and they were also shouting to the captain that they had elected him, they trusted him, and he should lead them to the State Duma.

Many were wearing ridiculous red scraps he couldn't stand to look at.

Nelidov was still quite tense from holing up yesterday in that cell—which had suddenly expanded to this entire disorderly parade ground. And now there was this comedy of a march to the Duma? Neither his heart nor his head had time to find their balance.

"How am I going to walk so far, men?" Nelidov replied, indicating his stick to the company. "You know very well one of my legs doesn't work."

The company fell into raucous debate, and offered a solution:

"We'll saddle up a horse for you!"

He could ride a horse, of course, but he wouldn't admit to that.

"No, men, I'd fall off a horse. Go without me."

They agreed. Soon their wobbly column began exiting onto Sampsonievsky, and Yakovlev rode in front.

The parade ground emptied out and the barracks became quite sparse.

Only then did Nelidov have an idea: Where was Fergen if he'd been elected by the 4th Company? And where was Dubrova?

Nelidov's quarters were in the officers' annex, next to the club. But before going there, he went to the club. He could tell from the outside that it had seen quite a lot of gunfire.

But what had gone on inside! A mob of vindictive foreign savages could not have done worse. There wasn't a single surviving portrait or painting. They'd all been sliced and stabbed. The regiment's 106-year history had been disgraced and sullied. The crystal chandeliers had each been smashed by many blows and the shards were on the parquet. All the furniture was spoiled. The cloth on the billiards table had been ripped up by bayonets, the cues snapped, and all the balls disappeared—stolen, probably. The wind instruments had been crushed and twisted and the drums split. The regimental museum had been jumbled into a pile of trash, historical regimental objects, uniforms from the Borodino era—all of it dragged off. The library had been scattered into piles on the floor.

This desecration was nauseating—as if they weren't Russians, as if their own glory were not dear.

Right then three regimental clerks approached Nelidov. First, in the middle of this rout, slowly crunching underfoot what had been smashed and crushed, then taking them to his chancellery, and they told him a great deal.

How the day before yesterday there had been a battle for the officers' club. And all this smashing and rout had been the night after that. Soldiers from the 3rd Company joined by many workers had done the smashing.

Colonel Mikhailichenko? He'd left for headquarters before the uprising and never returned to the battalion. Instead, he'd gone from there to his apartment on Vasilievsky Island, where he'd been seized this morning and taken away somewhere in a truck.

Staff Captain Fergen? He was here somewhere. Captain Dubrova? He'd had a stroke and been carried to the regimental infirmary on a stretcher. But the doctor didn't want to leave him there, he was afraid, too—so they moved him to the children's hospital, next to the barracks. But he didn't stay there, either. They transferred him to the city hospital on the Vyborg side. Where he was found. The crowd burst in and dragged him straight from his bed to the street—and spat on him, mocked him, beat him, and were about to execute him when a motorcar drove up, saved him, and took him to the State Duma.

Everything was topsy-turvy, and Nelidov's head was spinning.

But the clerks recounted their own steadfastness with a certain pride. They had not given the battalion committee just elected or their representatives who came a single report, had not explained a single way to solve practical matters. This was why, in the last twenty-four hours, the soldiers had thought better of it and today had started electing their own officers to their former posts.

The soldiers wouldn't have been so obstinate and enraged if the civilians from the Vyborg side hadn't come to spur them on.

And again in a certain dizziness, having lost any thread of meaning, Nelidov went to roam through the club's rout, crunching with his boots.

And he saw another such sad man wandering solitarily—Staff Captain von Fergen!

"Aleksandr Nikolaich!"

They hadn't seen each other since the morning of the day before yesterday, in the predawn dark, when they'd parted with their detachments for various locations on the Vyborg side. Was that just the day before yesterday? . . .

Now they met as if at a morgue.

Fergen's eyes watched him tensely, glassily, as if he'd lost his closest friend.

"They didn't make you go to the Duma?"

Fergen was unshakeable:

"I told them I wouldn't go anywhere or command them until they removed those red rags and accepted the proper order."

"What did they do?"

"They started hollering and got very angry. I left."

They were standing on shards.

"Let's go to my place, Aleksandr Nikolaich." Nelidov suddenly remembered he himself was never going to get to his own quarters. "We'll rest up and plan what to do next."

Fergen's apartment was in the city.

They reached the annex near the regimental church. They knocked, but Luka didn't open up right away. He greeted them with a sleepy face. He started justifying himself by saying they hadn't let him sleep for days, they'd come to search. But before the raid the soldier had managed to hide the gold and silver items and whatever was more valuable in the stove, so there was nothing for them to take. If the captain hadn't come today, he was thinking of going there, where he was hiding. Yes, Luka was truly devoted.

The rooms weren't heated, and Luka had been sleeping well covered. One moment, one moment and he would get the heat going and feed them. He got a glass holder, spoons, wine cups, and a ring out of the ashes—and before you knew it had it lit and the wood crackling pleasantly.

Devastated and somber, the officers sat down at the empty table facing each other. They started sharing the things they'd lived through and known in the past few days.

Fergen told him how for three days, in various places on the Vyborg side, Moscow guards, which no one was relieving, had continued and were stubbornly standing there today and wouldn't leave. But here in the battalion were soldiers no different—and look . . .

Warmth wafted through both rooms.

After they'd eaten something hot as well, they were suddenly bone weary. It was still daytime—scarcely halfway through—and they'd accomplished nothing—but it was as if the longest and hardest day of their life were drawing to a close, they couldn't take it any more, their very souls were weary.

Nelidov said:

"Maybe we should get some sleep? Eh?"

They didn't undress. They just took off their boots, pulled up the covers, and fell asleep in broad daylight.

[2 6 1]

Right there, at the top of Ostozhenka, was the headquarters of the Moscow Military District. Vorotyntsev headed straight there. They should know the entire situation, and everything would become clear. True, the headquarters' staffing had changed greatly since '14, and there was no one he knew left, but he did have acquaintances among the officers, and there were senior clerks who knew what was what.

He went just to find out but ended up spending a few hours there—it was impossible to put together and understand the complete picture any faster, and anyway it kept changing.

The impression was stunning. Something simply incredible had happened, and in such a short time that Vorotyntsev found it doubly unbelievable that he had walked right through it without a scratch. On Sunday, when he was leaving Petrograd, it had been completely quiet. On Monday, Moscow had seemed calm, he'd noticed nothing. But on Tuesday . . .

Learning from the headquarters staff what had happened in Moscow yesterday and today, Vorotyntsev, of course, did not reveal to them that he himself had already been here for more than two days and that he himself had come from Petrograd. He couldn't admit that he'd missed out on everything in both places.

Anyway, Moscow hadn't had any particular events of its own yesterday: no clashes, no shooting, no building seizures, no arrests of officials. Even today, the water supply was operational, as were the lights, telephone, banks, commercial and official places, everything as usual, there just weren't any streetcars or newspapers. It was all just an echo of Petrograd and the agitation of anticipation. But impatient male and female students had started converging on Resurrection Square. City duma members had gone out and made speeches. Then workers and ordinary people had been drawn in, the crowd had thickened, and then there'd been other gatherings around the city. In the duma itself, though, all the speeches seethed from the legitimate public, not the revolutionaries, and why should the sensibly minded segment of the population be barred? On the streets, neither the police nor the mounted gendarmerie tried to prevent anything anywhere; all the pickets let the marches with the red flags pass. Near the duma, a gendarme squadron on horseback shifted in place, not knowing what to do. Then why should the military authorities act? The troops had been led back to barracks and were sitting there.

It seemed right.

But then university students climbed over the fence of the Aleksan-drovsky barracks and burst into the reserve infantry regiment and the ensign schools to persuade the soldiers and first-year cadets to support the great Pet-rograd events—and no one had tried to stop them? Agitators had already burst into the Spassky barracks. But even this didn't rouse District headquar-ters to action! Late yesterday evening, a ragtag party had come directly to greet the mutinous duma—and all Mrozovsky could come up with after that night was his decree about a state of siege? By this morning everyone found it laughable. You couldn't enforce it without military power.

Information had flowed from Mrozovsky, who had refused to leave his home, to his assistant general, and on through the colonels—through head-quarters. Mrozovsky did not want bloodshed and therefore had rejected any actions by the troops whatsoever! Martynov, head of the Moscow Okhrana, suggested to Mrozovsky that he declare a blockade of Petrograd as having been seized by enemies of the fatherland and use reliable units to create a barrier between the capitals—but Mrozovsky could not bring himself to do so without instructions from the Supreme Commander.

Suddenly, that night, news came that the Emperor himself had left for the mutinous capital, so that everything was decided, it was marvelous, he himself would take measures there, so why blockade Petrograd? Then a rumor came in saying that Evert was moving on Moscow with troops—also marvelous. Evert would arrive and order would be restored. That very night a telegram arrived at the City Duma from Petrograd saying that Chelno-kov would not be the mayor now but had been appointed *commissar* of Moscow—a terrible, paralyzing word—but Mrozovsky did not wish to quar-rel with the new leadership. Early this morning, an ominous telegram had arrived from Rodzyanko for Mrozovsky himself saying that the old govern-ment no longer existed at all! Power had transferred to the Committee of the State Duma under Rodzyanko's chairmanship, and all the Petrograd troops had recognized the new government, and Mrozovsky, too, was or-dered to obey, otherwise all the responsibility for bloodshed would fall on his head.

It was enough to drive you mad.

Mrozovsky, evidently, got scared. And started calling the new commissar, Chelnokov, begging him to come and talk. But Chelnokov wouldn't.

After sitting at headquarters for a while, the assistant general himself was quite inclined to recognize the reality and submit to it, and submit to it quickly, while the new government was still represented by respected and distinguished citizens and before it passed into the irresponsible hands of extreme leftists. All the mediocrities meeting here, in the rear, at headquar-ters were even more willing to join in with this reassuring position. At the starting hour of mandatory activities, everyone arrived at headquarters—and was even more inclined not to intervene in anything today when the new government in Petrograd was becoming increasingly defined and strengthened. Why confront it? A delicate situation.

The strength and weakness of a military hierarchy! Invincible power when there is a firm command on top. And limp dough when there isn't.

There was also the Emperor's journey to Petrograd. . . . What had moved him to leave GHQ at such a moment? Had he really gone to establish order himself? The trip was superfluous but made an effect: to go into the thick of the revolt himself!

But no. No. He was too meek. He couldn't have brought himself to do that. He had probably gone to make peace with everyone. That was more like him.

But today—today Moscow was aboil with marches, from one hour to the next—while Vorotyntsev was just wandering through headquarters, perching first here and then there. People said the rebels had seized the city governor's offices, the city governor had fled, and the provincial governor had been put under house arrest! The police force had vanished from the streets altogether, and apparently policemen were being placed under arrest at no one knew whose instruction. Crowds were greeting the new government, which no one had seen yet or understood—while there was still an unabolished old one . . .

Mrozovsky hid in his apartment as if the events in this city and this country didn't affect him. (My God! And there had been such decisive generals in this post. Malakhov, for one! Why had Mrozovsky, who was decisive only in his rudeness to those lower in rank, so unfortunately turned up there now?) When other unit commanders requested permission to act, the beheaded headquarters told them to bide their time and muddle through for now. The District was falling apart, becoming just troops in individual barracks, which were being run as they saw fit. And streams of soldiers with red flags were already flowing from those barracks to the duma.

Yes, act! Act quickly and boldly! The hope of headquarters, that someone would come to his senses or Evert would come to Moscow's rescue, was not the military way. They couldn't expect others to hold their sector for them. At the height of war, the country's central garrison, its second capital, the main road and railway hub, was falling apart and would perish. This was a direct betrayal of the army in the field.

But who was to act and how? No one here was contemplating anything. So how could Vorotyntsev intervene? In what capacity? No one had summoned him, and there was no one here to whom he could offer himself. Here headquarters was so self-absorbed they had no room for a stray colonel. At the Spassky barracks or the Manège—there they, too, had their own commanders everywhere, so why some outsider colonel? The army's strength lay in each man being in his place. No one needed D'Artagnan's rapier.

There was also his own Aleksandrovsky Military School, and he called a teacher he knew there, who replied that the school saw its mission as preserving its cadets from being touched by these events.

This was where Vorotyntsev found himself: seemingly right there, in the thick of events—and unneeded by anyone.

It was true, if you thought about it. *How* could he act? How could the army act against a peace-loving crowd when no one was shooting, everyone was merely rejoicing, even some infantry there were rejoicing, too? By what forces and means could anyone disperse this joyous crowd to their homes and work? No one had even bared cold steel, and there had been no battles.

Maybe this would all resolve itself quietly?

Right then, everyone rushed to the windows onto Prechistenka. Vorotyntsev followed them. And he saw a large detachment of gendarmes—maybe a whole division?—slowly riding from Volkhonka onto Prechistenka wearing full dress uniform, in perfect order—but not undertaking anything, moving away from the center.

People hooted at them from the sidewalks and boulevard—but didn't touch them.

Had they quit the Manège? Then the center had no police forces at all.

Meanwhile, the time had come to take a break—and headquarters calmly dispersed for its midday meal. Vorotyntsev should have gone, too.

But where?

Where else but to his own Ninth Army? . . .

He needed more time to think. He couldn't undertake anything—but he couldn't leave here now, either.

He went out and was simply baffled, as if he too wanted to join the universal, crazed exultation. He started out down Volkhonka.

The weather couldn't have been better for a universal outing: a sunny day, a light frost (colder in the shadow of buildings).

Red flags on the roofs of streetcar stations.

But there weren't any streetcars or cabs. Occasionally a carting sleigh would go by and on it a party sharing the ride, some even standing. An overladen truck drove by crowded with soldiers carrying rifles, university students, and modern school and high school boys, all waving red at the public. They shouted "hurrah!" and the street shouted back—"hurrah!"

But the people! The people had flooded the streets and the thoroughfares, mostly the thoroughfares! In winter, yardmen cleaned the sidewalks, but not the thoroughfares, which was why they leveled out higher than the sidewalks and were gleamingly smoothed out by the sleighs, white when not marred by trucks. And now everyone was thronging down that strip, warming the snow up and mixing it with dirt. The crowd, scattered here, thick there, as if it were gaily dispersing after some gathering. All Moscow was in the streets! Young ladies in furs, servants in kerchiefs, artisans, soldiers,

officers. It was wild to see soldiers with rifles but out of formation, a strolling
jumble, some even with red on their chest. The majority saluted the officers, while others acted as though they'd forgotten. But it was inappropriate
to stop and call them to account. Although every man who did not salute
might as well have struck out at him. That was how it felt.

Walking along: a soldier and a university student arm in arm, the soldier
with a red flag and the student with a rifle.

A civilian crazily unbuttoned, his scarf dangling.

And on every face the joy of Easter, touching smiles—and not a threat in
anyone. If one were to act using an armed unit—then against whom? . . .

Vorotyntsev, carrying a small bag in his left arm, kept mostly to the
sidewalk.

Even stranger was it to come across officers, who saluted so irreproachably and passed by so calmly, as if nothing in particular were happening
around them—which made it look as though the officers were complicit.

This officer indifference given the crowd's mounting joy gave Vorotyntsev another jolt: What was this going on? What was this universal obscurity,
fascination, betrayal? Why wasn't anyone resisting? Why wasn't anyone
concerned?

There was no rebellion of any kind! No one was blocking anyone's way.
Was it just all of Moscow out for a stroll? Yet what was the merriment following? There had been no noticeable grief immediately preceding.

All the ordinary residents and servants had simply thronged here to get
an eyeful of what was happening. Over there a little boy was climbing an
iron streetcar pole. Here on that low fence a batch of smaller kids was huddled together and staring.

What was also notable was that strangers were striking up conversations
and introductions, delighted and congratulating each other for some reason. They were even embracing, even kissing! (This was the better-dressed
public, which was more delighted than anyone else.)

Understanding neither his route nor his objective, Vorotyntsev started
down Mokhovaya. Here the public got even thicker, and many male and female students appeared. They were especially lively, their teeth flashing,
laughing, and near the university they formed up into a column.

Hanging on the wall was a leaflet typed on a Remington. Near him, a
handful were reading it. Vorotyntsev walked up, too, waited his turn, and
read it. Shcheglovitov had been arrested. In charge of the arrests of enemies
of the fatherland was Kerensky. (He had never heard of such a thing.) The
military department had been assigned to Colonel Engelhardt. (And who
was that? What nonsense was this?)

Idle soldiers were entering and exiting the Manège freely. There wasn't
an officer in sight, and it was clear that the Manège was no longer resisting.

Of course, if GHQ were to send troops to both capitals, all this Moscow revelry and Petrograd self-styled government would blow away like the wind. Might they already have been sent? But the Emperor had gone to Petrograd for some reason, hadn't he? He'd abandoned the mighty GHQ and gone into captivity by the Rodzyanko government?

No, something wasn't computing. A crowd flowed thickly past the Manège toward Resurrection Square. Vorotyntsev knew the center was there and everyone was converging there. He, too, turned off, down the sidewalk, barely getting through the crush. Up ahead, coming this way, toward Aleksandrovsky Square and its particular hubbub. It was nearly a solid mass from here on. Behind the Manège, a large dark march of workers was thronging, also with red flags, of course, marching arm in arm, in rows—and this created an impression of force. They cut through the crowd confidently. And stretched a long way—some entire factory.

For some reason, Vorotyntsev didn't feel like going to the City Duma.

He passed down Mokhovaya to Tverskaya, where he did not miss seeing a march of infantry, a battalion. They were going down Tverskaya with a band, the regimental flag, and a large red towel on a stick—going swiftly, in rough formation, but they kept in step, and there was this: junior officers were marching in their proper places. Judging from their numbers this wasn't all of them, but they looked bold, confident, even cheerful.

The march of this formed-up military unit shook Vorotyntsev most of all. An army unit was marching in a rank to greet a self-appointed government when the old one hadn't gone anywhere!

No, they were reasoning without a master. . . .

But *what* could you call what was going on?

On Tverskaya, on the sidewalks, there were so many gawkers crowding around, you couldn't get through. Vorotyntsev went down Tverskaya, stepping into the thoroughfare, with its messy brown snow. The public was thronging thickly up the street and down.

All of a sudden he heard a powerful and strange rattling and rumble. The public staggered back. Finally they thought to look up. An aeroplane was flying along Tverskaya! All heads leaned back and everything came to a standstill.

It was flying low, a few hundred hundred feet up, clearly visible, a little lower, then a little higher. It wasn't tossing out anything, but it bore a red flag on its wing. . . .

And then that way, toward Resurrection Square.

The street shouted "hurrah" at it and tossed their caps.

But then following behind was another truck—with soldiers, workers, and university students—and they were tossing out leaflets right and left. Passersby were snatching them up. Vorotyntsev was curious to read it, but as a colonel he couldn't bend over and pick one up. Or ask for it from someone.

Also rolling by were two three-inch cannons—at which the crowd shouted especially ecstatically. Gunners marched lightly alongside and waved.

Several civilians were leading along an arrested policeman—a strapping man with a policeman's confident face.

There was also a red flag hanging from the governor-general's residence. Did you ever! The commotion alongside it, both motor vehicles and sleighs, showed that the new government had commandeered these places.

On the other side—a red flag poked up on the raised sword of Skobelev's monument. A speaker standing on something towered over the crowd. He was shouting, not speaking, and a couple of hundred curious people had gathered around and were shouting approvingly at him. (Vorotyntsev made out that he was shouting from a truck.)

But they turned onto Gnezdnikovsky, where the Okhrana had been sacked and anyone who wanted to was going in, carrying out documents, reading them, laughing.

Before Vorotyntsev reached the boulevard, he encountered something else new. Two university students were carrying a plywood shield on two sticks, and on the shield, slapdash, in crooked letters, with dripping red: "Long live the democratic republic!"

After this, Vorotyntsev felt he'd already seen everything conceivable today. There was no point in going to look, nothing more for him to do in Moscow.

But he was mistaken.

The Pushkin monument at the head of Tverskoi Boulevard was bristling conspicuously. One stick with a long red pennant was poking from Pushkin's shoulder—upward and high. Another along his bent right elbow—forward. Two more flags were coming from the bottom of the pedestal. The poet himself had a red ribbon wound slantwise across his shoulder. Attached to the front of the pedestal was coarse, solid red calico on which white letters had been rather painstakingly drawn:

> Have faith, comrade, in its rise,
> The dawn of captivating bliss!

Standing around the monument's chain were ladies, and old men of the merchant sort, old women with shawls wrapped around their fur caps. A few soldiers and a few of what looked to be servants.

Looking. And across the chain, in that direction, they were spitting seed husks onto the snow.

*   *   *

MOSCOW IS GETTING MARRIED! PETERSBURG IS, TOO!

*   *   *

[2 6 2]

On the approach to the Tauride Palace, marches were squeezing onto Shpalernaya from parallel streets, and people were waving and shouting at them from the sidewalks. Kutepov gazed on them with disgust. It was a workday, a Wednesday, the third week of Lent, the thirty-second month of the war, men were sitting in foul trenches at the front, fending off the enemy, cooling pots were being carried through the snow-swept communicating passages, Russia was at war, entrenched in the earth, and this degenerate riffraff in the capitals was exulting because they'd knocked out the policeman and so could carry on, drinking and stealing.

In the open space in front of the Tauride Palace there was already an indescribable crush, an eddying, and although the soldiers had rifles for the most part, they were so slack and turned every which way that they created the impression of prisoners of war herded together.

Kutepov and Kholodovsky, however, were walking with vigor and confidence — making their way toward the entrance.

In the entrance hall, Kutepov immediately recognized rifle cases and unassembled machine guns. In the next halls the thick was even more impenetrable and senseless: the same abundance of lost men facing in different directions, while above the crowd were various gesturing speakers and red.

But what enraged Kutepov was not even all this repulsive appearance of the soiled palace, the fake red flags when the Russian government had its own banners — but soldiers' seemingly recognized right not to salute. No one displayed any hostility toward the colonel and captain, no one said a harsh word, but their indifferent gazes slid over them as if they were equals. It was this brash indifference that choked Kutepov most of all, as if the hall's columns had collapsed. Without respect for officers, there is no army. As long as he'd lived, as long as he'd served — everything had rested on this.

There were sentries by many of the doors — cadets or Preobrazhensky men! — asking for people's passes. No one dared demand one from Kutepov, and he entered freely where he wanted but exited just as quickly, not finding the military headquarters he sought.

In one spacious room with velvet-covered tables he found what looked like a session, but it was disorderly, without rules, and the discussion was general — about forty well-dressed men, without their overcoats, wearing frock coats and ties, perhaps Duma deputies, perhaps public figures, and among them a few officers. They were sitting in armchairs and side chairs, also pretty much facing different directions, and discussing disjointedly . . . but discussing what? They ignored Kutepov and Kholodovsky, who stood there for a while and listened.

Here's what they were arguing: which is better, a monarchy or a republic? In Russia right now but also in the world, in general, always. They mentioned Athens, Rome, Charlemagne, and, of course, France, France in its various centuries and decades.

Kutepov stood there listening without saying a word. Listening—and filling with rage. He felt he could no longer leave without speaking. But as for a public speech—he'd never made one in front of an audience like this in his life.

And suddenly, ignoring the next speaker, interrupting him, he strode in military step to a space visible to everyone, in front, and in his imperious bass voice said:

"Gentlemen! You should be ashamed of debating when the government is perishing! What is Athens to you if there are drunken soldiers searching your apartment? I'm astonished at your frivolous conversations at such a time. The capital is in ruins. Your own palace is a three-ring circus. You should be talking about how to bring about order and rescue the situation. If this is not done today, right now, then it will be too late. The crowd is going to wipe all of you and your Athens off the face of the earth."

Everyone listened in amazement. But it rose in Kutepov's throat that it wasn't worth saying anything more, he wasn't going to convince them of anything, it was utterly hopeless. And just as useless to stay to listen to what they would reply.

He turned sharply, stepped away in military stride, let Kholodovsky go ahead, and slammed the door behind him.

They began pushing through again, and in the corridor they ran into Colonel Engelhardt.

Engelhardt was a rather weak, onetime Academy man, from the Guards Uhlans, who had for some reason been dragged through higher training and then had done well to retire early and go into agriculture. But he had been elected to the State Duma, and now during these revolutionary days he had once again pulled on his colonel's uniform—and acquitted himself rather poorly.

They shook hands, and Kutepov immediately asked what measures the colonel intended to take to institute order. Engelhardt replied he was no longer responsible for Petrograd, that Yurevich, a medical doctor, had just been appointed city governor of Petrograd, and he would bring about order everywhere.

"Who?" Kutepov couldn't believe it was a medical doctor.

But that was the case. A professor at the Military Medical Academy.

Kutepov looked at him as if he were insane. Nonetheless, he attempted to give advice. In the reserve battalions (he had gleaned this upon arrival) there were soldiers who for the last year had been on continuous duty with policemen at streetcar stops and intersections and had experience at instituting order in the streets. They all should be sought out right away, given commandant armbands, and posted to their familiar duties. The crowd would immediately sense that there was authority on the street.

Engelhardt flushed red.

"I would ask that you not lecture me!"

Kutepov looked down at him.

"Not only do I not want to lecture you, I don't even want to talk with you. But remember, no doctors are going to save you now."

He and Kholodovsky turned and left. They went outside, away.

On the front steps they encountered a crowd carrying the heavy Rodzyanko along, surrounded by red flags.

Kutepov was so exasperated, he decided to cut short his leave and depart for his regiment.

[2 6 3]

Anyone who has served in the army for a long time or who knows the people's life and has gleaned its wisdom knows that in any threatening and unclear situation that demands the impossible of you, you shouldn't reject it out of hand or even resist openly.

Iudovich could not directly renounce his position before the Emperor, could not shake the Emperor's merciful trust in him, could not open up in the simplest way and say, Let me go, Your Majesty, I'm weak, I'm unable, I'm not the hero you see in me. He couldn't bear to see the disappointment in the Emperor's eyes or shake his own honorable status as an adjutant general. How could he go on living without it? Perhaps he might be appointed to a higher post?

And here he had been appointed—dictator.

Not accept this assignment, not go to Petrograd and save the homeland—Nikolai Iudovich simply could not do that. But he could still delay.

He was assembling his own battalion, and making arrangements with GHQ, and scouting out the Petrograd situation—and that could take quite a while. He would travel late—and get started even later. Having finally attached his home-like train car to the St. George officers' train—even en route he hadn't fulminated at natural delays, hadn't demanded the station masters and military commandants come to him for a dressing-down, but had humbly accepted all the delays and difficulties of rail travel, the way a peasant at his work waits out bad weather. Yesterday, at seven in the evening, they'd passed through Vitebsk—and Nikolai Iudovich had fallen into his familiar soft bed, in his homey, well-appointed train car, to sleep. He didn't know what disturbances and dangers awaited him the next day, but for now, for the next few hours, his advantage was that he had no communication with and was reporting to no one.

The night passed very peacefully. This morning, a pleasant surprise awaited the dictator. In the night, instead of four hundred versts, they had gone only two hundred and were only at the Dno station.

This gave him great hopes for not arriving anywhere for all of 14 March and not getting down to business. Over this day in Petrograd, everything should come to some conclusion without him. Iudovich was much encouraged.

Right then he had presented to him Baron Raden, commander of the Dagestan infantry regiment, who was traveling via Petrograd from leave. What the baron told him of what was going on in Petrograd would take your breath away. Crowds of dissolute, drunken soldiers were firing guns and taking away officers' weapons, regardless of rank and battle service. They were putting barrels to heads. And shooting on the streets just like that, as if they were having a conversation.

This colonel recounted so much so colorfully that the adjutant general ordered the colonel to immediately write a detailed report addressed to the Supreme Commander's chief of staff.

Let Alekseev read it and realize how things were there, in Petrograd.

Meanwhile, they brought Nikolai Iudovich a badly delayed telegram from GHQ saying that yesterday, at noon, the remaining loyal forces had had to quit the Admiralty so the building would not be subject to attack. These units had been released to their barracks, but their rifles, machine guns, and gun-locks had been surrendered to the naval ministry.

There you had it.

And thank God it had all ended without unnecessary bloodshed.

It was now clear that there was no point thrusting oneself at Petrograd with a battalion. If you arrived there to command all the District's troops, they would simply put a barrel to your head, as they had to this baron.

Quite likely they had the machine guns there ready for that encounter.

But another telegram confirmed that troops sent from the Northern Army Group, and even further reinforced, were on their way to assist the dictator.

One could hope that they couldn't possibly arrive today, though; the earliest possible was tomorrow. And by tomorrow, with God's help, things might sort themselves out somehow.

However, it was also impossible to stop his movement toward Tsarskoye Selo.

It was also good that the royal trains were now taking a roundabout route, along the Nikolaevsky line. It would be very awkward for Iudovich to lag behind them on the same line or even meet up with the Emperor at some station.

They moved gingerly onward.

Right then, at the stations, complaints began coming in from commandants and the railroad police that many soldiers were traveling along this branch in trains from Petrograd, separate from their units. No one knew where they were going or why and many were drunk. At the stations up ahead, they were taking weapons away from officers and station police and committing various acts of violence.

Like it or not, they would now have to go into action. The dictator bore with him the ominous right of field court-martial—and could hold a trial right here at the stations and carry out executions. But these harsh extremes were the last thing he wanted, and he was hoping to pacify them in a paternal way, which would lead to a general pacification, although it would detain the expedition in transit.

At the next stations he ordered General Pozharsky to inspect the oncoming trains. He himself, with his Minin beard, pushed into one train car, hoping to overwhelm everyone and bring them to their knees—but he couldn't even get through the passageway, which was jammed with fare dodgers and a strange sort of public: many in civilian dress and all young men. Right then some of the passengers advised the general that it was soldiers in Petrograd who had robbed clothing stores and here they had changed clothes and were now dispersing to their homes. Why should they stay with their units? . . .

So the adjutant general left that train car having undertaken nothing.

After that, oncoming trains arrived with broken windows, and there was a crush on the platforms, all jammed with soldiery. St. George patrols began passing through the train cars, and passengers—sometimes women, sometimes old men—began pointing out which soldier-bullies had been taking away officers' weapons. They began arresting those bullies and taking them to their troop train and recovered as many as a hundred items of officer weaponry.

Right then, a soldier leaped out of a train car and ran at the adjutant general himself with three swords—one in each hand and one at his side, and also a rifle over his shoulder. The general managed to deflect the brandished sword, but the soldier was able to bite his hand. This scoundrel should have been tried quickly and shot then and there. But Pozharsky didn't feel like pouring oil on the fire, it being a dangerous situation as it was.

The situation—now it was clear what it was like in Petrograd.

If they were to bring order throughout, they didn't need to move forward, just meet the troop trains. But Nikolai Iudovich could not forget his combat assignment—so their train moved on. By dusk they'd arrived in Vyritsa.

Here they learned that there had been disturbances in Tsarskoye Selo the day before. The troops had refused to obey—and there was now a rebellion there.

So that's how it was! That meant the royal family was being held captive? Ay yay yay! The Empress! And the heir himself!

But if Tsarskoye Selo was already in their hands, how could General Ivanov move any farther?

It was reported to Nikolai Iudovich that even Pozharsky in Mogilev had told the officers that he would not allow shooting at the people, even if Ivanov so ordered him.

Thus, he had to be all the more circumspect now.

But he couldn't not continue on toward Tsarskoye Selo either. After all, the regiments were converging on that line.

Nikolai Iudovich gave orders for another locomotive to be attached to his train in back, facing backward, so that he could shift into reverse at any moment.

And with the utmost caution, they headed off.

[2 6 4]

What was the Minister of War to do with himself now that he was obviously a former minister but had not yet been arrested and so was compelled to make decisions and take charge of his own body? Yesterday, when he and General Zankevich withdrew from the Admiralty in a timely fashion, from the ruinous Khabalov detachment, General Belyaev had greatly extended his own existence at liberty.

Yesterday at the General Staff for the first few hours he had also sat by the direct line, sent dispatches to GHQ, answered their questions, and accepted their orders, all the while relying on their strength and saving intervention. During the second half of the day, full reports even arrived about the troops' movement on Petrograd, but the slow pace made it clear that if GHQ was going to come save the capital, it would be too late for Mikhail Alekseevich Belyaev. (Around the General Staff itself, machine guns were being fired very close by and very loud!)

What an amazingly swift, successful, and enviable career—and it was perishing! . . . (Two months ago had been another critical moment. He had lost his post under the Romanian king and was traveling in despair to his newly assigned division when the Emperor summoned him to Petrograd by telegram and appointed him minister.)

It was fine for Zankevich. He had his service at the General Staff and could stay on right there. He wasn't directly linked to the former government, and his unfortunate participation over the past few days in the Khabalov detachment's actions could be covered up. He was a neutral military specialist who could now even enter into negotiations with the new authorities.

It was also fine for Minister of the Navy Grigorovich. Although he held a post fully analogous to Belyaev's, he enjoyed the Duma's sympathy, had even won applause there, and now he had quite opportunely taken ill, had not participated in the government's most recent actions at all, and had even managed to refuse hospitality to the Khabalov detachment. All this had fortified his position enough that (Belyaev was in constant telephone communication with him, seeking a solution for himself) Admiral Grigorovich simply telephoned the Duma and requested that they send him a guard! And they did!

Belyaev was a lonely man, unmarried (always devoted to his service only, its decrees, directives, and instructions), and this would have eased the task of his personal salvation—had he had the same good public reputation

Grigorovich did. Unfortunately, he didn't. Since the New Year, in moving from irreproachable neutral posts to war minister, he had dangerously linked his name with this last doomed cabinet and also, by virtue of his post responsible for military censorship, he had answered as well for the censoring of certain Duma speeches. A dreadful position and a dreadful mistake! And who were you now going to convince, and how, that his whole appointment and promotion had come about not out of some particular devotion of his to the Emperor but simply because he spoke foreign languages and had the experience of foreign travel, which was important for the purposes of military provisioning. (Well, he had also very much pleased the Empress by transferring Rasputin's son from a Siberian regiment as a medic to Peterhof.)

One way or another, though, the entire second half of yesterday he had been seen at the General Staff, this news had already gotten out, of course, and it was dangerous to remain here overnight even in some general's apartment. (As it later proved: that night they did come to the General Staff to arrest him and did search for him.)

Where should he go? To his private apartment on Nikolaevskaya Street— but that was far away and dangerous—or take a risk, although it seemed like madness, and return to his official apartment on the Moika, to his ministerial residence, which he had fled the previous night under gunfire?

That was what he did, and it proved fortunate. The quirks of a revolution: the well-known apartment of the Minister of War in the very center of the city—and no one had attacked it, they'd just hijacked his motorcar. The direct line to GHQ was actually still working, so he could speak with Alekseev. Naturally, though, Belyaev not only did not make any such attempt, but he ordered his secretary, if a call came in, to say no one was there.

There had been no attack, but it could come, so Belyaev decided to make use of his return to burn as many documents as possible. He mobilized his secretary and assistant, and his batman, and the doorman—and they burned documents in two stoves and the fireplace simultaneously: files from the Ministry of War, and the Special Conference on Defense, and the Conference on Provisioning the Army and Navy, many materials that had no copies, the sole copy, many secret documents, and secret inventories, and the secret codes themselves, and records of telegraph conversations with GHQ, and materials from the recent conference of Allies in Petrograd. A great many papers, basically. And Belyaev, who had always so loved the very texture of papers, their shininess, their rustle, and the ink loops on them, he himself now was also shoving them into the fire frenziedly and with relief, as if freeing himself from his disgraceful connection to this government. The higher the shaggy piles of ash, the whiter he felt.

They kept burning like this until two in the morning—and no one attacked. It was so late by then that they could hope for a peaceful sleep.

In the morning, though, a relative telephoned with the bitter news that they were storming and looting his private apartment on Nikolaevskaya. A dreadful, tortuous state: knowing your apartment was being robbed and being powerless to intervene!

Again he conferred with Grigorovich over the telephone. Grigorovich was sitting it out safely under guard at naval headquarters—and he advised Belyaev for his own safety to move to the General Staff after all. Correct! Especially since a suspicious crowd, apparently, was gathering on the Moika opposite his gates. But they couldn't grab him at the General Staff during the day.

Putting on a more modest greatcoat without epaulets and pulling his large service cap down over his eyes, Belyaev exited via the back door and another courtyard—unnoticed, small, hunched over, unrecognized—and quickly reached the General Staff going down Morskaya.

There he felt much bolder and reasoned thus: he was no criminal as far as the new government went. He was the most honest of men but had been defamed in the general political uproar. During time of war he had done a tremendous job for the good of the homeland, and this should be taken into account. He was fifty-four years old and could be released from service with a large pension. He would very willingly shake off the dust of authority. How he now wished to begin the life of a private person! If necessary, he could sign an undertaking not to leave. But he had to ask for protection for himself and to save the apartment on Nikolaevskaya.

With this mood and these thoughts he sat down to the telephone after three o'clock in the afternoon and began trying to reach the State Duma and someone responsible. Nekrasov came to the phone.

"I am former Minister of War Belyaev. I have offered up no obstacles to you, nor will I. Only give me the opportunity to become a private citizen immediately. And protect me and my apartment, which they're looting. . . . I can sign an undertaking . . ."

"I advise you," Nekrasov replied, "to head to the Peter and Paul Fortress as quickly as possible."

"What's that? What for? If you please, I am the most honest . . ."

"There, in a casemate, you will be safest of all."

His heart sank. But he also managed to squeak to his heartless mocker:

"Then you'd better arrest me, please, and take me to the Tauride Palace!"

[265]

*　*　*

The Polytechnic Institute on Lesnoi. Above the building, white as a palace—a red flag. Around it, a crowd. Inside, the coatroom no longer had attendants, people weren't removing coats, and there was mud on the stairs and in the corridors. Signs on the auditorium doors: "Social Democratic faction," "Socialist Revolutionary" . . .

*   *   *

From the outside, the Sea Cadet Corps on Vasilievsky Island seemed dead; all the gates and doors were locked tight and there was no one at the windows. The crowd wasn't leaving, though, it was making noise, threatening. On the other side of the gates, the attendant was told the terms: the corps in full, including officers and with band playing, must pass through the city and thereby demonstrate its solidarity with the revolutionary people.

The terms were accepted. The youths lined up in the courtyard and went out with the band. The crowd greeted them gaily.

*   *   *

The crowd grabbed a nondescript police clerk, who shouted:

"I've joined!" Joined the people, he meant.

A motorcar pulled away from a building with an arrested admiral. Onlookers said: "Just an old man."

*   *   *

A crowd surrounded a short, compact, ruddy, bourgeois-looking man in a dark overcoat with a karakul collar and a soft, pie-shaped karakul hat. People shouted: "He's a minister!" The frightened man denied it. A young lady came to his aid: "What are you talking about! This is my co-worker from the Blinken and Robinson store." The crowd laughed; the finger-pointers were embarrassed.

*   *   *

To the well-known liberal Professor Bernatsky, as they were unseating him from his motorcar:

"Bourgeois! Used to riding around in motorcars? Now you can walk and we'll ride."

*   *   *

Soldiers brought Colonel Chetverikov of the 1st Riflery Regiment to the Technological Institute and demanded he be tried then and there for his sternness toward soldiers. With university students' help, they began the trial. But another soldier ran in—grabbed a sword, and hacked the colonel to death.

*   *   *

They drove Colonel Mikhailichenko, commander of the Life Guard's Moscow Battalion, around the city in a truck the entire day, showing "this bloodsucker" to the people. They would lift him up—and throw him to the floor of the truck's flatbed. After a few hours of that they took him back to the Tauride Palace badly beaten up.

*   *   *

In the City Duma, the lawyer Kelson sat at the desk of the chief of police. A hefty civilian came in with a saber, rifle, revolver, and hand grenade and machine-gun belts across his shoulder, leading in two old women he'd arrested who were scared to death. But he had barely begun reporting that they had spoken against the new order when he took a good look at Kelson, stopped short, and vanished. Kelson had recognized him. Just yesterday, if the revolution hadn't prevented it, he was to have defended the man on his ninth indictment, for another robbery. This was Rybalev, who had been stripped of all his rights, a burglar and recidivist.

*   *   *

There were no instructions on who was subject to or had the right to carry out an arrest.

Some policemen were arresting others for illegally bearing arms.

There were lots of drunks on the streets. Sleeping vagabonds were sprawled out here and there on the sidewalks.

Sometimes soldiers would sling over their shoulder, over their greatcoat, not machine-gun belts but broad general's ribbons—Orders of Saint Stanislav and Saint Anna.

*   *   *

On Millionnaya Street, revolutionary soldiers burst into General Stakelberg's apartment (he had kept them out for a long time, barricading himself in with his batman). They charged that a sailor had been killed on the street by a shot fired from this private residence. The tall general, not yet an old man, put on his greatcoat with a shoulder cape and beaver collar. They led him out. People shouted: "Stop, general!" They grabbed the greatcoat by its pelerine and tore it off. "Who killed the sailors, general?" "I'm not required to keep track of who is loafing about here"—with contempt. Voices: "Kill him! Shoot him! To the embankment!"—and they dragged him down Moshkov Lane. Some of the crowd disputed this and pulled the general toward them. All of a sudden, one swarthy soldier fired two shots directly at the general. But no wounds could be seen—and the stream bore the wounded general toward the embankment's parapet.

The general begged for mercy. But the crowd was already drawing back in a semicircle. A moment's silence. Someone shouted: "Fire!" The general made a warding gesture with one hand. A volley. He fell on his side.

Now, without a command, they fired excitedly at the lying man. A strapping Preobrazhensky soldier with a ruddy, almost maidenly face and smile tested his nice new hunting rifle, stolen from a store, on the fallen man.

Right then, sailors ran up from the Trinity Bridge—and two were wounded in the belly by a ricochet off the parapet.

They searched the murdered man and took a massive gold watch from his pocket. Four soldiers swung the corpse and tossed it over the parapet onto the Neva ice.

* * *

The crowd's ovation gushed down Nevsky for a procession of officers, in several long ranks, arms linked, taking up the entire thoroughfare. (They were coming from the assembly at the Hall of the Army.)

All were wearing red bows. Some were laughing and nodding welcomingly to the crowd.

* * *

"Enough, brothers!" a soldier shouted from his horse. "We're going to be eating off a silver platter!"

An enthusiast passing out proclamations:

"We need things to be good for us and our children!"

* * *

A local police inspector had once evicted a Jew lodging without right of residence in Petrograd. These past few days the inspector had been hiding at home. The neighbors knew but didn't denounce him; he was meek. Today that Jew showed up with a militia armband and two soldiers, arrested the inspector, and led him away.

* * *

The mother of a young Izmailovsky officer who had been killed the day before yesterday by the barracks gate arrived from Kaluga. She found his body in the box-room naked: he'd been well dressed and they'd stripped him completely.

No one helped bury him. But the crowd hooted.

* * *

At Kronstadt, workers exited the shipworks gate in the middle of the day, at an unusual time—in crushing silence.

They were joining the sailors.

The sailors were dragging cases of wine bottles from a restaurant wine cellar and smashing them in the courtyard, intoning: "This damned rotgut destroyed us in '05!" The wine poured out over all the snow in the yard, like blood.

People spread out over the city to arrest officers—army and navy—but first whoever was on dry land. They went around not spontaneously but according to lists—someone had drawn up lists of officers.

Some were killed immediately, in their homes or barracks, on the spot. Others were executed on Anchor Square. Still others were led to the edge of a ravine, so they would fall into the ravine, where Admiral Viren already was.

Staff Captain Taube saw his own men among the arriving soldiers, and he asked them loudly:

"Soldiers! Who is dissatisfied with me?"

No one said a thing. Then they took him to prison rather than executing him.

[2 6 6]

Hardly anyone had known this grand duke before today—only those who kept track of the grand dukes and didn't get confused about their genealogy. Today, though, his name was learned throughout the capital and even preceded him: Kirill Vladimirovich! His column was still marching, not having reached Shpalernaya yet, but people already knew and were waiting at the Tauride Palace. Grand Duke Kirill Vladimirovich was leading his Guards Crew to the Duma! (Before this they hadn't even known what he commanded.)

The eye had grown weary of the soldier's greatcoat cloth; its rusty gray filled all the streets to the point of tedium—and the black sailor column seemed joyous and fierce. The black color set off especially sharply the preserved evenness. Only the ribbons on the seaman's caps fluttered at will, and there was a regulation-breaking scattering of crookedly attached red— in bows, at angles, on chests and on shoulders.

The grand duke got ahead of the column and in his gorgeous blue motorcar with its little red flag arrived at the Tauride Palace ten minutes ahead of it—tall, black-mustached, with a stern, very intense face, along with an auxiliary admiral and a small escort of sailors. A large red bow stuck out from the breast of his naval coat.

Rodzyanko (Kirill had telephoned to say he would be arriving, then telephoned a second time as he led his column out of the barracks) came out to greet him in the Ekaterininsky Hall. There was a dense jostling that spoiled the solemnity; everyone had crowded in for a look.

The grand duke was unaccustomed to this kind of democratic crush so his feathers were slightly ruffled; nonetheless he maintained his bearing as a revolutionary honoree. And delivered a prepared tirade:

"I have the honor of appearing before Your Excellency. I am at your disposal. Like the entire people, I wish Russia good! This morning I went to all ranks of my Guards Crew and explained to them the significance of ongoing events, and I can now state with pride that the entire Guards naval crew is at the full disposal of the State Duma!"

Everyone liked this, and the ragtag public around him let up a "hurrah!"

Rodzyanko held himself like a large ceremonial stone sculpture, constantly at the ready to greet parades and deliver speeches. A few minutes later on the front steps, towering over Kirill, he was thundering exclamations to the crew about the homeland, loyalty, and victory over the enemy—the words were at the ready and rolled out of his mouth as loudly as cannonballs.

After this, the crew, apparently, had left or remained in part; it's not so easy for someone who has come to the Tauride Palace to part with it—and the grand duke felt the same way, wishing he could stay on in the present welcoming atmosphere.

First, he and Rodzyanko went to the President's last cramped refuge. There he showed himself to be anything but joyous but rather powerfully shaken and greatly alarmed. Rodzyanko, too, no longer triumphantly proud but rather abashedly, frowning and looking around to make sure no one was listening, told Kirill something unpleasant:

"Your Imperial Highness, forgive me, your presence here under the current circumstances is highly inappropriate. Not only that, you are an aide-de-camp. I do not advise you to openly demonstrate . . ."

After that the grand duke was taken up by newspaper correspondents. Correspondents? Yes! It was impossible to imagine that they existed here since not a single well-known newspaper was coming out and the Soviet of Workers' Deputies had not given permission, but correspondents remained in the flesh—and where would they be if not in the very thick of the Tauride Palace? How could they help but rush at the greatest sensation: following His Majesty's Convoy—the Tsar's cousin had gone over to the side of the revolution! A crew is one thing, they were sick of these combat columns, but a grand duke? The Tsar's cousin? He was more important than his entire crew. This was a symbol that the entire royal family had recognized the revolution! How could they help but ask the grand duke for an interview (even though they had no idea when it would be printed)?

And how could the grand duke refuse them? Having taken this irrevocable step, he had to at least show it presentably to Russian society and history. He had to allow everyone, himself included, to contemplate what had occurred.

Grand Duke Kirill followed the correspondents into their room—yes, they had such a room here.

There, nervously and handsomely smoking cigarette after cigarette, he responded to their curiosity.

"Now I am free and can say openly everything I think."

Revolutionary young ladies brought the grand duke tea and cookies.

Yes, his entire tragic life was passing before his mind's eye—and he felt he could reveal some of its wrenching peripetiae to the press.

"You see, I am one of the few who survived after the *Petropavlovsk* blew up. There were so many interesting details I could have reported to the supreme leader of the army and navy. But he never questioned me. Evidently, he had no time for all that."

An unforgivable lapse in government administration. And so, in essence, had gone his entire life.

"I am the Emperor's cousin and groomsman, and I had the daring to marry cousin Viktoria without the Tsar's permission. At Tsarskoye Selo they fretted and cast about. Aleksandra Fyodorovna suggested the most severe punishments to her royal spouse. I hurry there myself—to inform him of the changes in my family life, and they won't receive me. The next day, an order: three years abroad stripped of ranks and orders. And so I would have had to live in exile if not . . ."

You may well say, how many mistakes in the country's leadership:

"What an excellent ministry he could have composed for himself if he'd come to his senses earlier. So many remarkable and worthy men in the State Duma! . . . Even quite young ones, like the talented Kerensky. . . ."

It was a great pleasure to speak with the press and perfectly candidly. But eventually the interview was over, too. And the grand duke hurried on.

"Where would you have me take you, Your Imperial Highness?"

"I would like to go to the Military Commission."

Being a military man, naturally.

But wasn't it unnatural that this Military Commission yesterday had already tried to remove him from the Crew? What to make of that? Who was in charge there? Kirill had hoped to see Guchkov, suspecting that Rodzyanko was not the principal actor. He needed Guchkov in order to discuss . . . a rather delicate circumstance . . .

The problem was that when *these* events started, Kirill had given quite a lot of thought to his ambivalent position. He dashed first to Khabalov, then to the Preobrazhensky Regiment's club, trying to find that right thing for him to be. Support the throne with every last strength (he had sent a training detachment to Palace Square), or merely preserve his Crew (he had recalled the training detachment) and his own position?

But yesterday it had become clear that the throne had lost the capital (Kirill had offered the deputies his own motorcar), that movement had begun in favor of the Duma Committee—and Kirill had hurried so as not to lag in this movement: *he* of all people, ever the injured party, could not be caught under the throne's wreckage, he had to free himself first! Just himself? Not enough! And his entire Guards Crew? Also not enough! He had a marvelous thought on how to have his revenge on Aleksandra. He would take the entire Tsarskoye Selo garrison away from her! So he composed and sent such a note to the commanders of the Tsarskoye Selo units.

But although Rear Admiral Kirill switched so very quickly, so extremely quickly, to the side of the new government, the mood in his own Crew spilled over even faster. Yesterday the news that the grand duke had been dismissed had unnerved them. And this morning he was awakened by the news that several officers from his Crew had already been arrested by the sailors, others had been threatened, and everyone was inflamed by rumors of how Kronstadt had massacred its officers. Kirill had had to take this triumphant march to the Duma not out of his own growing desire but in order to save the Crew from collapse.

Kirill could only be relieved at Nikolai's fall. Nikolai had merited all this by his injustices, mistakes, bad advisors, and unbrotherly attitude. But who would take Nikolai's place? Kirill learned that there were secret movements afoot in favor of Mikhail, to make him regent. This news stung, singed Kirill. This was absolutely unbearable! Nikolai had been on the throne by right of inheritance, and a quarter-century already, no matter what he was—but why Mikhail? How could he bear that nonentity over him?

It was known that all this time Mikhail had been secretly communicating with Rodzyanko (Rodzyanko was not to be believed for a minute!) and been keeping it secret from Uncle Pavel and from Kirill, hadn't spoken of his own intentions, but had settled in Petrograd—for what reason? Waiting to occupy the post?

So this was also why Kirill had come to the Duma, in order to knock Mikhail from this position and overshadow him.

And he wanted to speak frankly about this with the practical Guchkov.

[2 6 7]

You could read a hundred books about different revolutions and still only experience it yourself for the first time: the revolutionary denseness of events, events that neither the heart nor the mind could keep up with digesting—though it is in those very hours, when they are most needed, that they fail you. Afterward—you have fifty years for regrets.

Only yesterday evening and this morning it had seemed that the main thing was to repulse the troops headed for Petrograd. It was natural to go against the old and not let the old smother the new. And Guchkov and the young Prince Dmitri Vyazemsky—his favorite intrepid aide, whom he had come to appreciate at the front a year ago, in his travels for the Red Cross, and in these past few months had brought into his conspiracy as an active participant and organizer—had now rushed off to inspect the regiments. In one place he gave speeches and they shouted back "hurrah" and the Life Grenadiers even carried him out on their arms; in another, he merely clarified the situation and tried to get the lost, beheaded units to fall back in the hands of their officers. If not create a defense for the city, then at least know well the forces present—that was exactly what he had to accomplish. Among

Duma deputies he was considered the most martial and bold, the one who knew the army best and was in constant contact with it.

Increasingly, though, Guchkov had seen officers running away from their units, mostly hiding in places unknown and even at the State Duma, for fear of being torn to pieces. And the battalions that had shouted "hurrah" to Guchkov—had an hour later or earlier shouted "hurrah" to the delegates from the Soviet. Thus, while Guchkov was assembling a defense against an outside enemy, an even more brutal force was assembling behind the Duma Committee's back. Perhaps he ought to have turned around quickly and found the forces to go and arrest someone from that unholy Soviet. But such forces most surely did not exist.

And while he was running around on these trips, in his own Military Commission, his own aide Engelhardt, out of fright, together with Rodzyanko, issued a wild, unthinkable decree ingratiating to the Soviet and dissolute soldiers and threatening officers with execution! Raving nonsense! But once printed up, it was scattered throughout the city faster and in greater numbers than Guchkov could catch up to—ruining everything irrevocably. Now there was no possibility of returning officers to their units or posting units in Petrograd's defense.

In the middle of the day, Grand Duke Kirill produced substantial encouragement with his appearance at the Duma. Although he had come out of definite calculation—to remain at the head of his Guards Crew—he was afraid they would replace him—and generally to hold on as a grand duke in the spontaneous chaos of these days, this deference to the Duma by a prominent member of the dynasty made a sharp impression on them all. And Guchkov, receiving Kirill in his office at the Military Commission and uttering hypocritically polite and reassuring words (this grand duke would apparently have nothing against taking the throne himself), could not conceal his triumph. This was the first from the dynasty, but contemptible as the dynasty was, they would all follow suit. On the one hand, everything around him seemed to be collapsing; on the other, what a force the Duma was!

What also made an impression was the fact that the Guards Crew did not lose its bearing and arrived with officers. Would the grand duke not take on the defense of the train stations against Ivanov, if only for the next few nights? Would he! He did. (He had thus proved useful.)

Guchkov was not alone in running himself ragged during those hours. So were all the Duma Committee members. But they were all running wherever immediate necessity called—to give a speech, to save detainees— and caught up in putting out fires, they were forfeiting their ability to grasp the entire situation and figure out how to guide its main aspects.

No matter what he did, Guchkov tried to keep these main aspects in view and to use them before they were diffused. There were victims even now, but if he did not decide quickly, there would be incomparably more: there would be civil war.

The turn of events had begun to eddy down a very dangerous slope, and he had to hurry to rein it in through a legitimate transfer of power. Guchkov's thoughts found their accustomed channel, which they immediately occupied: abdication and a regency. He had formulated this a year ago, if not before (in his soul, earlier, detesting this Tsar). He wanted this, thirsted for it, and led toward it as best he could. If abdication had been essential this past autumn, if it had already come to that then, then now it was past due—but all the more urgently necessary. He had to change the situation decisively and swiftly. Rather than defend itself from the Tsar, Petrograd would itself pounce on him! When the Duma Committee's legs went sprawling—due to the regiments' disintegration and the Soviet's ripening malice—instead of slipping, they should leap to capture the throne.

Guchkov understood the regency such that he himself would occupy the decisive place in it. Guchkov sincerely loved Russia. He was a patriot. But as such he understood that he should occupy the leading position in the *patria*, based on his political talents.

However he had no one, nowhere, ever to sit down with and discuss what was to be done. They all constantly had to go somewhere, be on their way, shout.

That's what revolution was.

[2 6 8]

This aging, one-track line with sidings stretched unbearably from Staraya Russa to Dno, knowing no expresses, and now the magnificent blue imperial trains had squeezed onto it. The rail line could not let it through any faster, but it did the best it could. The railroaders and local inhabitants gawked at the unprecedented trains, timidly talking among themselves, obviously: Where's the Tsar?

Naïve, sweet, and trusting were their common-folk faces. The Emperor did not show himself to them, but he did look out from behind the curtains—and his heart warmed. This was how he had imagined his subjects. It was for such as these that he had ruled, only never before had he, as now, through double windows, been able to hear them and explain to them directly; rather, he had always heard irritated, prejudiced, educated voices and clamorous newspapers that twisted everything until it was unrecognizable.

His heart had been heavy today, even though the sun had peeked out on the snow occasionally. Not as a conscious gloomy reflection, but in and of itself, an unbearable condition gnawed at and seized his chest. Even yesterday morning, the train's seeming peace had been entirely fictitious. There was nothing he could do, nothing he could read, nothing to distract him, no getting lost in his thoughts.

He was impatient to reach the Dno station quickly—first of all because this was the direct turn to Tsarskoye, and secondly because a meeting with Rodzyanko awaited him there, a meeting that seemed more and more like a relief, a solution: to peacefully arrange for everything to calm down and go back into place. Nikolai had already reconciled himself to the proposed concession of some of the ministers. One way or another, since the fateful and unlucky 30 October 1905, his course had been a chain of inevitable concessions.

It was as if the concession had already been made. And the pressure on his heart let up. Eased.

But he would not give up the principal ministries. And naturally, the ministers would be responsible to him, not the Duma. This monarchical principle was the bedrock of the government. If ministers were responsible to the Duma, then what was the monarch? A stuffed scarecrow?

Of this, Nikolai was confident, and Alix was fervently in accord with him.

His suite had information from somewhere that Rodzyanko was already en route.

At the small stations, the suite also picked up other rumors, and Voeikov would occasionally report. First, apparently there was an impudent order from that same comical Bublikov to detain the imperial trains! What's that? But no one was carrying it out, naturally. Then, that the rail line had already been blocked, but after the turn from Dno, or that some bridge had been damaged on that line.

They pulled into Dno after four o'clock in the afternoon. The hub station was orderly as usual, in no way disrupted.

There, though, a great deal of news awaited them, all of it unpleasant.

First, they learned immediately from the station supervisor that General Ivanov and his battalion had passed through Dno not yesterday but just this morning.

This morning? My God, why so slow? What had he wasted time on? But then, had he reached Tsarskoye Selo this minute?

Who was watching over the Empress and children?

But they knew even worse at Dno, terrible news: last evening, the Tsarskoye Selo garrison had joined the rebellion, too!

The Emperor's heart plunged into gloom. His light dimmed, and his buttress of these past few days came crashing down. He listened with a calm expression, but inside him despair was churning. Only he didn't have the right or freedom to show this in his face or words.

Meanwhile, Voeikov brought him a dispatch from Rodzyanko addressed to His Majesty that had arrived less than an hour before. Rodzyanko informed him that he was now (only now?) leaving for the Dno station to report on the state of affairs and measures to save Russia. He asked him to wait for his arrival, for every minute was precious.

Yes, but when would he reach Dno? In no less than another five hours. And also, the line had apparently been damaged. Was that so?

Voeikov was able to speak with the Vindava Station in Petrograd, and he learned that the train Rodzyanko had ordered was under steam—but as of that moment had not left.

Every minute was of the essence, but even more so in Tsarskoye Selo. Even greater was the torture of sitting at this backwater station—and not knowing what was happening with his family burned all the more!

My God! What was he to do?

Tiny, remote Dno. One railroad gendarme. One village constable. But it had a factory and factory workers, an inopportune spot.

The sensation was clear that they were in the wrong place. Not where they should be.

Voeikov was also able to learn over the telegraph that just before Tsarskoye Selo, the Vindava line had been occupied by revolutionary troops, and General Ivanov and his train had stopped in Vyritsa before ever reaching Tsarskoye Selo.

Nikolai looked nervously at the map.

Four lines crossed at Dno. They had arrived on one of them.

The other, to the left, led back to Mogilev. And called nothing to mind.

To the right—the short and desirable line to Tsarskoye Selo—had, it seemed, been cut off for him? Rodzyanko was expected along that line, and it would look weak to go to meet him. And if it was cut off, you couldn't get to Tsarskoye anyway.

But look: a direct line led to Pskov, and that was close. The headquarters of the Northern Army Group was there, and it had a Hughes wire. Maybe from there he would be able to speak with Tsarskoye (and GHQ) and quickly learn all. From there, it would be relatively easy to follow the two-track Warsaw Railroad to Tsarskoye via Luga.

Pskov had military forces and a railroad battalion. From there he could always ensure passage for himself.

This was his decision: go to Pskov!

It was actually good that Rodzyanko hadn't left Petrograd yet. Send him a dispatch to travel directly to Pskov!

But what could have held him up? Why hadn't he hurried? Perhaps there was a reason for his delay. Perhaps he was holding onto Petrograd and not surrendering it to unruly forces.

Right then the Emperor was handed one more telegram, from ten o'clock in the morning, and such a circuitous one! Once again the chief of naval headquarters had telegraphed from Mogilev (for some reason not Alekseev again), not on his own behalf but conveying a very strange telegram from Admiral Nepenin, commander of the Baltic Fleet—and that was also not on his own behalf but reporting two telegrams he had received from Rodzyanko the day before, 13 March—and then only with a delay. Only by this roundabout

route was it confirmed for the Emperor what was on a random leaflet in Bologoye: yesterday Rodzyanko had informed all army groups that his provisional Duma Committee had taken over all governmental authority in view
of the removal of the former Council of Ministers. He was inviting the army
in the field to preserve calm and hoped that the struggle against the foreign
enemy would not be weakened. Sensible words. He had blamed the old government for "general collapse" but had quickly set about restoring calm in
the rear and the correct activities of institutions.

Nepenin added that all this he had announced to his crews! (My God,
who gave him permission?) And he was reporting to His Majesty his own
conviction that the State Duma must be met halfway.

Of this the Emperor himself was increasingly convinced. In the past few
hours, Rodzyanko had moved to a new place in his perception and awareness:
he'd grown. The Emperor was no longer not only agreeable to receiving him
but now wanted him to come, though he was annoyed that he wasn't in Dno.

Oh well, if it was to be Pskov, then it was to be Pskov. They let them
know there and headed off.

The suite rejoiced: a quiet provincial town and reliable troops nearby.

They had their leisurely evening tea.

They rode—away from Tsarskoye Selo for now, having been delayed too
long by the detour.

Night was falling.

The Emperor had traveled to his Northern Army Group before—but not
in this situation.

He had another unpleasant thought: The chief of staff in the Northern
Army Group was "Black" Danilov. Two years before, the Emperor had considered him a great strategist and himself had instructed that Nikolasha take
him on at GHQ. But then he and Nikolasha got used to each other there,
and Nikolai removed him after Nikolasha, freeing up a place for Alekseev—
although not angry with him and still considering him a major strategist.
Neither Nikolasha nor Alekseev ever explained what Danilov had cost. Only
this winter had Gurko revealed to the Emperor how many cruel and bloody
mistakes Danilov had made in the first year of the war and what his mistakes
had cost our army. Nikolai was so bitter that he'd been deceived and had
even been grateful to him, rewarded him. Galicia, for example. . . . Nikolai
had considered it such a success. It was shameful how poorly Russia's troops
had been led.

And now he would have to encounter him, for the first time since then.

*　　*　　*

ROUGH THE ROAD TO DNO, THE ONE AND ONLY ROAD

*　　*　　*

[2 6 9]

Reports came into the commissariat saying that people were looting Kshesinskaya's mansion—so Peshekhonov sent Ensign Lenartovich to stop the looting and, if necessary, post a temporary guard there until the crowd ebbed.

Lenartovich didn't know the house and wasn't sure who exactly Kshesinskaya was. Peshekhonov explained that she was a famous ballerina who had been the Tsar's mistress in his youth and later had passed from grand duke to grand duke.

It turned out to be the first house on Kronverksky Prospect, where it started to curve, right by Trinity Square. It was nearby, and Sasha and two of his soldiers quickly covered the distance. The house's semicircular wing faced the square.

But at that moment there was no looting, and no crowd, not even a single person nearby or inside. The windows of the asymmetric, two-story house with the tower and half-cellar, which gave out directly onto the street, were all unbroken and shuttered. On the second floor was a small balcony, also lifeless. But you couldn't even tell how to get into the house—it had no door. Ah, over there, a gate to the courtyard.

The gate was locked, but Sasha saw a button in the stone column and rang it. The house was pleasantly finished with colored tile, and it was attractive for being asymmetric.

Servants came out, a man and a woman. Seeing an officer and two peaceful soldiers, they let them in, but warily. Indeed, in the past twenty-four hours there had been two robberies, both under the guise of a search. The servants couldn't not let the searchers in, but when they did, they behaved outrageously, stole openly, put things in their greatcoats, under their shirts—and what would their mistress say upon her return! Yesterday, an armored car had let loose a round on their house.

And their mistress was where?

The day before yesterday, in the evening, their mistress and her son, who was fourteen, and his tutor, had left the house, carrying a small bag—and told them to prepare tea, she would return soon, but she didn't. That same night, the two motorcars were driven out of the garage and hadn't been seen since.

They ascended the formal staircase to a hall with a marble floor. It wasn't particularly messy; they'd probably straightened up.

Sasha went to inspect the house, out of curiosity now, not need. The half-cellar floor was for the services. On the mezzanine, in the dining room, there had been some disturbance, but the silver, the servant said, was in place, or nearly so. They'd stolen very little and the china hadn't been smashed. Here there were parlors with luxurious furniture, including a small white marble hall big enough for a ball; you would never guess from the outside. The hall's large plate-glass windows gave straight out onto the Peter and Paul

Fortress, across Kronverksky. While the semicircular projection itself, surrounded by palm trees and with a small grotto in the middle, where water streamed across a bluish background—its windows looked out on Trinity Square and the Trinity Bridge. The furniture in the hall was upholstered in white silk matching the general color of the white marble, and the piano was the same hue.

All these luxurious design statements did not excite Sasha; on the contrary, they actually irritated him. Before the revolution—maybe. Right now, though, his attitude had turned around. The mistress had fled her amusements, but this large place and great wealth, all this should be preserved, especially from a foolish, pointless pogrom.

Sasha decided to post a guard here and keep it for now.

He went upstairs, alone. Here was where the pogrom had been, and the chaos remained. In two rooms, the floor was littered with photographs and papers, photographs and papers, and all the drawers of the desk and bureau had been pulled out.

Hanging untouched was a large photograph under glass of the young Tsar in a naval uniform, with an inscription below, apparently in his hand: "Nikolai, 1892."

Other portraits—grand dukes, generals, actors.

The furniture and furnishing had suffered little.

Under a glass case lay a wreath, some kind of award—was it gold? Sasha removed the cover, turned the wreath over, and underneath discovered a distinct hallmark: "96 carats!" The looters had simply had no idea.

Yes, a guard would have to be posted. And then a great deal taken out of here, rescued.

Bundles of letters, bundles of letters tied with ribbons.

And a stack of small morocco leather notebooks.

Diaries. . . . From the past twenty years. . . . If only he could read them right now. . . .

How old could she be? Past forty by now? And still dancing and entrancing?

Expensive toys, train tracks and train cars were scattered over the nursery floor. By whom had she had her children?

The situation was clear now, and affairs awaited him at the commissariat, so he had to leave. But he kept roaming from room to room.

Drawn along.

In the dressing room he pushed a door aside—and there were a great many dresses, blouses, and skirts hanging—two hundred, in all colors, woolen, airy, knitted, lace.

Looking around—no one there—quietly, he slowly ran his hand across this excess of garments.

Like over strings. And the dresses seemed to resonate.

And they smelled good.

He opened yet another door.

A bathroom. But not simply with an oval bathtub, but with steps leading down — into a marble pool. On the top step there were very small slippers of unknown purpose. Ballet slippers? Bathing slippers?

Sasha stopped over them and froze.

Likonya, whom he had pushed back all these days, now appeared before him lovelier than all these ballerinas — still enigmatic, still not completely understood, still slipping away.

He was drawn to her, tortuously and sweetly.

He stood for a long time looking down at the slippers.

[2 7 0]

Peshekhonov had been dogged for hours by concern over what he was to do with the Pavlovsky Military School. They'd locked the doors and hadn't come out in support of the new regime, but they could come out against it at any moment — and it was on the Petersburg side, after all — and what would be left standing there then? Fortunately, though, the Tauride Palace took up negotiations with them.

The Soviet of Workers' Deputies sent an order: *by one means or another,* the commissariat was to acquire the necessary number of vehicles (what did it mean by *one means or another*?), and if there were extras, to hand them over to the Soviet.

So his idea yesterday of seizing vehicles had been correct. One seizure differs from another morally, of course. This wasn't greed but the revolutionary justice that satisfies a new government's needs.

Right then there came crashing down as well on Peshekhonov's muddled head the billeting officers of the 1st Machine-gun Regiment immediately demanding lodging be provided for their entire regiment.

Their two machine-gun regiments had come on foot from Oranienbaum to Petrograd to help make the revolution. They'd spent one night in someone's barracks on the Okhta, but they hadn't liked it there and wanted to move to the Petersburg side.

He could scream. How many of them were there? The reserve regiments were swollen, perhaps four thousand?

Not so! There were 16,000!

And they'd all come here on foot!

But why so many?

The billeting officers couldn't say. (Later it was explained to Peshekhonov that there were no other reserve machine-gun regiments in all Russia, only these two trained machine-gun reinforcements for the entire army — and now they'd mutinied and migrated here.)

The billeting officers' main demand, though, was that the soldiers were categorically opposed to being dispersed to different places, in small parties; they wanted all to be together without fail.

An ominous force! And a poor force. Everyone feared them, but they were more afraid than anyone else, as if, dismembered, punishment might be visited upon them for their rebellion.

But there were no such large buildings on the Petersburg side. The sporting palace nearby hadn't been heated all winter, and its sewage system didn't work. The biggest building—the House of the People on Kronverksky—couldn't hold 16,000.

One of the comrades reminded him of the newly built palace of the Emir of Bukhara on Kamennoostrovsky.

Peshekhonov hesitated. Turn a palace into a barracks?

But they explained that this was simply an apartment building with twenty large apartments, as yet unoccupied.

The billeting officers hurried to meet their regiment, which had already arrived on Trinity Square and was standing there menacingly.

After negotiations and remonstrances, one battalion was tempted to live in the palace and allowed itself to be separated from the regiment. The remainder went to the House of the People.

While Peshekhonov was busy with the billeting officers, moving a little away from the Elite and giving them directions through the streets, intense gunfire rang out behind him. In the past few days, his ear had become so used to shots fired, even nearby, that Peshekhonov wasn't terribly surprised. But he was surprised that the public in front of the commissariat immediately vanished, entirely, no more crowding or forcing their way into the building.

Right then he saw—oh, horror!—that on the square in front of the commissariat, soldiers had lain down and were firing on one of the buildings down Arkhiereiskaya Street.

That was why the whole crowd had scattered!

And housed in that building they were shooting at—Peshekhonov realized—was an infirmary with wounded soldiers!

What was this? Had they lost their minds? He rushed from behind at the soldiers lying on the snow. Ran up and grabbed them by the shoulders.

"What are you doing?"

Somehow he stopped them. And they told him that people were shooting on the commissariat from that building, and they had no less than a machine gun hidden there.

Peshekhonov became furious.

"Who exactly saw it?"

He stood up among the scattered line and no machine gun struck him.

The soldiers started getting up, too. They couldn't find anyone who had actually seen it. And there wasn't a single man killed or wounded on the square.

He shouted at them, shamed them—and sent a detail—there being no officer or sergeant at hand—to check to see whether they had killed anyone in the infirmary. And if they did have their suspicions, let them check as well that there was no cursed machine gun. Hundreds of these machine guns had been fired by invisible hands from all the attics, but no matter how many times they climbed up to look, not a single one of these machine guns was found in all Petrograd.

The crowd had already flooded back toward the Elite and inside, so that Peshekhonov himself could barely squeeze in.

Once again he was beset on all sides by denunciations, demands for requisitions and searches, and proposals for new forms of public activism.

[271]

Readers came, quite a few, but none of them read anything, even if they borrowed books, not that they all did. On the main staircase, in the spacious entrance hall above it, near the book counters, near the doors to the halls, and in the halls themselves, small clubs gathered—and violating the sacred silence inherent to these places, some audibly droned in their normal voices. There were delighted female gasps, men's laughter, and cheerful interruptions. Others, faithful to discipline and habit, even now expressed their delight only in a whisper and crossed the halls on tiptoe.

The issuing of books came to a halt. The library came to a halt. And the meek employees were drawn out of every secret remote corner—here, to the people, to the lively discussion.

Vera had never seen so many happy people together at once—outside Easter matins. Sometimes one or two people's eyes would beam—but for everyone's to beam at once?

Many took note of this who had no notion of church: the Easter mood. Someone even joked, upon entering: "Christ is risen!" People said that strangers on the street were exchanging Easter salutations.

As if there had been a long—not a fast, not abstinence, but a dark nightmare, an utterly cheerless life—and all of a sudden something brighter than the sun had flooded everything. All men were brothers and felt like embracing and loving the whole world. Dear, joyous, trusting faces. This Easter mood, which was conveyed from one to another and back then to the first, kept building. Alone by herself, Vera hadn't experienced the dark nightmare of the past so much, but when people gathered here like this, then that nightmare formed an increasingly palpable cloud over them—so too today the unexpected liberation became palpably brighter and brighter. They had lived to see it, these happy people, a time when one almost couldn't gaze at life without squinting. From now on, everything would be built on love and truth! The future was opening up—incredible, impossible, undreamed of, unattainable. Something had to be done! Something in gratitude! But no one knew what.

Vera thought that perhaps, indeed, the principles of brotherhood—this brotherhood already tangible between total strangers—would now legitimately come to life and spread—and people would begin to act unselfishly toward one another. And in this unexpected way, Christianity would triumph.

They recalled the names of freedom lovers, since the time of Radishchev and Novikov, they recalled the Decembrists, Herzen, Chernyshevsky, the populist socialists, People's Will—generation after generation giving of themselves with faith in a future freedom. You see, despite everything, they had believed it would come! And here it had! What holy belief, what holy fulfillment!

Many had tears in their eyes.

Everyone found each stroke of freedom and each stroke of the past's demise so interesting. They passed on the names of the arrested figures of the old regime, each name like a sinister falling column. The latest news was that this morning Nikolai Maklakov had been arrested. They passed on a piquant detail, that the ferocious anti-Semite Purishkevich had been seen with a red carnation in his lapel. They were bowing their heads, bowing them, the scoundrels! . . .

And a sensational new rumor arose—but the newspapers weren't keeping up and there was nowhere to verify it—that there was also a popular revolution in Berlin, for a second day!

My God, was world brotherhood really beginning? Would this terrible war be broken off? Would Europe be transformed, would the entire planet?

And also a rumor about the royal train crashing. No one knew whether He Himself had survived.

And naturally—there were troops moving on Petrograd.

Of course, the danger of counterrevolution was still very great. It could not be that the old would be immediately smashed and die altogether, just like that. Of course, it would take cover and wait to attack our bright holiday. Of course, it would also dart in the street crowd as spies and eavesdrop. Of course, it was still hiding in attics with machine guns and was going to start firing on the streets at any moment.

But they were powerless and doomed! . . . People passed along with love and hope the names of the Duma Committee members, the remarkable figures who would now be leading Russia. The European-educated Milyukov, a genuine scholar, he would introduce scientific methods to administration! The Emperor's longstanding antagonist—the indomitable and militant Guchkov! And Kerensky, with his passionate thirst for the truth and sympathy for the oppressed! Yes, this would be for the first time in Russia—the power of the people, all for the people.

Thus, the day passed in these harrowingly joyous conversations, a happy, painfully nonworking day. Vera felt unusually warm and light, but it gnawed at her: Why were they killing officers? Our defenders, our army's heroes—what were they guilty of and before whom? (She was glad Georgi had left.)

She timidly attempted to express this in two groups, but it was as if they didn't hear her and didn't even object seriously. It didn't fit into the general flow of joy and was flung onto dry land as something heterogeneous. Well, random things happen, and what kind of revolution is without extremes? One couldn't break through to the bright future without at least small sacrifices.

The day passed, and once again Vera cut across the ebulliently ecstatic Nevsky, the same beaming faces of educated Petersburg on it mixed in with the most common crowd and soldiers, and everyone was wearing red. Red.

A group of prisoners was being led to the Mikhailovsky manège—ordinary citizens, to judge from their clothing. Someone denounced for something. Some in policemen's uniforms, too. And the women and children trailing behind kept being driven back.

She entered her building, still retaining this singing, springtime mood, with this same weightless smile—but her nurse greeted her gloomily, noticed this smile, and immediately drove it away:

"The dirty dogs! I don't want to hear it! Villains! Roaming all the floors to do their searches and cast an eye on where they might snatch something left lying about. And they keep coming, handful after handful, ugly-faced convicts, probably from the prisons but in different clothes. Not a shred of shame. Don't know how to hold a gun, one in the courtyard nearly shot a babe, came within a hair."

They came to search them, too, but her nurse stood on the threshold and didn't let anyone in and slapped their ugly faces with a rag. And the slightly better places, over there at the Vasilchikovs', next door—the doors never closed. More and more kept traipsing in to search, and women were roaming with them so they wouldn't tipple. But their shameless servants put on red bows—and off to town with them. Finally they found a few good soldiers, sat them down in the kitchen, and fed them—so they would keep off the gangs.

"They're rejoicing! The fools are rejoicing! And you, you fool, rejoicing with them. What's to rejoice about ruin? And the lines, over there, they're even worse! Now we'll live to see there being nothing to put in our mouths."

Vera was truly struck dumb in front of her nurse. She couldn't seriously repeat to her even the simplest words that had been spoken today at the Public Library—about the cherished fairytale, the dreams of generations, and certainly not Christ's Resurrection.

But because these words all seemed invalid in front of her nurse, they immediately became small, small and pallid. Could Vera keep them now even for herself? It was like a kind of hypnosis, the spell of society talking.

"What's going to happen to Yegor? Have you thought about that? If they take away his sword, he'll kill himself! He won't live!"

[272]

Following along, Vorotyntsev started down Strastnoi Boulevard and then Petrovsky, where there were no red marches. Rather there were the invariable nannies, prams, and children running in their colorful caps and mittens, and here the same red was entirely different and not annoying.

Did that mean Guchkov was right? He had to hurry to *warn* them?

Or the opposite: Did this mean they had *come to grief*?

Come to grief if this were now to roll over the country.

And to the front?

Meanwhile, if what was going on could be called a **revolution**—was this the revolution?—no, this was not yet revolution! It had no forces whatsoever. Right now, one good, solid regiment could take control of this shaken Moscow.

But where was he to get that regiment quickly? Evidently, there was no such regiment in Moscow.

What kind of revolution could there be here if the entire multibarrel, bayonetted, and hooved force was with the army in the field? If the army didn't recognize it, then there was no revolution, it was a fizzle.

Now, within hours, GHQ could decide everything. (Only why had the Emperor left it?) Loyal men would undoubtedly converge on GHQ from every direction.

Rush to GHQ?

The more disgracefully he had spent these past few days, the faster he needed to take some kind of action.

Go to GHQ! Suddenly it seemed so obvious and even immediate!

That meant to the Aleksandrovsky Train Station! But he was already going toward Trubnaya Square, only he'd made a detour.

He'd turned.

Right then he saw newspaper boys running down Trubnaya with ecstatically gaping mouths, shouting and waving. People rushed to them immediately, clustered around them, tore the papers from their hands.

Vorotyntsev, too, rushed over. This he could do; these weren't leaflets. Pushed through and bought one. The buyers read them then and there, and exclaimed, and the boys shouted, too.

They shouted that the Tsar—on his way to Petrograd—had been *detained*?

Some small, upstart little paper—*News of the Moscow Press.* Small though it was, though, one main thing followed solidly under the bold headlines, each of which grabbed the eye. The fall of the Admiralty! . . . The Preobrazhensky Regiment and its officers gone over to the revolutionary camp! . . . So . . . His Majesty's Personal Convoy gone over to the side of the revolution! . . . Tsar Nikolai II's journey . . . His train detained on the Nikolaevsky line. . . .

It wasn't stated clearly: What? Arrested? . . .

By whom? When? And where was he now?

This was exactly that vulnerable traveling by the Tsar that Guchkov had taken aim at. . . .

Vorotyntsev slowly pushed his way out of the crowd and back to the boulevard. And sat down with the newspaper right there, on the snowy, frozen bench.

This desperate journey by the Emperor, broken off no one knew where, was stunning.

What about GHQ then? Alekseev without the Tsar? GHQ was feeble without the Emperor's name. It could not take decisions or initiate military actions if the Emperor was in rebel hands.

There was no point going to GHQ.

But what then would happen to the army? (And the entire war!)

He couldn't make up his mind.

Honor demanded he intervene. Reason was not indicating a path.

Not for the first time during this war, and especially these past few months, Vorotyntsev, despite his belief in the power of a single will, for some reason felt a bewitched, a fateful impotence. Even in the thick of events, in the most necessary place, and no matter how hard you tried — there weren't the forces to turn events around! Why was this so?

Couldn't they race back down the Nikolaevsky line? Even straight to Petrograd? Maybe there was something more there? . . .

This was an adventurous thought, extreme perhaps, nonetheless the center of events was there, and maybe not everything was as irrevocable as they were writing. Were any actions possible after all?

No matter what sort of warrior you were, shot at a hundred times — here something completely unexpected approached and overpowered you and you were inside your uniform, a weak and helpless man, such as each man is.

Whether or not he actually went, at the Nikolaevsky Station he could find out something precise from arriving passengers.

Vorotyntsev rushed off to the Nikolaevsky Station, putting everything unspent inside him into his walking. He jostled along, crossed Trubnaya, ascended steep Rozhdestvensky Boulevard, and in order to avoid possible pandemonium at the Myasnitsky and Krasny gates, cut down Uhlan Lane and down Domnikovka.

In the side-streets he noticed nothing out of the ordinary. Crossing Sadovaya, he cut through the same kind of deliriously joyous multitude. As he was approaching Kalanchevskaya Square, he himself began to use the word "revolution."

A revolution during time of war! Even if it had the goal of exiting the war — this meant a total loss of the war. That was much worse than dragging the war out longer.

The same maddened, ecstatic, and roving rabble engulfed him at Kalanchevskaya Square.

But trains were running from the Nikolaevsky Station as if nothing were wrong. He could leave in a few hours.

But it was right then that the absurdity sank in. If the State Duma was at the head of the revolution, then what could be done against it in Petrograd? And with whom? The worthless Petrograd reserves?

Here a train had arrived from Petrograd. In the oncoming stream of people, Vorotyntsev began to look for people he knew, especially officers.

He didn't see any, but he did notice that all the officers were unarmed. He stopped one captain. And then another staff captain ran up.

They were in a desperate mood, not that superficial dismay like the officers in Moscow. They drew a picture of the hell in Petrograd, the pursuit and murder of officers. That he mustn't go there under any circumstance. He would be dealt with right on the train platform. He could only go in civilian clothes and unarmed. They recounted various instances. He was seriously taken aback.

Vorotyntsev was used to danger calling to him. But this danger wasn't.

And the royal train? Had they heard anything, encountered it? Where was it?

They hadn't encountered anything. There'd been nothing of the kind en route. They would have noticed.

Vorotyntsev had absolutely no idea what he should do.

No, he dropped the idea of returning to Petrograd, of course. It was a foolish thought.

And the Emperor's journey, too, was foolish, incomprehensible, suicidal! These past few days he had known of events from the very beginning—and what had he decided? Where had he gone? . . .

Vorotyntsev couldn't bring himself to leave the train station yet, either. Perplexed, he lost himself in the station crowd. He went to the restaurant to eat, to ponder, to gain time, to settle down, to keep from taking futile steps.

Right here, over the plates, he suddenly thought: Was the Emperor just going to see his wife? Was that all there was to it?

Then he was lost.

And all was lost.

They were walking through the station—two university students shouldering rifles on a strap. It struck him, it hurt him to think it: of course, they didn't even know how to shoot. Yet *they* had seized a weapon. And the officers were surrendering theirs.

Kalanchevskaya Square, awash in people, was already lit by evening streetlamps.

No, an officer apart from his unit is nothing. A military man is strong only in his proper place. What could one isolated, solitary sword do once it was taken away? He had to return to the 9th Army, to his place, simply and unpretentiously.

He went into a telephone booth and tried to call a captain he knew at District headquarters who was on duty there that evening—to learn the latest news.

The captain replied that the Kremlin, the Arsenal, and all the last units had gone over to the side of the revolution. General Mrozovsky had just been arrested in his apartment.

Well, he'd dawdled long enough.

[273]

It had been a difficult day for the Executive Committee. After a brief break, they again met in the second half of the day, to the drone of the disorderly Soviet through the door—and under threat of that desperate soldiery breaking in at any moment in search of justice. (They'd been wrong to allow one man elected from each company; too many soldiers were gathering.) But no, Sokolov was still coping with them somehow, and good for him. They were hollering there but not breaking in here.

Meanwhile the EC had roused itself to discuss the terms of a handover of power to the bourgeoisie, and Himmer was sucking the sweetest part out of the theoretical marrow.

In the new conditions of democracy, beginning with the struggle to the death against the bourgeoisie, they shouldn't rob the bourgeoisie of its hope of winning this struggle. Therefore, as they started out they mustn't set overly harsh terms of power. On the contrary, the bourgeoisie had to be lured to take power. There was one main condition: ensure absolute and unlimited freedom to agitate and organize in the country! This we need more than anything else! Right now we're scattered. But in a few weeks we'll have a solid network of class, party, professional, and soviet organizations, and if we also have full freedom to agitate, then the bourgeoisie can never take us and the liberated masses will no longer capitulate to the propertied clique. The forms of a European bourgeois republic will not take hold here, and the revolution will intensify.

At the same time, this demand—freedom to agitate—was so much a generally recognized democratic demand that the bourgeoisie simply couldn't refuse us. And if we add to this a general amnesty? And, in principle, a Constituent Assembly? How can they refuse? They themselves have been proclaiming this since '05! And for us, this is quite sufficient! For now we need nothing more, even about land, even economic demands. We mustn't frighten the bourgeoisie! We mustn't even demand a declaration of a republic. That will come of its own accord. And we especially mustn't breathe a word about a policy of peace. That would frighten them off for good. We can't demand Zimmerwald of Milyukov. That's *nonsense* plain and simple. If we unveil our entire peace program, Milyukov won't take power. And if we unveil just a part, Western socialists will be amazed at how truncated our program is. But there is no reason to worry. Given freedom to agitate, we will achieve everything necessary afterward.

"Comrades, who doesn't know that I myself have been a defeatist and internationalist throughout the war? But right now I advise us to keep quiet about that! Zimmerwaldist slogans could scare off even the deceived soldier mass, even in the Soviet itself. Among those simpletons it is still accepted that the war must be prosecuted to the end. No, for now we will furl our Zimmerwaldist banner!" Himmer got more insistently wound up in his monologue, carried along by his great thought, and even rose to his tiptoes at the meeting table. "We need only one thing from this government: that it complete and reinforce the coup against the tsarist regime! Then we will throw them out, too!"

He himself was trembling from the profundity of his own foresight. Somehow it was easy to say all this, unafraid of spies from Duma circles or that many would hear behind the curtain. Revolutionary truths have a great quality: even hearing them with their own ears, the doomed don't understand.

Right then the EC members began to make noise, several voices. The Bolsheviks: down with everything, defensists, moral midgets! Share power with the bourgeoisie? While robust Nakhamkes, who was coming into his own power and influence by the hour, sized up the situation with an attentive, sideways glance. Was it perhaps right to adopt the Himmer platform? Anxious to acquire this powerful ally and gather a bare majority, Himmer with new stridency, straining his weak throat:

"We don't need agreement with the bourgeoisie right now, just to pull out the poisonous fang of plutocracy against our class initiative! Their government won't last then and will quickly break under the press of popular forces! Their government will soon be victim to our intensified revolution!"

Himmer didn't remember ever speaking so convincingly and shrewdly. He sensed that this was simply his great moment, his ascent to the peak of revolution! A stormy petrel!

But they didn't understand, the cowardly loons. How was that? Not join the coalition and not have any agreement either? They wanted *agreement*! Chkheidze:

"We'll spur them on."

The dizzying complexity of the Himmer speech rested in the fact that all these subtleties about power, once said aloud, were merely the foreground for his intention, and hidden behind it was this: despite the preponderance of the swamp and defensists on the EC—already now, on this question, and later on every subsequent one, to synthetically and skillfully create a leftist majority out of the small Zimmerwaldist striking core on the leftist flank. But these leftists were foolish and incompetent and failed to understand all the subtlety of Himmer's intention. They wanted to shout about "peace" out in the open and scare the bourgeoisie to death. They wanted to seize power here and now.

It was especially hard to get anywhere with the Bolsheviks, who heard and saw only themselves. At the most important point in Himmer's report, Shlyapnikov slipped off somewhere, and then ran in, and demanding on a point of order, immediately, began in his Vladimir-inflected speech:

"While you're caught up in your academic questions here, they've confiscated our party literature at the train station! The Executive Committee must take emergency measures!"

Academic questions! Stupid man. The Bolsheviks had a comic singularity, that only their party literature was worthy of attention, only their proclamations contained correct slogans, and only their proposals could be adopted.

Through the door, soldiers were hollering. Oh, they were hollering—and just about to burst in with bayonets and curses! The soldier question roared—and demanded priority. If they did burst in, though, what would they tell them? The officers were returning? Then rub mustard into that return!

If they were to demand full freedom to agitate and organize the popular masses, did that mean in the army as well, the soldiers? How could that be? Yes, this was the undoubted, remarkable, and most productive continuation of Himmer's thoughts—and here he and Nakhamkes already saw eye to eye. Extending full democracy and the freedom to agitate to the army would create intolerable conditions for the bourgeoisie, paralyze it, and untie our hands. Extend to the army all the gains in civil rights, freedom of unions, strikes, and assembly—at least out of ranks—along with the freedom of self-government, and the army would be entirely on the Soviet's side!

But Nakhamkes had come up with and proposed one more specific step—and Himmer admitted it was congenial to his own proposals, and without this concretion, all our gains would come to nothing: *Do not disarm or remove from Petrograd the military units that took part in the coup!*

Correct! Correct! With this demand we can bind the capital garrison to us and to the revolution—and decisively take it away from the bourgeoisie!

Himmer and Nakhamkes could see more and more that the two of them had to take relations with the bourgeoisie into their own hands, that the rest of the Executive Committee would only spoil everything. The defensists still could not bring themselves to reject even a coalition and had been debating this however many hours since the morning.

Finally, sometime before six o'clock in the evening, they took a vote and decided, thirteen to seven, not to send representatives of democracy to Milyukov's ministry.

The minority were not pleased. Rafes mumbled that the EC decision was only preliminary, we would still be consulting with our parties, and tomorrow we would bring the question to the Soviet's plenum.

Not on your life! To move such a delicate question to a headless crowd, look at how they were hollering through the door.

The rightists even went so far as to say that the EC decision could not be considered authoritative because the Executive Committee had selected itself.

A dangerous argument! A dangerous tactic! It was revolutionarily and ethically impermissible to make that argument!

Everyone felt this almost immediately. The door from the Soviet's room was suddenly flung open, and from it thronged—no, not the entire Soviet, not a horde of savage bayonets—from it strode the unbuttoned, steamed Sokolov, still heading up the movement, and behind him about ten of the most common soldiers with highly inexpressive physiognomies. What was this?

Sokolov confidently announced that with him was a new addition to the Executive Committee—a group of ten soldier deputies!

This was unauthorized! Unenvisioned! Unbelievable! How could this be? To bring them in without asking anyone?

"This is quite unexpected, though, Nikolai Dmitrich! This changes the entire situation!"

"But this changes the Executive Committee's entire party and social structure!"

Nonetheless, they had tramped in and here they stood!

Actually, there weren't any chairs for them anyway.

The atmosphere was badly spoiled. How could they discuss anything serious now? What would become of the Executive Committee now?

Ah, Nikolai Dmitrich! What have you done!

He had irrevocably ruined the party representation.

Entering, Sokolov himself had felt this, of course. He now tried to justify himself:

"We chose them provisionally, for just three days. Primarily to resolve the issue of soldier rights. We're submitting the desires of the Soviet's plenum to the Executive Committee . . . not to give the officers back their weapons. And not to allow any officers who have behaved disloyally to the revolution to take command. And to ensure soldiers all democratic rights. . . ."

Nakhamkes assessed the situation and immediately accepted this:

"This is wonderful, Nikolai Dmitrich. Wonderful! Now you take your party and go occupy some room and work out a document. And we on the Executive Committee will approve it. I'll come to you later."

They exchanged looks. Oh, all right, fine, agreed, let them go.

This was all the soldiers wanted, their own need.

And Sokolov, not yet exhausted, was ready. Off they went.

They left, everyone superfluous. And the EC was left in its former sitting complement.

Scandalous! They'd had to get rid of this "addition" somehow.

Thus, a coalition with the bourgeoisie was rejected.

What about talks? The swamp and the rightists didn't dare refuse talks. They had to attach Soviet terms to a bourgeois government. And present them.

Rafes: First of all, get them to lift nationality restrictions!

Nakhamkes decided to take the matter increasingly into his own firm hands and bring this to completion; it can be hard for the proletariat to organize. He took a scrap of paper and started writing down which conditions had been cited and accepted.

All of a sudden, they were arguing very little. Land for the peasants? An eight-hour workday? War and peace? Even a democratic republic? All this could be shifted to the Constituent Assembly, if the franchised would agree. So that Milyukov would worry less, it could be called the National, or Legislative, Assembly, as this had all already been with the French.

But there was a loophole to remove: don't let them reach an agreement with the Tsar! That meant preventing them from preserving the monarchy. Forbid them a monarchy!

Himmer: But we'll frighten Milyukov, and he'll refuse power! And why insist so if even the Menshevik Organizing Committee in today's proclamation didn't mention a republic?

Let's put it this way: the bourgeois government should not predetermine the form of the future rule.

They passed it. Good.

And the government's makeup? Basically, let them choose who they want. Let their little friends divvy up the portfolios. It's not for long, after all. We won't interfere in this. Of course, if there are excessively odious individuals, we'll remove them.

But the remaining demands, whichever came to mind, they were all the same old ones, from '05, shared by the entire liberal and democratic movement. The Kadets couldn't have lost their conscience to such a degree as to reject them.

Only what Sokolov and the soldiers there were preparing now—that, too, remained to be presented.

[274]

In the afternoon, crowds of soldiers walked unimpeded through the streets of Luga under the command of no one knew what types of men. Two policemen were killed near the firehouse. Several stalls were looted. Drunks started turning up among the soldiers.

But following the chosen tactic, cavalrymen did not leave their barracks to suppress.

Cavalry Captain Voronovich remained in his detachment's barracks, nervous, but Vsyakikh had not returned from the "military committee" and there was no one else to send, it being a delicate matter.

At about six in the evening it was reported to the cavalry captain that Count Mengden was inspecting the barracks and giving speeches. That meant he hadn't stayed put and had decided to intervene. What could this harebrained old man spew out if he didn't understand anything about the situation or the soldiers' feelings? Voronovich hurried to find him and overtook his suite at the Horse Guards regiment detachment.

The old-fashioned, gray-haired general, confident of the irresistibility of what he was saying and with uncooled fervor, appealed to the soldiers about the regiment's glorious traditions and their loyalty to their oath. The soldiers heard him out in silence, did not let out any "Willing to do our best!," and were still silent as the general left.

Mengden wanted to go to the next barracks, too. But Voronovich thought to ask him to stop in at the administration to sign some urgent papers. The general agreed, and the entire suite turned around.

It turned out that in the previous few hours the general had already been detained in his apartment by gunners and taken off by these boys to their division, but there he was freed and they even apologized. This arrest may have been what had shaken Mengden. He was once again invigorated and confident as usual. Entering his office with Voronovich, he rebuked him, gazing with his reddened, nearly teary eyes:

"I regret very much that you dissuaded me this afternoon from going out and speaking firmly with these scoundrels. I made a mistake yielding to you. We cannot be idle. Tomorrow, or the day after, all the upheavals in Petrograd will be over, and we will only have disgraced ourselves before the army for this day."

For that one single instant even Voronovich had his doubts. Maybe it was true that he had suggested a false line and the old man was right.

But at just that moment people ran in and said that a crowd of soldiers had gathered in front of the administration building wanting to arrest all the officers.

All of them? Without distinction? His heart skipped a beat. Now he was trapped. Why had he left his own barracks? He could have gone on sitting there.

The banging of rifle butts was heard from the chancellery next door.

Tall, black-mustached Voronovich walked out of the general's office and saw that the chancellery was overflowing with soldiers from different units, mostly those gunner pups from the division. He made an effort to maintain calm, although he felt a trembling penetrating him—and indignation, and also worry. Hell! This was beyond bounds.

"What do you need, men?" he asked kindly.

Several voices answered:

"To arrest all the officers!"

Right then, though, Voronovich noticed several soldiers from his own detachment trying to squeeze through. Hope had appeared.

"All right, arrest us if you like." He lit a cigarette, and his hands were shaking noticeably.

"No, not *this one*!" his own men were shouting. "Don't touch this one!"

"This one"! Not "cavalry captain," not "his honor."

"Who do you want to arrest?" Voronovich asked with greater firmness.

A tipsy, forelocked sergeant stepped out from the crowd, cavalryman Gusev, who'd been released from lockup by the crowd, and declared with gloomy confidence:

"The ones of the Germans. 'Cause there're lots of gentlemen officers who're Germans and spies."

Someone slipped him a note and he began to read. First on the list was Count Mengden.

Voronovich lost his officer confidence. Rather than interrupt the sergeant or cut him off, he cautiously murmured something about the general's many years of service and his age. But a boy gunner stepped forward and declared that the "military committee" had ordered them to arrest General Mengden because he didn't recognize the new revolutionary government and was calling on his soldiers to do the same.

Here's where it was, the committee!

Gusev and a few others were already heading ominously to Mengden's office.

Voronovich went up to the new recruit who had spoken on the committee's behalf and gently asked whether they couldn't subject Mengden merely to house arrest; he wasn't going to vanish from his apartment.

But they could hear a loud voice, from his office:

"Ah! Drag him out!"

Gusev ran there. He was already taking down the general's warm overcoat, which was hanging on a hook, and handed it to him with an impertinent grin: "Wrap up in your nice coat, Your Excellency. It's going to be chilly in lockup!"

He insisted on leading all the prisoners to lockup, where he himself had only just been confined for disorderly conduct.

The general looked around helplessly, slackly, in hopes of someone stepping in.

But neither his cavalrymen, who were here, nor the chancellery clerks, nor the sole officer here, Cavalry Captain Voronovich, did.

Then the count himself turned to the latter and said in French:

"Captain, tell my wife I've been arrested."

"Don't you dare in German!" they rushed at him.

And led him off.

The captain stood there, inscrutable. Everything was balancing on a knife's edge. One wrong move and they'd arrest him, too. Events had surged much further than could have been expected that morning.

Gusev took out the note and read the following names: von Seydlitz, Baron Rosenberg, Count Kleinmichel, Colonel Egerstrom, Sabir.

They detailed detachments to search for them, arrest them, and take them to the guardhouse.

Among themselves, the cavalrymen and clerks were droning on and proposing that they bail out Seydlitz, Rosenberg, and Sabir.

The gunners agreed.

There was no mention of the others.

At the first opportunity, Voronovich cautiously slipped out of the chancellery with his soldiers.

He did well. It turned out that Gusev had been trying to talk the gunners into taking Voronovich. As senior adjutant, this cavalry captain had signed the order on the guardhouse for Gusev.

In his barracks, Voronovich felt he was in quasi-safety, nonetheless it was still alarming.

Soon after, Vsyakikh returned and reported that the "military committee" had indeed been meeting continuously in the motor company but felt lost without a single officer. All the officers were in hiding and afraid to show their faces. Actually, some of them had already been arrested. The committee had posted guards for the treasury and the wine stores, but the guards had dispersed of their own accord and looting had begun.

Oh, that was just what Voronovich had felt! How the committee needed him, and vice versa!

He sat down to write an official note to the committee saying that if the committee so wished, he would immediately lead his detachment into town, take over for all the sentries, and base himself with his duty platoon at a train station as the central most important point.

He sent an expeditious orderly with the note.

He himself began pacing nervously.

Right then terrified clerks from the administration ran in and told him what had happened. Count Mengden, Egerstrom, and Kleinmichel had been taken to the same cell Gusev had emerged from the night before. The hussars from Kleinmichel's detachment and others had gone up to the lockup doors and mocked the prisoners. The half-drunk Gusev more than anyone. Count Mengden remained silent, but those two responded. Egerstrom supposedly said: "Just wait, you scoundrels. Today you're full of yourselves, but tomorrow we'll give you a good thrashing."

He didn't realize how serious the matter was!

The crowd broke into the lockup and rushed at the prisoners. General Mengden was killed by the first rifle butt to his head. Egerstrom and Kleinmichel were skewered on bayonets and then tossed to the floor and finished off with rifle butts.

The cavalrymen in the barracks crowded around to listen; they felt sorry for Mengden. They blamed those who had been at the administration during his arrest. Why hadn't they bailed him out? Voices rose up. They had to find the old man's killer right away and punish him! But Voronovich held them back. This wasn't the time. This could only increase the bloodshed and upheaval.

Especially after this excess, we especially need close contact with the committee, otherwise in a few hours a general beating of all remaining officers will begin.

It's so easy to perish for no good reason.

[2 7 5]

Within an hour of each other, two telegrams from Mrozovsky were delivered to GHQ, one saying the troops were going over to the side of the revolutionaries, even with weapons, and there were large crowds of strikers all over Moscow and no reliable troops to disarm the mutineers.

The second was brief and to the point: there was total revolution in Moscow.

Thus, the hidden word that had still not broken through was sonorously stated: revolution!

What? Already? . . .

The Northern Army Group, having received reassuring Telegram no. 1833, amazed and nervous, was now questioning where their higher-ups had obtained this information. Their commander-in-chief, General Ruzsky, asked for immediate guidance in view of the passage through Pskov of the imperial train expected in two hours. According to their information, Petrograd had cut off all communications and they could not bring up the troops from the fortress artillery in Vyborg that were coming to help. And in Kronstadt, as was already known, officers and admirals were being killed.

Alekseev was feeling so poorly that in the middle of the day he took to his bed. Lying there, he ordered Lukomsky to pass on to Pskov, for the approaching Emperor, the Moscow news, the Kronstadt news, the Helsingfors news, and the fact that Admiral Nepenin was not hiding Rodzyanko's telegrams from the fleet and had recognized the Duma Committee. And once again to convey for the Emperor the morning's entire eloquent and persuasive letter that had been sent to Tsarskoye Selo.

Oh, why was the Emperor so stubborn? . . . In a year or two, after the war's end, autocracy would in any case have to agree to self-limitations and could not avoid granting a responsible ministry. So why not concede now? Why stir up excessive animosity and turmoil? . . .

But Alekseev himself couldn't change anything. He couldn't even call off the pointless movement of fortress artillery from Vyborg.

Lukomsky and Klembovsky took turns in the transmission.

"But, Mikhail Vasilich, what should the response be to Telegram no. 1833?"

Indeed, given the telegram confusion, what should the response be? He was ashamed to admit that he'd simply trusted and obeyed Rodzyanko. Although, actually, there had been confirmations from naval headquarters, too. And from foreign agents. Evidently, the situation was highly volatile.

"Say that the information included in the telegram was received from various sources and was considered reliable."

Alekseev was exhausted by illness, and immobility, and the impossibility of getting from here to Pskov to persuade the Emperor himself. That would resolve everything.

"Say that everything must be reported to the Emperor immediately upon arrival. If the letter trains' arrival in Pskov gets delayed, then they can send an officer from the General Staff to meet them with all the dispatches. By express train. And if there's disrepair on the line, then send a railroad detachment to repair it."

The sweat of impotence beaded up on Alekseev's forehead. Russia's entire fate came down to that stretch between the imperial train and Pskov. How could they be joined, clarified, and helped?

A report came in that General Ruzsky and Danilov had already left for the station to meet the imperial train.

So ask headquarters to chase after them immediately and bring all the telegrams to the train station!

The Emperor had to be informed of everything before he turned toward Petrograd!

Right then, Alekseev was visited by Grand Duke Sergei Mikhailovich, Inspector of the Artillery, who had also barely recovered from illness, dry, hunched, darkish yellow. Alekseev rose to greet him. And showed him all the telegrams.

Sergei Mikhailovich bore himself simply among the headquarters officers. He had long looked on affairs of the rear pessimistically. But now he was gripped by alarm for his Malechka Kshesinskaya, and her home in Petrograd, which rumors said had been ransacked.

Now he expressed full agreement with Alekseev's persuasive arguments about a ministry of public trust. And he gave his permission to convey his agreement to the Emperor.

Alekseev was very glad for the support and fortified all the more that he had been correct. He ordered clean-shaven Klembovsky to telegraph Pskov that Grand Duke Sergei Mikhailovich had unconditionally endorsed the necessity of the measures indicated in Alekseev's telegram and considered Rodzyanko himself the most appropriate as the essential *person*.

Not that Rodzyanko was that good, but no other candidate had come up. And also:

"Express my hope that Commander-in-Chief Ruzsky holds the same views. Therefore he will have no difficulty defending them to the Emperor and will be successful."

All reasonable men are always united by arguments for moderation.

Moscow had with its own uprising gone over to the side of the Duma Committee, too. The Baltic Fleet had gone over to the Duma Committee's side. The last possible moment was approaching for the Emperor to meet his population halfway and issue a pacifying *act*.

From the Caucasus Army Group, Alekseev received laconic encouragement from Grand Duke Nikolai Nikolaevich: "Read Telegram no. 1833, wholly and entirely endorse your opinion." (He used the familiar "you.")

By a roundabout route too clever by halves, a telegram arrived at GHQ from Brusilov—addressed to Count Frederiks, that is, for direct delivery to the Emperor. Out of his duty of honor and love for the Tsar and fatherland, the lively Brusilov ardently requested that the Emperor admit the fait accompli and peacefully put a speedy end to the terrible state of affairs. Internecine invective could threaten unconditional disaster both for the fatherland and for the royal house. Every minute's delay in the crisis could mean pointless victims.

This new telegram also fortified Alekseev in his peacemaking efforts. Once again he lay on the sofa with a temperature and weighed the facts. What had been taking shape? The peace-loving tendency was now openly supported by three army group commanders-in-chief and one naval commander, four out of seven, a majority.

Only Evert as yet had made an attempt to oppose. Not that Evert himself was important, of course, but behind him stood the Western Army Group, it was right nearby, thousands of officers, and all in place. While Evert himself was only frightening because of his appearance. In fact, he wouldn't take a step without an order.

Meanwhile, the Western Army Group hadn't forgotten and hadn't dozed, but at seven o'clock in the evening Kvetsinsky once again summoned him to the telephone. He wanted to know the answers to the Western Army Group commander-in-chief's questions. We have received telegrams of notification from GHQ. But the army group was being inundated by telegrams and rumors from all sides, and it was impossible to tell where the truth lay and where the gossip. The commander-in-chief was worried about the disturbances spilling over to the army group and thought it essential to obtain a definitive decision as quickly as possible. Where was the Emperor? And Ivanov? And the departed troop trains?

Again those suspended, unstopped troop trains. Events were not waiting, of course.

Steady, round-faced Lukomsky walked to the telegraph. Generally speaking, he irritated Alekseev, and he could not work with him for long. However, unsuited to military affairs, a ministerial purchasing agent who did not know the front, he had fortified Alekseev greatly during these crisis days by virtue of the fact that he sympathized greatly with society, the Zemgor, and reforms and sincerely supported Alekseev's latest steps.

Somehow he himself begged off from the Western Army Group, rumbled bulkily toward the recumbent Alekseev, and reported:

"Mikhail Vasilich. They must be informed of your afternoon telegram to Rodzyanko. And in general, they're insisting on a *definitive decision*."

A telegram of reproof to Rodzyanko? About the recklessness of his telegrams, the interruption of communications with Tsarskoye Selo, and the detainment of the royal trains? Bringing these up for discussion meant clouding over his relations with Rodzyanko—but Rodzyanko himself was asking for it. Fine, inform all the commanders-in-chief.

At this moment, our unity with them must be consolidated, and without concealments. Indeed.

But a *definitive decision?* Mikhail Vasilich himself would have liked to get that from someone!

[2 7 6]

No sooner had they—three sailors, two soldiers, and a bespectacled intellectual carrying a Browning—led General Sukhomlinov into the thick of the Tauride Palace than the news raced through the halls. Excited soldiers craned their necks: Where? Where have they taken him? Threatening to finish him off as well.

Who else had been led in as prisoners these past few days, the soldiers didn't know. They'd seen gendarme uniforms and general's uniforms, beaver hats and expensive fur coats, all alien to them. They'd seen people with revolvers leading some bishop, and that was a sin, he couldn't even walk, they brought him a chair and he collapsed onto it, and they carried him on the chair, and he bestowed blessings as he went. But Sukhomlinov was the sole name that even ignorant soldiers knew. All the newspapers had been writing about him for a year and newspaper readers had clarified that he was the chief traitor general responsible for the death of so many of our brothers at the front, for there being no shells and the war not coming to an end! At last they'd caught the true guilty party and enemy! (Some had also heard they'd already put him in the fortress—but then he'd been freed at the hands of other traitors just like him.)

They managed to lead him to a wing of the building, to some unknown room—but the soldiers caught up, the clamor mounted, they congregated like a vehement wall and demanded he be handed over, and they knew there was no way to take him to the prisoner rooms other than through them and then through the large hall. They shouted:

"Hand over Sukhomlin!"

Two Duma deputies came out and reassured them that the court would sort this all out, that there should not be reprisals.

"Give him over! Traitor!"

The crowd reluctantly yielded to their remonstrances. Taking retribution with their own hands—oh, that would truly be good, and quick, and for sure. Otherwise they'd hide him, take him away, and set him free again, and he'd get off. Who should do the deciding if not soldiers? Who died if not soldiers? You weren't the ones who died!

All right, someone quick-witted tossed out:

"Rip his epaulets off and bring them here to us!"

Epaulets, gold-entwined epaulets, were more hated than anything.

"No! Rip 'em off in front of us!"

"Can't we all go in? Fine, then in front of our messengers."

(A messenger was called a *delegate*, as other gentlemen in the other wing had taught them.)

Two of the soldiers went in. Went into the room, where this bald, droopily mustached general was sitting by the wall, hunched over, an empty sack.

Some gentleman approached him with scissors. But the general wished to cut them off himself. He nimbly removed the greatcoat and put it in his lap. Took out a penknife. And deftly cut off the epaulets without damaging them.

But by doing this he revealed his uniform.

"Take 'em off the uniform, too!" the soldiers ordered.

They helped him cut them off the uniform.

But he hadn't brought any medals on his chest, just his St. George Cross.

One of the gentlemen present said that he should remove the cross as well. But a sailor-escort stepped in:

"It's okay. The George can stay. Take it away when the court says so."

The soldier messengers brought the general's epaulets and held them high. The small crowd thundered "hurrah!"

"Show it here! Show it here!"

There can be justice on earth after all!

Some began to disperse. Others remained, expecting to be led somewhere.

The Duma deputies in the room didn't know how to transfer him safely to the ministerial pavilion.

And the general was trembling.

Right then the ubiquitous Kerensky showed up, burst in as if winged. He made the decision: take the general straight to the Peter and Paul Fortress, from which the Tsar had illegally released him! Kerensky himself agreed to lead him out. He walked in front with a theatrical stride and another two or three sailor escorts behind. Coming out to the already dissolving cluster, Kerensky, himself thin, shouted in a high and thin but ringing voice:

"Soldiers! Former Minister of War Sukhomlinov is under arrest. He is under the protection of the Provisional Committee of the State Duma. If in your legitimate hatred for him you permit yourselves to use violence, then by doing so you will only help him avoid the punishment he is subject to by trial! And you will disgrace the revolution by shedding blood within the State Duma's walls. And you will meet with the most energetic opposition from us, even if it costs us our life!"

His voice quaked from the beauty he was experiencing.

Although he expressed this in a learned way, the soldiers understood: All right, hands off, they'll try him.

And no one raised a hand. They just hollered:

"Traitor! Turncoat!"

A pale Sukhomlinov summoned up the strength to reply:

"That's not true."

"It's true. It's true!" they shouted on all sides.

So they led the general away and sat him in a new place not far from the front steps while they looked for a vehicle. Soldiers and civilians walked past him, armed and with red armbands, saying "Comrade, how do I get to this place?" and "Comrade, where's the information room?"

These "comrades" everywhere sounded strange.

Arrest was new to other dignitaries but not to Sukhomlinov. In the past four months alone he had been under house arrest, and before that'd sat in the Trubetskoy Bastion for half a year, in the Alekseevsky Ravelin, the sole prisoner there. He'd already spent a year with his thoughts and his insult. How many had he and so many others moved up the captivating ladder of government ranks, which went on like a charming and unending game? And why had it suddenly been decided, in his old age, to ask so much of him alone?

Sukhomlinov had advanced for a long time without reaching any shining heights. Only after forty had he become a general, whereupon his most vivid and happiest years had begun. The governor-generalship of Kiev since revolutionary October 1905, and, now a two-time widower, at sixty years of age he had fallen madly in love with a twenty-three-year-old married woman and had set himself the greedy task of having her for himself! In his lofty position, and with the memory of his second deceased wife having been a divorcée, and given the desperate resistance of her current husband, the three-year struggle for this new divorce had been shattering, but the marvelous prize was worth it, and Sukhomlinov was not despondent. He fought and gratefully accepted assistance from anyone who offered it, from the Austrian consul in Kiev, from General Kurlov, from the gendarme officer Myasoedov or the Okhrana chief Kulyabko. The scandalous trial had gone on for three years, and the cherished divorce had been wrested by appealing to Supreme authority, after Sukhomlinov had become Minister of War. The masculine victory gained had entailed losses—unpleasantnesses at Court, his wife's imperious whims, trips abroad to resorts, the search for money—but none of this had clouded his exquisite victory.

In Kiev he had learned to combine the incompatible: to be popular in society, to be liked by the educated public, the theatrical world, and the bishops of the church, to assuage the Jews, and to win higher and higher posts from the Emperor. He had capably avoided the Japanese war, preferring reliable promotion in the rear. As governor-general he knew how not to anger the revolutionaries or the liberals. Only the rightists had taken a powerful dislike to him, and in one public speech they had spoken of their governor-general as follows: "His windmill blades, or, as they're called in the local territory, *sukhom-lyns*, are sprinkled with golden dust and turn whichever way the wind's blowing."

At one time, Sukhomlinov had taught tactics to the young heir to the throne. In his mature years he had been able to revive a proper tone with the Emperor: the constant good cheer he liked so well! He had always tried to convince the Emperor of the very best course of military affairs. Thus he had printed in *Stock Exchange Gazette*, right before the war, that Russia was fully prepared for it, that it would forget all about the concept of "defense" and its artillery would never have to complain of a shortage of shells. (The Emperor found this so pleasant!) In 1914, the Emperor had wanted to appoint the Minister of War to be Supreme Commander, but Sukhomlinov had declined that honor.

This was in fact what he was like: life-affirming, life-loving, a teller of funny stories. (Which was why he could be rash. A clash threatened with Austria, but he placed military orders there and took his wife there to a resort.) A golden dust windmill, he kept grinding and grinding, not accepting anything too hard and so not risking cracking his teeth. If occasionally he was overtaken by the fearful feeling that his whole life he had been accepted seemingly not for who he was, and to keep from being exposed, his grinding grew more and more lively and florid. So cheerfully had his blades turned that when August 1914 came, he had neglected to draw up a reserve option for partial mobilization.

He was not a traitor. But he was on the highest hill—a windmill that had also swept us into war and brought down the best Russian force for nothing.

[2 7 7]

*   *   *

The meeting of printers at the Kalashnikovskaya Exchange had decided not to print the bourgeois newspapers for now. By resolution of the Soviet of Workers' Deputies, only those newspapers which did not run counter to the revolutionary movement were allowed to see the light of day.

*   *   *

They were carrying a fresh issue of *Izvestia of the Soviet of Workers' Deputies* out of the Tauride Palace to a vehicle for driving around and spreading them throughout the city. The public rushed toward them, begging them to share. The carriers began tossing them out. In a scuffle, one soldier exclaimed:

"Hey, stop it! Hey, calm down! I'm holding a bomb!"

He barely got out of the crush. And it was true, it was a bomb. A naval mine.

"Just look at 'em scramble, the dimwits!"

*   *   *

Men had been firing on a tall building from the street and had wounded the building's owner. The bullet had passed through his chin, drilled through his face, and exited above his eyes. "Did you fire?" "No!" A soldier wanted to shoot him dead, but a civilian in a black coat said: "Why waste a bullet on a brute like that?" He grabbed a log from a stove and cracked him over the head. They dragged the dead man downstairs to show the people and dropped him by the gate. And the civilian recounted to the crowd how he'd killed him, his eyes rolling wildly.

The man's wife ran up, weeping: "An innocent man is dead!"

*   *   *

Grand Duke Igor Konstantinovich telephoned from the Marble Palace to Princess Lidia Vasilchikova on the Fontanka. But scarcely had she picked up the receiver when another soldier gang burst into her home

"to see where they were shooting machine guns from"—and a sailor grabbed the receiver from the princess and asked:

"Where are you calling from?"

Had he answered "the Marble Palace"—the princess would have been done for. But hearing the rough, strange voice, Igor Konstantinovich grasped the situation:

"I wanted to find out whether you're all well there."

The sailor grinned:

"Thank you. We are well! And just how are *you*?"

*   *   *

All the pharmacies on Nevsky were shut. And above each pharmacy hung a two-headed eagle, as it was supposed to.

And here some worker had had a good idea, or had been given one. He found a ladder, propped it up, and smashed the eagle with a hammer. Shards sprinkled onto the sidewalk.

Two foreigners were walking by with a very satisfied look, conversing in English. They looked around, laughed, and continued on.

*   *   *

There were no yardmen standing by any gates anywhere or maintaining order any longer. Each was free to do as he pleased.

The infirmary soldiers were also running off to town, spending the night, and either not returning or returning late. The nurses begged them at least to telephone to let them know how they were.

*   *   *

A truck was moving slowly down the Palace Embankment past the Summer Garden in the red rays of sunset. In it were mattresses, bundles, things taken from the apartment of a policeman, who had been arrested, or killed. His uniform poked up in the air, having been put on a sweep-broom, and the empty sleeves flapped as they went. Ahead of the things, up in the cab, were two soldiers without belts and their hats slapdash. Between them was a drunken young woman wearing a bright yellow kerchief made from a tablecloth and a red sash slantwise over her coat and holding a bared saber. She was singing in a wild, hoarse voice, quite evidently not for the first time:

You fell victim in a fateful struggle —
and waving her saber in time.
They were driving right past the spot where Karakozov shot Aleksandr II.

*   *   *

In the evening, soldiers from the 1st Machine-gun Regiment, billeted in the House of the People, realized that there had been a reason for taking them to such an odd building that wasn't like a building and that stood so separate that it would be easy to blow up. They'd been brought there to be annihilated. In a large hall where everyone sat on one side they discussed for a long time whether they should leave. They sent out reconnaissance to inspect the cellars. So it was! There were machines of some kind there, and pieces of the floor had collapsed under them, and thunder had started from one of them without lightning. They were badly frightened, and everyone ran, panicked to get outside. Good thing there were lots of doors.

Nonetheless, they stayed. But there weren't enough latrines for the more than ten thousand that they were. The lads blocked up and filled all the holes in one go. They started cleaning out the holes with their bayonets — and poked through the pipes, which started leaking, which meant sewage — and the ceilings started getting wet.

*   *   *

That evening, the Petrograd streets were pitch-dark, many streetlamps had been knocked out, buildings were shut tight, windows curtained, and stores boarded up. Everywhere there was an awful emptiness. There were blocks where you didn't come across anyone except maybe a frightened figure flashing by.

The only strong light and movement was from headlamps when vehicles drove by. But some vehicles had one headlamp draped in red fabric, and so they drove, one eye red, one pink beam forward.

*   *   *

(*Schlüsselburg*) — Today workers from the gunpowder factories went on a big march up Neva, carrying red flags, trampling the snow on the ice. In the upper open windows of the Schlüsselburg Fortress, the prisoners were already awaiting liberation, waving and shouting. The guards made no attempt to resist and unquestioningly handed their rifles and pouches over to the workers. In the prison corridors, hammers appeared, and chisels, and the convicts themselves struck off their irons, tossing them on the floor like dead snakes. Someone took his for a souvenir. In the storeroom they changed their linen and shirts, but their gray robes and shoes remained the same. Through the yard, loading the sleighs with case files in blue covers, they dragged them to the boiler house—and threw them in, and after that in the furnace's maw. From other sledges where the guards' confiscated weapons lay, Comrades Zhuk and Liechtenstadt gave fervent speeches. And they all pushed through the gates and down the Neva—to the other bank, leading their sick by the arm.

In the town of Schlüsselburg they mingled with the residents, and there were more speeches. People brought the prisoners warm footwear, caps, and gloves. Then they stretched out in a long march toward the Gunpowder Factory. In the evening, the workers took the prisoners to their apartments, fed them, and put them in the best beds.

There had been sixty-seven men in that prison bastion in all, politicals and criminals. Among them was Pyanykh, a former Duma deputy and SR, who had been cashiered for his part in a murder.

*　　*　　*

(Moscow) As evening fell, the Kremlin surrendered, and soldiers thronged through Nikolsky Gate.

In the night, two thousand criminals were freed from Butyrskaya Prison—and headed off to carouse through the city.

*　　*　　*

(Kronstadt)—The Half-crew comprised the worst and even criminal sailor element, those who'd been taken off vessels and could not be sent into battle. That night they were the first to rush out. From the pier, they burst onto moored vessels and tied up the officers. The harbor was brightly lit by electricity, and you could see them throwing murdered officers overboard and the ice turning red from the blood.

Midshipman Uspensky, who that fall had survived the explosion of the *Empress Maria*, had in February been sent to Kronstadt to take mine classes. That night he was assigned to the watch on the minelayer *Terek*. From shore, a gang of armed sailors wearing the ribbons of the Half-crew burst in. They twisted Uspensky's arms and were putting a revolver to his head when a watch sergeant stopped them, saying that this one had come from the Black Sea and was taking the mine classes. They threw him down, tied up. They themselves took the officers' watches and rings, stole their wallets, and looted their cabins. The wave of ransackers was repeated five times.

The officers not killed were led onto the pier, their cockades and epaulets were torn off (with bits of sleeve fabric), and they were led to Anchor Square, to show them the bodies of the dead officers and the dead, tortured admiral, and then once again they led them onto the ice. "We don't want to soil Kronstadt earth with dog's blood. We're going to shoot you on the ice." Triggers were cocked, and they aimed—but then they took them to the Naval Prison and put them in cells without bunks, to sleep on the floor.

[2 7 8]

Who wouldn't be ground down by this stupid, exhausting overturning and battering! How could anyone retain an elevated soul in this mess? Everyone around looked knocked out, lost—but for the monarchist, for the patriot, for the conservative Shulgin it was bordering on the unbearable. Something *wrong* was happening, even compared with his audacious but successful trip yesterday to the Peter and Paul Fortress. The few lovely petals that had fluttered just yesterday morning had today been torn off pitilessly and trampled. Shulgin and all of them had ended up *in the wrong place,* and in their dizziness and loss of will they had no place or application for themselves.

They had no one's breast to throw themselves at in horror, no one left around with whom to share this.

It was a nightmare that had gone on for a day and a night, a day and a night, and a day and a night: momentary flashes of clarity, when suddenly you are keenly and hopelessly conscious of what has occurred, and then a gray, monotonous delirium, this viscous human sludge that filled the entire palace and tied up all movement both in his waking hours and in his dreams. Just as it was physically impossible to get through the palace, so it was impossible to act and impossible to come up with what to do. The half-dark of the nights, where Russia's exhausted new masters dozed in hunched poses on couches, chairs, and tables, alternated with the gyre of gray days, the ringing of telephones with complaints, summonses, and pleadings, the string of prisoners brought in and up for verifications of some kind or led into offices for hide-and-seek followed by release; an entire line of humiliated policemen who had changed clothes wound around the Duma's inner courtyard; pale, lost, questioning army officers; and instructions from the Duma committee, and trips to the regiments, and speeches, speeches, speeches right here, in the Ekaterininsky Hall, which was like a stable of bristling bayonets in a grayish-brown jumble, and in the former White Hall of sessions, where the empty frame of an imperial portrait now gaped; and the "hurrah, hurrah" of the unending rallies, interspersed with spoiled Marseillaises, occasional commands to "present arms" in honor of Rodzyanko, though the troops could no longer pass themselves off as troops but rather were armed bands to whom Chkheidze was singing about the shining majesty of the revolutionary soldier's deed and the dark forces of reaction, for some reason about the *old regime,* the Rasputin clique, oprichniks, gendarmes, the authority of the people, land for laborers, and freedom, freedom, freedom. There were also civilian deputations thronging into the palace, and only a lazy man could fail to give them a speech. Tables were set up between the soiled columns of the Ekaterininsky Hall, and young ladies—pharmacists and midwives to look at them—were passing out leaflets and brochures heretofore illegal. Party slogans on red calico stretched across the walls. It would take considerable repair to return everything to its former presentable Duma appearance. On the room doors were pieces of paper that said "bureau," "bureau," "SR Party CC," "RSDRP Military Organization"—they'd besieged and overwhelmed the Tauride Palace.

What caught Shulgin's ear especially painfully was this "old regime." It would be fine if by a change of regime they understood parting with Stürmer, Protopopov, the irresponsible ministers, and the untalented appointments. But by these words they also meant parting with the monarchy itself, didn't they? Along with all of historical Russia? Who had determined this? Who had resolved this?

And when? How had this come about? All his life, Shulgin, along with others of like mind, had fought revolution. They'd joined the Progressive Bloc in hopes of turning the Kadets into patriots—and where had they themselves ended up? They, they themselves were accomplices in the ill-starred Bloc's destructive work. Under the protective cover of governmental authority, they had eloquently threatened—governmental authority. And now that it had finally been toppled and was no more, now they were all facing the beast from the abyss.

Shulgin remained one of the few Duma deputies who had not given a single speech to this arriving herd. He had not aspired to such honor. Anyway, his throat was weak in the face of these bristling bayonets and his independent tongue was mute. All the faces in the crowd had started to run together into a single foul-brutish-dull expression, and he had no desire to see it, he turned away to where it wasn't, and he clenched his teeth in mournful revulsion.

As can happen, you completely forget an impression that you already know but isn't ingrained—and all of a sudden it comes through again. So too now, his old hatred of revolution rose up in Shulgin, that inner shuddering from 1905 Kiev. After many years of a restored, peaceful life, after the noisy Duma debates and revelations of the government—he'd completely forgotten that feeling. But now it was mounting by the hour deep inside him, now reaching the point of fury. If only they had machine guns! Bring a few machine guns here! *Their* language was all *these people* would understand!

How joyfully they were galloping along! Freedom to the point of stupor and retching! Ah, Shulgin had begun to see what this soldiery was so happy about. They were hoping now not to go to the front! That was why they were assaulting, humiliating, and killing officers—so as not to go to the front!

And where were these vaunted troops of Ivanov's dragging along? Why couldn't they get going? Why couldn't they come in?

Not even a battalion—the Duma Committee didn't even have three decisive bouncers to at least clear the corridor in their last Duma wing! You couldn't even push through these ugly mugs!

Actually, was the fallen government any better? What had it done with its troops, its police? They'd thrown policemen out on the streets by ones and twos to be beaten and slaughtered. They should have collected the entire police force into one big fist and waited this out. When all the units had mutinied and lost discipline—that would have been the time to move. But who could have figured this out? Protopopov? He was the first to flee.

And where was the Guard, that legendary *Guard*, that alone remained loyal to the Tsar in his worst hour of ruin, when all around was rebelling and burning? It was one or the other: either they needed the Guard, or there should be no Guard at all. If they needed it, then they shouldn't have sent it to war to be ground up, and its soldiers had to be chosen not by their height or the shape of their nose or by their place of residence close to the reserve battalion, but by their loyalty and mettle.

But there was no such Guard. The Guard had been cobbled together senselessly. And ground up.

And now all that was left was to pray to God that this whole upheaval had given birth merely to a constitutional, parliamentary monarchy, but *no further.*

For all this was already unfolding—*further.*

Shulgin had tried to formulate—before this ominous turbulence—what the Tsar should do. What would Shulgin do in his place?

Most correct would be to disperse this entire rabble with salvoes.

Or? Or else then . . .

He couldn't say the words even to himself. They were slipping into a chasm.

The Emperor had no supporters left, no loyal subjects—Rasputin had wiped out the last of them. He was even worse dead than alive. Had he been alive they could have killed him now and there would have been a respite.

The monarchy was in jeopardy!

How in this insane jumble was a monarchist to save the monarchy?

Shulgin wanted to find some lofty, handsome, swift—and aristocratic mode of action. But he could come up with nothing. He had lost his usual vitality and was languishing in a narcotic impotence.

The revolution was waiting for a few crowd-worn Duma deputies to exercise authority. What authority! . . . The Duma Committee was not only not an authority, it didn't have the forces to retain for itself even Rodzyanko's spacious office. Rodzyanko wanted to argue over the rooms, but Milyukov and the others gave in immediately, saying the Duma should avoid conflict with the Soviet of Workers' Deputies! And now the Committee had moved to two tiny rooms at the end of the corridor, opposite the library, where offices previously unknown to the Duma deputies themselves were located.

There, in that cramped space, and then only at intervals, when no one was rushing through the door and no one was being dragged outside, Milyukov and company discussed the makeup of the new government—whispering in the corners of rooms, at the edges of the table, and then loudly, several voices at once. What a time and place they'd found! How many times had Shulgin suggested that they firmly determine in advance and even publish a list of those "invested with the trust of all the people"—and they had always responded that it was inconvenient and premature.

And now, apparently, it was too late.

Milyukov had been the most undoubted candidate. He had confidently guided the negotiations, and he held the main list in his hands. Guchkov had firmly joined it. Although he wasn't a member of the Fourth Duma, his position had always been so notorious and militant that he had grounds for laying claim to a ministry. On the other hand, shying before the socialists, two portfolios—justice and labor—already turned out to have been conceded to Kerensky and Chkheidze. The inspired Kerensky, shaven like an actor, had become so essential to everyone these past few days that they could not contemplate a government without him.

But after that, something puzzling had begun. Some unnamed, secret collusion had entered into negotiations and people whispered more and more frequently—and Shulgin found out for himself—that wartime Russia's Minister of Finance would not be Shingarev, as expected, but for some reason the thirty-two-year-old perfumed dandy Tereshchenko, who was very rich and drove a motorcar wonderfully. Shulgin took a closer look and was astonished. Just as the old government was destroying itself, clutching at the Stürmers, while these very people were prodding it—so now these very people at their very first step were drowning themselves, burdening themselves with the nonentities Tereshchenko and Nekrasov. The century of the "liberation movement" against the tedious Historical Authority had taken a prize for itself at the finish—a cabinet of semi-nonentities.

All this was hurtling into a chasm. . . .

Shulgin was not offered any portfolio whatsoever. He was too rightist for the new government, in the new environment. Not that he was longing for a portfolio. He didn't even know what sphere of government he might lead. Not a single ministry suited him. By his nature he loved not material authority but spiritual avant-gardism.

With his perpetual vibrancy and wit he was, above all, an orator. Perhaps a writer. Not a worker of politics but an artist of politics.

And right now, as everything had started falling into a chasm, and growing dark, and his soul ached, and perhaps he should be preparing for death, all Shulgin longed to do was prove himself by some great deed.

An artistic deed. An aristocratic deed.

[279]

Rodzyanko had become a stone sculpture not only outwardly; he was in fact turning to stone. Turning to stone from the incessant speech-giving. Turning to stone from doleful thoughts. From the lack of sympathy around him from Committee members and because they'd deprived him of the right to act. All of them together had risen up against his journey—and he could not sunder this ring. The decisiveness was seeping out of his large body.

It wasn't so offensive when that horrible Soviet of Deputies hadn't allowed him to go. It was offensive that his own people hadn't, either.

Sometimes, from the height of the rostrum, he would gaze out over the Duma deputies as his own, protected and under his care, practically like his own sons.

But here they . . .

If he went, he would be prime minister. That was why they weren't allowing him, to get around him. They came up with a pretext, saying that "the leftists wouldn't allow" Rodzyanko.

For more than a day they'd been readying an illegal government—without the President.

How many years had he protected their freedom of speech with his own breast. Last night he'd saved them from punitive troops. And they still wouldn't let him go. They were scheming. . . .

All had been readied! A historic meeting! And it wasn't to be!

A telegram arrived from Voeikov in Dno saying that, rather than wait there, the Emperor had invited Rodzyanko to Pskov.

And they kept telephoning from Bublikov that the train at the Vindava Station was under steam. When were they going?

They were depriving themselves, depriving everyone, of one last opportunity for peaceful mediation.

It was a terrible surmise: Did they need peaceful mediation? Did they even need a peaceful outcome?

In Milyukov's cattily malicious eyes, Rodzyanko read that they didn't.

Apparently, they didn't want anyone to negotiate with the Emperor. Did they want a total break? . . .

But even in this bitter hour, he had to be noble and think about the hapless Emperor, who was having a rough time of it casting about like this, while meanwhile they wanted to detain him like a common thief. (Rodzyanko was ashamed that he hadn't managed to put an end to this right away this morning.)

Barely keeping himself from sobbing, Rodzyanko ordered Bublikov over the telephone:

"Appoint the imperial train for Pskov. It should proceed with every formality inherent to imperial trains."

His voice shook.

"Meanwhile, prepare a train for Pskov from the Warsaw Station."

Perhaps he would go yet.

Or someone else?

A decision yet to be made.

If you go, you will get an appointment from the Emperor, but here they'll consider you a traitor and an underling of reaction, right? That won't do, either.

There were also rumors from Dno that gendarmes there had arrested unreliable railroaders. The journey was not without danger for the President. It might be a good thing if he didn't go. Look out—they could arrest you, too.

And then, was the line to Pskov free? Had they reported about some mutiny in Luga? Ask Luga.

Right then, Guchkov arrived and began hinting that the journey was necessary, yes, not to win approval for a responsible ministry but rather for the abdication of the Emperor himself.

Ab-di-ca-tion already?

Perhaps, indeed, the President had failed to understand something here, was lagging behind.

No, he could not make the journey *for that*. Let someone else.

Although after Kirill's appearance—indeed, it was a shaky situation. The dynasty had split.

His swollen head buzzed from three days of spinning. From the impossible pandemonium in his dear Tauride Palace. He'd been lifted up by the regiments' exultant cries. And wounded by his Duma colleagues' treacherous behavior. And insulted by the boorish insolence of the Soviet of Deputies.

Some soldiers had sought to kill the President. And the Soviet of Deputies—if it could detain who it wanted, then could it arrest him as well? (He learned that they had spoken out harshly there today against him and Engelhardt.)

All this human spinning was ungovernable.

The Emperor's train was already in Pskov, and the Emperor was waiting for his President.

Obviously, though, they weren't going to let him go.

Rodzyanko telephoned the Ministry of Roads and Railways again and asked them to send a telegram:

"Pskov. To His Imperial Majesty. Extraordinary circumstances prevent me from leaving, about which I am informing Your Majesty."

This was his farewell to his Emperor.

[2 8 0]

It would have been amazing if the revolution hadn't come, it would have meant that the people had already fallen hopelessly. But for the people, unfortunately, revolution was only a practical means; the people had no feeling for its inner beauty as it unfolded from day to day and hour to hour. Only a strong personality could absorb this beauty.

In a country that a faceless ruling gang had stripped of personalities, Aleksandr Bublikov was an unusually intact and strong one. Here he himself had discovered and found and secured himself a place: running the Ministry of Roads and Railways. Had Bublikov not come here, not designated for himself a field of battle, this ministry would have remained in a state of torpor through these days of revolution, as had ten other ministries. But he had come, and he had lit a fire in its moribund governmental veins, and from here, from a few adjoining offices, he had accomplished a revolutionary act of greater significance than anything going on in Petrograd: he had sprayed the Petrograd revolution all over Russia using just his railroad telegrams, in a single night.

After this they'd started tracking down and cornering the royal train. Food supply trains kept moving freely toward Petrograd along all the lines. And on top of this Bublikov came up with one more game: how to set a trap for Grand Duke Nikolai Nikolaevich and force him to enter into talks with and recognize the new government. For this, Bublikov had sent him a telegram saying the main engineer on the construction of the Black Sea Railroad had to be replaced (as if during the days of revolution the ministry had no more urgent tasks)—and State Duma Commissar Bublikov was asking approval from His Imperial Highness, the Caucasus Viceroy, for this appointment. By giving his gracious consent, he would be recognizing the new government!

Pacing nervously through the spacious offices, rubbing his hands and catching up to events and people at great distances, Bublikov for the first time in his entire life felt he had genuine scope. He had always longed for action! He sometimes could barely breathe in driveling intellectual company constantly going on about morality but incapable of masculine action— compelling the disobedient, crushing the defiant, and directing the movement of masses. If, a few days later, he was appointed to this building as a full-fledged minister, Bublikov knew what grandiose transformations he would launch: they would floor the timid officials of the old breed but would be profoundly revolutionary in their engineering-technical essence. Our intelligentsia could not be reeducated with words; the ideology of industrialism had to be revealed in action. Russia faced a path of titanic development of its industrial potential and the magical development of capitalism—and this was the only way to avoid the fatal path of socialism, which was so ruinously close to the popular ideals of justice. But one had to know how to *call on* the people. Bublikov's first telegram was just such a call, and history would appreciate it one day as the start of a creative revolution.

Overflowing with these thoughts and with admiration for what he was accomplishing, Bublikov kept pacing through the adjoining rooms, in between telephone calls, and meanwhile he keenly took note of what was happening nearby. Rulevsky's strict watches had been organized (it turned out he was a Bolshevik) with shift changes. Each of them was given four student runners per watch for errands (they had nowhere to go; their institute

had been occupied by the infantry regiment that had come from Peterhof).
Cavalry Captain Sosnovsky, a very lively and pleasant man, tried in vain to
get sustenance for his Semyonovsky soldiers from their battalion; they
hadn't brought anything, so they started bringing it over from the railways
school. The cavalry captain himself made a habit of walking upstairs to the
empty ministerial apartment, which he had safeguarded from a soldier attack, and there, in gratitude, the ministerial servants treated him to wine.
Sosnovsky, as head of the guard, and Bublikov together signed various passes.
All the leaders—Bublikov, Lomonosov, Rulevsky, Shmuskes, and others—
were fed by the wife—a Latvian and socialist—of one of the couriers. Fewer
than half the usual employees had shown up, but the pulse of revolution
beat even more clearly in the ministry without them. They had failed to detain the royal train at Bologoye and along the entire route to Dno, and then
Rodzyanko had yielded and ordered them to let the imperial train through
to Pskov.

The podgy, worthless fatman! Is a revolution ever made with the likes of
him? The lost Russian people! Russia had no iron men!

Telephone negotiations with the Duma, both official and through acquaintances, took up Bublikov's time and energy more than anything and
caused the greatest irritation. Total disarray, bewilderment, and incessant
talk reigned in the Duma. The cancellations of the Rodzyanko trips alone,
from three stations, said it all. And he hadn't been able to go because obviously no one in the Duma had any authority but there was constant talking
with the Soviet of Workers' Deputies, which had outmaneuvered them all.
This enraged Bublikov. All of them there had been gripped by an intellectual helplessness, but he couldn't race off and and infuse them all with hot
steel—and vanquish the Soviet of Workers' Deputies.

This incessant talking in the Tauride Palace could be the ruin of the entire revolution—and indeed had begun to ruin it. They had just learned that
the Duma Committee was appointing commissars to run all the ministries—
and what had they done? Appointed as Commissar of Railways not Bublikov
but Dobrovolsky!

They had completely lost their minds! Not only had they forgotten about
Bublikov, who had given them all of Russia, not only had they forgotten
that he was already sitting there running the ministry and holding Krieger
prisoner—they had ungratefully forgotten even that it was Bublikov who
had come up with the very idea of commissars! For himself personally, Bublikov would have achieved more if he'd spent these two full days chattering
in the Tauride Palace's senseless crush!

He resolved not to cede the ministry!

For reinforcement, he appointed Lomonosov Deputy Commissar.

His relationship with Lomonosov was complicated. At one time Lomonosov had scuttled Bublikov's plan that was under review. But now Bublikov had rightly called him up to the revolution. Of course, his sharp eye

and keen nose were only attuned to ensuring that he would end up among the victors. He was no fighter. But right now, in this situation, he was wonderfully useful.

"And when I become minister, do you want to be my senior deputy?"

Lomonosov lightning fast (he had already thought about it):

"What about Voskresensky?"

"He won't agree. After all, he'd been predicted for a minister, and his nose is out of joint."

There are handsome gestures: I want no rewards for my participation in the revolution! Or: I'm used to working. Appoint me head of the Nikolaevsky Railroad or head of one of the administrations. But to let it slip at such a moment? Later, Bublikov would move on somewhere, be promoted, and you would immediately become minister.

"As you would have it, Aleksan Aleksanych."

"Let's sit down soon and discuss the lists of first appointments and dismissals."

But for now, the shorn kettle that was Lomonosov's head flitted by, from room to room, and the confident deep baritone of his telephone conversations inspired everyone here:

"What's happening there in Gatchina?"

"Twenty thousand loyal troops."

"What does 'loyal' mean?"

"Not revolutionary."

"Get this through your head once and for all that these are *mutineers!* The loyal men are the ones on the side of the people!"

[2 8 1]

This war had crested and then crashed for General Ruzsky, first carrying him aloft, then hurling him down. His initial appointment to army commander had been a success, followed immediately by the triumphal capture of Lvov. Nikolai Nikolaevich had been furious, though, that Ruzsky had not surrounded them and had let the Austrian armies get away, and even threatened to bring him up on charges. But then came gratitude from the Emperor himself, and Ruzsky, leapfrogging Alekseev, had brilliantly risen to adjutant general and the Supreme Command of the Northwest Army Group instead of Zhilinsky. (And who could have anticipated given his lowly beginnings, or who could now recall, that he was that Krever, the son of the palace department's linen-keeper, whom aristocratic servicemen saw as some Finnish outsider, who had changed his name to be more euphonious.) Thus two thirds of all Russian armies had come under his charge. Immediately after this had come the cruel trials in Poland, which might have ended in total catastrophe but instead ended in new glory: a St. George 2nd class (his third George!) "for the repulse of the foe from Warsaw." Then came a string of failures, especially in East Prussia, the rout of the 10th Army, and dissatisfaction with Ruzsky was aroused at the highest levels, and the Empress schemed—he and Zinaida Aleksandrovna believed it best for him to take leave for health reasons. And just in time: the entire great retreat of 1915 happened without Ruzsky—and from Kislovodsk he could allow himself to advise an energetic counteroffensive. But right then Alekseev, who had taken the army group from Ruzsky and responsibility for the entire retreat, was given not a demotion but a promotion—as the Supreme Commander's chief of staff, and under this Tsar, essentially Supreme Commander—and had now irrevocably circumvented Ruzsky. The Northwest Army Group was divided up, and Ruzsky was given only a part of his former army group—the Northern Army Group—and at a difficult moment, after the surrender of Kovno. Not for long, though. Again there was a string of failures, and right then he suffered a bout of pleuritis and his health truly was compromised—and for a second time in this war he requested leave for health reasons. They released him in December 1915 without trying to dissuade him. But when at winter's end he was back on his feet and quite ready to resume his army group command, and was even pushing for this insistently, they were reluctant to bring him back. A wall! The Empress and the Tsar himself. However, his leave had become indecently long and unexplained, and he, a combat general, could never make up for missing these months of war! He had to resort to the most various means. First, he made roundabout requests for favorable articles in newspapers, which started to come out: such diverse newspapers as *Stock Exchange Gazette* and *New Times* always reported with attention and sympathy on how General Ruzsky was, how he was recuperating, how he had come to Petrograd full of energy and prepared for a new appointment. This laudatory chorus resounded even in Germany, and the German press also wrote about Ruzsky as the most talented Russian general. Second, he sought out intercession from a few of the grand duchesses and dukes and, quite confidentially, Rasputin's prayers, which helped perhaps more than the other. In July 1916, Ruzsky was given back his army group command and even with an important addition. Now under his control was the Petrograd Military District and all of vibrant, seething Petrograd, and that meant the censorship of Petrograd newspapers. The general basically became the capital's chief, defender, and father. However, he did all this with such tact (with the advice of Zinaida Aleksandrovna, who knew Petersburg life and all the figures here so well) that he was able to establish excellent relations with the capital's public circles, and the major newspapers liked and praised him very much. This winter, even, the figures who arrived in Pskov had tentatively sounded out the general's attitude toward possible governmental changes—and Ruzsky, in exceptionally circumspect form, confirmed his sympathy with them.

This natural and vital connection with Petrograd had been broken by the recent detachment of that district, with Khabalov, into an independent unit. At first Ruzsky was very sorry and was insulted, but when in these past few days the Petrograd upheavals had broken out, Ruzsky could only rejoice that the executioner's role of suppressing them had not fallen to him.

By no means could he remain on the sidelines, though. On Sunday evening, Rodzyanko tactlessly sent Ruzsky a telegram trying to convince him to intercede with the Emperor to create a ministry of public trust. A prickly situation arose. It was unprecedented for a military rank, incited by a civilian figure, to go to his superior with a political request. However, given the sweep of Petrograd events, a general so popular with the public could not remain impartial to an appeal from the Duma President.

All Monday, Ruzsky agonized over his choice. He realized that this was a desperate step in his life, and he could lose his command, without which neither he nor Zinaida Aleksandrovna could imagine living. But on Monday, at almost eight o'clock in the evening, a copy of the Minister of War's telegram to GHQ arrived. It stated directly that they had not been able to put down the military rebellion in Petrograd, many units had joined the rebels, and only a few were loyal. This sweep of events justified intervention, and an hour later Ruzsky sent his own telegram to the Emperor in which he explained that events were beginning to reflect on the army's status, and this meant the prospects for victory, too, which was why the general was being so bold as to most loyally report to His Majesty on the necessity of taking urgent measures to calm the population, in preference to repression. Ruzsky did not repeat Rodzyanko's extreme words about a ministry of public trust, but he couldn't help but send a similar telegram at this hour, for in these very minutes his headquarters had received an order from GHQ to send four regiments to Petrograd. And Ruzsky had to assign and send those regiments by midnight. (However, the sending of the regiments was delayed by a shortage of rolling stock—a good thing.)

All yesterday, Tuesday, events had teetered on an alarming edge. Petrograd had not calmed down in the slightest, the last government troops had surrendered, and victorious telegrams were coming thick and fast from Bublikov—but troops against the capital were already assembling from three army groups, and GHQ had warned that even more regiments might have to be mobilized—so Ruzsky irreproachably transmitted all instructions and took all measures.

The Northern Army Group's proximity to Petrograd, previously advantageous, had now become exceptionally disadvantageous. Ruzsky found himself in the unwanted position of principal punisher, at least after Ivanov.

Today, since early morning, telegrams had been arriving from Petrograd— from Rodzyanko himself and from agents saying that the Duma Committee had taken on the functions of the government. Ruzsky was caught increasingly between Scylla and Charybdis: whom had he been preparing military actions against—the new legitimate government? . . . But he could not fail to obey the legitimate military leadership, either.

It had been a long time since Ruzsky had exhausted himself the way he had these past few days and especially today. He'd smoked innumerable cigarettes and sniffed cocaine to gather strength. Never before, not in any military operation, had his reputation and career converged at such a single point and tottered so.

Right then he learned that the imperial letter trains had turned away from Bologoye and were on their way to Dno and apparently going not this way but toward Pskov. Then a direct telegram from Voeikov arrived saying yes, to Pskov!

Very unpleasant! And so untimely.

First of all, it is unpleasant for any military leader or officer when his superior comes to where he is. No matter how superficially and formally an emperor slides over military matters, he can easily make a censorious remark or give an order drastically changing the entire established order of business.

Secondly, right now specifically, when these fateful events were going on in Petrograd, and the State Duma's Committee had taken power from the imperial government, right now even a brief stay by the Tsar at Northern Army Group headquarters could stain General Ruzsky's public reputation. Why had the Tsar gone to see him specifically at this difficult moment? Was there some calculation here on some particular loyalty of Ruzsky's? Later it would be hard to justify himself, to prove that there could not have been even a shadow of such a thing. After all, the royal trains' route obviously did not run through Pskov—but for some reason they were coming here.

Thirdly, it was unpleasant that now, no matter how quickly the Tsar passed through Pskov, there was no avoiding having a difficult conversation with him, after that telegram in support of Rodzyanko. . . . It hadn't been that hard to send it—at a distance. Now, though, Ruzsky could not allow himself to obsequiously repudiate his own point of view simply because of a personal meeting. No, he had to force himself to say the same thing. But this was a great emotional trial, intense, heightened emotional work. He had to demonstrate his character. Actually, the Emperor was not much of a rival for such a clash.

Fourthly, this threatened him once again with the loss of his post, which he had already lost twice. It was a kind of curse.

A few hours remained until the Emperor's arrival, and Ruzsky had to strengthen his own position for the impending conversation. Convenient reinforcement of this kind was provided by Alekseev's telegram no. 1833 sent to Ivanov yesterday and today, in the middle of the day, to Northern Army Group headquarters. This telegram drew the situation in Petrograd as remarkably calmer and disposed toward conciliation and agreement. From his own direct sources, Ruzsky knew something completely different, that the disturbances in the capital had not stopped and were only heating up in the suburbs and Kronstadt. Tactically, though, it was advantageous to argue from the official document from the Supreme Commander's staff. Ruzsky ordered that Alekseev be asked for clarifications. Where was he getting this information?

A torrent was flowing toward him from GHQ—the news, and Alekseev's own telegrams, which had been delayed in getting to the Emperor for a full day. But the answer to Ruzsky's direct question was evasive. The information about Petrograd calming down was from various sources (although he did not name them) and was considered reliable.

Ruzsky realized that Alekseev was embarrassed and had nothing to say to him. This information was utter nonsense, especially given the revolution unfolding today in Kronstadt and Moscow.

Ruzsky ordered a private telegraph conversation with Alekseev—and GHQ replied that Alekseev was unwell and had lain down to rest. This could well have been the truth; it could also have been a form of evasion. Relations between them were almost hostile. It was hard not to feel frustration. Alekseev was a gray workhorse who had only succeeded through persistence and diligence. Ruzsky only needed a couple of hours to grasp and understand something, whereas Alekseev needed entire days. Ruzsky's fate was to be revived in insult every day, receiving orders from Alekseev as if he were the Supreme Commander himself. (Even retreating into illness, Alekseev had intrigued and put Gurko in his place at GHQ instead of Ruzsky.)

Right now, over the telegraph wires, he could feel how worried Alekseev was there, how he was rushing to correct his miscalculations. GHQ was impatiently trying to find out whether the Emperor had arrived and all those outdated telegrams had been delivered to him.

Alekseev was clearly distraught and debilitated, but this wasn't a situation where Ruzsky could act contrary to him. Given the shock for both capitals, that subtly trembling moment had reached Pskov as well, when he had to mobilize all his emotional forces—and he could not lose his balance. During these hours, he could not fail to send telegrams to Rodzyanko saying the shock of Petrograd upheavals, the destruction of train stations, and the vagabond element coming in from there were threatening the calm and provisioning of the Northern Army Group. Alekseev could not be denied alliance: the chaotic turn of events had made them allies. There, even the grand dukes had joined them.

But ultimately one had to feel a general sympathy for changes. It was now or never: was he going to perform an immortal and unforgettable service for society?

However, Ruzsky would have preferred the Emperor turning off for some reason and not reaching Pskov.

GHQ kept sending instructions—to repair the lines, if necessary, for the royal trains—so that they could reach Pskov and continue on to Petrograd.

To Petrograd, indeed; and the sooner the better.

Alas! Right before the royal trains' approach, an unexpected communiqué arrived from Luga saying that the garrison there had mutinied, too. That meant the Tsar could not leave Pskov immediately and go through Luga.

So the Emperor would inevitably be stranded in Pskov. The matter was not limited to quick passage through a train station, either.

Ruzsky made an effort to muster moral resistance. He had to find the courage to reject the usual etiquette and not post an honor guard at their meeting. He had to shift the entire arrival to another tone immediately, in keeping with general events.

Yes, the Tsar was constantly hiding behind insuperable barriers. But now he had to step onto the ground of reality.

Now, since Ruzsky had been unable to keep his favorite Bonch-Bruevich, the army group's chief of staff was General Yuri Danilov, known as "Black" Danilov. He was a difficult man. Early on in the war, under Nikolai Nikolaevich, due to a play of circumstances, he had essentially led all military operations for the entire Russian army, which led him to understand a great deal about himself to this day as an incomparable strategist. In the specific military respect, he perhaps did have abilities, but in general he was rather dense, stridently prejudiced, and devoid of any creative gift or ability to quickly assess a situation. He was an implementer but not a leader of a great cause. And he had absolutely no humanitarian skills. Therefore, for Ruzsky he was not an equal, an interlocutor, or of like mind. However, there was one moment in the past that had made Ruzsky's relations with Danilov unnamably difficult. Ruzsky couldn't forget that Danilov, of course, would always remember how one November night in 1914, during the Lodz operation, Ruzsky had flinched and asked GHQ—specifically, Danilov—for permission for a major withdrawal the next night. He was given this permission, but he ended up not needing it. Over the course of the day, the situation suddenly straightened out, and instead of a grandiose rollback, they completed a passable operation. But this stain before Danilov remained—and compelled Ruzsky to be cautiously obliging toward his chief of staff. So now he was inviting him along on his meeting with the Tsar.

Danilov, for his part, had been deeply insulted when, in 1915, Nikolai Nikolaevich turned his back on him and the Emperor removed him from the GHQ's general quartermastery and sent him to lead a corps. Therefore he was now a good fit based on his mood: to meet the Tsar without the ringing honors that had always been rendered before and to downplay the significance of the royal arrival. This would set a precedent in Russia's history, but circumstances reinforced their decisiveness. They wouldn't take the Tsar to army group headquarters, to town, but would meet him at the train station and reduce his visit to a passing-through. Of all the indispensable figures they only informed—unavoidable procedure—the Pskov governor.

Thus, the public would not reproach Ruzsky for fraternizing with the autocrat.

They cordoned off the entire station, not letting anyone on the platforms, so that it was utterly deserted. The station was also quite dark, only a few lamps. The governor arrived with several administration officials.

Ruzsky, however, was very nervous. It was unclear where the Emperor would go from here. And in these fluid conditions—could he bring himself to do it?—wrest from him the concessions society demanded? Not an easy task, if you knew the Emperor's character: unimaginably unreasonable and injudicious obstinacy. And a fear of precise formulations. A fear of definitive decisions.

Only at half past seven that evening did the first of the two trains pull in. Here, too, there was this game every time: of the two indistinguishable trains, which was the Tsar's and which was the suite's? It was good that Ruzsky didn't demean himself by going out to the platform beforehand because the first turned out to be the suite's, where there was no one to greet.

Only twenty minutes later did the Tsar's train pull in. Curtains were drawn over its wide windows, and strips of light only came through the cracks. Then the door to the lighted carriage opened and out jumped a tall aide-de-camp. Rug-upholstered steps were brought to the door and two Cossacks appeared. This was the Tsar's car.

The generals entered. A footman took their greatcoats. Count Frederiks, the sad, bent Minister of the Court, invited them into the parlor car with its furniture and green, silk-covered walls.

The Emperor came out wearing a dark gray Circassian coat, the uniform of Caucasus foot scouts.

His face struck Ruzsky—two months after he'd seen him at the meeting at GHQ. The Emperor had always been so young, in enviable health, though he didn't do anything and went for a walk every day. Now, though, he looked badly exhausted and anything but young, and he had deep, dark crow's feet.

Unable to conceal the tone of awkwardness (due to his embarrassing position and the meaning of what was being said), but trying to carry on as usual, insofar as he could, the Emperor explained that his train had been detained at the Vishera station by the news that Lyuban had been captured by rebels. Now he wanted to proceed to Tsarskoye Selo. But he had not taken the direct route from Dno, assuming he would be less impeded by making a detour through Pskov.

He spoke not as a sovereign. His tone held something lost, if not suppliant. He spoke—and nervously touched his collar. This winding around in a harried train had left its trace on him.

Ruzsky had always felt a superiority over this monarch, but never so great a one as now. As if returning the distraught Supreme Commander to the rules of the service he had forgotten, Ruzsky in a monotone, even querulous voice reported on the status of his army group and the events in it—the last thing that interested them all. There hadn't been any events whatsoever, but by doing this Ruzsky strengthened his position and bewildered the Emperor all the more.

After this, though, he expressed doubt about passing through Luga because the garrison there had mutinied.

Nikolai II was a master of self-control and not expressing his feelings on his face, but even this mastery had abandoned him today. At the news about Luga, his face expressed vulnerability and defenselessness. Nowhere was there passage for him! His eyes, deep set to begin with, cut even deeper across his cheeks. His mustache was already drooping.

Not just a less than intelligent face but a primitive one.

Ruzsky sensed himself gaining firmness.

Actually—the Emperor corrected himself—he was not proposing to leave immediately. He intended to wait in Pskov for Rodzyanko's arrival, as the latter had promised.

("Promised!" Now he was waiting for Rodzyanko's gracious arrival!)

Was that how things were? This cheered Ruzsky. Then his problem was eased. He and Rodzyanko together. . . . And the Tsar meanwhile, apparently, was fully prepared to be cultivated for a responsible ministry. . . .

Not all that simple, actually! Ivanov's punitive corps was converging meanwhile.

Not indulging himself to incline toward mollification, Ruzsky forced himself to maintain his firm tone and bring up the most unpleasant point: whether the Emperor had received his telegram from the day before yesterday supporting Rodzyanko's petition for a ministry of public trust.

"Yes, yes," the Emperor hastily confirmed, self-consciously even. Not having the strength to show his disapproval.

The confluence of circumstances and his intellectual advantage placed an incomparable role and task on Ruzsky's shoulders and aiguillettes: to overpower the Tsar? Everyone was far away, and he was here, and all educated Russia was waiting for him to drive the monarch into the final impasse with an undeniable wall of arguments.

Black Danilov beside him confirmed everything with his bulk and immobility.

Through his simple spectacles, Ruzsky looked at the Tsar with a glassy gleam: there were also several news items from GHQ to cover.

They were both invited to the Tsar's table. The news from GHQ would be after dinner.

[2 8 2]

Grand Duke Mikhail Aleksandrovich thought at first, before dawn yesterday, that he had stopped by the Putyatins' to bury himself for just a few hours. But what had unfolded in the city was such that there could be no thought of going onto the streets and getting all the way to Gatchina. Any motorcar would be confiscated (it could be taken away where it now stood, under cover, on Fuhrstadtskaya, too), and he himself could simply be killed. It was also good that he'd been able to get a call through to Gatchina while the lines were still intact and hear Natasha's voice and reassure her. Naturally, she could not leave their young son and come here at such a time either.

But even here, in a private building, in a private apartment, there was no safety. Possibly because this street, Millionnaya, had especially attracted the crowd's envious attention, occasionally he could hear gunfire nearby, and through the servants he learned about looting in the form of searches in various neighboring buildings. This afternoon, at 16 Millionnaya, one building away from theirs, they had broken into the apartment of General Count Stakelberg with just this kind of arbitrary "search," led him outside, mocked him there, and killed him. During the subsequent hours they invaded their building as well—the family of the Synod Procurator and the Stolypins' family on the fourth floor—probably drawn by the name, though this was not the murdered minister's family—and routed and looted them—which was probably the only way the Putyatins were spared.

Today was an ominous date for the dynasty. On this date, terrorists had killed his grandfather. And on this date they had nearly killed his father.

With his "native" cavalry division, not sparing himself and not thinking of his own imperial origin, Mikhail had gone into deadly attacks under shrapnel fire. But right now all his daring and all his military ways were of no avail; he was like a silly, squeezed chick: sitting and waiting like a coward for them to burst in. It was a helpless, defenseless, unmilitary situation, and it was this that weighed most. How could he fire at and cut down a Russian soldier?

The Putyatins' governess had been on the embankment, and during her walk, before her eyes, in the middle of the day they had killed an officer for no reason at all.

He had to take advantage of his position to telephone Rodzyanko and summon a guard. Although the Preobrazhensky barracks were nearby, something was very wrong there, and the guard arrived from the ensign school. Five officers were placed in Putyatin's office and twenty cadets on the first floor, in another apartment.

Now, in his conversation with Rodzyanko, Mikhail had revealed where he was, and there was no point hiding any longer. It had leaked out. He telephoned his closest acquaintances. They came over. Through visits and telephone communiqués, an overview emerged of everything going on in Petrograd—and the unfortunate trip of his brother, who had not been allowed through to Tsarskoye Selo. He learned from Rodzyanko that he was preparing to go meet the Emperor and obtain a new government and new constitution—and Mikhail sincerely sympathized with this intention. Thus he truly wished that everyone could reach agreement and all would end well! Today he had hoped that by evening his brother would reach Tsarskoye Selo and would be well, and that he would sign everything and approve Rodzyanko for a responsible ministry.

But Buchanan arrived—on foot from the embassy, which was nearby. He had just spent ten days in Finland on leave and had himself not observed the mounting of Petrograd events, he had arrived to find the upheaval accomplished. But he wasn't the least surprised, he said, and this was just as he had predicted, and it could not end sensibly. Now, he was certain, it would not end without the Emperor's removal. (Oh, God forbid!) The sole means of saving Russia was to reject all its present politics and turn sincerely to society. The English ambassador reasoned and felt not as an outsider but as a staunch member of our society. And he grieved and even frightened the grand duke by trying to convince him that he had to prepare to accept the regency for the heir in the next few days.

But that was the last thing Mikhail wanted! All over again? Again the responsibility he had so happily rid himself of thirteen years ago, with the heir's birth? No, not that! He wasn't prepared. That would be a shattered life.

Then Uncle Nikolai arrived—dressed like a commoner in a drab peasant overcoat—although he only had to cross the street from his palace on the other side of Millionnaya. Uncle Nikolai had just returned from his exile in the country. He had expected nothing other than events such as this since they had not reined in the witch Alix. He had predicted this to the Emperor. But as a passionate historian, he was not so much oppressed as cheered by events. That he was present during them and could later describe them. And time did not wait. He had to act, and act correctly! And afterward correctly depict the events in history, so that their descendants wouldn't garble them the way they had cruelly garbled Nikolai I, for example. Uncle Nikolai had once written a long letter to Tolstoy shaming him for being swayed by superficial gossip, and Tolstoy had thanked him, but this had gone unpublished.

Although Uncle Nikolai was aware of his full responsibility to history, he hadn't come up with what to do. He left as he had come, wearing the peasant coat.

The idle, troubled, and wearisome hours of captivity dragged on.

Mikhail was prepared to help Rodzyanko and the State Duma as best he could in something; in this moment all the members of the dynasty had to help in some way. No matter how he had been punished over the years.

The offensive oppression from his brother and mother—as if he were not a grown man—stood vividly in memory. And how at Gatchina, by his Mama's order, they had eavesdropped through the palace telephone station on his conversations with Natasha, something he did not know for a long time. And how much his Mama had shamed him by saying that Natasha was twice divorced and had children, while his brother assigned Mikhail to serve in Orel, far from Gatchina. For four years they persecuted his love and themselves pushed him into a battle of wills. There could be no thought of marrying in Russia, so much were they followed and hampered. They went abroad—where they were both watched and prevented from being united. But Mikhail came up with a way to trick the surveillance. He took his motorcar supposedly to Nice but en route secretly boarded the Vienna train, while Natasha awaited him in Vienna—and there, in the Serbian church, they were finally wed. How many more years would they have had to remain abroad had war not broken out!

Can one really fight love? Are there such forces on earth? After all, even his grandfather hadn't been able to fight it—and had become intimate with

Princess Dolgorukova while the Empress was still alive, and had kept his lover right there, in the Winter Palace, and had sired a son and two daughters by her. And that had not shaken the dynasty!

But Mikhail's feeling of insult was not all that persistent; he did not tend to hold a grudge for long. But how could he help? He didn't know how to help. Sandro had always believed that their help was in the grand dukes holding all the principal posts in the government! God forbid such a fate.

His brother was just about to arrive in Tsarskoye Selo, and they would see each other, and they would talk.

But Rodzyanko hurried him on the telephone and asked for his assistance before that. Battling awkwardness, sincere resistance, and the full inappropriateness of any new interference, Mikhail decided to send his brother a telegram that would find him somewhere along the train's route:

"Forgetting all that's passed, I beg you to follow the new path indicated by the people. In these difficult days, when we all, Russians, are suffering so, I send you this advice from the bottom of my heart, advice dictated by life and the moment in time, as a loving brother and loyal Russian. Mikhail."

He was certain Natasha would have approved.

What he missed most of all right now was Natasha's advice!

Then Uncle Pavel telephoned from Tsarskoye Selo, also having learned where Misha was. Uncle Pavel spoke solemnly, saying they had to save the throne promptly. Kirill had gone to do this today, to the Duma, the true center of public life right now. A threat to the throne! Mikhail had to be prepared to become regent. But before that, he had to try to save the throne for the Emperor. Uncle Pavel also hinted that soon Mikhail would receive it, would learn what it meant.

Oh, again this shadow of a regency! Melancholy and a bad presentiment made Mikhail's tender soul ache. Oh Lord, how could he avoid this lot and not assume this unbearable burden. He felt so sorry for his brother!

How awful this was for Russia! Oh, if only he could keep the Emperor on the throne!

Soon after, a young man in civilian dress arrived with a packet from Uncle Pavel.

Inside it was a typewritten draft Manifesto. On the Emperor's behalf. Room was left for his signature. And at the very top it said that this act, presented by the grand dukes to His Imperial Majesty for signature, had their full approval. And below—Uncle Pavel's signature. And above that—Kirill's. Room had also been left above for Mikhail.

Kirill was nearby, much closer than Uncle Pavel, but due to his usual hostility had not let his presence be known in any way. Actually, Mikhail hadn't been seeking him out, either.

The draft Manifesto had been composed quite cleverly, as if the Emperor had long since decided to introduce a broad constitution and had only been waiting for the day the war ended. But the government, now the *former* government, had not wanted the ministers' responsibility to the Fatherland and had delayed the project. Now the Emperor, making the sign of the cross over himself, was establishing a new state regime and proposing that the State Duma President immediately assemble a new cabinet. And revive the Duma sessions. And immediately convene a Legislative Assembly.

Uncle Pavel probably wanted Misha's signature in order to better convince Nicky—and send it to him right away for signature.

There could be no delay. A messenger was waiting.

Well, all right! This was good! Save the throne and not be regent.

Mikhail quickly signed.

He thought that no, here Kirill had been forgiving: he had not denied Nikolai his help.

And that there should immediately be a new state order—well, he did have to concede something. It was difficult to determine what.

The messenger left, hiding the packet in his inside coat pocket. One copy, not yet signed by the Emperor, would now go to the Duma to pacify them.

He left—and Mikhail walked round and round in his confinement and loneliness, to the sound of street shooting—and for some reason began to consider whether it was really his business to sign. Was it his business to interfere in these important counsels? Why should he be interfering in this horrible political furor? And a copy to the Duma right away?

What was worse, there was no telephone to Gatchina.

He walked round and round the room, agonizing, even cracking his knuckles.

He didn't know what was right to do!

Therefore, the best of all was to telephone the Duma right now, to whoever had the packet, and have them remove his signature. There was no reason for him to be poking his nose in here.

And the telegram should not be sent. Or had it been already? . . .

[2 8 3]

Sokolov wanted to take his soldier deputies and set up right there, with the EC, behind the curtain, but no, you'll interfere with the Executive Committee's session. They could have gone back to the large Room no. 12, but no, the people there hadn't dispersed yet; they were standing around, gawking, enjoying themselves. They went to find a different room. They found a secretary's room, which had a table and a few chairs; the others could stand awhile, that's all right. And now you could smoke anywhere.

It was stuffy, and he was perspiring! Sokolov removed his jacket altogether, draped it on the back of his chair, and sat at the table in his vest. He had paper and an inkpot and he checked the pen, which was fine. Now we were getting somewhere. Beside him he sat Comrade Maksim—that is, the journalist Klivansky from *Day*, a socialist, who would be his most necessary assistant here.

But nearly all the soldiers were left on their feet. There were no chairs. Among them was that volunteer Linde—tall and thin, a sagging greatcoat with a university pin, and a burning gaze.

Now we were getting somewhere—be that as it may, be that as it may, but you couldn't just begin. How to write? Whom to address? The unusual nature of the proposed document gave even the hardened Sokolov pause.

He had composed his fair share of lawyer's documents in his life—petitions, appeals, protests, and even quite a few different socialist ones. But right now he didn't entirely understand the form. What was this going to be? A resolution of the Soviet of Workers' Deputies? A proclamation? An appeal to the garrison?

And as long as it wasn't on paper, then there wasn't anything, and everything would have been said for nothing.

He expressed his doubts to Klivansky. They discussed and sorted through things.

The soldiers were growing impatient, no longer quite believing their leader was going to cope smoothly now with writing it all down on paper.

All of a sudden, Linde leaned his head back like a bird swallowing water collected in its beak and with half-closed eyelids uttered in a low voice, casting a spell:

"An or-der! . . ."

Because he was a civilian, Sokolov didn't grasp this: How could there be an order? Whose order?

Right then Nakhamkes lumbered in to check on them. He stood by the wall, taller than everyone, his hands behind his back. He located the difficulty and said:

"As a former military man, I support 'order.'"

The soldiers liked this and started buzzing:

"Our order—to Rodzyanko's order!"

By their lights, only an Order was carried out, so what was this Appeal? Soldiers were used to being addressed with orders, that was true.

Not bad then, revolutionary creativity. An order? But an order from whom? Orders were signed by generals.

"Ours will get signed by the Soviet of Workers' and Soldiers' Deputies," Nakhamkes calmly let drop.

"But how do they get written, these orders?"

Nakhamkes thought about that. His military service in a local Yakut detachment was so many years ago, although in his company he had been the best front-liner, and an officer had helped him escape exile.

And there were no other officers, or senior noncommissioned officers, or junior officers here. But the soldiers themselves remembered a thing or two about orders. And the most impudent one, his face pock-marked, doughtily poked the paper with a rough finger and dirty nail:

"An order's got to have a number!"

What number? They hadn't published a single one yet.

"That means it's the first."

Sokolov wrote out in large, handsome letters: "Order No. 1."

The soldiers came closer, and the pock-marked one leaned his chest against the table and breathed a tobacco-ish stink:

"Put the date!"

"Does the date really go at the beginning?"

Fine, what was it today? Oh, they'd been through so much, yet apparently it was still 14 March?

The soldiers puffed away a little and from their fresh memory, as if from the printed page:

"For the garrison of the Petrograd District. . . . To all soldiers of the Guards, Army, Artillery, and Navy . . ."

It sounded good and loud, but it didn't seem like enough. The soldiers were thirsting to see their first-born order along:

"For immediate and precise execution!"

They themselves knew that was no way to write. But words like this— they'd heard them. And this order was defending their heads.

Sokolov pushed aside the soldier leaning on his elbows, whose smell and breath was so very astringent and unpleasant:

"Don't, comrade. . . . Where are our comrade workers here? This has to refer to workers, too."

"Does not!"

"Workers have nothing to do with this!"

There was also a strapping soldier with a mustache, such as they draw on Wilhelm:

"An order means an order! This is about us."

But they couldn't cede proletarian positions to the soldiery. Klivansky tried to explain to them that it just wouldn't do without the workers. But the soldiers were sorry to let go of having it be an Order. They argued and argued, and then, fine:

". . . And to the workers of Petrograd for their information . . ."

What came next in orders? Next came: I order!

But who was saying "I order"? Who was "I"?

The soldiers had no idea. Of all those present, no father-general had lined up who could issue commands in defense of the mutinous soldier— and basta! He cut them all off. They faltered.

From the wall, Nakhamkes dictated in his baritone:

"The Soviet of Workers' and Soldiers' Deputies has resolved."

Well, all right.

Then came the crux, which had been drawn up that morning at the EC, and Sokolov and Klivansky had already shouted and voted it through at the noisy gathering in Room no. 12. Klivansky even had it on paper: how to treat the return of officers and the Military Commission and what to do about the weapons. But it had to begin with the soldiers' committees. They were Archimedes' lever. How to put that in the Order, though?

"In all companies, batteries, and squadrons . . ."

Linde, lowering his eyelids, listened as if to music and smiled very faintly.

"Write: and battalions."

"Write: and regiments!"

"What about for sailors?"

There was one sailor there:

"On military fleet vessels."

. . . Immediately elect committees of elected representatives from the lower ranks. . . .

"But what about sergeants?"

"They're lower rank, too."

But these committees . . . what were they supposed to do?

Oh, everything. So that every last thing was subordinated to them.

"That won't work! What about formations, commands?"

"Fine. Formations, commands!"

"Oh, no! Can't manage without an officer."

The soldiers started to argue. They'd been shouting all day, and everything was still unclear.

Meanwhile, to this din, Sokolov wrote out for specificity:

. . . one representative from a company . . . with written certifications . . . to the building of the State Duma . . . on 15 March by 10 o'clock in the morning.

Remove the army from the State Duma. And remove it by tomorrow morning!

Nakhamkes added weightily:

"Nikolai Dmitrich, emphasize that in all their political statements, the military unit is subordinate to the Soviet of Deputies and its committee. And no one else."

Sokolov wrote quickly, his pen didn't blot or shred, and he had already moved on to the second page.

While Klivansky carefully continued from his own paper:

"The Military Commission's orders shall be carried out only if they do not contradict the resolutions of the Soviet of Workers and Soldiers . . ."

Nakhamkes quietly left.

While the soldiers, without interfering with Sokolov's pen, meanwhile had gone back to arguing about what they understood to be the main issue: Who would have weapons? The room filled with shouts not to give them to officers. And for their freedom they should take them for themselves. But this wasn't about revolvers or swords. If an officer wasn't in charge of regimental weaponry, or cannons—what kind of army would it be? What good would it be?

But the educated men at the table:

"There's nothing to debate! Weapons are not to be surrendered to officers under any circumstance."

That makes it safer for us, too. Only, what about the army? . . .

. . . Any kind of weapon . . .

"Then write specifically: machine guns, rifles . . ."

"Hand grenades, don't leave anything out!"

"Armored vehicles, too. . . ."

"And all the rest! And in general, all the rest, or we'll miss something."

". . . must be at the disposal and under the control of company and battalion committees and under no circumstance can be issued to officers even at their demand. . . ."

"But at the front?"

"That's at the front. Look out you don't get riddled with holes here!"

"That's right, brothers, and so? Or else they'll cast a spell over us again."

All sorts of things got heaped up in the day's shouting match: officers shouldn't live outside the barracks, remove their epaulets, and anyone the company didn't confirm went to the left flank. How else could things work?

Linde, straightening his arm out like a wing, as if banking down toward the soldiers:

"Yes! Yes, comrades! If the committees are elected, then the officers should be elected all the more!"

The soldiers shied at this: "Who is it we're going to want for officers for ourselves? You mean like him?"

Well, not from the soldiers exactly, Maksim explained. From the better of the officers. And the ones who are bad to you—sweep them out.

The soldiers shied at this.

But the educated men at the table didn't one bit. And that got added.

The soldiers started stamping: No! No! There's no way we can wipe out military discipline clean. We've still got the German on our land. How can we be in an army without rules? The soldiers asked them to keep the word "discipline."

"Fine," Sokolov conceded, amazed at the herd's susceptibility to fear. He repeated what he'd written out loud:

. . . When in formation and in discharging their service duties, soldiers must observe the strictest military discipline. . . .

That's it, that's it—and they smiled. Without order—what kind of army was that?

"And if they've scampered off from the line—that's it, freedom. And soldiers enjoy all the rights of citizens!"

Well, well, of course. Fine.

He added:

". . . in their political, general civil, and private life, soldiers . . ."

"And no more saluting!" Maksim added from his paper.

Again the soldiers felt awkward.

"What kind of service is it without saluting?"

"No saluting!" Linde's entire body shook, he threw his head back, and his pale cheeks flushed.

"Well, maybe so," the policemen at the table granted this privilege, "not to salute outside direct service. Take a step out of barracks and stop saluting. On the streets—no saluting."

Well, that was right. That had already started on the streets. They'd taken away officers' swords, they admitted that.

"Brothers, they seemed like a force, our commanders, a force! But in actual fact they're weaklings."

"What about 'your honor'?" Sokolov followed up. "Even in service. What was the purpose? Abolish it!"

"Indeed, brothers, what was the point of 'your honor'? Why was it?"

He wrote: Abolish it!

"And abolish addressing soldiers with the familiar 'you'!" Linde exclaimed.

"Abolish it how? What are they going to say?"

"Abolish it unconditionally!" Maksim insisted. "It demeans your human dignity."

They hadn't felt that! Look at the sheep!

"But what are they going to say?"

"The formal 'you.'"

"But what if we're alone? You mean I'm going to be all formal with him? I'm going to laugh until my jaw hurts."

They laughed. I've lived and I've breathed and all of a sudden we're all formal? A wonder . . .

While Maksim drove on, and Sokolov wrote:

. . . use of the informal "you" is forbidden . . . and any violation . . . must be brought to the knowledge of the company committees . . .

By now they were beat. Not having eaten all day.

End it here—it was already the way it was supposed to be. Right then the pock-marked one knew:

"The present order to be read out in all the companies, squadrons, batteries, crews, and other detachments, both combat and noncombat. . . ."

It was done.

Sokolov released the soldiers. And gathered up the pages.

Right then, Himmer ran in. He hopped around, took a look, checked it, and now the pages were taken to the EC for approval.

"And what then? I send it to Goldenberg at *Izvestia* and by morning we'll print out a separate leaflet. It's off and running!"

Because if the revolution didn't bring down the old army, the old army would bring down the revolution.

☆   ☆   ☆

YOU CAN'T KNEAD DOUGH
AND KEEP YOUR HANDS CLEAN

☆   ☆   ☆

[2 8 4]

The Maklakov children were eight, and although one of the brothers had followed in his eye doctor father's noble footsteps, it was not he who became the continuer of the line, rather only the names Vasili and Nikolai were heard everywhere, one in admiration, one in abuse.

Rarely does one find between brothers such hostile estrangement, such total distance, as between those two. Lost were the days of their childhood long ago, when they had grown up in the same home on Tverskaya, next to the eye clinic, and with just a year's difference between them, they chased each other around the large courtyard. Even back in their student years one could not have predicted what would sour them so. Vasili was studying law and Nikolai was in the school of historical philology, university students like any others, they taught young ladies the art of skating. But Vasili was looser and more eager for acquaintances—and it was he who took Nikolai to apartments where freethinkers gathered, and everything there jarred with Nikolai and offended him—so he stopped going, shrank back from all of them and then from Vasili, too. The brothers saw different meanings and circles for themselves in Russia. Vasili Alekseevich became a famous lawyer, a favorite of Petersburg society, a charmer of Petersburg ladies, a clever, well-known man, and even the premiere orator in the different Dumas. Nikolai Alekseevich had no such brilliant abilities, but he would have succeeded quite well with average ones had he followed a liberal line. Instead, he went into government service without patronage, beginning as a tax inspector in the back of beyond, and then in the Tambov and then Poltava treasury chamber. There, the Emperor paid a visit on the bicentenary of the Battle of Poltava—and with the joyous feeling of an intoxicated monarchist, Nikolai Maklakov so ingeniously decorated the city and the provincial reception that he received the highest notice and soon after was promoted to governor of Chernigov. (Perhaps this came about not without contrast to the impudent Vasili; "from the same family, you see, the brother of *that* Maklakov," the bad one—not everyone in Russia is depraved.) During the September 1911 celebration, just as ecstatically, the Chernigov governor greeted his monarch, who had sailed down the Desna. This was the very day of Stolypin's death, and as the Emperor later told the story, at the very moment when he was worshipping at the reliquary of Feodosi of Chernigov, the thought came to him that he should appoint Nikolai Maklakov Minister of the Interior. A year later, he did. The young minister rushed zealously and clumsily to establish order in the midst of the disruption. He offered his inexperienced chest to block Duma attacks, immediately bringing down on himself animosity and ridicule, unable to position himself well. The Duma canceled all his appropriations, without which the ministry couldn't function, and jokes spread freely through society about how Maklakov was holding on to his post by portraying for the royal family a besotted panther in a cage, beasts, birds, and other dignitaries. Meanwhile, Vasili Alekseevich was delivering his polished, erudite speeches in the Duma, smiting everything around the throne.

Each of them was ashamed to have such a brother and was ashamed of his name because of his brother, disdaining being confused with him.

So, too, now, perhaps, Vasili was striding through the Tauride Palace with his measured gait, a little ducklike—but the news that the disgraceful

Nikolai Maklakov had been arrested and was sitting in the ministerial pavilion could only bring him relief.

During the arrest, he'd tried to beat them off (athletic habits) and was injured in the head by a soldier's bayonet and brought here under a strong convoy that threatened to finish him off en route. At the Tauride Palace his head was bandaged.

He was arrested and led to the stuffy, unaired rooms of the ministerial pavilion, to a fantastic combination of a session of the government's top dignitaries and a disorganized prison. He immediately saw a great many acquaintances, in a pitiful state, and learned that it was forbidden to talk with them. On a table he saw an unappetizing pile of unfinished cheese and fish sandwiches, empty tea glasses, and ashtrays. He saw the exhausted, moaning Protopopov, the second on the sofa with Bark. He saw Goremykin with his wispy side-whiskers and weary eyes, as cold-blooded and philosophical as ever. In the mute eyes of some he saw relief that now he, too, Maklakov, had been arrested. And from a distance he saw still other mute eyes—of Shirinsky-Shikhmatov, with whom he had composed a desperate plan the day before yesterday, but seemingly nothing impossible—throwing a bomb at this Tauride Palace and end the whole revolution in an instant—but he was sitting far away now, and you can't say a lot with your eyes.

Standing by the walls were armed Preobrazhensky sentries frightening these old men out of running away and conversing. Ensign Znamensky was pacing smoothly back and forth with his incorruptible face and rich voice. The Jewish female students carrying the trays around rebuked them: "See, when we were in prison, you put shackles on us, and we're offering you sandwiches and cigarettes."

Maklakov stewed that he'd let himself be taken and hadn't managed to shoot himself.

Like everyone, he had to stand when Colonel Peretz, the palace commandant, entered. This colonel was apparently a journalist from the Kadet *Speech*. Small and insignificant, he feasted his eyes on the sight of yesterday's high and mighty, the generals who'd run to fat and the old men now desiccated, standing before him. He held his face not levelly, toward them, but half leaning back toward the ceiling and responded the same way, saying that it was in no way possible to permit conversation if they were to avoid a plot among the prisoners. So why had Karaulov said it was? Karaulov was no longer palace commandant and the question was not in his purview. But what if we don't touch on domestic politics? I've said no.

And the frightened, empty-eyed, big-eared, himself small Minister of War blurted out a pathetic statement to the commandant, saying that he, General Belyaev, had committed no crime, had been minister a very brief time, and didn't understand why they had arrested him.

Evidently, a competition could now begin among the prisoners as to who was less guilty before the new government.

They were also all brought to their feet and led around the table in tottering single file "for a walk." Octogenarian Goremykin, too.

They were all brought to their feet again before that arrogant shrimp Kerensky surrounded by his democratic suite, Kerensky, who was pleased to proclaim that they had all been arrested because he, Kerensky, wanted to spare their lives. In other words, given the popular anger against servants of the old regime, each of them risked being a victim of popular reprisal.

And once again they sat in tension and silence. A few times the robust Admiral Kartsev exclaimed wildly:

"Air! Some air!"

His lungs were used to fresh air, but when they opened the window vents the old men complained that there was a draft on their legs, so they had to be closed again.

Dr. Dubrovin, as a physician, asked them to send in ice immediately for his neighbor the general.

Suddenly they led into their room a gendarme colonel who had been captured in incredible attire when his apartment was routed: trousers, his son's evidently, bare ankles, his undershirt visible under his vest, sleeves that wouldn't let him lower his arms, and a standing collar without a tie, on a single stud. But the ensign quickly started shouting that they'd brought him to the wrong place; they should take him upstairs, to the galleries. They did.

All the rest of the time was silence and contemplation on an upholstered chair.

But Maklakov was not thinking about his three sons, two of whom were at war. Rather, why had God allowed him to live to see the collapse of everything he believed in on earth? He was present at the death of the state order—like being present at his own death.

Had he himself helped very much?

Yes, he had been inexperienced and unprepared. He himself had been largely to blame for the biased relations with the Duma. But it wasn't society's hatred that was surprising, but rather in the Council of Ministers itself he had not encountered well-wishers, and even among the rightist ministers Maklakov had felt lonely. Everyone was playing their cards close to the vest, but Maklakov was direct and fervent and only spoiled things. Despised and condemned by all, he spread his wings only with the Emperor's constant support. But what could the youngest of the ministers do—and in isolation?

After many reports to the Emperor saying that Russia's domestic condition had been exacerbated, they could not doze, they had to act. The year before last during Holy Week, during those days of focus, Maklakov had taken it upon himself to write a passionate letter: Honest Russian people are dismayed by the direction the government has adopted; the heart of loyal subjects senses disaster, the monarch's bright countenance darkens; your trust in me, Sire, has been undermined, and people and circumstances will in any case later compel you to dismiss me—so dismiss me now. The Emperor was agitated and just as ardently persuaded Maklakov to remain. But in the Duma, Maklakov was harassed more and

394 \ MARCH 1917, BOOK 2

more roundly, and three months after that touching outburst, the Emperor dismissed his beloved minister.

Maklakov wept. Not at the loss of the post. In service, he had not sought anything personal, his life belonged to the Tsar, and he saw the homeland's glory only through the Tsar's majesty, whom he adored to the point of tears and from whom he had seen only good. He wept because the Emperor had sacrificed him for the Duma, he was abandoning those loyal to him if public opinion was fired up against them, and the righteous cause would perish. This was hard for all loyal men. The Emperor's decisions were taken so unemphatically, were always put into such a lenient form, all that remained of the most energetic report was a crumb. Forgotten was the Holy Scripture, which says that the king is given the sword to punish evildoers and protect good people. From the Tsar's love of peace and softness of heart, Russia was on its way to collapse. The Duma reports spread throughout the country, undermining the state order. Russia was bewildered. Society was being reared in permanent anger at the government, in the idea that the Russian government was not simply wrong, it was *hostile* to the people and even the sole obstacle to Russian happiness. Given these kinds of Duma attacks, how could the army remain calmly in their positions?

Maklakov may not have had sufficient governmental intelligence, but as much as he could, for two and a half years, he had tried to hold back this destructive course. And when he was removed, destruction followed even more swiftly. Shcherbatov, Khvostov the nephew, and Stürmer had dug domestic policy's grave. Domestic policy was no more, essentially. There was no notion of where the country was headed. Movement was with eyes shut, like a drunk man walking from wall to wall. There was no system or program to the country's governance.

The rightists' weakening was so great and so general that even in the friendly confines of the State Council they no longer had a majority. And Maklakov, who was also a member there, had been *alone* in daring to vote against the ridiculous Special Conferences, which were already tearing the business of defense out of government hands and into the hands of society. In addition, he received crude, threatening letters from leftists professing the rightist way of thinking had become not only unpopular but even unsafe. Everyone who believed in Russian autocracy and tried to support it was hopelessly dispirited. Slanders of all kinds had come raining down unimpeded on rightists. Rightists were beaten, not allowed to get up, and beaten again. The rightist faith had been reviled, ridiculed, made fun of, and sullied in public opinion.

That December, Maklakov had once again written the Emperor an impulsively emotional letter. In this difficult, unprecedentedly acute time, it was the obligation of any loyal subject to tell the Emperor the full truth of the situation. The direction of the Duma's activities and the nature of the speeches delivered there since November were finally knocking loose the last remnants of respect for governmental authority. Although the country was not expressed by Petrograd and what upset the highest levels did not affect Russia, nonetheless, in the capital, along with the congresses and unions, *the storming of authority had already begun,* and it threatened the dynasty itself. It was difficult but still possible to halt an imminent disaster.

Maklakov had never considered himself smarter than the Emperor. He had happily recognized the superiority of the Tsar's soul and his farsightedness, but how could he add to his strength of will and authority?

He wrote the letter and left for the country for Christmas. And there, only in January, did it reach him that a royal courier had come to his Petrograd apartment to deliver a letter in response and that the Emperor had supposedly summoned him. But they hadn't sent the summons to Tambov Province. Evidently, the moment passed.

Indeed, at New Year's Golitsyn was appointed prime minister—in a vain attempt to find reconciliation with the Duma.

At the news of the courier, Maklakov returned to Petrograd embarrassed and almost guessing why he had been summoned and his adored Emperor had not reached him. He had no desire to join a government in such a defeated position. But he also did not have the right to decline.

Soon after, the Emperor's wish was conveyed to Maklakov: write a royal manifesto in the event he stopped not at the Duma's postponement but at its complete dissolution.

That was late February, three weeks ago, and Nikolai Maklakov's final service for the Tsar. He had invested all his modest powers of language and all his intact, never broken monarchist feeling into three days of writing this manifesto. He tried to listen with his soul to how this should thunder for any Russian ear, everywhere over Russia's expanse! He explained that our domestic enemy had become more dangerous, more impudent, and more hardened than our foreign enemy! He appealed to them: God is master of the bold! He blessed the sweep of the Tsar's will, which, like the striking of a church bell, instills all faithful Russia with the fear of God to make the sign of the cross. He called on everyone to close ranks around the Emperor. He had prepared the document for a turning point in Russian history!

Elections for the new, Fifth Duma were scheduled for 28 November 1917. The time until autumn had been gained without dissension, without vilification of the government. If the war ended victoriously by autumn, then all would be saved in the general enthusiasm.

He was granted permission to bring the manifesto to the Emperor personally. He blazed that night, and that morning—and in this state went to the train station.

But something had happened with the trains, and they had all stopped—and Maklakov was beside himself in his train car. The train was an hour and a half late to Tsarskoye Selo. In this time, the Emperor's schedule had already passed and he was rushing off somewhere. Maklakov had hoped to read it out himself inspiredly, but the Emperor took the document without reading it, looked at him with his entrancing gaze, and lightly—too lightly!—said:

"This is just in case, Nikolai Alekseich. It still has to be discussed from all sides."

That had been his last audience.

And his last unutilized step.

And now, surveying this room with its feeble old men, Nikolai Maklakov keenly regretted that he hadn't beaten them off today and couldn't leave to fight.

Or that no desperate man today would fly at the Tauride Palace with a bomb.

[2 8 5]

The Emperor rode the last few hours to Pskov with restored hope both for a swift agreement with the Duma, which would lift the weight pressing on his soul and the entire nightmare of the past few days, and for speedy passage to Tsarskoye Selo.

An honor guard had not been lined up to greet him in Pskov; he glimpsed a solitary soldier on sentry duty at the end of the platform. Never before had the Emperor arrived this way not just at an army group headquarters but even at a regiment. The Pskov governor had two officials with him, without the usual assemblage of local officialdom. Nonetheless, the Emperor did not take offense and did not ascribe any significance to the loss of ceremony. It was a dark time and affairs awaited, it was true. He immediately received the slender Ruzsky and the squat Danilov.

His first surprise was that they had heard nothing about Rodzyanko's anticipated arrival. Then a blow—about the mutiny in Luga. What was going on in Tsarskoye Selo was only the half of it! His train couldn't even get through to them! . . .

He sat on after dinner, with the generals and governors, in total abstinence from events, at the cost of distressing pauses, which the Emperor covered over by questioning the governor in detail about his life.

Oh, if only this dinner would end quickly and he could learn something, even something unpleasant. Even about what Rodzyanko would bring.

No, he still hadn't come. Then, after dinner, the Emperor was handed this telegram from Petrograd:

"Convey to His Majesty that the State Duma President cannot come due to changed circumstances. Bublikov."

Again his heart fell. (In the past few days, how fragile everything inside him had become.) These *changed circumstances* could mean many things, but all of them sinister. The change could have been due either to Rodzyanko becoming more arrogant or to a worse mutiny such that Rodzyanko could no longer cope with it.

And there was the ever enigmatic, never before heard of, and increasingly strong Bublikov like a wall blocking all the lines.

How things had changed in a day. This morning the Emperor was still trying to decide whether to receive Rodzyanko or not. And now he was anxious for his visit, but in vain.

This refusal of Rodzyanko's held a sinister break. Nikolai felt how several times since the autumn that had been rolling along inexorably, no longer obeying his will—and even making an object of him—and nothing could be corrected. Fate. In moments like these, his faith in his mission slipped—but this was a sin, and he couldn't, he couldn't give in to it! He had to fight off this new blow as well.

But how was he to get to Tsarskoye Selo? What was happening in Tsarskoye Selo? They weren't being jeered at, were they? His entire being, his entire core, his entire intimate inner self was drawn there and longed to be reunited with his precious Alix. However, not only could he not go, there weren't even telegraph communications. Insurrectionist Petrograd had commandeered them and cut them off.

He couldn't even send an ordinary telegram to his family saying he'd arrived in Pskov.

After dinner, the Emperor summoned Ruzsky to his train car study, while Black Danilov went to headquarters to pick up new telegrams and news.

Only now did the Emperor truly hear and see for the first time just what a self-confident pedant this Ruzsky was. Not the old Ruzsky—respectful, currying favor, imploring him to restore him to the Northern Army Group command—but edifyingly delivering his long monologue and, when interrupted, always returning to finish his sentence. In his movements as in his speech, a mechanical regularity manifested itself that the Emperor had never before noticed. And this combination of a gray crewcut and black mustache, doubtless dyed, seemed odd. Without vivid lines—he had the lifeless face of a small animal, but with spectacles fastened on. And sickly at the same time.

How strangely his relations with his subordinate general had changed in an hour or two. An inevitable, unrelenting interlocutor had arisen—and the Emperor knew no means against this change.

Ruzsky began with qualifications that his present report went beyond the bounds of his official competence, for this was not a military question but one of state governance. Perhaps the Emperor did not have sufficient trust in him, inasmuch as he was used to listening to Alekseev, and the two generals often did not agree in their assessments.

Naturally, the Emperor proposed that the general express himself with candor.

After this, Ruzsky's monologue unfolded. He said that Rodzyanko, though he hadn't come, was awaiting an answer, and this answer could be none other than to concede and allow a ministry responsible to the Duma. And why this should have been done a long time ago. And how all the events, whether mutiny at Kronstadt or the calming in Petrograd, all pointed to this very thing. And how on all sides all understanding and knowledgeable people were asking specifically about this. Duma deputies. Zemstvo representatives. The Union of Towns. Look—even General Alekseev and his forwarded telegram, more than a day old already. And look—even General Brusilov, the telegram sent via Dno, which did not reach you there. And look—Grand Duke Sergei Mikhailovich, even he, even the members of your dynasty.

Yes, unfortunately. Unfortunately, all this was present and laid out in front of him. Yes. In his two days of wandering, the Emperor had not received many things, and now everything had converged. From Alekseev. Yesterday's old and not at all bad information from Moscow. Everything terrible that had happened in Moscow today. And in Kronstadt today. (How painful and shameful for the navy, the Emperor's pride and joy!) The head of the Kronstadt port had been killed. Admiral Nepenin had recognized the Rodzyanko committee.

Alekseev's concern, as he had written, was to save the army: to save it from agitation, as there were many university students and young people in it, and to save its food supply transport. Alekseev felt that suppressing the upheavals was dangerous—especially for the army itself. The upheavals would spill over into the army, and that would lead to a disgraceful end to the war and even all Russia to its ruin. The State Duma was trying to institute order, and rather than fight it, they should help it against radical elements. Herein lay the sole salvation, and there could be no delay.

Was that so? . . . Was it really? . . . Terrible words.

But why was he so sure that *this* could spill over into the army in the field?

Uncle Sergei Mikhailovich—he was no longer saying "someone" but outright: appoint Rodzyanko, and only Rodzyanko, prime minister.

(He himself had made how much of a mess in the artillery.)

And for some reason from Brusilov. Unprompted, he had sent a telegram in Frederiks's name. To save the army, recognize an accomplished fact and end this *peacefully*.

But what was most striking was that Ruzsky and Alekseev, who always disagreed on everything and were rivals—here they were both saying the same thing. This gave him pause.

Perhaps he had no trust in Ruzsky—but why were they all at one?

However, could it be that a single truth had been easily revealed to everyone—and closed to the Emperor?

"But what would Russia's South say? What would the Cossacks say?" he wondered.

How could he agree to such a change during time of war, without waiting for its conclusion? As long as the German was on Russian soil, what reforms could there be? First they had to drive out the German.

Ruzsky clarified: exactly. Reform was essential for the war's salvation, for its successful conclusion.

Was the Emperor really opposed to consulting? Always and willingly, but with people of good will and devoted to Russia, not with these embittered men. Could party factions, narrow in their reasoning and programs, really open up a genuine path for the people and even genuine freedom?

How many years had there been of debates and battles—and all about this "responsible ministry"! How many irreconcilable points had clashed on exactly this rock! How much slander and insult had been born around it! How many meetings with public figures, how many scandals in the Duma.

But where did this assumption come from that under a parliamentary ministry the Army would fight better?

At the last winter conference the Allies as well had tried to wrest the same thing from Nikolai: a "responsible" ministry. (As if this were *their* business; they couldn't let it rest.) And Gurko had added to this, saying otherwise we would lose the Allies' favorable disposition. The English general attached to GHQ had written the same thing as a friend of the Emperor.

Everything had hammered at the same point.

However! The Emperor alone was responsible before God for everything that had and would happen to Russia.

For it is said: If the People sin, God will hear the Tsar's prayers for them. But if the Tsar sins, the People's prayers will not be heard.

Only he could not utter these lofty words to Ruzsky just like that, across the table.

Ruzsky was becoming more and more insistent and explaining in a lecturing tone that it was the Emperor's business merely to reign; the government should govern. *Autocracy* had in any case not existed since 1905. Under the State Duma it was a fiction and it made more sense to sacrifice it in a timely fashion.

For all Ruzsky's cultured gloss, something dull had come out in him. That rectangular brow. And his lifeless, superimposed ears.

Reign without governing? His great-grandfather Nikolai Pavlovich had said: I can understand a republic but I cannot understand a representative monarchy. That is an oxymoron.

The Emperor objected that he did not understand this formula. Most likely, to do so he would have had to be reborn and raised differently. He himself did not need power in the least. He didn't like it and did not cling to it in the least. But he could not suddenly believe he was not responsible to God.

Ruzsky shut his eyelids behind his spectacles, as one does at the mention of God—some sincerely, some in jest.

An Emperor could not divest himself of his responsibility before the Russian people. As if he had the right to hand over Russia's governance to people who had not been called to this, who today might bring Russia harm and tomorrow retire—and where was all their responsibility then? . . . How could he leave Russia without a reliable succession? How could the Emperor regard the careless activities of such men and pretend that it was not he, the monarch, but Duma voting that was responsible before God and Russia? Even though he had restricted his rights in 1905, or if he did so again right now, all the responsibility would still rest on him.

Ruzsky seemed to be openly losing patience—and began speaking in a tone as if it were not the Emperor in front of him at all. He began to cite the many truly unsuccessful and unfortunate appointments over the past few years in many ministries, from internal affairs, foreign affairs, and justice to war and the Chief Procurator of the Synod—and the Emperor listened and was himself horrified at how much truth there was in his reproaches and how many failures there had in fact been.

But had Ruzsky, or Alekseev, or any outspoken public critic, or anyone at all other than his loyal wife and the deceased Grigori ever shared with him that tortuous sorting through of names, that poignant days-long search in the human wilderness, when your head feels like it's going to burst but no ideas for a candidate will come? And finally: But all the candidates the public proposed—in what way were they more capable, or better suited, or more experienced than those chosen by the Tsar? They weren't. The Emperor then went through them in front of Ruzsky and tried to show how they lacked intelligence and experience. Russian society right now did not have the elements that would be prepared to govern the country and capable of carrying out the duties of governance.

But Ruzsky asserted that there were, and many of them.

However, Ruzsky did not seem to have attempted to understand anything in depth. He had not tried to convince the Emperor. He had simply put before him on all sides the fact that there was no other solution whatsoever.

So that's how it was. . . . For some reason it had come to pass that it was these two men, in a single conversation, over a small table in a train car study, and in Pskov, who were to decide Russia's fate.

Constrained, the Emperor had the implacable sense that even when not conceding he was already—conceding.

He smoked. He smoked his favorite amber meerschaum pipe and stubbed out half-burned cigarettes and immediately lit new ones.

Here is what he could agree to: let Rodzyanko form a cabinet and choose whoever he wanted, but four ministers—war, navy, foreign affairs, and internal affairs—would be appointed and overseen by the Emperor himself.

On no account! Ruzsky said indignantly as someone who had the right to be indignant and in the same lecturing tone: In that form, this is not consent. The distraught, droning Duma will take this as an insult! And who can take foreign affairs if not Milyukov? Does this mean shunting Milyukov aside?

The Emperor was prepared to agree even to Milyukov. He had left a reserve out of caution, so as not to concede too much immediately. He had put up barriers because he knew this weakness of his—conceding too quickly and easily.

Fine, here is what he could agree to: Let Rodzyanko form the entire cabinet, but to be responsible to the monarch, not the Duma.

No! Ruzsky rejected this in an imperious and raised voice.

Right then Danilov arrived from town, even more morose than at their meeting (openly reminding the Emperor of his insult at being removed from GHQ). He brought a new telegram from Alekseev.

Faced with the danger of anarchy spreading and the impossibility then of prosecuting the war, for the sake of the integrity of the army and Russia, Alekseev diligently implored His Majesty to vouchsafe the immediate publication of the manifesto whose draft he was sending by telegraph right now and which they had written at GHQ. (They had sat there and written something he had not ordered!)

And here it was in the manifesto: for the speediest attainment of victory, this very same ministry responsible to the people's representatives. And that it be Rodzyanko—a figure enjoying the confidence of all Russia—who should form it.

It was like a torture chamber had surrounded the Emperor and was getting narrower and narrower.

What if anarchy arose from exactly this? . . .

But he could not agree with Ruzsky, he could not agree with Alekseev, he could not agree with Brusilov—so what should he do? Replace the entire high command?

And at the height of a war? . . . For that he surely did not have the strength.

Yes, here lay a fully prepared manifesto, very clearly and even touchingly composed: about the loyal sons of Russia united around the throne; that Russia was indestructible as always and the enemies' intrigues would not overpower her.

All that remained was to sign.

The manifesto lay there, convincing because it was already written. Nikolai fought the relieving temptation to up and sign. If this was necessary for the good of Russia, how could he not sign? . . .

Oh, Nikolai had known this diabolical temptation since October of '05: such a seemingly simple step. Just sign—and instantly things would be so much easier! He knew, from his twenty-two-year reign, the seductive, blissful relief that always attends a concession. But only in the first moment.

Under a responsible ministry, he himself would have so many fewer cares! How much easier his own life would be.

But Nikolai remembered all too well that fateful concession of '05: it was since then that everything had gone badly. And it was **this** that he had conceded then. That Manifesto still ached in him.

Oh, where was he to get the strength for one little piece of his heart to cling to that slope and hold back the avalanche himself?

Only, where had this farsightedness come from in the foolish Rodzyanko? How would he find the individuals who would each enjoy the trust of *all* Russia? . . .

"No," the Emperor objected gently, even timidly to the general. "No. I cannot." And he quickly softened this: "For now. . . ."

Ruzsky soured greatly. But with new hope: Perhaps he could for now inform GHQ and Petrograd that the Emperor, while still not having signed, had consented to such a manifesto *in principle*?

No. Not yet. Let's wait. Not right away.

But about the army, the spirit of the troops and of Russia—who else? Ruzsky pleaded.

"If not," he said harshly, "what other measures? What are you hoping for, Your Majesty? If not, that means you have to bring the troops closer to Petrograd. And you are taking on a terrible responsibility. For the first time in the history of our army, are Russian troops to enter into internecine strife?"

The Emperor shuddered. The truth and power of this argument stunned him. Oh, anything but that, truly! He'd had enough with the memory of the unfortunate, unwise shooting on 22 January and the sticky epithet "Bloody" that the leftists had aimed at him. After *that* day *he* did not have the right to order Russian troops to fire on Russians. . . .

My God, what torment and what hopelessness! The torture chamber was pressing up against Nikolai's chest.

"So perhaps," Ruzsky suggested, seeing success, "for now we can order a direct telegraph conversation with Rodzyanko overnight? Agree on when he might come to the telegraph?"

"Well, of course. That's possible. That's all right. Since he couldn't come here."

They sent Danilov back to headquarters to make arrangements with Petrograd.

While the manifesto lay in front of the Emperor and called out for his signature. . . .

While Ruzsky, pitilessly, allowing neither time nor retraction, pressed. Demanded. That he immediately and honestly state his definitive decision before the army was rocked by the disturbances.

And the Supreme Commander, the Emperor, with his head tossed back and a drained, tormented face, asked him for mercy:

"I have to think. Alone."

Displeased, Ruzsky exited the suite's train car to wait.

Nikolai was left over the hopeless manifesto. He was left unfortified by anyone, unprotected, alone.

He propped up his head so it wouldn't fall. And nearly collapsed chestfirst on the document.

They had all come together. Everyone, united and all around . . .

Oh, how he needed his darling Alix right now, so she could advise. And guide.

Hadn't she written in a telegram that concessions were needed? Would she understand that this concession was inevitable?

Oh, how was it for her! How was it for her to suffer through all these events alone! . . .

No! No! Signing this document would mean betraying his duty as emperor.

Signing this document would mean abolishing the ages-old monarchical principle in Russia and abandoning the country to all the unstable fluctuations of a parliamentary regime. And directly to anarchy.

And at the same time, betraying his own son. No, *this* was something Alix could not approve!

What on earth had happened that in a single day he was supposed to concede the monarchy in Russia?

But what was the solution? Send troops into internecine strife? Dismiss all the senior generals?

My God, what agony! And You have sent it to me when I am alone.

When in his life had Nikolai been free to decide? He had always been constrained by circumstances and people's demands.

Perhaps this was what the good of Russia required? And God would forgive them all? What sincere relief there was in a good concession! . . .

Should he let these clever men form their own cabinet? We shall see how they labor and cope.

My God! Give me strength. Give me reason.

[2 8 6]

The subtly responsive Lili Dehn, like a silent, helping angel, was always herself either around the ill children or near the Empress in her moments of greatest need. There were always whims and complaints with Anya, and now that she was ill, they were not telling her about Petrograd. Lili was wholly there to listen and help, and only to her could the Empress speak as she would to herself.

"As it is, Lili, the entire situation is in the Duma's hands. Let us hope they will now come to their senses and be able to fix something."

Two palace carriages had been sent to the train station to meet the two awaited deputies.

But the carriages returned empty. The deputies had ignored the palace's invitation and anticipation and instead had taken a motorcar of the rebels to the singing of the Marseillaise and gone to the town hall to deliver speeches to the garrison assembly—evidently in the spirit of revolution.

The carriages returned empty—but this, too, was a humiliation she had to bear. The Empress asked Commandant Groten—the paragon of a general, all these hours a calm, confident, precise, truly military man and her main protection now—to go to the town hall and ask the deputies to come to the palace and give the guard encouragement.

Groten got there toward the end of the meeting, where the deputies had been greeted ecstatically. The deputies sensibly objected:

"General, what can we say to your guard? That the Tsarist government is no more and they must obey the State Duma? What will your position be? If we came to you, that would mean you had submitted to the Duma."

Groten could not find anything to say in reply, nor was he so authorized. He returned to ask the Empress.

The meaning of the deputies' visit proved to be not at all what had been promised. From the town hall they set off for the barracks of the mutinous regiments—apparently, with reassuring statements that their mission was to preserve the front.

Actually, a certain neutrality had already been established. The rebellious garrison had not approached or touched the palace guard.

On the other hand, Groten brought a Petrograd leaflet with absolutely incredible news: Yesterday, apparently, His Personal Convoy, in full, had shown up at the Duma. This was nonsense because not only was it about the noble Convoy soldiers but also because two hundreds were here, at the palace, and loyal, and hadn't gone anywhere, and two were in Mogilev, with GHQ, and could not have ended up in Petrograd. There was only a half-hundred and a noncombatant detachment in Petrograd.

Nonetheless! The Empress thought anxiously that if this treacherous news were to reach the Emperor, he might even believe it, for he knew nothing of the Tsarskoye Selo hundreds. My God, how quickly, in twenty-four hours, had an avalanche formed of things left unsaid and uncomprehended! What a horror!

Meanwhile, Grand Duke Boris had shown up like a meteor and swept through. He seemed to be in a terrible hurry, and was pale, and was biting his lips, and his entire message consisted in the fact that he had been urgently summoned to GHQ, which was why he could not do anything here, and all the troops under his command were there.

Coward. The Empress let him go contemptuously. She wasn't even offended at this "Cossack ataman"; she had expected nothing good from him. She was actually surprised he had come to register his departure at all.

But Pavel? What had become of Pavel now? This morning he had promised to meet the Emperor—and now he hadn't. So why hadn't he gotten concerned, why hadn't he come, and what was he going to do with the Guard?

He hadn't come and had sent no word of himself.

All was clarified soon after, that evening, but before dinner, Benckendorff and Groten having requested an audience. Grand Duke Pavel Aleksandrovich had in fact gone to the train station that morning and not met the Emperor, but even before this, last night, he and his family had been forced to hide in someone else's home for fear of an attack on their own unprotected palace. The grand duke was prepared to go to GHQ immediately and join the Guard at the front—but he couldn't have gone through Luga, where a revolt had begun as well. Not only that, though, the grand duke was upset by the rumors that had reached him that Duma circles were preparing for Mikhail's regency.

What was this now? The Empress had heard nothing of the kind! What nonsense was that?

Driven by these rumors, all these hours Grand Duke Pavel had been seeking out a way to save the throne for the Emperor.

What was he talking about? Save it? The throne needed saving?

The grand duke had composed and was proposing a draft manifesto that the Emperor had to sign—and all would be saved, and everyone satisfied. But as long as the Emperor wasn't here, perhaps the Empress would sign it to pacify the public? For assurance, as it were?

Astonished, the Empress took the document. The sole living son of Aleksandr II, who had been killed by terrorists, with one brother killed by terrorists and one other who had barely escaped the same fate—after all the harsh things he had listened to yesterday from the Empress, and instead of going to bring the Guard under his command here, how had he made amends? What had he proposed?

A perfectly idiotic document in high-flown, confused verbiage, alleging that the Emperor had always intended nothing other than introducing a responsible ministry, but previous ministers had prevented him. And now, in sorrow that domestic turmoil had overtaken the capital, but placing his hopes on the help of Divine Providence, with a wave of his hand he was offering the government a Russian constitutional regime and proposing that the State Duma President put together a provisional Cabinet of Ministers, and after that there would be a legislative assembly and a new constitution.

Despite her agitation, insomnia, and worry, though, Aleksandra Fyodorovna retained her statesmanly clarity of mind, as always. Immediately evident to her was the hypocrisy of this clumsy, utterly unjustified movement— and the degree of capitulation the grand duke had dared ascribe to the Emperor. Not even she could have brought herself to advise this, although the sweep of events had convinced her that some concessions were now inevitable.

Disappointed, she set the document aside. There could be no thought so foolish as her signing.

However, for some reason she wasn't angry at Pavel and actually pitied him. This document was hypocritical, but Pavel's impulse was sincere. He truly did want to save the throne for the Emperor. He was not secretly plotting with Rodzyanko, as Mikhail obviously was, hence the rumors of a regency. Pavel had shown himself to be not wise, but loyal—and the Empress was no longer angry at him. It was a mad—but also noble—notion.

Terrible hours had passed—hours marked by a stunning lack of news! No one knew where the Emperor was, and that was the most dreadful part. *Where* he was, at one point on the map, she had always known. (Even when

he had traveled to the different army groups, he had warned her of his itin-
eraries. She had even followed hour by hour what he might be doing in the
course of the day.) Now, though, there was no connection with GHQ. All
that remained was the single connection with the Winter Palace—which
had nothing to give. They had established only for certain that a crowd had
attacked and burned down Frederiks's home, and his poor family was in the
Horse Guards hospital, his wife unconscious.

Aleksandra had lived her entire life with Nicky, continuously, for twenty
years they had shared everything equally, big and small, consoling and
difficult. At one time, his departure for Italy for a brief time had seemed like
a nightmarish tragedy. She had always felt it as unnatural that he would
leave, and literally every one of his departures had been a terrible trial—to
see his big, sad eyes at their parting. She hated being apart! (Right now she
was passing with a shudder through the lilac room, where they had sat together so cozily.)

Ever since the Emperor had taken charge of the Supreme Command,
he had often had to remain at GHQ, and so for the first time in their twenty-
first year of marriage they had spent their day of engagement and birthday
apart. (At one point she had tried to persuade him to move GHQ closer to
Petrograd so they could see each other more often.) This separation, this
chain of separations, was their personal sacrifice, which they bore for their
poor country in this difficult time.

During their separations, Aleksandra suffered for him more than for herself, though. She suffered over *his* loneliness, how *he* was bearing their separation, and especially, when difficult trials befell him, he could soften and
lose faith in himself, and everyone around him there was always giving him
bad advice and exploiting his goodness, and he was exhausted by these internal questions. Every woman has something maternal in her feeling for
her beloved. Aleksandra seemed to carry Nicky inside her, in her breast.
This was how the Lord had arranged it. He wanted his poor little wife to
help him. What she advised him she did not consider to be any wisdom of
her own, but her God-given instinct. She had always been able to encourage him, had always been capable of inspiring faith in him. (This was why
those others feared her influence; she had a stubborn will and saw through
things better than others did.)

So it was today. She might have been able to avert something, but here
she had been forced to cast about and didn't even know his locations, to say
nothing of his circumstances—and anguish was gnawing at her heart.

At dinner—with Lili and her one healthy daughter Maria—they barely ate.

It had become too agonizing to pretend in front of the children and to
conceal from them. Eighteen-year-old Maria had already seen enough
herself, had heard snatches, and understood. But the older children lying
in their dark room and even Baby had to be gradually explained to and
prepared.

That afternoon there had been muted rumors that General Ivanov was on his way here from GHQ with troops. It was hard to believe. But late that evening it was suddenly reported from the train station that he had arrived. He was here!

Lord, what joy! Glory to You, thanks be to You! Lord, what unexpected joy! And to find out about the Emperor! (Might the Emperor himself be following behind?) Help and protection.

How she felt it! How she felt that she had always liked this general, calling him "grandfather," advising him to be taken in at GHQ, advising him to be the war minister. How he would have captured the hearts of the Duma! How tactful it was on Nicky's part to send Ivanov specifically!

The Empress ordered someone to rush to the station and summon the general here!

[2 8 7]

The train made it safely to the Tsarskoye Selo station. No one fired on or detained them.

Darkness had fallen long before, so it was all the more dangerous.

General Ivanov issued orders to the St. George battalion not to let anyone off the train and to keep everyone at full readiness, but inside. He himself sent for the garrison chief and the town commandant.

They appeared quite distraught and disturbed and confirmed all the worst news: the garrison was not obeying them, was in ferment, and was obeying their *committees*.

So that's how it was. . . .

Nonetheless, there had been no serious rebellious protests, either. And today, Duma deputies had been there and reassured them. All the taverns had been robbed—and in such numbers that not only was it enough for the garrison, but baskets of wine and beverages greeted the various newly arriving units, groups, and military trucks. Arriving from the Putilov factory in Petrograd, too, were armored vehicles with machine guns and soldiers—possibly for hostile actions against the Palace.

But what was Petrograd like in general?

There had been no resistance in Petrograd since midday yesterday. All military actions had ended.

And so, on the one hand, it was unquestionably dangerous for the St. George battalion to disembark. But on the other, inasmuch as there was no manifest revolt in Tsarskoye Selo, the garrison leadership could handle it themselves.

The Tsarskoye Selo palace? But its guard was not part of General Ivanov's direct assignment; his assignment was more general.

And then, a direct clash near the palace could indirectly threaten the royal family.

Fortunately, the revolutionary detachments had yet to attack the newly arrived troop train. But in the dark, in the depths, certain movements were taking place, and one got the impression that they were surrounding the station. Drunken songs were heard far off as well.

Based on his experience, Nikolai Iudovich could well imagine what it meant when four armed regiments had had too much to drink.

What to do about it was a conundrum. Nikolai Iudovich had never had occasion to act in such irregular circumstances.

Right then a newly arrived junior officer from the Tarutinsky Regiment reported to the general that his entire regiment had arrived, in its full complement and battle readiness, and was located five versts from here, at the Aleksandrovskaya station. That is, on the Luga branch.

Was that so? For long?

Since early morning.

"And no one has attacked you?"

No. The regiment is twenty versts from Petrograd on its own branch and is prepared to move along by troop train, or immediately disembark and proceed at a march.

"Under no circumstance!" General Ivanov decisively saw to and prohibited this. "Under no circumstance are you to provoke the people! Everyone is to remain on the troop train until my specific order."

And how had they traveled?

Via Gatchina.

And Gatchina hadn't detained them? Was there a large garrison there now?

About twenty thousand, all loyal, and they could also be summoned to assist.

Was that so. Good. For now, though, remain on the troop trains. And attach a liaison to me.

The general thought it over. The arrival of the Tarutinsky Regiment and the loyalty of the Gatchina garrison actually complicated his personal assignment.

He seemingly should have redeployed toward his main forces, but that was five versts to the side along a dark, undefended route—and how could he abandon the St. George battalion?

Military actions, when you don't wage them against a true foe but in your own native country, can create an exceptionally complicated situation.

However! They also had this fortunate characteristic: the possibility of direct intercourse with the so-called opponent. Before Nikolai Iudovich could frown over the map sufficiently, Colonel Domanevsky and Lieutenant Colonel Tilly came to his train car and asked to be presented. Was that so! The general had heard of the former, who had served in high posts in the Guards, and Nikolai Iudovich knew the latter directly from the Southwest Army Group. They had come not for themselves—these were not random officers—but had been sent across the transitory, so to speak, battle line by their superior, General Zankevich, head of the Chief Administration of the General Staff.

"General Zankevich is in position?" Iudovich rejoiced.

Naturally, why shouldn't he be? The entire General Staff was in position. Well, then this did not resemble a rebellion at all.

All day today, General Ivanov had thought he was traveling toward a dark horizon; events were impenetrably blocked off from him and he from them. Now it turned out that Petrograd knew perfectly well about his movement toward Tsarskoye Selo, and here Colonel Domanevsky had been sent to him as nothing more or less than his chief of staff, to help General Ivanov in his command of the Petrograd Military District and to clarify the situation.

This was marvelous! The screen of hostility had fallen away, and on either side there were disciplined officers of one and the same army!

But more and better than this, these two officers had been sent simultaneously as well at the behest of the Provisional Committee of the State Duma.

How, though? Did this mean it was all the same thing?

Yes, it did. A Military Commission was functioning under the Duma Committee, and General Zankevich was maintaining continuous contact with it. Here they had all jointly sent these two officers to conscientiously clarify to the newly appointed dictator what the situation was in Petrograd and to fully orient him as to Petrograd events.

Quite marvelous.

So there, in Petrograd, everyone was already fully backing the Provisional Committee of the State Duma and there was no more struggle. Even the Guards Crew and Grand Duke Kirill Vladimirovich today had offered themselves to the Duma, and even His Majesty's Personal Convoy had sent delegates, as had the Tsarskoye Selo palace guard. Many officers, by the power of the State Duma, had already returned to their units and were commanding them unimpeded. Khabalov and some of the ministers had been arrested. The entire struggle was over, and it was now hard to count on restoring the former order by military force. However, this was not required because the Duma Committee was loyal to the monarchical principle and to the prosecution of the war. Now, therefore, all the highest headquarters and military ranks of the capital were calmly continuing to work, recognizing the Duma committee. And in charge of it all was Rodzyanko.

The general listened and was amazed and at the same time relieved. His most difficult assignment had nearly ceased to exist. Rodzyanko? Well, Rodzyanko on the surface, but behind his back, of course, was Guchkov, and Guchkov, naturally, would be Prime Minister. (He and General Ivanov secretly had quite good relations.)

This meant, the sent officers explained, armed struggle would only spoil the entire situation. The most sensible thing for the new Commander of the Petrograd District was to support the moderate Duma Committee against the exorbitant claims of the Soviet of Workers' Deputies.

Oh, there were workers' deputies, too? No, all this was not so clear. He could not make any promises, but on the other hand, he could not spoil relations with the new government.

Nor could he fail to please His Majesty, though.

Oh, he'd landed in it! Oh, a difficult situation.

Clearly, Petrograd was a force to be reckoned with, with a garrison of nearly 200,000. What could he do with a single battalion that lacked any sort of combat frame of mind, that was straight out of GHQ's formal guard?

Not only that, it was also extremely dangerous to remain overnight in Tsarskoye Selo in a drunken revolutionary encirclement; the general had thrust too far forward.

Outwardly, Nikolai Iudovich did not let the newly arrived officers sense his alarm; his broad-bearded, broad-browed, simple-hearted face shielded such details.

But a precautionary measure gave him a guarantee: attached at the end was an engine facing backward.

The palace? He had not received direct instructions from the Emperor to defend the palace. And the more he learned now—if even the palace guard had sent its deputies to the Duma, that meant everyone was reconciled and no clashes were envisioned.

But more than an hour was spent on all these conversations and clarifications. The rumor of the troop train's arrival spread through Tsarskoye Selo and reached the palace—and now an officer came from there and handed General Ivanov a telegram from General Alekseev, which had come in at the palace telegraph office early that morning and had lain there.

Telegram no. 1833 was long, and the general went off to his study to read it and to think things through calmly. This telegram might complicate the situation greatly. But no. Fortunately, no! On the contrary, everything coincided with what he had been told by the sensible colonel and lieutenant colonel. Alekseev also informed him that there was perfect calm in Petrograd, the troops had sided with the new government, and the government with the monarchic principle. If all this information was accurate—and it was, General Ivanov was convinced—then his means of action had to change toward reconciliation, having avoided disgraceful internecine strife. The matter could be led peacefully to a good conclusion that would strengthen Russia.

Well, this was absolutely correct! So it was! This coincided with Iudovich's presentiment! This was what combat experience meant! How correctly he had behaved, without a single misstep, as if he had foreseen this telegram.

Now it was all easy; negotiating was not waging war.

And the negotiations would not be hindered in the least if they went back to Vyritsa for the night.

Standing firm a little longer, the general was preparing to issue this order—when another Guard officer arrived from the palace to tell him that the Empress was summoning the general.

How inopportune! He hadn't managed to leave!

In the new circumstances this could cast a new stain on him.

But in the old, there was no way he could fail to go.

He wasn't going to take his battalion along, so how was he to travel through the Tsarskoye Selo streets before these drunken brigands had gone to bed and calmed down?

He had to stall a little longer.

His half-century of service experience suggested that for now, covering the slight shortage of military actions, it would not be bad to write an order. Saying the general had arrived in Tsarskoye Selo and had his headquarters here.

* * *

"Comrade Soldiers!

. . . In order that the gentry and officers—that Romanov gang—do not deceive you, take power into your own hands! You yourselves must choose your platoon, company, and regimental commanders. . . . All officers must come under the oversight of the company committees.

Accept only those officers whom you know as friends of the people. Now that you have risen up and won, not only your friends, but former enemy officers, who call themselves your friends, will come to you. Soldiers! A fox tail scares us more than a wolf's fang!

. . . Your representatives and workers' deputies must become the people's Provisional Revolutionary Government, and from it you will receive land and freedom!

Soldiers! Discuss this in your companies and in your battalions! Organize rallies!

Long live the Soviet of Workers' and Soldiers' Deputies!

Petersburg Interdistrict Committee of
the Russian Social Democratic Workers Party
Petersburg Committee of Socialist Revolutionaries

* * *

[2 8 8]

The entire war, from the very beginning, and from the famous Tarnavka—up until January of this year, Staff Captain von Fergen had spent in the Moscow Life Guards Regiment, at the head of its 14th Company, which was devoted to him, had not missed a single battle, had gone on countless attacks, forays, and reconnaissance missions, had been beset by all the bombardments, had had all the bullets whistle by. Among the combat officers, every single one had been wounded; only he didn't have a scratch on him. To the superstitious front-line eye this was an out-and-out miracle, beyond the bounds of all likelihood. In January, the regimental commander, General Halfter, had called Fergen in and said:

"I do not feel I have the right to test your fate any further, my good man. I want to preserve an officer like you. Go to a reserve battalion for a few months and train them there. Someone needs to do it anyway."

So Fergen went to Petrograd and was given the 4th Company, fifteen hundred men. Even this vast, fluid company quickly learned his imperturbable, unexcitable nature, his refusal to find fault over trifles, even his meekness. There was nothing German about him except his name. And so the soldiers had not said anything hostile to him, and during the days of the revolt, when he returned with his sentry from the Sampsonievsky Bridge, they took him in to spend those two nights in company quarters. Yesterday evening, the company had once again chose him to be their commander—and today he would have joined the battalion march to the State Duma, if he hadn't replied abruptly that he wouldn't lead the company unless the soldiers removed those red scraps from their greatcoats.

But the scraps remained on the soldiers' chests and sleeves—so what next?

All that remained, in the devastation of his soul, was to take an afternoon nap.

He and Nelidov slept through until evening, until dark.

Suddenly they were awakened by an ominous knocking by several fists at the door and a continuous ringing of the electric doorbell.

They immediately understood this was bad. They had nothing to barricade themselves in with. And they couldn't not open up.

They put on their boots, and Nelidov himself limped to the door and opened it.

A band of soldiers, ten or so, piled in, and with them were workers. The company men found no familiar faces—what a public thoroughfare they'd made of the battalion!

But these men had not come blindly. They knew who they were after. They immediately poked a finger into Fergen's chest: he'd refused to command the company.

Was he supposed to deny he had? . . . He remained silent.

They were going to take him to the State Duma right now.

That was good, to the Duma. But the faces and voices were quite malevolent.

They began finding fault with Nelidov, saying that if his company had recognized him as commander, why was he here?

Luka, the nimble batman, darted out:

"Go to the company and check."

But they crowded around and started searching the rooms for weapons, they said, and they confiscated Nelidov's revolver (Fergen had left his at the company), and meanwhile they were openly slapping his pockets for anything valuable there.

"Collect your things!" they ordered Fergen.

He couldn't think of anything to do.

Nelidov and Fergen embraced and bid a solemn goodbye.

"Farewell," Fergen whispered to him. "They're going to kill me."

He felt his lips turning to ice, as if he were already passing away.

"Farewell, Sasha," Nelidov said, not disputing it.

Nothing had been announced, nothing had been said directly, but the clear sense of his impending end overtook Fergen as it never had before with a single incoming shell.

He had been prepared for the end long since — but why here? Why at the hands of his own?

He tripped and stumbled on the threshold.

While outside, under a streetlamp, a clutch of workers with bayonets let up a howl — and it was dark already, and there was no time to make out faces, more like animal masks.

"Let's go!" They showed him to the gate onto Sampsonievsky.

He started off surrounded by a disorderly convoy — not a military party where they obey a single man, but each one leading him and shouting whatever he wanted — and setting him straight with their bayonets.

There was no sentry or guard master at the gate, and no one tried to stop them.

Sasha Fergen wasn't afraid of death — but why at the hands of his own?

Pictures flashed before him with uncommon speed — his father and mother (he wasn't even married yet), his improbable escapes at the front, the triumph of his promotion to officer, the Emperor congratulating him with a gracious smile, then further, the Corps of Cadets. . . .

"So you don't like red scraps, swine?" they shouted.

They stopped. There was nowhere else to take him. They prodded him to turn and turn with their bayonets — to show himself and see everyone.

The light of the gate lamps reached them here. On all sides there was an evenly malevolent, teeth-baring, gray-black crowd. But he said nothing and saw nothing more. He felt a piercing through, like when you have a cold in your lungs — and was deafened by a blow to the head.

His extinguished consciousness had already freed him from knowing that his body had been thrust through by several bayonets and lifted off the ground, into the air, for show — and the crowd guffawed gleefully.

[2 8 9]

If one were to think back on Pavel Nikolaevich's fifty-eight-year life: his glorious scholarly activities, later transferred to the public arena; his knowledge of the West and even America and his role there as the harbinger of the coming Russian revolution, his successful, highly influential lectures there — about the inevitability of Russian autocracy's demise—this broad Western outlook that made Russia's general weaknesses especially well visible; and then with the glory of a "fierce revolutionary," his return to Russia in the most fluid, transitional months of 1905 and his immediate plunge into politics (they correctly predicted that he would become the historian of Russian autocracy's fall, but he longed to be a participant in that fall as well!); and in Russia's primitive political amorphousness the feeling out of firm ground, the drawing of dividing boundaries, the assembling of men of like mind; and with an ever firmer hand the formation of Kadetism as an ideology, a movement, a party—the very same party that would uphold the future constitution, a party of firm discipline and the most leftist among analogous Western European parties; and in response to the concessions of the Tsar's Manifesto of 30 October, to find a successful combination of liberal tactics and revolutionary menace, never to permit the public condemnation of terror, to be ready and unsqueamish with regard to the physical means of struggle while trying to achieve the immediate removal of the government gang that had seized power in Russia; and in that very same October 1905, to pass the entrance exam for leadership among the Kadets and, in the past few years, leadership in the Progressive Bloc as well. If all were remembered, then one might say that no one in all Russia was so well prepared for the country's present upheaval, for understanding and governing it, as was Milyukov.

He had given over his entire being to the process of Russian political struggle. He had dissolved his entire personal life in the Sisyphean work of politics (so that he rarely had a chance to relax with a lady friend on his brief European outings). And he never altered his convictions.

It was the first revolution that, at its conclusion, had lain the path for Milyukov to become a minister, if not Prime Minister. He had been invited for talks first with Witte, then with Stolypin on Aptekarsky, and his terms had actually been weighed and reported to the Tsar—and he would already have gained power if not for the Tsar's evasiveness, Stolypin's coldness, Muromtsev's ambition, and the painful sensitivity of Shipov, who saw in Milyukov autocratic ways and a weak religious consciousness—which also turned out to be a hindrance to occupying a ministerial post. (Moldy Slavophilism—"People, not institutions," "Morality, not politics"—suspicious formulas that masked reaction.)

It goes without saying how much Milyukov had grown over the past few years, occupying such a unique position that he had no opponents, rivals, or competitors, anyone in the system who could compete with him and his political experience, discursive thinking, and ability to lead. Maklakov could shine in oratory and juridicism, but he was not well adapted to practical battles and had neither a chest of steel nor legs of stone. The fiery orator Rodichev, although of a provincial scale, the derisive paradoxalist Nabokov, and the sharply cut formulist Kokoshkin had each been irreplaceable in their own personal place, on the Duma dais or over the painstaking preparation of documents, but they could not lay claim to party leadership. Ardent Adzhemov and hardworking Shingarev were merely individual rays of light emanating from Milyukov. Only Petrunkevich and Vinaver could still lay claim to the leader's seat, but as a result of Vyborg they had gone off the rails. (Milyukov had also helped them compose the Vyborg Appeal itself. And before its signing, he had convinced them not to retreat.)

Thus, his entire life and his experience of many maneuvers had prepared Milyukov better than anyone for the stormy situation that had befallen them now and for holding on

to the helm of the ship of state. More than anything else, though, he was especially prepared for negotiations with the socialists, such as were coming up for him tonight. His
main book, published in the United States, had proven this very thought, that only a rap-
prochement between Russian liberals and Russian socialists would bring Russia political
freedom. This was his favorite, long-held, and even crowning idea. In order to implement
it, in the autumn of 1904, during the Japanese war, Milyukov had headed to a Paris conference together with Russian socialists and terrorists. An alliance of constitution and revolution! His persistent dream had been to become the leftists' ideological leader, the supreme
designator of their path. While keenly seeing to the precision of his boundaries on the
right, Milyukov had been good-natured toward the blurring of boundaries on the left. Even
if there were none at all, this was what would achieve a stable alliance with socialists for
taking over the government; they would merge in their struggle with the regime.

Unfortunately, the socialists' intolerance had already destroyed this hope how many
times! Even the sensible Mensheviks, who frequently took a specific position that was fully
in line with the Kadets, nonetheless out of prejudice and shame always staggered back as
from the *bourgeoisie*. This went without saying for the Bolsheviks, who projected geometric
lines into an empty future. And since the Stolypin years, the SRs, Milyukov's old friends,
had become increasingly weak and pale and were melting away. The choice of the nature of
their mutual relations for some reason always belonged to the leftists—who always chose a
drastic, insulting repulse. Facing the leftists' front, there was always the danger of discredit-
ing oneself with one's moderation—but no daring could merit their praise. Nonetheless,
Milyukov never tired of patiently trying to convince the leftists and building bridges.

This persistent crack of mistrust between Kadets and leftists was all the more regrettable
and dangerous because the main danger to all society always threatened from the rightists
and Black Hundreds, and here analysis was not enough, but the only type of person who
could comprehend the strength of the threat was someone against whom they had raised
their dirty hands. In some distant year, in the window opposite Milyukov's office, certain
mysterious preparations were under way that were explained by friends as poising a firearm
to shoot at him. Then a telegraph communiqué was received saying that at the German
border they had detained a certain medic, a shady gunman traveling with orders to kill Milyukov, Gessen, and Gruzenberg—so that government agents had to stay in the kitchen for
a while protecting Milyukov's person. Later, on Liteiny, a solidly built petit bourgeois type
leaped at Pavel Nikolaevich, struck two blows to his neck, knocked off his bowler, and
broke his spectacles. The series of assassination attempts threatened to continue, but Pavel
Nikolaevich went on a trip abroad.

And now, eleven years later, the same situation and the same concentrated, acute questions had arisen in Russia anew. The revolution, with its
violent heaving, was a terrible and beautiful storm in which a new system
was being born. It was a unique correlation of forces that was placing the
reins of government in the Kadet leader's deserving hands of their own accord. Placing the rightist, Tsarist counterrevolution advancing in Ivanov's
brutal troop trains, too. Again the leftists' misunderstanding, mistrust, and
wariness! They had occupied the Duma wing very close by and they had no

wish to unite! Certain vague, chance contacts flashed by between the two wings of the Tauride Palace, ad hoc reports, someone told someone something, whispered—but the Soviet of Workers' Deputies stubbornly maintained its self-sufficiency, disdaining the anxious Duma wing, deciding and organizing something of its own there. (Even though Milyukov and Skobelev had slept one night on a table under the same fur coat.) Every hour this schism was incredibly dangerous, repeating the schism between revolutionaries and constitutionalists that had been the ruin of all of 1905.

And now *this* schism, *this* misunderstanding today tormented Milyukov more than all the other concerns of the day, especially since the real time to take up the fallen government had drawn nigh. Right here, in Petrograd, without any sanction from the useless monarch, to seize power de facto. The Duma's Provisional Committee had become ridiculous; in no way was it leading, nor could it succeed at doing so, and it consisted half of rot. (Milyukov had taken the other, competent half into his government.) Here, too, were the clumsy plans of that bumpkin Rodzyanko, his vain impulses to become dictator of the Russian revolution, his transparent intentions to reach agreement with the Tsar and the commanders-in-chief, to travel to an unmonitored meeting—and seize the prime ministership for himself in a cabinet of public trust. (In these past two days, Rodzyanko had become a played-out figure, eliminated by a mere wag of the finger. Milyukov had cleared out tougher heads than that in his day! There was a time Rodzyanko had come in very handy for constraining the rightists in the Duma, and for the past two days he had done useful work, but that time was now over.)

Prince Lvov had not shown up at the Tauride Palace today, and the government's entire formation had proceeded without him. All the better.

Also secondary were all the combinations around the withering Emperor Nikolai, the pathetic manifesto by the three grand dukes that was brought to Milyukov for signature and that he put in his pocket without showing it to anyone. This emperor would never reign, of course, but the Aleksei-Mikhail combination had great chances, and in that way the baldachin of monarchy would be preserved without which the people would be dismayed.

What did disturb him was this standoff with the Soviet of Workers' Deputies. The standoff made no sense historically, for the first Petersburg Soviet of Workers' Deputies had been pushed to the surface by Milyukov's allies, who had hidden it in their apartments. And it was awkward in a practical sense, in today's complicated, stormy situation.

When it was learned late that evening that the Soviet of Workers' Deputies was proposing talks, Milyukov exulted. This was the creation of a genuine foundation for the government being formed! Stablest of all would be if the socialists warmly joined the cabinet. But even if they didn't, then these negotiations were the basis of a cabinet.

Here was the highest meaning of the leftward orientation: given proper dealings with the leftists, leaning on them, one could emerge into power.

And Milyukov knew how to negotiate!

He realized, naturally, that they were coming here again with mistrust, again with bias—not as they would simply to see people, not as they would to see their comrades, but as they would to see the franchised bourgeoisie, before whom they could not show weakness.

But Milyukov was prepared to outfox them! He was prepared for all their mistrust, and he was tolerant in advance toward all the impending vexatious twists. What was important was starting a dialog! He had done so much in common with them in the past—this could not fail to affect the negotiations. It was no disaster that the third sleepless night was coming on. When negotiating, Milyukov would withstand even a third, and even without coffee.

So much he'd done with them in the past—but with prominent, vivid leaders, not with these who had just come. Of these he had long known only the lawyer Sokolov, back from the League of Liberation—a talentless and limited man capable only of conveying party directives. The others were, similarly, the second tier of party political journalism.

He was even disappointed that coming to oppose the lion of the Kadet party were not prominent socialists—though where were they to be found in Petrograd?—but rather just anybody.

Oh well, these were the *wrong* leaders, but circumstances had put them in the place of the *right ones*. He did not have to respect these men specifically but leftists in general, the revolutionary upthrust in general, without which a radical liberal could not persist.

But he did know how to negotiate!

Some disheveled, crazed soldier ran into the Duma Committee's room. And without introduction, rudely:

"Here, we need to print up this order right now. Who's going to do that?"

They smiled and politely refused him.

He looked at them, his mouth hanging open, and with a sweep of the arm: "Well then, we'll print it ourselves!"

[2 9 0]

Gradually, the Executive Committee wore itself out and spilled away— and no one was given authority to negotiate with the Duma deputies; it was just whoever was left: Nakhamkes, who had not let go of the points, and Himmer. Nakhamkes, though, was very prudent. No matter what Himmer had ever gone to do, Nakhamkes hadn't been idle. He'd gone to the half-empty Room no. 12 and read out his nine points before what was left of the undispersed assemblage—and just try to prove later that they weren't approved by the Soviet.

Himmer's small body possessed an excess of dynamism; he was small but could leap higher than anyone tall. So swift were his thinking and actions that he ran circles around everyone.

No matter how much they'd discussed the problem of negotiations with the Duma deputies all day, he still wasn't satisfied, and his brain kept nagging at him that they hadn't reached agreement on everything even in their narrow circle. First of all, weren't the bourgeois government's supports bent too far in his own formula? Never had he had a class-based world in mind. He was not about to repeat 1848, when workers pulled the chestnuts from the fire for the liberals, who later shot them; oh no, better we not waste our time and just shoot the liberals ourselves. Nor was he proposing renouncing drastic opposition; that would be capitulation to democracy. No! He had in mind only secret contacts with the bourgeoisie—only for these brief days of upheaval not keep the Duma government from doing its work, since under a franchised government there would be no military suppression from GHQ—and keep their claws retracted, at the ready, to be shown soon after. The nine points Nakhamkes wrote down made no mention of this question of government support, but there was a danger that in the negotiations the Duma deputies would come back at them with it. The second question and second danger was that the Duma deputies bowing before their State Duma would be unwilling even to hear of any Constituent Assembly alongside it.

In the last half-hour before the talks, Himmer and Nakhamkes agreed to do everything they could to slur over the question of support, and on the question of a Constituent Assembly, if people really dug in their heels, then not to insist.

Himmer had established communications with the Duma deputies faster than anyone. No matter how busy he was in the Soviet, he always managed, the way people ran out to the washroom, to dash out and jostle through the Tauride Palace to gather information and contacts. Over the course of this evening he had already managed two or three times to inform the Duma wing and also to repeat and pump up the message that he was *preparing.* That *there would be contacts.* That they would come to the negotiations. This was required in the practical sense, too, for the meeting to take place, so they wouldn't disperse over there, but also, for the opponent's psychological suppression: in a few bursts the repeated statement should give rise to concern in them as to what kind of negotiations these would be and what kind of ultimatum they would be brought.

Here, Kerensky could be an exceptional help, and with his help these Duma deputies could be hoodwinked—but he had succumbed to the neurotic disease of power, the desire to become a minister. He had lost all his revolutionary democratic reason, and it was impossible to talk to him about any practical matter of the Soviet, but when in these last few runs Himmer had encountered him—he had been summoned somewhere and was wearing his fur coat, prepared to leave—he had listened and understood poorly, and replied nervously and disjointedly about one and the same thing, that the leaders of democracy were showing their mistrust of him, that they wished to have him quarrel with the masses, they were undermining him, intriguing, and initiating persecution. Himmer, himself one of the main leaders of democracy, looked with pity at his former friend, who was definitely of no use for the upcoming negotiations.

This made Chkheidze even more essential for the delegation to take along for the negotiations, although even he was a casualty of the surfeit of events: sleepy, languid, soft, indifferent.

And then there was someone who was just as active and indefatigable as Himmer, but in a foolish way: Sokolov. Sokolov was sitting in the first room of Duma deputies, in the connecting room, over tea and sandwiches, with the new city governor, Yurevich, discussing the objectives of the city governor's office. But Himmer had an upset stomach and immediately rushed toward them and the tea, which had been served with little spoons and sugar, and interrupted heatedly about how to rout the police apparatus and create a select police force. Then Sokolov latched on to him and ferreted out his intention—and asked that he be taken to the negotiations, too. Then Himmer started talking to Nekrasov. He could see from Nekrasov that the Duma Committee had been prepared and was waiting and worried.

"What do you propose discussing?" Nekrasov asked warily. (Actually, he was a fool, too.)

Ah, so that was what was eating at them there now! This was what they had feared, that they might be presented now, for example, with a Zimmerwaldist "Down with the war!" This was just what Himmer needed, to frighten them and soften them up in advance; herein lay his tactic.

He paced in front of Nekrasov with arms akimbo:

"We're going to have to talk about the overall state of affairs."

Nekrasov huddled up, went through the door to report to his principals, and returned to say that they were expecting representatives from the Soviet of Workers' Deputies at midnight.

[2 9 1]

General Ruzsky left the Emperor tense and vexed that he hadn't carried the matter through to the end, although during the few minutes of the conversation it had seemed to him that he had done well in his arguments: the Tsar was nervous, one hand had twitched, and apparently he had been about to pick up his pen.

Where was he to go now in this constraining state of anticipation if not to the compartment of some member of the suite? Ruzsky found himself in the open compartment of the decrepit and bent Frederiks with the teary eyes; but there was someone both inside and in the corridor close by, and people were passing through the corridor. Agitated conversations were passing there between them but died down in Ruzsky's presence.

Ruzsky infinitely despised the entire suite as a whole and each member of it separately. There was not a man among them of any use for the government, nor was anyone engaged in any useful activity; they were too many, but nonetheless there had to be that many around the sacred person. He now found it humiliating to be equal with them, having ended up in their company against his will. In addition, he was by nature unsociable. But where was he to wait this out? He couldn't leave for his own train at the station.

Sleepy Naryshkin was there. Cute young Mordvinov. The fussy and foolish historiographer Dubensky. Once the low-slung Admiral Nilov walked by with an ominous and irreconcilable (as was obvious to Ruzsky) look. And the stupid, self-enamored Voeikov, not deigning to speak to them, merely walked by firmly, proudly.

But the rest very much wanted to speak with the army group's commander-in-chief! The rest crowded in to join him from the other compartments—one other young general, one other aide-de-camp, a duke apparently, and another Convoy commander, a count apparently—to learn the news, what the talks under way were about, even for his help:

"Your Excellency! You alone can help! . . ."

Master of the situation, Ruzsky leaned back in the corner of the sofa and looked at them all sarcastically. The only thing left to do was to shock them, insult them, and irritate them in the extreme. They had been nothing before, and were especially nothing after the events that had taken place, gripped by fear for themselves, and even all their combined hostility could not hurt Ruzsky, who had already decided to take a harsh tone with the Emperor himself. Leaning back on the sofa and shutting his eyes in genuine exhaustion, he sighed:

"Yes. . . . Russia has been brought to the point of . . . No matter how much talk of reforms or how the entire country insisted . . . I myself warned many times that we should proceed in agreement with the State Duma. . . . No one listened. . . . The voice of that Khlyst Rasputin had more weight. And then the Protopopovs started in. . . ."

"What does Rasputin have to do with this?" ancient Frederiks objected, having suddenly heard through his deafness and with sudden force as upon awakening: "What influence could he have had on government affairs?"

"What do you mean what influence?" Ruzsky opened his eyes, astonished.

Frederiks replied with dignity:

"I, for example, never saw him and did not know him. And I did not notice his influence in anything."

"Well, Count, perhaps you did keep out of it," Ruzsky conceded respectfully. (Especially since he himself was not without fault; at the difficult moment of his dismissal, people had petitioned for him through Rasputin as well.) "But the duty of those surrounding the Emperor was to know what was going on in Russia. The entire policy of the past few years has been a bad dream and thoroughgoing misunderstanding. Popular anger will not forgive Shcheglovitov, Sukhomlinov, Protopopov, or protectionism in the appointments . . ."

It was *they* he had in mind, the courtiers, but they weren't the least bit shocked and crowded around offering him cigars—but Ruzsky didn't smoke cigars and held on to his cigarette. And they haltingly prompted Ruzsky to further explanations.

"What will happen now? . . . What should be done now, Your Excellency?" several voices asked. "You see, we're standing over an abyss. All hope is on you!"

They already knew from Danilov that even Alekseev had sent a telegram asking for a responsible ministry.

"What now, now that it's come to this?" Ruzsky sighed, as if beset. "Now one can only surrender to the victor's mercy."

"The victor?" The suite floundered in fright. "But who has won? . . ."

"Who do you think!" Ruzsky grinned. "Rodzyanko. The State Duma."

Oh! The suite was not only not opposed to a responsible ministry, it turned out to have been waiting for concessions to the Duma! They were now all in favor of a responsible ministry.

(Ruzsky didn't know that the angry little Admiral Nilov, having called the historiographer away, was trying to prove to him the necessity of proposing to the Emperor right now the he remove Ruzsky, execute him, and appoint an energetic general to take troops against Petrograd. However, neither one nor the other had the courage to address the Emperor directly, and they didn't know who could.)

"Well, then," Voeikov's swollen snout suddenly appeared from behind the other heads. "I'm prepared to discuss this with Rodzyanko by direct line."

At this Ruzsky could grin especially venomously:

"If he finds out it's you who wants to talk, he won't even come to the telegraph."

And proud Voeikov moved aside.

They smoked and talked—but the Emperor did not summon Ruzsky. And the hands of the clock were approaching midnight.

And crossing it.

This was becoming untenable, humiliating. What kind of spectacle was this thinking alone, without consultations or telephone anyway?

Ruzsky was starting to wonder whether he should leave. No, let them report definitively for the last time whether he should leave or wait. Right then Voeikov approached him once again. And spoke before Ruzsky could:

"General, I have a telegram from the Emperor for transmittal. Allow us to use your Hughes wire."

"No!" Ruzsky's voice broke as he shouted. "I'm in charge here, and only I have the right to send telegrams!"

He should not have started shouting, but one could lose one's balance: they wanted to circumvent him with an unknown result, and even if he was successful, to crowd him out, as if it wasn't he who had achieved all this.

Voeikov strode back to the Emperor with the telegrams, but even Frederiks wended his way there, upset by the breach of etiquette.

(What's this? Are we captives here? This passed through the suite.)

Voeikov returned quite displeased and held out the telegrams to Ruzsky.

Ruzsky straightened his spectacles and read the top one:

"Arrived here at dinnertime. Hope everybody's health is better and that we shall soon see each other. God be with you. Warmly embrace you. Nicky."

He shuddered and shuffled it to the bottom.

But when opened, the main one, to Alekseev, said that he agreed to the proposed manifesto and agreed to a responsible ministry.

Perhaps overly irritated by the previous confrontation, Ruzsky now found that this was expressed insufficiently clearly. Although everyone had an identical understanding of what "responsible" meant, nonetheless, responsible to whom? He had to indicate this specifically, that it was to the Duma, to the people. Wasn't this the type of clever, evasive maneuver by the Tsar, so characteristic of him?

Ruzsky insisted that the Emperor receive him again. He did.

How long since Ruzsky had seen him? Forty-five or fifty minutes. It was unimaginable that in that time a person could grow that haggard, lose his very recent stubbornness, that his gaze and face could spread so thin, the bags under his eyes sag so, and the skin on his face turn brown.

But Ruzsky's pressure was all the more confident. There was a mistake in the text of the telegram, and this was either not quite right or quite wrong. It had to be corrected!

The Emperor looked at him uncomprehendingly.

He asked how he should express himself more precisely.

And rewrote it then and there.

Frederiks sat dozing in the corner, occasionally shuddering.

The Emperor raised his big eyes from the paper with hope:

"Tell me, general, but they are also sensible governmental forces, after all, right? Who we're handing over to."

"Naturally, Your Majesty," Ruzsky encouraged him. "Quite sensible, indeed."

Now Ruzsky proposed that the telegram be sent not only to Alekseev but also, for speed, reported immediately to Rodzyanko in Petrograd.

The Emperor meekly agreed.

And wouldn't His Majesty himself like to go there for this telegraph conversation?

The Emperor looked, poorly understanding. What for? Where? In the middle of the night?

"I'm charging you with negotiating."

Ruzsky was flattered that he would be the first to report this thunderous news to the State Duma.

But having invested so much of his strength over the course of this evening, having achieved so much, such that no one could have dreamed of in Russia—how could he stop? For the umpteenth time this evening, still studying the ring with the elongated green stone on the Emperor's finger, and the reddish hairs on his hand, and the brown spots like large freckles,

Ruzsky led his broken interlocutor on further. Now, after this main concession of principle, how could he continue the senseless operation of sending
troops against the capital? The troops very soon might amass and clash—
and in the name of what was it all? And bloodshed, too?

If he was reconciled, then what troops? Against whom?

The mollified Emperor immediately agreed to halt the troops from the
Northern Army Group.

And the Vyborg fortress artillery, of course?

Yes, that, too.

But Ruzsky didn't feel like leaving yet! He sensed he might get something else.

Yes, this: then General Ivanov should be stopped as well?

The Emperor looked with his enlarged, doleful eyes, not understanding
immediately.

Ivanov? Yes, Ivanov, too, of course. Send him orders to halt, too.

"But this only you personally can do, Your Majesty. He answers to no
one else."

The Emperor immediately sat down. And immediately wrote in his own
hand. And passed the telegraph form to Ruzsky.

And then, all of a sudden, a very forced and embarrassed smile appeared
on his big lips under his thick mustache:

"And what do you think, Nikolai Vladimirovich? May I now continue on
to Tsarskoye Selo? You know, my children have the measles."

"But of course," Ruzsky agreed. "Once this is confirmed. Once the ministry of public trust is approved and things calm down everywhere—you'll
be on your way."

He left clutching his telegraph spoils.

[2 9 2]

Those stray bullets were flying in all directions—up, but also along, and
also across, and some part of them were bound to get caught somewhere
and sink in.

But Guchkov and Prince Dmitri Vyazemsky kept going, kept racing
through Petrograd, from battalion to battalion, from barracks to barracks,
where they soothed passions, where they gathered forces to repulse the government troops expected to attack the city.

Objects moving chaotically have a likelihood of crossing paths.

At around midnight, they were driving past the Semyonovsky Regiment
barracks, and in the snatches of light, shouts, and gunfire they saw and
guessed that Semyonovsky soldiers or other ones were looting, eviscerating
officers' quarters. The officers themselves may have hidden away beforehand, but the women were shouting and protesting, and since there were

four of them sitting in the motorcar, the motorcar pulled up short—hesitant whether to get caught in a minor everyday scuffle or to drive on farther—and at that moment Vyazemsky gasped and grabbed his back:

"Oh! I think . . ."

He was sitting next to the driver, while Guchkov and his adjutant, Count Kapnist, were in back.

"Hit? Got you?"

"Ooh!" he moaned. "Badly, I think. . . . Rats, I'm done for!"

What bad timing! . . . But when is it good? They'd been racing on wings—and been stopped.

Dmitri took his hand off his back and brought it forward—and it was drenched in blood.

Whoever fired—you could look and look into the darkness, whether it was aimed or not—wasn't going to fix anything.

Where to now? Home? Asya wasn't home in any case, she was out of town. To his mother's on the Fontanka? No need to disturb her yet. The hospital? But maybe wait and see if we can get by? Why not one of these apartments? We can defend it at the same time. . . .

In the heat of the moment, Dmitri took a few steps and then nearly fell; Guchkov and Kapnist caught him on either side. They wondered whether they should return to the motorcar—but no, they'd proceed as decided.

Vyazemsky hung on their necks; he couldn't move his legs at all. The driver took Guchkov's place.

Through a well-lit, wide-open door, two soldier looters flung themselves from the steps in front of them into the darkness. Guchkov shouted at them, in warning.

A woman in the door started to close it—but the three-headed monster advanced on her.

Guchkov identified himself and asked to enter.

Another woman was there as well, and both were so upset that their hands were trembling—and now they carried in the wounded man, an impossible encumbrance, and all on a single family in a few brief minutes.

They removed his greatcoat. His wound had to be examined, but his lower back was so thickly soaked through his trousers and tunic, they could tell it was grave.

They had to lay the wounded man down—and they thought of doing so facedown, so the blood wouldn't flow as much.

"Cover the sofa with an oilcloth, please. Do you have one?"

The restrained Dmitri was moaning loudly, and looking on, you could tell that putting him down would hurt even more. Whether he himself or they supported his legs, they pulled him back—and every way was worse. Clearly something had been damaged in his back.

They laid him down—and the pain eased. Bathed in sweat, he let his face fall. They brought a pillow to prop up his face.

Then, all at once: What had happened in the apartment? What was going on in the Semyonovsky? And where was there a telephone nearby?

"Aleksandr Ivanych," the injured man asked not yet weakly. "Call Dilka. She's at home and will do something quickly. But don't let her tell Mama."

Dilka-Lidia was his only sister, quite a decisive woman who happened to be born a girl. The entire Vyazemsky family was at the center of society, intersecting with the Vorontsovs and Velyaminovs, his older brother Boris was married to a Sheremetieva, Dmitri himself to a Shuvalova, his younger brother to a Vorontsova-Dashkova, and all of them were friendly with the young Konstantinovich grand dukes. Lidia herself ran a front-line hospital and knew many surgeons, and she surely would, right away, quickly . . .

One woman threw on a fur coat and led Guchkov. He spoke with her distractedly.

Dmitri was so unlucky! This was his third injury. Last autumn a bullet passed straight through his chest, and he hadn't completely healed from that. Released from military duty due to a heart defect, he decided to run a flying medical detachment from the trotting society, in the most forward position, always in the thick of things.

Guchkov felt sorry for Dmitri and couldn't shed his irritation at how inopportune it was to lose him in these very hours, when he was so needed by his side, and to lose these most historic hours, when what was most intense was flowing and flowing away somewhere.

Dmitri Vyazemsky was his favorite and a loyal fellow champion from the failed coup. By his nature, he reminded Guchkov of himself. Dmitri was glad at any danger, he seemed to seek it out and advance toward it. (Thus he and his detachment would creep forward where others wouldn't go, but that is what allowed them to collect the wounded promptly.) Whether it was from some permanent inner disquiet (as if "proving" himself over and over), he was utterly fearless and swift in his decisions. And inasmuch as he was not under police surveillance, as Guchkov was, and himself was so nimble and had such wide acquaintances among Guards officers, he was the best liaison and had traveled through the reserve units along the railway and sounded out the officers' mood. (True, he had recruited only one cavalry captain.) And now, during these Petrograd days, he had boldly entered raging soldier barracks.

And here he'd been pulled up by a silent, stupid little bullet.

Lidia Leonidovna was reached by telephone immediately, and she went to find the best surgeon, Zeidler, and arrange an examination right away.

Ah, how wrong they'd been to get out of the motorcar; they should have gone straight to the center and the hospital. They'd hoped it was a light wound.

At the Semyonovsky battalion things were very uneasy.

Guchkov never did organize barriers for the Vindava and Warsaw train stations. In the evening, he was still rushing to the palace to see Kirill

Vladimirovich—who turned out to be all bluster. He hadn't been able to send detachments from the Guards Crew, which no longer obeyed him.

Not that the Tsar's troops had approached the city. Only the Tarutinsky Regiment had stood all day today outside Tsarskoye Selo; as yet there were no others. Ivanov himself was already in Tsarskoye Selo, they knew, but Guchkov did not sense any threat from him.

Nonetheless, with every half-hour, boundless events were seeping away into all the breaches.

He had lost a great deal of blood, but Dmitri himself hadn't seen it and did not suspect. They applied iodine to the edges of the wounded area and covered it in bandages.

They didn't find an exit wound. It was lodged there.

How could he be lifted and taken farther? Guchkov sent Kapnist to the telephone to try to summon an ambulance.

Dmitri lay with his cheek on the pillow, his long, narrow head—with its perpetual look of surprise, though now harsher—turned on its side toward Guchkov.

He was terribly pale.

"Looks like my luck's run out," he said quietly. "And from a Russian bullet. . . ."

What was most annoying right now was the bullet's chance nature, its unintentionality. Why? What was the point? That was what hurt the most.

And the inaction.

But there were no grounds for thinking ill. He himself had always inclined to think positively. Nonetheless . . .

"If I knew no critical organ was hit . . ."

But the bullet was lodged somewhere.

And the blood hadn't stopped. It was running off the oilcloth into a bucket.

"Lidia will arrange everything right away," Guchkov reassured him. But he himself was somber. "How do you feel?"

"My ears are ringing badly. Speak louder, Aleksandr Ivanych."

They had just been racing around together, in the same sphere, in the same circle of thoughts—but a piece of lead went flying, and their spheres quickly started moving apart. Guchkov's, apparently, was still expanding and straining, in a vain effort to grasp what was slipping away due to this delay. He was sitting by the injured man's head and frowning. But Vyazemsky's sphere of action had begun to thin out, lighten, stretch into a shining ellipsoid, less and less weighed by the cares of this night, less and less sprinkled with the litter of revolution. The leading edge of the ellipsoid went into a future no one knew; the trailing edge, into the dear, bright past.

"I'm so sorry you never visited us in Lotaryovo, Aleksandr Ivanych. . . . Steppe all around, and every road an allée. How Boris and I loved to ride to the herds, to the meadows, to sit there in the grass. . . ."

That was where he had grown up, trying out young trotters on the race-course, taking trips to the herds, to the far end of the estate—a rider, a horse-man, a sportsman. He had cultivated hunting with hounds as well. Once, riding a half-Arab through the plowed fields, he had set off after a full-grown she-wolf, galloping twenty-five versts after her, and the she-wolf had flung itself on the horse's neck and scratched Dmitri's jacket. And in the forests of Aspen Grove, his maternal estate, here, outside Petersburg, on the Fin-land side, they'd hunted bobcats and set up a menagerie: bison, moose, and Ural goats.

If a moment had been missed, then it was not even over the disposition of detachments in the train stations or in tightening the reserve battalions—but over the Tsar's abdication. It was the abdication that would put everything on course. It was the abdication that would lift the danger of civil war. Only ab-dication could unite insurrectionist Petrograd and the quiet front. It was now, when things had got so out of hand in the capital, that was the strongest posi-tion for an ultimatum to the Tsar. They could set any terms for him and de-mand not just a responsible ministry but much more. Rodzyanko wasn't up to this, of course, and it was a good thing he hadn't gone to see the Tsar; he would just have spoiled everything.

"One time we caught a bear cub. And in the autumn we brought it to Pe-tersburg and donated it to the zoological garden. He grew up there for a long time, and they called him Mishka Vyazemsky."

The insoluble sphere around Guchkov's gloomy head whirled and thick-ened, ever darker and heavier; Vyazemsky's oval stretched out ever brighter and more naïve. As if it were Guchkov, not Vyazemsky, who had been wounded and was in danger.

"When we were just children, our father would pull us around the park in a low-slung donkey cart. There was an old peasant who mowed the grass in the park, and my father asked him whether he knew what kind of animal it was. He replied: 'Assuredly I know. It's a lion, the very beast the Savior rode.'"

This sudden immersion of Dmitri's into his childhood memories was frightening. Without knowing anything about where the bullet was, in what organ, the wounded man knew more about himself than an educated sur-geon could express.

Was he really? . . .

It might have been Guchkov in the front seat. Or the bullet could have missed.

So many times, with an almost pathological desire, had he sought not to miss out on danger anywhere on earth. Did Guchkov fear death or had he just not given it much thought? But he had always wanted to die—hand-somely! What he feared was dying insignificantly. There had been instances when he had crossed the line—in the Caspian Sea, in a vicious storm, in a tiny old boat with tangled sails, which he didn't know how to straighten out, and he wasn't a good swimmer. In the sea's fury he had experienced his first genuine total terror. But even at that moment he hadn't prayed—and there, having crossed the line, he hadn't sensed or believed in God.

Dmitri said in a bright voice:

"And at Korobovo next door, two versts from us, my father built a hospital as good as any in Petersburg."

And he'd donated it to the zemstvo. There was a small, ancient church there, too, and his great-grandmother remembered finding Tatar arrows in it. So his father built the peasants a spacious new church. And to train the chorus he brought in a chorister from Moscow's Archangel Cathedral. Engraved on the bell was this from Schiller: "I summon the living. I commemorate the dead. I drone in the fire." They added: "I save men in the blizzard. . . ."

". . . And under the church they put a crypt for our entire family. My grandmother and grandfather, father, and two aunts are there. Will I perhaps be the first of the younger ones to go there?"

"What are you saying, Mitya? Come to your senses. I don't recognize you. You'll sit out events in the hospital, yes. Then you'll get back up."

Guchkov tried to invest as much feeling as possible in his voice and force himself to be felt by this pinned body. But no, it wasn't his body that was wounded, and the tenacious, clawed, coiling sphere of action would not let go of his mind. Such a moment, such hours! But he was tied by circumstance, by sitting here. He was burning to race to the Tauride Palace as quickly as possible to see what had been happening without him.

"Here's the vexation, that Asya's not here, she could have brought the children. . . ."

"Well, she will tomorrow, to the hospital, Mitya. . . ."

As far as Guchkov knew, things were not all that straightforward with Asya either. Dmitri felt that the Shuvalovs had trapped him in reckless courting. For a long time Asya didn't know he thought so, and when she found out, their relationship cooled. But there were already two little ones.

"No, seriously," Vyazemsky said with mounting amazement on his steadily paler, long and narrow face. "If I die, tell my family, so they know, that I must be buried in Korobovo. It's not at all indifferent where a man lies."

Kapnist returned. With all this going on everywhere, he came up empty-handed for an ambulance.

Then Guchkov walked over to the telephone again.

Dmitri had attached himself to the leader of the Russia-wide opposition—but from the wrong side somehow. He had always been the perfect conservative, always opposed to any kind of liberal impudence, and never shy about saying so, and in the county zemstvo he had taunted the leftist majority. He had attached himself so it wouldn't all go to rack and ruin.

After all, even Guchkov was reproached for being a monarchist. And even Guchkov, after the Third Duma's declaration on Poland, had awaited his death from the Poles.

Once again he reached Lidia Leonidovna. She had found Professor Zeidler at a session of the City Duma, and he had promised to go immediately to the Kaufman community hospital and told her to take the wounded man there. Lari was looking for an ambulance right now. (Prince Illarion Vasilchikov, Lidia's husband, was also a prominent rank in the Red Cross.)

There, that's fine. It won't be long to wait now.

(Did Guchkov even have to wait around?)

Meanwhile, Dmitri was starting to hallucinate. Huge, enigmatically solitary oaks in the steppe. . . . The steppe flowering with yellow and blue flowers. . . . And outfalls in pink almond trees and white blackthorns. . . . The beauty, the Baigora River. And the peasants, the peasants. . . . Both those close to him—and strangers. . . . And some other language—and the main vital part of his native expanse. . . . An old woman, a centenarian, asking to kiss Dilka's hand and offended that they wouldn't let her: "They're proud now." . . . But in '05, in Arkadak in Saratov province, when the herd was set to roam—the swarm had revolted. At nineteen, Dmitri reared his horse on its hind legs and rode at the crowd. The troublemakers removed their caps. . . .

"Assuredly I know: it's a lion. . . ."

[293]

Ever since the Duma Committee, pressed by the crowd, had retreated from Rodzyanko's spacious office to more remote rooms in their wing, they had been set up quite uncomfortably, increasingly provisionally—and now there wasn't even a connecting room for negotiations with the Soviet. There wasn't the kind of long table where the two delegations could sit properly on two sides facing each other. Rather there were variously situated office desks (on them, alongside the documents, were empty, uncleared plates, bottles, and glasses), ordinary chairs, as well as a few armchairs, but the most inappropriate armchairs—low and with backs that tilted steeply, so that whoever sat in the armchair had no way to be at the level of the negotiations; on the other hand, given the universal exhaustion and insomnia, he could almost sleep.

Having stretched out on tables for the two revolutionary nights, Milyukov was extremely tired and, like everyone, was in great need of rest by midnight of the third night. However, he more than any other Duma deputy was aware of the importance of the impending moment—for the entire new Russian era. And for himself as well. Therefore he had to summon all his stamina—and he had incredible stamina!—in order to overpower the Soviet's deputies using the advantage of his intellect and experience.

None of the Duma deputies present could be his ally in the negotiations. Rodzyanko—better he not butt in to speak at all; his time had passed.

Kerensky was utterly unpredictable and alien. Nekrasov looked out rapaciously but was capable only of tripping them up. Shidlovsky was a placeholder, a zero. Shulgin had wit but no restraint, and he was a rightist and alien. Who would be irreplaceable was Maklakov, but he wasn't here and so be it. (Maklakov had gone off to be commissar of the Ministry of Justice, to expedite the first laws of the revolution.)

Not that anyone could or should be Milyukov's colleague in these negotiations. He alone should meet them, however many came, and alone grind them down.

As so they did not prepare out loud among themselves; all the preparation went on in Milyukov's head. He was anticipating serious pressure, even a direct attempt by them to grab all the government seats. Ever since '05 he'd known how hard it was to negotiate with leftists, how insistent and uncompromising they were. But Milyukov had no equal in apodictic dialog.

They went in. Four of them. Sleepy, weary, hoarse Chkheidze, tripping on the even floor—he too was a member of the Duma Committee, but these past few days he had avoided them like the plague, hadn't come here, and had only been seen as an orator above the troops. Tall, handsome Nakhamkes-Steklov and sturdy, short Sokolov. And—but not "and," rather before them all, like a boy ahead of the grownups—the frail, keen, shaven Himmer-Sukhanov. Shaven, or else his beard hadn't grown, he had bald spots near his large ears and high on his crown, and even higher, like a wig that's slipped back, he had a mat of gray hair rolled out flat.

Except for Chkheidze, no one tried to hide their importance and satisfaction at coming here and now shaking hands with the Duma Committee. But Himmer was especially transformed. It was impossible to recognize in him that fidgety individual they would come across in the corridors, who sometimes liked to horn in with a cheeky comment but was constantly finding out or reporting something—now, despite the same figure, despite the same sharpness of facial features and the turns of his head, this was an important, highly significant diplomat who shook hands or bowed his head with a special, calculated ceremony.

The new arrivals seated themselves importantly on the chairs, and an armchair was found for Chkheidze, who lowered himself into it weakly and ceased to exist.

They hadn't thought of how to begin, and now in addition the seating had turned out to be inconvenient for negotiations, and as it was there was no chairman or procedure, and a very general and unhurried discussion began—at half past midnight of the third sleepless night!—about how matters were going in the city in general. The great word "revolution" was not uttered, nor was any other significant word, but just: how matters were going in Petrograd. Look: clashes, misunderstandings, and excesses. And look: breakdown in the reserve regiments and violence against officers.

It wasn't an indifferent topic that had come up but rather the most opportune one for the Duma deputies. For them, this was exactly what they needed from the Soviet of Deputies, to give the Soviets a scare and compel them to tame the whirlwind.

But that wasn't what the Soviet needed! Seeing that the conversation had taken a dangerous turn toward diffusing and obscuring the central issues, Himmer abruptly went into action and announced he would like the floor. There was no one to give it to him, or not to, and it had been stated in a timely fashion—so the floor was his.

Milyukov hadn't anticipated his opponents speaking quite this intelligently and tactfully. To tie in to what had come before, but as if merely by the way, Himmer said that the struggle against anarchy was one of the Soviet's technical objectives, and one it was not neglecting, and right now a special proclamation to the soldiers was being printed about their attitude toward the officer class. . . .

"Ah, is that so?" The Duma deputies were pleasantly surprised.

. . . but the present conference should take up the central issues. As they knew, the creation of a new government was in the works. The Soviet of Workers' Deputies did not object and was even offering this right to the franchised elements, and even believed that this flowed from the current overall state of affairs.

A marvelous beginning! The direct struggle for power had immediately fallen away. The Soviets hadn't tried to seize it altogether. Milyukov relaxed a little. Bona fide negotiations had become possible.

However, the Soviet of Workers' Deputies, as the popular movement's ideological and organizational center, as the sole organ capable now of leading this movement into any given framework, the sole one possessing real power in the capital—as Himmer advanced, understanding perfectly the strength of his position—wished to express its attitude toward the new government being formed. How it viewed its objectives. And (expressively)—to avoid complications—to set forth those *demands* which might be presented in the name of all democracy—to the government the revolution had created.

It could not be denied that this was intelligently stated, as if it were feasible assistance rather than a confrontation or haggling.

His grasp was cold and firm, all the Duma deputies felt this immediately, but none of them would have to debate this and they could remain spectators. Milyukov tensed his strong neck, however, anticipating the blows. The situation was this: The State Duma had given the overthrow unity and strength, but now others had come from the outside and felt empowered to dictate!

Now the floor passed to Nakhamkes. The situation was unofficial and the speakers did not stand. But Nakhamkes, who had in his lap his points, which he had written on an uneven scrap of random paper, began speaking with great pomposity, formally even.

Once a youthful revolutionary, expelled from the seventh grade of his Odessa high school, and a Yakut exile, then in émigré wanderings, then in the first revolution under Trotsky, and arrested in this very same Petersburg Soviet of Workers' Deputies, and once again, once again the pointless émigré years—Nakhamkes couldn't have imagined for himself this height and significance, that here he was proposing a government, that here the most renowned bourgeois leaders were sitting listening to his conditions. He didn't just read them one after the other and didn't even state how many there were, in order to have a stronger effect, but reading one point in a calm, restrained voice, not in any hurry to clarify or give his reasons, as if condescending.

All this put together came out long.

But the first point, which could have been immediately devastating, was merely a general amnesty. For all crimes, including political ones, including terrorist ones, including military uprisings and pogroms against landowners.

In good conscience, the Kadet leader could make no objection to this! A general amnesty had always been the trump card of the Duma and the Bloc against the government and had always been the favorite slogan of the entire intelligentsia, ever since the First Duma.

The second point was just as indubitable and just as intellectually acceptable: freedom of speech, assembly, unions, and strikes. Who could oppose this?

True, with an extension—extending those rights to the army. (But after all, democratization of the army had always been in the Kadet program. And it had been put forward even in 1906 at the negotiations with Stolypin.)

Immediately, though, Milyukov began to object. He believed that in the present situation this would give rise to chaos in the army, which would lose its battle-readiness *en masse*. Nakhamkes, on the contrary, argued with great calm that this demand was perfectly compatible with preserving the army's battle-readiness. That giving the soldier mass all these political and civil rights would cleave the army to the revolution's objectives and its battle-readiness would, on the contrary, strengthen. He cited examples plucked from his own service as a private and supposedly from European armies.

Himmer spoke as well, and the debate stretched on. But from the Duma deputies' side, only Shulgin, who barely sat but nervously paced, occasionally butted in, exclaiming agitatedly. Everyone else was silent, as if it didn't affect them at all, and Nekrasov was absolutely implacable. He was very good at being silent when doing so was advantageous. And Kerensky was completely silent.

Rodzyanko was drinking soda water and wiping away perspiration. He had a mournful look, as if his head hurt badly or his whole self was ailing.

Milyukov calculated that it was more important for him to hear the full list of points than to argue over each one in turn. Leaving the argument unresolved, he asked him to go on.

But the third point was for the government to refrain from all actions that could predetermine the form of governance.

My my! That meant opening the way to a republic!

He couldn't help but take a stand on this! Especially since the Soviet's delegation was proposing that all these points, after their passage, the government had to publish in *its own* name—simultaneously with its declaration of its own creation. What was that? In the complex conditions of a government being started, to start as well from a total shattering of foundations?

He had to take a stand! Introduce a republic immediately? That would summon up the most terrible troubles in the country!

He couldn't lay out all his arguments openly, though! For many long months the Kadets had been trying to storm the throne, and the more widespread the opinion that the dynasty had rotted away, the better it was for their political movement. Nonetheless, the Kadets' program called for a constitutional monarchy. But right now, when real power was already flowing into their waiting fingers, there was no more stable foundation for it than the hereditary dynasty. Yes, the throne was constantly tottering—that was true. But now that it had tottered too much, it had to be supported. Herein lay the dialectic. In order to take power, it was not at all necessary that the previous authority come crashing down. Then chaos would ensue and it was entirely unknown to whom the authority would obtain. Seize power—but gently, without letting the previous one fall. Simplest of all would be to replace just the monarch. The current one was very stubborn, and over the past twenty-two years he'd learned to dig his heels in, and there would be no working with him. Public opinion was already strained, though, especially among the socialists, so that Milyukov would be ashamed to stand before them with an explication of these arguments, as if he were the defender of the universally hated, cursed, and condemned Romanov dynasty. Thus, he had to construct complex sentences with complex jurisprudential and governmental arguments in order to surround his position with these spectral bastions. You must understand, gentlemen, the monarchy will do nothing to destroy our *modus gubernandi*.

Or rather, he could have spoken to them comprehensibly had there been only four of them here—three from the Soviet and Milyukov. Given the numerous Duma deputies here, he felt uncomfortable expressing this simple argument too simply: "You must understand. The heir is a sick little boy, and the regent Mikhail is a very foolish man. What could be more favorable for all of us? A minor heir under a weak regent will not exercise his authority as full bearer of power—and this will give us the opportunity to gain strength!"

However, as a master of political-juridical speech, he composed this into sentences about the personal dynastic situation being most favorable to the strengthening for us of constitutional principles, which needed time to strengthen. The monarchy simply could not be restored at its former strength.

They objected, citing the universal hatred for the monarchy, saying that it was discredited in the eyes of the popular masses.

Yes, Milyukov understood how shameful this would look from the outside, that he was coming forward as a defender of this dynasty. As a practical politician, though, he could not concede this support to his own future government.

Well, apparently everyone understood his euphemisms, everyone except Sokolov—they weren't stupid men.

And Nikolai? Milyukov had not defended Nikolai. Abdication was now inevitable.

Kerensky was sullen and even demonstratively scornful. In the presence of Duma and Soviet deputies, it was important for him to maintain a balance and not show whose side he was on. He was above all sides.

Rodzyanko was sucking out of his glass, quite ill and unfortunate, a handkerchief to his forehead.

Shulgin was apparently having a fit of hysteria. He imagined that something two-headed was rising up in these negotiations, not the usual two-headed eagle, but the two heads of the new government—and he seriously disliked that second head. But did it seem to be rising over all Russia? Who were the Duma deputies here? Russia-wide names, famed politicians. Who were these newcomers? Scribblers no one knew and chosen to come here by no one knew whom. And here they had come to dictate conditions, even the dynasty's overthrow! And they had the power; that could be felt. And the Russia-wide figures were supposed to implore them?

One time Shulgin still reproached them in a restrained way for undermining the State Duma, the hope of the entire people. This didn't affect them in the least. Another time he shouted at them:

"Fine! Arrest us all! Put us in the Peter and Paul Fortress! And govern yourselves! Otherwise, let us govern as we see fit!"

Red-bearded Nakhamkes, with his calm magnanimity and, what was outrageous, his genteel intonation, responded to that nervous exclamation:

"We have no intention of arresting you."

But it had come out: we have no intention, although naturally we could.

All of a sudden—no one was expecting it—Vladimir Lvov burst out from his black-bearded and burning-eyed silence. He broke in at a pause, not asking anyone, and began stormily, nearly exploding from emotions. But what emotions?

Himmer had vaguely counted him among the strong rightists and was stunned: this ridiculous, bald, wild, and rather foolish man, from his deep armchair where, it turned out, he had not been sleeping, began to speak, lashing sentence after sentence, saying that he was a republican! He considered Tsarism's return worse than death! And the new government wouldn't bring it back for anything! But. But! But returning Tsarism was exactly what the Soviet of Workers' Deputies wanted with its insane policy of breaking down the army during time of war. There would be a military defeat, and Wilhelm would impose Tsarism on us.

Lvov piled on so much nonsense that no one took him seriously. Nonetheless, he had shaken Milyukov.

Right then Engelhardt came in and reminded Rodzyanko that the time had come for him to go to the direct line for negotiations with Pskov.

Rodzyanko picked up his handkerchief, girded himself, put on his fur coat and cap, and went out, only to return very quickly, again with an un- happy look:

"Let the gentlemen worker deputies give me a guard! Or come with me themselves! Otherwise they'll arrest me along the way or there, at the tele- graph office."

Nakhamkes began to rock with good-natured and pleased laughter. Now it wasn't he but Himmer, with a stinging smile and even insinuatingly, who began reassuring the Duma President that they had no intention whatso- ever of arresting him.

They instructed Sokolov to go find escorts for Rodzyanko.

But they had to move on through the points. Himmer and Nakhamkes exchanged glances. Right now was the point they had agreed to concede to Milyukov immediately: a Constituent Assembly. Either call it something else or remove it altogether.

They pronounced: take immediate measures to convene a Constituent Assembly on the basis of universal, equal, direct, and secret voting.

And Milyukov nodded.

Nodded?

He wrote it down and nodded, as at an easy point, waiting for the next.

How were they supposed to understand this? Himmer and Nakhamkes again exchanged darting glances. Having just spent half an hour arguing against not predetermining the form of governance, how had he yielded so easily to a Constituent Assembly? He had let the form of governance hang while the Constituent Assembly decided—and of course not in favor of a monarchy! When a revolution spreads broadly enough, a republic is assured.

He just nodded? He conceded right away?

Himmer now saw even more perceptively the correctness of his tactic. If the demand had been thrust forward about the immediate cessation of the war, the rejection of territorial acquisitions, and loyalty to the Allies, even the harsh imposition of any domestic undertakings, Milyukov might have immediately spurned them. But tomorrow, no one knew what there would be. After all, Tsarist troops were on their way toward Petrograd, and in the Soviet itself the unreconciled Mensheviks could dispute the actions of the self-styled delegation and the as yet unsettled points. No, they had to hurry specifically to install the franchised elements into a government.

But why this calm about a Constituent Assembly?

Either it was something very clever, or the famous parliamentarian's mind had failed him.

[294]

It is the duty of the chief of staff not only to submit an idea to his com- mander but also to draw up a prepared document so that all that remains is to sign. During the course of the day, it had become increasingly incontrovertible to General Alekseev that the Emperor could not fail to allow a responsible ministry. And by evening he realized that it was up to him to compose the requisite manifesto right there, at GHQ—and deliver it to the Emperor for signature while he was still in Pskov with all due haste.

With the help of the diplomatic office attached to GHQ the necessary manifesto was written, and meanwhile Alekseev composed as well a final, decisive, convincing telegram to the Emperor that included the manifesto being prepared as a component part. If the previous night it had become clear to the general that the publication of such an act stemmed from the calm established in Petrograd, then here it became all the more necessary, due to the danger of anarchy spreading through the country and the army. In order to save the army and prosecute the war, the only solution was to call for a responsible ministry and entrust it to Rodzyanko. And to hurry, so that the Duma figures would be able to safeguard the regime from extreme leftist elements.

He was nervous while they were composing the manifesto—and even more nervous after ten o'clock in the evening, when they transmitted the manifesto to Pskov. It was not clear whether the Tsar was still there or whether Ruzsky had maintained contact with him. How had the Emperor reacted to all the day's previous telegrams sent on to him? And how had he taken this last one?

But it was hard to find out anything properly. All the leadership there had left headquarters for the train station, the only person left being Quartermaster General Boldyrev, who then stopped coming to the telegraph, and it was headquarters colonels instead. They themselves were not initiated into what was going on, and when they did find anything out they neglected to immediately report to GHQ, as they had been ordered and asked. Several times Alekseev queried Pskov on the fate of the telegram with the manifesto and insisted that it be taken immediately to the Emperor at the train station. There it went through the duty officer, through Quartermaster General Boldyrev, through Chief of Staff Danilov—and finally, at around eleven o'clock, it reached Commander-in-Chief Ruzsky at the station, and he would personally report to the Emperor.

Also at around eleven o'clock Northern Army Group headquarters did not know when the Emperor intended to quit Pskov.

Alekseev was beside himself from worry. He would lie down and get up again, and sit at his desk with his greatcoat draped over his shoulders, trying to deal with the latest papers—but there was no ease for his soul; right now the entire fate of Russia and the front hung on the manifesto.

Meanwhile, new, quite remarkable information was trickling in from Petrograd. That His Majesty's Convoy, in full, with the permission of their officers, had today appeared at the State Duma! That the Empress herself had tried to gain a meeting with Rodzyanko! That Grand Duke Kirill

Vladimirovich had personally arrived at the State Duma to welcome it! And which prominent dignitaries had been arrested in Petrograd. And the Petrograd officers had resolved to recognize the Duma Committee!

This important news had to reach the Emperor as soon as possible if it was to influence his decision! It was after midnight when Klembovsky conveyed all this to Pskov.

When major events begin, they invariably come together for some reason in the night or, at least, in such a way that military leaders have to come up with all their decisions and all their actions at night.

Alekseev discovered an oversight: for a full day they had not informed Ivanov of all the events in Petrograd and Moscow or of the steps taken by the chief of staff—and it was more urgent and important for Ivanov than anyone else to know, or else something might begin there. Klembovsky started to prepare a telegram for him.

After one in the morning, Pskov telegraphed—not about the Emperor's decision yet, but that His Majesty had authorized the commander-in-chief to discuss over the telegraph with the State Duma President and that this conversation would begin at two-thirty in the morning.

Here was when everything would be decided, then. May as well not sleep, just wait.

Pskov also telegraphed that the Luga garrison had mutinied and gone over to the Duma Committee's side, and a question had arisen about returning the troops sent from the Northern Army Group, about which its commander-in-chief would have a report with the Emperor.

Oho! A serious decision was coming to a head, much bigger than would be given rise to by a single Luga garrison, where there wasn't a single competent combat unit. There were other roads to Petrograd, too. But that meant Ruzsky was taking advantage of the occasion to convince him to stop advancing troops altogether.

And that was correct. That eased Alekseev's burden as well. For a full two days his order on sending troops and troop movement had been developing, and Alekseev formally had not violated it in any way, other than stopping the Southwest Army Group, but he had also moved those regiments himself, without the Emperor. Formally, he had not violated the order in any way, but he felt less and less sympathy for the plan. Sending troops against their own Russians was unthinkable!

Lukomsky fed his doubts, too. Lukomsky believed that sending troops to suppress an uprising was extremely dangerous. It made no sense to act in small numbers, but assembling large forces could take ten days, and by then all the cities and the entire rear would have been overtaken by revolution. Thus they would have to wage war against the Germans and against their own rear, and that was impossible simultaneously. Stripping the front—did that not mean stopping the war with the Germans? Having spent so many lives on this war? . . .

So there was consensus that the revolution had to be stopped peacefully. That is, with concessions.

But it was too late for small concessions.

And where did the major ones begin? And *what* were the major ones?

This was left unsaid among the three of them, the heads of GHQ, but there was something tortuous weighing on their minds.

But in Pskov there was immediate success! They hadn't reported directly about the Emperor's decision, but at half past one in the morning a copy of Danilov's telegram was sent to his Fifth Army, where, with supreme assent, he ordered the return to the Dvina District of the troops headed for Petrograd! And he asked GHQ to inform Ivanov, if possible, because the Northern Army Group headquarters didn't know his location.

So swiftly and easily, evidently, had the supreme assent been obtained!

Despite his infirmity, stooped, his greatcoat draped over his shoulders, Alekseev began to pace. Now an altogether different telegram would go out to Ivanov. Although he wasn't subordinate to GHQ, and you couldn't order him.

Now, though, if the Northern Army Group had been recalled, how could the Western move?

There were no instructions about the Western, though. Since the Emperor had left, in those two full days, he had not responded to his chief of staff with a single word. Was he angry over something? . . . Alekseev had the feeling that, yes, he had left displeased. But now—now he had to strike while the iron was hot. He had to immediately request (he'd already instructed Lukomsky) supreme instructions as to whether the regiments of the Western Army Group could be sent back, too.

Lukomsky went to telegraph, but Alekseev was left feeling there would be no reply to him from the Emperor. There would be no reply, and Evert's regiments were moving toward an irreparable clash—and this now hung on the conscience of Alekseev alone.

As of yet, there had been no shooting anywhere. He had to be in time to stop it.

But he didn't dare stop troops without permission!

Nor could he permit a bloody clash!

Right then they slipped him one more telegram. What was this? Nekrasov, Rodzyanko's deputy, informed him with alarm that, according to a message from the Duma Committee, the Emperor's train was in Pskov and evidently had not been sent on to Tsarskoye Selo.

This was what they called fresh news? In the Duma they obviously knew even less about events. Nothing at all. But what gladdened him was the amiability of the very fact of this telegram. That they had addressed Alekseev as they would one of their own, as an ally.

And that was right. That had to be supported.

It was already two in the morning. The telegram had gone to Pskov, but they had other things on their mind there: the conversation with Rodzyanko was just about to begin. Couldn't they now race to the station to see the Emperor, and would their Emperor receive them so late? He had probably gone to bed already. So wait until tomorrow morning?

Troops don't wait, though, and the troop trains move even at night—and all of a sudden, at an unexpected hour in an unexpected place someone somewhere could clash and Russian blood could be shed—and that would mean civil war! And it was General Alekseev who had allowed it to go this far.

Much had fallen to his lot these past two days. His inflamed chest breathed heavily. However long he'd served, forty years, he had never acted without permission, without his superiors' assent—and now he himself was supposed to decide? . . .

But hadn't he already stalled the Southwest? He himself had offered all these regiments to the Emperor and could have offered others, fewer in number, couldn't he?

His heart was breaking from the unprecedented tension and his own audacity. Hastening to catch up with the nighttime minutes, he again summoned the ruddy-cheeked but cold Lukomsky and ordered him to telegraph the Western Army Group to hold back all troops! Any not yet dispatched should not embark. Any en route should be held at major stations. Additional instructions would follow later.

He didn't bring them back entirely. But he did stop them.

And this felt like the correct step.

Would he have to answer to the Emperor? . . . But even the Emperor had abandoned him without rudder or sail.

Now he just hoped Ivanov wouldn't blunder into battle!

[2 9 5]

The trials that came crashing down that day would have wearied an even greater giant than Rodzyanko. The entire day spent either burning up or freezing. The long day had begun with him stopping eight regiments by brute force. Then he and Engelhardt had saved Petrograd from a new soldier insurrection (and the people who had threatened to kill the President—they remembered that now), which could flare up again at any hour. Five times, on three trains, he had tried to go to see the Emperor—without success. At the mercy of other people, he had felt the ground crumble beneath his feet the entire day. And while he greeted the soldier formations as the chief here, behind his back silent gnawers were gnawing away at his senior and singular position. Mighty though he was, he could not think of what he should undertake.

They were digging not only under him but under the Emperor as well. At first, Guchkov and then others tried to explain to him that Nikolai Aleksandrovich was obviously not to reign in Russia any longer. This had been decided by certain underground forces, without the President.

And at first this was inadmissible. But later, after he thought and sorted through everything—Rasputin, Protopopov, the evil Tsaritsa, and the disrespect for the Duma—then perhaps it had been inevitable.

The day's cauterizations did not end here, though. The President had been finished off by the nighttime negotiations between his Committee and the Soviet of Workers' Deputies. All day, from one hour to the next, Duma deputies had been talking about the Soviet with dread, constantly looking over their shoulders, so that eventually even Rodzyanko himself was a little afraid. But now, tonight, three "workers' deputies" of whom no one had the faintest idea, not a clue, who were not known for anything in Russia and had no significance, had come with Chkheidze and had sat as equals across from the best-known members of the Duma, to say nothing of the President—who did not say a word to them and sat to the side and shot them wild looks. He'd been gripped by unrelenting spasm, for something of a great Eclipse had befallen Russia. (As one of the prophets had said, apparently, but you weren't going to mention that in the State Duma.)

These deputies sat there—one, a redhead, sprawling, while the other two kept twitching—and they weren't embarrassed in the least by their lack of eminence or their appearance from the ashes. Only now, at this nighttime session, did Rodzyanko examine these brigands and get an earful of them. Nothing embarrassed them, and they explained to Milyukov with derision, condescension, and confidence that their side was going to win out.

The brigandish points they advanced were beyond the pale.

The negotiations didn't even mention the State Duma, or even any constitution, and the Emperor was assumed to be dead altogether.

The President, who just three days ago had been the number two man in the government, sat here, at these negotiations, as if swept aside—and for the first time understood his own impotence. Not this afternoon, when Milyukov and Nekrasov hadn't let him go to Dno, but right now.

What would it cost these voluble bandits, at any moment, to order everyone here, the Duma deputies, arrested?

Even Rodzyanko himself?

Just as the President of the State Council had been arrested and nothing could be done. And the former ministers. However bad they were, and however much we had argued, nonetheless, they weren't murderers. Meanwhile, they were being kept under lock and key, with fierce precautions, all together, and weren't even given beds, worse than a prison cell. And the plan was to send them on to the Peter and Paul Fortress.

So couldn't they arrest Rodzyanko himself at any moment?

Hang him even?

And he couldn't go home. He couldn't escape these rooms. So the summons conveyed from General Ruzsky to the General Staff for a telegraph conversation came as quite a relief.

This was marvelous! And this would be like a substitute for his trip to Pskov.

With the difference that if you went you'd be a guest there and even a captive of the generals, but from here you speak as the head of revolutionary Petrograd.

His soul was still scarred from Alekseev's reproof, and he felt a need to smooth it over. And also to get away from these horrible *points*, this vile meeting. He barely lasted until the appointed two o'clock in the morning.

He had already left when he suddenly thought: How would he get there? Through these wild streets, completely unprotected, when someone was seeking to tear him apart. His own Russian people—yet here they could stop you in the middle of the street and you wouldn't know how to talk to them, in what language.

There was nothing to be done for it. He returned to the meeting and asked those villains to provide him with some kind of guard, from them specifically, so that he wouldn't get arrested en route. Not just someone with a rifle, but someone *from them*—then they wouldn't touch him.

Yes, he had to admit that all the power had suddenly shifted to *them*.

They gave it. Some loudmouth, a sergeant. And two sailors.

For the second night in a row, Rodzyanko was riding to the General Staff. As if it were a regular undertaking. Today, it was even later and more deserted.

He rode, despising his escorts.

There was a wrinkle: Ruzsky would ask why Rodzyanko had still not formed a ministry.

But he had to look beyond that. This conversation was to stop the troops for good. And pacify everything. And save everyone.

Once again—save everyone.

But there was hardly any way to help the Emperor.

Now that it had been decided that Rodzyanko would not be the government, evidently only abdication could save him.

Oh, Emperor, Emperor! You yourself are largely to blame! How many times had the loyal President cautioned and warned you!

The General Staff—enormous, semicircular, dark from the shuttered windows, filled with military men, officers, and duty officers—had stood through the days of revolution neutral and untouched by either side.

Herein lay the universal respect for the war. It was a symbol that the Fatherland could withstand anything, including these upheavals.

He walked down the Staff's endless, curving, electric-lit, parquet corridors and thought that even *he*—what could one man do against the universal stream? Was he to perish now personally defending his unreasonable Emperor?

After all, the heir would have Mikhail as regent. The President had great influence over Mikhail.

If the State Duma stood, Russia would abide as well.

[2 9 6]

General Ivanov was met at the palace by two counts—middle-aged Apraksin and dried-up old Benckendorff—with great hope and delight.

The more insistently they approach you, the more importantly you must comport yourself, so as not to be degraded. And say as little as possible.

While they were waiting for the audience, for about ten minutes, the general didn't let a thing slip. But from them he heard that the Guards of the Combined Regiment and the Convoy's Cossacks had been assembled in the extensive palace cellars in order to be summoned at the alarm at any moment. But around the palace, by arrangement with the rebels, a neutral zone had been created where neither one went with weapons. That evening, though, there had been a panic that the neighboring Lycée had been seized by a gang of unknown soldiers that was about to fire on the palace. Then they'd sent a scout there, and the rumor turned out to be empty. There was no one there.

The two counts, on either side of Iudovich, vied in their worry about what would happen to them and the palace, and they looked into the general's eyes with hope. But the general was the commander-in-chief of the capital District, and even the dictator, and could not give them private explanations.

The Empress had always regarded General Ivanov with extreme approval. She had received him very graciously last autumn. Through her he had occasionally petitioned the Emperor indirectly for what he could not directly. Nikolai Iudovich had to be extremely obliged to her—and this constrained him all the more in the current difficult circumstances.

The Empress received him wearing a dark gray dress and a nurse's kerchief, her only jewelry some large amber stones in several loops on her chest. Her face was crumpled and weary, but at the same time it retained an assertive energy, even a proud and cold beauty, with her large eyes.

She walked through the room with unceremonious speed—as if she were rushing toward Nikolai Iudovich, as if she were prepared to embrace him. She held out both her hands at once, to both of his:

"General! What happiness! What happiness you've come, our deliverer!" she said in Russian, almost entirely correctly, but tensely, the way foreigners speak. She was very welcoming, but no smile touched her lips. "How we have been awaiting you! I was afraid you wouldn't get here!"

Iudovich knew his own captivating look and captivating voice, and he knew how to make everyone like him with his good nature. He had always been liked at royal tables. Added to his advantageous appearance was also the broad bass from his broad chest:

"What do you mean, Your Majesty! How could I not come here? It was an order. But yes, there were obstacles."

"Please, do sit!" she pointed impulsively to an armchair and herself sat not far away on a banquette, as if in no need of a prop for her tall, even back—and held on to the banquette's handles as if they were a ship's handrails when you ascend through a ship, and also her hands were trembling:

"The Emperor telegraphed me that he was sending troops. Do you have many troops? And the cavalry from Novgorod? Where are they assembling?"

Come to the point this quickly, and soon there would be nothing left to talk about. Nikolai Iudovich drew it out:

"We're fine for troops, Your Imperial Majesty. An infantry brigade and a cavalry brigade apiece from each army group. But until everyone assembles . . ."

He knew he had taken on a martial look. Only strategic obstacles could restrain a courageous general from an offensive.

"When was the last time you saw the Emperor?" the Empress asked even more impatiently, overtaking herself.

"When? . . . The night before, Your Majesty."

"When was that?" Concern ran nervously over her directly displayed face. On her face he now saw reddened areas, like large spots of an unjoyful flush.

The general spoke from the depth of his graying beard:

"The night before last. Life has started to be more at night."

She didn't notice the reproach, or there might not have been one:

"What kind of mood was he in? How did he view events?"

"His mood was calm."

"Before that night, the day before yesterday, I sent him three desperate telegrams about the situation in Petrograd. Did he really not receive them? . . . How could he not reply? Had they already been intercepting them then?"

Behind the curtain of his shovel-shaped beard, with his broad, low forehead, the general was in no hurry to reply.

Chasing after his nonforthcoming words with a harsh, searching gaze, leaning all the way forward from the corner of the couch, with her long Roman nose, she burst out impatiently:

"Tell me. Where is the Emperor right now? He should have arrived here this last morning! And he didn't! . . . Is he not following behind you? Why didn't your trains proceed together?"

"Not at all, Your Majesty. The Emperor saw fit to take a different route, through Bologoye."

"Then he's been detained!" The Empress's eyes glittered. "Where has he been detained? By whom? I have no contact with him!"

"I cannot know, Your Imperial Majesty. I came thinking to find the Emperor here. And who would dare detain him?" Nikolai Iudovich was genuinely surprised. "Is there really insurrection everywhere along his route?"

The Empress's tautness relaxed. She clutched at her heart with one hand:

"Oh, now I don't believe anything. I don't know anything. If someone dares *stop* the Emperor, I no longer understand anything!"

Should he tell her or not?

"The Vyritsa stationmaster told me that he had information that the royal trains had passed through Dno today."

"Dno?" The Empress perked up with new hope. "But then he should already be here, shouldn't he? Already approaching?"

Nikolai Iudovich spread his large peasant palms.

"I have no way of knowing. Maybe he went somewhere else?"

"But where else?" The throat under the Tsaritsa's long, imperious face shook. "Where else if not to his family?"

"GHQ perhaps?" Nikolai Iudovich murmured implacably.

"GHQ?" the Tsaritsa repeated thoughtfully. "But he has to come here!"

The old general was bitterly perplexed.

"But I can't imagine they would dare detain the Emperor."

It was as if the Empress's very bones had softened. It had become hard for her to sit without a backrest. She rose (and the general leapt up) and walked over with a none too confident step and sat down in an armchair (while the general lowered himself).

"Oh, general!" she said. "We have long suffered from being surrounded by insincere people. So few loyal ones remain!"

Nikolai Iudovich looked at the Empress devotedly.

"I don't want to believe it," she said in a powerful low voice. "But they brought us news that today Grand Duke Kirill Vladimirovich and his Guards Crew had gone to the Duma to pay homage! If grand dukes are leading the Guards like this, judge for yourself who we can rely upon!"

The old general's face darkened, poor thing. He could not even imagine such treachery.

But he confirmed that he did have this sad information about the Guards Crew.

"And I didn't believe it! It's not to be believed! We always loved the Guards Crew so! And two of their companies are here now, in the palace, guarding us!"

Sparks blazed up but went out in her expressive gray eyes. Her stern, decisive face had lived by faith alone. And with the loss of faith, it had lost its form.

However, the honest general could do nothing about these traitors.

Less agitated now, shifting to a practical tone:

"When do you think you will enter Petrograd, general?"

Nikolai Iudovich exhaled powerfully with his heroic broad chest:

"It's difficult to say, Your Majesty. After all, I now have eight hundred men. What can I do? I have come to command the District's troops—but they might simply arrest me."

The general's rather simple face expressed his racked mind.

"Yes, but the regiments are on their way to you!" The Empress was now sitting not tensed, leaning against the high back and clutching her heart. This was not a gesture of emotion but apparently actual pain, and her undying eyes blazed anew: "There are horrors being perpetrated in Petrograd! They're looting apartments, destroying homes, here they've set fire to Frederiks's, they're drinking with abandon and killing officers. All this must be stopped immediately! But without bloodshed."

"Everything has already calmed down in Petrograd," Nikolai Iudovich objected, handsome and bright-eyed.

"What do you mean calmed down? When?" The Empress was astonished. "Where did you get this information? I know, for example, . . . Only just now . . . Even here in Tsarskoye . . ."

"Not at all, Your Majesty"—the broad-browed general swayed. "We know that everything has calmed down in Petrograd."

"And where is this coming from? That's just not so!"

"Kindly see, I just received a telegram from GHQ. There is a new government in Petrograd. The former ministers have, of course, been arrested, and this is deeply grievous, but the new government has adhered to the monarchical principle, and I've been ordered to enter into negotiations."

"What negotiations?" the Empress gasped. "Those are brigands, thieves, enemies of the Emperor there! What negotiations with them? This is a drunken gang or traitors to the fatherland and must be immediately dispersed! And all of them arrested!"

She threw that out precisely, and such a decisive, harsh expression came over her face, and the necklace on her chest jumped—you'd think she was ready to lead the troops now herself.

"But GHQ—"

"What can GHQ understand from there? The Emperor's gone, and Alekseev is still ill. What can he decide?" the Tsaritsa raged, and rage suited her face very well.

However, her agitation did not convey itself to Iudovich, who remained quite pacific: respectful but not agreeing.

"Kindly see, Your Imperial Majesty, it is an order. It has been ordered not to initiate internecine strife." He answered her with sorrow, even, that they were not letting him wield his general's authority. But after all, they could not lay down their own people with such a war under way.

"Internecine strife? Of course not! Bloodshed? Under no circumstance! But you will assemble all your regiments and enter the city in a triumphant march with music! And that's all! Some will scatter immediately, while others will immediately obey and calm down. And that's all. Just so the authority of the government is made manifest! Bloodshed—of course there must be none, under any circumstance!"

Well, that was exactly the same thing the general had said. Exactly what he had been ordered.

"But what negotiations? What 'new government'?" The Empress rose in vexation—and the general rose immediately as well. She started pacing around the room, and he turned toward wherever she was.

This "new government" seared her most vexatiously of all, and she had no desire to hear about it (although she had been compelled to ask Rodzyanko for protection). Pretenders! Duma scoundrels!

She cracked her knuckles impotently. Her accent became stronger:

"But this order doesn't come from the Emperor, does it?"

"The Supreme Commander's chief of staff," the general reminded her respectfully. "I have no communication with His Majesty."

Yes! It all came back to that! There was no communication with the Emperor! The Emperor had to be found and rescued!

She stopped. And folded her hands over her chest, as if prayerfully:

"You're right, general. Before acting, right now the most important thing for us is to find and free the Emperor."

The most important thing right now was for the Emperor and Empress to be united. Right now, under the general's protection, the entire family could go to him. But she couldn't tear the sick from their beds, given the mishaps of a journey, and no one knew where to go, and the general's detachment was not larger than the defenders they had here in the palace.

"The Emperor must be rescued!" she decided finally. "And the way here opened to him. Can you bring the Emperor's train here?"

The hero's broad, tested chest sighed, and his ash-gray beard fluttered:

"Your Imperial Majesty! I am at full readiness! If I am able to break through to Dno, I will go on to search for His Majesty's train and free it— and he will come to you!"

The general stood there without swaying and looked without blinking, a wise old commander.

(Then he would be released—not only from the campaign against Petrograd but even to base his headquarters in Tsarskoye Selo.)

He truly felt sorry for the Empress with her sick children and two versts from insurrectionist regiments. But the guard here was decent.

The Empress looked hopefully and gratefully at the dear old man who had gradually come to comprehend the situation. She brightened at a new thought:

"General! I have a letter for the Emperor that cannot fall into *their* hands. In it I write frankly about our circumstances and plans. . . ."

She finished speaking as she was already on the move. Lifting her long skirt slightly, she quickly exited the room. A rustle was heard from behind the portiere and a conversation in English.

Iudovich quickly got the idea. God forbid he take such a letter. After all, he could be seized and searched at any moment, like the most common officer, even now, in deserted Tsarskoye Selo, even before he reached the station. They weren't going to pat him on the head for a letter like that: a participant in a conspiracy.

The Empress returned holding the letter, presenting it with a smile. She held out to him—her fingers beringed and with the Emperor's wedding ring—an envelope.

Iudovich, with the same nobility of an old general, informed her with heartfelt loyalty:

"Your Imperial Majesty, this is utterly impossible. I might fall in battle. I have a detachment in my hands. And I'm not certain I'll reach the Emperor quickly myself."

"Then send someone!" She still would not take back the proffered envelope.

"Absolutely not, Your Majesty. I do not have a reliable man like that with whom to send it."

In regal disbelief, the Empress tossed her head back, in a gesture that showed her breeding.

Iudovich turned himself inside out, explaining:

"Your Imperial Majesty, my service as an officer is alien to any sort of self-seeking. . . . Forty-seven and a half years . . . After all, this is not for my sake. How can I risk your precious letter? How can I allow your most august plans to fall into the hands of some scoundrel? . . ."

General Ivanov was in a great hurry to get away from the palace, but in the bright entrance hall he was chased down by the duty officer and given from the palace telegraph office another new telegram—in a sealed gray envelope with the palace coat of arms—which had just arrived.

Annoyed that he hadn't managed to get away, the general opened it.

The thick paper was the same, with the palace coat of arms, and written on it in a handsome calligraphic hand:

"Pskov, 0:20. I hope you arrived safely. Before my arrival and your report to me, I ask you not to take any measures. Nikolai."

Well! The last shackles had fallen from the burdened general's arms. He did not have to enter Petrograd! He did not have to assemble the troops! He did not even have to take any decisions. Nor did he have to rescue the Emperor, who would come himself!

Excellent! Splendid! Nikolai Iudovich had envisioned it all—and all correctly! It was good he hadn't started firing, that would have been a mess. It was good he hadn't stuck his nose into Petrograd.

Cheerful, he rode through the drunken or frightened desertedness of Tsarskoye Selo. Nowhere were there any crowds, patrols, sentries, or pedestrians; everything had been cleared away into the houses and barracks. And there was a crisp frost! He reached the train station safely.

In the poorly lit station was his dark troop train of fifty train cars. Ivanov ordered them readied for departure. Both locomotives had already been attached behind. For better concentration it was clear he needed to pull back.

And take the stationmaster with him as a hostage — so that they wouldn't start something with the switches or connections.

He ordered them to start immediately using the two locomotives — back, to Vyritsa.

*　　*　　*

A HERO'S BEARD, A CONSCIENCE OF CLAY

*　　*　　*

[2 9 7]

Evert had been beside himself all day. There were no events at the front, but the wind of alarm was blowing on his back — and there was nothing left to do but sit and reread, reread and try to make sense of this stack of inexplicable telegrams.

But they were not to be made sense of.

Nor could Alekseev be reached by direct line — either he was sick or Lukomsky would come to the line instead.

Revolt was spilling through Russia with brazen impunity — and GHQ was making no effort to prevent it, actually reporting a calming.

The abruptness of the change was striking. What had cracked? What had broken? Three days ago, all of this was criminally punishable — and here it was proceeding without anyone trying to prevent it.

Evert sat over these telegraph tapes, holding his large, uncomprehending head in his large hands: never had he thought that he would have to engage in politics. All his life he had served in the imperial army, this was his third reign, and his third major war, and he knew he served the throne and the homeland, and everyone around him served the throne and the homeland, and there were no cracks where doubt might creep in about anyone or anything. But what was this going on now? And what should be done?

In and of itself, he, the Western Army Group, the central group of the front, the Second, Third, and Tenth armies, was a huge force — but he himself didn't know how to wield it. Did the fact that Evert stood, broad-shouldered, from the Western Dvina to the Pinsk swamps mean he could shrug his shoulders and turn everything around? But he was weakened by a feeling of total isolation. What if he'd had direct contact with his right-hand neighbor Ruzsky or his left-hand one, Brusilov? But no such communication ever took place, and both were completely alien to him. He could not turn to them directly even when it was a matter of acting to the throne's benefit.

Now, had the Emperor come here, to Minsk, and ordered him to act, Evert would have acted.

But outside of a direct order, Evert's long service had taught him that it was better not to take on anything extra. He had to serve faithfully—but also not to shake his position recklessly. Thus, last year, he could have decided to attack with the forces of the Western Army Group, and he could have decided not to—and Evert decided not to, pointing out that the enemy's positions were very strong and he preferred to lend some of his troops to Brusilov. An offensive is a very unsure thing. One can gain great fame and one can fail badly.

Thus, for an entire day Alekseev had not come to the direct line. At seven o'clock in the evening, Evert ordered Kvetsinsky to ask GHQ one more time what he was to do with the telegrams, reports, rumors, eyewitnesses, and gossip flooding the army group from all sides. The front could not stand like this. GHQ itself, in Klembovsky's telegram that had just been sent out, had confirmed that there had been a complete uprising in Moscow and Kronstadt and that the Baltic Fleet had gone over to Rodzyanko's side, and for now General Alekseev was asking the Emperor for a pacifying act—but for Evert's army group, a delay could be fatal. Give instructions on how we are to act! Kindly inform us where the Emperor is. Where is Adjutant General Ivanov? Where are the troop trains we sent?

Again it was Lukomsky, not Alekseev, who replied. He apologized that some important telegram from Alekseev to Rodzyanko had not been passed on to the Western Army Group. The staff officer had confused them. It would be sent on immediately. General Alekseev asked Rodzyanko not to give orders that bypassed GHQ. You will see that the planned reply to Rodzyanko from the Western Army Group's commander-in-chief does not contradict the view of the chief of staff. The Emperor was in Pskov, and General Ivanov was already three stages from Tsarskoye Selo. And the Western Army Group's troop trains were evidently passing freely.

But again there was no decision. And again no instructions.

And so it went until late in the night. Everything was spinning, shaking, turning over—and no instructions.

It was like walking a knife's edge, and you couldn't decide anything yourself. Too much was unknown.

Finally, after one in the morning, Evert ordered Kvetsinsky to send one more telegram to GHQ saying that he could not allow these destructive telegrams to reach the troops! That General Evert had given preclusive orders for his district, but he considered unity of measures in all the army groups to be essential—and he was asking for instructions!

Whether anyone at GHQ read it or they were asleep—there was no reply. But no, they weren't asleep because half an hour later a telegram arrived in Kvetsinsky's name from Lukomsky—and of absolutely stunning content. It said that in consequence of the impossibility of the troop trains headed for

Petrograd moving farther than Luga (where there was also a revolt); and in consequence of the Tsar's permission to the Commander-in-Chief of the Northern Army Group to enter into relations with the State Duma President (an unmitigated traitor!); as well as in consequence of the supreme assent to turn around the troops sent from the Northern Army Group—the chief of the Supreme Commander's staff was also asking the Western Army Group to give orders not to let embark those troops that had yet to be sent, and to halt those that were en route, detaining them at the large stations.

Now that was a bang! Look at how things had turned around!

However, with permission, if the Emperor had ordered the troops of the Northern Army Group turned—had he not given orders about the Western? And was this perhaps so they could occupy a single perimeter? In these decisive hours in the regiments' movement—had General Alekseev stopped them by his own decision, by analogy?

He was taking his oath very lightly. A dodgy formulation.

But there was nowhere to get through: the Emperor was with Ruzsky and there was no connection.

And in the Supreme Commander's absence, the chief of staff is Supreme Commander.

My God, what was happening?

He could not fail to carry it out.

He didn't understand politics, Evert didn't.

And he had to be cautious.

His own army group had already been shaken and pecked at from behind.

Evert thought and thought—and came up with nothing.

At three in the morning, Kvetsinsky began stopping the sent regiments.

And they had only just properly gotten going! . . .

[2 9 8]

Milyukov calmed down as they went from one point to the next in the negotiations. What he had most feared was that the socialists had changed their minds and decided to form a government themselves—and here they had no such intention. They weren't talking about the war or the Allies. Very good. A Constituent Assembly? Why, this had been the intelligentsia's most popular slogan since the turn of the century, and there was no way to repudiate it now. That would look like open betrayal of their own positions. A Constituent Assembly was everyone's favorite mirage. But if wishes were horses, beggars would ride. It was important for the Kadet government to obtain real power today and consolidate—and then a Constituent might not be needed.

No terrible points of any kind came up, and this was such a pleasant surprise for Milyukov that he couldn't restrain himself and said:

"Well then, your terms so far in general are acceptable and can lie at the base of our agreement. I'm listening to you and meanwhile I'm thinking how far our workers' movement has advanced since 1905."

Not yet extinguished in his memory were those intolerable, insolent leftists, for example the ones in the Union of Unions, with whom discussing anything had been wretchedly impossible. But he also said this on purpose in order to flatter and mollify them. After all, any negotiation and agreement is a matter of mutual support as much as it is mutual struggle. Troops were on their way to Petrograd, they had no one to defend themselves with, there had been no government of any kind for more than two days—and both sides were in a dicey position. The negotiations had to be moved along toward success, and quickly. They had to obtain power quickly and moreover not allow the army and monarchy to be undermined as a principle—which was also for the convenience of the transitional period.

Milyukov was beginning to feel better and better. He still found Himmer disagreeable, but Nakhamkes-Steklov had simply won him over, what a positive individual; he was likely to advance among the socialist leaders. Milyukov tried to be maximally gracious with him. Finally he simply asked Nakhamkes to hand him the list of their demands so that he could see it with his own eyes and refine it.

Nakhamkes himself read it some more and then handed it over. Milyukov set it next to a blank piece of paper, copied the points for himself, and continued to discuss them.

As it seemed to him, he had disputed the point about not predetermining the form of governance, so they let him strike it out. There were now eight points, not nine. In order not to change the numbering, they moved from the end to honorable third place the abolishing of all class, confessional, and ethnic (essentially, Jewish) restrictions. This was simply music, not negotiations! The Soviet of Workers' Deputies did not even have to propose this point; the Kadets themselves had always cited it above all others.

Nor did he dispute the point about replacing the government police subordinate to central authority with a decentralized popular militia with elected leaders. Naturally, in some sense this meant the temporary destruction of the country's system of public safety, but this, too, was already happening spontaneously. The police were already being harassed and driven out. On the other hand, this was straight out of the old 1905 program of the Liberationists and Kadets, that the government would not have in its hands a centralized force against the people. A sensible system of public safety would gradually sort itself out. Ultimately, all of us, after all, all of us come from the same intelligentsia.

He was surprised and quite pleased to find more agreement than argument between them. And it occurred to Milyukov to wonder whether he hadn't made a mistake at one time in creating a Progressive Bloc in alliance with the right, instead of a Leftist Bloc.

There was one more point that had particular, temporary, completely nongovernmental significance but was evidently important for the Soviet of Deputies, which depended on its soldiers: Do not remove from Petrograd or disarm the military units that were there at the moment of the revolution. It was odd, of course. Did this mean the war was already over for these reserves? Of course, here *petitio principii*, one could argue, but realistically, at the given moment, there was really nothing to be done with this dissolute soldier mass, so that this point was easy to accept, especially since it was set as a condition for the handover of power. How could the ministers be left without a garrison in the face of a Tsarist counterrevolution?

However, the list of points ended with a bombshell: self-governance for the army! Elections for officers! And this at the height of war! This insane demand could not have been made by normal people. Obviously, the Soviet's delegates had not given proper thought to this or understood its full significance.

But they were adamantly insisting!

Well, well. Now Milyukov was trying to argue with them that never before in the world had there been elected officers.

While Nakhamkes took up the argument that the only strong army was one in which the officer enjoyed the soldiers' trust.

As usual, Kerensky had gloomily stayed out of the discussion, and at that point he dashed out altogether.

Chkheidze was dozing in helplessness.

Sokolov had left and not returned.

And these two socialists had latched onto this point.

The Duma deputies dropped out. Vladimir Lvov had put everything into his one outburst and did not explode again. Shulgin woke up and lashed out, saying that elected officers would mean total collapse—and he fell back prostrate.

It was after two in the morning. No one could take it any longer. But Milyukov knew that he could and would. He did nothing better in the world than this slow wearing down of his interlocutors. He knew this art: suddenly abandon the main area of disagreement and start grinding away, grinding away with his jaws at some peripheral, secondary point—and from there gradually gnaw his way back to the main point. Also in reserve he had the art of finding reconciling verbal formulas that would satisfy his opponent and open up a new line of action for himself.

Milyukov had already noticed how poorly and repetitiously the Soviet's list had been compiled: the point about the people's civil rights being extended to the army and the point about the army's self-governance were in different places and largely repeated each other. He took up the former and insisted, insisted while he was trying to copy it down, that political freedoms did extend to servicemen but within the limits permitted by technical military conditions. In the same way he began eating away from the edges at the point on army self-governance. If he ate away at it some more, it took on a form already acceptable: assuming the preservation of strict military discipline in the ranks and assuming the performance of military service. . . .

Himmer debated intelligently as well. He did not say that it was they, the Soviet's leaders, who had come up with and were insisting on this. But rather that such were the masses' radical demands: the soldiers would only put up with elected officers, and the Soviet would do what it could to moderate and keep this within a rational framework. But if the masses' demands were neglected altogether, then the the movement was so big, it would sweep away all governmental combinations. And he reminded them:

"Do not forget that only we have the real forces. Only we can hold back the elements!"

(He had already noticed that the franchised believed this, here this was a strong point, and he pressed it. He and Nakhamkes knew that "Order No. 1" had already gone to press and there was no turning back.)

Yes, Milyukov did understand this, that without the Soviet there was no governing the masses. Or repulsing counterrevolution from without. But as if not hearing these threats about the elements, without a flinch of the ear or eye, and himself reminding them about the danger of General Ivanov, he methodically nibbled and nibbled at the edges. They told him that the demands were minimal as it was—but he nibbled away at them.

As soon as he had bitten off the election of officers and he thought the point about the form of governance had been won, he, following the highest rules of negotiations, at that same moment himself went on the attack diligently and unexpectedly:

"These are your demands for us. But we have our own for you."

"Is that so!" Himmer thought privately. They were just about to be tied down with the obligation of supporting the new government and the war— thus shackling the Soviet's entire initiative and destroying democracy.

Not quite, but something like that. The soldier anarchy had frightened the franchised people to such a degree that all their thoughts were about soldier anarchy. Indeed, Milyukov asked for a reciprocal declaration from the Soviet to be printed simultaneously with the government's declaration approving the Soviet's points, while the Soviet would confirm that the government had been formed with its consent and should be legitimate in the eyes of the masses.

One step away, apparently, from participation in the government?

(But he hadn't thought to ask them to support the war! . . .)

No, Milyukov was not asking for the Soviet's direct participation but rather for another declaration of confidence in the officer class. And a condemnation of robbery and the looting of private apartments.

That again? Not only were we not supposed to elect new officers, we were also supposed to trust the old ones? But wasn't that class counterrevolutionary? Wasn't it loyal to the Tsarist regime? . . .

Meanwhile, Sokolov burst in, newly agitated. Here is where he turned out to have gone: he'd learned that the Duma's Military Commission was preparing a proclamation to the troops and he was now reading its proof-sheet. Here, you see, it talks about so-called "German militarism," "total victory," and "prosecute the war to conclusion"! . . . How about that?

This was infuriating and perfidious on the part of franchised circles—to publish such a proclamation behind the Soviet's back! (Sokolov, however, had the wit not to point out that they themselves had drawn up "Order No. 1.") This was at the least an indecent thing for the franchised party to have done. In the negotiations, the Soviet had tactfully skirted the issue of prose-cuting the war—and here the franchised circles were asking for trouble! The Soviet had made a hard sacrifice and exposed itself to a blow from European democratic opinion—and now the Duma deputies were exacerbating it!

Of course, this had been done by Guchkov, who wasn't here. Milyukov immediately condemned his lack of tact. Milyukov valued the agreement they had nearly reached among the sleeping corpses.

The Soviets asked pointedly who the government was, individually? The Soviet's deputies weren't terribly interested, but still? For example, what about Guchkov? He aroused great mistrust.

Even Milyukov, his well-known foe, had to say that given Guchkov's or-ganizational abilities and his extensive connections in the army, he was irre-placeable in the present situation.

They laughed at Tereshchenko. But Milyukov himself looked askance: what crack had they pushed this Tereshchenko through?

Right then they brought in the proof-sheet of the Guchkov proclamation—in enormous letters, for pasting up on the streets. Scanning it, Himmer personally did not find it all that terrible. It was a perfectly acceptable ap-peal to a warring army during time of war. But it could not be counte-nanced. He said that if the Duma deputies did not stop it, the Soviet would stop it by force.

This time, stubborn Milyukov apparently was not going to insist. He kept returning to the same thing, that they had to write up a reciprocal declara-tion from the Soviet.

Meanwhile, the members of the future government should put in order and draw up the points that had been gone over.

All this could come out tomorrow, that is today, in the morning, in the Soviet's *Izvestia*.

It was after three. They decided to disperse for an hour for editing and then reconvene. No one had any more strength, or ability to think, and they will-ingly would have left it for tomorrow. However, Milyukov insisted, under no circumstance could they delay. The population would get the impres-sion that the government simply couldn't form itself, that there was some fatal obstacle.

And without this agreement, neither side would have any way out.

[2 9 9]

SCREEN

A painstaking red boutonniere, the silk kind made by patient, deft fingers,
   even during these insane days —
a flower or a rose, more perfect than nature's — six petals? eight? ten? —
   so strictly, so precisely symmetrical, these identical petals with
   paired flaps, —
turning slowly, slowly on its axis, as if admiring itself or letting us admire it.
But nowhere does perfection last long, and we see the boutonniere only
   four-pointed, and not painstaking now, its edges nipped unevenly
   here and there,
and it doesn't turn quite evenly, either, first slower, then faster, as if something were getting in the way.
Larger.
=   This is a two-pointed red bow, caught nearly in the middle, where a
   random pin gets stuck, and widely ramified in two directions,
an intentionally large bow, the kind officers who join the revolution pin
   next to their medals so they can be seen a block away.
And it shifted sideways — and pulled sideways,
no, this was it starting to revolve,
and faster, although the bow was still distinguishable.
And in its very revolving it changes and loses its shape —
larger
=   this large, torn red scrap snatched from somewhere, as shaggy as fire,
   pinned on willy-nilly,
is revolving around the pinning point in angles, tears, and wisps.
Full screen
   wild spinning,
   and frightening, for some reason.

[3 0 0]

General Ruzsky had never felt as strong and proud as after his talks with
the Tsar, which stretched from evening into night. Never could he have
imagined that he would dare speak this way with the monarch. The unexpected advantage of his strength, deep down he had known quite a few de-
feats and the superiority of others.
   Proud because Ruzsky alone had been given a few hours to complete
the decade-long objective of all Russian educated society, what so many

Duma sessions and hundreds of appeals, petitions, and resolutions had not achieved—and now Ruzsky could stagger Rodzyanko and all Petrograd.

With his limited health, he barely endured the entire nighttime stretch, and at the army group headquarters telegraph office he sank with pleasure into a deep armchair. He was so tired that he conducted the conversation while reclining in the armchair, and Danilov held the tape from the telegraph up for him.

It was two-thirty in the morning. One can just imagine the extent to which there were no nights in Petrograd now. What was going on there in general! . . .

Rodzyanko had appeared at the other end; the telegraph tapped that out.

However, Ruzsky was upset by the cancelation of the President's scheduled arrival—especially since he had been invited by the Emperor. And in order to understand more accurately the correlation of individuals and forces, Ruzsky first asked for an explanation as to why Rodzyanko had not come to Pskov as promised. Moreover, the general wanted to know, in total candor, the *true* reason.

Rodzyanko, with *candor*, said that the first reason was that the troops sent from the Northern Army Group had mutinied in Luga, joined the State Duma, and decided not to let through even the royal trains, and Rodzyanko was busy now trying to open up the line for them.

The tape flowed, and Ruzsky understood that this was incoherent. The upheavals in Luga were of the local garrison, not the troops sent, and were obviously directed in favor of the Duma; they were not preventing Rodzyanko from going. No, Rodzyanko was not prepared to reply, he was hiding something.

But the tape flowed, and Ruzsky did not object. The shortcoming of a telegraph conversation is that you can't see your interlocutor's face. Its advantage is that they don't see yours.

And the second reason: the President had received reports that his trip to Pskov might entail undesirable consequences.

Now we're getting somewhere. What consequences? There was something to this, of course, and Ruzsky accurately sensed it!

"The impossibility of putting a stop to the popular passions that have run rampant in the capital without my personal presence, since they still believe only me and carry out only my orders."

Well, now that made perfect sense. The evenly tapping Hughes wire served up only a tape with letters. There was no device for hearing Rodzyanko himself. But anyone who had ever once heard and seen him had practically no need of a repetition. This giant, who had finally acquired power commensurate with his capabilities, rose above his own words. This raging Petrograd could be imagined—but so, too, could Rodzyanko's thick hands pulling hard on the reins.

The reasons indicated held no refusal or change of heart, and that meant Ruzsky could report his magnificent news.

"The Tsar initially proposed suggesting you form a ministry responsible to His Majesty. But then . . ."

It was awkward to say outright: "as a result of his conversations with me." But this would become obvious itself. . . .

"As he was releasing me, His Majesty expressed his final decision and authorized me to bring the following to your knowledge: allow a ministry responsible to the legislative chambers, with a commission that you form a cabinet!"

Ruzsky pictured Rodzyanko's flabbergasted and joyous face at the other end. And meanwhile, never to be forgotten was the first person who had brought this joyous news. And, now showing off a little:

"If His Majesty's desire finds a favorable response in you, then a manifesto has been drafted about this which I will now transmit to you."

It had come to pass.

The conversation dragged on voicelessly to the even tapping.

But the tape from Rodzyanko somehow did not bring reciprocal joy.

"Obviously, you and His Majesty do not realize what is happening here. One of the most terrible revolutions has come, a revolution it will not be that easy to fight."

Then—how for two and a half years he had been warning the Emperor of the threat. How now, at the very beginning of the movement, the ministers had lost their nerve and taken no measures of any kind. . . .

". . . And little by little such anarchy has ensued that the State Duma in general, and I in particular, have been left with no choice but to try to stand at the head of the movement so that the state does not perish."

Ruzsky rejoiced once again that he was now not responsible for Petrograd.

"Unfortunately, I have not succeeded very far in this. Popular passions have heated up so much that they are scarcely to be restrained. Not only are the troops not obeying, they are killing their own officers. Hatred for the Sovereign Empress has reached extreme limits. To avoid bloodshed, I have been forced to lock up all the ministers in the Peter and Paul Fortress."

Oh my! The picture had gone far beyond what had been imagined. But Rodzyanko had dealt with it vigorously!

"I'm very worried that the same lot will befall me, too."

What? This didn't fit into his cranium!—Ruzsky raked it with his fingers, and the unflappable Danilov also became agitated. What must the scale of this unprecedented revolution be if the *sole* person whom they trusted and whose orders they carried out—might be thrown into the Peter and Paul Fortress at any moment!

While Rodzyanko kept moving mountain after mountain:

"I believe I must inform you that what you propose is now insufficient and *the dynastic question has been posed point-blank.* I doubt this can be avoided."

All of Ruzsky's efforts, all his victory and pride had now been spurned! . . .

His exhaustion passed and he sat up straight in his chair.

"Your information, Mikhail Vladimirovich, truly . . . This will reflect above all on the war's outcome. . . . But the war has to be prosecuted to an end appropriate to our great homeland. . . ."

General Ruzsky did not forget that he would have to show this tape to the Emperor tomorrow, and perhaps even send it to Alekseev, so the adjutant general had to express himself very cautiously. Nonetheless, he could not ignore or omit what was going on in Petrograd. There it was all clear to everyone; to us here, not yet. A path had to be paved in a safe but probing way between the abyss of ending up a traitor and the abyss of ending up a reactionary:

"Couldn't you tell me in what form the solution to the dynastic question is being contemplated? . . ."

It was not easy for an imperial court chamberlain to say this:

"I will answer you with pain in my heart. I repeat yet again that hatred for the dynasty has reached extreme limits. But the entire people, no matter who I have spoken to in going out to the crowds, has decided firmly to take the war to a victorious end. All the troops are on the Duma's side, and the ominous specter of a demand for abdication in favor of the son, under Mikhail Aleksandrovich's regency, has arisen. It is with terrible pain that I tell you this, but what can I do? While the people were shedding their blood, the government was positively mocking us."

And once again, the cursed names—Rasputin, Stürmer, Protopopov—the constraint on society's ardent impulses, the failure to take measures, the investigations into a then-nonexistent revolution. . . . Ruzsky let all these familiar repetitions slip through his fingers and past his eyes, and he burned to understand how the dynasty question stood so that he himself would not misstep. Petrograd's one and only master had said "extreme limits."

". . . The Sovereign Empress has done things for which it will be difficult to answer before God. . . . Sending General Ivanov only poured oil on the fire and will lead to internecine fighting, since there is definitely no possibility of restraining the troops. . . . The heart bleeds. Put a stop to the sending of troops. They are not going to act against the people. . . ."

Ruzsky did not dare reply to the extreme statements against the Empress on the printed tape. He spoke of certainties: what was needed was the homeland's swift pacification and in such a way that anarchy did not spread to the army. The indicated mistakes must not be repeated in the future. A responsible ministry had been proposed, so think about the future. And the troops going toward Petrograd, Ruzsky was happy to clarify, had been sent by directive from GHQ, not him, and they were already being recalled:

"Two hours ago, the Emperor gave Ivanov orders not to undertake anything. . . . Similarly, the Emperor graciously expressed his assent, and a telegram was sent two hours ago to return to the front all units that were en route."

Two hours ago. That meant that Ruzsky had achieved this, understand! And once again to his main achievement:

"On the part of His Majesty, all possible measures are being taken. . . . It is desirable that the Emperor's initiative find a response in the hearts of those who can halt the conflagration."

An irreproachable tape from the adjutant general and army group commander-in-chief. Having learned enough for himself (and in a new solid position with respect to the Emperor), Ruzsky remained a loyal subject, having made not a single dubious statement.

He had also transmitted the full text of the Emperor's draft manifesto.

"Mikhail Vladimirovich, I have today done everything my heart so prompted me. Spring is coming, and we are obliged to concentrate on preparations for active steps."

And from there a thundering:

"Nikolai Vladimirovich, you have utterly tormented my already tormented heart. From the late hour at which we are having this conversation, you can imagine the tremendous work that rests on me. I repeat to you, though, I myself am hanging by a hair, and authority is slipping from my hands."

This was simply unimaginable: Rodzyanko threatened with the Peter and Paul Fortress?

". . . Anarchy has reached such proportions that I was compelled tonight to appoint a Provisional Government."

Ah, here it was! What tricksters! He'd saved it for last! Yes, of course, why did he need a responsible ministry then from the Tsar's hands if he himself had already *appointed* a government! . . . At this remove from the capital, you lag constantly behind and strike the wrong tone.

". . . The manifesto came too late. It should have been issued after my first telegram. The moment passed and there's no going back. I repeat, popular passions have heated up to the realm of hatred and indignation. We hope that after the Provisional Government's appeal the peasants and all inhabitants will bring grain, ammunition, and other pieces of equipment."

There were sufficient reserves because the public organizations and Special Conferences had made sure of that.

"I pray to God that He allow things to remain at least within the limits of the present disarray of minds and emotions, but I fear things might get even worse. I wish you a good night, if anyone can sleep well at all in these times."

It wasn't hard just to sleep well but even to move away from the telegraph. What did "even worse" mean? General Ruzsky was struck by a bad premonition.

"Mikhail Vladimirovich! Bear in mind, however, that any violent overthrow will inevitably leave traces! What if anarchy infects the army and leaders lose their authority? What will happen to our homeland then?"

This neither one of them could even remotely imagine.

Ruzsky was still trying to convince him how sorry he was to part with what he'd achieved. The goal, after all, was still a government responsible to the people. And so, what if a normal path to this were opened . . . ?

Something about this abdication, so unexpected for him, frightened the general.

But not Rodzyanko in the least. There, in the revolutionary element, Rodzyanko had already made peace with the idea:

"Don't forget that a coup can be voluntary and quite painless for everyone. Then everything will be over in a few days! I can say one thing: there will be no bloodshed or unnecessary sacrifices. That I will not allow!"

This confidence from a powerful man began to be conveyed to Ruzsky as well. If in a few short days and without any bloodshed—truly, why not . . . ?

It was still not growing light but morning was not far off when they ended their slowly flowing telegraph conversation.

He could go wake up the Emperor and report to him that there would be no reconciliation of any kind. The State Duma President intended to overthrow him—so perhaps the halted troops should be sent back to Petrograd?

Absolutely not. The thought didn't even occur, to report such a thing to the Emperor. (In any case, he was asleep.) Without even saying yes to Rodzyanko about anything, Adjutant General Ruzsky seemed to have made a deal with him. He had already been caught and carried away by the new turn of events.

The person who needed to be informed of all this immediately was Alekseev.

Then we would see.

As it was, GHQ was in a flurry and losing its decorum. They kept asking for guidance more often, whenever there was something important.

He instructed that they be told that, by order of the Emperor, a manifesto about a responsible ministry must be published.

And a summary of his discussion with Rodzyanko.

At four o'clock, he headed for bed.

[3 0 1]

Tonight's conversation, like yesterday's, once again gave Rodzyanko wings. Good fortune again! Success again!

He raced lightly through the General Staff's semicircular corridors as if his hulking body was weightless and a light wind was turning him.

A double success! A triple success!

It was true: it was he whom the Emperor had appointed, he on whom it had been laid to form a responsible ministry!

A little late.

A little late, but an honor nonetheless, and a recognition of his services. The manifesto he was now carrying in a wound tape could not help but flatter!

A little late.

Perhaps he should just go ahead and accept the offer?

Rub Milyukov's nose in it along with all the other intriguers'?

But he had said: I've appointed a provisional government. That meant he himself hadn't joined it.

And they really were forming it.

Then: Rodzyanko learned for sure that all the troops had been stopped altogether! Ivanov had been stopped, and just outside the capital!

This was his personal victory! In two nighttime conversations Rodzyanko had saved freedom-loving Petrograd!

He had expressed himself well to Ruzsky, saying that the Petrograd troops could not be restrained, so eager were they for battle against Ivanov! (Though there wasn't a single battle-ready company.)

In general, he had unwittingly exaggerated here and there—including about the extreme limits of the hatred for the dynasty. But he'd wanted to convey to Ruzsky more vividly just how dreadful the situation here was.

Print the manifesto now? This was what he had said to Ruzsky toward the end:

"To be honest, I don't know what to tell you. Everything depends on events, which are flying with head-spinning speed."

To be honest, I don't know.

It's a little late.

Oh, why did you tarry so, Emperor?

Now nothing like this is going to satisfy the revolt.

Unfortunately, abdication is inevitable.

But for some reason that wasn't frightening. It would pass easily. A swift changeover to Mikhail's regency.

But bloodshed, victims, and upheavals—that the President would not allow. The people's defender. The people's hope.

God, help Russia!

[3 0 2]

The Duma deputies had been lied to at the negotiations about the Soviet supposedly composing and printing a pacifying proclamation to the soldiers. In fact, an inflammatory proclamation was being printed—Order No. 1— and in a few hours half a million copies, freshly printed, would flood the capital, and they would bring it here, to the Duma building, at which point all the nighttime work of the negotiations might collapse. Right now, the situation was favorable. They had stopped Guchkov's patriotic proclamation— and needed to hurry up and finish and reinforce the negotiations' results. To keep them from breaking off altogether, they would have to agree to a concession: be in time to delete from Order No. 1 the point about the election of officers, since they'd already conceded this in the negotiations. Nakhamkes went to telephone Goldenberg at the press.

Himmer took a seat in the connecting room of the Duma wing, taking a blank piece of paper and wetting his pencil in his mouth, hurried to draft the Soviet's declaration that Milyukov had requested. He'd even written something:

"Comrades and citizens! The total victory of the Russian people over the old regime is nigh. But this victory still requires tremendous effort. We cannot allow disunity and anarchy. We cannot allow excesses, robberies, and looting of private apartments. . . ."

He scribbled a few more words with his unsharpened pencil but suddenly felt his brain's utter exhaustion—from his empty stomach, from his lack of sleep, and from the arguing he'd been through.

Right then Kerensky walked in, more cheerful and delighted now, and again pestered him, saying that here they were offering him the portfolio of Minister of Justice, and what should he do—accept or not? He'd dropped all his revolutionary principles and ideas over his personal ministerial problem. Himmer gave him a look of reproach. He didn't need advice, he'd obviously decided to accept the post, but he was worried about how his comrades in the Soviet of Deputies would look on this.

No, writing the declaration was too much for Himmer, and sticking what he'd begun in his pocket, he went to the Soviet side; they might be able to compose it there together.

There were many fewer soldiers in the Ekaterininsky Hall than on the previous nights. People were no longer worried about sleeping in the barracks and had dispersed.

In the empty corridor, Himmer saw Guchkov coming toward him in his fur coat. Aha! He was on his way to see his franchised colleagues. Guchkov didn't know Himmer by face or name, of course, but all Russia knew Guchkov. Himmer could have walked by in silence, but he had an urge to provoke him:

"Aleksandr Ivanovich! We were compelled to halt your proclamation, the Military Commission's proclamation, to the army. It is full of martial tones that do not correspond to the revolutionary state of affairs."

Guchkov was deeply somber and at first seemed not to even notice that someone was walking toward him. He heard what he said, stopped, and gave him an abstract look. Whether he'd understood what had been said, or even if he hadn't, whether he looked at this man or more likely didn't, he didn't ask who he was or who "we" were, moved his lips oddly, saying nothing, and walked on.

Himmer watched Guchkov go with hostility. These were the kinds of gentlemen who should have the stuffing knocked out of them; herein lay the revolution. But they were trying to get in on the revolution.

Even though it was four o'clock in the morning, there were people awake everywhere. In the Executive Committee room, Nakhamkes was telling the SR Zenzinov and the Menshevik Zeitlin about how the negotiations had gone with the Duma deputies. Telling the tale was good, and the support of another two members—that was fine, but they had to work flat out and write the Soviet's declaration, and Himmer egged Nakhamkes on. But for some reason, Nakhamkes didn't take the bait.

Suddenly, Fleckel, a young SR, ran in, shaking still other papers and shouting with indignation about a new provocation.

What was this? Another new proclamation, already printed and signed by the Interdistrict group and the nonexistent Petersburg committee of SRs represented by Aleksandrovich alone. Just yesterday there was their joint leaflet about a workers' government—and now this one.

No, you weren't going to show up in the Duma room with this proclamation. It was written in Pugachev-like tones—not only against autocracy but against noblemen, that they'd gone mad sucking the people's blood, against the treasury and the monasteries, and then even against the officers and the Romanov gang, calling for them not to be recognized or trusted, to be hunted, everything short of destroyed outright.

And where was this leaflet? It was already spreading through the city, and there were stacks of them in the Bolsheviks' storeroom here in the Tauride Palace.

The Bolsheviks and Interdistrict group had always been mutual supports, and this complicated the matter.

It was indeed unsatisfactory—both because it called for pogroms and even more because contact with Duma circles was being disturbed at the crucial moment. They expected a reassuring leaflet there, and they were going to get Order No. 1—and even before that this one here, which was worse.

Those there, four or five from the Executive Committee, began to confer. The question was very complicated. Whether they could still stop the leaflet in time, but also as a matter of principle: this would mean putting a ban on the socialist group's free speech. Did they have that right? (Guchkov's chauvinistic leaflet was another matter.) On the other hand, even distributing this leaflet throughout the city right now was truly dangerously explosive, could enflame this mood, and the Soviet itself would go flying upside down and, of course, no new government would be created whatsoever. Naturally, the few here didn't like the idea of accepting full responsibility and quarreling with the Interdistrict group and the Bolsheviks; of course it would be better to wait for the daytime session—but they couldn't wait. The leaflet was already set to fly through the city this morning. This afternoon at the session they could pose the question in all its fullness as to what extent each party faction had the right to act without the Soviet's knowledge. Right now, though . . . ?

Whether or not they were going to decide to, right then, fortunately, Kerensky flew in like a squall. He flung himself around the room, flung himself at each of them with fury. His fury was about this very leaflet. He had just read it and accused Krotovsky and Aleksandrovich of provocation and being successors to the Tsar's Okhrana. And when they started objecting that he couldn't speak so harshly about his party comrades, about his own revolutionary democrats, he started attacking the members of the Executive Committee as well, accusing them of complicity.

"What are you going to say now at the negotiations? How do you expect to face them when you come to write a declaration about pacification?"

Kerensky's abuse gave them courage to risk stopping it before the Executive Committee's afternoon session.

The bales of leaflets were piled here, across the room, very close by. Himmer, as always the swiftest to act, headed off on reconnaissance to see what forces the Bolsheviks and Interdistrict group had there.

It turned out, they'd left only the bungler Molotov sitting there. Himmer flew at him boldly, and the others joined in, and Molotov at first objected but then became flustered and released the bales without a scandal.

Fleckel and his assistants immediately snatched them up and sequestered them.

Very few had been distributed yet. They'd intercepted them in the nick of time.

Phew, Himmer took a deep breath after this disaster. But the hour's break was over and the declaration still had not been written.

[3 0 3]

Although he was wearing a civilian's fur coat, Guchkov entered the Duma office with the step of a commander. Everyone was sprawled or slack, bleary, even the very sturdy Milyukov was badly dazed at his little table, and everyone was short on air—whereas Guchkov was fresh, straight from the cold.

Short and stocky, he stopped soon after the door in an open space, wiped his fogged pince-nez, looked around to see who *wasn't* there (not there from the Duma Committee, fortunately, were the fidget Kerensky and the sourpuss Chkheidze), and asked, rather menacingly, asked them all but primarily his age-old enemy, wakeful Milyukov:

"So, you're giving the army up to plunder, to breakdown? And you think you can hold on yourselves? You're going to go flying head over heels! How many concessions have you made on the army? What kind of government is it going to be? The workers' deputies' plaything? I refuse to participate in a government like that!"

(He really was prepared to refuse, preferring to become a member of the regency and then President of Russia.)

Imperturbable Milyukov was taken aback. He understood that Guchkov was speaking about the agreement they had reached with the Soviet and was astounded at how Guchkov, before he'd taken off his coat, having barely set foot in the Tauride Palace, already knew everything. However, a quick shove could not knock Milyukov off the position he had defended all evening. He was proud of the negotiations he'd held and of keeping the Soviet in a conciliatory mood:

"Aleksandr Ivanych, you are casting aspersions on our position. We have no thought to handing over the army. On the contrary, we think the points on the army have been formulated quite satisfactorily."

Guchkov (cap in hand, but still in his coat) furrowed his brow over his pince-nez:

"What *points*?"

And then it became clear that he was talking about his forbidden proclamation to the army. Forbidden? On whose authority? The Soviet's?

Milyukov had forgotten all about this proclamation. He had conceded it as of little significance. Was it worth spoiling relations with the Soviet on a secondary matter when such an important overall agreement was being reached?

An agreement? Where was it?

With a brusque movement, Guchkov threw his coat on an empty table and quickly sat down across the table from Milyukov. He was as energetic as if it were daytime and not four in the morning.

He sat on just the chair where Nakhamkes had been sitting before this, smiling haughtily at the Kadet leader's objections.

And as the new opposition across the table, Guchkov put the plan Milyukov had achieved in a new and unattractive light.

He wanted to read it with his own eyes, but these were Milyukov's barely legible scratchings, copied from the Soviets' paper, and Pavel Nikolaevich had to read them out loud.

And once he began reading in front of his tense, demanding, and perpetual foe, then even "technical military conditions" no longer seemed such an actionable limitation on soldiers' political freedoms.

A police force with an elected leadership seemed unreliable.

The decision not to remove revolutionary units from Petrograd was a shackle.

It was entirely incomprehensible how soldiers were going to make unlimited use of all their social rights.

And how did this look to Guchkov? He could barely conceal his disgust.

Milyukov felt extreme vexation at it being with Guchkov rather than someone else that he saw his plan's weaknesses.

How much had they clashed in life—comrades at university and then forever divided. How much had they argued, beginning with the Polish question in 1905! And when Witte invited them to join his cabinet. And when they were creating the two rival parties, the Kadets and Octobrists. And their contests in the Third Duma. His perpetual rival, the perpetual obstacle in his path—before him alone did Milyukov secretly shy. At one time there was even a duel set between them, and Pavel Nikolaevich, in his gloomiest presentiments, had already started singing Lensky's aria—but they managed to get by with a vindicating explanation. And their diametrical positions around Stolypin's activities and death. Fate had somehow always brought them forward and facing each other, in view of all Russian society, which left no room for neutrality or indifference; they always had to vie.

In this rivalry Milyukov had known his own persistence, patience, methodicalness, and firm tie with Western sympathies, while Guchkov rolled up and back like some Slavic sphere, first from the Duma tribune to Mongolia, and then back, as Stolypin's avenger, then in a disgraceful failure in the elections for the Fourth Duma, then with the Octobrists' unmitigated revolt against the government. There was so much strength in this unpredicted, wild rolling back and forth that he nearly knocked strong-legged Milyukov off his feet. Thus, yesterday afternoon he had rolled irrepressibly onto the Duma Committee as an unofficial fourteenth member, as Minister of War in the government being formed, and had taken over the Military Commission—where he had burst in to annul the agreement. He had not been at the exhausting negotiations, and Milyukov had had to do the kicking alone against the three Soviet representatives—and now Guchkov was obstinately overturning and wrecking everything.

Quite so! He raised his muffled voice, rousing those heedlessly dozing, and with all the bitterness of their festering disagreements, sharp wrinkles by his eyes, he now laid out for the quailing Milyukov that this was God knew what but not an agreement! If the Soviet was so feared, then of course they would grow in strength! They had to be squeezed before they became a force. How much could be conceded to them? The army itself? What would the government's buttress be then?

While some in the room still dozed lethargically.

The agreement was broken. Or in any case, put off until tomorrow, until the next negotiations.

Actually, they still had to write a declaration in the name of the Soviet. But the draft brought from the Soviet was useless. Unembarrassed, Milyukov himself sat down to write this declaration in the name of the Soviet—and saw fit because of this to postpone the negotiations until tomorrow.

Kerensky hadn't returned and one could speak openly as before—and Guchkov woke up Shulgin, Shidlovsky, and the others:

"Gentlemen! The situation is deteriorating by the minute. The anarchy is not only not abating, it's mounting. We can expect the complete and utter slaughter of officers! The Soviet has cast off all restraint; agreements like this must not be concluded. Meanwhile, troops are advancing on Petrograd from without, troops we have no way to repulse. We must take an important decision immediately, here and now! The new government cannot be founded on sand. We must accomplish something major that yields a general outcome, makes an impression, saves our situation, and saves the officer class—and the monarchy!"

In front of these men, who had slackened in the sleepless stuffiness, he preserved all the advantage of a brisk, very confident man.

"We must emerge from our ominous situation with the fewest losses and even with a victory. Establish a new regime, but without upheavals. Save the monarchy and even strengthen it! But at the price of the Emperor's abdication. In any case, Nikolai can no longer reign. But it's very important that, rather than being overthrown by force, he voluntarily abdicate in favor of his son and brother. You can see precisely from the Soviet's demands that we have to hurry with the abdication—and not wait for the moment now imminent when this gaping revolutionary rabble starts looking for a solution itself. End the revolution by legal means."

The Emperor's abdication! Who hadn't thought, whispered about this. Strangely, though, in the turmoil of these past few days, the Duma Committee hadn't once sat down to discuss this separately and seriously. They'd swept away the previous government, but Tsarist rule still existed, as yet not rejected by anyone (though no longer recognized by nearly anyone). And they still hadn't met to decide this question in principle and in practice! With all the greeting of troops, all the speeches and congratulations, the Duma Committee's members had forgotten that they were temporary, self-appointed, and, seeing that no punitive troops were coming, they had discounted any negotiations with the Supreme Power. In the enflamed Tauride Palace, new things kept coming up that were deemed important, while the old government receded as *former*. Everyone around kept talking about the danger of reaction, but they themselves no longer believed in it. Their heads were spinning with the idea that power had to shift entirely to public figures, that Nikolai II had to go, of course, but somehow they awaited this like the falling of a ripened fruit.

Perhaps not all of them had thought about this, but Guchkov had thought of nothing else the whole time. This nail had been hammered into his head: Emperor Nikolai. This afternoon it had been too early to insist. Rodzyanko had still been preparing to travel for a responsible ministry. But they hadn't let him go, and he hadn't gone, and the moment had been let slip. And now, since the recent evening hours, there could be nothing other than abdication, and every hour that passed was lost for good. Rodzyanko hadn't gone, and now Guchkov was demanding the authority. He would go!

With the advantage of confidence and energy, he had no doubt that these sleepy men would give him the authority right away.

Milyukov, embarrassed by the rebuke to his agreement, was chewing his lips and didn't have the strength to object.

But right then Rodzyanko returned from the telegraph unrecognizably cheerful. Occupied by Guchkov's vigorous plan, though, they somehow paid little attention to his return. His conversation with Ruzsky seemed secondary, a detour. Rodzyanko had got a hold of the conversation's tapes and wanted to read them out, but they wouldn't listen to him. What had he learned that was new, completely new, from Ruzsky?

A manifesto on a responsible ministry!

They just snorted: the Tsar had come to this too late.

Rodzyanko understood this himself. But there was other stunning news: the Emperor had halted Ivanov's troops.

Now that was marvelous! Magnificent news!

But! If the Tsar had halted the punitive troops, that made it all the clearer that he was weak. And knew it.

And that meant Guchkov was all the more correct about abdication?

Rodzyanko sat down to the side as yet another listener.

Guchkov proposed that they authorize him to go immediately to obtain the abdication.

Nonetheless, they hesitated. Nonetheless, this was too decisive a step. Must we? So urgently? Wouldn't direct dealings with the Tsar discredit their Duma Committee and the nascent government? How would the Soviet of Workers' Deputies exploit this?

The Duma opposition's most decisive orators, who had scattered the state order to dust, now could not bring themselves to take the simplest action without which all the rest made no sense. If we're putting together a government here ourselves, independently . . .

Or did it seem more important who would take which portfolio? . . .

"Fine!" Guchkov declared firmly. "If the Duma Committee doesn't have the nerve to authorize me, I'm going at my own risk and peril! I'm going as a private individual. Simply as a Russian man wishing to give the Emperor salutary advice. I've long been convinced of the necessity of this step, and I've decided to take it no matter what!"

Long, indeed. Before—and more steadfastly than—them all. And of course, he was the first candidate for accepting this abdication. He hadn't simply taken another political step, he'd sensed that he had come to the culminating point of his life.

This turned the matter around completely: whether the Duma deputies agreed or not, Guchkov was going!

Who else? Who was better connected to the army generals?

But what about the Soviet of Workers' Deputies? Would they allow any of our negotiations with the Emperor? Would they allow sending a delegation? Did the Soviet really want a peaceful abdication and the monarchy's preservation?

Guchkov lowered his voice, in militant style:

"Of course, acting only in secret. In no case should they be informed, and no one should be asked. And not a word to Kerensky now! An agreement with the Soviet would only bind us and spoil everything. We will present them with a fait accompli! Let Russia wake up a day from now with a young Emperor! And under this banner we will quickly begin to assemble resistance against the Soviet and its gangs. For now, the Emperor is in Pskov, which isn't far, a very quick trip."

Pskov headquarters were under the Duma's strong influence. This was incomparably better than GHQ. Pskov was an excellent place. And for now the Emperor had not continued on. (And secretly tell Ruzsky to detain him? . . .)

Seeing that he'd shaken up everyone and Milyukov, too, was distraught:

"Gentlemen, there is nothing more to discuss. I'm going! Will anyone else come, a second?"

Right then young Shulgin, now long since wrested from sleep, increasingly gripped and enchanted by this courageous voice and this courageous plan, as well as the idea of circumventing and deceiving the despised Soviet of Deputies, exclaimed loudly and jumped ecstatically at the chance:

"Gentlemen, I'll go! Gentlemen, permit me!" There was even a youthful supplication in his voice, hope that his elders wouldn't refuse. He was on his feet and vigorously turned to them all. And to him: Will Guchkov take me?

Shulgin sprang to life. He was no longer the least bit tired. What a unique historical event, to be present at the abdication of the All-Russian Emperor and even to take this abdication himself!

One might have wondered at such an inveterate monarchist responding. But there was no one to wonder, they were tired of wondering, tired beyond belief.

Guchkov did not object. Let him, this wasn't bad.

And so, were they warranted? To bring back the abdication? Did the Provisional Committee of the State Duma consider abdication the sole solution? Under the heir, with Mikhail as regent.

And the text of abdication itself?

Oh, how could they at such a late hour? Their heads were dropping, refusing.

All right, compose it en route.

But how to arrange the journey? Contact the railroaders via Bublikov.

Everyone collapsed to get some more sleep. While Guchkov and Shulgin went to Sergievskaya, to Guchkov's home.

The streets were dark and deserted. That brief predawn hour when even the Revolution was worn out.

[3 0 4]

Night had fallen, but no one in the Luga cavalrymen's barracks had any thoughts of going to bed.

After midnight, Cavalry Captain Voronovich had decided to act. He lined up his detachment and, exacting from it a promise to obey unquestioningly, led them in formation through the town.

The inhabitants had all crammed into their apartments, not even poking their noses out. Crowds of soldiers were roaming the main street in a cheerful pogromish mood. But the sight of three hundred tall armed Guards in exemplary formation—the platoon commanders counting out the cadence and barking commands—made a huge impression on the reveling soldiers. They stopped and looked in surprise. Inhabitants began looking out of some windows.

Voronovich and his detachment reached the train station, where he found utter depravity. The buffet and halls of all three classes and even the formal "royal" rooms that were never opened were packed with soldiers. Most of them were new recruits in the artillery division, with rifles that had been taken away from other cavalrymen. They stood, sat, and lay on the floor, chairs, tables, even the buffet counter. In the formal rooms the band from the fire brigade, surrounded by a crowd, was playing a seriously flawed Marseillaise, starting over immediately when they finished.

These sounds carried the sleepless celebration over the entire station.

A soldier-driver in a leather jacket was rushing around; it turned out he was a member of the "military committee." And he replied, perhaps speaking for himself:

"We received your note, your honor, and are very grateful. The committee is asking you to step in as garrison chief, at least for a while."

He said Luga was awaiting some important special train from Petrograd with members of the State Duma, and the place was such a mess. The cavalry captain was the only officer here, and their hopes were on him.

Voronovich thought about how to clear out the station. First of all, he led the fire brigade band out onto the platform—and the crowd of soldiers all surged after it. This emptied out the formal rooms, which were then locked, and sentries were posted at the doors.

Now the cavalry captain made a speech to everyone on the platform, saying that they were now going to prepare for a formal welcome, and he asked those who so desired to line up in order and the rest to step aside and not get in the way.

Everyone so desired. But the old-time cavalrymen lined up quickly, while the new recruits did their best: they dragged their rifles clumsily and immediately fell out of formation, sat on the platform, and lit up. Accordions started playing instead of the band.

Voronovich had an idea. He began shouting commands, rehearsing the welcome, "Attention! Present arms!" The armed recruits got flustered; they didn't know a single rifle position. Then he started teaching them, calling on the sergeants and then the old-timer soldiers to show them and execute the positions.

The tired recruits willingly gave them their rifles and thus ended up disarmed.

Now that all the rifles were with cavalrymen, Voronovich suggested that the recruits go home and go to bed.

They began protesting noisily that now there was freedom and the recruits should enjoy the same rights as the old-timers.

The old-timers didn't like that, and they asked the cavalry captain's permission to drive the youth back to the barracks.

So the recruits were sent back, accompanied by cavalry patrols.

Then it became clear that the train from Petrograd had been canceled. But worse was the confusion: the entire "military committee" arrived, and its chairman, Sergeant Zaplavsky, informed Voronovich that a telegram had been received saying that the lead troop train of the Borodino Life Guards Regiment on its way to pacify Petrograd was about to arrive in Luga. So look: how could the Borodino men be stopped?

According to the reports, the troop train had 2000 men and eight machine guns. In all Luga, armed soldiers numbered 1500, but no more than those who were here now, three or four hundred of the best, could be assembled at the station. And the machine guns didn't have belts. The brigade intended for France didn't have a single cannon or rifle, and they hadn't joined the revolution; they were just roaming. In the artillery division, all the cannons were for training; not a single one was any good for firing.

But one of the weapons and two of the nonfunctioning machine guns, which gunners had brought here out of mischief, were now on the platform.

On this alarming night, Voronovich, shaken by the evening's experiences, had kept a clear head. His mission was the same: to serve the revolution with excellence. His head was working. What was needed was more and more daring. Two officers, a lieutenant and an ensign, offered their services to the military committee that some drivers had formed. Voronovich began to devise something with them.

This hauled-in gun would be their threatening artillery—quickly, manually, point its barrel toward the approaching train, at an angle.

The cavalrymen hid in and behind the station.

They could already see the blinding triangle of the locomotive's white lights.

Always ominous in the night, now the troop train seemed especially ominous because it was carrying a crushing force.

The three officers, spread out on the platform and pumping up their courage, walked up to the approaching train cars and in a loud, commanding tone shouted to the soldiers not to get out of the train cars because the train was being sent on immediately.

If the Borodino men had spilled out right then, everything would have fallen apart and then no one knew what they would do. But it was the dead of night, nearly four o'clock, and none of the sleeping men showed any intention of crawling out of their warm cars.

For those minutes the military committee blocked the exit from the officers' car, but they were asleep as well and didn't try to come out.

Voronovich and his aides returned from running the length of the train—and now confidently entered the officers' car, followed by the military committee.

The sentries by the entrance and by the flag saw officers entering and let them through unquestioningly.

The military committee jammed the passageway. The officers found the regiment's commander and presented him with an ultimatum not from themselves but from the State Duma attaching the entire 20,000-man garrison of Luga to Petrograd, saying any resistance would mean pointless bloodshed. There were guns here and they would open fire on the troop train point-blank. It was suggested that the regiment surrender its weapons. They would be returned to the regiment in Pskov as soon as they returned there.

Borodino Life Guard Colonel Sedachev was indignant. But in the face of such numbers and the visible outline of the cannon he yielded to the superior force.

The Luga officers immediately asked the Borodino Life Guards to surrender their revolvers—but they could keep their cold steel. This concession calmed the Borodino officers, and some were prepared to go explain to their soldiers—to surrender their weapons.

(Meanwhile they moved a shunting locomotive to the tail of the train, unhitched the last car with the machine-guns and hand grenades, and quickly drove it off into the darkness.)

The soldiers took this very calmly. After all, their own officers had come to explain it to them. They started carrying their rifles out in bundles onto the platform.

Voronovich called up his own men and posted a guard by the bundles.

That was it. The troop train had been disarmed.

This is how a revolution wins! It always wields a special wiliness against the established rules. Voronovich was proud he'd been able to do it all!

The soldiers returned to their warm cars. Their locomotive was turned around and reattached to the tail.

They suggested the regiment's commander leave a small group here to escort the weapons for their return and for the rest to go to Pskov.

Dawn was just about to break, and the Borodino men were going to see the sole cannon without a gun-lock, two machine guns without belts, and no force whatsoever at the station.

*   *   *

PLENTY OF ROOM FOR ANY THIEF

*   *   *

15 March
Thursday

[305]

Just after three o'clock, they woke up Quartermaster General Boldyrev and summoned him to the telegraph room. Tobacco smoke filled the air. Ruzsky was sitting in an armchair exhausted, his tunic unbuttoned. Heavy-shouldered, broad-faced Danilov was standing by the telegraph and concentrating on the tape, reading aloud to the commander-in-chief, or looking over at the telegraph operator as he was typing from Ruzsky's weary voice. He nodded at Boldyrev that a summary of the conversation had to be swiftly composed for GHQ.

Boldyrev took the first part of the tape and he and the officer went into Danilov's office. Later they were brought the continuation.

The conversation's historical importance was immediately obvious, and his annoyance passed at having been wakened. Under his major general epaulets and General Staff aiguillettes, Boldyrev sympathized whole-heartedly with events, as did any cultivated person, and secretly he wanted them to roll along faster, more terribly, and more irrevocably. He was very pleased that the Petrograd events had exceeded the notion of them here, and even a responsible ministry had become nothing for revolutionary Petrograd.

However much he sympathized, though, the quartermaster general tried to make the conversation as impartial as possible. Ruzsky and Danilov had already arrived and at the last lines were hard on his heels. Ruzsky wanted to throw out any details regarding the dynastic question and alter it in the main tape:

"They'll think I was an intermediary between Rodzyanko and the Tsar."

And he asked that what had not quite succeeded in the conversation be expressed in greater relief in the account: now the troops sent were already returning to their army group, and it was hoped that the Emperor's initiative would find a response in the capital among those who could put out the fire.

The commander-in-chief steered the most pointed conversation about the desired abdication in such a way that even ardent legitimists couldn't catch him out. Everything remained perfectly in place, but Petrograd wanted too much too soon.

He was insuring himself.

He had left the conversation, though, removed himself from it, and now, not hobbled by a record on the tape, he began understanding the situation more broadly than he had an hour or an hour and a half before.

Alekseev's telegram of yesterday evening, which had heaped up all the horrors and deaths, spoke . . .

"Wait a minute, where is the text?"

Yes, it spoke directly of the *danger for the dynasty.* That meant even at GHQ, independently of Rodzyanko, they had also been thinking **that way**? But in his evening conversation with the Emperor, Ruzsky somehow had not stressed this at all, had let it go, had simply not taken it as a reality. But was that right?

"What other nighttime telegrams were there about the situation?"

Pock-marked Boldyrev with his short, pointed beard readily brought them. Received from Klembovsky after midnight: Did Northern Army Group headquarters know that His Majesty's Convoy, in full, had arrived at the Duma and submitted to the Committee? And the Empress, as it were, had also recognized the Duma Committee? And Kirill Vladimirovich had seen fit to go to the State Duma himself? And how many ministers and dignitaries had been arrested?

Ruzsky read it through attentively, listened to Boldyrev's addition about Kirill—and on his tired, aching face, his eyes glittered with a flicker, and a smile barely grazed his slack lips.

Boldyrev eagerly imitated his smile.

In fact, despite the difficult, sleepless night, a rather cheerful lightness had overtaken them.

What kind of Supreme Commander was he? Hadn't all three of them seen Nikolai II as a mediocre colonel who hadn't even graduated from the General Staff Academy?

Danilov picked up on this. And said in a similar tone:

"Here GHQ is so worked up about the free movement of the letter trains."

Ruzsky sighed in agony.

"Well, I have to get some sleep. I have to report to the Emperor soon."

They parted. Boldyrev sat down to transmit his summary to Mogilev.

After that, a qualification, that inasmuch as the Tsar's manifesto about a responsible ministry had been deemed obsolete in Petrograd, and the Emperor would be reported to about the nighttime conversation only at ten o'clock in the morning, it would be more perspicacious not to publish the signed manifesto before additional instruction from His Majesty.

So he went to get a little sleep; it was already after five.

Just as he was nodding off, though, his adjutant woke him. The military censor was demanding an audience immediately.

This time he so firmly didn't feel like getting up or dressing that he went to see the censor in his house slippers and greatcoat thrown directly over his undergarments.

Before he could apologize for his attire, the censor began apologizing:

"Forgive me, Your Excellency! But there are instances when even a *simple soldier* is compelled to disturb a general."

He said this not without irony. He had a military rank far from the lowest, and in the civilian world he was a state councilor.

This joke of his restored to Boldyrev that cheering lightness that had been interrupted by his oblivion. Given events such as these, truly, it was a sin to be angry that they wouldn't let you sleep.

The censor's urgency was the fact that the local *Pskov Life*—he had the fresh issue in his hands—taking advantage of the absence of preliminary censorship, had printed here all the agency telegrams from Petrograd and all the appeals of the Duma Committee.

What were they to do now?

This news leak was to have been expected, of course. An entire public volcano was erupting so close by. How could it not throw sparks and ashes on neighboring Pskov? All kinds of wild rumors had arisen in Pskov about twenty telephone operators sitting under the Pogankin Chambers and transmitting something, maybe to the Tsar, maybe to Wilhelm. But here the newspaper had already been printed. It could be banned in its entirety. Or let be?

But then the revolutionary news would begin to make its way victoriously and openly through Russia, wouldn't it?

He was besieged by total uncertainty. Everyone in Pskov already knew of the existence of the Provisional Committee of the State Duma, but there was no official recognition of it on the part of the military authorities. And here Grand Duke Admiral Kirill had recognized it. Perhaps the Empress as well? . . .

No preliminary instructions had been provided for this situation. In Riga, by its authority, the headquarters of Radko-Dmitriev's 12th Army had prohibited any news from Petrograd. What about the army group headquarters now?

The fact that the commander-in-chief had just spoken with Rodzyanko meant that the Duma Committee had received de facto recognition from the Northern Army Group. And since the conversation had been with the Emperor's permission—then did it also have the Emperor's recognition? . . . In addition, the ban on printing news would inevitably give rise to public indignation in Pskov against army group headquarters.

Boldyrev himself tended to think that it should undoubtedly be permitted. However, he could not take that permission on himself.

He left the censor to wait and went to wake up Danilov.

Danilov groaned heavily and bellowed and simply would not wake up. But when he grasped the acuteness of the matter—he didn't want to risk a minute himself, they went together to wake up Ruzsky. Danilov hadn't dressed either and was wrapped in a blanket—and sat on a chair just like that next to the commander-in-chief's bed.

Ruzsky woke up easily but did not get out of bed. He picked up his spectacles from the nightstand and started reading the newspaper lying down.

Now fully awake, they tossed sentences and opinions back and forth—the cheerful, soothing tone they had found had come to their rescue. An incredibly interesting little paper.

"There hasn't been anything like it since the demise of the Pskov Town Meeting!" Boldyrev quipped.

And why suppress it?

The commander-in-chief understood that. They agreed.

"Only there's no need for official authorization," Danilov rumbled. "It's as if we simply didn't know, hadn't noticed."

"I agree," Boldyrev chimed in. "Nonetheless, we have to pluck up our courage and inform GHQ and say we hadn't known but now we did and we think . . . Let them scratch their heads there."

They liked it. Danilov, an old hand, understood this as a protective measure. They agreed. Ruzsky stayed to get a little more sleep; his report to the Emperor was already pressing on him.

Boldyrev let the censor go, got dressed—and went to help Danilov compose a telegram to GHQ. Danilov was already sitting at his desk in his tunic and boots and writing.

They wrote so that the Northern Army Group's commander-in-chief wouldn't see any reason to impede the dissemination of those statements of the Provisional Committee of the State Duma that aimed at the pacification of the population and an influx of food.

"Yuri Nikiforovich," Boldyrev said cheerfully, "what does the communiqué on the arrest of the former ministers aim at, for example?"

"The influx of food," and Danilov laughed resonantly, as did Boldyrev, more loudly.

[3 0 6]

On this short and overwrought night, General Alekseev wasn't the least sleepy. He lay down with the burden that for the first time in his entire military service he had taken a tremendously important decision without permission: he had halted the regiments of the Western Army Group. Most agonizing of all in his position was not even the difficulty of his unusual, seemingly completely nonmilitary tasks, complicated by his chill and the distraction of illness, but the fact that in these hours he had been abandoned by both the Emperor's presence and even the Emperor's telegrams—and had had to—could not help but—act arbitrarily! He could have easily made the calculations, reported, and given orders had he just had someone with a decisive yes or no over him.

He lay there without undressing, all the while waiting for consent to come from the Emperor to the halting of the Western Army Group regiments he had authorized.

It didn't come. The Emperor must have gone to bed.

They couldn't find Ivanov, either—and God forbid Ivanov got up to any mischief.

Alekseev shuffled his boots to the telegraph room. Maybe there were telegrams they hadn't brought?

No, all was quiet. The duty officers and telegraph operators were in place, but the telegraph was silent.

Silent about the most important thing: the manifesto on a responsible ministry. Had the Emperor signed it? Had he not?

Again he lay down. And struck matches from his bed to see his pocket watch set out on the nightstand. It was a quarter to four—and they still hadn't come to awaken him, hadn't come with news. But Ruzsky had been talking with Rodzyanko since two-thirty. Could they still be?

It was four-twenty—and they hadn't come to awaken Alekseev.

How he awaited the feather-light ring of boots.

It was ten to five—and no one had come. Silence.

Then a tense muddle came over him, and Alekseev was late somewhere, and he was down on all fours in despair, and some incredibly bizarre faces leaned out and said meaningless, puzzling sentences, and everyone was bitterly reproaching Alekseev. Finally, Alekseev was pulled out of this difficult dream by a saving shake of the shoulder . . .

. . . by Lukomsky. Holding a candle.

Alekseev gave his head a shake, relieved of those ugly faces, and without asking anything, for some reason glanced at his watch.

Six o'clock exactly.

"About the regiments?" Alekseev asked hopefully.

"It's all here," Lukomsky replied, holding out a roll of telegraph tape.

Alekseev took it straight from sleep, as if to read it right there in bed—but his fingers, still clumsy, dropped the roll on his soldier's-cloth blanket. He was lucky it didn't go farther and didn't unwind a long ways and get tangled.

He lowered his feet and pulled on his boots. And went to his desk.

Separately, Lukomsky handed him the telegram from Pskov saying that the Emperor had given his permission to publish the manifesto about a responsible ministry.

And separately, advice from Northern Army Group headquarters to refrain.

There was a lot to read, and Lukomsky left. Hunched over as usual, Alekseev sat down at his desk, on the surface of which his entire life had passed, put on his spectacles, and began patiently unrolling the tape in his fingers.

Here, in brief, was the essence of the conversation between Ruzsky and Rodzyanko. The troop trains sent to Petrograd had mutinied in Luga and joined the State Duma. . . .

What was this? It wasn't the weak Luga garrison that had mutinied? But the troop trains? Which ones? All that could be there was the one Borodino

Regiment. . . . And it had mutinied? Oh ho. . . . Then on whom could he rely? Well, naturally, yes, this game of sending troops to our own capital could not lead to any good.

. . . Popular passions have run rampant. . . . In Petrograd people now believed only in Rodzyanko and only carried out his orders. . . .

Here they had laughed at Rodzyanko, but he'd turned out to be a firm, courageous man who wielded an imperious strength over the crowd and the anarchy.

. . . Ruzsky had conveyed the manifesto's text to Rodzyanko. . . . But in reply there had come one of the most terrible revolutions, and even the Duma President had not been able . . . Hatred for the Empress had reached extreme . . .

This he could understand. Alekseev himself could not stand the Empress. Who could? . . . But still, a responsible ministry, won in such agonies, had become irrelevant without having appeared? What then? . . .

The tape replied terribly: the dynastic issue had been raised point-blank. The crowd and troops were presenting a demand for **abdication**! . . .

His hands turned cold and again the roll unwound more than he wanted. It took some untangling and straightening. . . . This word, concealed in whispers and dark corners, had cut through GHQ's official tape! The idea may have been distilling in many breasts—but here it had been blown out in Rodzyanko's strong exhale.

. . . **Abdication** in favor of the son under Mikhail Aleksandrovich's regency.

Rodzyanko was in the thick of events; he knew better. And at the same time:

. . . The crowd and troops have decided firmly to take the war to a victorious end. . . .

So, a sensible crowd. Sensible troops. What we're obligated to save given all the circumstances is the army and the victory.

. . . Rodzyanko demanded a halt to the sending of troops against Petrograd! And Ruzsky replied that this order had already been given for the Northern Army Group.

Alekseev felt a little easier about his own order. Yes! Fighting our own rear cities was unworthy of the army.

Nonetheless, he wished he could get confirmation from the Emperor.

The tape was all there was. Signed—Danilov, 5:30.

But—the same painful confusion had spread in his head. And the same darkness outside, no dawn to be seen under lamplight.

What was to be done now? What decision to be made? . . .

Yes, a sworn military man cannot allow such an idea. This wild and unusual, rebellious thought had lain and warmed itself in some breasts—and here it had broken through the Duma President.

A military man cannot let that idea . . . It had been proposed not to him, though, but to the Emperor himself.

It was for the Emperor to decide—and what else was he to decide if this was the mood of the two capitals, and Kronstadt, and Helsingfors—and the Emperor had already rejected the idea of sending troops?

No matter what governmental upheavals we were fated for, the objective was for them to proceed as smoothly as possible, without upsetting the front. If changes were inevitable, then as smoothly as possible.

God preserve Russia!

A believer always had this solution, and it was very understandable and accessible to Alekseev: pray. He knelt down on the rug in front of the icon— and prayed.

He asked the Lord to send the Emperor understanding, so that he would accept the best saving solution. Preserve our army's sovereign power before the enemy. And send his servant Mikhail relief and liberation from this impossible situation.

He rose from his knees calmer and lighter. But alone, by himself, he could not think further. He invited Lukomsky via his orderly.

Lukomsky arrived now not sleepy but fresh, daytime, ruddy, solidly healthy, with the Russian army's sole Order of St. Vladimir on a St. George ribbon (for the mobilization), a content look even. Even his eyes were shining. It was health that the exhausted Alekseev now needed most of all. He asked in anguish:

"What do you think, Aleksandr Sergeich?"

"I?" Lukomsky replied with a confident, solid voice. "In my opinion, Mikhail Vasilievich, there is nothing to think here. There can be no other solution. Now that we have come this far—it means abdication!"

He said this just that bluntly. And this ease of his made Alekseev feel much better. A communicable thought! Never would he have thought this, never would he have borne this—and now he had assimilated this thought. And its saving nature was plain.

"How could one agree to a conflict with public forces?" Alekseev responded in kind. "After all, the Zemgor and volunteer organizations could deny us any and all supplies, it's all in their hands."

"Conflict is out of the question!" Lukomsky exclaimed with his comic positivity. When he wanted to say something with particular authority, it always sounded slightly ridiculous. "The conflict has been reversed with the recall of troops. Thus there is no other solution than a peaceful agreement. The Emperor in particular has no way out. After all, the royal family is in the revolutionaries' hands, so what choice does he have? Judge for yourself!"

"If internecine strife begins"—Alekseev nodded—"then Russia will perish under Germany's blows."

"As will the dynasty!" Lukomsky proclaimed animatedly. "The dynasty—he won't save that in any case. Thus the only sensible thing now is for him to cede his place—and save the dynasty!"

Yes. Thus it came out, on all sides, amazingly whole. Truly, what a solution! Both easy and painless. And swift, all of a few hours, one quiet signature—and the army stands, does not move. And the war continues as if nothing has happened, and Germany will have won nothing.

But then Alekseev had another thought: What was Ruzsky doing? Had he begun to act? Reported to the Emperor?

There was no longer any doubt that Ruzsky thought the same way they did. But he had to act. He had to hasten events in Pskov. It would also take the Emperor time to get used to the idea.

Lukomsky went to the telegraph to awaken Danilov, to awaken Ruzsky, so that he would quickly awaken the Emperor and report his nighttime conversation to him. All etiquette had to be cast aside. The situation's present indeterminacy was worse than anything and threatened the army with anarchy.

So it was conveyed from General Alekseev that he was asking him to act without delay. And then, having no instruction from the GHQ chief of staff but already convinced of his consent, he telegraphed Danilov:

"That is the official message. But now I ask you to report to General Ruzsky from me personally that, based on my deep conviction, there is no choice and the abdication should take place."

As it was transmitted from one set of lips to the next, this idea imperceptibly strengthened. Rodzyanko said only that the ominous specter of a demand for abdication had arisen more and more; he was still not saying that it was certain and inevitable.

But of course it was inevitable. Lukomsky passed along that if the royal family was already in the hands of the rebellious troops, and those troops had occupied the Tsarskoye Selo palace, danger threatened the royal children. And the dynasty would perish under internecine strife.

"It pains me to say this, but there is no other solution."

Rodzyanko's idea was picked up and grew stronger and firmer, was now already howling.

For his part, Danilov guarded Ruzsky, whom he would not awaken. Danilov had only recently gone to bed and would soon be getting up. His report to the Emperor would take place at nine-thirty. And Danilov had expressed great doubt as to whether such a decision could be drawn out of the Emperor. Hardly! If a responsible ministry couldn't be dragged out until two in the morning. Time would merely drag on and on hopelessly. But on the other hand, they could not count on the Emperor preserving himself on the throne.

As always, other events kept clouding the main event. Right then, Danilov had complained of the sending of General Ivanov, which had complicated the entire situation. He reported that Ruzsky had ordered that the Northern Army Group not hold up the Duma Committee's notifications—

the floods of which could not be stopped anyway—especially if they inclined toward maintaining the peace and the influx of food.

Lukomsky headed off to Alekseev with the results.

More than once, Lukomsky had noticed a certain characteristic in Alekseev. If several questions arose at once, Alekseev rushed to deal with the minor ones first; he needed to tidy up the overall picture. So it was now, reading the tape of the conversation, he added nothing on the trembling question of abdication—actually nothing depended on them right now. However, he viewed with great alarm and diligence the matter of letting notifications through from Petrograd and holding back Ivanov—actually, only here could he act.

With respect to revolutionary news, they had had Evert's completely opposite telegram since the previous night: hold back this entire flood! And now Ruzsky had gone and let it all through. He had to choose a line.

In the spirit of good will toward the Duma Committee, and if they could expect from the Emperor further concessions and even abdication, then, of course, Ruzsky was right.

Alekseev instructed that an order be issued immediately to the Western Army Group and the Southwestern to authorize and allow to be printed those statements of the State Duma Committee which inclined toward calm, order, and strengthening the delivery of food supplies.

And Ivanov? . . . Although Ivanov reported only to the Supreme Commander, based on the Rules for the Administration of the Army in the Field, in the event of the Supreme Commander's illness, the chief of staff was to direct the armed forces in his name (and in the event of his death, to take his place). The Supreme Commander's present separation apparently resembled illness. In any event, if Ivanov were to overlook anything anywhere or enter into conflict, it was Alekseev whom Petrograd, the Duma, and society would not forgive.

But Ivanov had ominously disappeared, without a trace, had not sent a single dispatch and was in some unknown location—and might already be undertaking the irrevocable.

Ivanov could be found and stopped only with the help of Northern Army Group headquarters, though. Alekseev took this up immediately and handwrote a telegram to Danilov to send an officer via Dno to establish contact with General Ivanov.

But the Northern Army Group was not responsible for Ivanov's actions and did not hurry to implement, and even expressed doubt as to the utility of such an action. Then Alekseev tediously instructed that a second order be sent. Then Boldyrev, delaying, asked, but what exactly should the instruction to the officer be? And what if he couldn't reach General Ivanov?

Then for a third time GHQ ordered an officer sent to find Adjutant General Ivanov and obtain from him all information about his intentions and situation.

General Alekseev also ordered verified the strange communiqué from Rodzyanko which claimed that Luga had been seized by detachments of troops sent from the army group. And not by the mutinied Luga garrison?

[3 0 7]

A politician's career takes shape differently from the life of an artisan, scientist, or writer. For the latter, their type of activity doesn't change at the beginning and end of life but goes from ware to ware, from book to book. They can be more or less successful, they can bring the author money and fame or not, but from his youth it is clear what this person will be doing and what he is going to be called: tinsmith, botanist, or poet.

Whereas the birth of political careers, apart from the unfair hereditary monarchy, is utterly unpredictable. A boy cannot say: "I'm preparing to be prime minister." Nor can his family say: "We're going to make him a deputy in parliament, the opposition leader." Many unknowingly start out from a direction not at all political but from something related or adjacent—and then suddenly, mysteriously, in part due to a favorable confluence of circumstances, but more often, of course, due to the candidate's personal qualities and internal predestination, the fragments of fate reconfigure kaleidoscopically—and the person almost suddenly (for others, not himself) becomes a well-known political figure.

A boy can grow up in the family of a failed architect; be witness to his mother throwing plates at his father; grow up without any emotional connection to his parents so that later he might not notice his father's death or see his mother and be reconciled. The boy's school nickname might be "Kangaroo," he might have little to do with his classmates and might even tattle on his brother (from whom he is estranged as well). When they forbid him to play with the children of their poor neighbors, he doesn't, and when his agemates climb the fence to shake the apple trees, he sensibly stays on this side of the fence. Our little boy can write poetry as a child and willingly studies the violin. For a brief while, he can even be lured by church ritual, and attend the Church of John the Baptist on Starokonyushenny without being forced—but without anyone's support, he quickly abandons this, especially since it's so easy to obtain the certificate of confession and communion needed for the high school authorities. The priest has no time to hear his sins, and covers the pupil's head with his stole. In high school, our boy is drawn by classical antiquity and he will do well in it, although he graduates with only a silver medal. What will affect him most irresistibly will be Voltaire's irony and sarcasm, which will help him view religion's formalities intelligently and negatively. Spenser, too, will increase his doubts about traditional religiosity. The life of the intellect will elevate him over the life of emotion, and the youth will take little notice of proximate female beings. For a while he will share society's general enthusiasm for liberating the Southern Slavs—and during the Turkish war he will go to the Caucasus as a medic in a rear hospital. So far, he has not been at all inclined toward politics; apparently he has never yet engaged in any political activity—but he was expelled for a year from the university at age twenty-two for a speech at a student gathering. Inwardly, he was simply glad that under Aleksandr III the studentry's political activities ceased, they having drastically impeded his engagement in scholarly work. In the opinion of his supervising professor Klyuchevsky, though, the classical and Western stream he had mastered was preventing our young man from being permeated by the spirit of Russian history—and the young man found he could remain at the university's department of Russian history only despite his teacher. His emotional longings, unsatiated during his young years and dried up before they could even get started, the young man marries based on a compatibility in their freedom-loving and violin inclinations, and then, in time, one son and a second are born to him, little noticed. At his first lessons at the high school and his first lectures at the university, the young lecturer is agitated, and he still flushes thickly—though afterward this quality wears away. Over the years he buys a great many books on history, so that his apartment resembles an antiquarian bookseller's. He is thirty-five and the ways of his private world have been permanently set, and now the only variable is precisely what research he is able to complete and how original that research is.

But no! In a third of a century we might not see through to our own political ambitions. The kaleidoscope's shards haven't even begun to arrange themselves. Being a historian, how can one guard against comparisons, judgments, and prognoses, now political—especially in the face of such a politically avid public as the Russian intelligentsia in the provinces (in Nizhni Novgorod, on a lecture tour of various cities). And the investigation begins, and just having raised all of liberal Petersburg to its feet in his defense, he manages to get sent to the quiet provincial capital of Ryazan for his exile—and the professorial *Russian Gazette,* Russia's most intelligent and progressive newspaper, now appreciates the exiled man, proposing permanent collaboration and a fixed salary. Two peaceful, happy years of his Ryazan exile.

Meanwhile, the elements of fate are latching on to one another and reconfiguring. The concluded investigation threatens a year of prison, but permission is given to choose two years of foreign travel instead of prison. Naturally. Once you begin your exile (lectures in Sofia, journeys through the Balkans, overseas, lectures in Chicago and Boston, research in England), you yourself change, and so does the view of you everywhere. You open the United States' eyes to Russia's crisis, that there is even a catastrophe maturing in it, that its culture is primitive and Russia's weaknesses innumerable, Slavophilism has died, and the national idea has collapsed and is not going to rise up. You share this opinion with your English colleagues as well, that the Russian path differs from the European only in that it is delayed.

You sail to the America you've come to love over and over again and sometimes you return to Russia, where, during the time of your exile and absences, you seem to have acquired considerable fame as a politician and there is no way now for you to be the modest professor you once were. You yourself no longer feel like shutting yourself in with rows of books brown with age, you are too worked up by the public arena you've entered, and you're already searching for exactly what to call yourself. In stable, freedom-loving England you can allow yourself to be a liberal, but in cataclysmic Russia, radicalism is inevitable. You also discover in yourself a quality that your fellow champions and people of like mind just don't have: your virtual destiny as a leader. No matter where you turn up, you're promoted almost effortlessly to the first rank and the first place, the first lecturer, the first respondent, the first organizer. Never having been a zemstvo man, you suddenly become the ideologue of a zemstvo movement transformed by revolution. Never having been a revolutionary, you sit in sessions with them as well. (Is it not to the revolutionary movement that we owe our most important gains in freedom?) None other than you does the first congress of the Kadet party toast with a glass of Champagne, anticipating celebrating the 30 October Manifesto—but you pour cold water on your listeners when you say that nothing has changed and the war with the government continues. And here you are among the first to whom Witte offers a ministerial post. You are the invariable progressive of the Kadets' *Speech*. You are the first speaker at Kadet congresses and only by an administrative trick were you deprived of getting into the First Duma. You are still nobody in 1906 and 1907, but you are summoned over and over again to secret talks about the formation of a government—and you explain magnificently to the figures of reaction: "If I offer five kopecks, society will be prepared to take that for a ruble. But if you offer a ruble, they won't take it for five kopecks."

A miracle seemed to have occurred! The unforeseen had been fixed! The glass shards had arranged themselves if not into a prime minister then into a minister of foreign affairs! Nonetheless . . .

Nonetheless, by the same inexplicable caprice of history, before the pancake has grazed the lips, it disappears, and there's not even a skillet, let alone a first pancake. Everything vanishes, and for a good ten years.

During those ten years someone else in his place, uncalled, might have long since lost his courage and hope and passed from the circle. But he who is truly born a politician, even though he found this out only in his later years, he will take the smallest steps on patient feet and step over, wiggle through, or wait it out, won't disdain the work of the Duma commissions or the most tedious speech topics, in rivalry with his party colleagues will hold onto the reins of party leadership and become leader of the Progressive Bloc and the entire Duma and . . .

And once again nothing may come of it! Sixty is coming fast, and the debility of old age is not far off. All your efforts, talents, and patience—all of it might go clattering off in vain, such being the depths of the political gulf. All of it might snap, disappear, be erased, unless at the fateful moment you feel a sudden gust of wind at your back.

Just such a red gust came on 12 March—and by the first night Milyukov was nearly at the head of the Duma's Provisional Committee and at his urgent request had compelled them to take power. For the past three nights and two days, though, cautiously stepping out from under Rodzyanko's protective back, all he could think of was how to seize power Russia-wide.

He understood with surety that the loftiest days of his career had come, the crowning point of his life, now or never. And today, 15 March, had come and defined itself as the greatest day in Milyukov's life. He had lived fifty-eight years for this day!

The revolution that had begun could have been suppressed by outside troops, but when this had not happened by the end of the third day, yesterday, he could say definitely that it was not going to. Resistance could have been expected from the old government in Petrograd itself, but that government was blown away and scattered the very first day. Ruinous dissension could have arisen with the revolutionary Soviet wing, but at today's agonizing but inconclusive nighttime negotiations, Milyukov pushed through and sensed that there was no genuine resistance.

Just after four in the morning he fell on the table, on his fur coat spread out there. Even his iron endurance couldn't take any more.

He awoke after eight—and lay there a little longer, pretending to sleep, so as not to enter into the discussions right away—and clarity entered his awakened mind. As of this night, as of this morning, there was nothing preventing him from creating a Russia-wide government! It didn't matter that they hadn't finished their negotiations. Nothing now impeded the formation of the government itself. All obstacles had fallen away. The only thing left was to settle on the ministers.

The only thing! This was among the most intricate tasks, in a continuous tangle with what someone had secretly contrived, someone had openly expressed, conjectured, hinted at, supposed—and one had to slip in and between all this, lopping something off here, assenting there. You might say that these past three days, since the revolution began, Pavel Nikolaevich's mind had been engaged with only this: how to compose a government. How to arrange this entire train of candidates correctly and who to put in which seat. While outwardly participating in other discussions with the Duma deputies, too, mentally, Pavel Nikolaevich was focused on this one thing. The nighttime negotiations with the Soviet had been so easy to sit through because the Soviets were making no claims to a single ministerial post.

The previous plans for a government of popular trust, plans from the days of the Progressive Bloc, had been devised for an abstract situation and could not come through revolutionary days unscathed. All the forces, scattered in a new way, were pulling every hour, pushing and pulling—every hour changing the government's proposed makeup—up until the official hour when it would suddenly be announced and come to exist.

All these constant changes and all the burning plans and candidacies lived and moved in Milyukov's mind. This was all he had been whispering about all these days, while about some he decided in silence.

The most unfortunate legacy of previous plans, of course, was now Prince Lvov, because now, since his arrival the day before yesterday, it had become painfully clear that he was a milksop and because he was occupying Milyukov's legitimate prime ministerial seat. But it would be a major public inconvenience to change him now due to the pressure of public opinion, the tradition of the Union of Zemstvos, and that paradoxical circumstance that it was Milyukov who had nominated him, chucking out Rodzyanko. Oh well, he would have to be wise and reconcile himself to this for now. Nonetheless, the deciding seat in the government would be occupied by Milyukov, and in a few months he would likely move Lvov aside altogether.

In any case, these past few days, even if he, Prince Lvov, was here, in the Tauride Palace, glimpsed fleetingly, he did not have the influence to prepare a government. Milyukov did not consult with him and merely muttered something out of politeness.

Rodzyanko was also playing out his role to the end, a role of considerable use in the preceding days, and with each hour he withdrew further into the background. Fortunately, thanks to his good nature and incapacity for intrigue, he was neither a foe nor an obstacle for Milyukov.

Then: Guchkov's confident entrance. Guchkov arrived at the Tauride Palace and was coming into power without actually asking anyone, but as the historical fighter against the old government and also, as everyone knew, five minutes from a would-be palace coup. Milyukov's longtime antagonist and even personal enemy, Guchkov promised to be a difficult companion in the government, but there might be certain pluses here, too. Two strong antagonists, like two magnetic poles, they could create stability for the government. Milyukov was a realistic politician, and when necessary for the cause, he could change both his attachments and his repulsions.

The inevitability of accepting the Konovalov-Nekrasov-Tereshchenko-Kerensky combination had turned into a relief for the able politician. Now, distressing though it was, he would have to reject his dear comrades from the party and not invite Maklakov, Vinaver, or Rodichev. There was no way he could say no to his comrades-in-arms, with whom he reached the pinnacle of victory—but what if insurmountable circumstances were such? As long as the Kadets were fighting the old government, each such orator, figure, and fighter was worth his weight in gold. But now, no matter how Pavel Nikolaevich considered these individuals, rather than see them in their correct governmental seats, he saw in them an obstacle to his own future activities. Each of them was too individual, with his own quirks, caprices, or deviations, his own pretensions to shine, sparkle, and accrue popularity (and they were very good at this)—but that kind of uncoordinated popularity could only weaken a government team and lead to redundant disputes and mutual arguments for which there would not be time, more likely creating instability and discord inside the government. Of course, it would be striking to lend the future government the glamour of introducing this pleiad, but the government's functioning would not be the better for it. And right then, one wedge knocked out another: forced to accept these strangers—not out of caprice—they had to push out their own Kadets.

Was there even a place left for the unfailing Shingarev? He was presumed for Minister of Finance—but Tereshchenko, all of whose virtues, besides his knowledge of ballet, came down to his wealth, what post could he occupy besides Minister of Finance? It was too bad to leave out Shingarev because he was a decent worker, but it was hard to carve out something for him.

Kerensky had actually become the key figure for the newly created government. In his person the government wrested away the revolution's ringleader, acquiring stability by expanding to the revolutionary wing of democracy. Kerensky was all the more essential because Chkheidze had declined.

The negotiations with Kerensky were top secret; he hid carefully from his comrades in the Soviet. First he gloomily predicted that they wouldn't let him join. Then he ardently promised but demanded secrecy until the last moment. And until the final hours, the entire picture depended on Kerensky's final decision.

It was this morning that he summoned Milyukov to the telephone. He had finished out the night somewhere, not at home, and now with a cheerful voice spoke from there, saying that yes, he agreed irreversibly. However, as before, he asked that no one be told until the last minute, while he was still neutralizing his opponents.

What remained now was to wait for this. There would be a signal.

His head was freed from the final calculation—and Milyukov looked at himself in the mirror. Crumpled, unshaven, an unfresh shirt, he did not at all suit his great day. He should go home to Basseinaya, wash up, and change clothes.

Outside it was a bright and sunny, frosty, cheerful day.

[3 0 8]

Not only had General Alekseev remained in place of the Supreme Commander, but he was supposed to resolve or help resolve all of Russia's fate. But he had never prepared for this.

He was sick as well. Perhaps in good health he could have grasped this more clearly.

Now, there, in Pskov, the persuading of the Emperor had begun—and of course the process would be long and tedious, as Danilov had predicted.

Alekseev felt the burden of undertaking something, of helping matters from GHQ, of helping along a successful resolution. But how? If the Emperor were here now, Alekseev would be going to his residence with telegrams and would have tried to help with advice, would have cautiously encouraged him. But the Emperor had left—as if he had deserted. And left everything on Alekseev's shoulders, obliging him to take his own actions at each event.

Although every day Alekseev did everything as he saw fit and had met with no objections from the Emperor, now it turned out that all alone—he couldn't.

He needed to share this burden with someone.

Whom? Independent and equal in rank to the GHQ chief of staff were only the commanders-in-chief of the army groups and fleets.

That was an idea! In the past few days, Rodzyanko had already gone directly to the commanders-in-chief; he had already drawn them into the discussion of affairs of state. So wasn't it natural to continue this discussion specifically with them? This was a way to ease his task. Ruzsky already knew anyway, so why hide anything from the others?

Alekseev liked this idea very much. It eased the unbearable pressure of responsibility.

When Rodzyanko, a civilian and outsider, appealed to the commanders-in-chief, it was outrageous interference in the army hierarchy. But if they were to do the same from GHQ itself, it would only mean honor and respect for the commanders-in-chief. Indeed, why not turn to them now with the impending fateful question? To obtain from the commanders-in-chief that senate, that supreme council, that special military parliament whose combined opinion would both help the Emperor with advice in a difficult moment and to some degree require him not to hesitate endlessly.

Based on yesterday's negotiations and expressions, Alekseev could be certain that Brusilov, Ruzsky, and Nepenin viewed the situation soberly, without a loyal subject's excessive timidity.

No sooner had Alekseev thought of this than he immediately approved it. He told Lukomsky—who very much supported it. Work began to seethe for them: compose a circular letter to the commanders-in-chief. Make it convincing, and quickly.

Rodzyanko's mighty voice, winded by Petrograd fears, was instilled in this letter. The thought of the capital's most intelligent men conveyed to the GHQ generals the absolute inevitability of abdication. How had they themselves not seen before this morning that this was not a matter of a responsible ministry but of posing the dynastic question point-blank? That the war could be prosecuted to a victorious conclusion now only if the popular demand for abdication was met.

Mixing his own voice with Rodzyanko's, Alekseev, without perceiving it, was now himself clarifying and adding that the situation evidently permitted no other solution. The very existence of the army in the field and the operation of the railroads was in fact in the hands of the Petrograd Provisional Government. If they were to save the army and save Russia's independence, costly concessions were needed.

Fiercely intent and feeling much better, Alekseev very quickly wrote out a sheet of paper; he had always written quickly and had no difficulty choosing the right expressions. While Lukomsky leaned his elbows on the desk beside him and supported him with timely and well-placed advice. With every sentence written, Alekseev not only gained confidence in himself but even warmed to the idea of how easily one might emerge from this terrible difficulty without shedding a drop of blood.

His pen transformed Rodzyanko's nighttime bucking nearly into a military order: Would the commander-in-chief be so gracious as to telegraph post-haste his most loyal request directly to His Majesty in Pskov, copy to the Supreme Command's chief of staff?

Once again, for fear that the document was not fully intelligible: the loss of each minute could be fateful for Russia's existence; unity of thought must be established among the high command of the army in the field. Such a decision would rid the army of possible instances of betrayal of duty and from the temptation of taking part in a coup—which, however, could be achieved painlessly by a decision of the Emperor himself.

Now this. To Ruzsky—who knows everything—the first prepared telegram. To the Caucasus Army Group and the fleets, due to communications difficulties, telegrams. And divide the three remaining army groups among us three, so as not to lose time, and simultaneously conduct with all three a persuasive telegraph conversation with the commanders-in-chief themselves.

But Alekseev was so tired that he passed on the interlocutors expected to be difficult—Evert and Sakharov—to his aides. And for himself chose the easy Brusilov.

From his very first words, Brusilov supported his hope:

"It is my honor to greet you. What is your order?"

In transmitting the text, Alekseev followed the one written for everyone but here and there added something of his own, as in a live conversation. He stumbled in one place and changed it:

". . . The situation is foggy. . . . However, it obviously permits no other solution. Every minute of further hesitation can only elevate the challenges. . . ."

He also added in confidence that he was worried about intrigues by the vanished Ivanov, who could spoil the entire peace-loving intention. At that point he was brought a paper saying that Ivanov was returning to GHQ, but the chief of staff didn't really believe it.

And a reply flowed in from Brusilov that was like hearing his cheerful, delicate, ever-at-the-ready voice:

"I agree with you completely. We must not waver. Time is of the essence. I will immediately telegraph your most loyal request. I completely share all your views. There cannot be two opinions here!"

"Yes!" Alekseev rejoiced. "We will act in concert. Herein alone lies the possibility of surviving the illness Russia is suffering from with the army intact, not letting the contagion touch the army."

An easy man Brusilov!

"Yes, there must be complete solidarity among us. And!"—the other did not forget to add—"I consider you by law the Supreme Commander in lieu of another instruction."

Well, this was too farsighted. But Alekseev had not had a chance to think about this since morning. After all, if there was an abdication, what would happen to the post of Supreme Commander? . . . In this entire action, though, Alekseev had by no means sought the post for himself. Indeed, not having straightened his back for many months here, inwardly he was wholly reconciled to the idea that when the streak of military successes came, he would be replaced by someone more prominent and brilliant.

When others were promoted, he retained a tranquility of spirit.

*　　*　　*

OH, SAY IT LIKE YOU MEAN IT, SAY IT LOUD AND CLEAR!

*　　*　　*

[3 0 9]

The night was a patchy business and deceptively peaceful. For a few brief hours, sleep encased you, and you could sleep as if nothing bad were happening. But at the very first wakening, the chest was defenseless and so badly gnawed, it was as if it had no shield in front all the way to the neck, nothing but a torn, aching cavity. You wished you could save yourself and go back to sleep—but it wouldn't take you back.

Even before you were fully awake, even more explosively and tortuously than when fully awake, with open eyes, sorting through already specific questions: What was happening in Tsarskoye? Alix and the children were in danger. You couldn't get to them. Yesterday you capitulated and granted a responsible ministry. But actually (a fearful presentiment stirred) it would still be fine if everything calmed down at this.

Although his nighttime conversation with Ruzsky seemed to arrive at universal reconciliation, by morning, he saw how hopeless it was.

Getting up was very hard as well because the day would not bring people who were close to him, people he could confer with. His suite was a void; he had no one close in it. How had he lived with this suite all these years? . . .

And from Alix, no news. The trip was supposed to unite them, but he'd been torn away.

Prayer. In his abandoned, hopeless state, prayer alone fortified him. You stood there and felt it restore your strength, which had leaked from your toppled body in the night.

How many misfortunes had there been in his life? What else might he not be prepared for?

Since early morning it had been overcast, and it was unclear whether there would be sun.

Overnight, snow had swept under the royal train on the reserve track.

Opposite the window and across two platforms was a water pump. Beside it was a gray stone outbuilding. And an unhitched cistern barrel.

He drank his coffee without tasting it.

At the station, close to the royal trains, all was calm: no threatening assemblages and no additional guard. Trains were coming from and going to Petrograd. Only those coming from the capital (the suite was intercepting them) were recounting that officers were being disarmed there, there was occasional shooting, and there were masses of troops on the street and many going to the Duma.

On the side of the royal train away from the station, long freight trains passed pulling their freight, so essential to everyone.

There was no sense of the front in Pskov, which was far from the front-line Dvina positions.

The Emperor would have liked to take a stroll down the platform, but he felt awkward about attracting attention.

His lot remained to sit in his car and wait for news.

It didn't take long: Ruzsky arrived now with a report.

Restraining any expression as always, the Emperor also restrained any expression of the hope with which he greeted this strange general with the tin eyes and the sharply jutting face who was, meanwhile, an intellectual straight out of Chekhov. Had Rodzyanko gone wild with joy over the responsible ministry? Was the fatman himself going to arrive soon with an eccentric Council of Ministers?

Ruzsky comported himself pompously and guarded his words. He presented the Emperor with pages pasted with the telegraph tape from his nighttime conversation. (He was amazed at how overnight the Tsar had become even browner and how his oval eye sockets had sunk even more, like grooves, in the gray light of the train car.)

They sat down. The Emperor began reading to himself. Slowly, so slowly, the sentences wouldn't come together. The simple work of literacy—reading printed letters—was suddenly hard for him.

"No," he asked. "You read it, Nikolai Vladimirovich."

Ruzsky began to read—in a monotone, with pauses, like a teacher, so his words would be absorbed.

Oh, Nikolai had had a foreboding, and now it sunk in. His supreme sacrifice, a responsible ministry—rejected! Too late . . .

One of the *most terrible* revolutions? Could anyone imagine what was going on there!

And what about in Tsarskoye Selo? . . .

But he fortified himself, saying that, given his tendency to exaggerate, this clown Rodzyanko might be making more of it than was there. This horror might not be that great, and he was amplifying it so that he could add to his own merits later for managing so well.

But when Ruzsky read that the dynastic question had been posed *point-blank*—and he uttered this word poignantly—this *point-blank* pierced the Emperor's chest.

Nor did it remain a puzzle for long. Here was the explanation: abdicate in favor of his son under Mikhail's regency.

Abdication?

All of a sudden they expected abdication?

He simply could not take that in. Given a living, healthy father—an artificial regency? To what end?

For some reason, it became even harder to penetrate. But there was no more sense to be made of it—one could go no further.

The Emperor stood up. (Ruzsky stood as well.)

He walked over to the window. He looked at the meaningless platform.

At the water pump. The gray building. The lonely cistern.

All of a sudden, it was as if the chilling canopy of a vast, immense tent had unfurled over him. Full abdication? My God, there was even a sanctity to this.

You've wanted this for a long time? You've needed this? Well, take it.

Rule. If you think that this is a delight. Whoever is so lured by power. Whoever is so thirsty for it.

Abdication? A sweep of his generous hand. This wasn't petty trading over a responsible ministry or the bowing of a monarch's neck under the Duma's yoke.

Abdication was liberation. Of others from yourself. Of yourself from a monumental burden.

Now, while agreeing to a responsible ministry, wasn't it natural to step away, too?

He staggered back. No, this was a temptation. A blissful temptation. He was the anointed sovereign. How was he at liberty to do this?

What about Mikhail? What good was Mikhail? His entire licentious story with Brasova, his inability to fight his passion. After Georgi's death and before Aleksei's birth he had been considered the heir, but he had never seriously prepared for the throne. In these past few days, though, someone had instructed him to interfere.

Georgi! How unluckily and early! And in Georgia's mountains, almost like being abroad, in Abastuman, where he died of suffocation, there is a black marble chapel with gold Slavic ligature under the cupola: "Blessed are the pure in heart, for they shall see God." A sad and lonely death. But a shining destiny.

Blessed are the pure in heart. . . .

We had grown accustomed to his death and didn't think of him. But now it swelled up again: Oh, why was he gone? He was older than Mikhail and more serious, and he might have been able to do what hadn't worked out for Nikolai: govern not at odds with society.

If there had been someone to hand it over to, would Nikolai have refrained? He would have done so willingly. What was there to this power, other than perpetual disquiet?

But would Russia be saved by his abdication? . . . Wouldn't the throne totter in the people's eyes?

"For the good of Russia," he spoke in a parched voice, "for the good of the people I would always step aside. But if my departure were announced right now, all of a sudden, would the people really understand? Would they really accept it?"

But General Ruzsky had not said that. He'd said nothing of the kind, not now and not last night with Rodzyanko. He? He had only brought the tapes. This was what was written on the tapes.

After yesterday's grinding away over a responsible ministry, it could not have occurred to Ruzsky that the Emperor would agree to discuss something even greater—abdication. But since he had brought it up, then . . . Say it? . . .

General Ruzsky could add that this morning Lukomsky had telegraphed. And he . . .

Lukomsky had said—*on his own behalf.* But this did not look as if it was "on his own behalf." And it could not be "*on his own behalf.*" It would mean nothing "on his own behalf." . . . Here a starker relief was needed.

. . . GHQ, too, persisted in thinking precisely this: abdication was inevitable. No one wanted bloodshed, and everyone wanted to save the army from this anarchy. Save it for victory.

Did they think Nikolai wanted bloodshed? Oh, my God, anything but to allow the shedding of precious Russian blood! . . . Or did they think he wanted victory for Russia less than they did?

And also this: the news conveyed by GHQ for His Majesty in the night. Many former ministers and presidents of the Council of Ministers had been arrested—Goremykin, Stürmer, Golitsyn.

Poor, innocent old men.

In Moscow, too, there had been rallies all over, and it had been suggested to General Mrozovsky that he submit to the new authority. In Petrograd there was a continuous flow of people welcoming the Duma, including Grand Duke Kirill Vladimirovich at the head of his Guards Crew, who presented himself personally and put himself in the power of the Duma Committee.

The Emperor shuddered. A painful betrayal. Not Kirill—envious and vindictive, who had always lived in the competition between the two branches of the dynasty, offended—Kirill wasn't a surprise. But the Guards Crew! Especially beloved. Those marvelous sailors who had sometimes accompanied them on the royal yacht.

The Empress had expressed a desire to hold talks with the chairman of the Duma Committee.

Ah, Sunny! Ah, my dearest! How desperate for her! How humiliating.

And also: yesterday, His Majesty's Personal Convoy had shown up at the State Duma—and had also taken the side of the insurrectionists. They asked to arrest their officers.

What? Even **they**? . . .

Even the Convoy? . . .

This was a blow Nikolai had not expected, and he could not hide that fact. His face and voice changed, his legs buckled, and he sat down. Everything taken together that had happened in the capital gone mad these past few days did not shake him the way this small added news did. The night before he had steadfastly borne the Tsarskoye Selo garrison's betrayal. Unsensibly, random units, many reserve ones, had been posted there. He could be betrayed by all the grand dukes (which was nearly the case), the entire nobility (this was not at all the previous high-minded nobility but fallen, greedy people), the entire State Council, half of which had been appointed by the

Emperor himself (while the State Duma was made up entirely of his ene-mies)—but **how** could His Personal Convoy betray him, those marvelous, courageous, and good-natured Kuban and Terek Cossacks in whom their Emperor had taken such pride? They had lived almost as part of the royal family—each of them known by name, their families showered with gifts, Christmas parties held with them and triple kisses exchanged with each at Easter—*how* could they have gone to greet the Duma? What had driven them there? (And what about his family now? Were they in the hands of the rebellious rabble? . . .)

Everything inside him collapsed. He became morose, as if deafened, barely understanding.

Right then Ruzsky was handed a telegram from Alekseev at headquar-ters. Naturally, he had to read it out loud to the Emperor.

Was that so? His chief of staff, without asking him, had advised all the commanders-in-chief of his abdication? But why? Who had authorized him?

There was a great deal to be surprised at, but for some reason Nikolai wasn't. Over these past few days he had become accustomed to events rolling along without asking him.

The situation evidently permits no other solution. . . . The loss of each minute could be fateful for Russia's existence. . . .

My God! Was that really so?

But perhaps it truly was? . . .

My God, how hard it was to think. Nor did one want to.

He had the good idea of asking Ruzsky:

"And what do you think?"

Ruzsky? Had he ever dared express anything of the kind even last night, even now? He had not said anything of his own up until this moment.

Caught unawares by the drastic words in Alekseev's telegram, Ruzsky now tortuously sought an answer that wouldn't trip him up—but would also not overlook the Tsar's hesitations, which he had never anticipated, but here he'd noticed!

"Your Majesty. The question is too important and even horrible. I ask permission to be allowed to think it over."

The Emperor was touched at the general's agitation. He graciously suggested:

"Then stay and have breakfast with me."

But Ruzsky's remote eyes turned glassy behind his spectacles:

"Your Majesty, the reports and telegrams have piled up at headquarters."

So the Emperor let him go to think. Telling him to return after break-fast. Ruzsky asked permission to come not alone but with the other gener-als. Fine.

Since this was so, since Alekseev had sent this telegram, we would wait for the replies from the commanders-in-chief. This was actually a relief—to think not alone but in council.

The Emperor was left alone—and his soul ached even more. It had been easier to talk with the mechanical Ruzsky than to be left alone again.

Most important to his heart was what Nikolasha would say.

Truly, should he perhaps concede after all? What a relief for himself and for them.

After all, they were asking him to abdicate the throne, not the principle of monarchy. Or the dynasty. The abdication was personal. It was a personal step.

To admit that he was a failed tsar.

Personal abdication did not mean a parliamentary system. There would simply be another Tsar. Aleksei, before his time.

Nikolai himself could easily stand aside. Only he did not have the right to let the crown collapse. Therefore, yesterday it had been much more difficult and dangerous to agree to a responsible ministry than it was today to abdication. Yesterday was entirely against his conscience, entirely against his feeling.

Moreover, if he were to abdicate now, wouldn't yesterday's concession of a responsible ministry be canceled automatically? How good!

It was hard only to take the first concessionary step. And then—immediate relief.

Oh, how hard it was to bear this all alone!

There was something bright in this decision.

It was a decision of conscience. To step away from evil.

[3 1 0 '']

(FROM *IZVESTIA OF THE SOVIET OF WORKERS' DEPUTIES*)

CAN THE ROMANOV DYNASTY REMAIN?
 . . . If power is going to be handed over to a monarch, even a constitutional monarch, he could shackle the people in the chains of slavery. . . .

NOTICE. On this 14 March, a rumor spread among the soldiers of the Petrograd garrison that the officers in the regiments were confiscating soldiers' weapons. . . . I declare that the most decisive measures will be taken to prevent such actions on the part of officers, up to and including execution of the guilty parties by firing squad.

Engelhardt

FEWER WORDS, MORE DEEDS. It is still too soon to be shouting "hurrah" and "bravo." In 1905, everyone talked too much, waited, conferred, assured each other and themselves that everything was going well. . . . Now the government, its servants, and a few thousand savage landowners are not napping but organizing around Petrograd in order to turn everything around and above all to revel in bloodthirsty revenge.

THE FATE OF TSAR NIKOLAI II. According to reports from the Soviet of Workers' Deputies, the royal train has been stopped between the Bologoye and Dno train stations; a wreck has been arranged behind it and revolutionary troops ahead. The question of arresting Nikolai has been raised. According to other reports, Nikolai is headed to Pskov. All this time, the Empress has been in hysterics, and the heir has a temperature of 39°, measles.

ORDER No. 1
14 March 1917   For the Petrograd garrison. . . .
The Soviet of Workers' and Soldiers' Deputies has resolved . . .
....

STORES MUST BE OPENED. The victorious people must have all necessities. No danger whatsoever threatens stores. In the daytime, stores can calmly trade, but at night they must be well guarded.

RATES. Set rates for all objects of consumption according to the prices that existed up until the revolution. Put an immediate end to speculation!

THE PETROGRAD ORGANIZATION OF THE BUND invites all members to a general assembly. . . .

. . . the Okhrana's papers have burned up; the people have dealt with these ulcers. Destroy everything that might help the stooges of the old regime!

SHOOTING. The bloody government still does not want to reconcile itself to the people's victory. Its stooges, provocateurs, policemen, gendarmes, and spies have hidden on building rooftops and in attics—and are shooting at the people. The revolutionary army and people are easily dealing with these attempts by sinister forces.

FROM THE TELEGRAPH—
IN BERLIN, A BLOODY REVOLUTION HAS BEEN GOING ON
FOR MORE THAN TWO DAYS.
Kronstadt is in the power of the revolutionary army

STOP THE ROBBERIES!—. . . . gangs of hooligans, who are robbing shops and inhabitants' property . . . are casting a shadow on the sacred cause of freedom. . . .

[3 1 1]

Every separate nerve in Captain Rengarten was alive, and the tension and splintering made it impossible to concentrate or calm down. The past night had escaped him entirely. He'd barely dropped off at seven in the morning, and at seven-thirty he jerked awake. Later in the morning, worn out by exhaustion, he dozed a little more—and then again for half an hour, and it was a painful kind of dozing. Everything was boiling over in him.

Most inconceivable of all was the pace of current events, with which neither actions, nor plans, nor intentions could keep up. Just two days ago they had contemplated how to *spur it on*! But by the time something was being contemplated and starting to be done, it was too late and pointless.

The steady alternation of moods, from the latest news: first joy, then alarm, then hope, then disquiet.

In the morning, a telegram had arrived from the commandant of the Reval fortress about disturbances in the city and saying that the commandant feared ominous complications unless he told the demonstrators categorically which side he and the garrison were on.

Nepenin was already so entrenched in the line he had adopted that he did not think long and immediately dictated a reply: "If the situation leaves no other alternative—announce that I am joining the Provisional Government and am ordering you to do the same."

He immediately asked Rodzyanko for assistance: send Duma deputies to Reval to calm the population.

In the morning, there was again a meeting of flag officers, and Nepenin told them the news—the terrible news from Kronstadt but also Guchkov's consoling intervention: Duma deputies were being sent there, one of them would take over the commandant post, and Kronstadt was apparently already starting to calm down. The admiral was even certain that order had been established.

But if it had, then anarchy flaring up was absolutely unfathomable. That was clear to everyone here! People said sixty officers had been killed! What was going on? They were killing us all in short order! What sinister forces had been stirred up! This was the end of the navy!

But Nepenin had control of his face, his firm voice, and the situation. Stop the hysterics. There were no revolutions without excesses. This had all come about from the ships being kept in the dark, so that the slightest wild rumor or appeal could blow up everything. But with a broad, fearless explanation of events and an open announcement about everything going on, nothing like that would happen anymore.

What if it flared up in Helsingfors, too? Shouldn't we change our line? Maybe we're making things worse? Maybe we should . . .

Old naval relics! Reactionary prolixity and stiffness! Nepenin was already breathing a different air—of freedom. But while preserving his love of freedom in his overall worldview, these past few days he seemed to have toughened; he spoke with the flag officers in an ironical tone and did not permit discussion:

"We must not interfere in internal affairs of state. We must recognize that the State Duma's actions are patriotic. And if circumstances so demand, I am openly stating that I recognize its Committee. I will order all of you to do the same. I"—he paused briefly, not in hesitation but for dramatic effect—"I will answer alone. I will answer with my head, but I have firmly decided. I will not allow discussion of this question here! I'm prepared to hear your opinions—but individually, for which you may visit me in my cabin."

Captain First Rank Gadd, commander of the *St. Andrew the First-Called*, looked beaten. Rear Admiral Nebolsin managed to interject:

"But our sailors are not at all that simple-minded. Many are half-educated, and this is a dangerous element. And there are lots of workers."

The other flag officers and leaders maintained a concentrated, gloomy, and reserved look.

Nepenin himself ordered the crews be given another detailed announcement about events. Only total candor could support the officers' firm position.

After the meeting, the Decembrists came to see him and spent all the remaining time with him. They sorted through who of those called to the meeting were hopeless conservatives, like Gadd. There were lots of them. But we'll overpower them! They sorted through the whole stack of cutting news that continued to pour in over the telegraph wires. The manifesto of the Central Committee of the Social Democratic Party (the so-called Bolsheviks) made a very difficult impression with its call to end the war, divide up the land, and establish a democratic republic. Left among his intimates, the admiral relaxed and expressed himself more candidly. Before this, at the meeting, to a question put to him as to whether the Duma Committee's actions already contained a definite predetermination of the form of governance, Nepenin replied with the same weighty voice that it didn't. Now, among intimates, both he and everyone admitted that the pillar of the dynasty was already tottering if not collapsing in these very hours.

Their hearts contracted once again with joy and alarm both. How intense and new! What unexplored expanses!

How should they understand their oath now? After all, its categorical, unambiguous nature did not allow a sudden switch to the Duma Committee's side, did it?

But the oath's formal, dead words could not be placed above the Homeland's interests!

Cherkassky and Rengarten admired the Fleet Commander's firmness. Having crossed a line by declaring he would not recognize his removal by the Tsar, he showed no sign of stepping back, but rather took a bold step forward: Wasn't it time to remove the Tsar himself?

[3 1 2]

Although the Executive Committee members had assembled in their room, no one could find the strength not just to finish the talks with the franchised but even for a simple conference among themselves. The over-heated nighttime acceleration had been lost, and now, dampened, they moved around listlessly, sat willy-nilly on chairs, someone picked up the telephone and tried to answer some question.

What had enlivened everyone and freed their tongues was the scandal in *Izvestia*. The Soviet's own newspaper had written something completely different from what the Executive Committee had decided yesterday! And now half a million copies had been distributed throughout the city and could not be stopped. The EC's leftist majority, which had come together yesterday, had passed a resolution, 13:7, saying that revolutionary democracy would not participate in a bourgeois enfranchised government! But this hadn't been published anywhere yet, this was still being batted around in the negotiations with Milyukov—but meanwhile, the insidious conciliatory minority in the crafty, clever article by the Menshevik Bazarov had sent the exact opposite out over all Petrograd and all Russia: that democracy should join a bourgeois government. This was simply a shocking and outrageous fact! They hadn't taken a vote, they were resorting to subterfuge. How dare the editors print such a sensitive article without asking the Executive Committee's position?

Some were outraged at Bazarov, Bonch, and Goldenberg; others were confused; others did their best to avoid suspicions; and still others openly laughed at the majority. Himmer suffered terribly from this failure; it was as if he had been personally and publicly disgraced!

Izvestia had other surprises for some EC members as well. For instance, not everyone had seen Order No. 1 yesterday. And the report on a revolution in Berlin? It was enough to make you gasp and your heart take a leap— but Bonch had already called from the editorial office to say this was an unfortunate error.

There was no physical opportunity whatsoever for meeting. Since yesterday, another ten of those unbidden soldiers had sat on the EC itself—and here they had showed up early this morning, they hadn't forgotten, anticipating their own participation, they sat like alien stumps. How could they discuss in front of them, how could they work with them, how could a majority be formed? Outrageous! And soon, at one in the afternoon or perhaps a little later, the din of the entire cumbersome Soviet was supposed to start up again nearby, in the next room. If yesterday it numbered nearly five hundred deputies, then today they could expect a thousand. How were they going to cram them in?

Of course, policy isn't made at general meetings; all these populous plenums had no practical significance. But today this Soviet could not be left unattended and unsupervised. The entire issue of entering government was to be formally pushed through, but their position could become unstable and unconvincing in the face of a wild, noisy assemblage. The very idea of a peaceful agreement with the bourgeoisie could be beset by the shouts and battle of recklessly leftist demagogues like Shlyapnikov, Krotovsky, and Aleksandrovich, given the alarming mass of soldiers able to apply street-fighting methods, outrageous methods when they were directed against our own Social Democrats. They would shout: What has this bourgeoisie done for the revolution? Why hand over power to it?

Whereas the Mensheviks and Bundists wanted to join the government.

No, today, the majority of the Executive Committee itself had to climb on the tables and steer the unbridled assembly so that the leftists didn't lead it astray.

But here's what! A great deal depended on the speaker Nakhamkes—and Himmer moved over to talk with him. On this point they both understood the matter identically. They simply had to shut down the debates and not let all their opponents speak. Nakhamkes himself was actually inclined to speak at length—so now he had to at even greater length! Even more fully! He had to take up an hour and a half's time for his report! Two hours! But the crowd was impatient, on its feet, it was crowded and stuffy, and in that time it would tire—and then the debates wouldn't get out of hand.

Right then, Kerensky didn't just walk but raced into Room no. 13 accompanied by his sidekick Zenzinov. Somehow he knew how once again to look full of strength, and not only had he had some sleep but he'd had time to see the barber! His very neat crewcut stood up in a rectangle from his temples. But he didn't smell of cologne and wasn't wearing a starched shirt and had no white collar at all, wearing the standing collar of his dark tunic. He looked triumphant and excited: all the days of the revolution were great, but today, apparently, Aleksandr Fyodorovich anticipated an especially great day!

He didn't indicate why he'd come and didn't enter into the loud discussions. He had come here by rights, as deputy chairman of the Soviet—but not to fulfill any specific functions. First he sat down abruptly (so did Zenzinov) and looked at everyone. Then he stood up abruptly (so did Zenzinov) and paced nervously. Then he started calling the most influential individuals into the corner one at a time.

Himmer guessed what this was about: naturally, he was again conferring about the Ministry of Justice. Oh, how he wanted to be minister!

Yes, that was it, it was finally Himmer's turn. Confidentially, slightly embarrassed, Kerensky asked whether there was any possibility at today's session of the Soviet of securing approval for him to join the government.

No, *this* was something a Soviet meeting might not be able to digest. At this, in response, some Bolshevik or Interdistrict man could jump up and demand that the people take all power into their own hands. We could lose all the maneuvers we've won! No, it was impossible! Kerensky could act as a private individual, and then nothing need be discussed in the Soviet.

No, he didn't like it like that! With a sharp glance, throwing back his long, narrow head, he himself, in front of Zenzinov, who approached on his sign, began accusing the Executive Committee of not focusing its attention properly, of trembling pettily over there not being a single socialist minister, but meanwhile yesterday in the negotiations they had completely surrendered the very republic to Milyukov! On this most heated point, they had left a misunderstanding—and Milyukov had been allowed to behave in such a way that the monarchy would remain!

Kerensky became lightning quick and swept out with Zenzinov, like the wind.

[3 1 3]

* * *

The Petrograd day started out fairly gray but stretched into a light frost with a bright sun. And because no factory smoke stretched over the city, the air was unprecedentedly, festively clean. Nor did you hear the factory whistles or the streetcars. A holiday! Even the shooting had let up, it was almost quiet.

Red banners were hanging everywhere—on apartment buildings, office buildings, and the Mariinsky Palace, with several on the Tauride Palace. The Russian national flags had disappeared. There wasn't a single one anywhere.

* * *

On the walls and fences: Order No. 1 of the Soviet of Workers' and Soldiers' Deputies. In the barracks, too, they read it out loud, in great numbers.

But it was safer on the streets for officers than it had been the past few days.

Although here and there another leaflet hung, half torn: "Soldiers, you still have not heard whether land will be taken away from the landowners. . . . The gentlemen-noblemen have gone mad on their wealth, sucking the people's blood. . . ."

* * *

The vehicles racing madly were now many fewer (maybe broken down?). But there seemed to be even more people on the main streets! Even on the small streets there were clusters of people. But the red ribbons and bows on everyone were now familiar and no longer seemed like anything unusual.

There were the same lines at the bread shops. The stores were shut, nailed up; a few were opening tentatively. In some shops handfuls of loudmouths were threatening, forcing the tradesmen to sell at unthinkably low prices.

And the yardmen were ignoring their duties; in many places the sidewalks hadn't been cleared of snow and there were mounds and holes. People were tripping.

*   *   *

On a narrow street, a mangled motorcar. Wheels broken, the windows of its square cab smashed. Gawkers stood there looking for a long time.

*   *   *

Incompetent militia at street posts: first-year cadets, even older high-school pupils, Scouts ages ten to fifteen, with white armbands. People were obeying them—with a smile.

Anyone who asked got a sign: "This building is under protection of the militia." Many buildings sported them.

But this did little to stop anyone. Throughout the city, armed soldiers were continuing to search and rob private apartments. Institutions, too.

*   *   *

Down Nevsky, the wealthiest public, and officials, and ladies, with broad gestures of joy, were reading *Izvestia of the Soviet of Workers' Deputies* and the *Izvestia* of Petrograd journalists—and discussing and exulting.

There was a long line of all ranks for a fresh newspaper.

*   *   *

In *Izvestia*, in some of the print run, someone, evidently afraid of revealing a military secret, had deleted the word "Kronstadt" from the report on the bloody revolution. And in the blank space, someone had put—"Berlin." (The result: a revolution in Berlin, and Admiral Viren had been killed.)

A ravishing, soaring rumor raced through the city about a revolution in Berlin as well! Revolution everywhere! An end to the war! The shining heavens thundered.

And countering this, another rumor: the heir Aleksei was dead of scarlet fever!

*   *   *

An exultant crowd! Unbridled joy! If the indestructible regime had fallen so easily, then how easily and happily things would continue! Down with the old, insane, tongue-tied rulers! Let them be replaced by energetic, wise, and honest men! A general state of ecstasy, everyone hoping, for no apparent reason, only for good. People were lounging on the sidewalks; people were waving kerchiefs at them from windows.

Zinaida Gippius: The angels are singing in the heavens.

Pyotr Wrangel: The wild merriment of slaves who have lost their fear.

*   *   *

On Sampsonievsky Prospect, across from the Landrin Factory, two engineer companies, no longer young soldiers, had formed up. The unit commander and several officers walked up:

"I congratulate you, brothers, on this great fortune! The government everyone hates has been overthrown. Now we must worthily defeat the foreign enemy. The new government is asking you to obey the gentlemen officers as before. I ask you to go to your places in the barracks."

The soldiers replied: "Willing to do our best!"

Nearby, though, a smart aleck with a rather foolish face (the Bolshevik Kayurov) crept out from among the gawkers and broke in loudly:

"Allow me to speak, commander sir!"

The commander hadn't expected this and was confused. He gave his permission.

Kayurov cockily took a step forward and confidently (they had already indoctrinated the entire Moscow Battalion):

"Comrade soldiers! Did you hear? Return to barracks and obey your officers again? Is this really what blood has been flowing for in Petrograd for three days? Is this really what thousands of proletarian fighters died for? No! The proletariat of Petrograd will not go to the factories until they win the land back from the landowners. Comrade officers! You must join us, too, if you wish happiness for the people! No, they're silent, you see. That means they have another goal. I propose you arrest them, comrades, and choose a new command for yourselves! . . ."

*   *   *

Down Shpalernaya, lines of units that had come to greet the Duma. While waiting, the soldiers drifted out of formation and stacked their rifles in pyramids.

Directly in front of the palace there was a crush, like in church on a major holiday. Everyone was raging to get inside and take a look. But they were demanding passes on the front steps.

Everyone was trying to get into the Tauride Palace! A mother trying to find her children. A delegate from the overseers of the burned-down Lithuanian Fortress prison had come with a list of its wardens, to legalize their residence. Someone was asking for a guard to be posted for his valuable collection. A cabby came: his horse had been stolen. A soldier came: where should he take the horse he caught on the street? A servant came asking permission to walk his gentlemen's dogs in the Tauride Palace garden. (Refused: that would be tactless during the Great Revolution!)

A gentleman came to complain: soldiers had broken into an apartment supposedly searching for weapons, right here, at 44 Shpalernaya, but there was only a single ill woman in the apartment. They stole a massive gold clock and silver spoons. They corrected him: those were hooligans dressed in soldier's uniforms; revolutionary soldiers can't steal.

*   *   *

A mama took her little daughter's head in her hands (a memory):
"You're going to be happy! Hap-py!"
She took her daughter to the demonstrations.

[3 1 4]

A specialist in fortifications and geometry, Lieutenant Stankevich now found himself in military administration.

He was junior in rank, but he had been given a voice of confidence in the sapper engineer battalion by his constant communication with the Duma and in the Duma by his status in the battalion. The sappers were quartered on Kirochnaya, which was quite close to the Tauride Palace, and Stankevich managed to go back and forth several times a day.

A few brave officers in the battalion had been killed during the first few minutes of the uprising. The rest were utterly lost in the new situation, facing the mass of soldiers who had killed those first ones. They couldn't tell them apart by face or eyes and suspected a killer in each. The officers now moved about timidly and didn't dare speak up or have an opinion about battalion affairs. The soldier uprising—was now supposed to be referred to as a great feat of liberation more and more loudly, officially, and obligatorily for the officers. (Now, since the great feat, they had joined—but could they be trusted? . . .) What else could officers do? They would have been happy to vanish altogether from this Petrograd, but they were forced to move over it specifically, using the pass issued them: if from the community governor, that the bearer was not subject to search or arrest and had permission to reside in this city during the month of March; if from the commandant of the Assembly of the Army and Navy, then he had permission even to bear arms. All the battalion's officers held their tongues and could only gaze hopefully at the expeditious Stankevich. They told him that only in his presence did they feel calm in the battalion.

When Stankevich came to the Tauride Palace, because he so firmly belonged in his unit, it was as if gunpowder smoke formed a halo around him, and people put their hopes in him. He himself had hopes, too, as before, of uniting the Duma and Soviet wings, the liberals and socialists. But in the Duma wing, Stankevich did not meet quite the same joyous excess and triple-kissing as on the streets. He encountered worried eyes: what will this great feat of liberation spill over into and how can the soldiers be calmed and guided? Out loud, everyone was required to rejoice and greet, to greet the arriving delegations, but people were already starting to be concerned that this flow was carrying them too powerfully—and where was it going? Even bulky Rodzyanko, who delivered his speeches with such dignity and enthusiasm, would return from them with an expression of suffering and despair. Even he, a powerful man, was being carried off somewhere like a twig.

Privately, Stankevich repented that then, on the 12th, on Kirochnaya, he had folded, obeyed his sergeant's cautions, and hadn't rushed flat out to his own battalion, hadn't attempted to take command of it in time and lead it to the Duma as Kerensky had asked.

Alone in the entire Duma, Kerensky was apparently afraid of nothing and did not tremble in the face of the ominous revolutionary stream but boldly joined it and encouraged Stankevich. Probably because he himself still didn't realize what he was getting into.

A former commander of the sapper engineer battalion had been killed in the first minute of the insurrection—when he led his training detachment to meet the insurrectionists. He had been replaced by someone senior in rank—but the soldiers didn't like him and the churning began. Stankevich was chosen to be the battalion commander's aide, and he had to replace the commander with a lowly ensign who should not have raised objections.

All this Stankevich had done early that morning, now with great confidence and very clearly. Had he had the least bit less confidence, nothing would have come of it. He led the entire battalion into the yard in full battle formation. Here he began speaking in the name of the State Duma, reconciling everything, accusing no one; he presented the new commander and heard no rumble of indignation.

For reinforcement, he proposed proceeding immediately, with the band already in place, to the Tauride Palace. The soldiers liked this! It was all too short a distance, and they willingly would have wound around a few more blocks. The officers, too, obediently took their places. Red banners were carried ahead of the companies.

Very formally, with the thunder of their band, they approached the palace—and Chkheidze came out on the front steps, fell to his knees, and kissed the red banner of the first company. Then, in a rattling mumble, he uttered ecstatic words about the victorious revolution—and said they shouldn't believe the new provocation by the as yet undefeated Okhrana, which yesterday, in the name of the two socialist parties, had released an infamous proclamation calling on soldiers not to obey their officers. But here he was, Chkheidze, a State Duma deputy and the chairman of the Soviet of Workers' and Soldiers' Deputies, ardently calling on the soldiers to trust their officers, to welcome them as citizens who have joined up with the revolutionary banner, and to remain brothers in the name of the great revolution and Russian freedom.

And they hoisted Chkheidze on their shoulders.

Outwardly, everything had worked out excellently. (Although Stanke-vich did realize that the leaflets were from the socialists themselves. And gloom blanketed his soul: we ourselves are going to ruin everything.) They returned to barracks not quite as excellently. Along the way, a number of soldiers peeled off to have a good time and started out through the city. At least, though, the lowly ensign was approved.

An hour later, Stankevich was back at the Tauride Palace. Alone now, in-side. The same Sodom-like closeness and the steam from people's exhala-tions. Young ladies, university students, civilian intellectuals, officers, Duma deputies, soldiers arm in arm with nurses, others lying on the floor between bundles, and still others leading an arrested dignitary.

He came across Kerensky, this time preoccupied, wearing a dark work-ers' jacket rather than a suit. Kerensky led Stankevich to a corner of the room and asked confidentially:

"You know, they've offered me the Minister of Justice portfolio. What do you think? Take it or not? The democratic parties don't want to participate, and I don't want to go against the will of my comrades. But on the other hand . . ."

From his face, Stankevich could tell that he wanted to hear "yes," he was just restraining his joy.

And suddenly Stankevich answered more hopelessly than he had ex-pected of himself:

"It doesn't matter, Aleksandr Fyodorych. Whether you do or don't take it—all is lost."

"What?" Shocked, Kerensky recoiled, losing his languorous veneer. This was someone he'd never expected this from! "On the contrary, everything is going superbly. What are you saying!"

Stankevich's knowledge of mathematics demanded he express himself more precisely:

"Whatever is going is doing so out of the inertia of the old regime, not the new one. All we see that's still holding on—it's from the old regime. But will this inertia last long? Now I'm a soldier and can't help but consider how this is reflecting on military operations. I've come across the following formula: in ten years, all will be well, but in a week, the Germans will be in Petrograd."

"What are you saying! What are you saying!" Kerensky flapped his arms femininely. He didn't even try to argue. "But should I take the justice port-folio or not?"

"Oh well," Stankevich agreed. "Maybe you'll still save this. Take it, of course."

They were close, and Stankevich kissed Kerensky in parting.

And Kerensky dashed off, very pleased. A happy exception.

More and more, Stankevich was seeing worried eyes.

But people wouldn't admit this face to face.

[3 1 5]

One of Peshekhonov's aides, a university student, came up and informed him of the following news: the 1st Machine-gun Regiment, which yesterday had been posted at the House of the People, had placed machine guns on all sides of it, set sentries, and wasn't letting anyone in. But the administrator had called in despair, saying that the sewage system was out of order as of last evening. It was built for two or three thousand men, and ten thousand had barged in. Because times were such, there was no one to call in for the repair, and the soldiers wouldn't let them in anyway, so for as long as they were staying here—there was nothing you could fix.

The architect from the home of the Emir of Bukhara came with concerns that the beams wouldn't hold the weight of so many guests. Nor would the sewage system.

So he had to abandon his commissar concerns and go find a place to put the machine-gun regiment.

He and the student went to the House of the People.

Indeed, the machine guns were there in a semicircle, and the patrols, the soldiers, feared an attack. They didn't trust and so checked and reported—and barely let the commissar inside.

And what was going on inside! The House of the People had known overflows at large celebrations, especially on Easter night, when they held public matins, but there was never this kind of crowding on the staircases, in passageways and galleries; everywhere there was nothing but soldiers, without rifles (having left them by the walls), with no semblance of organization—and no trace of the Petrograd joy on their faces. Some removed caps—and they were close-cropped, unwashed, rural, and rough-hewn. The enormous, alarmed hive droned and droned, and it was hard to imagine where such numbers put themselves at night, lying down.

Peshekhonov, a populist to the bone, even before searching for the leaders, started talking with the soldiers themselves to see how they understood what their regiment should do. The people should know their own good.

But although his appearance was quite modest, if only without a greatcoat—they answered him with ill will, harshly, the way they would a gentleman:

"We're gonna take all the palaces!"

"Yeah, we'll take our machine guns and clean you all out!"

Peshekhonov almost turned to ice. After all, it was true: the regiment had three hundred machine guns, and all in working order! And if this avalanche moved across Petrograd searching for a place for itself . . .

But he learned from the soldiers that attached to the regiment there were also officers, newly elected. There was also a regimental commander who'd been chosen, a captain. They started searching for him.

All the officers invested with the soldiers' trust turned out, in essence, to be under arrest. A single small room had been set aside for them, and they filled it to bursting. The soldiers wouldn't allow the door to be shut even at night for fear of some trick from the officers.

The officers were exhausted by their situation: the outburst of the Oranienbaum revolt, which had spared their heads but with a senseless decision had dragged them along as well—to Petrograd. Here they had no influence whatsoever, they weren't allowed to use the telephone, and they just ran the sentry service. Their captain couldn't decide anything, but only advise going to the regimental committee.

They jostled and searched—and found the committee. Sitting at a table in the room were about fifteen soldiers and one ensign discussing agitatedly. They paid no attention to the men entering. Absolutely sovereign on the whole Petersburg side, Peshekhonov the populist stood close to the door and in his unpretentious voice made several attempts to interject—but there was no pause to slip into, and they weren't listening to him.

Then a university student stood up and shouted forcefully:

"What's wrong with you? Don't you know who this is talking to you? This is *Comrade Peshekhonov!*"

That made an impression!

"Ah!" they exclaimed and jumped up. "Comrade Peshekhonov? Hurrah! Hurrah! Lift him up!"

They nearly started to, although, as Peshekhonov realized, they were hearing his name for the first time.

On the other hand, now he could speak and they were listening.

He started explaining to them the difficulties with both of the buildings they were using. But they couldn't find anything roomier either. What would be best would be if the regiment returned to its barracks in Oranienbaum. They stopped listening and started exclaiming:

"You have room for others but not us?"

"You mean others in Petersburg are going to be put up while we go sit in Oranienbaum?"

"Why don't you set aside a palace for us!"

"Give us the Winter Palace!"

Peshekhonov began explaining that he wasn't in charge of the palaces, that it would be even worse in the Winter Palace, where the toilets weren't at all equipped. And there weren't any other large buildings on the Petersburg side.

They asserted as one:

"That can't be!"

Their eyes were burning. They were aching to spend just one day in a palace and see what it was like to live there.

Fine, Peshekhonov suggested that they appoint billeting officers to go with him right now and survey the Petersburg side and be convinced that there were no such large buildings.

They agreed to go, but only tomorrow. Right now they had to finish discussing something else, and clearly they felt like staying here a little longer.

All right. Surveying with worry and sympathy all these clusters, gatherings, and strings of disheartened, lost soldiers putting on a brave face one more time, Peshekhonov and the student went out through the machine-gun posts and drove away.

At the commissariat there was the same crush and commotion, but an hour later a specific noise was heard, shouts. The sentries tried to hold the intruders back, but some broke through. Peshekhonov hurried toward them. It was two dozen menacing soldiers, some having lost their weapons, some armed, and at their head—like that recent red-headed, insane high school pupil, an equally mad university student, short, with the audacity of the man who decided to take the Bastille, and the soldiers had trustingly closed ranks with him, and even just a few of his armed men were enough to sweep everything away here. The student demanded that they arm the remaining men.

But this morning, the commissariat's weapons upstairs had just been supplemented by grenades and bombs, and all of this lay in a heap on the balcony.

But how could he have a conversation with an entire crowd? Twenty throats were shouting and demanding weapons—and at any moment they could start hoisting the commissariat staff on bayonets, a skirmish between free citizens.

Peshekhonov proposed that the student and three soldiers come inside for talks, behind the partition obstructing the entrance.

At first they didn't want to separate off for anything. Then they went in, all the armed soldiers. But not a step farther! That is where the conversation would have to take place, in the thick of the public, by the entrance.

Peshekhonov was afraid of this mad student and wanted to ease his tension and speak with him in a more kindly way. He began gently explaining that the commissariat carried out other functions, that only the recognized militia could bear arms, and he paternally placed his arm on the student's shoulder.

But the student jerked as if from electricity, reared back, and let out a heart-rending wail:

"Comrades! Come to me! They want to arrest me!"

There was a menacing metallic click as rifles were cocked, revolvers were cocked—and a dozen barrels were immediately aimed at Peshekhonov's head—both right here and across the partition.

All it took was one man firing.

Peshekhonov became flustered and fell silent.

But right then Comrade Shakh, the commissar's sensible aide and head of the publications section, stepped forward. He had such an insinuatingly persuasive and soft voice, he immediately eased the tension and made the men turn toward him. He said that both the commissariat and those who had come were doing a great, united, common revolutionary deed—so why should they quarrel?

The barrels began to lower and hands relax.

But Peshekhonov started retreating and retreating and made no further attempt at conversation.

Only a few minutes later did he fully realize the danger he had survived.

What if they'd broken through and found the bombs? The commissariat might have been swept away along with the entire public.

But Comrade Shakh convinced the furious student to search for weapons elsewhere.

[3 1 6]

At Princess Golitsyna's women's agricultural courses, the students had begun discussing noisily back on Monday as to whether to continue classes or interrupt them and fling themselves into events. Naturally, they didn't ask the professors' opinion, or even the courses' director's, the universally beloved Professor Pryanishnikov, but only each other. And the multiple and loudest voices said to interrupt and fling!

And fling they did.

Ksenia Tomchak hesitated. She would have willingly continued classes. She loved them and excelled in all subjects. But she didn't have the mettle to raise her voice against the majority. Oh well, if they were flinging, so would she! It had a good cheer of its own, and she only had a bit of her fourth year and then her fifth left of her Moscow life—after which she was to drown in the Kuban steppe for good.

So on Tuesday they began dribbling out of their courses, ranging through Moscow in herds and rushing about first in a sunny frost and then in a slanting, windy snow. In the beginning, it was just their own fellow students, but then they joined up with students from other women's courses, the Gerier and the Medical, and then with male university students, and at some point even with older high school boys who had somewhere cleaned out a weapons depot and offered all the female students pistols—to arm themselves in the event of a counterrevolution. (None of them took one; they just laughed.)

On the streets, strangers were embracing as if the closest of friends. Everyone was intoxicated by this unprecedented festivity. If only they could take it all in! Orators were shouting something from the City Duma steps, words that didn't reach the depth of the crowd but that everyone received approvingly. There, cutting through the thickness, entire battalions marched past with banners and bands. Some people—there were no streetcars, cabs, or carriages—thronged over the packed, snowy, now brown sidewalks and filled the streets so that there was no getting through. People said there hadn't been crowds like this even at the coronation ceremonies or Muromtsev's funeral. There wasn't a street in the city center without this black sea. Perhaps half of Moscow, maybe even a million, had been coming the entire day, standing, looking, waving, and shouting hurrah. (The first traffic to appear was freight sledges, which were making a little extra on the side, and anyone who was in a hurry climbed on, even in expensive fur coats, dangling their feet.) Policemen vanished from all their posts, and student "militiamen" appeared wearing armbands (and even Scouts with their staffs) and cheerfully began to sort out the crowd: "Conscientious citizens! Don't congregate here. You're slowing traffic!"

"Conscientious citizens" suddenly became the favorite public address, as if a mutual compliment. All faces were shining, and everyone had red on their caps, chests, and sleeves, like pieces torn from red banners.

After all, revolution, as it's drawn in history, is always linked to barricades, shooting, and dead bodies. But in Moscow there was none of this. Three soldiers had been randomly killed, and people said that on the Yauza Bridge some old man had been calling the crowd to order and they'd drowned him in an ice-hole. The entire revolution had proceeded on nothing but joy, smiles, and radiance, and people had even begun to wonder what they'd been thinking up to this point? Why had they waited and lived otherwise? What had prevented them from living well before? Apparently, no one had any regret for the old days, or even the thought that they might return. On Wednesday, policemen and gendarmes drew together in Carriage Row—but surrendered to the crowd. Many policemen were led to the City Duma, but not hostilely, as if only half-arrested, and the crowd whistled at them as they passed. And if the Aleksandrovsky Military School hadn't joined immediately? On their doors, Ksenia had read a notice: "Citizens! Allow the cadets to continue their work calmly, to the glory of Russia!"

People may not have seen something themselves, but rumors were passed along, one more touching than the next. That the physician Kishkin, now Moscow's commissar, had broken down in tears during a speech at the City Duma and been unable to go on. That the Moscow merchant class had donated 100,000 rubles for the poorest of the poor. Or that an ancient general, a veteran of the siege of Sevastopol, covered in medals from the previous century, had uttered on Resurrection Square: "I thank You, Creator, for not letting my homeland perish!" That the university council had already petitioned for the return of professors dismissed during the years of reaction.

But the most touching rumor going around Moscow was about the honest men from the Khitrovy market, who had been exceptional swindlers and thieves until today, how at the Khitrovy market policemen had promised thieves vodka if they helped them hide, but although they did take the vodka, they led the policemen to the City Duma: "Believe us, gentlemen. On days as sacred as this we Khitrovians don't disturb the peace." And at the Khitrovy market there reportedly really was astonishing peace, all the corners sported red flags, and some tramps were walking around proudly with the emblem of revolution on their rags.

These past few days, Ksenia had also been to a meeting of the Upper Women's Courses, in their entrance hall with the glass ceiling, and there they'd begun to say that they shouldn't be spectators, they shouldn't be running around town looking but should do something practical to help the revolution. On Wednesday, she, Edichka Faivishevich, and a whole group of male and female students went to the medics' cafeteria on Devichie Field, where they cleaned vegetables and made cabbage soup and macaroni in incredible quantities, while the students delivered this food in trucks through Moscow and fed the troops and the crowd. At first it was fun, but they were peeling potatoes hour after hour, hour after hour (something Ksenia had never done at home or for her landladies), and she was beginning to find this kind of revolution boring. But she'd missed the time to leave, it was late, and she only managed to phone her landladies to say she wouldn't be coming back for the night (also an unprecedented scandal!).

The young people had a great time of it, vying with each other singing revolutionary songs, whoever knew which song. How did they know them, or had they learned them along the way? Ksenia tried to chime in, but more out of politeness. The words to these songs were crude, as were the melodies, and she began to feel demeaned and sad, as if she were playing a part foisted on her. How natural it had been to leave classes with everyone, and to run around the city with everyone—but all of a sudden something began to ache, ache deep down, and she felt very lonely. But she felt uneasy showing this to anyone; she had to maintain a cheerful countenance.

In the next building, they were reproducing leaflets on a collotype press, bringing them here, damp and foul-smelling, to proofread, and then taking them somewhere to paste up or pass out. In the big cafeteria hall they slept catch as catch can—on chairs, on tables shifted for two—so Ksenia and Edichka lay down like that, holding on to each other so they wouldn't roll off. They didn't put out the light, but all the lamps were covered in red material—both so they wouldn't shine in their eyes and as a sign of revolution.

But the effect was a perfectly awful, bloody lighting. Sleeping was harsh, and she had nothing under her head. And she felt so sad. Ksenia had landed in something that wasn't for her. And to what end?

This morning, rather than stay to peel more potatoes, she had set out on foot across the entire city, as far as the Salt Building, where home was. She walked in guiltily, as if she'd done something bad or against her landladies.

She was actually frightened of them. These were two sisters, spinsters, impoverished gentility, very strict in their life rules, so that Ksenia couldn't even have a party there, and they didn't like it when she returned late, so they were even more shocked that she hadn't spent the night here. Now they were telling Ksenia that the previous evening two thousand criminals had broken out, together with a handful of political prisoners, from Butyrskaya Prison, and now they had spread through Moscow and were already robbing buildings and on the streets, so now the door had to be bolted and chocked and in the evening not opened even on the chain.

There was also a warning about this escape in today's newspapers (the newspapers had started coming out yesterday). Indicating the same degree of danger, they had printed next to it that members of a Moscow monarchist organization had been arrested, but their Black Hundred documents had not been seized; they'd managed to take them out of Moscow during the first few days of the disturbances.

The sisters waxed indignant at this comparison. They forgave this revolution only for the fact that, unlike in '05, the electricity and water had not been cut off. And wouldn't you know, the only shooting in all these days in Moscow had occurred nearby, on Bolshoi Kamenny Bridge, which had frightened and repulsed her landladies even more.

During the first year of her life in this apartment, Ksenia had found their strictness a burden. Was this why she had come to Moscow, so she wouldn't have freedom of movement here either? But somehow she'd grown used to it. She didn't want to rent an apartment in Petrovsko-Razumovskoye. She preferred traveling far to her courses. On the other hand, living in the center of town, close to everything, it was good coming home from the theaters and her ballet group. In fact, she liked their strictness. It had been the same with the Kharitonovs, too. This way you studied better and felt cleaner. And they didn't keep her from dancing.

Now, swallowed up by this revolutionary spring, it was so pleasant to take a shower at an odd hour and nestle down on the couch with a volume of Strindberg.

[3 1 7 '']

(FROM THE FIRST NEWSPAPERS)

NOTICE FROM THE HEAD OF THE PETROGRAD GARRISON

. . . officers in the regiments were confiscating soldiers' weapons . . . I declare . . . measures . . . to prevent such actions on the part of officers, up to and including execution of the guilty parties by firing squad.

Engelhardt

OFFICERS' APPEAL TO THE SOLDIERS

Our fighting comrade soldiers! The hour of popular liberation has tolled. And we, your fellow comrades in forward positions . . . who have mixed our blood with yours on the battlefield . . . You must believe that our homeland's freedom is dearer to us than anything. Let the old autocratic regime, which in two years of war has not been able to deliver a final victory, vanish forever. Along with you, we consign the old regime to perdition. Comrade soldiers! Do not throw down your rifles. Return to your units to work with us as one. . . .

Your comrade officers. State Duma.

RUSSIAN BASTILLE FALLS The fearsome squall of the Great Revolution has reached the walls of the Peter and Paul Fortress. . . .

According to information from the State Duma Committee, in Petrograd and the capital's surrounding areas THERE IS NOT A SINGLE MILITARY UNIT THAT HAS MAINTAINED ITS LOYALTY TO THE FALLEN AUTHORITY.

. . . The power of the State Duma Committee is absolute, for there is no one objecting to it. Its dictates are law, it is beneficent, and it is popular. . . . The State Duma is our national leader in the great struggle that has roused the entire country.

BEWARE OF PROVOCATIONS. The black spawn of yesterday's tyrants have crept away, the lackeys of the defeated government, and they are calling on the festively inclined crowd to attack stores and shout wild slogans of dangerous rebelliousness. But the plans of the servants of darkness and disgrace have come crashing up against the pure conscience of the enlightened people.

THE ARREST OF N. MAKLAKOV

REPRESENTATIVES OF ALLIED COUNTRIES IN THE STATE DUMA. . . . Military agents and diplomatic representatives of England, France, and Italy were received. They stated . . . Upon the arrival of the Italian delegation, the huge masses of people who had overfilled the Ekaterininsky Hall since early morning, greeted them ecstatically: "Long live Italy!"

. . . We will not be traitors toward the French. And we will do our utmost to keep the promise we gave England. . . .

WHERE ARE MARKOV AND ZAMYSLOVSKY? . . .

GENERAL N.I. IVANOV. On 14 March in Petrograd, rumors circulated that General Ivanov was on his way to Petrograd, leading a corps of government troops. Upon verification, these rumors proved groundless.

TELEGRAM TO PYOTR ALEKSEEVICH KROPOTKIN in London from Burtsev: "At this historic moment, your presence is essential."

TELEGRAM TO PLEKHANOV . . .

STREAM OF GREETINGS. From every end of Russia . . . telegrams from the populace, city dumas, zemstvo assemblies . . . The State Duma Committee's decision to stand at the head of the popular movement is being greeted with ecstatic exclamations. . . . Many touching telegrams from individuals at the head of major enterprises . . . A representative of the Nizhni Novgorod millers proposes offering all their mills for the homeland's needs at no cost. . . .

COUNCIL OF CONGRESSES OF INDUSTRY AND TRADE. Bowing to the great deed presented to the country by the State Duma . . . it is pouring fresh forces into the country for the total repulse of a hostile invasion.

APPEAL OF THE SOCIETY OF THE FATHER DEACONS OF PETROGRAD
And lo, I am with you always, even until the end of the world. Amen. . . . The Orthodox clergy of Petrograd and all Russia have been called upon to unite with the people. Delay threatens Orthodoxy with the people's wrath.

In Moscow, the Bolshoi and Maly theaters have been occupied by troops, who are sleeping in the foyers and on the stages. . . .

In Tsaritsyn . . . A wave of joy and enthusiasm. "The Duma is Russia's savior" rings out everywhere. The arrest of sinister forces has created a tremendous impression, an outburst of ecstasy.

DETAILS OF BAGHDAD'S CAPTURE by English troops . . .

ON THE FRENCH FRONT . . .

ON THE BALKAN FRONT . . .

[3 1 8]

Although the Military Commission was created to guide military events, the most it managed to do was to follow competently how events themselves were playing out and to comment intelligently on them internally. It already had typewriters and excellent clerks on hand, and there was a guard of Preobrazhensky soldiers deflecting the press of idle visitors; and on its authority officers sat in the Tauride Palace and the Hall of the Army and Navy filling out thousands of passes for officers for the right to be, the right to live, the right to leave, the right to bear arms. (Officers were brought who had just escaped being killed in their units—and how delighted they were to obtain revolutionary safe passage!) The Commission undoubtedly ran the defense of the palace itself: the evacuation of the mass of explosive material that had been brought here during the first few days of the revolution, and especially the guncotton, which was dangerous to transport when it was cold (they submerged it in a well).

If anything serious happened, for good or ill, the Military Commission could only learn and wonder, as they wondered today at the event at the Luga station. How was a noncombatant, unarmed, inexperienced, and disorderly garrison able to disarm a military unit as excellent as the Borodino Regiment without shedding any blood?

If a military order was issued in Petrograd, then it turned out that it hadn't come from the Military Commission. The Military Commission did not associate itself with yesterday's order from Engelhardt about how officers would be shot for any attempt to bring about order using weapons, or with the demobilized Engelhardt himself, who had graduated from the Academy due to a misunderstanding and was no longer the Commission's chairman. (No one knew who the chairman was: Guchkov was constantly on patrols, and here Colonel Polovtsov had inserted himself in an indeterminate position.) The irrepressible Cossack Karaulov was flinging out orders more and more. Yesterday he had issued orders for all of Petrograd, as Tauride Palace commandant. Today he wasn't the commandant but just as a member of the Duma's Provisional Committee he had again issued for all Petrograd Order No. 3, which was published and posted everywhere, in the most decisive language (actually, even Polovtsov would have signed this: arrest and even shoot robbers and looters). They laughed (and didn't) that Karaulov had his sights set on becoming dictator.

The Tauride Palace's new commandant, yet another demobilized man who happened to have colonel's epaulets, the liberal-sentimental journalist Peretz, today so far had limited himself just to residency permits and passes for going in and out of the Tauride Palace, but he definitely longed to be issuing high-profile orders for the whole of the Petrograd District.

Now, perhaps vainly copying Karaulov, the Soviet of Workers' Deputies suddenly took to writing military decrees. Just tonight, when the General Staffers had dispersed and sheltered somewhere to sleep, some soldiers from the Soviet had apparently broken into the Military Commission, said they wished to read the order, and were told to wait till morning—but in the morning it had already been printed in newspapers and leaflets, distributed and pasted up everywhere, nearly a million copies of their Order No. 1—for the entire Petrograd garrison.

It was already after their morning coffee that the General Staffers read it. Order No. 1 was a crude and pretentious parody of the military orders for the District, and in essence it spouted all kinds of nonsense, reflecting what was already going on in the city: elections of soldiers' committees, the barring of officers, and the fact that many of Petrograd's battalions were holding elections for officers, without which no one dared take command. They could even wonder at the fact that the order called on soldiers to observe strict discipline in their ranks and in service. If only that were so! Then there would be some benefit from this order.

But a particular sensitive point was aimed precisely against the Military Commission: not to carry out its orders without the Soviet of Deputies! Thus the Military Commission was left with even less authority and fewer opportunities.

The reserve battalions were a world unto themselves, catch as catch can, and so Order No. 1 was brought to each battalion. Duma deputies went there, to deliver a contrary message, but only to the calmer battalions, whereas they couldn't bring themselves to go to the Moscow battalion, for example.

The General Staff was bustling on its own, supervised by Zankevich.

The General Staff Academy, on the other side of the Tauride park, was getting used to the new regime. A general, its chief, came to complain that his motorcar had been taken away, and Polovtsov mocked him:

"Your Excellency, thank God you still have a head on your shoulders."

The offensive by outside troops had ended completely. The sole regiment delivered to suppress—the Tarutinsky—had stopped not far from Tsarskoye Selo. The Borodino was turned back. The rest, apparently, were not supposed to show up.

But the danger did not threaten from there. Among the General Staffers' commission the following *mot* appeared: if we stand up to the revolutionary authorities, we'll save the revolution.

To say nothing of Engelhardt, Karaulov, and Peretz—who else commanded under their leadership and in their circle? Engelhardt assigned to "Guards Lieutenant" Corneille de Batte two companies "for the defense of the populace" and made him commandant of the City Duma, where he went about giving energetic orders—but he turned out to be Private Kornei Batov, who had no other goal than stealing, which is what his detachments were doing. He was arrested. Meanwhile, someone named Baron had ensconced himself while the arrested dignitaries were being fed in the ministerial pavilion, announced that he had been elected troop ataman for the Kuban—and then disappeared before he could be unmasked.

The chaos in the reserve units was already spreading from Petrograd to all its outlying areas.

There was no single strong hand over all this. Since Khabalov's arrest and Ivanov's failure to arrive, there was now no one at all at the head of the Petrograd Military District!

An army cannot exist that way.

The General Staffers' conversations made it increasingly clear that they had to search for and suggest a strong and very popular general not connected to the throne as District commander. None of them, all colonels, could take the post due to their rank. (Privately, Polovtsov was sure that in the revolutionary atmosphere this post was just right for him; that was the entire point of his coming here. But through the neglect of GHQ or the Emperor himself he had not yet been promoted to major general.)

They came up with a candidate: General Kornilov. A soldier. All Russia knew and loved him for his escape from Austrian captivity. He had never been among the throne's favorites—and the public would welcome him.

They wanted Guchkov's consent—but he didn't show up all day. They decided to report directly to Rodzyanko.

[3 1 9]

The Empress's morning did not start until eleven o'clock. Long before this, though, Count Benckendorff collected a great deal of news, all of it unpleasant.

The first and early rumor was that an attack was being readied on the palace.

And then even that 30,000 soldiers with machine guns were moving toward Tsarskoye Selo.

But none of this happened and no one was coming to storm the palace. However, although the outside Cossack guard with their white armbands remained, the palace seemed to be guarded from the outside against itself—by soldiers from mutinous units, that is besieged, and that meant they could verify those entering, and only women passed freely; Count Apraksin removed his court uniform and got through in civilian dress.

News also arrived that the company of His Personal Railroad Regiment guarding the royal pavilion, a separate station for royal arrivals and departures, had mutinied in the night, killed two of its officers, and left.

Later it turned out that in the night, from the cellars of the palace itself, the two Guards Crew companies guarding it had left without a word—left with hardly any officers, and without a banner, but obeying the order of their superior, Grand Duke Kirill Vladimirovich.

The palace's guard was melting away.

All the news was hard, but Count Benckendorff knew that the Guards Crew's departure would hit the Empress the hardest; they were much loved by the royal couple as their own.

But there was one good piece of news. A nighttime telegram sent to General Ivanov over the palace telegraph was reported to Count Benckendorff: The Emperor had been found! He was in Pskov and intending to arrive soon. (Up until now, all the telegrams the Empress had sent to various towns at random had returned with a note in blue pencil from the Tsarskoye Selo telegraph office: "location of addressee unknown.")

With all this news, Benckendorff, the High Chamberlain, waited for the Empress to awaken and summon him in order to report to her everything bitterly essential and the single consoling item.

Well accustomed to the Empress, he could see today from her listlessness, the circles under her eyes, and her tone of voice that she had slept very little that night. She received him lying on a sofa. But no sooner had she heard that the Emperor was in Pskov and had sent a reassuring telegram to Ivanov and intended to be here soon himself than she abruptly and joyously rose on an elbow, so that the count took fright that she would harm herself and bend the wrong way somehow.

"Thank God! Thank God!" The Empress crossed herself, half-sitting. "That means he hasn't been arrested! He's with his troops again! All is saved! He will come here in force!"

She grinned at her own weakness:

"Count, I've been lying here and wondering. Outside today there's a joyous sun, so how can everything be so bad? But the sun did not deceive me."

She rang and told her lady's maid to pull back the delicate curtains, which were blocking some of the light.

Inevitably, though, he had to report further. In his respectful familiar way, Benckendorff told her about the departure of the Crew companies at Grand Duke Kirill's summons.

First, a wounded moan tore from the Empress's breast. She held her hand at her brow. And dropped back to her pillows. And using her hand to block the the overly bright light, she spoke intermittently:

"Cowards. They ran away. There's some microbe in them all. They understand nothing. My sailors! My own sailors! I can't believe it." She writhed with new force and exclaimed: "All the officers, too?"

"No, some remained, Your Majesty, and are awaiting your audience."

The Empress no longer took in the other news. She couldn't lie there for a few hours anymore, gathering her strength. She had to get up. Everyone was waiting for her.

And so, without collecting a clear mind, she launched into her new, insane day.

What undercuts more than a chain of betrayals? Everyone had betrayed them! Although the Convoy had not betrayed them in any way. But it was bitter that all Russia was relishing its betrayal. . . . (They weren't at all to blame, though. A convoy member had arrived from the Petrograd half-company: there was already a rumor that the Aleksandr Palace had been destroyed and the entire royal family had perished under the ruins.)

Even before visiting her sick children, she received the loyal Crew officers in her pink boudoir.

The stalwart naval officers stood there with tears in their eyes from the disgrace. The one thing they had managed to do was preserve the Crew's banner. Now they were all asking whether they would be allowed to remain with the Empress. They placed this above their obedience to their own commander and were transgressing his order.

The Empress was touched by their devotion and preservation of their banner and for this forgave the Crew in part.

"My God, what will the Emperor say when he hears of this! . . ."

Soon after this she was brought a direct telegram from the Emperor himself, the first in two full days!

From Pskov, today at midnight. The joy at words addressed directly, the tenderness, inexpressible through a stranger's tapping of telegraph keys. But no news, not even an intention of arriving at Tsarskoye Selo soon, as had been expressed to Ivanov.

She had taken just a few steps, precious telegram in hand, when General Groten reported several new pieces of shocking news.

That in Luga there was revolution and the loyal Borodino Regiment, which had come to rescue him under orders from General Ivanov, had been disarmed. (This stung: Luga was on the direct line from Pskov, so how would Nicky get through?)

That General Ivanov himself and his troop train had headed toward Vyritsa last night. (Obviously he'd gone to rescue the Emperor!)

That the disturbances, robberies, and drunkenness had started up again in Tsarskoye Selo.

The palace telephones could no longer communicate with Petrograd. Several times they tried to call—and finally the telephone operator whispered into the receiver: "I cannot connect you. The telephone is not in our hands. I beg of you not to speak. I'll call you myself when it becomes possible."

The direct line to the Winter Palace was still open, but nothing was happening there, and the staff couldn't tell them anything.

With this news, the Empress ascended the ornate staircase to see her ill children on the second floor in their darkened rooms. Everyone except for the still healthy Maria had a temperature of between 37 and 38, but there had been no complications, only Tanya's ear had started to hurt. Everyone was very weak, but Aleksei was quite cheerful.

Just yesterday their mother had started telling them some of what was going on; it was too agonizing to go on pretending. And today she told them nearly everything as it was. The two older daughters already had much experience working in hospitals and on committees for the wounded and refugees, they'd learned to observe people and their faces, had developed spiritually through the family's suffering, which they understood, and so had known what the family was going through these last few months. They already possessed thoughtfulness and heartfelt emotion. Let them know everything. Even about the Crew.

And they took it like troopers. Marie—because she was still healthy— was especially angrily indignant at the Crew's departure. The elder girls were reconciled to Divine Providence.

Yet another lesson in knowing people.

Now, having ascended to the second floor, the Empress stayed right there. Her heart ached badly again, the usual dilation, when even drops didn't help. She would have to bear more than her heart could.

The Empress was exhausted but forced herself not to show it, so that people wouldn't think she was dispirited. She smoked to dull her emotional pain. Right now she had to find the strength to go to the other side of the palace and inform Anya. Aleksandra Fyodorovna was very touched that for more than three days Lili Dehn had not wished to abandon the royal family and hadn't gone to see her own son in the city.

The Empress felt that she should figure something out and do it, that something kept slipping away from her imagination—but she kept being interrupted, either by Apraksin, or by Commander Resin of the Combined Regiment, or by her intimates—and she couldn't stand it when people broke in and made her lose her train of thought.

Yes, here's what! Why not send an aeroplane to Pskov with a letter for the Emperor? The simplest solution. She sent to the flight crew to find out whether this was a possibility.

Her head was spinning, whirling, she couldn't put together an accurate relationship among things. How would it end? How would this be resolved? What should she do?

What was he doing in Pskov? Had going there been in fact a free choice? What if he had been compelled? Did they want to keep him from seeing his loyal little wife—and maybe slip him some vile document?

A colonel reported that there was an aeroplane in working order, but all the aviators had vanished.

Everyone had betrayed them! Everyone had vanished!

How could she send a letter? How could she let him know? How could she break up this plot? Her heart was breaking that he was all alone and they knew nothing about each other.

One means was a courier. A loyal officer could go. He could go by train through rebellious Luga and secretly carry a letter. They'd lived to see it! The royal couple's letters had to travel secretly.

Right then, General Groten handed her a packet from Pavel.

Pavel informed her that he could not let yesterday's draft of his "manifesto" lie there without action. Since the Empress hadn't signed it, and the Emperor's name had to be affixed and supported in the present circumstance, he had seen fit to collect the signatures of whatever grand dukes he could, from the three of them—him, Kirill, and Mikhail (which would simultaneously destroy the pernicious rumors that had arisen about Mikhail's regency—a kind of guarantee issued from the dynasty). Late yesterday, this manifesto had been delivered to the Duma and submitted to Milyukov, who had approved it.

Once again he attached yesterday's typewritten text, which the Empress had tossed aside.

Her woman's eye could not fail immediately to notice the first thing, what united these three grand dukes—that all three were morganatic apostates from the dynasty. A morganatics' manifesto! Unheard of!

Now these three, who had no power over themselves, over their passions and weaknesses, were suggesting to their Emperor in what form it would be best for him to cede state power! That was the best they could come up with!

And the contemptible Milyukov had *approved*! Well, naturally! And Grand Duke Pavel had written about this with pride.

Oh, God, how far had we fallen.

But for some reason she felt no anger toward Pavel.

But the *others*, the Milyukovs? They were still thirsting for power—so let them impose order, let them show what they're good for! They had set a large fire. How were they going to put it out now?

As if there hadn't been enough blows this morning, they had brought yet another. But it was brought by the brave Groten, whose bearing and purity seemed to purge these betrayals. He brought a note from Kirill—"Rear Admiral Kirill"—that had been sent to the chiefs of all the Tsarskoye Selo units saying that he and his Guards Crew had wholly joined the new government and hoped that all the remaining units would do the same! . . .

The morganatic! Along with his "manifesto." Not only had he himself betrayed, he was convincing others to do the same.

Oh, God, where was the limit to the betrayals?

It was all repugnant! But the Empress forced herself to believe that everything would still be fine!

[3 2 0]

With respect to the corrupting revolutionary telegrams that General Evert had so vigorously forbidden, GHQ sent a refined response after nine in the morning that Adjutant General Ruzsky had already given permission to let pass those inclined toward pacification, order, and transport. (As if! . . .) Adjutant General Alekseev, too, recognizing as essential an identical decision for all army groups . . .

Marvelous! But if it's identical, then why not Evert's decision, which he had given before Ruzsky, to hold *all* telegrams and forbid them as coming from the rebellious center and an unrecognized government! GHQ had been notified in the night. And it could take as an example specifically Evert's military decision as legitimate commander.

Calls for pacification and order from the rebels? Or were they going to transport food supplies to the army? No, they were going to send those supplies to themselves, to anarchic Petrograd.

What was this? Evert rubbed his thick forehead. Ruzsky and Alekseev, was it? They'd taken the side of the revolt? But then Evert would like to have a direct order from the Emperor.

The Emperor, though, had been isolated and silenced. And could have fallen into Ruzsky's trap.

Agitated, Evert strode, paced around his office. What could he do? Disobey his immediate superior? That would be a new mutiny! Any action assumed a clear order from above. The way Evert's subordinates carried out his orders. The only strength was in the unity of subordination.

But what was to be done if the subordination had fallen apart above Evert? He had begun to suspect as much, for he could not ascribe such orders to the Emperor. Nor had Alekseev referred to the Emperor's will.

Alekseev also had obviously taken it upon himself to order the halt of the Western Army Group regiments. And now the regiments were there, uncertain which way to go.

But could he choose to drop out of the army structure and act according to his own conviction? Evert had neither the awareness nor an advisor to guide him.

He spent a difficult hour this way. Everything seethed inside him, unable to break out into any action.

But nothing comes of waiting. An order is an order. He had to assemble the provincial and city elite (and the Zemgor's then?) and convince them not to let telegrams destroy the calm.

Outside headquarters, the square and streets were still peaceful. But in a few hours these kinds of telegrams could electrify the city into disarray.

That is, of course, Minsk already knew a lot—from people passing through and from rumors—but as long as this wasn't in the newspapers it was as if it didn't exist and the dam held.

Right then Kvetsinsky knocked and entered walking like a drake, with puffy, listless eyes and twisty eyebrows, and reported:

"Aleksei Yermolaich! GHQ wants you on the direct line."

At last we'll clarify matters! This alone was a clarification! He would have preferred Alekseev himself, and to speak resolutely with him!

Evert practically ran to the telegraph room, kicking up dust.

But at the other end not only was there not Alekseev, or even Lukomsky, there was only Vladislav Napoleonovich Klembovsky.

He wished Aleksei Yermolaevich good health. And that man transmitted the following on instruction from the chief of staff: His Majesty was in Pskov, where he had expressed his consent to meet the popular wish that he establish a ministry responsible to the chambers . . .

Well, if the Emperor so deigns. But why in Pskov?

. . . having entrusted his office to the State Duma President . . .

That scoundrel. So.

. . . However, according to a communiqué of this decision by the Northern Army Group commander-in-chief to the Duma President tonight, the latter replied that this act had come too late. . . .

Well, if he doesn't accept it, then drive him out!

. . . now a terrible revolution has come, popular passions are hard to restrain, and the dynastic question has been raised point-blank. . . .

The dynastic question? My God! About what?

. . . and a victorious conclusion to the war is possible only if he abdicates the throne in favor of his son under Mikhail Aleksandrovich's regency. . . .

The slow tape was streaming out too fast! Faster than Evert's mind could understand, connect, and digest it all! It was like a bomb thundering from the ceiling: abdication? More kept coming and kept coming:

. . . The situation evidently *does not permit any other solution*, and every minute of further hesitations . . .

Evert was utterly staggered and absorbed the rest of the tape poorly. He was shell-shocked, he felt his forehead and wouldn't have been surprised if blood had been trickling down. It was strange that all the objects in the room stood and hung as before and the plaster hadn't sprinkled down.

Not only the thought of abdication, but that it did not permit any other solution? . . . And even all the hesitations—someone had already been through them, they were in the past?

The tape informed him:

. . . save the army in the field from collapse . . . save Russia's independence . . . bring the dynasty's fate to the fore. . . .

He could not take this in at all, could not even understand what it was about. Save Russia at the cost of the dynasty? That is, destroy it? Everything was layering over itself, turning in on itself, rolling out of control . . .

. . . If you share this view, then would you please be so kind as to telegraph post-haste . . . to His Majesty through the Northern Army Group commander-in-chief, after informing the chief of staff? . . .

So it was still not decided? It really depended on Evert? He was supposed to telegraph post-haste—but what did His Majesty think? The most important piece was missing! What had the Emperor decided?

. . . The loss of each minute could be fateful for Russia's existence . . . —the tape threatened—. . . establish unity of thoughts and goals among the top leaders . . . and save the army from possible instances of betrayal of duty . . .

Stop this, damn it! No mind can take this in!

. . . an overthrow, which will be brought about less painfully given a decision from above . . .

An overthrow—but from above? What balderdash was that? And not allow *betrayal of duty*? And permits no other solution? . . .

"That's all," Klembovsky concluded. "If you have a question to ask, I'm at your disposal."

"This will be painless for the army only if it comes from above? . . ." Evert muttered, and the telegraph operator understood that this was his reply, and he tapped it out.

Get a hold of yourself! In the same dismay and disbelief, but more firmly:

Hostile elements will be found . . . and maybe people wishing to catch a fish in muddy water as well . . . ?

He thought rather than said this, but this diabolical machine snatched it away and took his words with it. No, he couldn't respond like that right away.

"Have the other commanders-in-chief been asked?"

"All the commanders-in-chief have been informed of the same thing."

Well yes, because they were all in concert: Alekseev. And Ruzsky. And Brusilov, of course. And Nepenin, of course? They were the majority, and they'd already decided? And we're disunited? Or is it only me?

He had a saving thought: If they could make inquiries, then couldn't I now do the same, all the way down to the corps commanders?

"Is there time to consult with the army commanders?"

But not only was there no time for that, there wasn't even time to think:

"Time is of the essence. Every minute is precious. And there is no other way out. The Emperor is hesitating, and unanimous decisions from the commanders-in-chief could rouse him to take a decision, the sole decision possible for the salvation of Russia and the dynasty."

No other way out? This decision is the sole possible one? And not a moment for a decision! He started sweating under his tunic and into his hair. And they drove him on more, and worse:

". . . If a decision is delayed, Rodzyanko can make no promises, and everything could end in ruinous anarchy. It must also be borne in mind that the Tsarskoye Selo palace and the most august family are being guarded by mutinous troops. . . ."

GHQ did not reply about the army commanders.

But GHQ also could not demand that Evert bark out a "Yes, sir!"

"I have nothing more," Evert cut him off.

"I send my highest regards." Klembovsky smiled unseen. Evert was left with the unswallowed hulk of a question—a bigger hulk than he himself was.

And for the briefest time.

What if he were to turn several divisions around right now and go from Minsk to Mogilev? . . . It wasn't that far, and tomorrow he could take Mogilev.

And after that? But there was a revolt in Moscow. Had the Emperor been in Mogilev and expressed his approval—but how could he take this on alone? Against everyone?

Ask the three commanders? Gorbatovsky, Smirnov, and Lesch? . . . Maybe just to play for time, but what would they say?

Yet he was to provide his answer immediately!

And look how they had put it: For the preservation of the army. For victory over the Germans. For the salvation of Russia! For the salvation of the dynasty!

Nonetheless, the Emperor was hesitating?

Who could verify this, tear it out of glass-eyed Ruzsky?

But also, the royal family was in the rebel hands!

Never before had Evert been obligated to decide anything so difficult so quickly. Something so lofty, wide-ranging, and in general unmilitary—with his simple army head.

No! He summoned Kvetsinsky:

"Ask GHQ. Let them tell us how Ruzsky and Brusilov responded."

Not give any answer at all? But the request was supposedly from the Emperor? (This could not be verified.) How dare he not respond to the Emperor's request?

But what would he write?

Not about his own confusion. Not about his own helplessness. Yes, saving Russia from enslavement by Germany came first, that was so. And saving the dynasty—yes, that was understandable. Evert was taking all measures to safeguard the army against any information about the situation in the capitals. But look what was going on there! And on the Baltic Sea! This was terrible! This was an anarchic gang, not a normal, proper opponent; there is no military experience against this. Evert didn't have this kind of experience. What if the army got infected, too? . . .

How could anyone decide on military actions independently? . . . He had to act as everyone else did. Like all the rest.

But here was Kvetsinsky in the doorway:

"They've answered. Ruzsky and Brusilov—they're both in agreement with the proposal. The chief of staff is asking you to hurry with your decision."

Again hurry, oh, God, even faster!

Support the petition if he agrees . . . And if he doesn't? . . .

There, in the south, Sakharov and Kolchak might be thinking differently, but it wasn't as if he could jump over Brusilov or send a carrier pigeon.

So maybe . . . ? Maybe it was true? . . . The disturbances had to be stopped somehow, didn't they?

Given the current situation . . . finding no other *way out* . . . his tortured mind . . . a way out that it was impossible to utter or write in pen, but you, Your Majesty, you know . . . you understand. . . . Limitlessly devoted to Your Majesty, your loyal subject can only implore you . . . In the name of the salvation of the homeland and the dynasty . . . If this is the sole way out? . . . And can it save Russia from anarchy? . . .

If he answered like this, His Majesty would understand!

How much better he felt right away! In concert with the others.

After all, the royal children were in rebel hands, so what could he do? . . .

This is how we get cornered sometimes. . . . Might wins out. . . .

Evert may or may not have written all this, but while he was agonizing and sketching it out, confirmation arrived from GHQ supporting Alekseev's nighttime willfulness:

"His Majesty the Emperor has ordered the troops headed for Petrograd from the Western Army Group to turn around and has canceled the sending of troops from the Southwestern."

Was that so! There was a lesson! The Emperor hadn't hesitated at all, that means!

He himself had just stopped the struggle.

He knew what he was doing.

All Evert had left to do was . . .

And he felt so much better! . . .

[3 2 1]

Brusilov's instantaneous reply gave a good start to the consultation among the commanders-in-chief.

But after that things flagged, and no one was in a hurry to reply. General Alekseev was worried. Having begun this survey, he couldn't drag it out. If no one responded anymore, the inquiry would fall as a stain on Alekseev. He wouldn't dare come out in favor of abdication unilaterally.

Why was Grand Duke Nikolai Nikolaevich silent? One might expect a swift and welcoming reply from him.

More than an hour passed, and Lukomsky sent a follow-up telegram to the Caucasus.

Yanushkevich responded: his answer would come soon and be in the spirit of General Alekseev's wishes.

Good! The grand duke hadn't let him down.

For his inquiry to the fleets, Alekseev called in Admiral Rusin, naval chief of staff under the Supreme Commander. Alekseev placed the telegram in front of him—and saw the admiral's gaze cool.

"What a horror!" the admiral moaned. "What a great misfortune! . . ."

Yes, that was so. Yes, that might well be so. But ever since Alekseev took up this reasonable consultation among the commanders-in-chief, he had been in motion and had shed his initial timidity. This was a question of saving Russia and the dynasty, and it was not the time to indulge in sentiments.

Evert stalled. He wanted to learn the opinions of the other commanders-in-chief.

Alekseev considered Evert's idea of also asking the opinion of the army commanders. There was a logic to this. But involving another twelve men? That would be cumbersome and time-consuming, and what would come of it? What was the purpose? The situation inside the Empire was little known to the commanders, therefore asking for their opinion was superfluous.

But Sakharov extricated himself most cleverly of all: he cut communications with the Romanian front altogether, turned them off!

Lukomsky shouted in the telegraph room and demanded communications be restored immediately with Jassy.

They thought of asking the Southwestern to contact Jassy as if for itself.

Right then there arrived from Pskov the Supreme Commander's wish to return the regiments of the Western Army Group to their places and not to send the Southwestern.

How Alekseev had burned waiting for this telegram last night! Now so much had changed in those twelve hours that it was almost unnecessary, taken for granted.

However, Alekseev had now shed the ultimate shame before society for sending those troops against Petrograd! This was a good sign. The Emperor was sensibly inclined. Thus, he would probably be amenable to the abdication as well.

He ordered telegrams sent to Evert and Brusilov to halt the troops.

Assent was finally wrested from Evert, too.

Communications were restored with Sakharov—who now asked for replies from the remaining commanders-in-chief. He, too, was being circumspect, afraid of losing.

They telegraphed him that they had all replied positively. They hurried him.

Three replies arrived, and looking through them, Alekseev decided to compose from them a combined telegram to the Emperor—and as quickly as possible, before everything got decided there.

But he also had to think further. Where would the Emperor get the actual text of an abdication manifesto? It had to be formal and expressive, preserving the tradition of the Russian throne. It had to be composed here, at GHQ.

Lukomsky took on the writing, but Alekseev tried to find more experienced pens. Why else was Deputy Chamberlain Bazili, chief of the diplomatic section and Sazonov's protégé, attached to GHQ? They also found the help of a military lawyer. And also the smart GHQ Lieutenant Colonel Baranovsky. They withdrew to write.

While Alekseev once again hunched over his desk and once again pursued his wide-ranging telegram.

. . . I most loyally present to Your Imperial Majesty the telegrams I have received . . .

The first, naturally, from Nikolai Nikolaevich, both because he was a grand duke and because it was so very expressive.

Then from Brusilov, because of the finality of its formulations.

Then from Evert, which ultimately came out rather well.

Ruzsky—he was already there.

Still nothing from Sakharov. Or Nepenin. Or Kolchak.

Four we have, three we don't. The eighth opinion had to be reported by Alekseev himself.

But after the three telegrams already included in which a decision so terrible for the Emperor had been spelled out in so many words, Alekseev had no need to exacerbate the Emperor's wound yet again.

He felt sorry for the Emperor. He could see in front of him his noble, bright, kind gaze unlike anyone else's.

So Alekseev avoided saying directly the terrible word "abdication" or what this was about.

He said only that he implored the Emperor to take the decision the Lord God instills. His Imperial Majesty fervently loved his homeland and would take the decision that would provide a peaceful and safe outcome.

[3 2 2]

How out of sync we can be with the passage of time, sometimes burning up in minutes, sometimes dozing through months—and in the same way our unruly body can often be unprepared for events that catch us unprepared. Only once things have settled in us, shifted around, can we be fully conscious to take any blow, surprise, grief, or even joy.

So it was now on the Kiev train, with limited opportunities for doing anything, in no danger of being late anywhere, Vorotyntsev surrendered to this inner slowing down.

There had been powerful storms, and not everything had been cleared everywhere, so the train dragged along, dragged past snowdrifts and country women carrying wooden shovels. It waited for long stretches at the stations, forgetting its schedule. And in this slowed, dragging journey and idleness, in the crampedness and silence of his compartment—fortunately his neighbor slept the whole time—Vorotyntsev slowly came out of his daze.

The shame! The disgrace over the week he'd just spent! He could not have spent this week more senselessly and idiotically. He'd lolled from one lady's bed to another—without waking up, without guessing he'd fallen into the very thick of incredible events. All his life he'd dreamed of ending up at the most dangerous and necessary place, on his own Pont d'Arcole, and now he may have been sent an incomparable action—but he had trailed along like a rag, defeated by inner infirmity—and missed it all. Had anyone ever predicted this for him, he wouldn't have believed it.

Yesterday had been lost in a very particular way, for he'd been open for movement, his eyes had been open—and he'd come up with nothing. And today? Unknown, elusive, unstoppable events had gone on somewhere at every hour, and Vorotyntsev had only traveled farther away from them, in ignorance and inaction.

And the Emperor? What about him? Hadn't he borne the shining crown, hadn't he accepted the popular crowds' ovations for twenty-two years, for just this moment?

And he had gone off to be with his wife and children? . . .

Nonetheless. See how easy it turned out to be to get confused. But family weakness—oh!—it can seize anyone.

No, Georgi did not have his former anger and hard feeling for the Emperor now. He hadn't even noticed when that had happened. Since yesterday, when he'd learned the Tsar had been detained? Or from Olda's arguments, back in October, and now? Last autumn Vorotyntsev had been vexed and troubled that the throne was destroying the army in an unnecessary war, and he saw the Emperor's will as an obstacle to a sensible exit from the war. And now it had come crashing down—and he fervently hoped the front wouldn't collapse.

Lay one finger on the throne, Olda had said. But the same went for the front, too.

Now it wasn't the former threat—that soldier forces would be worn down—oppressing him, but that everything had gone haywire behind the active army's back. This was much worse than what Vorotyntsev had been so anxious to warn of.

His ranging autumn search now seemed pathetic.

But what was the right thing? . . .

Dealing with such massive historical events, you couldn't be nervous and jumpy. Had Svechin been right?

But where was the Emperor? Until he recognized the Petrograd rebels, they were no one, and nothing had happened in the country. Was he in their hands? Or had he broken free?

Or had he not been detained at all, and that was only a rumor?

Oh, it was becoming clear now. He hadn't thought it through, he'd been wrong. Yesterday should he have raced from the Nikolaevsky station to find the Emperor's train and perhaps be useful?

His train peace was over; he got a splinter whichever way he turned.

Too late now? It was ridiculous. Things there were already coming to a head.

The Kiev train was dragging along, away from all the events. It stood there, remote, languishing.

Vorotyntsev stepped out to walk around the short, snowy platform—and maybe learn some news? Not likely! For the locals, events had stopped at yesterday and the day before. In fact, it was the locals who surrounded the passengers with questions and even hopped on the train cars asking for newspapers, newspapers, any news at all! What was going on there, in the capitals? Russia lay in its remoteness and knew no revolution whatsoever.

[3 2 3]

Shingarev had gone to the Food Supply Commission on 13 March and had sat right there for three full days, taking little time for sleep or food. This whole time he had not taken part in the political passions, intrigues, designs, and hopes and hadn't even followed them, as if he weren't in the

Tauride Palace at all (though he did spend one night there). The Food Supply Commission did not at all feel the soaring of the revolution but rather worked the abacus, bills of lading, commissions, and columns of figures. This was also perhaps the sole place where the Duma Committee, not confident of itself, and the insolent Soviet of Workers' Deputies didn't vie with each other, didn't suspect each other, but cooperated.

Shingarev had always been drawn to active work, and there was hardly anything more active and important in Petrograd right now than food. As before, everyone got hungry during revolution, too, and lines formed at bread shops early in the morning.

Not that there wasn't plenty of flour in Petrograd!—as Shingarev now discovered with amazement from the incoming documents—and military stores as well. The entire danger had been greatly exaggerated. And since the storms had ended, new train cars of flour continued arriving at the Nikolaevsky Station as if nothing were the matter. But because of the revolution, they weren't being unloaded. Hundreds of thousands of pounds! And they needed to be unloaded immediately and transported, stored once again, released to bakeries, and baked—but no one was so inclined. They had to persuade the drivers and bakers, appeal to their consciousness as citizens.

But who was going to guard the flour deliveries to the bakeries? (There hadn't been any attacks on flour or bread yet, which meant people weren't hungry, but given the general disorder, there could be an attack at any moment.) Who now was supposed to feed the soldiers who, in the defense of the cause of freedom, had left their barracks? And what about all the additional regiments that had flooded into Petrograd from the surrounding areas? Apparently a fodder subcommission had to be appointed and something decided regarding Petrograd's cab horses, which were eating bread for lack of fodder.

Something the extinct old regime would never dare, the present Food Supply Commission could now do: appeal to the honor and dignity of every citizen who had now gained his freedom, asking him to limit his consumption of essential foods and make purchases only according to actual need, and not just in case.

On the other hand, they had to introduce ration cards for bread. It was a pity, but the revolutionary era would have to begin with the institution of bread ration cards. And with setting the ordinary citizen's daily ration at a pound and a half a day—no, even a pound and a quarter. For the soldiers, though, considering their turbulent revolutionary spirit, they would have to make it two and a half.

With his governmental experience, though, Shingarev saw that the matter could not be limited to Petrograd's bread concerns alone. The entire country appeared before his eyes. Based on its position, who if not Petrograd was obligated to continue reliably supplying Finland, the Baltic Fleet, and also the Northern Army Group? Given the revolutionary role Petrograd had declared for itself before Russia, it was obviously Petrograd and no one else that had to provide bread for the entire army in the field and all the cities of the Empire. Until a new government came into being, who was to take on all these concerns now if not the Food Supply Commission? Shingarev tried to persuade his chance revolutionary colleagues that the revolutionary government had to live tomorrow and the day after, too, and therefore their concern had to be not only about the bread Petrograd already had but about bread everywhere in Russia, and it was essential that people decide to take it to Petrograd and other places.

Shingarev was putting his hopes in the good will and good consciousness of the people themselves! For centuries, our people had been deprived of the precious gift of freedom. And now that the revolution was offering them freedom in all its breadth, the populace as a whole, our Holy and Long-Suffering People, would find the correct path. The reason insufficient grain had been coming in so far was that the peasants didn't trust the old government. But if we were to openly call on the peasants to selflessly surrender their grain, it would immediately start moving, in a broad-hearted movement, in a string of wagons, to the new revolutionary authority. And so there was no getting along without an appeal to the entire country, the revolutionary authority's first appeal to Russia, and it would be about grain. Something like this: "Citizens! A great deed has been accomplished. The old regime, which was destroying Russia, has fallen apart! Our main task now is the provision of food. . . . There are very few grain reserves left from the old regime, and we must hasten to prepare . . ."

But who was this anonymous Petrograd Food Supply Commission to be calling on Russia?

And who in general could, had the right, to call on Russia now? There was one such undoubted name: Rodzyanko. They had to convince Mikhail Vladimirovich to sign it. There was no doubt he would.

But first they had to compose those powerful words, that resonant appeal to Russian hearts.

Shingarev sought them, agonizing that the wrong ones kept coming, not the best ones; he sat at the corner of some table and sketched out the appeal, himself so agitated that he had to hide his swimming tears from his neighbors:

". . . all as one man, hold out a hand of assistance during these ominous days! Let not a single hand drop!"

When Andrei Ivanovich thought about the people—the people as a whole and all the noble hearts that comprised the people—he was always prone to these teary eyes, this teary voice, and his face and voice always expressed more than intractable spoken or written speech could:

"Quickly sell your grain to representatives! Give up everything you can! Quickly take it to the railroads and wharfs! Quickly load it! . . . Time does not wait! Citizens! Come to the homeland's aid with your grain and labor!"

He had written it. And broken the resistance of the dry socialists Groman and Frankorussky, who didn't believe in heartfelt appeals but only in economic laws. Rodzyanko easily added his sweeping signature. And it was printed in news leaflets and went flying!

A few hours later, though, the socialists pressured Shingarev in return. Landowners vary, and some have large plowlands—and their grain has to be requisitioned, not called for voluntary surrender. A revolutionary government was so obliged.

After the appeal's emotional sweetness, this was like a knife to Shingarev. He resisted them as much as he could, but they had the power and pressure behind them. The Food Supply Commission sent out the following telegram to all ends of Russia (at telegraph speed it should have caught up to and in some places overtaken the appeal): Requisition all grain stores (without a reduction in price—this was all Shingarev could get) from all landowners with plowlands of more than 135 acres (and this was not at all a large holding!). As well as the stores of commercial establishments and banks.

An anonymous Petrograd commission neither chosen by nor known to any Russian had telegraphed this command.

Truth be told, in the midst of these upheavals and struggles, Shingarev had forgotten that in some other room a government was being formed and he was just about to move over there as Minister of Finance.

Suddenly he was invited to see Milyukov.

In the room where Milyukov was sitting, extra people were crowded, too, and not only trusted ones. Shingarev took a seat closer to him and they spoke in lowered voices.

In these last days Pavel Nikolaevich's features had sharpened. His eyebrows had become costally angular and his mustache now looked as stiff as wire. He was tense—and at the same time rather scattered; he was talking to Andrei Ivanovich but apparently thinking about something else.

Not that it was a long conversation. The Kadet Party leader informed his faction co-member and deputy that he would be given a portfolio in the new government.

All right, Shingarev nodded.

Although this was and wasn't so, Pavel Nikolaevich expressed his concern and with an expression of unpleasantness and severity. There was a somewhat more complex combination that went beyond intra-party calculations. Andrei Ivanovich would have to be minister of—agriculture and land tenure.

As the expression goes, Shingarev's eyes popped out of his head. How is that? What is that? Why? After all . . . after all, not he himself but the entire Kadet faction, the entire Duma, had grown used to the idea, predicted that he would be Minister of Finance!

Not that he was a financier or finance specialist, he didn't have that education, but the Kadet faction was so exhaustively legal and humanitarian, no one possessed any practical experience and no one even knew how to calculate; but someone had to deal with finance—so Shingarev had taken it up. For years he had sat over the estimates and learned from finance officials, and studied their methods—and had apparently acted rather brilliantly as an opponent to Kokovtsov. All that labor, study, and analysis—and for what? . . .

Shingarev's open brow could not conceal his feelings. But never in his entire life, probably, had Pavel Nikolaevich been wide open or emotionally soft; even his close comrades in the party did not expect sentimentality and sympathy from him. Milyukov didn't even have an urge to express the appropriate regret. Although he did reply in the following words, as if dictating:

"Unfortunately, this is absolutely unavoidable. This is not subject to discussion. It could not be arranged otherwise."

Apparently, he knew a great deal he could not say. Shingarev was used to seeing in Milyukov a grand-scale politician to whom he could not compare. He'd believed him, followed him, was prepared to agree and let himself be convinced—but he still had to explain, didn't he? How insulting! To suddenly have the goal of so many years fall from your hands.

Then Pavel Nikolaevich explained to the somber Shingarev in a quiet voice:

"Look here, Andrei Ivanych! You could be considered a specialist in naval affairs, too, since you chaired that commission. In the end, have you really gone deeply enough into the state's productive forces to run the economy? Your concerns were about the fairness of direct and indirect taxes and were dictated by your marvelous love of the people. So in this sense you will have even greater range by taking on the food supply. You've been involved in this for the last few months and you acted successfully as Rittikh's opponent—so now go and take his place."

Yes, there was some truth in all this. Pavel Nikolaevich did know how to speak convincingly. Although, still, so many years of work and effort and . . . ?

But the situation did not permit objections. In these days, no matter what post the party appointed you to, you had to accept it. Even before, Shingarev had been used to taking up a new matter, making an effort, and learning from that. He had not been that well informed in naval affairs, it was true. He'd also given quite a lot of thought to the food supply, that was true, too.

Why all this had been shifted around, Shingarev did not insist on knowing. But so disappointed and insulted was he that he didn't think to even ask who *was* going to be Minister of Finance.

On his way out, he wondered why hadn't they discussed this earlier, but instead had gone behind his back, decided without asking him. How oddly and uncollegially this longed-for ministry of public trust was being formed! . . .

For Shingarev this was the choice of his life's path for the entire revolution now. With regard to agriculture he was no kind of specialist other than from his criticism of the Stolypin reform.

But as he was returning to the Food Supply Commission (without having said anything to the socialists), he reread his appeal from yesterday—and was again struck by the purity and sentiment of its feeling. Here the figures had lined up, figures of it didn't matter what ministry, whether in rubles or bushels—behind them rose handsome stalks of wheat, and popular life itself swayed, a life that had to be lifted out of ruin and allowed to flourish.

An hour or two later, Andrei Ivanych felt that he had forgiven the insult. And reconciled himself.

He now even liked becoming Minister of Agriculture.

This feeling of revival, renewal, and uplift nestled in the very essence of his soul. How many times had that feeling quickly lifted him anew, out from under any landslide, fire, or ashes, toward stability and the light!

[3 2 4]

These past few days, Shlyapnikov had been incapable of coming to rest anywhere. He didn't know the right place for him to be.

As a member of the Soviet's Executive Committee, he ought to have been attending their endless sessions. But it made him sick to be there, among the Mensheviks, defensists, and quasi-defensists who dominated. To hear them speak, there were quite a few internationalists here, but they were impossible to knit together: they feared a schism and so tagged along behind everyone else. Shlyapnikov was surprisingly vexed at the Soviet, at how it had come to be that the Bolsheviks here were so constrained, they were so few, and they did not have the main voice. In the underground he wouldn't have lowered himself to a comparison with these men who had quietly sat out the war. But here they had immediately horned in, obstructed, and taken over. Shlyapnikov was simply suffering at how they had summoned their nerve so quickly and no longer seemed to reckon with the Bolsheviks.

For years he had applied his efforts to the main enemy, autocracy, where those efforts were needed, where it would not give way. He had never expected that the moment he eased up, all these would jump in from the side and be first!

Theoretical windbags like Himmer had swarmed in, and what had they tried to prove? That power should be given to the bourgeoisie! How absurd! Give all the real power, now in the hands of the masses, to the bourgeoisie? While they, ensconced in the Soviet, did not want to take power! So why had they taken up all this space if they were just getting in the way? (Or were they just pretending not to want to take power? Maybe they did, only without us?)

No, sitting on the Executive Committee, the biggest thing Shlyapnikov did was just to strengthen the Mensheviks. This was not to be endured!

Time was whirling, and every hour was carrying off some unused, unique opportunity. He didn't have the intelligence to think, grasp, and do!

Right here, close by, he had let opportunity slip in the Ekaterininsky Hall and on the Tauride Palace steps. Yesterday among the soldiers here he'd tried to speak against the war—and they wouldn't let him, they shut him up. The Bolsheviks were just finding their voice, they didn't mean anything yet, they didn't have the power to push either up or down, and the Bureau of the Central Committee, foisted on them from Switzerland, was barely recognized.

So you didn't know where to begin.

This morning, Shlyapnikov had swept into the Tauride Palace, but there wasn't even an Executive Committee session, so they sat there, listless, in the common room, passing on gossip about yesterday's negotiations with the Duma deputies, how they had ceded power, the bumpkins! These negotiations were nothing but a betrayal. In the negotiations they hadn't said a word about the war, about land, or about the eight-hour workday. Conciliation and capitulation! Nakhamkes wouldn't take Shlyapnikov seriously and threatened to tell Lenin about Shlyapnikov's un-Marxist conduct, that he'd forgotten who was supposed to carry out the objectives of bourgeois revolution.

Lenin wasn't about to start talking to you Liquidators, either!

There was also grumbling on the Executive Committee about the Krotovsky and Aleksandrovich leaflet; even the SRs were all against it, keeping away from it. And in the Ekaterininsky Hall, out loud, Chkheidze even called the proclamation provocative.

Actually, it was a fine leaflet! It soberly called on everyone to struggle with the officers until the end! Not to let the class struggle die out in the army—that was right! Shlyapnikov roundly cursed Molotov for getting cold feet and surrendering bales of this fine leaflet to the defensists without a fight, the driveller.

Well, all right, a few things still got through. Bonch was a sad sack, but he'd quickly released the Bolshevik Manifesto (the Mensheviks could only gape—and rush to compose their own). And following that, Order No. 1. Was there no getting away from the Executive Committee's signature?

What Shlyapnikov realized in time and did do was to revive *Pravda*. They commandeered a large building on the Moika, the marvelous *Village Herald* press, and its nice new rotary presses. Now they were cobbling together an editorial office—but once again was there no one to write? Put Molotov there?

He longed for action! Drastic action! Powerful action! Action to scorch everyone! An authentic cause: to create his own strong, local government and armed militia made up of workers; they were already collecting weapons and bullets.

Today, as of three o'clock, here, in the Tauride Palace, a large plenum of the Soviet had assembled. And it had to be taken under control! He had to speak at it and toss out slogans.

But which ones?

After all, Shlyapnikov had already acclimated to the Petersburg underground! He felt fully capable of controlling the capital's worker masses, as he had last autumn—to make them work or take them out on strike. But now everything had burst out to the surface and spilled through the streets—and could no longer be controlled. It seemed now that only correct slogans could be the new reins. But how to find these slogans? He didn't have the mind for it. This slogan was racing around or lying somewhere nearby, and it could be composed of the simplest words—but the cursed words wouldn't come together. He had to confer and use the collective mind.

For now, before the Soviet began, he decided to go see his people on the Vyborg side; it was good he had a motorcar at his disposal.

The Vyborg District Committee now used a room in a shattered police station on Bolshoi Sampsonievsky, where he met a lanky sailor, Ulyantsev—one of those sailors who had stood trial in October. This one was fresh from Schlüsselburg and wanted one thing: to rout the vipers! These were the kinds we needed. Send him to Kronstadt.

The fellows on the district committee were headstrong if not educated. Shlyapnikov explained to them: "Men, we can't sit here being patient. We have to start the struggle! Didn't we proclaim a revolutionary government? We did. Well! What are we waiting for?"

The men were in full agreement. The men were already preparing large posters like that: "Confiscate Gentry Land!" "An Eight-Hour Workday!" "A Democratic Republic!"

What about the revolutionary government, though? And the Soviet of Workers' Deputies? All at once it became clear that this Soviet should simply become the government. Let it seize power!

But how to promote this? Roll out a new flyer:

"Citizens, soldiers, and workers!"

There was a tested Bolshevik device:

"The mass meetings of soldiers and workers assembling in Petrograd have adopted the following resolutions. . . ."

No such resolutions had been adopted at any mass meetings yet, we were only composing, printing, and distributing them now—and we'd have mass meetings and resolutions afterward.

". . . All power into the hands of the Soviet of Workers' and Soldiers' Deputies as the sole revolutionary government! The army and populace must carry out instructions only from the Soviet of Deputies and consider instructions from the State Duma Committee null and void! The State Duma was the bulwark of the Tsarist regime. . . ."

War on Rodzyanko and Milyukov! Break up the schemes of the franchised classes and their separate government!

Now to print it on the rotary press and . . .

[3 2 5]

Only a passion to see and learn something totally unheard-of could drive so many soldiers into this crowded room and be packed for hours like sardines such that they couldn't stretch their arm out or scratch their nose—and only the lucky few could smoke. No one brought rifles here any more, to keep from scratching each other. Workers with red pins crowded in, but not as many.

There wasn't a single chair left in the room; some had been broken and some carried out. There was only a large, trampled table, and on that table since the very beginning different people had climbed up to take the floor or seize control; they'd sat here in the back room in advance, they'd come from there.

First and foremost among them was a rather old, balding, short man with a fibrous beard wearing a spattered, worn jacket who spoke almost unintelligibly, who emitted gurgles sometimes instead of words and then would start scratching, and you could tell he was a poor, weary man. He said that now here the Soviet wasn't just for Workers but for Soldiers' Deputies, too, and it was taking its bright future into its own mighty hands. That the time had now come that everyone had dreamed of all their born days, and the people themselves would show their power. And the soldier would show that he understood army affairs even better than some officers. But not all their enemies had been defeated yet, there were still dark forces, and they needed a government that was orderly and there was no getting by without the *yelements*. They'd talked to those yelements yesterday, they were ready to stick it out, and the very best terms for all of us. Right now our comrade from the Executive Committee was going to lay this all out in detail for your judgment.

Then next to him, his shoulder higher than the first's head, this ginger-bearded fellow who looked like he could butcher a carcass in one fell swoop started talking. But he spoke agreeably, reassuringly, as if he were offering fine goods, as fluid as a burbling stream—he was very appealing to listen to, and people did. Who ever talked to us lowly folk this way before?

He said all kinds of things, so many, you couldn't keep it all in your head. And it was all about freedom. Now there would be all-out freedom. Anyone languishing in prison—freedom for them all. And even more freedom for all free men. And for the soldiers, the most of all. Now, in all the companies and battalions, the soldiers were supposed to elect committees, and all power would now be with the committees, not the officers. The officer's business now was just, say, have them line up in formation—and then right, left, order arms—though even a sergeant could do that. If any officers tried to block the committees, they would have to answer to the new authority. The moment a soldier stepped out of formation, he was the freest respected citizen now, and all rights were given him. He could walk down the street and there'd be no police, no one would stop him or forbid him anything. There would be light oversight by university students and there, too, everyone elected. But above all, no one would drive the soldier to war. After the great revolutionary deed, the entire Petrograd garrison would be on leave and in the event defend Petrograd from dark forces.

His sweet speech flowed so, you couldn't get enough of it. Such a fine man, such a good life had now ensued!—and look how all it took was to dare leave the barracks once, and now you could leave as much as you want. All this new sweetness the soldiers seemed to have sensed themselves—but it was precious to hear it again from this fine man. They listened hard and long, though their sides had started to be pressed on and they felt like having a stretch.

Well, this ginger beard's speech ended, and whoever could slip his arms between the other people's sides clapped for him sincerely, without regret.

Right then there was a hitch among the main people at the table. At the other end of the table, someone quickly began climbing up, grabbing on to his neighbors and swaying. Climbed up hand over hand, pushed everyone aside, and thrust forward—and they recognized him: that narrow-head who'd been racing around the palace more energetically than anyone else, who only knew how to run. And ringingly, confidently, with the voice of a youth:

"Comrades! I have to make a report of the most extraordinary importance!"

Strong words: extraordinary importance! And they started turning more toward him.

He was so pale! Whiter than canvas. His sincerity touched them—he was tottering, could barely stand. And his voice—suddenly he lost it entirely. And only out of sympathy, by holding their own breath, could the crowd hear him:

"Comrades! Do you trust me?"

He asked like a condemned man. This was what they'd come to! Here was our leader, he was on our side, they didn't know his name, but they'd seen him loom up tirelessly. They took pity and started shouting on all sides:

"We do! Well! . . . And so? Of course, we do!"

But he was dragging, gasping, faltering:

"I speak, comrades, from the bottom of my heart! I am prepared to die if need be!"

What kind of villains were these? Who had brought him to this?

"Come come! Live on!" They encouraged and clapped for him. Chills went down their spines for this dear, sickly, pale man, who had tried so hard and one could tell, for our good.

Gathering a touch of strength, out of breath:

"Comrades! A new government has just been formed. And they have offered me the post of Minister of Justice. I was supposed to give them an answer in five minutes. Therefore I did not have time to obtain a mandate from you. I risked taking this upon myself and accepting this offer—even before your final decision!"

Well then, all right, well. Sometimes a man just has to.

"So be it!" they shouted to him. And clapped some more.

He stood up, stood tall, "at attention," and rolled his eyes back. And told them:

"Comrades! In my hands, under my lock and key, we are holding representatives of the vile old regime—and I have not been able to bring myself to let go of them. If I hadn't accepted the offer made to me I would have had to give back the keys. So I decided to join the new government as the Minister of Justice!"

And rightly so! Because you can't let them go! They kept shouting and clapping for him.

This spurred him, and with more energy and good cheer:

"Comrades! My first step as minister was an order to release all political prisoners immediately! And to bring our comrade deputies from the Social Democratic faction back from Siberia with special honors!"

Also poor creatures, you see. Freedom for everyone means just that.

"But in view of the fact that I risked taking on the duties of Minister of Justice before obtaining formal authority from you"—and he tossed his reconciled head back and his neck stretched taut—"right now I am relinquishing before you my duties as deputy chairman of the Soviet of Workers' and Soldiers' Deputies!"

They didn't understand what it was he was relinquishing. Was he going away somewhere?

"You stay on, fella! Hogwash!" they shouted at him.

Then his lively eyes darted and he was spurred on and the color returned to his face:

"But I am prepared to take up this title from you once again if you deem it necessary!"

"We want you to! We want you to!" they shouted at him and began to clap. All right, so be it, this one's not bad for us.

Then he beamed and bowed, bowed in different directions and lay his hands on his chest. And practically wailed:

"Comrades! While joining the new Provisional Government, I remain what I was—I remain a republican!"

Well, good.

"I told the Provisional Government that I'm a representative of democracy! The Provisional Government must look on me as an expresser of the demands of democracy! And it must especially consider those opinions which I am going to defend as a representative of democracy! For it was by the efforts of democracy that the old, intolerable regime was overthrown!"

What he was talking about—they couldn't tell, but he was fresh! He spoke without being boring, to the heart. They approved of him. Anyone who blathered something against got shut down. Be quiet—he's for us!

While he, sincere, vibrating like a string, stood tall in all his slimness:

"Comrades! Time doesn't wait! Every minute is precious! I call on you to organize! To be disciplined! To lend support to us, your representatives! Who are prepared to *die* for the people! And who have given *their entire lives* to the people!"

They listened and very much approved, but when he mentioned death a second time—it struck them hard, chilled them to the bones.

"Live on!" they shouted at him. Hands up front reached out to him, grabbed him, pulled him down, he was so light—and started swinging him from arm to arm, onward to the door.

And the whole room shouted:

"Hurrah!"

They didn't pass him along that well, and sometimes they forgot and let go of his leg, but close to the door they got a firm hold of him—you could walk there now—and carried him through the doorway, and the entire room droned long in his wake:

"Hurrah! Hurrah!"

*   *   *

TOSS A KOPECK, CATCH A ROUBLE!

*   *   *

[3 2 6]

They'd thought to leave early—and didn't come close. First of all, it was nearly five in the morning when they went to bed—and they were out cold, so that all Russia could have gone up in smoke, but getting up was impossible. And when they did get up, it was no longer early, and they pumped themselves up with coffee—and then they had to make several telephone calls, Guchkov not wishing to appear today at the Duma, where they were supposed to say he was going around to the different barracks. From the first calls, though, through Obodovsky, he learned of Vice Admiral Nepenin's request from Helsingfors to help establish order at Kronstadt and saying who should be appointed the fortress's new commandant to replace the murdered one. Not yet declared Minister of War and the Navy, Guchkov was already unanimously presumed to be such. Thus, he had to give orders, immediately, on what to do for Kronstadt, a not unimportant place, and Nepenin himself had to be supported.

Meanwhile he telephoned Mitya Vyazemsky's sister and the Kaufman community hospital. He still had to go say his final farewell, but Dmitri was already unconscious. He'd been asking the professor since yesterday what organ of his had been hit, and the professor had honestly replied that none had. But his sacrum and pelvis had been shattered. He'd lost a lot of blood and would not survive.

And between Guchkov's two telephone calls he died.

Just yesterday his closest associate, the most essential person—and now he was gone, and now Guchkov had to go on.

Maria Ilyinichna, too, despite the general joy, was extremely somber right then, spoke reluctantly, and had to be convinced of the importance of his departure and of her answering correctly over the telephone.

Leave home as soon as possible! Somber, Guchkov broke off and went with Shulgin to the Warsaw Station.

It was getting on toward two o'clock in the afternoon, and in that time the Soviet of Workers' Deputies could have found out ten times about their departure and prevented it.

But no! Despite the fact that they had openly telegraphed Ruzsky about their journey and had telephoned the Warsaw stationmaster, such was the general turmoil that evidently it had not reached the Soviet—otherwise they wouldn't have allowed this sort of private, secret trip to see the Tsar. The special train designated for Rodzyanko yesterday, consisting of a salon car and a sleeping car, was still there awaiting the deputies, and a locomotive being held in reserve for it was now attached.

The last thing that Guchkov thought to do in time and that had to be done before departure was taking General Ivanov in hand. Although he had already withdrawn from Tsarskoye Selo, and although Guchkov knew, due to their long acquaintance, that this was a sad sack, not a combat general, and also shy of public opinion—all the more reason he had to be wholly taken in hand and made to see reason. Since he hadn't left the Warsaw Station yet, it was most convenient to send him a telegram via the Tsarskoye Selo station, along the Vindava rail line, telling him to come to Gatchina for a meeting, set for four o'clock in the afternoon. Or else he could go to Pskov. Guchkov had no doubt that Ivanov would be happy to obey and slip out of his difficult position.

Finally they did leave, at three o'clock. The Soviet hadn't stopped them! Hadn't found out.

The engineer got the order to move at top speed. Two railroad engineers from Bublikov boarded their train car—to eliminate any possible obstacles along the way.

The early morning had been bright; now it was gray. The sun wasn't shining on the snowy fields.

There were compartments and they could lie down, but that didn't occur to them, they were so agitated. Young Shulgin, pale from exhaustion, always with glittering eyes, now beamed specially somehow, sensitively.

They were sitting side by side in the salon car—and barely talking.

Guchkov's underslept mind was filled with an alarming but also joyous buzz.

Had it been long since the Tsar had forbidden him to travel to army group headquarters? And here he was traveling precisely to an army group headquarters, and why? To wrest abdication from him!

What was his necessity in going? He had a badly organized Military Commission, the Petrograd regiments were in a terrible state, and in a few hours he would be accepting the Ministry of War. He was hopelessly short of time to do and see to everything in Petrograd—and here he was racing to Pskov, not a trivial journey.

But the revolution they had wanted to avoid had come to pass—the handiwork of the rabble. Both power and any kind of order were drifting out of the hands of the educated class, those called on to govern the people. In this muddy, swift stream making off with everything but blundering for the moment, there remained a few hours when he could chase down the throne that it was carrying away and drag it to a firm bank.

It was for Guchkov to go. This was his personal, longstanding destiny. This was his reckoning with the Tsar. Guchkov was on his way to carry out a matter of state. This felt like the crowning moment of his life.

It was also revenge for his failed coup d'état, a kind of recompense for what he had failed to do. (Let it be considered thus, so handsomely and tragically would it go down in history: the plot would definitely have been carried out, but the revolution forestalled it by two weeks.) To justify himself—to himself. He had nearly managed to overtake and correct it!

This might be a weightier step into the future Russia than becoming Minister of War. Right now, Guchkov was on his way to obtain an abdication in favor of the heir with Mikhail as regent and Lvov's confirmation as prime minister. Right now, for now, in this storm—both to save the throne as such and to put a government firmly in place.

With Russia's free and extensive development in the future, the monarchy might very well become too constricting for it and Russia would free itself altogether in favor of a republic. Then it would need a president. Russia's first president.

And then it was not at all indifferent on whom the reflection of today's abdication would fall. It was like the shadow of a succession.

Russia loved Aleksandr Guchkov! As his illness this past year showed: who else was so popular?

His arms were already stretched so far. And a place had been set aside in his soul for this action. Not succeed? Utterly impossible. This was rolling on irrevocably. That this might not succeed—he hadn't even accounted for that possibility.

His former plan had been to place a prepared text of abdication before the Emperor. Seemingly the simplest part of the task was to draw up the text. But this had never been done. They kept thinking they would have time for this, the easiest part.

But as of last night, when the trip was decided, he still hadn't written it, didn't have a handle on it. Here they were actually en route and there was no text. And his brain was absolutely refusing, especially with the train shaking, at the train car's little table. His thoughts wouldn't collect, the sentences wouldn't coalesce.

"Vasili Vitalich! What about the text? We don't have one. . . . Perhaps you might try to sketch one out now?"

Shulgin, with his lunatic appearance, distracted:

"Eh? Yes. Right! I'll give it a try. . . ."

He took out his pen and started right in.

After all, not everything was clear and only now did it come to him:

"Do you know, Vasili Vitalich, whether any fixed form of abdication exists?"

With a sweet distracted smile from his separate thoughts, Shulgin said:

"I have no idea, Aleksandr Ivanych. I never gave it any thought. I don't think so because . . . No one here has ever abdicated, have they? None of the Romanovs and none of the Ruriks."

"Is that really so? Wait a minute. . . . Ah . . . and Peter III?"

"Well, maybe Peter III. But that was a pretty dodgy case and can't be a basis for us."

"But is there any legislation about this? Any dynastic rule?"

It was strange that Guchkov, in discussing the plot, had never given this any thought before.

Shulgin's blue eyes shone celestially:

"Oh, I don't know, Aleksandr Ivanych."

[327]

For all that, the train's crampedness was exhausting; there was no way to stretch your legs. He wished he could leave the car. Before breakfast, Nikolai stepped out to stroll along the platform.

Past the brick water pump with the frozen crest of ice. The separate cistern. They would be etched for life like no other landscape in Russia.

The day was rather gray and turbid. Not cold.

The men of the suite were strolling, some behind him, some to the side. The odd passerby was different from before: not standing with mouth agape, but walking past.

So the Emperor found himself without his own space, without authority. Just yesterday it had been clear: sending a telegram somewhere, even home—could only be done via Ruzsky. (But there had still been no reply to what he'd sent where Pskov was indicated. My God, what's happened to Alix?) Only through Ruzsky could he receive or learn anything. But he even felt awkward asking for a motorcar for an outing. Did he actually have the right to go anywhere?

A strange status, one might say, like having been sentenced. The holder of a great Empire, one would think he could decide, choose freely, but in actual fact . . .

Somehow over the past two days all his power had apparently leaked away from him. Though reckoned as Emperor and Supreme Commander, he had no one to whom to give orders. He could only agree to whatever document they might bring. During these past few days of traveling, telegraph offices somewhere had been in contact, telegraph conversations had gone on, but everything had bypassed him, others had picked up the line and others had responded, but he had been brought only final results.

Somehow, imperceptibly, the remnant of power had drifted away from him to Alekseev—who was himself already asking about abdication?

How would the commanders-in-chief respond?

Dare he give up power, even a power he did not love—how could he face his ancestors? Nikolai had always feared not measuring up to his calling, in particular, proving unworthy of his father and his great-grandfather Nikolai, who had led so boldly and confidently.

How would the commanders-in-chief respond?

And did all Russia itself want him to abdicate? If it did, then, yes, certainly, immediately! If the Tsar had become an obstacle to national unity, then he would go. And he would thank God if Russia finally became happy, without him.

But how could he learn Russia's true will?

Ruling is a cross. A heavy burden. The Tsar takes on the full weight of state decisions, all the fuss and pettiness of administration, in order to free his subjects' souls from this muddle, so that they can rise up toward God unconstrained.

Everyone was always after him with reports and opinions; some wanted one thing, others the opposite, and it all had to be heard, read, and signed. No matter what you decided, though, society was always whistling and hooting, dissatisfied.

How nice it would be to give all this up and go live the rest of his days in Livadia! What refreshing air! What a soothing spot. Was there anything in the world to equal the southern Crimean shore? To sit high above the sea behind a small marble table, on a marble bench, looking at the sea's sunny glint or the fairytale moonlight. To take the royal path as far as Oreanda. To ride horseback to the vineyards. To live out the rest of one's life like this as a family, nothing better needed, and raise his son. And Crimea was very good for Aleksei's health.

Yes! After all, he would have to reign! . . .

Breakfast without guests.

Had the suite guessed what question had been raised? Heard something? Worried? This did not reflect on the ritual of taking sustenance.

Immediately after breakfast, the Emperor, wearing his favorite dark gray Caucasian undertunic with the epaulets of the foot scout battalion and his colonel's stars, a narrow dark belt with a silver buckle and a dagger in a silver scabbard, in this military garb, his soul subdued, in the green salon car with its spinet, received three generals—three not even by seniority in the Northern Army Group, since as the third, for some reason, they brought the supplies chief.

The Emperor invited them to sit and smoke. Ruzsky sat down and lit up, but the other two remained standing, putting him on his guard. In a mechanically even voice, Ruzsky reported the day's news about the recalling of the troops sent to Petrograd. Then he placed before the Emperor a pasted-together telegraph tape from Alekseev.

The Emperor accepted it with agitation and felt his forearms get hot.

. . . I most loyally present to Your Imperial . . .

Followed immediately by Nikolasha's reply.

This time it all did reach his consciousness, it all sank in keenly.

. . . Alekseev has reported . . . unprecedentedly fateful situation . . . and asks you to support his opinion . . . the taking of *extraordinary measures* . . .

To support his opinion . . .

And—*as a loyal subject, by the duty of my oath, by the spirit of my oath,* Nikolasha on bended knees implored him: Save Russia! Make the sign of the cross and pass on the throne to your heir. As never in his life and with an especially ardent prayer . . .

No, why this "as never in his life"? This already happened once, in October 1905. When he extracted the Manifesto. . . .

And Nikolai lost all his agitation. He even lost interest in reading further. He now understood.

In the same way, Brusilov's most loyal request had been based on his devotion to the royal throne: relinquish it in favor of your heir, otherwise Russia will perish. *There is no other way out,* and haste is imperative in order not to incur innumerable and catastrophic consequences.

There was also Evert. More or less the same thing. There were no resources whatsoever for stopping the revolution in the capitals. Finding no other solution and limitlessly devoted to Your Majesty, he implored him in the name of saving the homeland and dynasty to accept the suggestion of the commanders-in-chief. . . .

How quickly all the telegrams had come. And how unanimous they were.

And all three were, after all, commanders-in-chief, all three were adjutant generals, that is, the generals brought closest, cosseted, sincerely trusted, who wore the royal monogram on their epaulets.

And all spoke as one.

Their unity shook the Emperor.

This meant it was God's will.

Only the good Alekseev had added his own comment so warmly. He hadn't insisted or instructed exactly what to do. But take the decision the Lord instills, toward a peaceful and favorable outcome. The Christian way.

This mild conclusion of Alekseev's reconciled him to the generals' harsh document.

While facing him, here, was Ruzsky. Tripled to be convincing by the broad-faced "Black" Danilov, who had a marked gray streak and a blank, obstinate look, and Supply General Savich.

All three, one after the other, reported their cruel belief that the situation evidently permitted no other solution. . . . The loss of each minute could be fateful for Russia's existence. . . .

Could every last one of them be mistaken and only the Emperor alone thinking correctly?

The Army, his Army, couldn't be against his authority, after all! If now the entire Army was turning its back, was slipping out of his hands—that meant . . .

What did refusing, taking a stand now, mean? It meant provoking bloody internecine strife, and with a foreign war in full swing. Did he really want that misfortune for his people as well?

No, anything but a civil war!

Keep the Army as far from politics as possible. It was enough that they had drawn in the commanders-in-chief.

For the good of Russia . . . To maintain the Army in peace . . . For final victory.

Here Rodzyanko was saying that hatred for the dynasty had reached the extreme limits—but the entire people were filled with determination to prosecute the war to the end.

They wanted that. Everyone wanted exactly that. And for that alone was domestic conciliation needed.

So that goal was worth this! For the good of Russia—with what heart could he oppose it? After all, he was the people's Tsar, for his dutiful people's good. That marvelous people who had knelt on Palace Square at the outbreak of war. Or the people exulting in Novgorod at the Empress's arrival.

For this people, how could he not concede?

"But who knows?" Nikolai still objected in his reflection. "Does all Russia truly want my abdication? How can I find that out?"

Ruzsky—no longer the frail man of the morning but fortified, smoking a lot—replied that now was not the time for questionnaires. Events were racing along at too horrifying a speed, and any delay threatened disaster. And other generals thought so, too.

Three generals. Not with bared sabers, not conspirators who had burst in, but with the most loyal conviction as to how abdication would immediately rescue Russia from both turmoil and military disgrace.

The Emperor wearily shook the ashes from his cigarette. And looked at the speakers sadly, sadly.

Each person is imprisoned in the cell of his own personality. He couldn't jump up, shout, and drive them out. He could only sit and smoke, smoke hard, listen hard. An unfortunate characteristic: always to trail after the arguments of one's interlocutors and find them convincing and not having the strength to cut them off.

It was these besetting arguments that were hardest for the Emperor to withstand. He could not withstand these arguments! If he was to mount a refusal, it would have to be by gaining time and, through this, strengthening his resolve. If only Alix! . . . If someone had restored his faith in himself! . . .

There was no time left, though, that's what they were saying. The Emperor had been caught in such a way (smoothing his mustache with his thumb and middle finger, thumb and middle) that concession was clearly inevitable. These generals were his subordinates, but at the same time he seemed to have fallen into their power.

What an unexpected form the common good can assume, and right in front of us.

How hard it is for the human mind to comprehend how things were situated. How could you be sure you understood circumstances better than the others?

Maybe it was true and a new government would govern more successfully. After all, the Emperor had not been able to find good ministers in the whole of Russia—but maybe they would. That would be a blessing for Russia.

If society wanted so badly to govern itself, why not let it?

Should he sign the abdication for them then? . . .

But would he have to stop being Supreme Commander? That hurt most of all.

Should he ride around to all the armies and say farewell to the soldiers?

And let the adjutant generals do what they want.

(But first, break away to Tsarskoye Selo! Sign the abdication for them—and break away.)

The tranquility of inevitability descended on him. Evidently this was foreordained. And if that was so, then all the easier.

In any case, the dynasty had been preserved: his son, his brother.

He rose. He crossed himself assiduously in front of the icon in the upper corner.

"All right. I'm prepared, gentlemen. To abdicate."

According to form the generals crossed themselves, too.

According to form he should have thanked them for their service, and especially Ruzsky. After all, they had not come here as enemies. According to form, given this kind of gratitude, one was supposed to exchange kisses.

Although his heart dodged at kissing this little animal in tin spectacles.

The Emperor cleared out, with a hitch in his gait, as if it were hard to tear his feet from the floor. As if he'd changed his mind and wasn't leaving.

Ruzsky did not open up to the generals but he hadn't found the words, he was so surprised. Was it really that easy? Would he really bring it? He didn't believe it.

The Emperor returned with the same clipped eyes and slumped shoulders. And handed Ruzsky two telegram blanks.

One to GHQ. The other

"To the President of the State Duma.

There is no sacrifice I would not make in the name of the true good and for the salvation of my beloved Mother Russia. Therefore I am prepared to abdicate the throne in favor of My son in order that he remain with Us until his majority, under the regency of My brother the Grand Duke Mikhail Aleksandrovich.

Nikolai."

It was five minutes after three in the afternoon.

Ruzsky expressed nothing outwardly. He folded both blanks in half together and slipped them into his pocket as if they were the most ordinary pieces of paper.

[3 2 8]

And so, the stars had aligned to create and declare a government! Since now it *could* be created, it *had* to be created because every hour the entire stream of events demanded a cabinet of ministers over it. The fact that Nikolai had not yet abdicated was no obstacle for Milyukov at all; the Tsar's abdication was now a matter of mechanics and a few hours. True, Guchkov had been delayed in his departure, but the abdication would be in his hands today nonetheless. The former Tsar had no choice.

All the ministerial posts had been agreed upon, there remained only to await the final sign from Kerensky. He intended to obtain some kind of sanction from the Soviet—and then everything would be open. Kerensky ran off, ran back, and indicated with his eyebrows that he wasn't quite there.

An agreement had yet to be reached with the Soviet over terms, too. They hadn't finished last night, and in the morning no one had had the strength to continue. But there may have even been something advantageous in this: declare a ready-made government in a revolutionary way, *by spontaneous action*! The Soviet would have to reckon with this fact and this would strengthen his position in the negotiations. The main thing had been clarified yesterday: they made no claims to joining the ministers.

Pavel Nikolaevich even felt a chill of anticipation. He couldn't remember feeling this kind of inspired agitation for many years. Today he felt like the man of the hour. He could barely contain this secret—and had to declare it as soon as possible, let it splash out—and have the right to publicly call himself a minister.

The appointed ministers themselves knew the secret, but even the Duma deputies around them didn't or didn't all, and the government was not discussed out loud at the Duma Committee with Rodzyanko either, but only in corridor whispers. Everyone knew this was in the works but they didn't know its exact makeup. And now all this was about to be announced publicly, quenching the general thirst—and Milyukov, naturally, would not give up this right to declare it, to Lvov or anyone else. (It was lucky, too, that Guchkov had left.)

But *where* to announce it? It was fine for the Soviets; they had somewhere to make announcements, at the Soviet. But where was Milyukov to announce his new government and to whom? It no longer made sense to gather a semblance of the Duma for this, to make a show of things and busy himself with its remnants. Created entirely for other circumstances, in the present revolutionary ones the State Duma would only be a clumsy obstacle

to the new government's actions, and there was no point artificially resurrect-
ing the Duma authority now.

Wait to publish the government's makeup in the newspapers? But that
would mean the loss of another full day and would destroy the truly historic
moment of the announcement.

But there was a simple solution. Why think about where to go out to the
people if the people themselves had come here and were jostling in the
thick of the Ekaterininsky Hall today, too? Just go out into the hall, climb
on a table, and announce to everyone who happened to be there. And
thereby carry out the first official act, giving the new government its public
investiture.

Pavel Nikolaevich waited, and waited, not losing his enthusiasm, silently
pacing through the Duma rooms, flashing his catlike spectacles at those
around him, when suddenly a joyous noise and loud tramping was heard
from the corridor. They looked out, and it was Kerensky being carried along
and lowered to the floor.

Festively crumpled, like an artist after a triumph, exhausted and happy,
he took flying steps right up to Milyukov and didn't even say but whispered
on his final happy exhale:

"You can make the announcement!"

And with this faint exhale, he conveyed to Milyukov the excess of his
happiness—and now a bursting excess of happiness formed in Milyukov.
He was filled to overflowing and could no longer stand there, put it off, wait
for anything else, but like a billiard ball jolted by another billiard ball, he
rolled firmly out the door, down the corridor, and into the Ekaterininsky
Hall, taking no one with him as entourage. In this great moment, no one
was worthy of being around him and sharing this historic pinnacle. (Only
earlier he had ordered there to be stenographers in the hall.) Like a billiard
ball, a balloon even, he rolled into the Ekaterininsky Hall, and easily made
his way through the crowd to a higher staircase landing.

Keen to the sense of history, he looked at his watch. It was five minutes to
three.

He had a surprise: a rally already under way, quite a leftist one, it seemed,
and snatches of phrases reached his ears. All kinds of demonstrations were
constantly going on.

But they noticed Milyukov's imposing figure, let him go up the first steps
of the staircase—and the previous speaker either finished up or ceded the
floor, so that no one got in his way, and everyone crowding nearby was now
looking with interest. Waiting.

Pavel Nikolaevich also had a minute to look around from above, at the
hall. Those closest were looking at him from all sides, and farther away
heads were turned every which way, they were looking in all directions,
some were talking, some far away had their backs turned, while others even
far off looked this way. Many were wearing tall fur hats, Volynian caps,

seamen's caps with ribbons, and the flat fur hats of respectable residents, and some without any hat at all, as it was warm here, somewhere there was a group of female students, somewhere ladies, somewhere people of common status, standing by the far columns a lot higher than the others, evidently on settees, disorderly, disorganized—but precisely the way the **people** should be.

Accustomed to public speaking and easily taking in the hall's size, Pavel Nikolaevich, without clearing his throat, began in a stentorian voice:

"We," he began, without any term of address—because nothing united this hall, "gentlemen" not seeming appropriate, and he couldn't bring himself to utter the word "comrades"—"we are witness to a great moment in history!"

He fell silent for a moment with his head leaning back because this moment had pierced him.

"Just three days ago we were in the modest opposition and the Russian government seemed all-powerful. Now this government has collapsed into the filth"—and he had a triumphant thought and added: "with which it had long since associated. And we"—here it was important to add for strength: "and our friends on the left have been brought forward by the revolution! By the army! And by the people! To a place of honor as members of the first Russian public cabinet!"

He punched out each of those last words, delineating each separately, and then left a pause for clapping.

When the crowd realized this, they responded with applause. This was what the public had come here for—to listen and applaud. It had come to observe, agape, the miracles of the revolution—and here it had just been shown the greatest miracle. The words came easily, threaded themselves:

"How could this event, which so recently seemed incredible, have come about? How could it have happened that the Russian revolution, which has overthrown the old regime for good"—Pavel Nikolaevich had no doubt of this—"turned out to be nearly the briefest and least bloody of all the revolutions history has known?" (This was evident to everyone.)

What he had not quite been able to say over the years in the official hall next door he could now hurl at his old enemy full force:

"This has happened because history has never known another government so foolish! so dishonorable! so cowardly and treacherous as this one!" His voice reverberated more and more powerfully through the hall, and more and more people were turning toward him and listening. "The government that has now been overthrown has covered itself in disgrace, deprived itself of any roots of sympathy and respect that connect any even somewhat strong government with the people!"

Oh, how singularly well this was said—not to Chicago teachers on summer vacation who listened as to something exotic but by autumn would forget, it was spoken in his own conquered capital—and Milyukov was flying above the people, above these two or three thousand heads, and wondering at his own suddenly metallized voice:

"We overthrew the government easily and simply. But this is far from all that needs doing. Half our work remains—the bigger half. It remains to hold onto this victory that came to us so easily. For this, above all, we must preserve that unity of will and thought that led us to victory! Among us, the members of the *current cabinet*"—and the words spilled warmly through his heart—"there have been many longstanding and important debates and disagreements." He mostly had in mind Guchkov, partly the socialists. "These disagreements may soon become important and grave, but today they pale, effaced, before this shared and important task of creating a new people's government to replace the old one that has fallen!"

He spoke very well and they listened superbly; the audience turned out to be prepared beyond his expectations.

"You, too, must be united. . . . Prove that the first public government advanced by the people will not be easily overthrown!"

He said this with faith in the crowd, and the crowd responded to him with their faith and noisy clapping. Oh, how fine it felt to fly over the crowd, over Russia, over History!

"I know, relations in the old army were often founded on the serfdom principle. But now even the officer class has understood full well that we must respect the lower ranks' sense of human dignity. The soldiers who have won this victory know full well that only by maintaining their connection with their officers . . ."

Apparently they didn't know this point as well, and some even completely disagreed. While some kept clapping at every pause, others started shouting, and even hostilely. And someone shouted distinctly to the entire hall, in an untimely and tactless way:

"And who elected you?"

Pavel Nikolaevich had still not moved on to the makeup of the government. Pavel Nikolaevich was thinking he would speak a little more about the obligations of the crowd to freedom, but this tactless outcry derailed his speech. You couldn't pretend you hadn't heard it. It was that loud, and this wasn't a simple listener but a demonstration regular with bellows for lungs. Milyukov quickly sorted his thoughts and without the slightest confusion adjusted his speech:

"I hear someone asking me who elected us." He could have hidden behind the Duma. But that now embarrassed him. "No one elected us, for if we were to wait for a popular election, we couldn't wrest power from the enemy's hands! While we were arguing about whom to elect, our enemy would organize and vanquish you and us!" He thought he'd said this powerfully and definitively. And he added for effect: "The Russian revolution elected us!"

He shuddered at how suddenly and powerfully this had come out, you could put it in a textbook. In that moment, he honestly didn't remember that his goal had always been to avoid revolution; and now it was from revolution that he had naturally appeared and risen to this point.

Once again there was noisy applause and that loudmouth was nowhere to be found. Who wouldn't the historical process shut up?

"How fortunate" (for them, the masses) "that in this moment, when we could not wait, this handful of people were found who were sufficiently well known to the people by their political past and against whom there cannot be the shadow of those objections under whose blows the old government fell."

Every crowd always likes sentimental notes:

"Believe me, gentlemen, we are taking power now not out of a weakness for power. This is not a reward or pleasure but a service and sacrifice! The moment we are told that the people don't need these sacrifices anymore, we will go with gratitude for the opportunity given us." Another speaker might nearly have broken down, but that was not in Pavel Nikolaevich's character. On the contrary, even more firmly: "But we will not give up this power now, when it is needed to reinforce the people's victory and when, if it drops from our hands, it could only fall to our enemy."

Again they clapped eagerly, but shouts rang out:

"Who are the ministers?"

These shouts snatched away his initiative and prevented Pavel Nikolaevich from building his speech, forcing him to respond not according to plan:

"For the people—there can be no secrets! All Russia will learn this secret in a few hours. Of course, we have not become ministers in order to keep our names secret. I will tell you them right away. At the head of our ministry we have placed a man whose name"—he had to say something here— "stands for organized Russian society."

"Franchised society!" a loud and brash but different voice interjected.

This was bad. There turned out to be too many leftists here and not *friends on the left*, but irreconcilable leftists. He needed to hold onto the helm of his speech:

". . . society, which was so irreconcilably persecuted by the old government. Prince Georgi Evgenievich Lvov, head of the Russian zemstvo . . ."

"Franchised! Franchised!" they shouted again.

It was getting very hard to speak. Yes, the popular situation was alarming:

". . . will be our Prime Minister and Minister of the Interior and will replace his persecutor. You say the franchised public? Yes, but that's the only organized one! And it will later allow other strata to organize."

And quickly, not dwelling too much on Lvov, who wasn't worth it, to the most winning figure (and it turned out disproportionately so, as if the number two in the government):

"However, gentlemen, I am happy to tell you that the nonfranchised public also has its representative in our ministry! I have just received the consent"—he had spilled the beans about being the actual prime minister— "of my comrade Aleksandr Fyodorovich Kerensky to take a post in Russia's first public cabinet!"

At this, applause broke out—stormy applause, such as there hadn't been since the speech began. Here was who was truly popular! Linking his surge to the surge of this soaring clapping, Milyukov involuntarily expressed himself more ardently than he felt:

"We are endlessly pleased to put in the faithful hands of this public figure the ministry in which he will hand out just retribution to the underlings of the old regime, all those Stürmers and Sukhomlinovs!"

The surest place for his blows. No matter how much you struck at these, there would be no disagreements.

"The cowardly heroes of days that have passed for good, by the will of fate they will end up in the power not of Shcheglovitov justice but of the Ministry of Justice of Aleksandr Fyodorovich Kerensky!"

Again they clapped stormily, tempestuously, and shouted, but also approvingly, and in all this approval Milyukov was once again fortified.

But for some reason they were still shouting:

"And you? . . . Who? . . ."

"You want to know the other names?" Pavel Nikolaevich responded more modestly and not as loudly. "I have been instructed by my comrades to take the helm of Russia's foreign policy."

They clapped well, well on all sides, and Pavel Nikolaevich also bowed, bowed to all sides. For these moments he forgave the crowd its previous acts of insolence. It was for the sake of these moments that he had ascended to this landing. He didn't feel like spoiling them with arguments about the Dardanelles or the war's prosecution. But he did have an urge to strengthen the feeling between him and the crowd, and his voice shook:

"Perhaps in this post I will turn out to be a weak minister. . . . But I can promise you that *on my watch* the secrets of the Russian people will not fall into our enemies' hands!"

But he couldn't dwell entirely on himself, and Milyukov moved on:

"Now I will name for you someone who, I know, will arouse objections here." And he paused. With a heavy feeling Milyukov proceeded with this inevitable recommendation. "Aleksandr Ivanovich Guchkov was my political enemy . . ."

"Friend!" shouted some class analyst, who had no desire to discern the individuality of their positions behind his franchise hatred.

" . . . enemy throughout the entire life of the State Duma. However, gentlemen, we are now political friends. Yes, and . . . and one must be fair toward one's enemy." (Once again, a winning moment when a good word about an enemy creates a good impression.) "Guchkov lay the first stone toward the victory with which our revived army . . . Guchkov and I are different types of men. I'm an old professor used to giving lectures" (you understand, of course, that this is an ellipsis), "while Guchkov is a man of action. And now, as I speak with you in this hall, Guchkov is on the streets of the capital organizing the victory!"

This was not entirely easy to say, he even had to tell an outright lie. An hour before, Guchkov had telephoned from the Warsaw Station to say he was going to leave at any moment. But amazingly, the Soviet had still not roused, and he had to conceal this secret mission from them so that Guchkov wouldn't be arrested en route, and then our heads would be in jeopardy. Now one more, very disturbing reef:

"Then we have given two seats to representatives of that liberal group of the Russian bourgeoisie who were the first in Russia to attempt to organize an organized representation of the working class. . . ."

A sharp voice:

"And where is it?"

Milyukov deflected that: "So you see, the Workers' Group was put in prison again by the old government, and Konovalov helped . . . and Tereshchenko helped . . ."

"Who? Who?" they shouted. "Tereshchenko? Who's that?"

"Yes, gentlemen," Milyukov grieved. "This name is well known in Russia's south. Russia is great, and it is difficult to know all our fine men everywhere. . . ."

The misunderstanding was felt in the crowd. They hadn't asked what posts they were occupying, and Milyukov hadn't said. On the contrary, they shouted out about farming—and he had to mention the honest and hardworking Shingarev, who . . . They shouted out about the railroads, advantageously:

"Nekrasov is especially loved by our leftist comrades. . . ."

They clapped harder. They didn't ask about the other ministers, and Milyukov didn't bring them up.

But in all these shouts, which could not be ignored, Pavel Nikolaevich lost his speech's structure and plan and inwardly was somewhat disheartened. They had even shouted to him a question about the government's program.

"I very much regret that in response to this question I can't read you a paper where this program is set out. The fact of the matter is that the sole copy of the program discussed yesterday at a nighttime meeting with representatives of the Soviet of Workers' Deputies" (here he did well to hide behind the Soviet) "is now undergoing their final review" (to say nothing of the fact that they had composed it). "I hope that in a few hours you will learn about this program. But of course, right now I can tell you the most important points. . . ."

The entire audience blended together for Milyukov. He couldn't single out good sympathizers, or clamorous offenders, but only heads, heads, he shuddered at every new shout and started agonizing over how he was going to end all this and get out of there. Gazing abstractly at this grayish black muddle, he might still have concentrated and mentally restored that crumpled, uneven, poorly recorded document of Steklov's, remembered all its eight points, if he hadn't been interrupted once again:

"What about the dynasty?"

Right then, exasperated by these shouts and unprepared for a new one, Milyukov blundered. He suddenly didn't remember how well all this had been maneuvered for a Constituent Assembly to decide, and the EC deputies had ceded to him on the delicate point of not predetermining the form of governance, and that had to be appreciated, and kept quiet about right now—however, confused and interrupted so vexingly by these shouts, Milyukov suddenly lost his caution, his balance, all the qualities of a political fighter. And responded impermissibly candidly:

"You ask about the dynasty. I know beforehand that my answer will not please all of you, but I give it. The old despot, who brought Russia to the brink of disaster, will voluntarily abdicate or be deposed!"

They clapped. All this was so. Here, Pavel Nikolaevich might have lingered a little longer and moved on to something else, after all, he had nearly answered! But an ossification of thought had deprived him of his ease at skipping around, and he continued in a reckless and direct way.

"Power will pass to a regent, Grand Duke Mikhail Aleksandrovich. . . ."

That part of the crowd which had clapped delightedly at every announcement kept clapping, but an ominous noise also rose up, especially very close, to one side, from the remnants of the former leftist rally. But Milyukov hadn't come to his senses, hadn't realized, and continued what he was saying:

"The heir will be Aleksei. . . ."

"That's the old dynasty!" they shouted at him.

Rather than spin his head or bat an eye, but like a man being held back, forward in single file, stubbornly:

"Yes, gentlemen, that is the old dynasty, which you may not like and I may not like myself. But who likes whom is beside the point right now. We can't leave the question of the form of government organization without an answer and decision. We are picturing it as a parliamentary constitutional monarchy. Others may imagine it otherwise, but now, if we are going to argue about this instead of deciding immediately, Russia will find itself in a civil war and the recently destroyed regime will be reborn."

He hadn't managed to sort out all the moods here, but this was what he thought and one doesn't easily concede one's convictions. So, too, had the Progressive Bloc thought like this at all its sessions for more than a year now: In order for a constitution to take root in Russia, why destroy the monarchy? That had never been envisaged. Without understanding why they didn't understand him right now, with mounting perplexity, Milyukov made a slip:

"This doesn't mean we've decided the question without any control. As soon as the danger passes and a stable order is reborn, we'll set to preparations for calling a Constituent Assembly. The freely elected popular representation will decide who more accurately expresses Russia's shared opinion: we or our opponents."

Here, "opponents" turned out to be not the old, vile, overthrown government, but somehow those in the hall here shouting against Milyukov.

They demanded harshly:

"Publish your program!"

Right then Milyukov's acumen returned:

"Deciding this depends on the Soviet of Workers' Deputies, which holds the power over press workers. Free Russia cannot get along without the public's broadest right to know. . . . Tomorrow, I hope, it will be possible to restore the proper functioning of the henceforth free press."

The dissatisfied drone against the dynasty continued. But now Pavel Nikolaevich simply appealed to them for mercy:

"Gentlemen! I'm hoarse! It's hard for me to talk anymore. Gentlemen, allow me to end my speech at these explanations. . . ."

Somehow, just to end it.

His opponents made angry noises, but enough jokers and enthusiasts were found to sweep up Milyukov and carry him to the edge of the hall.

Thus he made it out almost triumphally.

But he was shaken. And felt sullied. A nasty feeling.

[3 2 9]

It was remarkable foresight on the dictator's part that in the middle of the night he fell back to the south from Tsarskoye Selo, by not just one station but by several, by forty versts, to Vyritsa. And then learned along the rail telegraph that fifteen minutes after they retreated, a crowd burst into the Tsarskoye Selo train station and had even readied machine guns. (The machine guns, as Domanevsky and Tilly clarified for Iudovich, in the present Petrograd situation, had shown themselves to be most dangerous combined with armored cars or even simply with trucks seized by the soldiers, or even simply in the hands of private civilians.)

And so they arrived in Vyritsa at almost four in the morning, and everyone was whole, and the battalion was sleeping peacefully in the troop train. The dictator would have slept, too—in his familiar, comfortable, beloved train car, on which he had conducted so many campaigns on the Southwestern. But he couldn't sleep yet, his soul was uneasy, for he needed to decide whether to let GHQ know immediately about his new arrival or indulge in a few hours of oblivious rest. However, whom he couldn't fail to report to on his location was the Tarutinsky Regiment subordinate to him, which was at the Aleksandrovsky Station, on the other side of Tsarskoye Selo. Immediately afterward, at five o'clock in the morning, the commander of the Tarutinsky Regiment connected by railroad telephone and reported that an order had been received from General Ruzsky to put the regiment on a troop train and return to the command of his army. Tilly listened to all this—and brought it to Nikolai Iudovich.

Oh! Excellent! Magnificent! After this separate order, the sole possible meaning immediately came through to Iudovich. The Northern Army Group was returning all their troops! Otherwise that kind of separate order could not have been given to the forwardmost regiment. That would be a retreat then.

And if this was so, then Iudovich had no desire to stand on ceremony with Ruzsky, to flaunt his rights as dictator and demand that orders go through only himself. If this was so, then God be with them, let them go home. He sent Tilly quickly, while the line was connected, to reply: "May they go with God!"

Of course, there was no assurance that *all* the troops and *all* the army groups had been recalled, but Iudovich already saw clearly with his mind's eye this favorable turn of events. Thank God!

Now he firmly decided that it would be more honest to send GHQ a telegram about his own location. Not trusting GHQ or the telegraph with all his intentions and concerns, he wrote a single sentence: "Spending night of 14–15 March in Vyritsa." It was sent immediately.

And collapsed into bed.

When he collapsed it was already five thirty in the morning—and he didn't wake up until ten. The troop train was waiting quietly on a reserve track, untouched, in perfect order, and the St. George battalion entrusted to the dictator was intact.

After his solid, albeit brief sleep and a good breakfast, subsequent actions would be easier to conceive. Yesterday's hesitations—whether to drive to the Tarutinsky Regiment (yesterday this was a dangerous ride)—had now fallen away. But although the Emperor in a merciful nighttime telegram had released Iudovich from any actions until his supreme arrival, nonetheless the general's conscience demanded some kind of action, especially in Tsarskoye Selo. Then he and his advisors deemed it sensible to meet and speak with the commanders of the reserve battalions quartered at Tsarskoye Selo. He ordered them telephoned such that either he was inviting them to come to him in Vyritsa or else he was prepared to go to Tsarskoye Selo personally, without his battalion, so as not to arouse suspicions.

The communication went on for a long time while they connected with one and another, but the answer was unanimous: they themselves couldn't come, for that would arouse suspicion in the regiments, and they advised the adjutant general also to reject travel, which could lead to dangerous consequences and even an outburst.

Fine. Then he sent Tilly there instead of himself, by train, so as to defuse the untoward atmosphere of distrust there for General Ivanov.

A long time passed. With the overflowing trains passing through from Petrograd, the adjutant general was able to observe the following scene: The St. George battalion would run out excitedly, surround the train cars, and ask questions. And its martial spirit was definitely falling.

Nikolai Iudovich found himself contemplating and doubting and without decisive actions until, long past noon, they brought him a dispatch from the telegraph office. And who was it from? You'd never guess! Guchkov! Saying he was on his way to Pskov and was definitely expecting to see General Ivanov en route or in Pskov. An order had been given to allow him through in that direction.

Now that was a success! Guchkov was master of the Petrograd situation, of course, and of the entire new government, probably. Which, surely, is why he had written that he was letting Ivanov through! Ever since the Japanese war, relations between them had been good. (Also, something no one knew, a deep secret, it was actually Nikolai Iudovich—and not Polivanov, as many thought—who in 1912 had given Guchkov the secret document from Sukhomlinov that was later to cause a scandal.)

But then, was it permissible to go at Guchkov's summons? General Ivanov was not obligated by GHQ to stay put in Vyritsa, after all. He had to act according to the circumstance, which was very changeable. In a certain sense, the meeting with Guchkov right now was more important than any order from GHQ. Just so they didn't meet in Pskov, of course, where the Emperor was.

Iudovich hastened to reply to Guchkov that he would be happy to see him! He was in Vyritsa but would immediately leave on the Gatchina line. It was only about twenty-five versts to the Gatchina-Warsaw line station, over a connector branch. Of course, gather up his entire battalion and go immediately.

Those were his orders. And they left. But whether due to age or anxiety, Nikolai Iudovich felt weak, lay down, and fell asleep.

He awoke feeling as though he'd slept a long time. The train had stopped. But not in Gatchina. He looked out the window and saw an expressive sign: SUSANINO.

Just what was this, if you please, this was piracy! This was right next to Vyritsa! They hadn't gone anywhere? Had something happened to the train? To the railroad?

The general got very upset because, if he missed Guchkov, the entire matter might get derailed. He sent an officer to find out and give orders!

The officer returned to say that there was an order not to let them go anywhere. We're blocking trains and have been shunted to a sidetrack.

He felt a chill in his belly.

The officer also brought an indirect dispatch picked up on the side from Northern Army Group chief of staff, Danilov, to Dragomirov, commander of the Fifth Army, saying that the Tsar had given the Northern Army Group commander-in-chief permission to enter into talks with the State Duma president and had agreed to return to the Dvina District the troops that had been headed for Petrograd.

It was as if a ray of light had been shed on the murky environs! The light of peaceableness that Iudovich had predicted. Everything was developing precisely according to his prognosis, and he hadn't transgressed in any way and was pure before those who had sent him. Thank God!

Iudovich had just begun to grow warm inside when they came running from the telegraph office and brought such a graphic dispatch that it was like plunging into an ice-hole head first:

"Vyritsa. To General Ivanov. I have learned that you are arresting and terrorizing railroad workers under my jurisdiction. By instruction of the Provisional Committee of the State Duma, I warn you that you are thereby incurring grave responsibility. I advise you not to move from Vyritsa. Commissar Bublikov."

Bublikov again! And what kind of rank was that—Commissar? Who was it who had spread this slander against him? As God is holy, by the cross on his neck, no such thing ever happened! He hadn't terrorized anyone, and if he did arrest anyone, then yesterday the stationmaster, for the delay with the switches, in order to ensure the safety of his courageous battalion—but he had released him immediately. Now this abuse had been spread, and there was no avoiding responsibility before the Provisional Committee. They might even try him, a simple matter. All power was shifting to them. That much was clear.

General Ivanov had stood steadfast before the Tsar, GHQ, and his military duty—but he hadn't figured on being discredited before the new authorities. What was going to come crashing down on the old warrior's head now?

The dictator shuddered. He should have gotten to Guchkov with all due haste, before he had gone by, and through Guchkov obtained full mercy! But now he was so late, and this ominous Bublikov, this Commissar, had barred the way!

Iudovich shrank and didn't dare ask about anything else, so as not to make matters worse. He sat in his car. The battalion in its cars.

Like a new Minin—and together with Pozharsky, who had come over—he looked out the window and saw nothing but the "Susanino" sign and the railroaders walking back and forth over the platforms and tracks and the oily snow between the rails.

They wouldn't allow the train's departure.

The meeting with Guchkov was lost. His soothsayer heart ached that this would not end well.

In Gatchina there was a garrison of 20,000, and they hadn't joined the new authorities, which meant they were subordinate to the District Commander, to him—and these you couldn't call back anywhere, and what else could be done with them? He had to answer for them as well. Whatever mischief they got up to.

Suddenly he was brought a new dispatch from Bublikov, this time gracious, thank God:

"Your insistent desire to travel on poses an insurmountable barrier for carrying out His Majesty's desire to continue to Tsarskoye Selo. I earnestly ask that you remain in Susanino or return to Vyritsa. Commissar Bublikov."

Oh, that was so much better! A completely different tone. And here, after all, even Commissar Bublikov had not disdained His Majesty's interests. So perhaps they could all reach an agreement, little by little, bypassing the old general?

The best, while they were allowing him through, was to return to Vyritsa. The offensive had failed.

But from there, all the same, to report to GHQ about these railroad outrages.

Documents – 10

GENERAL SAKHAROV TO GENERAL ALEKSEEV
Jassy, 15 March

. . . the criminal and outrageous reply of the State Duma President to the Sovereign Emperor's most merciful decision to give the country a responsible ministry . . . My fervent love for His Majesty does not permit my soul to be reconciled to the possible implementation of the vile proposal conveyed to you by the Duma President. I am certain that it was not the Russian people, who have never laid a hand on their Tsar, who conceived of this evil deed, but the handful of brigands called the State Duma who have treacherously exploited a convenient moment to achieve their criminal goals. I am certain that the armies of the front would stand unwaveringly for their Autocratic Leader, were they not called upon to defend the Homeland from an outside enemy and were they not in the hands of those same state criminals who have taken into their own hands the army's lifeline. . . . Weeping, I am compelled to say that perhaps the most painless solution for the country and for retaining the opportunity to do battle with the external enemy . . . is to meet the stated conditions halfway so that delay does not provide fodder for the presentation of further, even viler claims.

[3 3 0]

The city offered nothing but danger and disarray, but it was demeaning and pointless to stay on at his sisters'. Kutepov regretted he'd come on leave at the wrong time. On his way to Petersburg he'd dreamed of meeting with a good woman—but what the devil did he need a good woman for now! Right now in Petersburg, he had no way of helping anymore, and he couldn't live for himself—but he could go back to his regiment early.

He thought some more until the middle of the day—and then headed for Millionnaya to announce his departure for the front. Despite the extraordinary circumstances, it would be tactless to leave without saying goodbye at the club, no matter how these officers had behaved.

There was still no way to ride through the city so he set off from Vasilievsky Island on foot. Although there were a great many people, like on a holiday outing, all apishly wearing those red scraps; nonetheless the rancor against the officers had somewhat abated and you could adopt an easy gait, look freely in all directions, and accept salutes from many (but not all) soldiers.

He reached Millionnaya safely. But right then he saw a chain of soldiers with rifles across from the Preobrazhensky barracks. They were standing spaced out. Kutepov walked confidently between two of them toward the club entrance.

A nearby soldier, embarrassed, stopped the colonel and quietly reported that they'd been ordered not to let anyone into the club.

The right thing to do would have been just to keep walking, but now the right thing was to stop, acknowledging discipline above his colonel's rank.

Kutepov stayed where he was, having already passed a ways down the chain, and told him to summon the chief of the guard.

The soldier did so. Black-bearded Kutepov waited as if made of stone, expressing nothing to the soldiers watching him.

A short, much too casual lance corporal came out of the club entrance, his gait unduly familiar, carrying a large officer's sword and a large revolver, none of it regulation, rather what had been picked up in the past few days. Swinging his arms not by the book, he walked up and without saluting asked the colonel in a pushy tone of voice:

"What do you need?"

He *needed* to give him ten days in the guard-house. But instead, pointing to the chain, he asked:

"What is the meaning of all this, corporal?"

This came out in a fine bass, and the lance corporal was happy to reply, saying that all the soldiers had left for the barracks on Kirochnaya to choose their new battalion commander. And all the officers had been detained here, at the club, therefore the cordon. And again with undue familiarity:

"And who would you be?"

Kutepov could not help but smile at this scoffer:

"I have the honor of serving in the Preobrazhensky Life Guards Regiment."

Amazed bravery registered on the lance corporal's face:

"Ah! In that case I must arrest you."

Then Kutepov aimed a lightning bolt at him and snapped at him commandingly:

"When you have fought in our regiment's ranks as much as I have and know all the gentlemen officers by face, then you and I will talk!"

The lance corporal was taken aback and could find no words.

And so they were all sitting here under arrest—his regimental comrades and the Preobrazhensky men who happened to be attached to them, whether keen combatants or the liberal dreamers who had so invited this rosy dawn—Maksheev, Priklonsky, Skripitsyn. He wished, Kutepov wished he could look at them now and listen to what they thought. But the correlation of forces did not permit him to pay the regimental duty of courtesy; at this point, that would be bravado.

He turned and deliberately, confident of himself, walked back in the direction of the Winter Palace. Privately he thought that if the lance corporal tried to detain him, he would lower his sword on his loathsome head, and that would be it.

But they didn't call out or chase after him.

Walking slowly now across Palace Square, Kutepov saw from a distance a Preobrazhensky sentry posted by the entrance to Military District headquarters. Kutepov turned that way and walked into the entrance. There he discovered Staff Captain Kvashnin-Samarin, who was in charge of the guard, which, he learned, had gone two full days without relief. Kvashnin didn't know what to do now but wasn't in a great hurry to get to the battalion given what was happening there.

The colonel entered the guard room, greeted the arrayed guard, thanked them for their fine service, and announced that, for the third day, he was transferring them from guard to detachment, from sentries to orderlies, and granting them permission to sit at their posts. He summoned the building superintendent and ordered him to be sure to feed the men better. They quickly brought the soldiers lots of fluffy loaves, sausage, tea, and sugar.

In this time, Kutepov learned that other Preobrazhensky guards had been standing at the Winter Palace without relief as well. They had to be reinforced; battalion elections and arrests might go on for a long time.

He went to the Winter Palace. A lieutenant and sergeant told him that several times the guard had had to keep certain sailors and workers out of the Winter Palace's courtyard, that suspicious types kept approaching the sentries and trying to propagandize them into abandoning their posts and storming the palace.

The guard was lined up. The colonel thanked them loudly and clearly, and they responded loudly and clearly. He also gave them permission to henceforth consider themselves a detachment, to remove a few outside posts, and to post paired orderlies at the gates. Downstairs by the telephone he found the assistant to the palace superintendent and asked him to give the guard more sugar and bread and to fit out the guard as well as possible. He was surprised to hear in reply that it would be hard to carry out his request since the issuing of sugar had already been increased above the law by a quarter-dram per person.

These rear rats, and at the palace to boot, didn't understand a thing about what was going on and what might happen to them in five minutes! After that reply, Kutepov ended his conversation with this gentleman and began telephoning to the Guards Crew, where, rumor had it, order was still being maintained. He asked whether they could send a guard to the Winter Palace. The crew's man on duty replied that he couldn't even think of it.

Then Kutepov telephoned the Pavlovsky Life Guard, where, apparently, they had already *elected* their new battalion commander. This new one, some staff captain, did come to the telephone. In a sad voice he confirmed that, yes, unfortunately, he had been chosen battalion commander, but he didn't know where his men were, or how many rifles they had, and he doubted they would carry out a single order of his—and he certainly couldn't send a guard.

There was also a Preobrazhensky guard at the Admiralty. Kutepov didn't bother to go there but headed home.

It had become so less tense to walk through the streets that he could be distracted and think. He thought how, despite the revolution, he had acted and moved around Petrograd freely these past few days. He had done little, but if of the thousands of officers here just a hundred had done as much, there wouldn't have been any revolution.

The Preobrazhensky reserve battalion had conducted themselves quite decently. They had performed excellently on Liteiny. The companies formed up on Palace Square had not joined the insurrectionists, and only Khabalov was to blame for not using them. And here the guards had been standing without relief in all the main buildings. Had the Preobrazhensky captains behaved differently, they would not have been detained and the soldiers would not have gone off to the elections.

He was so lost in thought that at the Nikolaevsky Bridge he himself didn't even see, but was seen by his younger sister and younger brother, who were waiting to warn him that in the hours he was gone, sailors had come three times to arrest him.

They had sniffed out who had acted on Liteiny after all.

His brother and sister wanted him not to return home but to go straight to the train station.

But why hadn't they collected his traveling bag? No, that kind of flight went against Kutepov's grain. Later he would long remember such a humiliation and not forgive himself. Fine, I'll leave, but let's go collect it and say goodbye.

There is a special taste—for testing danger. To pass so very close by with sang-froid.

Off they went. Before they got there, they sent their sister to scout out whether anyone was waiting in the apartment now.

No. They entered the building. The sisters begged him to hurry. But rushing was also a humiliation. He listened to the lament of Zakharovna, the old servant:

"All you have to do is look at their ugly faces! They'd kill their own father. Go, dear! While they were watching out for you, they took my sugar, fifteen pounds. I hope they choke on it! . . . I hope they get theirs in the next world!"

He packed. They all sat for a few moments' silence. He said goodbye. And he and his brother went to the Vindava Station, again on foot. A considerable hike, but without incident.

The station itself turned out to be entirely surrounded by soldiers, although no one tried to disarm him. (But this time he had his revolver in his bag, not to tempt them.) It turned out that the trains through Mogilev weren't running and no one knew when they'd start.

Then what? Go to Kiev circuitously—through Moscow and Voronezh.

They headed for the Nikolaevsky Station. It was already growing dark.

Trains were running from there to Moscow as if there hadn't been any revolution at all.

[3 3 1]

At two thirty, Alekseev sent the Emperor in Pskov a summary of the wishes of the commanders-in-chief.

And so the agonizing waiting began. Had they not sent anything, had they not initiated anything, there wouldn't have been this tension. But now they wished things would get going as quickly as possible. There was no other solution.

Alekseev felt that he and the Emperor could no longer meet as of old.

He could no longer remain under him as his former chief of staff.

They had only just given him good advice: abdication was the easiest and swiftest way to arrive at universal calm and accord. But for some reason they had crossed an irreparable line. The more time passed from the sent telegram, the deeper this was felt.

A telegram arrived from Nepenin, not in response but an indirect morning telegram—and it decisively confirmed once again that the Baltic Fleet was joining the Duma Committee. So that there was no doubt about his position.

Around three o'clock, they finally wrested a telegram from Sakharov as well. With various reservations, but he agreed. They sent it on to Pskov.

Only Kolchak remained silent. But nothing could be decided by him alone.

And then Nikolai Nikolaevich responded with full authority and decisiveness for them both.

Thus the alarming tension at GHQ still remained, but the decision had moved off to Pskov.

Pskov? And the Emperor was deciding? No! After three o'clock, suddenly, a rumor popped up somewhere that the letter trains had left Pskov!

His heart sank at the credibility of the news: This was our Tsar! Here he was! Evade, hide, flee a decision! This was he.

And where had he gone? Where had he rushed off? Not here, surely?

They immediately inquired with Northern Army Group headquarters: Where were the letter trains at this minute? In Pskov or gone? And following what route?

Northern headquarters asked the train commandant: the trains were still there.

But the rumor refused to die.

Alekseev sent Lukomsky himself to send a telegram: Are the letter trains in Pskov or have they gone somewhere?

In Pskov.

Then Klembovsky sent the following order to Northern headquarters: If a report is received saying the letter trains have left or even that just the instruction has been given—immediately inform GHQ!

Will comply.

(What, had Alekseev decided to detain them? No, not that directly . . . However . . .)

They calmed down, but not for long. A report came in that the Northwestern Railroad's Operations Section had already been ordered to send the letter trains toward Dvinsk!

That is, to the front line. To Fifth Army headquarters, to see Dragomirov. What was this?

Once again they rushed to question Northern headquarters. But you couldn't get a hold of anyone there who knew anything; they had all drifted off. Finally they found out that the letter trains hadn't moved and they hadn't heard of any such order. They knew something else, though. Guchkov had left Petrograd by express train. He was expected in Pskov after seven o'clock this evening.

Guchkov? That was news!

Not bad news. Alekseev brightened up. With his intensity, Guchkov would get what he was after.

Northern headquarters also explained what had happened with the frontline regiments that had been sent. The Tarutinsky had remained loyal, but it would be returned by a circuitous route via Estland, so that it wouldn't go through mutinous Luga, to avoid conflict. Luga would return to the Borodino Regiment the weapons that had been taken away and the Borodino would turn back.

Wait, did that mean the Borodino Regiment hadn't gone over to the rebels' side as reported?

Oh no, it hadn't. But details later, it's awkward over the telephone.

The simplest things were so hard to clarify. All day, based on an earthshaking rumor, GHQ had believed that the Borodino men had mutinied, and this unreliability of the troops had especially hastened the steps over the abdication—but it turned out they hadn't.

There remained an accursed uncertainty with Ivanov. Although at noon a telegram had arrived from him saying he had spent the night in Vyritsa—what about after that? What was he doing there? He was so close to the rebellious units that a clash could arise all on its own! He had to be kept from any active actions.

GHQ worried about Ivanov, while Petrograd had its own concerns. Naval General Staff drew a picture of the terrible Baltic situation and the rebellion in Oranienbaum, and Minister of the Navy Grigorovich gave orders to act in accordance with the Duma Committee. Meanwhile, from the General Staff, General Zankevich, on Rodzyanko's orders, had questioned Lukomsky *with all haste* on the situation on the fronts—and waited by the telegraph for an answer.

Apparently, they had had rumors, too, perhaps about the Germans breaking through our front.

They learned from Lukomsky that there was a lull at the fronts.

During these slow hours, everyone's nerves were tensed to the last string, including Alekseev's. It felt less and less possible to wait in ignorance. Everyone thirsted for a decision as soon as possible!

If so little was known at GHQ, absolutely nothing was understood at the army group headquarters and in the major front-line towns. (Especially nervous and waiting was Yanushkevich, chief of staff for the Caucasus Army Group.) Lukomsky enlivened them with his preliminary telegram saying publication was anticipated of a supreme act that would calm the population and avert the horrors of revolution. He asked them to inform the district chiefs of this.

Although the military districts seemed to be silent and not asking questions, for several hours Odessa had been very nervous. The district chief there had reported that the population's alarm was mounting and would continue to do so. At first there was a dearth of telegrams from Petrograd, then a flood of them had made the situation more dangerous by the hour, and order was being maintained with difficulty. When would the promised supreme act finally follow?

Klembovsky explained to Odessa that they were talking about *abdication*, and evidently it was a foregone conclusion, although the decision had yet to be made. But calm had been restored in Petrograd.

Headquarters' leading generals could not sit still, they were so agitated, as in a major battle. Meanwhile Actual State Councilor Bazili and his aides were continuing to improve the abdication manifesto's style, and Lukomsky had gone there to hurry them up. The matter could not get bogged down just because the manifesto wasn't ready!

Finally, at 4:50 in the afternoon, the expected did come through, but for now in a vague guise: a telegram arrived from Danilov, although not about the abdication! The evasive, obstinate, indecisive Emperor had expressed himself in an extended conversation with the generals saying that there was no sacrifice His Majesty would not make for the true good of his homeland. Which Danilov reported.

Of course, this might not conceal all that much. But Guchkov and Shulgin were expected by nightfall.

The hint about *sacrifice* gave GHQ the right now to spread reassurance more broadly. Almost immediately they sent out telegrams directly to the military districts, even the Irkutsk and Amur districts, and to the Don

Cossacks saying publication was anticipated of a supreme act that must necessarily calm the population. The GHQ chief of staff expressed confidence that the District troops would remain calm.

Actually, other than the Odessa District, no one had reported any disturbance.

However, sincerely sympathizing with the Emperor at how constrained and difficult this was for him now, Alekseev transferred the idea also to his mother, what she must be thinking in this hail of telegrams and rumors. He ordered Brusilov to make sure the Southwestern Army Group kept the Dowager Empress in Kiev informed of the situation as he, Brusilov, came to know it.

And also to ask Pskov once again whether the letter trains were still there. They were.

After all, these remonstrances of the Emperor, through his undoubted torment, had been undertaken only in order to save the army from anarchy! And now a few more worrisome hours, the last hours—and Russia would be saved from collapse and the army saved for the spring offensive!

On the path to Russia's salvation stood just the one stubborn heart of the monarch.

[3 3 2]

There had been no searches of Krivoshein's apartment since they'd taken Igor away the day before yesterday; they'd been able to post some semblance of a guard at the front door.

But Krivoshein had arisen over these past days as such a well-known yet by no means odious figure that other prominent individuals, members of the State Council, kept coming to him to hide, to be saved, or for advice, all Petrograd well aware that former dignitaries were being arrested. Yesterday toward nightfall a badly frightened Aleksandr Trepov had come. There was no avoiding letting him spend the night; Krivoshein had a debt of honor to their family.

The entire Trepov family—the father Fyodor, Petersburg's city governor, whom Zasulich had tried to murder, Police Chief General of the Kingdom of Poland, and all four of his sons had played a prominent role in Russia's administration, undeservedly, one might say, judging by their abilities. One son, Dmitri, Governor-General of Petersburg, had averted revolution and bloodshed in the capital in 1905 (he had been nicknamed "spare no bullets"), and he had patronized Krivoshein and brought his notes to the Tsar's attention; but he had been dispirited the following year and sought agreements with the Kadets and had panicked at the thought of the First Duma's dispersal. Another son, Vladimir, was Stolypin's famous opponent in the State Council, a senator and equerry, appeased in the past few years by profitable concessions in Siberia. The son Fyodor was a governor-general, in charge of the Southwestern Territory. Aleksandr had joined the government in the days when Krivoshein had left, was Minister of Roads and Railways for a year, and had led it with great energy, especially the Murmansk Railroad, and in November when his star soared to be prime minister, he immediately attempted to change his conservative course for a quasi-liberal one (demonstrating that neither one was kindred to him), sought popularity from the Duma and didn't find it, lost the throne's confidence, and by New Year's had come crashing down. He was harsh, imperious, and secretive but also experienced and successful in state administration, although perhaps moved only by his career. They had been wrong to dismiss him. He, truth be told, could have defended the throne these past few days. He had been sacrificed over his inability to ally himself with Protopopov and Rasputin.

Society knew that Trepov could not stand Rasputin, and the entire two months of his prime ministership he had tried in vain to dismiss Protopopov, and so it was unlikely anything serious threatened him right now in the Tauride Palace, but he was awash in fear, so unexpected given his strong nature, and he had hidden and was asking for protection. He had expressed himself so much, before, about drastic, decisive measures. How instantaneously can our situation in society and our character be shaken!

Not tall, solid, with thinning hair and a streak of red, an intense gaze and a ruddy face, he seemed to have repeated his brother Dmitri, who before his death had entwined his house with an electric alarm system against terrorists.

Nonetheless, this man had decided to take the post Krivoshein had never been able to bring himself to accept.

For the second time in the past few days fate itself had sent him an overnight guest to hold governmental discussions—about the secrets of the Council of Ministers and the fate of the Russian administration now.

An administration that was totally unclear. Because all at once the logical progression of service had been violated for everyone. All strata had shifted at once, and all the complications were irrevocable. Society, meanwhile, had no habits of governance.

Even today, Trepov was sure that if in November they had been rid of Protopopov, he, Trepov, would have saved both this government and the throne.

However, right now Trepov gave the impression of a finished, played-out figure. But Krivoshein saw his own fortune differently. The collapse had bypassed him, leaving him standing and getting even stronger. Russia right now had no more experienced figure of state who at the same time the public saw as perfectly unstained. It had to be clear to any unclouded gaze that the only new prime minister it made sense to invite was Krivoshein—and that would save everything.

In this insane, spinning, bullet-ridden capital, during these sleepless nights, Aleksandr Vasilievich had become more and more determined to take power. Something he hadn't been for so many years. He had let go of the helm when it had fallen into his hands.

But now he was determined.

Hour after hour, privately, secretly, he waited for a courier from the Duma. But no courier came.

Even though they still hadn't been able to form a government.

Trepov passed the night safely—but what was he to do next? He had the thought of getting to the Ministry of Roads and Railways, where his former official apartment, which Krieger had not occupied, had survived, and where a fellow railroad engineer, Bublikov, was giving orders in the name of the Duma Committee. Either they would shelter him there or else they would give him some kind of safe conduct; at least from there one could begin talks.

That would be all the better for Krivoshein; Trepov was a burden to him.

But how could he get there?

Now—only on foot, there being no other transportation. And under the protection not of his son, an officer—only old Krivoshein could defend him in the event.

"Well, let's go, Aleksandr Fyodorovich."

It wasn't a short journey. And you didn't know which was better—through the center or along the Fontanka. The time had come. Their fur coats were a burden, they would look rich, but they had nothing poorer to put on their shoulders.

They decided to go down Sadovaya, through its usual diverse commercial bustle. There would be fewer army trucks on that route. That was probably right.

They got through without falling under fire or being detained.

Krivoshein gazed around in astonishment. It was as if the air had changed. The red scraps, the dissolute smoking soldiers, and the looted shops here and there, many of them shut—both in Gostiny Dvor and in the Apraksin Market—stunned him. Though many were trading. Life was limping along, but it was not broken.

At one point they regretted not having thought to fasten red bows on themselves, it would have been easier. But they got by.

On the Fontanka, there was a soldier guard in front of the ministry. They sent a note to Commissar Bublikov—and ten minutes later were received and escorted upstairs to see him—in what had recently been Trepov's own office with its windows on the Yusupov garden. Up until this morning, the detained Krieger had been held here, but now he'd been led off to the Duma.

Bublikov was running, not walking, around the office, quite agitated and twitchy, having lost his usual plucked and tidy look, but was nevertheless very confident. After a few sentences the visitors understood from slips of the tongue that he was becoming the new Minister of Railways.

(Had the individual ministers already been so definitely appointed?)

For now, he received them joyously, as equals. He learned the purpose of their visit and promised safe passage and of course he could spend the night in the ministerial apartment.

For now he had them served tea and cookies, and the four of them sat drinking (Bublikov also had an engineer with him, also a commissar) in the spacious office where everything remained as before. It was both strange and pleasant for Trepov to be in his own office. The sky was growing light, and the pre-sunset sun poured through the garden from left to right, lending the office a reddish illumination.

They drank the tea and discussed Russia's fate. Since Bublikov was joining the new government, all the better, their visit took on the nature of reconnaissance. Krivoshein knew his own ability to charm interlocutors, and he felt no urge to restrain it.

"Has Russia not finally earned a strong government of talented men?"

Everyone agreed.

"However, in order to become a government, you're first going to have to establish order at least where you are in the Tauride Palace. Then in the city."

He told them how they had arrested his son and taken him away.

But Krivoshein knew much more than he had time to say. He knew the extensive and slow progress of statistical research, the combined results from which the first opinions were born, then the plans, counterplans, and precisely worded arguments, then the supreme consideration, the work of appointed commissions, new reports in the Council of Ministers, the debates, supreme approvals—for decades he had lived in that steady activity, and he could not believe that anything of the kind could be born out of today's chaos. (And without him.)

"Yes," he joked. "You've exasperated us with your mad resolutions, and now you and I are changing places. Now you'll become a minister and we'll be working in public organizations and desperately criticizing you. Only we have the long experience of government work, and your ministers have none whatsoever."

At that moment the telephone rang. Bublikov picked up the receiver and joyously shouted:

"The makeup of the government?"—and he began receiving and repeating to all those present out loud: Prince Lvov . . . (And it was all over for Krivoshein.) Milyukov. Guchkov. Shingarev. . . . He gaily repeated this but had a hard time concealing his agitation; as they got close to railways his face flushed.

That's all, Krivoshein surmised. That's all they could come up with. Lvov, Milyukov . . . hopeless Kadets. That's all? They didn't understand that back in early winter that kind of cabinet could have held on—but not in the throes of revolution. There was no government experience, this was the main thing. And without it, who are you?

Hundert fünfzig Professoren . . .
Vaterland, du bist verloren![1]

Tereshchenko made Bublikov stumble and everyone wonder. What? Who? This youth from the ballet, a patent leather dandy, as Minister of Finance?

But then Bublikov's voice rose to barely concealed anguish:

". . . Railways . . . Nekrasov?"

He uttered it again, out of inertia—and his voice broke, his face darkened, and he stopped repeating anything out loud and replaced the receiver. He plopped down in his armchair.

Tsarist Minister Trepov, who had found safety, gave vent to his onlooker's astonishment:

"Nekrasov has never worked on the railways. He's a lecturer on construction statics without a single scientific work. The last thing he might have is fifteen-year-old university lecture notes. And materials for a few Duma speeches. No practical experience of any kind."

"A total nonentity!"

But did this really express the full insult? The full blow to his heart? The full breakdown of his world? Did it?

Bublikov's rage seethed like molten lead and had to splatter out—but he still couldn't let his face change, still had to pretend—and not jump up right away and run to the next room and the other phone—to call them there! and vent his anger!

But call whom? He couldn't even vent to the perfidious Rodzyanko, that overblown, large, loud man, because for three days he'd been sagging like a sack of rags. Oh, it had come to pass! He himself was to blame for sitting here, leaving the Duma, seizing the railways for them. *Who had he been working for?* He'd pushed along the grain trains. He'd hurried the coal from the Donbass. He'd called on the depot workers to step up repairs. He'd replaced the murdered Valuyev. And now? . . .

He was shouting into the receiver, crazed, trying to free himself, to keep from smothering:

"I won't serve with those boors! . . . What does he know about operations? Can he really run a ministry? . . . If my services don't mean anything to anyone . . . Villains and boors! They're destroying Russia! . . . The purest demagoguery, a blatant mockery! . . . They won't last two months, they'll be driven out in disgrace! . . . There wasn't this kind of disgraceful cronyism even under Rasputin! . . ."

Lomonosov, with his rolling cauldron of a head and darting glance, was in that room. He heard it all, understood it all, and nodded angrily. Bublikov had burned out. But Lomonosov could still maneuver and get a good place. Leaning, he hunted over the railroad map:

1. "One hundred fifty professors . . . Fatherland, you are lost!"

"... So ... The train with the deputies arrived in Luga. ... In Pskov
soon. ... So ... The Tsar's caught—and a new era of Russian history is beginning! ..."

[3 3 3]

Himmer knew perfectly well that all these crowded meetings did not decide policy, that policy was made by a few men in back rooms; nonetheless
Kerensky's crafty maneuver stunned him, taught and showed him other
possibilities.

While Nakhamkes, in his soporific, unhurried voice and spilling speech,
took up the assembly's time, explaining to the masses that last night a great
victory had been won over the bourgeois elements, and our concessions
were insignificant and we had not promised the bourgeoisie any serious
obligations—Kerensky arrived in Room no. 13 with Zenzinov, twitched
nervously there, languidly sparred with a Bolshevik—and did not reveal by
word or glance that he was preparing for a leap. In fact, he seemed perfectly
normal. But as soon as the applause coming through the open doors of
Room no. 12 marked the conclusion of Nakhamkes's speech, Kerensky
rushed there irrepressibly—and a minute later began his own speech in a
state of exaltation, dropped to a mystical whisper, and announced to everyone that he was prepared to die. These were devices, unknown to our unprepared crowd, taken from French orators, capable of delivering a powerful
jolt: he was speculating in a calculated way on his audience's unprepared-
ness and herd instincts. And no matter what nonsense he went on about—
that his ministerial appointment had to be decided in five minutes, that in
the as yet unformed government he had given an order to free political prisoners (whereas this had been ordered by Maklakov and Adzhemov, who had
been sent as commissars over the old ministry)—and no matter in what half-
swooning state he uttered his half-illogical sentences—it was all very dema-
gogic and harmonious. But having gained his triumph and been carried
out, he immediately returned to his normal state and began a lively conversation with some British officers.

In and of itself, Kerensky's maneuver was instructive and dazzling, but it
contradicted interparty ethics—and this angered EC members: Kerensky
had simply ignored the entire Executive Committee, and its whole resolution; he had no desire to be guided by it or to get it overturned, and like
some little Bonaparte had upset everything with his prank.

During his speech, the majority of the EC, standing right there, behind
everyone's backs, from the doors of Room no. 13, had been indignant but
powerless to stop him. Given this kind of success, it was risky to start a public dispute with him.

But the Bundists Rafes and Erlich, supporters of the coalition with the
bourgeoisie, while outwardly indignant, inwardly apparently regretted that

Kerensky hadn't brought them in on his plan earlier, hadn't enlisted them, hadn't perhaps called on someone else to come along as a candidate for the government. The Mensheviks also hoped today to discuss joining the government—and everyone was stunned that in the night Himmer, Nakham-kes, and Sokolov, whom no one had authorized, had already announced their decision to the bourgeoisie on the EC's behalf! Now, how could they argue with this decision at a general meeting, when there was a threat of harsh statements by the Bolsheviks and the Interdistrict group?

The Bolsheviks and Interdistrict men climbed onto the table with speeches, and these new debates went on for another three hours, with fif-teen speakers. No one was promising to die immediately this time around, but the Bolsheviks did demand an immediate end to the war, the immedi-ate introduction of the eight-hour workday, the immediate distribution of landowners' land—and for this, allowing no contact whatsoever with the Duma Committee, and rather than letting a bourgeois government form, creating a revolutionary one.

"What happened?" the Bolsheviks shouted. "We went out on the street, our blood flowed, and what are they offering up today? Tsarist counterrevo-lution! Guchkov, Rodzyanko, the factory owners, and Konovalov are laugh-ing at the people. The peasants won't get land, they'll get a lump of coal!"

And as they did to any loud exclamation, the crowd shouted back joy-ously and loudly.

In that atmosphere, Rafes and Erlich didn't dare suggest joining the gov-ernment. The Mensheviks did, though, saying that a coalition government was essential for unifying the entire people.

But did this herd really understand the word "coalition"? Or "Con-stituent Assembly"? Or anything of what had been said here at all? For the masses, only "Executive Committee" had a commanding ring.

Finally, just before six o'clock, when it was already dark outside, the So-viet's members—worn out, perspiring, depressed, with swollen feet and even hands—were ready for a vote.

The Soviet's crowd—as if it itself didn't remember, wasn't aware of, didn't notice that it had approved Kerensky's joining—now with all their might raised 400–500 voices, too many to count, in the corridor as well—and waved their hands in favor of the decision of the secretive Executive Committee not to join a bourgeois government under any circumstance! But support it. And also—Nakhamkes had forgotten to read this small point yesterday—self-determination for all nations. They voted for it.

Had anyone else come out with any amendment—to create a second revolutionary government—they would have voted for that, too. The sol-diers were one thing, but it was as if the workers, who had a basic education, didn't understand anything.

But this historic standing session of the Soviet in the budget commis-sion's room had to be its last: it was unbearable to melt and suffocate here, and tomorrow another slew of deputies would show up, possibly as many as a thousand.

They had to commandeer the Duma's large White Hall.

The assemblage was finally decomposing, and someone was shouting out additional news and special announcements, when the Menshevik Yermansky climbed on the table and, shaking a piece of paper, announced that yes, it was confirmed that for a second day there had been a revolution in Berlin and Wilhelm had been overthrown!

And everyone still there—everyone knew Wilhelm—started stamping and clapping and barking "hurrah!"

Chkheidze in the chairman's post—what had become of him? He had completely nodded off, but now he hopped up on the table, rolling his eyes, windmilling his arms, in an unprecedented Caucasian dance—and also growling "hurrah!" as hard as his old man's strength would let him.

[3 3 4]

By his own assessment, Himmer had everything—tremendous theoretical baggage, a keen political nose, indefatigability in discussions—and he had apparently earned the top spot in the revolutionary movement, but he was impeded by being short and skinny and his unimpressive face, and the awareness of these defects had made him a timid speaker. He could say anything at all to a few people in a room, but to a crowd? Nakhamkes rose calmly and chatted with the crowd as if they were people he knew; he seemed to be able to scratch his head or stick his hand in his pocket while doing so. Kerensky soared like a rocket, and whether he shouted, whispered, sighed, or subsided, everything made a magnetic impression on the crowd.

But Kerensky's impudent concert at the Soviet today had utterly infuriated Himmer. He decided to test himself and speak as well. Only in this way could he become a full-fledged socialist leader.

He didn't stand around being bored the whole time in the Soviet, naturally, but often stepped out to check on events in the right wing, the left wing, and the Ekaterininsky Hall. He was sorry he'd missed Milyukov's speech. It would have been quite appropriate for him to speak out in opposition to him right there, in public. The speech, which had not been agreed upon by the EC, had been premature and controversial.

So Himmer was walking along in his jacket, pushing his way down the corridor, when he was told that some new delegation had come to the palace, a member of the Executive Committee needed to speak to them, and there was no one around.

His heart started to pound. The moment had come! Himmer knew he had decided! So he started for the exit.

They told him he should put on his coat. But he thought that in his coat he would look very homely, and it wasn't that cold. He went out as he was.

And immediately saw *his* crowd—and got scared. Heads and faces, heads and faces taking up the entire square and all of them turned his way, patiently awaiting a speaker—they were standing and looking his way.

Fear stabbed Himmer sharply, right above his stomach, as if such a crowd, as if he'd never seen such a crowd in his life!

The crowd stood there, not reacting, not realizing that this was its speaker who had come out.

Meanwhile, the chilly air gripped his head, which his patch of hair did not cover completely, and he was cold.

Someone nearby planted a tall fur hat on him that slipped over his ears and forehead, but his head was warm. In a protective motion, Himmer turned up his jacket collar and lapels.

But how should he begin? How should he draw their attention? Everyone accompanying him was taller than he was, and apparently they were expecting a speech from one of them.

Someone shouted out powerfully:

"Comrades! Here to speak with you now is a member of the Executive Committee of the Soviet of Workers and . . ."

But not a sound came from Himmer's throat.

Two soldiers near him had realized he was going to speak and hoisted him on their shoulders, easily, one hip on one epaulet, the other on the other.

"Comrades!"

Too weak. Stronger:

"Comrades!"

What was this? His voice turned out to be very weak. He was already speaking as loudly as he could—but this wasn't his voice. What was going on?

Even stronger! As loudly as he could!

Too weak again.

You live your entire life and don't know you have no voice at all! And to find out now, here, on strangers' shoulders, above the crowd.

Well, he'd make do. Himmer began to speak. His thoughts and their logic did not fail him: about the people's liberation that had come about, about revolutionary slogans, about the need to form a government, about the negotiations between the Soviet and the Duma Committee. He didn't forget in the least and followed his thought along the path of greatest resistance for the masses, saying that they needed not to take power themselves but to hand it over to the franchised classes and even oblige them with a minimal program. His arguments did not betray him, and he thought he said everything, and no worse than usual.

But he could tell that the crowd couldn't hear him past the sixth or eighth row. And it was an amazingly patient crowd—no signs of irritation. They stood there watching quite seriously.

But why so quietly and silently? Like fish crowded together in an aquarium, where sounds didn't reach.

Or was he like a fish in an aquarium for them?

The first rows may have heard—but what did they hear? Had his arguments reached them? Convinced them? Only when, while enumerating the ministers, he named Kerensky, did the crowd open their mouths and start shouting and applauding.

You might even have thought they were applauding Himmer.

They also shouted out asking whether the monarchy, whether the dynasty was going to stay.

But he wasn't prepared to answer that. Up until very recently he had given little thought to the dynasty's fate, a secondary issue.

But to answer that way was impolitic—so he pointed to his throat and felt his Adam's apple.

He managed to climb down from their shoulders and went into the palace, dejected.

With revulsion at the crowd. That senseless soldier crowd. Any crowd.

No, public speaking was not for him.

[3 3 5]

He'd arrived!

And summoned her. Again a note.

Fearfully, she took it (what if something was wrong?). But he had summoned her.

How bright the world was again!

How could she thank him for making her feel so good! If not for him, her soul would have remained forever empty.

She knew this second one by heart.

He was all large, powerful movement. People said that Volga ships, fast steppe horses, and something in Siberia were like that. And he himself in boots, field boots, not a soldier's. He was racing across all of Russia!

He had entered Petersburg's little theatrical world like one of Ostrovsky's best young heroes, more realistic than could be reproduced on stage.

It was entirely out of character for him to walk on as an admirer. But whatever his presentiment here, she, so little, would give him all of it.

Cling to his clothing like a piece of fluff—and race off with him before the four winds! Weightless and under his protection.

She had stopped hoping they would meet.

She wished she could explain to him why she had never lived before this moment.

She was drawn to him too soon, tearing her feet off the floor by force.

In a few hours . . . She could not imagine this meeting. . . .

[3 3 6]

And so, for various weighty reasons, the State Duma President could not approve the Emperor's instruction to form and head up a new government. Not even to join the cabinet being created as just a member.

But this did not mean Rodzyanko was left without affairs and obligations. On the contrary, if you thought about it, his special status had risen even more.

For who would be the source of power for this government? Who would hand over to it the authority of popular representation, if not the Provisional Committee of the State Duma headed up by Rodzyanko? In essence, this was the Supreme Committee, so that its President functioned virtually as Head of the Russian State.

Broadly embracing all circumstances, Rodzyanko understood that he *himself* could never join the government, no matter how much they asked. How could he? If he went over to the government, who then would lead the State Duma? Dissolved for an interval, deprived of its regularity, its deputies scattered, more defenseless and in need of leadership than ever—who was going to lead them? How could the President abandon his Duma in such a difficult moment? Not these intriguers, of whom there were a few, but the rest of the deputies, trusting and defenseless? Abandon the very cause of freedom? . . .

Who would watch over the new government, which was to be *responsible* for that very reason, in order to account for itself to the Duma?

Rodzyanko had become as one with his Duma. It had become increasingly clear to him by the hour that this was a mistaken notion in general—to move over to the government. He could not accept an appointment to the government.

He no longer regretted anything.

During this transitional period, before a government was created, to whom did all the major military leaders and everyone who had an important question turn? Grand Duke Nikolai Nikolaevich had sent telegrams from Tiflis—to him. Vice Admiral Nepenin had asked none other than State Duma deputies be sent to Reval to calm the population so that the residents would stop inciting the sailors. Former Minister of the Navy Grigorovich, who had not been arrested, had sent Rear Admiral Kapnist from the Naval General Staff with advice on maintaining order in the fleet and restoring order at Kronstadt.

People came running to the President for explanations on how to understand the Order No. 1 issued by the workers' Soviet, and Rodzyanko declared to them all that it should be considered null and void.

And to whom if not the Duma President did the telegrams of support, delight, and approval flow from all kinds of provincial, not always known and even unknown assemblies, institutions, societies, and associations?

Highly encouraging reading. This great country knew no government, no Soviet of Workers' Deputies—but only its hope, the State Duma, which held all power.

Who had to be quickly found when a terrible rumor raced through the capital that major German forces had broken through the Western front? (He instructed Zankevich to check with GHQ, and fortunately there was nothing of the kind.)

And then, who was the main figure obliged to welcome the military units coming to the Duma, if not the Duma President? Today the cadets of the Pavlovsky Military School (where in previous days there had been vacillations and disturbances, for which the general in charge had been arrested, and today there'd been a search) and the Military Topographical School. But without reproaching anyone for the delay in showing up, Rodzyanko fervently called on them to continue their studies and to gain military knowledge in order to rout the hated Germany.

Thus the President spent the entire day in cares and concerns and burdens; there was no time to rest. The last thing he was spending any time on was the new government's makeup.

He had been approached, and several times, by colonels from the Military Commission reporting that the chaos in the garrison was mounting and there was no firm military administration. They needed a *figure* at the head.

Well, appointing a Military District commander was well within the President's scope. It was an inspiring suggestion, to give the disturbed capital a firm military authority! Who? They had said they needed a famous hero, so perhaps Kornilov?

Kornilov? Not bad. We weren't going to wait for Guchkov; time is of the essence.

General Kornilov was at the front commanding a corps. Thus he reported to GHQ. But the Supreme Commander . . . was now facing abdication. And during these hours Rodzyanko was virtually head of state.

And so: simply send an order from the State Duma President to the Southwestern Army Group, to valorous Lieutenant General Kornilov, to hand over the 25th Corps as quickly as possible, in a matter of hours, and depart for the capital to take up his new high post.

But since the telegram was going to go through GHQ anyway, he had to politely inform GHQ of this somehow as well. There was no point offending Alekseev. It could even be couched as consulting with GHQ, or a request.

Meanwhile, the Emperor was a figure to be passed over in respectful silence.

All this took a great deal of intelligence and subtlety.

On the other hand, for the capital itself, hastening to gladden the inhabitants, the President could first announce Kornilov's appointment in the form of an Order of his own.

Even the colonels from the Military Commission could not help him now. These were not the lines of an ordinary dry military order; one had to live through and experience as much as was contained in Rodzyanko's broad chest.

"The difficult transitional period has ended. The people have accomplished their heroic civic deed and overthrown the old regime. Citizens of the country! First and foremost, citizens of the agitated capital! . . . Return to your calm working life. The Provisional Committee of the State Duma is appointing as Commander-in-Chief of the troops of Petrograd and the surrounding areas . . ."

All correct, all very good. But it was missing some final triumphant chord. Elbowing his way through the crowded rooms, Rodzyanko understood and added:

"Schedule a parade for the Petrograd garrison troops for 17 March. . . ."

The President was somewhat grieved that the Allies' envoys had sought out relations not with him but with the government in the making. However, Rodzyanko retained a very important connection—to Grand Duke Mikhail, who was to take Russia into his own hands at any moment. Since that evening when they last saw each other, the grand duke had been stranded in Petrograd, hiding in a secret apartment. In these decisive hours he needed spiritual support!

As much as he could given the cramped conditions, Rodzyanko removed himself, so that no one would look at his paper, and wrote something to His Imperial Highness to be conveyed by a trusted person.

. . . Everything was too late now . . .

(As was the appointment of Rodzyanko himself, which a month ago might have saved the country.)

. . . The country will be calmed only by an abdication from the throne in favor of the heir—under your regency. I beg of you to use your influence to see that this comes about voluntarily and then everything will calm down immediately.

Rodzyanko did not have much faith in Guchkov. Guchkov was quick-tempered and hostile to the Emperor and could only spoil things. It had been a bad idea, sending Guchkov to Pskov. But the grand duke, of course, had no direct link to his sovereign brother now, but might be able to send him a telegram indirectly somehow? Or send a note with someone? But Rodzyanko was certain that there was no other solution for Russia than the Emperor's abdication. The waves of popular passion had been unleashed! . . . (How else to say it, if people had threatened to tear the President himself to pieces! . . .)

. . . I personally am hanging by a thread and could be arrested and hanged at any moment. Do not take any steps or show yourself anywhere! . . .

God forbid they tear the grand duke to pieces as well.

. . . And know this. There is no avoiding the regency for you.

Rodzyanko was spiritually fortified by this secret closeness with the incoming monarch.

[3 3 7]

The Emperor had put his abdication in the hands of others. To them first, these three random generals, he revealed and conveyed his intention without having consulted with a single living soul.

But his own soul demanded that he talk to someone close. To fortify itself.

But he had no one, no one *close*, around him.

He had two or three people who were truly close, family. But he was cut off from them.

No, one person was warm and devoted, Frederiks, about whom Alix had been angry for more than a year, saying his mind was gone and he was dangerously unsuited to his position. But Nikolai did not like to dismiss old loyal servants and felt a tenderness toward Frederiks.

Now Nikolai summoned him. The stooped, ancient man with the tearful gaze came immediately. Frederiks, you see, had his own sorrow. News had come from Petrograd that his house had burned down and nothing was known of his family.

The first thing the Emperor did was inquire whether there was any news about the family.

Frederiks shook his bowed head sadly.

He had permission to sit in the Emperor's presence right away—and he did.

In slow sentences, with pauses, as if about something new and perhaps not yet accomplished, the Emperor began explaining to him.

That—here it is. . . . That if the army is in favor of this . . . Everyone had turned their backs on him. There was no other solution.

The yellowish-gray old man, his mustache still bristling, followed him with an extinguished gaze—and suddenly his eyes lit up, his head shook harder, his lips began to move, and a rasp emerged:

"I don't believe it, Your Majesty."

Nikolai was distraught.

"But it is so, count, unfortunately."

Frederiks's head shook in denial, as if he rejected this:

"No. This I hadn't expected. That I would live to see such a terrible end. . . ."

Nikolai felt it like a collapse in his chest. What had he in fact done?

Frederiks's head shook now affirmatively:

"Why am I still alive? This is what it means to outlive yourself."

And now there was also the Heir's fate, totally unknown. Nikolai felt the tears in his eyes and could not speak.

Had the Lord really abandoned him? . . . Then there was no reason to resist. He must surrender to God's will.

But right then they reported that General Ruzsky was once again requesting an audience. The Emperor wiped his eyes.

What was this?

The same nervous, mechanical general entered, with his even, rectangular hedge of gray and white hair and wire spectacles.

There was this news: a telegram had arrived from Petrograd saying that State Duma deputies Guchkov and Shulgin had left for Pskov to see His Majesty as delegates. (Guchkov was not a member of the Duma, but right now no one noticed this difference; naturally he was part of that company.)

So now Ruzsky had returned from his train car. He still hadn't managed to send the Tsar's telegrams—and should even he send them to Petrograd now, if people were on their way here?

The Emperor's heart started beating massively with joy. He was being raised from the well; only now did he feel how much he had already given away! They were coming? They could only be coming to negotiate. That meant there were changes for the better in Petrograd. Perhaps he might not have to concede so much quite yet!

(At that moment, even the fact that it was Guchkov coming was not oppressive. Guchkov, who had divulged the Emperor's intimate statements to a newspaper, whom the Emperor had told through Polivanov that he was a scoundrel whom *he didn't recognize* at the final reception for the Third Duma—now, on his way with good news, appeared in a somewhat softer light and was to be partly forgiven.)

"You've reasoned perfectly correctly, Nikolai Vladimirovich," the Emperor replied, pleased. "Why send it now? Let's wait." And although this was his perfectly natural and legitimate right, still he said shyly: "Please, then . . . give me back my telegrams. . . ."

Ruzsky went into the same side pocket of his tunic where he had put the telegrams, pulled them out—and gave them back.

However, this was just **one** telegram! The Emperor turned it over: to GHQ. The second, to Rodzyanko, wasn't there.

But they had been together in the same pocket and even, he thought, folded together—and now the other wasn't there?

"You're . . . mistaken, Nikolai Vladimirovich. I need the second as well, please. . . ." But at that moment it occurred to him that this might not be an accident, and his voice subsided into timidity. The Emperor was always distraught whenever it seemed as though his interlocutor might commit some tactless act. Had Ruzsky purposely put them in two pockets so that he wouldn't make a mistake in pulling them out?

But in order to speak with the Duma deputies, the Emperor needed the Rodzyanko one back.

Ruzsky rose up quite firmly and pushed the circles of his spectacles forward:

"Your Majesty, I sense that you don't trust me!"

The Emperor became even more embarrassed.

For Ruzsky, primarily:

"No, why? . . . Not at all. . . . I trust you completely. . . . It's simply . . ."

Trading reproaches with his own general would be a loss of dignity.

"Rest assured," Ruzsky punched out firmly, "I will not send it off before the deputies' arrival."

And he didn't budge. He did not give back the other one.

They both stood there, and the mute Frederiks, who may not have understood any of it, sat in his chair.

Due to the terrible awkwardness that had taken shape, it was difficult to insist.

Even when Ruzsky said in a monotone of certainty:

"If you will allow me, Your Majesty, I will receive the deputies first and prepare them for your talk."

The Emperor did not understand or object.

Ruzsky saluted and left for his train car.

As he went, the Emperor wondered why Ruzsky should receive the deputies first.

It irked him that Ruzsky had held onto the second telegram. A bargaining chip.

Actually, what difference did it make who held it? What was important was that it hadn't been sent.

Had they appointed Guchkov intentionally—to insult and remind him?

On the other hand, he had Shulgin with him, a longstanding and loyal monarchist. That was a good sign.

That meant wait.

He let Frederiks go.

Time passed.

The decision to surrender brought great relief in that first moment.

But living with that surrender now was a burden. Actually, maybe he wouldn't have to abdicate.

Meanwhile the entire suite had found out from Frederiks and a very agitated Voeikov had come with his snow-white aide-de-camp aiguillettes, his eyes popping:

"Your Majesty! Is it really true what the count says?"

And he began trying to argue forcefully, military fashion—on his own behalf and, as he said, on behalf of the entire alarmed suite, saying that the Emperor did not have the right to abdicate the throne merely at the behest of the Duma Committee and the army group commanders-in-chief. Abdicate simply like that, in his train car, at a random train station? To whom? Why?

"What choice did I have left, though?" the Emperor replied in a subsided, weakened voice, increasingly suspecting he had made a terrible mistake. "When everyone thought the same? If that is what all the commanders-in-chief want—that means the army . . . Otherwise there will be internecine strife."

With his usual heated force and powerful voice, Voeikov tried to argue that the exact opposite was true. It was abdication that would provoke internecine strife and might mean ruin for the war and Russia. The country's form of governance could change if there was legitimate, universal discussion, but not like this!

His insides were in knots. Oh, he was right! Had he missed this? Made a mistake? Done the wrong thing? . . . Oh no . . . But in any event:

"The Duma representatives are about to arrive and we'll discuss . . ."

"But you left a telegram with him? A document? How is this possible?" Voeikov was furious, and the whites of his eyes were flashing.

"Don't be so upset," the Emperor objected weakly. "He's not going to send it, after all."

Gloomy, angry, close to exploding, Voeikov left.

The solitude in the train car was quite distressing, and there was decidedly nothing to do. If only the deputies would come quickly. Why hadn't they come?

Right then Frederiks dragged himself in and with a weak and ailing voice, speaking for the entire suite, said that everyone was worried and asked the Emperor to take back the telegram from Ruzsky. This was some kind of intrigue. He would send it and bring about the abdication by deceit.

No, now he felt awkward asking for it. No, Ruzsky wouldn't send it. Why, the representatives were about to arrive.

However, when the Emperor went to the dining room for five o'clock tea—the entire suite was present, and only the suite, no outsiders, and the Emperor caught their unprecedentedly alarmed looks. However, none of them dared ask a question out loud or advise him. Only the Emperor could break the traditional silence—and every heart was waiting for this. But this was so unusual and improper, and what might they advise? What did they know more than the Emperor?

And besides, there were servants present, carrying the tea from the buffet.

Trying to behave as normally as possible, the Emperor kept to small talk. And was responded to in kind. This was punctuated by long, utterly blank pauses.

Tea was over and the deputies still hadn't come. He was informed that they were delayed.

It was close to twilight, and the Emperor decided to walk a little more on the platform. He invited the doctor, Professor Fyodorov, to join him.

The Emperor strolled steadily, moderately, as if nothing had changed, smiled or nodded occasionally at anyone he had not yet seen today.

There had been a thaw, and water was dripping from the roofs of the station structures.

With everything now being laid on Aleksei's shoulders, the Emperor's concern had mounted. How could the boy cope? He had invited Professor Fyodorov in order to have a conversation—oddly enough, the first candid one between them. For some reason, the full danger had never been made explicit and the question had never been asked entirely. Finding out was frightening, and why should he ask, when there was Grigori's prediction that at age fourteen the boy would cease to suffer, and he would turn fourteen in the summer of 1918, which was soon.

"At another time, doctor, I would not have asked you a question like this. But a very grave moment has come. And I'm asking you to reply with full candor. Will my son live the way everyone lives? And will he be able to reign?"

Fyodorov did not try to soften the blow:

"Your Imperial Majesty! I must confess to you that according to science, His Imperial Highness should not live even to the age of sixteen."

Cold pincers seized the Emperor's heart. The sentence was undeviating and without mercy.

What? This meant that all these long precautions and hopes, thirteen years of leading the Heir toward the throne—and all for nothing?

"But medicine could be mistaken!"

"Of course, it could, Your Majesty. God grant it be so. They live to an even greater age, but by warding off even the most minor of accidents. However, a cure for the Heir would be a miracle. His life can be extended only through extreme caution."

But if the unfortunate boy had so little time left to live, then why pass to him the bitterness of the crown? Just so that they can later turn their backs on him in the same way? . . .

In any case, what Fyodorov said confirmed the Emperor's decision. While inheriting the crown, the boy must remain with his parents. Especially since *their* plan might in fact consist of tearing Aleksei away from his mother. But neither his mother nor his father would consent to that! Fyodorov's diagnosis had given him just the right he needed not to let go of the boy.

But when he expressed this decision to Fyodorov, the doctor was astonished:

"Your Majesty, do you really think they will leave Aleksei Nikolaevich by your side even after the abdication?"

"Why shouldn't they? He's a child, and until he becomes an adult . . . For now Mikhail Aleksandrovich will be regent. . . ."

"No, Your Majesty. That would never be possible. And you absolutely cannot hope for this."

"But precisely given the state of his health, how can I let him go? If this is so, now I'll have the right to keep him with me!"

And the doctor had to explain to the monarch!

"Monarchical considerations are exactly what will not allow this. In order that there not be influences on the Heir's will. . . . They would more likely agree to place him in the regent's family. . . ."

In an illegitimate family? With that adventuress Brasova? Alix would never allow that!

"Nowhere are parents prevented from taking care of their children!"

"But what do you suppose, Your Majesty, where are you yourself going to live?"

"Well, in the Crimea, for instance."

"I'm not certain they will allow you to remain living in Russia."

"What? Even as an ordinary resident? Am I really going to be intriguing? I shall live near Aleksei—and raise him!"

Utterly astonishing! The Emperor had absolutely no doubt of this!

"And if they don't allow this in Russia—then even more so, how can I part with my son? Even more so, if he cannot be useful for the fatherland, we have the right to keep him with us!"

Parting with his son was much more difficult than renouncing his authority. Parting with his son was beyond his strength! No one could demand that of a father! How could he hand him over like a toy into the hands of these immoral politicians? What degenerate notions would they instill in him! How could he hand over not only him but his soul!

After all, that was what the telegram said: so that he remains with us until his majority. Otherwise it is null and void!

The Emperor returned from his stroll disheartened. He had simply not predicted such a turn. He had absolutely no idea now what to do.

To think as well that they would take away Aleksei and in his name carry out their own infamous policy?

Repulsive.

Not surrender the throne to them at all?

Better not to then!

Once again Voeikov arrived from the suite, very firm, saying that everyone was insisting the telegram be taken away from Ruzsky!

Indeed, it had now lost its meaning. It could not be implemented. It had to be taken away.

The Emperor agreed they should go take it away.

But Voeikov couldn't. He and Ruzsky had already argued and would argue again.

Then Count Naryshkin could go.

What now remained to be done with the throne?

If not to Aleksei, then to his brother Mikhail? . . .

Naturally, Misha was utterly unprepared for it. But becoming regent, wasn't that the same thing?

Three days ago, after all, Mikhail had presumed to give him advice of state over the telegraph.

Naryshkin went—and came back empty-handed. Ruzsky had not given the telegram back to the suite general. He had replied that he would give the Emperor private explanations.

But he hadn't come to explain.

All the Emperor's authority was suddenly repressed. And he couldn't compel him!

No matter. That telegram no longer had significance. It could be changed in the deputies' presence.

But they still hadn't come.

A passenger train arrived from Petrograd, but not theirs. The suite said it was a terrible sight. Even the officers and cadets had fastened red bows onto their greatcoats. And all were without weapons. In Petrograd they were beating up officers and taking away their weapons.

[3 3 8]

There had been a great many disappointments this winter. First the rumor that in a few days Switzerland would be drawn into the war, which was rather awful, so he had to make quick calculations: he himself would remain in the German occupation zone and Inessa would go to Geneva, where France would take her—and thus we would improve our connection with Russia. Then relief: there would be no war. Then Nadya fell ill— bronchitis, fever—and he ran for the doctor, so there was no chance to get to the library.

However, this was no time to twiddle his thumbs. What if we ourselves, directly, without any Swiss—get the Swiss army to mutiny? A plan arose to write a leaflet ("Let us kindle revolutionary propaganda in the army! Let us convert a hateful civilian peace to revolutionary class actions!"), but in absolute secrecy (one could suffer badly for this, be expelled from Switzerland), and sign it "Swiss group of Zimmerwaldist leftists" (let them wonder which of them, even Platten) and distribute it in a roundabout way, as if not from ourselves. Inessa would quickly translate it into French. Only absolutely secretly, burning drafts. (They were satisfied the post didn't check letters.)

They started in. But from this came a new plan: why not compose it again ourselves but sign it from others, a leaflet like this: rouse *the entire European proletariat* to a general strike on 1 May! Why not? Would the proletariat really not respond? And at the height of the war, what a force that would be! What a demonstration! And from the strike, look, mass revolutionary actions could begin spontaneously, too! One good leaflet and all Europe rises up, eh? Only we have to hurry. It's not long until 1 May. Quickly translate it into French, publish it, send it out. (And in utter secrecy!)

Before a Europe-wide strike could be thought through, however, when the leaflet's translations were still in preparation, a sudden letter arrived from that Kollontai woman, who had returned to Scandinavia from America. New fire to the gunpowder: there had been a *schism* at the Swedish party's congress!

What unexpected fortune! How could they forget their loyal Zimmerwaldist comrades-in-arms? And what devilish disarray and confusion there must be now in the Swedes' minds!

How could he influence this? How could he help? He had an idea: here was where the awaited task, the most important and noblest task lay: a revolution should be made in Sweden, not Switzerland! Begin *there*!

Kollontai went on to write that young Swedes had decided to assemble on 12 May to found a *new* party "on Zimmerwaldist principles." Oh, young fledglings, sincere and inexperienced! Who will explain to you that the Zimmerwald-Kienthal principles have been *betrayed*! Betrayed, drowned in the swamp by nearly all the parties of Europe! Zimmerwald was *dead*, dead and bankrupt! But you are sincere and pure, and no matter what, *before* the congress you need help sorting out the baseness of Kautskyism and the vileness of the Zimmerwaldist majority. (Oh, why am I not with you there?) The time had come to cut Branting's claws! I must send you my theses to help you immediately! We are morally and politically responsible for you. A decisive moment in the Scandinavian workers' movement!

All this temporary pessimism and the discouragement that overtook him after his failures with the wretched, spineless, hopeless Swiss leftists was now flooded by joyous impatience to *set Europe on fire from the North*! The time remaining was short and there was a great deal to do, but correspondence was having trouble going through Germany. It was an energetic, active, and purposeful struggle, though! Life had been reborn! New meaning had lit up the somber vaults of Zurich's church reading rooms, newspaper stacks, and rustling brochures in the Center for Social Literature: a leaflet by 1 May! Theses by 12 May and a coming to terms! All forces for a European strike and a Swedish schism! We should only be working on youth! We will never do or see anything. But the blood-red sun of revolution will rise for them yet!

On 15 March, he was finishing dinner at home when suddenly there was a knock. Bronsky. This was a bad time, though. (In this failure with the leftists, so much had been put on Bronsky and these elections-nonelections, that seeing Bronsky now was not very pleasant. And they still had not updated him on the new plans.) He walked in and, without sitting down, in his languid manner as usual, a little melancholically:

"You know nothing?"

"What?"

"In Russia—there's been a revolution . . . apparently . . . They've written . . ."

He also had a way of never raising his voice, and this dragging things out, as if he were uncertain—Ilyich lifted his eyes from his plate of boiled beef, having finished his soup, he looked at the quiet Bronsky—he had made no more impression than if he had said that a kilo of meat now cost 5 rappen less. In Russia? A revolution?

"What nonsense. Where did you get that?"

He kept eating, cut a piece crosswise, to get meat and fat. Where, out of thin air? That's the kind of nonsense people say. He dipped pieces in the

mustard on the rim of his plate. He also disliked having his meal interrupted, not being allowed to eat in peace.

But Bronsky stood there without taking off his coat, kneading his wet felt
hat, which he treasured greatly. For him, this was tremendous agitation.

Nadya ran her hands down the sides of her gray checked dress, as if wiping them:

"What's this? In what newspapers? Where did you read this?"

"Telegrams. From the German papers."

"Well! German papers about Russia! They're lying."

He calmly finished eating.

European newspapers wrote about Russia scantily and always distortedly.
Without accurate information, it was hard to discern the truth from that distance. And they almost never had letters from Russia. Two fresh Russians
who had fled German captivity had just appeared briefly—and he had run
to see them and talk. It was interesting. Russia was mentioned occasionally
in reports, but no more than the Paris Commune, which was a very long
time ago.

"How exactly was it stated there?"

Bronsky attempted to repeat it. And as usual for most people—though it
was shameful for a professional revolutionary!—he couldn't repeat the
exact sense, let alone the exact expressions.

"There have been popular disturbances in Petersburg . . . crowds . . . police . . . The Revolution . . . has won. . . ."

"What exactly does this victory consist of?"

". . . The ministers have . . . resigned, I don't remember . . ."

"Did you read this yourself? What about the Tsar?"

"Nothing about the Tsar. . . ."

"Nothing about the Tsar? What does the victory consist of then?"

What nonsense. Maybe Bronsky wasn't to blame but this imprecise item
itself.

Nadya fingered her worn dress—even more worn from the little light
in the room—into pleats on her chest—it had been drizzling since early
morning:

"But still, is there something to this, Volodya? Where is this from?"

Where! The bourgeois newspaper's usual canard, inflating an opponent's
least failure; how many times during this war had it all been blown out of
proportion?

"Is this really how one finds out about revolutions? Remember Geneva
and the Lunacharskys."

One January evening, he and Nadya had been walking down the street
when the Lunacharskys came toward them, joyous, beaming: "Yesterday,
the twenty-second, they fired on a crowd in Petersburg! Many dead!" How
could he forget it, the exulting evening of the Russian emigration! They
rushed to the Russian restaurant, everyone gathered there, they sat excited,

they sang, their strength replenished, everyone at once so revived. . . . Tall Trotsky, his arms extended, too, was off and running with toasts and congratulating everyone and saying that he would go immediately. (And he did.)

"All right, let's have some tea."

Or not?

To go back to the reading room and continue his regular work didn't seem to be panning out, either. For some reason he was stuck, blocked. He had to clarify something. Some obstacle to all his plans.

But the newspapers with today's telegrams wouldn't be in the reading rooms until tomorrow.

On Bellevue, though, they hung urgent ones in the window of *Neue Zürcher Zeitung*.

All right, let's go there.

Nadya had gone out very little since her recent bronchitis in February and stayed home. But Ilyich pulled on his old mended coat, planted his old bowler on his head like on a block—and off they went.

"Here lived the poet Georg Büchner"—on a neighboring building. They started quickly uphill along a damp narrow side-street where the crumbly wet snow had still not melted near the walls. Taking short-cuts down side-streets, to get closer to Bellevue.

In the Swiss manner, everyone was carrying umbrellas, barely avoiding poking each other's eyes out in the side-streets. But Lenin didn't like carrying one: sometimes it was useful, sometimes not. And everything he wore was old so he didn't mind. Bronsky likewise.

In the windows they found more or less what Bronsky had said. Only the ministers had apparently been arrested. Arrested? . . . And also: the Duma deputies were in power. And the Tsar? Not a word about the Tsar. It was clear then that the Tsar was at liberty, with the troops, and would now give them what for.

If it wasn't, in fact, all lies.

No, such a thing was impossible in present-day Russia.

And there were no crowds at the window; no one other than the two of them.

A fine rain was drizzling on the square and lake, blanketing everything over the lake evenly, and there was a milky gray shroud over Uetliberg on the other side. Cabs had their dark tops up, and dark umbrellas were moving steadily. What revolution? . . .

Still, one would like a thorough explanation.

They went to a newspaper kiosk on the Heimplatz in hopes of coming across something. Lenin never bought the papers, but for this occasion he could, out of the party treasury.

However, the simple-hearted news vendor admitted there wasn't anything in any of them—so they didn't buy a one.

Put a stop to this nonsense and go to the reading room and work. Bronsky relaxed, flustered, seemed prepared now not to lag behind, to drag through the streets or wait in the rain by the window for the next telegrams—the diffuseness of aimless men. He reproached him—and said goodbye. Again and again, by side-streets traveled a thousand times, not noticing the buildings, the windows, or the people—he headed for the canton reading room.

But in front of the Gothic windows themselves, he faltered.

Something wouldn't let him. As if he would get stuck in the doorway. As if something inside him had swollen up in the last half-hour—and wouldn't let him.

Meanwhile the rain had stopped.

He stood there, angry. Naturally, he could force himself, and he could sit there until evening, but . . . Direct and clear work called him—for the Swedes but . . . He'd been distracted, at a bad time. And the excerpts—"Marxism on the State" . . . But he couldn't do it.

On the contrary, an alien, uncharacteristic, even criminal thought slipped out: go to the Russian reading room. A nest of SRs, anarchists, Mensheviks, and all kinds of simply Russian rabble. He tried always to avoid it, like a nest of vipers, not to go to Culmannstrasse, not to breathe that air, not to meet or see anyone. But now he thought: After all, they've probably gathered, are gathering there. . . . Whether they know or not, they're talking, they'll talk. I might hear something. Not to speak myself but to find something out.

And breaking all his rules, drawn to that repugnant place—he went.

Culmannstrasse was across the river, not close at all. And significantly uphill. Off he went.

Indeed, about twenty people had already crammed into the small, heated room out of the cold damp and in their damp clothing, some sitting, some without a thought of sitting—but no one was silent, everyone was talking at once, buzzing and droning, and the general rumble crashed like waves over the room. Well, of course! The Russian love of baring the soul.

He'd been wrong about only one thing. He'd thought they'd rush at him, express amazement, greet him hostilely—but no. Some noticed his arrival, some didn't, but everyone accepted it so naturally, it was as if he were a familiar visitor here.

Lenin responded to someone (in such a way that he didn't respond). He had nothing at all to ask anyone. He sat down at the edge of a bench in a corner of the room and removed his bowler. He sat and listened as he alone knew how, selecting out the suspicious thing that others didn't even hear.

It turned out that no one knew anything more about those telegrams, except for this one thing: "after three days of struggle" the revolution had won. After three days. Herein was the mark of authenticity, yes, and they gasped and no longer had any doubt. Lenin did not consider it necessary to object out loud, to wonder why nothing had been communicated these past three days. Generally speaking, no one knew anything more than the telegrams, but a multitude of words spilled into all the available space around this information.

One man (whom he'd never seen), wearing a stretched and battered tie, ran up to one person and then another, flapped his arms like a rooster flapping his wings, and not saying anything completely or intelligently—moved on. One tall woman only knew to sniff a small bouquet of snowbells. No matter what anyone said to her, she just rocked in astonishment and sniffed.

Lenin felt contempt for the expatiations of the supposed revolutionaries, the way they sonorously discussed *freedom and revolution* without grasping all the chess possibilities under which these events could proceed and what kind of enemies they had and how deftly they could intercept them in progress or even at the start. They talked about it as if it were a universal holiday, as if it had finally happened. (But **what** had happened? And what **had to be** for it to happen? Who among them understood this?) What was the Tsar doing, though? What counterrevolutionary army was moving on Petersburg? How would the Duma more than likely turn coward and rush to make a deal with reaction? And how weak and disorganized still were the proletarian forces? They weren't thinking about this or searching for these answers. All of a sudden everyone, as if reconciling and forgetting their interparty disagreements, these lively ladies with their beribboned hats, were rattling this joyous gibberish, and now, after an hour or two, no longer feeling like forced residents of Switzerland but "united as Russians," they constructed unitedly Russian and groundlessly Russian surmises as to how they were all going to get to Russia as quickly as possible.

Well! . . .

They pushed up to Lenin with their overly friendly ways and starry-eyed plans, perched close to him, some knowing who he was, some not because it was a nonpolitical crowd here, too. He squinted at the arm-wavers, drunk without wine, at these twittering ladies—and did not respond harshly to anyone but also didn't respond at all.

Here was what they'd come up with: Now all émigrés could unite without party distinction (petty bourgeois heads filled with claptrap!) and create a Swiss-wide Russian émigré committee for the return to the homeland. And . . . and . . . and return somehow, but *how*—that no one knew, though they suggested all sorts of things. Even today they were convening a planning commission for this evening.

To return when they didn't know what was happening there. Maybe they were already putting revolutionaries up against all the walls.

Outside even more people accumulated, but not more ideas. Once again, everyone checked the news with each other—and again no one knew one word more. Lenin extricated himself from their idle chatter as imperceptibly as he'd entered.

Outside, not only had it stopped raining but it was brightening up and the clouds had thinned quite a lot. It was drying up, but as cold as before.

His feet started out quickly downhill, in the direction of the library and home.

The right thing would have been to go home.

Actually, he didn't know where he should go now.

He stopped.

Just two hours ago, before dinner, it had all been clear: split the Swedish party and what had to be read, written, and done for this. But here an unauthenticated, incredible, and unnecessary event had come in sideways and without even seeming to touch or sideline him—it already had. It had already diverted his powers and broken his routine.

It turned out to be impossible to go back to the library.

And he didn't feel like going home. Over the past year, it had somehow become boring to talk everything over with Nadya. In reply she would say something so obvious that it did not bear saying, and she would say it so pompously. He couldn't get any fresh, original comment from her, nothing to sharpen his thinking.

His feet dragged at going.

But he couldn't stand the streets, either, that was impossible. Should he go up the Zürichberg, which was right nearby?

The wind had come up a little—cold but not strong. Only it wasn't going to rain, it had already brightened, and the sun was just about to break through.

His coat dried out nearly completely in the reading room, Lenin now started steeply uphill. In the mountains your legs loosen up and your thoughts settle and you can understand things.

The steeper and shorter the side-street, the quicker he would get there, to the top. His legs were as strong as young ones. Little boys were hurrying there, too, with their knapsacks and their afternoon studies—and Ilyich did not lag behind them. He experienced no shortness of breath and his heart beat healthily.

He wished all were thus. But his head . . . Lenin bore his head like something precious and sickly. An apparatus for the instantaneous taking of unerring decisions, for finding incisive arguments—by the base vengefulness of nature, this apparatus was painfully and somehow stricken in new and different ways, constantly making itself felt in new places. Probably the way mold grows in a large piece of something living—bread, meat, mushrooms—in a coating of greenish film and in threads that reach deep: as if it were still whole and still untouched, unscraped, and when your head ached, it didn't all hurt, just individual surfaces and threads. You might think it hurt like everyone else's, and if you took a powder the pain would pass. But if you thought differently sometimes—that it hurt in a special way, irrevocably, that the powder was only a deception for a few hours, while *there* it was growing deeper in threads, then the horror clutched at you, and you couldn't break away! There was no getting away from this head. Everything in the world awaited your assessments and decisions! Everything in the world could be directed by your will! But you yourself were already in its clutches and you couldn't break away!

A healthy heart, lungs, liver, stomach, arms, legs, teeth, eyes, ears—list them and be proud. But before nature, like before an implacable and perceptive examiner, you have left something out, indeed you couldn't list it all—but the disease had already noticed the lapse and had crept in, crept in through secret gaps of destruction. All it took was a single wormhole to bring down an entire statue of health.

And this eased his regret about their silences and misunderstandings— all of it irrevocable for some reason when you made an effort to be close. In a year you can lose the habit. He needed Inessa. He did. But did she need him that way?

So close, yet not to come for a year?

Yes, of course. Someone else . . .

But he was cloaked in half-dead reconciliation.

From the canton hospital he climbed through the upland section, by twisting ascents, where the richer Swiss burghers—scrambling above the city, closer to the forest and the sky, with a view of the lake distances—built their homes, the bourgeois's small palaces. Each had thought how to adorn itself—one with figured masonry, one with ceramic tiles, one with a spire, one with gates, a veranda, a carriage house, a fountain—or with a name like "Mountain Rose," "Gordevia," or "Nicette." And they smoked! Smoke came from their chimneys—because of course their fireplaces were stoked for comfort.

This arrangement of beauty and comforts walled off by fences, gates, notary acts, and convenient Swiss laws, higher up, separated from the masses, reverberated in his chest with a seething irritation. Oh, if only the crowd could boldly throng here from below and storm these gates, windows, doors, and flowerbeds—with rocks, sticks, heels, and rifle butts. What could be merrier! Had the dispossessed masses become so bogged down and sunk so low that they would never rise up in revolt? Would that they recall Marat's fiery words: *Man has the right to wrest from another not only what is excess but what is essential. If he himself is not to perish, he has the right to slaughter another and consume his trembling body!*

This marvelous Jacobin worldview would never awaken in the proletariat of a lackey republic because morsels kept falling from the gentlemen's table, feeding the workers up. And its opportunists like Grimm entangled them in their web.

But what about Sweden?

And now, what about Russia? . . .

All kinds of things might happen in Russia, but there was no one to provide direction. Today all was probably lost there, and they were drowning in blood—but he wouldn't find out from telegrams until the day after tomorrow.

Not because it was higher on the mountain but because the sky was clearing—everything became brighter. Now underfoot the clean, never dusty, never muddy, smooth pounded stones of the sidewalks and pavement were dry. If a passing carriage's wheels did splash through a puddle, it was clean water. There were lots of trees on the streets of the mountain slope, and higher up even more, and higher still—forest.

Here people were simply strolling, not walking purposefully. One and then another slow, dignified bourgeois couple with furled umbrellas and little dogs on leashes passed by. Then two old ladies conversing loudly and smugly. And someone else. They were enjoying their neighborhoods. Rarefication emanated from the passersby and from all of life.

Just below the forest, one street ran flat along the mountain, neither descending nor ascending, coming out on a viewing platform surrounded by a railing, and from here—actually through the branches of the trees just below—one was supposed to admire the distant view of the lake's lip and the entire city in the slate-gray haze of the lower elevations—its spires, chimneys, and blue double streetcars as they crossed the bridges. A cold, mechanical, metallic ringing floated up from the monotonously gray churches again.

There was a little boulevard here under the great trees, with gravel and benches, and just ten paces long, leading to a single grave, for which it had been built. When he and Nadya used to come to the large oval Zürichberg, they would climb from other streets and to other places and had never passed by here. Now he approached this grave on the high, observation point.

There was a chest-high tombstone made of uneven, pocked gray stone, and etched into the smooth metal plate inserted into the stone it said: "Georg Büchner. Died in Zurich with his unfinished epic poem, *The Death of Danton*. . . ."

It didn't come to him right away where he knew this famous name from, Georg Büchner. . . . He knew all the Social Democrats and political figures. But a poet? . . .

Then it hit him. Yes—a *neighbor*. He had lived at 12 Spiegelgasse, next door, sharing a wall, three paces from door to door. An émigré. He'd been a neighbor. And died. With his unfinished *Death of Danton*.

This was devilish. Danton was an opportunist, Danton was not Marat, Danton was not to be pitied, but he wasn't the point. That point was that this had been his neighbor. He too probably longed to return from this accursed, constricted, narrow country. But he died in Zurich. In the canton hospital, though perhaps even on Spiegelgasse. It didn't say what he died from, maybe his head hurt the same way, and hurt . . .

Really, what should he do about his head? His sleep? His nerves?

And what was going to happen now more broadly? One man could not be enough for the struggle against everyone, to correct and guide everyone.

A grating encounter.

All Zurich, a quarter of a million people probably, native and from all over Europe, were crowded there below, working, making deals, exchanging currency, selling, buying, eating in restaurants, sitting in meetings, walking and riding through the streets—and all in different directions, and all possessing uncollected, undirected thoughts. Whereas he was standing here on the mountain and knew he would be able to direct them all and unite their will.

But he did not have that power. He could stand here above Zurich or lie down right here in the grave, but he could not change Zurich. He had lived here for over a year, and all his efforts had been in vain, nothing accomplished.

Three weeks ago, this city had exulted at its idiotic carnival. Bands in clown costumes pushing ahead, parties of zealous drummers and shrill trumpeters, figures on stilts, people with tow hair a meter high, hook-nosed witches and Bedouins on camels, entire floats with carousels, stores, dead giants, cannons firing soot, horns spitting out confetti—how many idle lazybones had prepared for this, sewed costumes, rehearsed, how much well-fed strength they'd lavished, freed from war! If only half of that strength could be set going for a general strike!

In a month, after Easter, there would be a holiday to say farewell to winter. The holidays were countless here. Yet another parade, now without masks and makeup, a parade of artisanal Zurich, just like last year: oversize sacks of oversize grain, oversize workbenches, bindery benches, grinding stones, irons, a blacksmith's forge on a wagon under a tile roof, and as they went they fanned the furnace and forged hammers, axes, pitchforks, flails (an unpleasant memory when once in Alakaevka his mama had forced him to become a farmer, revulsion at these pitchforks and flails); paddles over the shoulder, fish on sticks, boots as banners, children with baked breads and pretzels—yes, you could boast of all this labor if it didn't degenerate into something bourgeois and didn't insist so adamantly on its conservativism, if not for this grasping at the past, which should be destroyed completely. If only behind the artisans in their leather aprons there hadn't ridden horsemen in red, white, blue, and silver jackets, in lilac tailcoats and every color tricorne, and columns of old men marching in their old-fashioned frock coats and carrying red umbrellas, learned judges with outsize gold medals, finally also the marquises and countesses in velvet gowns and white wigs—pity that there weren't enough guillotines for them in the Great French Revolution! Once again, hundreds of trumpeters and dozens of bands and brass on horseback, horsemen in helmets and chainmail, halberdists and infantry from the Napoleonic era, their last war—so quick were they to play at war when they didn't have to march to the slaughter, and while their traitor social-patriots weren't summoning them to turn around and start a civil war!

And what kind of a working class did they have? A Bern landlady, a presser, a proletarian woman, found out that the Ulyanovs had cremated their mother, not buried her, and so weren't Christians—and evicted them. Another evicted them just because they turned on the electricity in the day-time to show the Shklovskys how brightly it burned.

No, there was no raising up these people.

What could five foreigners with the truest ideas do?

He turned off the boulevard and started steeply uphill, into the forest.

The clouds had thinned to a gentle light yellow, and you could tell where the evening sun was now.

Here he was in the forest. It wasn't groomed, but there were paths here and there. Interspersed with the firs were grayish white trunks of some kind, not birch and not aspen. The wet ground was thickly blanketed with old leaves. It was muddy here, and you could slip, but hiking boots, clumsy on a city sidewalk, were just the thing here.

He climbed steeply, straining his legs. He was alone. Tidy couples did not stroll in the damp and mud.

Every so often he stopped to catch his breath.

Nestling boxes, still empty, were blackly wet on the bare trees.

There is no ascent harder than that from illegitimacy to legitimacy. The word "underground" is no accident, after all: not showing yourself, always anonymous, and suddenly to emerge high up and say: Yes, it is I! Take up arms and I will lead you! What had made '05 such a hard year was that Trotsky and Parvus had snatched away the entire Russian revolution. How important it was to arrive at the revolution in time! A week late and you lose everything.

What was Parvus going to do now? Oh, he should have answered him more amiably.

So, should he go? If it was all confirmed, should he go?

Just like that? Right away? Drop everything and race there?

Past the mountain's first ridge there was a drop-off into a damp, dark fir grove, where the road was nothing but churned-up mud. But he could walk across the ridge itself without a path—it was dry—on the grass and under the sparse pines.

Here, onto another hillock.

Where the view opened up again, even more extensively. He could see a large chunk of the tranquil, tin-colored lake and all of Zurich under a basin of air that had never been torn by artillery explosions or ripped by the cries of a revolutionary crowd. And the sun was already setting, not below him, though, but nearly at eye level—behind the gently sloping Uetliberg.

What had driven him up the mountain on a workday, in this damp—the discomfort and agitation he'd experienced in the Russian reading room, the unified bleating about how the revolution had begun—resurfaced, as if after a restorative oblivion. How gullible all these professional revolutionar-ies were, so easily lured by any fairytale.

No, now was when he had to manifest the greatest skepticism and caution.

So he walked across the trackless dry ridge, across the brown grass and dry branches. Here, on the mountain, one often saw squirrels, and sometimes even very young roe-deer the size of a dog and larger flashed by in the distance, running across the road.

At this height and in this silence, in this clean air, this squeezing band around his head eased. All the irritations and all the irritating people fell away, were forgotten, left below.

The past winter had been hard and had worn him out. He couldn't live with strain like that, he had to take care of himself.

But for what? If he didn't do anything, what was he taking care of himself for?

You couldn't live this way for long, though. His head felt unwell. Bad.

The ridge he was following broke off when it came to an intersecting gravel road. Ah, a familiar spot. The obelisk. A path descended that way. It was a monument to two battles for Zurich in 1799 between the revolutionary French and the Austro-Russian reaction.

Opposite the obelisk, Lenin perched on a damp bench, tired.

Yes, indeed, they had fired here, too. It was terrible to think that there had been Russian troops here! The Tsar's paw had reached this far!

An even clatter of hooves over firm ground reached him from higher up, past the bend in the road. And right then, out of the dark forest, in the incomplete post-sunset light, he saw a woman's hat held on by a ribbon, and then the woman herself in red, and her light chestnut horse. The horse was going at a walk and the woman was sitting erect—and something in her manner of holding herself and holding her head . . . Inessa?

He shuddered, saw, and believed! Although this was utterly impossible.

Closer—no, of course, but there was a resemblance. The way she was so self-aware and held herself like a treasure.

Red, she emerged from the dark thicket, riding in the damp, pure, soundless evening.

It was, rather, the horse that considered itself the main beauty—verging from light chestnut to tan, perfectly harnessed, it fastidiously placed its little hoof-cups.

The rider sat imperturbably or sadly and looked only straight ahead, at the road's descent, without a glance for the obelisk or the badly dressed man pressed to the bench below, wearing the black bowler.

He sat there without stirring and examined her face and the black wing of hair that had escaped her hat.

If suddenly he could liberate his thoughts from all essential and correct tasks—it was beautiful, you see! A beautiful woman!

It wasn't she herself rocking her shoulders or at the waist so much as the horse rocking her and raising her boot tip by the stirrup.

She rode downhill, where the road turned—and only the faint tapping of hooves still reached him.

She had ridden by, plucked something off him—and carried it away.

[3 3 9]

One could not help but be absolutely astonished at how yesterday and today the brilliant and lucky Kerensky had jumped, leapt at exactly the right time—between two cliffs, two shores, two diverging icebergs—one leg there, one here, and now he was whole and unharmed, the victor, raised above all Russia!

All last night, that sleepless and incandescent night, instead of participating in events, one should have been disappearing and absenting oneself: fateful negotiations were under way between the Soviet and the franchised faction, and in the presence of both sides Kerensky was the most vulnerable: as a revolutionary democrat he was supposed to support his Soviet companions and with them portray intransigency toward the bourgeoisie and contempt for their government. But in fact he had been sawn to pieces by the insolent and senseless demands of Nakhamkes and Himmer, and so as not to support them—but he couldn't be silent the whole time!—he would gallop off on business.

His impetuous self was up to his ears in work; he could find something that needed doing in any corner of the seething Tauride Palace, but most important, for more than two days he had had in his charge the pavilion with the arrested dignitaries. A brilliant idea dawned on him, that this pavilion was the platform for his ascent!

In the whirlwind of historic events, brilliant maneuvers are born in us like lightning bolts! The situation when you act not even by calculation, not even by reason, but almost by instinct, almost by some magnetic attraction through the fog! And you come out at precisely that ladder leading up!

The resistance in the Executive Committee was quite persistent and dangerous, but did they, compared to Kerensky, really have the eminence of statesmen? He had overturned them all with a stunning blow! When he was carried out of the Soviet triumphally, he saw their faces in the back rows breathing vengeance, but they hadn't dared even open their mouths.

In any case, if it hadn't worked out through the Soviet, Kerensky had arranged insurance through his political party: he'd instructed Zenzinov and another good friend, the SR Somov, to collect as many SRs as they could today, seven or eight, which was all they could come up with in Petrograd— but without Aleksandrovich, naturally—and call them the Petrograd City Conference of SRs and approve a decision to support the new government and for Kerensky to join it as a form of oversight over the government for the laboring masses, as a defender of the people's interests.

In the end, no alternative plan was needed; all the reefs were crossed in a single, winged surge! At three o'clock, Milyukov had announced the government. From the moment of the announcement, new wings kept sprouting on his back, and Kerensky almost hovered above the crowd, accepting ecstatic looks from all sides and hearing ecstatic words.

Aleksandr Kerensky was a minister! Could long-suffering Russia ever have expected this, thought this? . . . Exhausted by agony, torment, and unprecedented persecution, here she had broken through to freedom in him, the first people's Minister of Justice!

Oh, what freedom he was about to let flow over the face of Russia! Oh, how wide Russia's horizons would open! And—oh, tremble in fear, enemies!

What scope for his activities! But also, how much energy he felt in himself! He kept forgetting, had forgotten, his last year's illness and operation. Oh, how young he had been, how quick and smart and exceptional! For the past three days the uncertainty about the government, these behind-the-scenes maneuvers, had held him back, but now his energy had been unshackled and he would show himself to Russia!

However, did everyone understand, had everyone heard the Milyukov announcement? They might not all have; the public here kept changing. It had to be repeated again. Also, they might not all know Aleksandr Fyodorovich by face—he had to show himself to the crowd.

Two hours had passed since Milyukov had stepped off the platform— and Kerensky, with the help of his wings, had flown higher and higher, to the gallery loft—and in his new democratic guise, in his buttoned-up black jacket with the standing collar, as he had dressed for this great day, for uniting with the people—and only his inspired face was white.

Some noticed and raised their heads from the bottom of the Ekaterininsky Hall, while others didn't see and jostled there below and buzzed.— Kerensky shouted out to the entire hall in a youthful voice:

"Comrades! Soldiers! And citizens! I am State Duma Deputy Aleksandr Fyodorovich Kerensky, your new Minister of Justice!"

Oh, what a storm of applause shot up! Oh, how the "hurrah" peeled out under the old hall's sculpted vault! Oh, there was no end to these raptures! And he hoped, he hoped there would never be . . .

The slender young minister stood through the storm of rapture and then picked up just as sonorously and distinctly, reaching the farthest corners:

"I am announcing to you that the new Provisional Government has entered into the performance of its duties—by agreement with the Soviet of Workers' and Soldiers' Deputies!"

What Milyukov, who himself had achieved this, had neglected to announce. What had been advantageous and simultaneously had strengthened Kerensky against the EC:

"The agreement reached between the State Duma Committee and the Soviet of Workers' and Soldiers' Deputies"—these words rang out like great oaths!—"has been approved by the Soviet of Workers' and Soldiers' Deputies by hundreds of votes to fifteen!" Kerensky was celebrating his victory over the EC.

The surge, the push of his voice told the crowd that stormy applause was expected here! And it came crashing down at the feet of his delicate black monument in an oncoming decuman wave! Seagulls flapped their wings over people's white crests: "Bravo! Bravo!"

After it ebbed, the youthful monument stood there still unharmed. Oh, what could be greater than this satisfaction! To aim words of freedom at a liberated people!

"The Provisional Government will immediately promulgate an act of full amnesty! Our comrade deputies from the Second and Fourth State Dumas who were illegally exiled to the tundras of Siberia"—he was all a-tremble at the coming justice, as if he himself had now been freed from the Siberian tundras—"will be released immediately and transported with special honors!"

Here he again waited for a storm of applause but hadn't given it a big enough push so there wasn't one.

"Comrades!"—he moved on to something else, again something advantageous—"I have in my charge **all** the old regime's prime ministers! And **all** the ministers of the old government! They will answer, comrades, for **all** the crimes before the people! According to law."

(A law not as yet created.)

They applauded. Black birds of vengeance were flying, not seagulls: "No mercy!"

It turned out to be easy for a natural to swim in this popular storm; the brave swimmer wouldn't let himself be washed away but handsomely built momentum:

"Comrades! Free Russia will not resort to the disgraceful means of struggle to which the old regime resorted. No one will be punished without trial. Everyone will be judged by an open popular court. Statutes approved by the new government will be pro-mul-ga-ted!"

Look how magnetically he controlled the crowd! He could drum up a storm in it and could also nobly calm it down. Stepping outside the realm of justice, he could also help his other colleagues in the government who lacked the daring to speak like this:

"Soldiers! I beg of you to render us assistance! Don't listen to appeals coming from agents of the old regime! Obey your officers! Free Russia has been born, and no one can tear freedom from the people's hands!"

Oh, what a "hurrah"! What a new storm of applause! And bowing all around, this time Kerensky descended over its waves and floated off to the working rooms of the governmental wing.

He had introduced himself. And enthralled them. And guided them.

Everything in him quivered, not only with joy at this admiration but also with a thirst for further action! The Minister of Justice could not wait and vegetate for hours more while the clumsy new government prepared to function.

Reval? He sent a telegram to rebellious Reval and instantly calmed the city.

He could immediately rush to the Ministry of Justice building—and stormily set about the ministry's reform. However, two Duma commissars were sitting there right now (Maklakov's miscalculation: he should have been here, not there). They had already worked out the most pressing popular reforms there: universal amnesty and the inclusion of all Jewish jurists in the estate of lawyers. They had to be forestalled! The act must be sent immediately, by telegram, from here, from the Tauride Palace, to all ends of Russia—from the vigorous new minister!

And so, the first step: immediately release all political prisoners and those under investigation from all Russian prisons—and all prosecutors from courts of justice must report on this to the minister by telegram! And especially: immediately release all State Duma deputies, five Bolsheviks. And charge the Yenisei governor, under his personal responsibility, with ensuring their return to Petrograd with full honors.

Second step: admit all Jews who are lawyers' assistants into the legal profession. (Oh, this will mean immediate popularity and stability!)

Then: put an immediate halt to political investigations and inquiries throughout the Russian Empire!

For now, for tomorrow's newspapers—this was enough.

But also—he still had his favorite prisoners in the ministerial pavilion. And his great personal favorite, Minister Makarov. Without Kerensky, he might not have been picked up, he would have left. On Tuesday he was detained and brought in but was freed as an enemy of Rasputin and Sukhomlinov. Yet human memory forgot that Makarov had opposed Kerensky's rising star in the case of the Lena goldfields shooting and managed to keep Kerensky's star from soaring in the decisive months before elections to the Fourth Duma. When Makarov was released it was late in the evening. Afraid to return through the revolutionary streets, he found a haven in a private apartment on the palace's mezzanine. Fortunately, though, this was whispered to Kerensky, who grabbed two armed soldiers, ran up the staircase, himself burst into the apartment, and rearrested Makarov!

However, there were already a lot of them, a lot of arrested dignitaries, in the pavilion, crammed in. This was no place for the most dangerous and pernicious. Kerensky decided that tonight, after the public left, they would be moved to the Peter and Paul Fortress, under a strictly reliable convoy.

That would have a popular effect!

What now awaited Aleksandr Fyodorovich himself filled him with yet newer liberation! During the first few days of the revolution, right here, on this couch, he had reflected that these unprecedented circumstances were freeing him from his tedious domestic captivity. It had become natural now that he simply could not go home to spend the night—and for a long, long time to come! On Monday morning he skipped out of his home, never to set foot there again.

And after that . . . he anticipated an intoxicating string of encounters. . . . At the moment of success there are always women delighted to accept us. As if, lurking, they had all been waiting for this moment—and now they would all declare themselves at once, smile, invite you to lighten your historic burden.

For now, he spent these nights curled up right here on the Tauride Palace couches, tables, and chairs, not that there were any nights. But he had to arrange his daily life on a bachelor footing in the Ministry of Justice: occupy the minister's office and a couple of other rooms—and for now leave the official apartment for the wife of the arrested Dobrovolsky. The necessary helpers would appear immediately for a historic individual such as Kerensky. Count Orlov-Davydov came forward (Kerensky was best man at his second wedding, to the actress Poiret), zealously prepared to serve and assist, offering his own chef to feed Aleksandr Fyodorovich and accompanying him everywhere, carrying out any intimate commission. True, the count's public reputation had suffered greatly after the scandal of his divorce trial with Poiret (he had divorced for her, but she had duped him with a false pregnancy and fictitious childbirth, and the count had figured it out only by accident, and all that disgrace). Nonetheless, he was a count! And what an ancient, resonant name! And wealthy!

[3 4 0]

*   *   *

Moscow was enjoying a light frost—three below zero. The streets were overflowing even more than yesterday. Universal celebration. People moving aside and squeezing together to let armed vehicles through. Military bands here and there. At the head of military detachments there were no longer just ensigns but also lieutenant colonels and colonels.

Near the City Duma, two English officers were telling the public ecstatically: "We knew that Russia was a great country, but we didn't know you had such marvelous discipline. At last the real Russia has found itself! We will convey what we have seen in England."

From the steps of the duma they were announcing that a detachment had been formed in Luga to arrest the Tsar.

In the duma itself it was so crowded that in the afternoon Lieutenant Colonel Gruzinov requisitioned the Art Cinema on Arbat Square and moved his *insurrection headquarters* there. He himself rode around the city in a motorcar giving speeches everywhere.

* * *

There were rallies and political speeches all day, in various parts of Petrograd: What kind of government would it be? What would happen to the Tsar?

One man in a worn little coat:

"Comrades! Can Rodzyanko and Milyukov really give us land and freedom?"

A university student:

"Comrades! This is a provocateur speaking!"

And the other man:

"They want to lull you so that you obey and don't demand anything more!"

A gentleman wearing a soft black hat climbed up and delivered a speech about Rodzyanko's honesty:

"He has defended the people's interests for many years!"

The faces in the crowd displayed the agony of indecision. Who should they trust?

* * *

"Russia! You are a slave no more!" Under red flags, with red bows, a lively mixed demonstration moved down Nevsky: men workers in black coats, women workers, university students—and along with them well-nourished, pale-skinned citizens wearing expensive fur coats and bowlers. Together they sang:

Long in chains did they hold us!
Long did we suffer from hunger! . . .

* * *

Fourteen-year-old Lena Taube recorded in her diary: "Telephone communication with Kronstadt has been cut, but there's still the telegraph. We received a telegram, we don't know who from: 'Master alive and well. Arrested.' Mama was in tears, then she fainted."

* * *

The apartment bell. Two mustache-less soldiers, red scraps on their tall fur hats.

"Let us take a look."

Cigarettes in their teeth. Leaving, they crushed them on the floor and spat.

". . . Searching everything, rummaging through everything . . ." the servants grumbled. "This never happened under the old regime."

*   *   *

The draymen carting food were attacked: "Where are you taking that? Pass it out here!" And it was dragged off.

*   *   *

In the Peter and Paul Fortress, many extra officers gathered — not part of any guard or garrison, but lounging about, discussing events, playing billiards. Hiding.

*   *   *

Late in the afternoon, fresh issues of *Izvestia* were read to the crowd from a truck, the makeup of the new government.

People were surprised: "What about Rodzyanko? He didn't make it in?"

The crowd swung down Nevsky, rejoicing.

Still other leaflets, pink, on the walls, not on Nevsky: "Don't believe the Provisional Government! Workers have to take power into their own hands."

People read in perplexity.

They droned that Milyukov had promised to return the Tsar. What did that mean? Were we all to be punished? . . .

*   *   *

During the days of revolution, at the palace of Grand Duchess Maria Pavlovna, the wine cellar, valued at half a million rubles, was looted and smashed.

*   *   *

In the evening a rumor arose that a crowd had stormed the university on Vasilievsky Island.

That black motorcars were driving around the city and firing on peaceful inhabitants.

That night, once again, people either didn't turn on or hid their lights. An uneasy feeling.

Near the bonfires on the streets were military and civilian patrols, new militia, and volunteers with rifles and revolvers. They stopped the vehicles that occasionally sped by and demanded their pass.

Here and there in the dark, black trucks and motorcars stuck in the snow.

By nightfall, large, sparse, picturesque snowflakes had begun to fall.

[3 4 1]

A rumor sped down the line that important State Duma deputies were on their way, Guchkov himself, and at the stations handfuls or small crowds gathered—railroaders, workers, individual soldiers, random people, passengers—and they demanded a speech, as everyone had gotten into the way of demanding these past few days, like their next meal. From the small platform of his train car, or from some box on the platform, having removed his pince-nez and squinting, Guchkov would deliver a speech; he already knew it by heart: obey your officers, support the new government, long live the revolution, and victory over the Germans.

There was a large crowd in Gatchina, and he spoke for longer, but the same thing.

After Gatchina he began thinking that the windmill was turning to no avail, draining him and for no benefit.

They were held up in Gatchina for an additional half-hour, anticipating the approach of General Ivanov along a connecting branch. But he wasn't there. The day was already coming to an end, the train had been held up, his mission had not been accomplished, and he couldn't wait. Off they went. (Later, en route, Ivanov's telegram caught up with him saying that he was in Vyritsa and would be happy to see him. Guchkov expected nothing else of him.)

In Gatchina, the 20,000-man garrison was calm. But Guchkov had known since yesterday about the Luga garrison, that there was a mutiny there and they were killing officers. Early this morning, at Guchkov's instruction, State Duma Deputy Lebedev and General Staff Colonel Lebedev had gone there to settle and calm the situation. Luga occupied too important a place on the Petrograd-Pskov line. Although it was by this very rebellion that it had served the revolution, having disarmed the Borodino men. But that was sufficient; beyond that it had begun to impede.

Many times Guchkov had had to travel to the front, although always on Red Cross business, but on these trips he had felt in himself a fine military liveliness, he even had quasi-military clothing—jacket and boots—and he was often photographed and put in the surveys. Today, too, was quite like a trip to the front. Here in Luga he was to plunge into a soldier sea, an outraged and possibly dangerous one, but Guchkov liked danger, and all he was missing now for his ease was that military attire. After all, he was going to see the Emperor, and he was wearing a good suit, starched collar, and tie, and over that a rather heavy civilian coat with an expensive fur collar and a fur cap.

The sight of the Luga train station was unusual due to the many soldiers—not in detachments or formation but roaming, looking, idle—actually, this could no longer surprise a Petrograd eye. Among these idlers there immediately arose movement toward the arriving train of just one car, and they began to crowd in, some inoffensively, some defiantly. The soldiers' defiance was especially striking.

Both Lebedevs immediately entered the train car, wanting to report, but the crowd was thick and it had to be defused with a speech. Guchkov realized this. He came out and repeated the same thing in the name of the sacred State Duma and the holy war against the Germans.

That helped. They listened and shouted "hurrah"—and thinned out, dispersed. The Lebedevs apologized for not having been able to arrange a proper greeting party with an honor guard, band, and soldiers filing by to the Marseillaise, as they themselves had been met by the local cavalry captain. But now the military committee, consisting of a single motor company, was in command and had definitely already entered into relations with the Petrograd Soviet, since it wasn't far from here: the same habits, slogans, and distrust for the Duma. Guchkov could not avoid dealing with this committee now as well.

Shulgin remained in the train car to write the draft abdication, and Guchkov went into the train station for talks with the committee, which had upheld its reputation by not sending its own representatives to meet his train.

Naturally, none of them knew that during these very hours Guchkov was to become the Minister of War. However, as an illustrious figure in Russia, he might have anticipated a more respectful reception from rank-and-file fellow citizens. When he entered the room, no one stood to greet him; rather they indicated where he should sit, at the same table with them, in the smoke of cheap tobacco. Everyone was smoking and spitting on the floor, smoking and spitting.

Guchkov plunged into the thick of it. Luga was the last thing he should be wasting time and energy on now, but he had no choice. Out of the entire new government, the man most offensive to the Soviet of Workers' Deputies was here, and recognizing the force of the situation, he had to lie to them that there were no contradictions in Petrograd between the Duma Committee and the Soviet of Deputies. His insides twisted up at their insolence, but Guchkov could not jump up, issue orders to them, or leave himself; rather, he had to sit and convince them to establish order—moreover, the kind of order that would allow the royal train heading to Tsarskoye Selo to pass through Luga tonight unimpeded.

Guchkov was on his way to complete the mission of his life, to take a historic step for all Russia—but he had to stew here with this disobedient mass and eye its slippery soul. He was on his way to a historic meeting with the Emperor—but he had to sweat, to crush and soil his starched collar in this stuffy air and cheap tobacco. He was on his way to give an ultimatum to the head of state—but found himself in the pincers of sergeants. There was a moment of suspicion: he wasn't certain they would let him travel farther.

How much they had argued about this People! Were they dispossessed, virtuous laborers whom the constables and gendarmes wouldn't let be good, while the intelligentsia could have led them out to the light, or were they happy, religious masses ever ready to sacrifice themselves on the altar of the Fatherland. But finding himself on a level with this People in a smoke-filled, spit-spattered room, on the same bench, made Guchkov very uncomfortable. Not one of the faces from the motor company committee reminded him of the noble Face of the People—every last one of them was unexpected, unapproachable, unwilling to be convinced of anything.

They didn't grab Guchkov by the shoulders or point bayonets at him— but he felt a melancholy and bitterness toward the whole dark force of this element, which had unfortunately been allowed to break out. What he had always feared.

Meanwhile, that same Cavalry Captain Voronovich arrived, a tall, robust cavalryman, very neat, excellent bearing. Smooth, soot-black hair, a sleek luxuriant mustache—and a completely closed face. An excellent diplomat, not just a fighter. He sat in on the general conversation, and Guchkov was struck at how free this cavalry captain felt among the rebellious soldiers, even right after the murder of officers from his own regiment, at the freedom (albeit cautious) and confidence (also cautious) with which he reasoned, finding subtle ways as well to let Guchkov know that he supported him, of course.

Guchkov had seen a great many army officers, but he had never noticed, never picked out among them this type, who would glide so easily over the revolution's waves.

With the cavalry captain's arrival, the discussion went more favorably, and there was no longer any hint that Guchkov might be detained or that they had the right to detain him, or might have suspicions about why he was going to see the Tsar. But Guchkov did not ask about the royal train; that would have been dangerous. He realized that the Tsar was only anxious to see his spouse, and he had the right to this recompense in exchange for his abdication. Oh well, he could go the roundabout way, through Dno again.

The talks—what about was unknown—the general situation, the victory over the old regime, loyalty to battle flags and the Petrograd authorities— ended, and Guchkov went to his own train.

But he didn't recognize it.

The engine's curved black chest was criss-crossed with red ribbons, and a red flag poked up from the engineer's booth; pine boughs were stuck in wherever they could be, as well. They'd also attached another train car, a suburban passenger car, which had its own stove firing, sparks from its smokestack, and a few soldiers and a few armed civilians, all in red bows, had taken seats there.

Guchkov had no power or will to destroy this revolutionary magnificence or uncouple the other train car; he was just glad they were letting him go unimpeded.

They would have frightened the Tsar and his suite at the Pskov station, but by now it was dark anyway.

[3 4 2]

The Empress had the idea of sending not one officer to the Emperor but two and giving each a letter, and on small pieces of paper moreover, so that they could be folded to a couple of inches, hidden in a boot, and if necessary burned. One of the two officers would get through!

Everything that crowded and seethed inside her—during these hours she attempted, in the interval between affairs to which she had to attend, to write this into first one letter, then the other.

The hours were terrible. A young lady-in-waiting, by age her daughters' friend, had made her way there from Petrograd, and what she had told her, what was going on there—it was beyond comprehension.

Aide-de-Camp Linevich, who had been sent to Rodzyanko, had not returned yesterday or today. From Petrograd, Sablin sent a secret note with a trusted man saying he was anxious to get here but simply couldn't go because everyone as prominent as he was *on the books*. General Groten had been sent to the Tsarskoye Selo town hall for talks with the rebels—and for some reason had not returned.

Her initial morning joy that the Emperor was in Pskov had gradually been overshadowed by mounting black clouds of alarm. Had he gone and stayed there voluntarily? Had he been ambushed?

A supremely base and vile deed, unheard of in history—to detain one's own Emperor! How humiliating to sense the Emperor in captivity! What horror for their allies! What joy for their enemies!

Oh, she now regretted not having told old man Ivanov to act in the most decisive manner to liberate the Emperor! Out of goodness, he might show lenience.

Why would they seize the Tsar? Clearly to keep him from seeing the Tsaritsa. And why was that? To force him to sign some intolerable responsible ministry. But that would be Russia's ruin. However deceived the Emperor had been and separated from his loyal troops, he dare not betray his coronation oath! He dare not allow the crown to become a subordinate decoration while giving authority to a government made up of self-appointed individuals that answered only to itself!

Or were they going to force him to appoint unbearable ministers?

What, indeed, was to be done? The capital could not be drowned in blood, especially during time of war. Yet, especially during time of war, rebellion could not be allowed to blaze. If Ivanov's triumphal entrance into Petrograd did not succeed, some concessions were perhaps inevitable, the only question being to whom, for how long, and in what form.

There, perhaps, in the Pskov muteness, a great spiritual single combat was taking place. Her spouse, with his far from strong soul, was defending a sacred principle—but during these hours she could not convey to him her own strength and firmness! And not to receive the least news from him! And how could she send her own through the air?

Oh, my holy martyr! What inexpressible humiliation I am experiencing for you! How heart-rendingly I'm pained for you—and I can do nothing to advise you. Just don't let them coerce you! God must hear our prayers and send us some success at last. This is the height of our misfortunes, and we will pass through it! My faith is limitless, and it supports me. God will not abandon you or our beloved country. Just now I wanted to include a small icon in the letter to you—but then the paper couldn't be crumpled. You're shy about wearing Grigori's cross—but how much calmer it would be for you!

Know that my mood is brisk and militant!

If, having no army behind you, you are forced to surrender to circumstances, God will later help and free you from them. If you are compelled to concessions, later you are in no way obligated to carry them out because they were obtained in unworthy fashion. If you do sign a promise, it will not have any force when power is once again in your hands. But almighty God is above everything, He loves his anointed, and He will save you and restore you to your rights. God will help, He will, and your glory will be restored!

Two currents, two snakes—the Duma and the revolutionaries. Might they gnaw off each other's heads and in this way save the situation? I feel that God will do something!

Might you show yourself to the troops in Pskov and gather them around you? When the troops understand that you aren't being released, they will become indignant and rise up against them all!

. . . General Resin arrived and reported that the revolutionaries had arrested General Groten in the town hall.

[3 4 3]

In Rostov-on-Don, a public outburst had been building up for more than two days. Rostovans were used to full freedom of any kind of speech, even angry speech—on the street, in the streetcar, in the university hallway, and at the market. But now something was being hidden from Rostov! For more than two days no agency telegrams of any kind had arrived from Petrograd, although the lines were intact because frequent private telegrams were arriving. And these private ones hinted at important events in the capital. People kept dashing one day and the next to the editorial offices of *Azov Territory* and *Rostov Speech*—but they didn't know any more than the ordinary inhabitants. The utter blockheads of the ruling authority had set their boot somewhere on the flow of news and stifled it. But the rumors, the rumors had implacably broken through the prohibition!

What university classes! Yesterday there had been just a floating sense of alarm, but today at both the university and the upper women's courses, the lectures had been haphazard, and many were absent, of course, including Sonya Arkhangorodskaya. She and a few of her law school friends roamed the city, stopping by newspaper offices, and simply down Sadovaya, making telephone calls to find out, to find out faster and sooner! But her heart had already guessed that an incomparable moment in their lives had come!

And spring was in the air! For a few days there had been a serious thaw, and brown streamlets ran down all the streets, boring through the snow, marking the inclines of all the streets, which were so steep in Rostov. By evening it had cooled off, and there was a thin ice crust over the bared sidewalks, street snow mixed in brown puddles. But as always happens in Rostov on March evenings, the springtime air held on, the mysteriously joyous air of spring that had flown in from somewhere.

Naturally, her papa might know more, and twice Sonya ran home to see what she could find out—but even Zoya Lvovna hadn't been able to reach him for half a day; he'd been summoned for an urgent session of the War Industry Committee. Her brother Volodya returned after university—he had sat through all his lectures—and Sonya lured him right away to go to the *Azov Territory* offices, too.

There'd been a crowd there for two hours because the office had promised news imminently, at any moment, and there would be a special bulletin—and finally, very late in the afternoon, the newsboys darted out with stacks of the bulletin—at first with desperate shouts and then they stopped shouting—they could just barely keep up with pocketing the coins, and the stacks they were holding tapered down to nothing almost instantly.

And what news! No one in the crowd regretted their wait. Nature's springtime had been joined by a tumultuous newspaper springtime! The black typographic letters confirmed more than even the rumors had before not simply the Petrograd disturbances but that all power in Russia had passed to representatives of the people!

What triumphant moments! What a burning moment! Now the tyrant's fall seemed inevitable! Russia would rise from its stinking grave! Down with the monarchy! Down with social classes!

By now all Sadovaya was jubilant, and the celebration was clearly going to go on for days! Crowds spilled out thickly; you couldn't get through on either sidewalk, only flow in a slow stream. Everyone was rejoicing, strangers (although there are few such in the Rostov public) traded opinions, here and there people started singing revolutionary songs. The Empire and Cup of Tea coffeehouses were filled beyond capacity. People there were reading the news out loud, delivering speeches, demanding that the band play the Marseillaise, and everyone stood up, and the officers saluted. Someone shouted: "Long live France!" And the idea was expressed that they should start a demonstration to the French consulate.

And the police? They stood at their posts—but indifferently, as if not noticing a single thing! What did this mean? Had they been ordered to do this?

But what if Novocherkassk sent Cossacks against Rostov? It would be a slaughterhouse!

The most important demonstration, which even impeded the streetcars going to the train station, so the streetcars in the city filled up—got very dense right opposite the Arkhangorodsky apartment at the corner of Pochtovy because directly opposite, across Sadovaya, rose the ribbed columns of Warsaw University, which had now moved to Rostov (and it was anticipated that the government would establish it as Don University any day now). A crowd assembled in the thousands, filling every space around the university entrance under the overhang of an enormous balcony, both the Sadovaya pavement and Pochtovy Lane.

They were eager for the university assembly to end. What would it decide? Although the course of affairs in Russia seemingly did not depend on it. It was dark when the university students started pouring out of the university's double-mirrored doors, into the crowd. It turned out that they had elected a student Revolutionary Committee, although there was an opposition, the student Progressive Bloc (Volodya was in that), and a few philologists without scruples stated that "they considered themselves generally incompetent in such questions."

What antics were these? Tomorrow the female students would elect their own deputies to join in!

Although the usual gas streetlamps were lit, spaced out, and windows in buildings were lit, the young people were carrying about a dozen torches, left over from some carnival, and their disturbing tar fires blazed here and there above the crowd.

Two or three torches had been raised to the university's broad balcony as well, where members of the Revolutionary Committee and professors from their own council had emerged—the latter, apparently, not altogether willingly. Also looking displeased were Chancellor Vekhov and the Slavist Yatsimirsky, while the short, thick-mustached mathematician Mordukhai-Boltovskoi simply looked angry. On the other hand, physics professor Kolli standing next to him beamed.

On the balcony, a bold speech rang out to the crowd from a youthful throat, a speech that would have been impossible that morning:

"The Bastille gets taken by a surge, not by reason! The victorious people have smashed their chains of bondage! The *old regime's* malevolent disdain for the sacred interests of the homeland . . . The whole regime was shot through with Prussian ideals. . . . But the handful of scoundrels who governed Russia against Russia have fallen! All the country's vital forces have joined together in revolution! Russia's long-awaited renewal has begun! . . ."

And the authorities hadn't tried to prevent anything! And the police—as good as having no police—had crammed into some dark corner.

Turning around in the crowd, through the weave of bare branches, Sonya saw her papa and mama on their small corner balcony, wearing their fur coats now, standing and looking this way.

Her papa knew something more and would tell her something!

A fairy-tale evening! Reluctantly, everyone dispersed.

Sonya ran up the stairs and flew into the dining room. There was no overhead light, supper hadn't been set out, and her mama was talking heatedly over the telephone by the lamp. She was so hungry! She and Volodya went into their papa's study. Ilya Isakovich sat at his large desk, his lamp in a matte white shade.

"Papa! Papa! First tell us in just a few words! Then in detail."

Ilya Isakovich looked at them almost guiltily. They thought they could see a tear behind his spectacles:

"My words can't keep up with my feelings."

"Well then, in detail?

"What did we say, papa, what?" Sonya exulted. "That little Nikolai is tossing and turning in his train! Clearly, his days are numbered. Now it's clear that in '05 Tsarism was dealt a mortal blow and these past twelve years have been just its death agony!"

"Yes, tell us, papa," Volodya stopped her.

With his usual moderation in his movements, which he had not lost even on this great day, still slightly turned toward them in his swivel chair, his fingers crossed at his belly, Ilya Isakovich instead of exulting said quietly:

"Now . . . now, children. . . . We must harness all our will so our heads don't just spin from joy. The most dangerous part is just beginning."

"What? Why? Maybe you don't know everything, papa? Did you read the bulletin? Here, we've brought it. . . ." She started for the hallway to her coat.

"Sit down, sit," Ilya Isakovich grinned. "I knew four hours before your bulletin."

The sister and brother sat down, a little closer.

Ilya Isakovich had been in a session of the War Industry Committee since midday. Their chairman, the well-known Paramonov, a stout but energetic industrial big shot, had been summoned along with the Rostov and Nakhichevan municipal heads and Zeeler from the Don and Kuban region Zemgor to see the city governor, Major General Meyer. The War Industry Committee continued to meet and discussed what they could guess at all the more. A couple of hours later, loud-voiced Paramonov returned to them with news, a host of decisions, and a look that said he took credit for practically the entire Rostov revolution and a quarter of Petrograd's.

City Governor Meyer, who before had been quite sympathetic to society, now opened up to it in a more than well-disposed way. He announced that it was he right now who had obtained permission from Ataman Grabbe to publish agency telegrams without redaction. Now decisively confident of the irrevocability of events (he had just returned from Petrograd, where he had managed to see the outset of the disturbances), he assured them that neither the ataman nor the head of the Rostov garrison would dare use weapons in support of the old regime. He admitted the following:

"What made the former state system hard was that no worker at the low end of the social scale could perform and act openly without donning a mask of so-called loyalty to the government. The mask was a condition of work. I'm now happy to take it off. Before, I did everything I could to relieve the lot of fighters for popular interests, you will recall."

In response, four of the figures asked to confer for half an hour without Meyer. Afterward they set conditions for him. Release those imprisoned for political or religious reasons. (Immediately. There were three of them.) Freedom of assembly without oversight by the authorities. (Granted.) They agreed to take on the difficult and important task of forming a Citizens Committee in Rostov, but only if the local government would carry out all the committee's resolutions without question. (The city governor approved.) In this way, the post, telegraph, telephone, and railroads would move under the Citizens Committee's oversight. (Agreed.) And the Okhrana wouldn't be a hindrance? (No, Cavalry Captain Pozhoga has typhus and is delirious.) Immediately shut down or at least put under strict censorship the Black Hundreds' *Rostov Flyer*, so as to prevent agitation for the old system. (We don't practice civil censorship, but in this instance I agree.) How will the authorities look on possible street protests by Black Hundreds? Will the government help neutralize their protests against the new order? Meyer promised he would not allow demonstrations with Tsarist and other provocative portraits. Right then, in front of them, he ordered the police chief not to impede any demonstrations other than monarchical ones and to be patient toward the expression of popular joy, even if they were hostile to police officers. Explain that, even before, the police served the population and now would not go against the people's will.

Paramonov had also been able to obtain copies of all the Petrograd telegrams in order to verify personally that military censors hadn't hidden anything.

All four dispersed to their places to ready the Civil Committee. It would meet in the Melkonov-Yezekov mansion on Pushkinskaya, where Paramonov also went, to chair his War Industry Committee. Meanwhile, among the very last telegrams there turned out to be a proclamation by the Council of Congresses of Industry and Trade saying that this leading group of industrialists and merchants had called on all stock exchange committees and merchant societies to forget any social discord and close ranks around the Duma Committee. And Ilya Isakovich, who later paid a call on the stock exchange committee, helped compose its telegram to Rodzyanko: ecstatically greeting in your person . . . we offer all our powers for organizing our fatherland.

"This is all magnificent, papa! This is just what you wanted! In a single day, all the barriers of tyranny have been smashed! They turned out to be so flimsy!"

They rose to go into the dining room. Ilya Isakovich embraced them both; he was a little shorter than Sonya and noticeably shorter than Volodya:

"That is all so, my dears. This may be the great beginning. But revolutions have the perfidious quality of getting out of hand."

The three took a step with their arms around each other and he stopped:

"But what has struck me in all this is City Governor Meyer. The Petersburg events haven't amazed me as much as Major General Meyer has. After all, if I had been city governor, in that high and trusted post, I would have held out to the last. But he's in such a hurry. It's unseemly."

"That just shows, papa, that their cause has been over for a long time. They are done for!"

[3 4 4]

The remnants of the Duma Committee, or the beginnings of the new government, under public pressure, had retreated from yesterday's room into the next, inner room—where three from the Executive Committee had horse-traded with Milyukov yesterday, and secondary individuals were now sitting, the chancellery, the temporarily detained, a kind of guard—so the Duma leaders were crowded into an even smaller room, where disorder loomed even greater than yesterday. They talked, walked, fussed, and conferred, and there wasn't enough room for anyone.

But now, just after seven o'clock in the evening, another delegation arrived from the Executive Committee, just two this time—Himmer and Nakhamkes.

The Duma deputies didn't try to counter with any semblance of a meeting. Milyukov simply went with the two of them to a small table in the corner of the room, where everyone sat side by side facing the wall, there wasn't even a table lamp, and their shoulders blocked out the overhead light. Himmer was in the middle, otherwise he wouldn't have been visible over Nakhamkes's shoulders.

Also the two Lvovs—one mellow, the other gloomy and lanky—attempted to pretend that they too were part of the meeting and sat off behind them, but after sitting for a while unnoticed, not intended for the conversation, they disappeared.

We didn't finish yesterday, after all, and haven't met all day; such is life now. What didn't we finish yesterday, do we remember?

The terms of activity of the new government were already approved. . . .

Not entirely. A few changes had been added at the Soviet's plenum.

Ah, was that so? (Milyukov regretted, regretted that they hadn't finished yesterday, and all because of Guchkov.) But one can't work this way either, comrades. . . . Do we still have to agree on the Soviet's parallel Declaration?

Here, on two sheets of paper, were their from yesterday attempts: one page, large and unevenly torn off, was offered by Nakhamkes, and on it was one paragraph from Himmer, but there was an arrow moving to the top a paragraph from Nakhamkes, which was supposed to go first. On the other sheet, Milyukov's, was a paragraph Milyukov himself had written in the Soviet's name.

Now they began to look at and blend the paragraphs from the two sheets of paper. And what yesterday their exhausted nighttime heads couldn't put together, their eyes now saw: it was all right, it would work. Himmer wrote that anarchy could not be permitted and the robberies and break-ins at private apartments had to be stopped—if only they could. Whereas Milyukov had written about officers, to whom the interests of freedom were dear, and how, for the sake of the revolutionary struggle's success, their insignificant transgressions against democracy had to be forgotten, and the entire officer corps as a whole could not be branded. There was sufficient mention of revolution and democracy to make it acceptable to the Executive Committee.

Himmer joked that Pavel Nikolaevich was moving to the left and before too long would be a workers' deputy.

But Nakhamkes wasn't joking (although in general, in the revolutionary milieu, he was very fond of funny stories). Most of all, he wasn't joking in his new paragraph, which was written legibly, with large, slightly slanted, clearly delineated letters. Milyukov hadn't seen this paragraph yesterday and now read it for the first time.

It spoke of the new government very abstractly—here, it said, the new government is announcing and requiring, some reforms (the very ones dictated by the Executive Committee) should be welcomed by democratic circles—and *to the extent to which* the burgeoning government acts in the direction of these obligations, democracy must render that government its support.

Pavel Nikolaevich very much disliked that *to the extent to which*. Yesterday, under our circumstances, you promised us unconditional support. But here you have it, and it's both conditional and quite restrained.

Nakhamkes, neither upset nor in a hurry:

"That was yesterday. Since then we've thought it through. We've listened to the Soviet's opinion. . . ."

Ah, strike while the iron is hot. We should have finished yesterday. Yesterday they were more prepared to reconcile. Now Nakhamkes was unbending.

But Milyukov was afraid to get into too much horse-trading for fear of destroying his power, so hard-won as it was. Without the Soviet, they could never cope with the masses.

And both Executive Committee members had already reproached and even attacked him: how could he speak publicly before an agreement? That was a violation of honest negotiations. Why did you suddenly talk about the monarchy if we decided not to predetermine anything?

(Ah, Pavel Nikolaevich himself regretted that.)

He spoke because we basically had a full agreement yesterday—and it was impossible to wait.

And now the Soviet today had advanced new conditions.

What conditions?

"Here"—and Nakhamkes, from another piece of paper, also uneven and crumpled, read the transcript from the plenum: "The government is obligated not to use military circumstances as a pretext for delaying implementation of the promised reforms."

Milyukov screwed up his head, lips, and nose under his round spectacles: "You simply suspect us of everything, every kind of dishonesty."

"The class instinct!" Himmer sniggered.

But Nakhamkes ran his thumb farther down the large lines, to another condition: the Provisional Government's declaration has to be signed by Rodzyanko as well.

"What is that for?" Milyukov was sincerely surprised and was not about to horse-trade over it. "Well, what is it for? What is Rodzyanko?"

They were foisting the Duma on him as his inheritance, with all its awkwardness.

His Soviet comrades understood this question and even agreed, but . . . that was what the Soviet had decided.

Himmer noticed that Milyukov was getting angry. There were too many changes. One misstep now and Milyukov would cut off the negotiations and the agreement would break off—and so would the great plan to foist powerless power on the bourgeoisie. The Soviet itself was in no way capable of creating an administrative apparatus. Everything would go down the drain, and the revolution would perish.

He picked up from the table in front of Nakhamkes those four conditions of the Soviet; two had gone unread. What difference did it make what they shouted there at the amorphous Soviet? These weren't genuine conditions. As the presenter, Nakhamkes stuck by the paper, but Himmer not one bit.

What about the government's obligations? Yes, we agreed yesterday we wouldn't be going back to them.

The scrap of paper on which Nakhamkes had taken notes during the Soviet's meeting yesterday was for now their most authentic transcript. There was also a piece of paper where Milyukov had repeated them for himself yesterday, but abbreviated. There was also a distinct and handsome list of the new government written by Milyukov—and before it a handsome preamble: "The Provisional Committee of the State Duma, with the sympathy of the population and the assistance of capital troops, has achieved such a degree of success over the sinister forces of the old regime . . ." And

Milyukov was very worried that they were just about to attack this formulation, asking where the Soviet of Workers' Deputies came in. Did you really do more than the capital garrison? And then again to argue and rewrite it and the whole effect was lost. But to his delight they kept quiet. After that came this: "A public cabinet made up of individuals who have earned the country's trust by their past activities"—and they kept quiet, too. That meant the list had survived. And only:

"So we don't forget, Pavel Nikolaevich, write it out now in your own hand."

Milyukov very much did not want to, and he wiggled his mustache:

"Completely unnecessary mistrust."

But he wrote it out, dipping into the heavy inkpot:

"The Provisional Government believes it its duty to add that it by no means intends to take advantage of military circumstances to delay implementation of reforms."

"And undertakings," Nakhamkes added.

"But would that be literary? Maybe put it like this? Reforms and undertakings?"

"All right"—and Nakhamkes confidently placed his paw on the document.

"All right," Himmer said. "We are all three writers, and with considerable experience."

That was it. Now to collect signatures from all the ministers—for the sake of ceremony, like an oath, and Rodzyanko's, too. That was it. (They all no longer saw, or had forgotten, that this document had begun as an announcement of the Duma Committee—and was now ending on behalf of the ministers; no one knew what document they had.)

But in a nonobliging, half-businesslike tone, Himmer did repeat his reproach of Milyukov:

"Even though we removed the form of governance for you, Pavel Nikolaich, you shouldn't have jumped out with the monarchy. You were wrong there."

"Not at all," Milyukov of course objected, of course insisted.

"I'll tell you something out of my experience," Himmer said pompously. "Recently, just now, I spoke before a large crowd. They greeted me wonderfully and I kept hearing approving shouts. Nonetheless, afterward they started to shout about the dynasty—and in a completely different tone. You overstimulated them, Pavel Nikolaich."

Where indeed did that come from? Neither yesterday nor the day before did anyone seem to have thought of this, and no one had shouted. Could it really have been all because of Pavel Nikolaevich's speech? You can't shut your eyes on the future: without continuing the monarchy you can't have normal constitutional development.

"Well, naturally," Milyukov surmised, "to the soldiers the return of any Tsar might seem dangerous. It puts them closer to punishment for the uprising. We have to clarify that this is not the case."

Himmer knew, first of all, that a venomous article against the Milyukov speech was being written at that very moment for tomorrow's *Izvestia*. Secondly, he himself had never focused on this issue before, had not ascribed to it such importance. The question of real power had been resolved independently of the Romanovs' fate. Anyway, the Soviet was secured from surprises by the point about a Constituent Assembly.

"Are you really hoping"—Himmer grinned, and his skinny cheeks stretched—"that a Constituent Assembly will leave a monarchy in Russia? All your efforts will be for naught in any case. . . ."

Milyukov seemed on the verge of puffing up: his cheeks and mustache lifted a little:

"A Constituent Assembly can decide anything it likes. If it speaks out against the monarchy, then I can leave. Right now I can't leave. Right now if I'm not there, there won't be a government at all."

He looked at Himmer, and he looked at Nakhamkes. Sufficient warning.

The Executive Committee members evidently still didn't know about Guchkov's trip! Or else would they have kept quiet? He had won time this way. In a few hours, Mikhail would be regent, and Russia would be faced with that fact. If there wasn't a monarch, then who, in essence, laid claim to being the autocratic power? Why, the Soviet: after all, it was the one setting the terms for the government's existence, it would be exercising oversight.

So what was this about that parallel statement from the EC? Three different paragraphs had been sketched out on three different pieces of paper—and now they were going to debate each other and rewrite it from scratch? This was tiresome, and Pavel Nikolaevich in particular had no patience: proclaim it quickly and begin full-fledged activity. Here's what. Since there were scissors and paste in the room, simply paste together these three pieces of paper of different widths and different handwritings. First Nakhamkes's paragraph, second Himmer's, and third Milyukov's. And all this together would be "From the Executive Committee of the Soviet of Workers' and Soldiers' Deputies."

Now it remained, on a blank Milyukov sheet, to collect the signatures of the members of the first public cabinet and Rodzyanko (Milyukov signed first), type it out, and send it to the printer, to be ready tomorrow . . . for the newspapers? But there weren't any newspapers. . . . To be ready for the *Izvestia* of that same Soviet of Deputies. And as a proclamation to be pasted up on the streets.

All three rose—and Nakhamkes unexpectedly embraced Milyukov and even leaned forward as if to kiss him. (Milyukov realized bitterly that this meant he had missed or lost something.)

Nakhamkes left. Milyukov collected the ministers' signatures while Himmer observed. Rodzyanko took a seat and signed, significantly and impressively—as if his signature decided everything. He was very pleased they'd reached an agreement. He did not want this to drag out.

Then Himmer took it all to the printers.

While Milyukov pondered it. Yes, obviously, he had accepted conditions too hard for the government. Yes, and behind the ministerial calculations he may have missed the fact that the monarchic question could resurface abruptly. Yes, perhaps he shouldn't have announced it out loud today. But everything had gone routinely and inevitably. In a few hours, Mikhail would be regent and the question moot.

Right then English and French correspondents dashed up to him: Europe, after all, and the Allies, after all, wanted and had the right to know what was going on in foggy, fiery Petersburg.

Loving the Allies with all his heart, Milyukov gave them the first governmental interview:

"Popular indignation was such that the Russian revolution was practically the briefest and least bloody in history. The present great events are augmenting popular enthusiasm, multiplying popular forces, and giving them, at last, the possibility of winning the war."

"But what will be the monarchy's fate?"

"The new government believes it essential that a regency be temporarily assumed by Grand Duke Mikhail Aleksandrovich. Such is our decision, a decision we do not feel it possible to change."

(By the time they printed this in Europe and these words became known here, the deed would be done.)

[3 4 5]

Only in books do you read about moments like this, never dreaming of falling into their delightful and terrible maelstrom. Rare are the people, lucky their whole life, marked out by the gods, who manage to lay their fingers on history's greatest events. Shulgin had done so twice, on two major ones: the day before yesterday he had taken the Russian Bastille without firing a shot; and today he was going to the Tsar for his abdication. This would be a legacy not only for your grandchildren, not only would those who know you be asking about it for many years to come, but it would go into textbooks and readers and be depicted in drawings, as for all great revolutions.

Here, so close, you see the thousand-maw rabble, the mud and scum, you race through these awful twists and turns. What can you do? There they are! You have to be prepared to be torn to pieces at any moment—but also to admit how light your feet have become, as if you were partly flying, you have to admit it.

Intoxicated by this unusual state, Shulgin wanted nothing for himself. He hadn't joined the government, they'd taken someone else, and it didn't matter. Even now he wanted not fame but only to be a part of this great and tragic moment.

As a falling star draws a shining line across the sky, so a clump of events was racing across the Russian sky, and Shulgin was intoxicated that he could be a shimmering spark there. He hadn't joined the government, but long live the new government, and we're all going to support it with all our powers, for the enemy is at Russia's gates. If we mightily support this handful of courageous men from the Tauride Palace, we will save the country.

Let our personal lot be strange, deafening and new. This isn't the time to think too hard, so we won't, we'll believe!

His mind refused to grasp this! Four days ago, on Sunday, when Petrograd mysteriously froze and was so marvelous before the collapse, Shulgin would have been offended if anyone had said that now—when? on Thursday—he would dare be on his way to suggest abdication to His Majesty!

But the overthrow had come about so unprecedentedly easily and unopposed that now he was doing just that, and it seemed plain to him that the Emperor could not go on reigning.

All this past winter, every once in a while, it had seemed to Shulgin, carried away by Purishkevich's furious speeches, by the whole wave of indignation even among noble circles, that this regime could not go on existing any longer! This way we'd hurtle on to the point of regicide!

How could the Emperor keep reigning if month after month society hurled all those harsh accusations in his face and his spouse's—and he never responded.

No one had ever responded to a single one of them.

By his silence alone he had nearly lost the throne before there was any revolution.

And now that the sky had opened and everything had come crashing down . . . ? There, under the Tauride Palace's vaults, next to the Soviet of Workers' Deputies, and seeing these pushing, hollering crowds—it was almost impossible to imagine that the Emperor still existed, that he still acted or ruled Russia.

Obviously, the hour had struck. . . .

Or was this perhaps due to an insufficient consciousness, a troubled mind, insomnia, weariness? Somehow no other outcome was in view. On the contrary, all searches for a solution for Russia were tending toward abdication—in order to save the throne itself and the dynasty.

Hadn't history known quite a few examples when shifting power from monarch to monarch—to a son, brother, nephew, or uncle—saved the throne, saved the monarchy?

Save the monarchy by sacrificing the monarch.

And, of course, many bureaucrats would need to go, as well.

That was the most sensible solution. If there was an abdication, the revolution would immediately cease to be, power would gently transition to the regent, and a new government would be appointed, all by legitimate means.

In 1905, there might also have been a terrible shock, but at the time the government's credit had not been as undermined, at the time it had at its unshakeable defense the entire Guards, the army didn't mutiny, the junior officers didn't have doubts about carrying out orders, and in the heat of the upheavals, and despite death threats, the rightist *Kievlyanin* was able to continue to publish. And when on the balcony of the Kiev Duma they started smashing the Tsar's crown, the crowd, having listened to the revolutionary rally, gasped in horror, and hands reached out to lift the fragments from humiliation.

Had that happened in today's Petrograd, they wouldn't have rushed to pick them up. . . .

Oh, how much the Emperor had lost over these years! And how much had the throne.

But the throne still could, still had to be saved!

Shulgin was on his way for precisely this, that was the idea maturing in him: precisely in order to facilitate abdication for the Emperor. After all, the Emperor well remembered Shulgin and spoke kindly to him at receptions. Shulgin was a natural monarchist, although a member of the Progressive Bloc, but on its right flank. He would accept the abdication with more tact than any leftist and would ease this bitter moment for the Emperor. His presence alongside Guchkov, a well-known despiser of the throne, would mitigate a great deal. It would be easier for the Emperor to hand the act over to a loyal, enthusiastic monarchist.

Only this act just wouldn't let itself get written. His thoughts and sentences wouldn't coalesce. Because of this weariness? Because his head hurt?

He and Guchkov spoke little en route, both overburdened by their own thoughts. Shulgin was trying to sketch something out, in the darkened train car, to candlelight, rocking—but he himself was quite dissatisfied.

Well, "in a trying year," this of course . . . "difficult trials for . . ." A tautology, but otherwise it didn't work. . . . "Lead the Empire out of trying turmoil in the face of a ferocious . . ." "We considered it a good that will satisfy the wishes of the entire Russian people . . ."

But was this really the wish of the entire Russian people? . . .

How else to motivate this, though? . . .

". . . lay down the burden of power invested from God . . . In the name of the greatness of our beloved Russian people . . . We call for God's blessing on our son . . . while as regent . . ."

No, this wasn't working.

And besides, the paper looked untidy.

Perhaps they should have worried more? But they had worried so much these past few days, they'd become dulled.

Once again, he surrendered to his dreams. Or memories.

Memories of meetings with the Emperor. At the reception for the Volynian provincial delegation. At a formal reception in the Winter Palace. At a service in the Tauride Palace. He recalled the Emperor's incomparably gentle smile, the shyness he had never overcome, the nervous jerk of one shoulder, his low, rather thick voice, his precise and clear speech with the slight Guards accent, and his strikingly calm gaze.

A Christian on the throne.

Shulgin was on his way—and he loved him. On his way—and he rejoiced that he would see the Emperor again. On his way—and hoping to mitigate, lighten this fateful and irrevocable moment.

And all of a sudden a memory pierced him: 15 March. The terrible 14 March had been avoided—but what had happened on the 15th?

Ah, on 15 March—exactly ten years ago—the Duma ceiling had caved in. So this was what that prophesy had been about!

[3 4 6]

GHQ's anxious, protracted anticipation of the abdication was interrupted in unexpected fashion. A telegram arrived from the GHQ telegraph office sent not to GHQ but bypassing GHQ—to the Southwest Army Group, and even bypassing the Southwest—to Corps Commander General Kornilov, saying that he had been appointed by Rodzyanko to command the Petrograd Military District!

What was that? How swiftly stable concepts were being toppled! The commanders-in-chief had barely begun irregular relations with Rodzyanko, and here he was already, disdaining GHQ, and directly appointing Kornilov, removing him from his army group?

They delayed the telegram, naturally.

But it was followed by an ameliorating telegram from Rodzyanko to GHQ. He explained again why the Provisional Committee of the State Duma had been forced to seize power and was now handing it over to the Provisional Government. That the troops, the entire population, and even members of the royal family had recognized only this authority. But for the complete order of the latter, as well as to save the capital from anarchy, it was essential that the valorous combat general Kornilov be seconded to Petrograd—in the name of the homeland's salvation and victory over the enemy, so that the war's innumerable victims would not have fallen for naught.

It was interesting that there wasn't even a hint here of what Rodzyanko had said in the night about abdication.

Before Alekseev could solve this rebus properly, a supporting telegram arrived from a general at the General Staff requesting the valorous General Kornilov's immediate secondment to Petrograd—to save the capital from anarchy but also from terror. . . .

Also from terror? What happened to the "calm"?

. . . and to prop up the Duma Committee, which was saving the monarchic order. The explanation given was different from Rodzyanko's: destructive work and propaganda was being carried out among the troops by the Soviet of Workers' Deputies, work that did not allow the troops to be put under officers' command, so that they were going over to the side of a radical leftist workers' party.

Oh! The picture in the capital presented itself as very very dangerous.

They would have to grant the request.

But where was the limit to circumventing regulations? If no one dared summon Kornilov by bypassing GHQ, then even Alekseev could not make such an important appointment without the Supreme Commander.

Who may have removed himself from practical leadership—but who hadn't rejected it either. And he was perfectly accessible at Northern Army Group HQ.

All that remained to be done was to send a most loyal request to the Supreme Commander in Pskov, on the basis of Rodzyanko's telegram, asking for his permission to recall Adjutant General Ivanov from his post (since Rodzyanko had forgotten that there can't be two commanders in a single district) and to second Kornilov there.

Meanwhile, give Brusilov a preliminary telegram to be prepared for such a secondment. The battle general with the popular name could lead toward the institution of order.

Brusilov quickly responded, and unsatisfactorily: Kornilov was ill suited for this post, too blunt and excessively fiery.

He was jealous, of course. But right, actually. They should be sending a diplomat like Brusilov himself into the present Petrograd situation.

But the appointment had been correctly contemplated. And they had to hurry with it and save the capital. And not even be squeamish about Voeikov and pass on to him the request of the Supreme Commander's chief of staff to speed up Kornilov's appointment.

Were the letter trains still there?

Yes, yes, Pskov confirmed, the letter trains hadn't gone anywhere, but during the second conversation between the Northern commander-in-chief and the Emperor the situation had altered, and it was wise to be cautious. There were as yet no instructions regarding the Manifesto of abdication. But Danilov himself thought they needed to prepare for its imminent release.

Why, the text was ready!

They had transmitted it to Pskov.

GHQ was helping in whatever way it could.

Northern headquarters was in no hurry to reply.

Once again an inquiry: Had they given it to the Emperor?

They'd given him everything. But there was a worry that the draft of this manifesto might be too late.

What? Even this was late? . . . Well, events had piled on! What else then?

There was partial information that this manifesto had already been published in Petrograd on instruction of the Provisional Government itself.

How could that be? Then it was a coup, not an abdication?

Yes, they truly had to hurry to make it a decorous abdication.

Even equable Alekseev lost his ability to deal with ordinary matters and just waited nervously.

Meanwhile, the freshest but also most desperate telegram was brought from Nepenin of the Baltic Fleet saying that he was having tremendous difficulty maintaining the fleet's discipline and of course he joined the petitions for abdication. If this decision wasn't taken in the next few hours, a catastrophe would ensue with innumerable calamities for the homeland.

This telegram lashed at Alekseev like a landslide, struck him in the face. The Baltic Fleet on the brink of anarchy!

If some doubt had gnawed at him a little all day, then this blow knocked him out. It was all correct! Only abdication! And as swiftly as possible!

But from the Black Sea, proud Kolchak sent not a word in reply.

Only at half past nine did the Emperor's consent arrive for appointing Kornilov and recalling Ivanov.

Not a word about the manifesto. . . .

When? . . .

Now, inwardly having carried out the mandatory official cycle, Alekseev could allow himself the liberty, in response to Rodzyanko, not to mention the procedure with the Emperor's signature, perhaps dubious and outdated. Instead: by *my* order, Lieutenant General Kornilov, commander of the 25th Army Corps, has been appointed commander of the Petrograd District.

Alekseev attempted to contact Ivanov through Rodzyanko to recall him finally to Mogilev.

And again he spoke with the Northern Army Group: When would they finally send liaison officers to Ivanov? And where was he?

We don't know where he is.

Suspicion crept toward Alekseev; after all, he was without guile, and the Emperor was evasive and secretive. Was he playing a double game? As he was promising a manifesto, was he perhaps moving Ivanov somewhere farther along? Was he himself about to slip out of Pskov and not give his abdication?

What was happening with the letter trains? Were they still there?

Yes, yes. Guchkov and Shulgin had arrived and been invited to the Emperor's train car.

Historic moments had begun.

The Army Group of the Caucasus kept trying to find out, on behalf of Nikolai Nikolaevich, whether the Emperor had abdicated yet or not. It was extremely important for the most august commander-in-chief to know.

GHQ tensely awaited every new communication from the telegraph office.

But the tapes coming in were terribly insignificant, in no way on the level of events. From Kvetsinsky: a delegation of as many as 50 from the new government was on its way from Velikie Luki to Polotsk and was disarming the railroad guards at all the stations. Then Pskov confirmed that three such deputations had started out from Bologoye in three directions and were disarming gendarmes. They said they were representatives of the new government.

Now Evert was asking GHQ to get in touch with Rodzyanko and arrange for some new rule so that commanders-in-chief were informed beforehand about any trips to the army groups. These could be imposters, after all.

This was not the time to deal with this deputation, and Alekseev wasn't in the mood, and Rodzyanko—but here was a train proceeding in the zone of military command and disarming military guards!

Alekseev had to telegraph Rodzyanko that indeed the order that existed in the armies was being violated, and the new government had to honor the army's rules. The Supreme Commander's chief of staff asked that he not be denied an indication as to what kind of deputation this was.

[3 4 7]

Well, if the new government had already been composed, and made public, and agreed upon by the Soviet of Deputies—why shouldn't it start exercising power? True, the day had been annunciatory, ceremonial, and it was getting on toward night again—but circumstances couldn't wait. It was also convenient that the members of government were mostly all there, they hadn't dispersed.

Of course, they weren't alone in the room. Sharing the handful of tables, chaotic chairs, and spots on the sofa with them, crowded members of the provisional Duma Committee. These past few days, people here had physically not separated; they were the Duma's united head, their secrets were shared and so were their conversations. But a government had been formed, and a new barrier ran between them, still glass for now, you could still see and hear through it—but it was a decisive barrier. Kerensky had ceased to be alien and Soviet, Tereshchenko had ceased to be alien, to say nothing of Prince Georgi Evgenievich—but now the Duma Committee members, who yesterday, even this morning, had seemed indistinguishably theirs, were already clearly perceived as alien and disruptive.

Now the members of government, prepared to begin a session, but not having a separate room for this—masters of all Russia, they didn't have a room for their sessions—felt rather awkward and exchanged glances. Even they didn't know what their session would be about or how confidential their conversations would be—but it would be a profanation of their new ministerial calling to hold a discussion in front of outsiders.

Apparently . . . apparently they should ask the others to go out, leaving to them this last, blind room.

But the heavenly eyed, most kind Prince Georgi Evgenievich could not bring himself to utter such an incivility.

Was it up to Milyukov to demonstrate firmness? He could, naturally, but it was sad that at the first and slightest occasion, barely off the mark, he had to do the prime minister's job.

Before he could frown sufficiently and wiggle his grayish mustache, though, the Chief Procurator of the Holy Synod, who had shortened his disheveled beard ever so slightly, and with the same spark of madness in his leaping eyebrows and glittering eyes—looking directly at the crumpled but still magnificent Rodzyanko, blurted out with less restraint than was even necessary:

"Gentlemen members of the Committee! We, the members of the government, would like you to leave us alone."

Crudely put, but it was worth noting that this second Lvov might come in quite handy in other instances.

Like a taunted bull, Rodzyanko looked at the troublemaker Lvov. At the others. Squinted. His large face displayed astonishment: the revolution, the turbulent crowds, had squeezed him in his own Tauride Palace building— but for his own Duma deputies to do so?

Although . . . there seemed to be no way to object.

He took his sorrow to another room.

All it took was pushing Rodzyanko out and the others were easily pushed out, too.

Now the new government was left to itself—and they took seats. Who wasn't here? Guchkov. Shingarev. The latter was still finishing up at the Food Supply Commission. Well, so be it.

Like a nice shiny silver ruble among dulled ones, the new Minister of Finance Tereshchenko stood out among them all—so fresh and young, dressed elegantly, a bowtie not at all awry on the freshest starched collar, the whitest possible corner of a handkerchief peeking from his chest pocket— among all those crumpled men and Kerensky's unseemly black jacket.

They took seats. Perhaps not at one big table, but wherever they could, and not very comfortably—but it was hard not to sense the great moment for Russia. The people's ages-old dream had come true! What the masses had dreamed of, what fighters had given their lives for: Russia's first public cabinet, endowed with the popular trust, and responsible to a parliament, not a Tsar—had finally assembled and begun its work!

This moment divided all of Russia's history into two eras: the era of bondage and the era of freedom.

So. Everyone could see and hear each other more or less. Good. But there was no secretary. Not one session, not one step of this government could take place without a transcript. When forming, somehow they hadn't given any thought to a secretary. They would need to find one—and he had to be a highly educated and talented, simply an outstanding person. But for now . . . ? They looked around at each other and couldn't find a secretary. The Minister of Education? He couldn't cope. Konovalov was sluggish and couldn't keep up, either. Vladimir Lvov? Too nervous. It was awkward to nominate Tereshchenko, to say nothing of Kerensky: the most leftist, and perpetually active, a bundle of energy, at any moment he might leap up and run away, thereby surprising no one. And it nearly ended up being—Milyukov again?

What was the session's agenda? It hadn't been drawn up.

Kerensky was sitting here out of decorum, to show his sympathy, but he had no need of the ministers' ideas about what he should do with justice. His program was clear—expand freedom limitlessly—and he'd already begun.

Likewise Milyukov, the most refined specialist in the nuances of international relations, had no need of his colleagues' advice; he himself knew.

That most tactful chairman, Prince Georgi Lvov, ran the session with the greatest inner turmoil. How terribly the conditions of taking power differed from how he had always pictured it before! Just this afternoon they had been shouting in the Ekaterininsky Hall that Prince Lvov stood at the head of only the franchised public. And how was he now to channel this public dissatisfaction? Extremely dubious conditions—and why was it he who had to bear responsibility?

However, seeing that his colleagues were in no hurry to speak out, Prince Lvov himself, in cautious form, expressed the thought that in taking up its activities the new government might need to define the scope of its authority. Looking down the line, this authority was limited by the upcoming Constituent Assembly.

Yes. However remarkable the fact that they had obtained power, at the Constituent Assembly their authority must inevitably come to an end.

But *until* then? Until then one would hope that their authority was as full and sovereign as possible. It had to be grounded theoretically: to whom precisely would the fullness of power be conveyed? It would be correct to believe that it went specifically to the government. It would be wrong to believe that it went to the State Duma. It seemed highly doubtful that the Duma could revive its activities in this situation, when the rightist segment of the deputies had been lost and wouldn't dare show up; and the entire Duma would be too rightist for the present current of events. Also, it was to be reelected this autumn anyway. Right now it would only constrain the government.

There were also a few delicate points—how the ministers were selected, to begin with, or how the government was formed, and what its relations were with the Soviet—and not all that could be divulged in the Duma. It was more convenient to act without Duma sessions.

Rodzyanko wouldn't stand for that, of course. He couldn't even be told this openly.

But if the State Duma would be constraining, then what about the Duma Committee? What was the Duma Committee for? This was a doubling of government that was entirely inadmissible.

This too, especially, could not be expressed to Rodzyanko right now.

Gentlemen, wherein lies the particular difficulty of our government's activities? In the fact that, as is clear to everyone, the entire makeup of the Russian state's basic laws ceased to exist in a single instant. And new laws take a very very long time to be worked out. So we are going to be acting in an airless space. This is why we especially need the fullness of power. We have ahead of us legislative as well as executive activities. We ourselves must develop the standards we are going to deem appropriate at the given moment.

It would be productive to arrange for a kind of extended, permanent Article 87: to pass laws without the parliament.

And if we also take into account the general anarchy? And the fact that we are going to have to deal with the opinion of the Soviet of Workers' Deputies?

Gentlemen, we cannot allow that kind of interference in our actions or we will cease to be a government.

However, real circumstances force us to reckon with it.

Well, then, we must somehow unofficially learn the desires of the Soviet of Deputies—even before the government's official sessions. Through Aleksandr Fyodorovich?

Look, we've just learned in private contacts that the Soviet of Workers' Deputies is in favor of deporting all the members of the House of Romanov from the Russian state.

Is that true? . . .

A heavy silence fell. How terrible this Soviet of Workers' Deputies appeared to be: after all, in the official negotiations they had agreed not to pose the question of the form of governance, but here in private contacts with our trusted colleagues . . . Someone we don't know, which makes it even more frightening, has expressed the opinion that . . .

Forgive me, but this looks absurd. How then can the dynasty continue to remain . . . ?

(A rumor had also just rolled through the city that the Heir had died. They telephoned Doctor Botkin—no, he was alive.)

Maybe for *certain* members of the dynasty? . . . Maybe limit their stay within known boundaries, but inside Russia?

But there was no one to answer: after all, this was a *contact* that had taken place and was over and now there was no face attached to it.

Nekrasov, with his hooked nose, sat there sharp-mustached and close-mouthed. Konovalov stuck out his thick lips and didn't move. Tereshchenko beamed like a birthday boy.

Since everyone knew why Guchkov had gone and where, then perhaps this question shouldn't be discussed today? It could wait a while.

But the relationship with the Soviet of Deputies would remain the government's most ticklish problem. . . .

Now what practical questions must the government discuss immediately?

The Minister of Finance raised the question of the right to issue paper money in the amount of two billion rubles.

Well, if it's essential . . . Indeed, after this kind of upheaval of the state . . .

But the dear, gracious prime minister was at pains (as might have been expected) simultaneously to play two parts, also as the Minister of the Interior. Therefore he would have thought to retain only the overall leadership but hand the direct conduct of affairs of the Ministry of the Interior, all its practical work, to his assistant at the head of the Zemstvo Union, the very promising Dmitri Mitrofanovich Shchepkin. . . . (In December, he had helped Prince Lvov make public the harshest of the antigovernment resolutions.)

The prime minister's first request could not be rejected.

Did that mean this clerk would now unwittingly become a kind of member of our government cabinet?

Well then . . . Well, we'll have to . . .

[348]

After nine o'clock, the Tauride Palace emptied out. Its main residents—errant soldiers—no longer feared returning to their barracks; they already knew they weren't going to be punished and their officers were more likely to be executed. Although the guard had left the palace entrance, no one was wandering into the palace anymore. The Ekaterininsky Hall, where a continuous rally had crowded in the afternoon, had also emptied out, as had the wing of galleries, where some speaker or other had been shouting continuously; the agitators' little tables had emptied of brochures, and the young ladies had gone home after handing out the brochures—and only on the columns, pasted up, were the names of the parties and the slogans, handwritten in large, crooked letters: "In struggle you will gain . . . ," "Proletarians of all countries . . ."—according to the new ways, they were sacred, and no officer or Duma attendant dared remove them. Not that there were any traces left of duty officers with a chain on their chest, or of attendants, no one was cleaning the building anymore, apparently, and it was good that the stokers hadn't left, they kept stoking—if the stokers left, the citadel of revolution would scatter, too. The red silk on the benches was ripped and badly stained, the white marble columns were pock-marked and covered in ashy black spots from extinguished cigarettes; the floors everywhere had been spat and snorted upon, butts and torn paper lay about, and everything was covered in mud from men's boots. There was scarcely any point in cleaning all this today; they would come pouring back in tomorrow. They'd turned off the large lamps, and the despoilment was less visible in the half-dark hall.

The Cupola Hall had been freed up some. They'd removed the explosives, some of the large weapons, and the meat carcasses from the Tauride Palace, some of it for a purpose, while some of it people were pilfering for themselves. But some sacks remained, and there was still diesel and two sewing machines.

The second floor, with the prisoners, was quiet, tightly packed in the different rooms, lying on the floor; police and gendarme officers and arrested officials rejoiced that, although they were in close quarters, they were safe.

Although there were still people darting down the corridors here and there, crossing the halls on the diagonal, and compared to the former peacetime this would have looked like a disturbance, a cause for alarm—right now it felt deserted, a respite of silence, the first such evening. The enormous, stormy, vast revolution that had raged here for four days had vacated the palace and thronged elsewhere.

In this first quiet and half-dark hour, its principal master emerged to tour the palace.

If all the Duma deputies had found the Ekaterininsky Hall's besmirched look offensive, then imagine how the President saw it! And he couldn't order these repulsive scraps with inscriptions pulled down. All the glory of Russian society, assembled in this Duma, in this hall, was now so vile and unsightly. The revolution had taken giant steps into the shining future but had left filthy tracks on the parquet.

The revolution had moved off! Here, right now, he felt it for the first time: it had moved on from the Duma rooms.

And from Rodzyanko himself.

At last the Public Cabinet had assembled that had loomed so long before Russia and that people had awaited with bated breath—but the most prominent, chief, principal person hadn't joined it.

Would people understand? . . .

Would they understand that he, who had brought about this entire revolution with his own large hands, who had defended it before the throne and saved it from suppression—now had taken nothing for himself? The first candidate before all Russia—and now he hadn't joined the government.

They should appreciate this.

Bitter though it was.

Slowly he crossed the hall. And tried to contemplate the future and how to lead the Duma, the first free Russian parliament, with glory now.

Suddenly a noise came from the entrance to the Cupola—loud steps and a criss-cross of voices.

It was a group of officers—heading straight for him, having recognized him immediately, of course.

They were waving their arms as they went and speaking so dissonantly and loudly, they didn't even look like officers. One tall dragoon, two Jägers, and three Izmailovsky men, none more senior than a captain.

"Who are you looking for, gentlemen?"

And without restraint, extremely agitated:

"Mr. Rodzyanko!"

"You once again, you . . . ! We can't live this way!"

"You see, you are putting us in an extremely . . . !"

They were speaking nearly all at once, and Rodzyanko, seeing nearly all their faces, could not distinguish individual ones, but they all had the same—desperate—face.

What had happened? What Milyukov had said—that the Romanov dynasty would remain—had spread through the barracks and set off a tumult: We won't stand for it! We'll kill our officers!

"Yesterday, Mr. Rodzyanko, your appeals to return to ranks were understood the same way, and they threatened to kill us, they drove us out of the barracks. . . . And now it's happening again. Gentlemen! Think of us! What are you doing? . . ."

Although the soldiers didn't know the word "dynasty," of course, and not one in five knew "Romanov," something had happened or these officers wouldn't have converged here from different regiments, at the same time. . . .

Rodzyanko was a human being, too, and could not think cold-bloodedly now. Since yesterday, his own sense of danger had not abated, when they'd threatened to kill him—so he picked up on the officers' alarm all the more acutely and sympathetically, and with a great surge of his mighty heart:

"What?" he nearly bellowed. "Again?"

The hapless officers could not live this way! The glorious army could not remain this way! Russia could not develop further this way!

"Let's go!" the old Horse Guard commanded the officers, and he headed off ahead of their handful, also swinging his arms and seething.

He sped as fast as he could, so that this seething wouldn't burst his chest, to throw this in Milyukov's face.

Several of them were sitting in the room there, all members of the new government, which had not taken in the giant Rodzyanko, and he, bursting in at the head of this handful of officers, himself a thoroughgoing officer, something these civilians couldn't appreciate—for all of them he hurled loudly at Milyukov:

"What on earth are you doing? Because of your announcement, officers can't return to their units! You're destroying the army! After your announcement . . . ! Now we have to save our officers. It's our duty!"

He experienced a bitter satisfaction as well in speaking to this circumspect, restrained, sinister cat Milyukov, because of whom so much . . .

Milyukov stood up. Never one to blush, apparently he did a little. He immediately understood what *announcement* of his was being referred to. He had been reproached for it already.

"But we cannot act to address individual situations," he objected firmly. "If we agree on this opinion in principle"—and he looked around for support at the ministers sitting at the table, who were so newly appointed that they themselves were not yet used to the sound of this title. "We all think this and cannot . . ." He already sounded less firm.

In the past few hours, this bumpkin Rodzyanko had rolled downhill like a stone, outstripping everyone in his fall: he had rushed the agreement with the Soviet and he had signed its conditions. Only two hours before he had proudly disclosed to the ministers that he was in constant contact with Grand Duke Mikhail and had already prepared him for the regency and could engage him immediately. And now he was already trying to shake off the monarchy?

Prince Lvov sat at the table on a velvet chair, erect and unconcerned, although he was facing the agitated group that had burst in. He looked at them with kind eyes. Not quite understanding. Not picking up on their agitation.

The other Lvov sat there, too, a spindle-legs with a bare scalp and a brigand's black beard—watch out, he might rush at you and bite or strike! He might blurt out the most injurious words at any moment.

Nekrasov bore his face like a printed photograph: you could examine it all you liked in its immobility and opacity. His mustache never moved and concealed any expression on his closed lips, there wasn't a single vital feature on his smooth face, and his mysterious eyes quite fixed.

Milyukov already knew that Nekrasov favored a republic. During the ministerial trading he had written this on paper and showed it to him, so the others couldn't hear, and had himself carefully torn it up. He'd already stated his opinion that the officers in fact favored the old regime, were agitating for the old regime—and now they were putting the ministers in an awkward position.

Milyukov realized that he wasn't going to get any support from these three.

Professor Manuilov, the Minister of Education, was also sitting there, but Milyukov couldn't expect anything from that one, either.

Lastly there was Kerensky swiveling on his chair, with his narrow, pressed head, first surveying the officer group with their hero Rodzyanko, then his dozing cabinet colleagues, and Milyukov, who was losing confidence. Kerensky was like a high school boy, maybe even a medal winner, but who had been immediately appointed principal and was intoxicated with that fact alone. As to the form of government? It was simply ridiculous because everyone knew that he was in favor of the most extreme republic.

So who then in the government still supported Milyukov and his unfortunate idea about continuing the dynasty? Guchkov? But while he was trying to accomplish something in Pskov, we here were losing everything.

Rodzyanko, the most loyal monarchist, here he was standing at the head of the angry officers! He reproached Milyukov as if he himself had rejected the dynasty a long time ago.

Milyukov sensed this sudden loss of any support—not just the floor and chair back but even the air. He could have lectured them at length about continuity of governmental authority, but it was hopeless to try to draw their support. A constitutional monarchy was dogma for him, an essential stage of development toward a republic, and he had never had to prove this to his fellow Kadets; everyone had always thought that way, and so had the entire Progressive Bloc—and all of a sudden, in a flash, in this shattered new world, Milyukov was the last man standing.

Yes, everyone thought he should retract what he'd said! . . . Why provoke new irritation, now, against the new government?

But he didn't want to disavow it. This was what he thought, he argued, unusually distraught. He had also just lost his voice, having completely strained it in the hall.

"Then announce that this is not the government's opinion but your own personal one," Nekrasov suggested.

How do you like that! He was faced with a disavowal at the very first step! . . .

And he had to hurry to give this announcement to the correspondents so that it would appear in tomorrow's newspapers.

[3 4 9]

With red ribbons across its iron chest and red flags, the locomotive pulled its two train cars into the Pskov station not long before ten o'clock and not far from the platform where the royal letter A train was. The paired sentries by His Personal train and the guard officers and suite were struck dumb when they saw under the station lamps several soldiers with red bows in their lapels hop out of the arriving official train car, so inept they were dragging their rifles as best they could—a visible manifestation of revolutionary Petrograd. The newly arrived train cars had stopped by the next platform cater-corner from the royal salon car. From the back platform of the second train car, a young civilian, also with a red bow, having inquired of the station officials and random passersby, handed them leaflets. They took them, some uncertainly, some willingly. They dispersed. Others wanting to take them came up.

General Ruzsky definitely wanted to catch the deputies and call them in to see him, bypassing the Tsar. He gave instructions to that effect and himself did not leave for town and sat in his own train car at the station, while Danilov from headquarters in town sent incoming documents to him here—telegrams of reply from Sakharov and Nepenin, the telegram about Kornilov's appointment, and then the draft abdication Manifesto worked out at GHQ. Ruzsky had sent all these documents on to the Emperor, himself avoiding seeing him, as he wished to hold onto the Tsar's abdication telegram—and held firm despite repeated demands and did not surrender his treasure. He feared an about-face in the Emperor's mood in these idle hours. Ruzsky had to be the first to see the deputies, in order to explain to them how much the Tsar had weakened and caved, so that their pressure did not relent. He was concerned that Shulgin—a well-known monarchist, although for the past eighteen months also a loyal member of the Progressive Bloc—was coming. The Petrograd situation kept swaying enigmatically, changing, and an about-face could be expected. Before Ruzsky could rush a reassuring telegram to Rodzyanko saying that, at his behest, Kornilov had just been appointed to Petrograd (he was not officially obligated to send it, but it was propitious to present himself to the mighty Rodzyanko), a rumor rather than a dispatch arrived saying that several armored vehicles, or possibly trucks with armed soldiers, were moving from Luga toward Pskov. How was this to be understood, and what was to be done? Ruzsky would never dare oppose the new government's troops, yet how could he let an aroused band into army group headquarters?

No matter how he sat on pins and needles in his own train car at the other end of the station, doing nothing, only waiting, though—he let the moment slip, was told too late.

Guchkov and Shulgin also wanted to see Ruzsky beforehand in order to determine all the circumstances and not take a wrong step. But before they could leave the train car and listen to the tense formal report by the station commandant (under Ruzsky's orders), the aide-de-camp on the lookout for them came up and invited them to see the Emperor. They couldn't refuse. Not only due to ages-old notions, but also because it would look unconfident and spoil their very mission.

Guchkov, ponderous, squat, and limping a little, wearing a rich man's fur coat, and the lightly dressed, slim, rather tall Shulgin wearing a sealskin hat—headed for the royal train car, as if that were how they'd intended to begin, and stepped down to the tracks and onto the other platform.

On the way, Aide-de-Camp Mordvinov asked Shulgin what was going on in Petrograd, and he, young and impressionable, responded candidly, not in line with his mission:

"Something unimaginable! We are wholly in the hands of the Soviet of Deputies, we left secretly, and they may arrest us when we return."

"Then what hope is there?" Mordvinov was astonished.

"We're hoping," Shulgin said sincerely, "that the Emperor will help us."

They entered the train car's dining compartment. A footman helped the deputies with their coats. They passed through the doors into the salon, which was flooded with bright light, despite the curtained windows, and glossily clean; the deputies had become unused to any cleanliness over the past few days in Petrograd. The walls were covered in light green leather. A spinet. A small decorative clock on the wall.

They were met by Court Minister Count Frederiks, a skinny, yellowish-gray general getting on in years with aiguillettes and a bristling gray mustache. For many years he had preserved his tall, erect figure, but now the bend in his back had twisted him. Nonetheless, he was faultlessly attired, and the portraits of three Tsars in diamonds on a sky-blue bow reminded the impudent deputies where they were. He had his own urgent question about Petrograd—about the attack on his home and his wife having been taken off somewhere—but he was carrying out duties higher than his own person and asked nothing.

As he greeted him, though, Guchkov told him this very thing plainly, even absent-mindedly, almost the way people pay an ordinary courtesy, saying that the minister's home had been attacked and that he, Guchkov, did not know what had become of his family.

Guchkov tread with heavy feet, like a victorious commander arrived to dictate a peace. But Shulgin was shy. He felt utterly unprepared for an imperial audience, was neither fully washed nor well shaved, and was wearing a simple jacket, having spent four days in the Tauride Palace insanity. Only now did he realize just how far they were from ceremony, just how unprepared outwardly they were to be present at Russia's great moment.

The Emperor had been in the next train car and right then entered—not with his usual light, youthful step, although as trim as ever, and still wearing his gray Circassian foot-scout coat with the cartridge belts and a colonel's epaulets. His face was darker and had the many deep wrinkles that had furrowed it in the past few days. He abandoned the ceremony of having them approach him and himself approached and greeted them with a very simple handshake; he had a firm hand.

That the Tsar had lived to see this! He had awaited his personal, familial enemy like a deliverer, and his heart had hastened the meeting all these terrible seven hours from his afternoon abdication to the deputies' arrival. In those seven hours he had endured tea and dinner with his suite. And read Sakharov's encouraging telegram. And Nepenin's despairing one, saying that if the abdication was not given in the next few hours, disaster would befall Russia. Alekseev's telegram brought Rodzyanko's confident announcement about the formation of the self-styled government and about how it had chosen a general for the Petrograd District on its own. Several times he reread the Manifesto of abdication expeditiously prepared by the diplomatic section of GHQ, quite a noble text, actually.

This time, more than likely (he feared), his eyes did not conceal his dismay, his hope that perhaps the deputies had brought him mitigation. He hurried to guess just what they had brought. He was prepared for a responsible ministry and prepared for his bitter enemy Guchkov to be made prime minister (and then work with him and endure his reports), just so this tortuous wrangling with Petrograd would end and the Tsar himself could proceed unimpeded to Tsarskoye Selo.

So well known were all the people here that the receiving side didn't even think to ask the arrivals what authority they had from the State Duma for this trip and these negotiations. Whereas the deputies had not given a moment's thought to such authority either in Petrograd or en route.

They had come together as unquestionable figures in unquestionable circumstances.

Unquestionable—but perhaps not sufficiently well known to the Emperor here in Pskov? . . .

The Emperor sat down at a small square table by the wall that sat two on each side, leaning gently against the green leather wall covering. Guchkov and Shulgin were on the other side, facing him, and Frederiks on a separate chair in the middle of the room. In the corner, at another small table, was General Naryshkin, head of the traveling chancery, who brought pencil to paper, ready to record.

Understanding that of the two, Guchkov was in charge, the Emperor nodded to him to speak.

Oh, how much Guchkov could tell this man! How many reports there had been between them, in '05 and '06, received in confidence, so that great hopes for action had been raised; later, as president of the Third Duma, his reports were misunderstood and rejected. On top of this, at various times, how many mental reports had Guchkov prepared for the Tsar, monologues to him, revelatory letters! Not one scar of the past decade had been smoothed over or forgotten. However, the reluctant monarch had evaded all those monologues, time had passed, and it was too late to say all that in reproach—except for the pleasure of revenge. Now Guchkov detected in the Tsar's eyes a lack of both hostility and confidence.

So he needed to take the shortest, straightest path and finish off his most august interlocutor, who had never completely surrendered before.

Guchkov began talking—simply, in order, the way it all was:

"Your Majesty. We have come to report to you about what has happened these past few days in Petrograd. And at the same time . . . to confer" (this was put very well) "on what measures might save the situation."

What he was not striving for was brevity. The path to the end and the desired conclusion was quite clear to him, but he himself could not state it without laying the groundwork—and the Tsar especially needed that groundwork. It was by being lengthy, thorough, and convincing in his speech that Guchkov could best push the Tsar through the impending morass of hesitations and doubts. Now he was recounting to him in detail about how it had all begun, first with the attacks on bread stores, the worker strikes, and various instances with the police, how it had spilled over to the troops, and what fires had been set, and it all really did appear before his eyes—the fires, and bonfires on the streets, the motorcars with bayonets, the deputations to the Tauride Palace. The paralysis of the former regime. How the Oranienbaum machine-gun regiments had marched in the snow. . . . And afterward, how all Moscow had joined amicably and without struggle. The fact that there had been no resistance in either capital was especially important for his argument and was in fact the most striking point: the regime had actually proved to be nonexistent!

"You see, Your Majesty, this arose not out of some plot or previously contemplated coup . . ." He hadn't given thought to how to express this, but his tongue did the expressing itself, involuntarily drawing him to the scene of the crime, the way it often draws the criminal. "Rather, this is a popular movement that burst forth from the very soil and immediately acquired an anarchic imprint. It was this anarchic character of the movement that frightened us, the public figures, the most. To keep the rebellion from becoming total anarchy, we formed the Provisional Committee of the State Duma. And began to take measures to return officers to their command over the junior ranks. I myself personally visited many units and tried to convince the junior ranks to maintain calm. However, besides us in the same Duma building another committee has been meeting—workers' deputies. And, unfortunately, we are under its power and even its censorship. Their slogan is a socialist republic and land to the peasants, and this has gripped the soldiers. There is a danger that they will sweep us moderates aside. Their movement is overwhelming us. And then Petrograd will fall wholly in their hands."

This revelation of the true state of affairs may have held an improvidence that Guchkov had not accounted for. After all, their Provisional Committee was here considered an all-powerful government, which was the only reason why they were conducting negotiations, otherwise who were they and why had they come?

Sometimes, though, meeting the Emperor's unconcealed, sincere eyes, Guchkov could tell that in his eyes certain faint sparks of hope that had apparently been there at first were now being extinguished. Obviously this complete truth had a surer effect on the Emperor: these men who had come were moderates, not fierce enemies of the throne, as once depicted, and an inclination arose not to obey them as the real authority but to help them as the quasi-allies they'd turned out to be.

Occasionally Guchkov would gaze into the Emperor's face, but for most of his speech he didn't even look, his head inclined downward, his eyes on the table—to concentrate better? Or hesitant to triumph too openly over his old enemy? For some reason he avoided a direct gaze.

He was agitated. He spoke in a muffled voice, pausing, not always in grammatical agreement.

While the Emperor, leaning sideways against the train car wall, had also lowered his head and stopped looking at Guchkov.

They conversed as if they were divided not by this small table but by hundreds of versts of telegraph wire.

And now came an unquestionably convincing and advantageous argument, to which they must be better attuned here than anywhere else: What if the mutinous movement spilled over to the front? After all, everything was flammable material, and any military unit, if it fell under the movement's influence, would immediately be infected. Therefore it was hopeless to send troops against Petrograd; once they came in contact with the Petrograd garrison, they would inevitably go over to its side.

There had not yet been such an instance, and what had happened with the Borodino Regiment was very different (actually, the Tsar probably didn't even know about that incident). However, Guchkov was not only trying to scare him, but was sure of it himself. He had also had occasion to see the dissolute Luga garrison—and this was no longer Petrograd. Why wouldn't it go on like this?

"Any struggle is pointless for you, Sire. Suppressing this movement is not in your power!"

Was it so, or was it not, or was it embellished to beat back the Tsar's hope and conceal what had provoked the Duma deputies' own dismay? The Emperor neither objected nor disputed. His bowed head was still and his face impenetrable. He sat there apparently the calmest of them all.

He only ever became agitated right before the decisive moment, but when it began he would calm down. Right now he was utterly calm, having learned that they had brought him no relief whatsoever. He lost his last agitation along with his last hope. He listened with indifference—as to something new? Or was he merely verifying what he had decided for himself?

He was also privately surprised at how decently Guchkov was behaving, not at all highhandedly. He had anticipated insulting behavior.

After excoriating someone outside the door for not sending the deputation to him first, Ruzsky walked in. He asked neither for permission to be present, other than a nod of the head, nor to join them as the fourth at their table—but sat down on the third side of the table next to Shulgin, fiddling irritably with the cords of his aiguillettes.

Hammer-like notes now appeared in Guchkov's even voice, as if he wanted finally to make sure he had gotten through to the Tsar. He recounted implacably how people had come to congratulate the Duma and recognize its authority—deputations from His Personal Convoy, from His Personal Railroad Regiment, from the Combined Guards Regiment, and even from the Tsarskoye Selo palace police. Everyone, all the trusted men who had anything to do with guarding the Emperor's person.

Indeed, it was noticeable that this had touched the Emperor; his brows twitched, his shoulder jerked.

Guchkov interpreted the Tsar's incredible tranquility up until now by his reduced awareness and reduced sensitivity to how all society thought of him. He himself never forgot the Emperor's stunning tranquility at his Peterhof audience in the summer of 1906: such imperturbable calm alongside mutinous Kronstadt! At the time, Guchkov concluded from this royal placidity that everyone was going to perish. Russia was going to perish. Now, too, he thought that a normal person could not listen so calmly to news so terrible for himself. The fact that at this fraction of a moment the Emperor had expressed agitation was proof of the same thing: in the midst of Russia's terrible days, was this the first thing to have struck him? Had it not been for the Convoy's betrayal, would he have understood what an abyss he stood over?

Developing this motif even more: All these units had been ordered to continue protecting the individuals assigned to them. However, other Tsarskoye Selo units were in rebellion, the common crowd was armed, and a *danger* (Guchkov did not say outright "for your family") of course did exist.

He was trying to jolt the Emperor out of his placidity.

But the Emperor, again, did not show anything.

Indeed, despite all his simplicity, something in him would not let it be forgotten that he was the Tsar.

And so, the Duma Committee consisted entirely of supporters of a constitutional monarchy. But the people had a profound awareness of the government's mistakes, especially the Supreme Power's. Therefore, some *act* was needed that would influence the popular consciousness. Like the lash of a whip that would immediately alter the general mood. Actually, for all the workers and soldiers who took part in the disturbances, the old regime's return threatened retribution against them. They no longer had a way out either. There was only one way out for everyone: a change of regime. The sole path was to put the burden of Supreme governance into other hands. Russia could be saved, as could the monarchical principle, and the dynasty, if, for instance, His Majesty announced that he was handing power over to his young son under Grand Duke Mikhail's regency.

At this, the Emperor interrupted for the first time, rather timidly:

"But have you given sufficient thought to the impression this will make on Russia . . . ? Where have you gleaned the assurance that with my departure even more blood won't be shed?"

Guchkov, who was stiffening badly, and Shulgin, who was quick with inspiration, in two voices and a single thought told him that it was precisely *this* that the Duma Committee wished to avoid. That through abdication Russia could, without any obstacles and with full domestic unity, end the war victoriously.

"If one even judges on the basis of Kiev," Shulgin broke his silence with conviction, "public opinion has now drawn far back from the monarchical. If there is resistance, then the numbers will be insignificant. On the contrary, we must fear serious internecine strife if the abdication drags out."

What? Kiev, too? The ancient capital, monarchical Kiev? . . .

The Emperor looked at this well-known, once devoted, and even outstanding monarchist, at his small, sharp, dandyish mustache, apparently for the first time in the conversation—and sadly. And asked not him but Guchkov again:

"Won't there be upheaval in the Cossack provinces?"

Guchkov smiled.

"Oh no, Your Majesty! The Cossacks are all on the side of the new order! This manifested itself clearly in Petrograd in the conduct of the Don regiments."

Ruzsky was growing nervous. Everything was being said all over again, and the Emperor could go an hour like this without saying anything, as if the abdication didn't exist at all. Guchkov was wasting his effort! Ruzsky had in his pocket the afternoon telegram written in the royal hand!

However, having no opportunity to interrupt in the Emperor's presence and make his own statement out loud (although it was high time this unbearable etiquette were broken!), Ruzsky fidgeted, leaned toward Shulgin, and defying decorum, whispered something supposedly to him but in fact so that it would reach Guchkov, too:

"*This* is a done deal, already signed. I . . ."

It was *he* who had broken the Emperor! That had to become known!

But Guchkov didn't hear or understand! Before this meeting two words would have been enough so that now he wouldn't have had to say this at all or lure the former emperor into the temptation that he might cling to a corner of the throne! Guchkov didn't understand and with enflamed eyes behind his pince-nez and a crooked tie, he once again insisted:

"Events are moving so quickly that right now radical elements consider Rodzyanko, myself, and other moderate elements traitors. Of course they are opposed to that solution because they see in it the salvation of the monarchical principle."

He did not say "which is dear to all of us," but that was the only possible meaning. Whether previously contemplated or of its own accord, the new arrivals' position had shaped up so that they had not arrived as opponents or as counterparts but actually as allies saving all things holy, together with the Emperor.

"So, Your Majesty, only under these conditions can we make an attempt" (still just an attempt!) "to instill order. This is what Shulgin and I have been instructed to tell you. . . . You, Sire, have no other choice either. No matter what military unit you send against Petrograd right now, I repeat . . ."

No longer able to restrain himself, setting his eyepiece more firmly, Ruzsky corrected him:

"It's worse than that. There isn't even a military unit you could send."

This was strongly stated. Who better to know than the commander-in-chief closest to the capital?

(But had anyone asked or, for that matter, given any thought to whether Petrograd had a military unit it could send against GHQ?)

Now, all of a sudden, quite out of the blue, the Emperor understood exactly what animal Ruzsky had always reminded him of. A weasel! A bespectacled weasel because of the strong cheekbones flattened over his temples. Or rather, a young weasel but with an old expression.

Frederiks sat there heavy and downcast, as if he were dozing and threatening to fall off his chair.

Guchkov missed Ruzsky's hint, but he saw with his own eyes that there would be no struggle, that the Tsar was close to capitulation.

Without noticing it, he was more and more speaking with this man, recently ruler and sovereign, who formerly could easily have had him exiled or arrested (but had not done so), more and more speaking down to him, lecturing him, like someone not fully matured or fully grown. When he had proven to him irrevocably that the only solution was to hand the throne over and heard no objections, he wanted to show his magnanimity:

"Naturally, before deciding on this, you should give it careful thought." Ceding to his psyche: "And pray." Though more firmly: "Nonetheless, you must decide no later than tomorrow. Because tomorrow we will not be in a position to give you good advice if you ask us for it. The crowd is extremely agitated and aggressive, and it is capable of anything."

Guchkov paused and then repeated condescendingly:

"Perhaps, Sire, you would like to be alone now? For contemplation, for prayer?"

The Emperor gave Guchkov a wild, astonished look.

Guchkov placed before the Emperor the creased draft of abdication that they had composed en route.

Yes, yes, Shulgin had sensed accurately why it was right that he had come. His presence here erased any hint of coercion or humiliation. Two monarchists—because Guchkov, too, was a monarchist—two well-bred men, without weapons, had had to quietly approach the Emperor and report on what was going on in weary, hoarse voices. In this situation, it was not humiliating for the monarch, who loved his country, to abdicate.

But the Emperor remained silent, occasionally smoothing his mustache with his thumb and index finger. His shoulders drooped in a decidedly un-Tsar-like way, but like the most ordinary of men. He looked with his large, blue, aching eyes. After this long hearing, he finally said:

"I have thought about this. . . . I have . . ."

Ruzsky was eating his heart out that he couldn't unfurl before the deputies the prepared abdication. Although the Tsar no longer seemed to be Tsar, his entire former authority lay there, folded in quarters, right here, in the inside pocket of Ruzsky's tunic, although etiquette's authority, inculcated since he was young, would not release him. He did not dare announce this himself. But this unsporting tone, this drawn out "I have thought about this . . ."—as if there were already an uttered agreement—revealed to Ruzsky a right (this is how he thought of it):

the right to pull it out of his pocket and as he returned it to the Emperor himself, handing it across the table, to say:

"The Emperor has already decided this matter."

This was a very successful move! Retreat was now cut off for the Emperor!

But Nikolai II, finally getting back what he had let go, what he had not been able to get from the commander-in-chief all day, did not unfold it or tell the Duma deputies anything but simply slipped it into his pocket.

He stole back his own abdication? What a mistake for the general! To surrender so foolishly!

Ruzsky himself prepared now to announce it, to say loudly *what* was in that document that had not been destroyed and was still right here, in the Tsar's pocket.

No, to Ruzsky's relief, the Tsar was not being cunning. Was he searching for words? Yes. He wasn't upset, though. Did he know how to be upset? Did he possess that ordinary human quality? He was calmer than everyone else, as if this episode concerned him least of all.

But he was frankly sad. And so looked at Guchkov, who was not looking for a meeting of glances.

Without addressing anyone, he clearly spoke to Guchkov alone, however, and his voice was very plain:

"I have been thinking it over. All morning. All day. And what do you think?" He retreated in the shy tone of the petitioner. "If he accepts the crown, can the heir remain with me and his mother until his majority?"

And he looked at him defenselessly and with hope. Guchkov shook his head confidently:

"Of course not. No one would entrust the future Emperor's upbringing to the person who . . ." — and his voice became firm, this was not about those present — "brought the country to its present state."

"What am I to do, then? . . ." the Tsar asked in a very quiet, cheerless voice.

"You, Your Majesty, will have to go abroad."

The Emperor nodded sadly.

"Here is my decision, then, gentlemen. At first I was ready to agree to abdication in favor of my son. It was this that I signed today at three o'clock in the afternoon. But now, having thought it over one more time, I have realized . . . that I am incapable of parting with my son."

Guchkov looked up abruptly at the Tsar.

The Emperor's voice was anything but statesmanly. But it was also not indifferent and shuddered with pain:

"I have realized that . . . I hope you will understand this . . . His health is delicate, and I cannot . . . Therefore I have decided to cede the throne, but not to my son. Rather to Grand Duke Mikhail Aleksandrovich."

And he cast down his eyes. He was having a hard time speaking.

The deputies exchanged astonished glances for the first time in the entire conversation. Shulgin stepped in — hastily, as if for fear they would beat him out:

"Your Majesty! This proposal catches us unawares. We envisioned only abdication in favor of the Heir Apparent. We came here to propose only what we have told you."

Such a simple alteration, such a simple exchange of two objects—but the deputies were completely unprepared for it, as were those who had sent them, and no one had contemplated this before. . . .

Guchkov, too, sought a rejoinder:

"It was felt that the image of the young heir would greatly alleviate . . . for the masses . . . the fact of the transfer of power. . . ."

Everyone there, in the new government and in the Duma leadership, was counting on Aleksei's minority and Mikhail's lack of independence. . . . Where did this leave them now?

"Then will you allow me," Shulgin was searching, "to confer with Aleksandr Ivanovich?"

The Emperor did not object. But he did not get up to go.

He wasn't the one to be going!

Were the deputies to leave?

But they, too, were distraught and didn't leave. Apparently, Guchkov did not seek Shulgin's advice; he would have presumed to decide himself.

But the Emperor had his own vastly difficult burden. And he had no one to go off and consult with, but here once again had to ask those hostile arrivals about the same thing:

"But I have to be certain . . . how all the rest of Russia will view this." And his distraught blue gaze sought an answer from them, avoiding Ruzsky: "Won't this cause . . ." he couldn't find a way to put it discreetly.

"No! No, Your Majesty, it won't!" This Guchkov knew firmly. "The danger is not in this at all. The danger is that others will declare a republic before us—that's when . . . That's when the internecine strife will begin. We must hasten to strengthen the monarchy before that happens."

To Shulgin, too, this question was clearer than this unexpected hitch with the succession. He had long since been trying to break in with a monologue, which was why he had come:

"Your Majesty!" he began heatedly and convincingly. "Allow me to provide an explanation of the situation in which the State Duma has been forced to function."

He described how the impertinent crowd had inundated the entire Tauride Palace and how the Duma Committee had just two small rooms.

"They're dragging in all their prisoners, and it's lucky for them that they are, since this frees them of mob law. . . . The Duma is hell! It's a madhouse!"

But apparently this heated characterization did not strengthen the arriving deputies' position. Shulgin took a new tack:

"However, we maintain the symbol of the country's administration, and only thanks to this can some order still be preserved. Look—rail movement has not stopped. But inevitably we are going to be entering into a decisive battle against leftist elements, and for this we need firm ground. Your Majesty, help us create it!"

They were simply pleading, not forcing him to do anything!

But the Emperor still could not bring himself to be convinced, could not grasp this:

"But I would like to have a guarantee, gentlemen, that as a consequence of my departure even more blood will not be shed. . . ."

Oh, quite the contrary! Quite the contrary! Only abdication will save Russia from the prospect of civil war!

Indeed, this would at least be peaceableness. It would at least mean no retributions whatsoever against anyone.

With respect to the Emperor's change in the draft, naturally, here we must . . . At least confer for a quarter hour.

But Guchkov accepted it more readily. After all, he had come here knowing this man's incomparable stubbornness, anticipating the most exhausting and perhaps unsuccessful single combat, so that he might have to return with only a responsible government and a small piece of a constitution—and now everything had snapped, the abdication had been served up on a platter, the goal of the long social struggle had been snatched away, and they had to take what was being offered.

He could not at this moment hate this man. He said magnanimously:

"Your Majesty! Naturally, I do not consider that I have any right to interfere in paternal feelings. In this sphere there is no place for politics, and any kind of pressure is impermissible. Against your proposal, any objection . . ."

Faint satisfaction appeared on the Emperor's long-suffering face.

They had found the point at which he would dig in his heels: the right to his only son!

The deputies were at a loss for words, and the Emperor did not force them to make their arguments. He rose quietly and went to his train car, leaving behind the draft brought by the deputies.

Without explaining whether he was giving them time to think. Or had he already made up his mind?

They dispersed around the train car and smoked. Broad-shouldered General Danilov, who had not been invited and who had been shifting from foot to foot enviously on the platform, joined them.

Then they started talking, and it occurred to them that there ought to be special laws of succession, and it wouldn't be a bad idea to consult them. Count Naryshkin, who up until now had been keeping a record of the conversation, went out and brought back from the chancellery the required volume of laws of the Russian Empire. They leafed through it, searching to find whether a father-guardian can abdicate in favor of his son. They didn't find anything.

Nor did they find types of abdication—or even a section on abdication in general.

They'd been fighting for twenty years in hopes of limiting or removing the Tsar, and no one had given a thought to the law. Wasn't that something.

Guchkov and Shulgin now conferred, or rather, each thought his own chaotic thoughts.

If Mikhail became the central figure, he could carry out an unexpected, independent policy. The monarchy might not take on the proper, desired form of the monarch reigning but not ruling. Such an outcome contradicted the Provisional Government's decision and desires.

They just hadn't gotten that far; you couldn't grasp it right away. Shulgin would have said, with a little romantic appeal: "Your Majesty! Aleksei is the natural heir, the embodiment of the monarchic idea, which everyone understands. He bears no stains or reproaches. There are quite a few people in Russia prepared to die for this little Tsar. . . ."

Might this way have its own pluses, though? If the Tsarevich remained on the throne, it would be very hard to isolate him from his father's influence and, most important, his mother, who was so hated by all. They would retain their former influence; the parents' exit from power would seem fictitious. If the boy remained on the throne but was separated from his parents in actuality, they would go abroad—and that would affect his weak health, and he would be thinking about his parents all the time, and he might nurture unkind feelings toward those who had separated them.

Criticizing was the easiest thing to do, and now Danilov offered Guchkov his criticism. Wouldn't it be dangerous to accept a system not envisaged by succession? Wouldn't abdication in favor of Mikhail give rise to major complications as a consequence?

Guchkov punted the tiresome Danilov over to Shulgin. And Shulgin, who'd been feverishly turning things over in his mind, was inspired to find and come up with something else: if, God forbid, the next monarch should have to abdicate (given the situation, this would be no great surprise), then Mikhail could peacefully abdicate, but Aleksei, a minor, could not abdicate, and then what? . . .

Meanwhile, Ruzsky, insulted that his entire role in the abdication had been blurred, rebuked the deputies. How could they come on such an important matter of state and not bring along a single volume of basic laws, or a lawyer?

But they hadn't expected this decision! You had to imagine the present Petrograd situation!

But here was an important argument: if the boy took the throne, then would his oath of loyalty to the constitution be legally competent? It was this oath that the Duma Committee had wanted, so that the new Tsar could not restore the throne's independence. They could demand this oath immediately from Mikhail. As regent, Mikhail would have to defend all the Heir's rights in full. As Tsar, Mikhail might be limited as he ascended, and that would facilitate . . .

Guchkov had no desire to accept the Emperor's alternative. But his weary brain could not find a serious argument against it.

He was quite stunned at the extent to which the Tsar had not resisted abdication! Those who had lived for decades under this cumbersome imperial regime could not have anticipated such a thing! This success had fallen into their hands—how could they not take it? In a single step, Guchkov had taken a unique step in Russian history. He may have reined in the revolutionary turmoil—and saved the monarchic principle as well!

Apparently no one was waiting for their decision: the Emperor had not returned. Did he consider the matter decided? Or had he gone off to ponder it himself?

Reasoning from the converse: if he did not now agree, did that mean there would be no abdication at all? That meant they would leave empty-handed. And given their status as Tauride Palace captives, would the matter of abdication simply be passed on to the insolent Petrograd rabble, the Soviet of Workers' Deputies? The worst calamity, which had to be avoided. That would mean the guillotine and a republic. . . .

So they had to take the abdication they were given. There was no choice here.

Most important, they had to get it quickly and leave in an hour in order to announce it as quickly as possible in Petrograd!

They discussed this in the salon car. Here, at the Court, they knew how to behave, but Frederiks was crushed and his head was hanging. Guchkov tried to cheer him up, saying he would inquire and take measures to rescue the countess.

In that hour on the platform, about a hundred people of all sorts assembled between the imperial and deputy trains, read the revolutionary leaflets being distributed, and shouted hurrah! The officer of the guard wanted to give orders to disperse this crowd, but the aide-de-camp stopped him. His Majesty had ordered that no one was to be touched or driven away.

By eleven, the shouts on the platform were still intensifying and they were coming closer to the imperial train. In the adjacent train car, the text of abdication was being composed to these shouts. Guchkov, taking advantage of an idle pause, went out on the salon car's back landing and announced to the agitated crowd:

"Gentlemen, calm down! Our father the Tsar wholly agrees with us. He has given us even more than we anticipated."

"Hurrah! Hurrah!" kept intensifying.

At a quarter past eleven, the Emperor returned—no more shaken than when he'd left, self-possessed as before, and held out two typewritten sheets of paper:

"Here is the act. Read it."

Everyone had stood up at the Emperor's entrance and they were standing now. And Guchkov, and Shulgin from the side, leaned over the table and tripped over themselves reading under their breath.

"In the days of the great struggle against a foreign foe . . . The incipient popular upheavals threaten to undermine the tenacious conduct of the war. . . . In these decisive days We have deemed it a duty of conscience to facilitate Our people's closest union and consolidation . . . and in agreement with the State Duma, We have considered it desirable to abdicate the throne of the Russian state. . . . Not wishing to be separated from Our beloved son . . . We leave Our heritage to Our brother . . . We call on all faithful sons of the Fatherland . . . to bring Russia into the path of victory, prosperity, and glory. . . ."

And—that Germany thirsted to enslave Russia. And—that the Emperor was withdrawing for the good of a Russian victory.

Ruzsky saw that this was far from the Manifesto that had been sent from GHQ. Had the Tsar really rewritten it himself so quickly and smoothly?

Guchkov did not object to anything. But Shulgin, following more precisely the constitutional spirit that had propelled them, suggested that Grand Duke Mikhail Aleksandrovich be instructed to offer up a national oath of loyalty to the legislative institutions.

The Emperor furrowed his brow, thought about it, and added: "taking the step with an inviolable oath."

Shulgin pursed his lips at the style: he hadn't added "national," and what other oath is there than an inviolable one? But he didn't argue.

He suggested that the time be noted—three o'clock in the afternoon— when the Emperor had reached his decision to abdicate even without them.

So that people would not later offer the reproach that the deputies had extorted the abdication.

For Guchkov, on the contrary, such a notation belittled his mission. But he held his tongue. They noted the time: three o'clock in the afternoon.

And the Emperor sweepingly signed the abdication—in ordinary pencil.

Guchkov thought that in such troubled times one shouldn't take risks with the authentic Manifesto. Could they type out a second original and leave it with Ruzsky?

They took it off for one more to be typed.

Now the three of them—the former Emperor and the two delegates of the new government—had twenty minutes of silence face to face.

Actually, he couldn't just drop everything as someone else's business. Order must not be violated. The throne to his brother, fine. But who was to lead the government? And who was to take on the Supreme Command?

The deputies approved: it was a good idea to make arrangements. Strengthen the succession of power. And date it an hour earlier than the abdication, so that it would have legal effect.

So who would chair the cabinet?

The Emperor didn't want it to be Rodzyanko. Here was who to appoint: Krivoshein.

The deputies advised:

"Prince Lvov."

Fine.

And the Supreme Command, of course, to Nikolai Nikolaevich. Who else?

Decrees were written to the Senate. This would strengthen both appointees.

They were handed over for retyping.

Now there was silence.

And then, then . . . The hardest thing was talking about oneself. What an unprecedented condition—without a crown. And where was he to go? . . .

The right tone had yet to be found. Who was subordinate to whom here now or not? It wasn't good to act without permission, but it was also humiliating to ask . . .

The Emperor jerked his shoulder.

"Will I not encounter obstacles if I go to Tsarskoye Selo now?"

Guchkov's brow went up like a barrier. That afternoon he had assumed as much, but . . . Behind the Tsar he saw his chief foe, with her imperious, sinister posture.

(Should he be allowed to be rejoined with his will? No. He might rescind the abdication.)

Out loud, he did not forbid it. But his entire tensed look, the redness of his brow. His silence itself.

A protracted silence.

Then he said there was an uprising in Luga. One could not guarantee safe passage.

The Emperor swayed ever so slightly—and sagged as if from a blow.

(He couldn't go to Tsarskoye Selo? But that's the only thing he wanted. That was why he had hurried to get through all these formalities quickly. And now he couldn't? . . .)

After all, he only wanted to go to Tsarskoye Selo for a while, until the children recuperated. And then take them all to Livadia, if he could . . .

So now where? To GHQ? . . .

He had to go to GHQ. He had to hand over affairs there, too.

And he could summon Mama from Kiev to Mogilev. To say goodbye.

If he was now going to have to quit Russia?

"To GHQ" was spoken and hung there: as a question? a statement? Was he asking permission? Not asking permission? . . . It was a confusing condition.

Guchkov took another look at the Tsar in his full pince-nez, barely concealing the way he saw him frightened.

(GHQ, the center of their forces? With Alekseev and without Alix? He wouldn't dare try anything there. He was incapable of anything.)

Permitted.

General Ruzsky actually cringed in bewilderment and protest. How could they let an abdicated Supreme Commander go to GHQ?

But he couldn't bring himself to object to Guchkov out loud.

They brought the second document.

The deputies suggested that Frederiks countersign both of the Emperor's signatures. The Emperor nodded. Frederiks sat down heavily and picked up an automatic pen. He spent a very long time tracing it out, with tortuous efforts, as never before.

Well, the Emperor also asked the deputies to sign, to acknowledge receipt of the document.

When you live with wolves . . .
The clock on the salon car wall said a quarter past eleven.
They said goodbye.
Ruzsky asked the deputies to come to his car.

And the royal train could start for Mogilev. Having completed a point-less, convulsive, three-day circle, having lost his crown, he could now re-turn to the place he should never have left.
The trains waited there for more than an hour longer.
They drank their night tea with the suite. But even here they didn't speak about the abdication.
In an everyday tone, the Emperor remarked:
"How long they've kept me here."

[3 5 0]

Nothing had changed in the ministerial pavilion's stuffy, smoke-filled rooms. Night was approaching, the first for some, the third for others, and once again they had to slumber through it sitting up, with the lights on and without undressing, as if it were an agonizing, badly organized train station. So many prisoners had been added today that having two lying on a sofa, like Protopopov and Bark, was now a luxury, and three had to sit up together.
All the arrested men were far from young, were mostly old men, as old as eighty even, and were not used to going several days without washing or changing their linen; they found all this excruciating.
Admiral Kartsev kept growling: "Air!"
Never in their lives had they been torn away from their families, and now their alarm was even more about their families and homes, whether they'd been looted. After all, revolution was looting first and foremost. What else?
In all these days, the arrested men had not been able to talk among themselves except for ten minutes when Karaulov, when he seemingly be-came the commandant, permitted conversations, but soon after, unfortu-nately, Kerensky came in and discovered this and in a dramatic voice told the guard that he was again forbidding this.
No matter who was replaced in the guard, or who was replaced as com-mandant, the true authority over all fates for some reason was Kerensky. The old men were afraid of him, this recent pest.
They were also in the dark about what was going on in Petrograd and Russia. As men of governmental habits, placed in this enforced inaction, they found it impossible not to think about the unfolding unknown, not to construct assumptions as to how events had gone, and whether a new gov-ernment existed, and how the Emperor viewed it, and how the Emperor was now to act.

From surveying who was present, they saw that there were no old authorities left in the capital. Everyone considered Protopopov a demon of evil and saw not without satisfaction that he, too, was here, recently such a prominent figure who here had immediately become as crumpled, frightened, and aged as a plucked fowl.

They asked an ensign for newspapers. He refused. Then they brought two issues of *Izvestia of the Soviet of Workers' Deputies* (what a wild title!), and the former dignitaries took this vileness in avidly, read the inexpressible language on the bad paper with muddy stains, and interpreted them for themselves, how to understand it and what stood behind it.

Naturally, they realized that they wouldn't be kept here in the ministerial pavilion forever, but what was next? Would they let them go home? Interrogate them? So excruciating was it to sit here that they would have preferred having something change, and soon!

That's what they thought, but at close to eleven o'clock in the evening the door opened wide and in walked Ensign Znamensky, and behind him a reinforcing detail of Preobrazhensky men with rifles, two more ensigns from the Mikhailovsky School, and then the taut and menacing Kerensky holding a document, and the prisoners' hearts started to pound. Everyone in the first room instantly realized that something irrevocable was just about to happen, and now they feared having to leave the warm and not that uncomfortable pavilion, their defensive little corner, even, in the face of the terrible future.

Such already was the atmosphere surrounding Kerensky's slender figure, and he himself looked so demandingly, so confidently, at no matter whom he'd been addressing these past few days, that the old dignitaries rose from the chairs and sofas—gray-haired and ramshackle, wearing general's uniforms—and stood in front of the until recently insignificant deputy.

Now, even more aware than all these old men of the majesty of the moment, and although he himself had only barely seen the inside of a prison in 1905, restoring from long memory and by the brilliant gift of his actor nature, Kerensky grasped both the voice and the significance and announced shrilly:

"Everyone I am now going to name!"—he was holding a list, but also for theatricality; he had no need of it—"shall be sent away immediately!"

And he had the sense to stop there, without saying **where.** That was the most frightening thing! They could be *sent* to the next world, too!

And Stürmer, the most unrestrained, most broken-down old man, with his bristly beard, tall, frail, four months ago a detested prime minister, in a pathetic, immediately tearful voice, asked:

"But who is going to guarantee that they won't behead us?"

Out of fright and awkwardness he had named a form of execution no one used any longer, but not only did this not sound funny, it was all the more frightening. One could just picture somewhere outside of town a scaffold under a streetlamp in the frosty night and the executioner's pole-axe.

Kerensky let the question pass with dignity and began reading out each name in full voice, and then left a pause, as if letting each chord finish sounding.

Some were in other rooms, and Kerensky went there to read the entire list, beginning with the introductory, "Everyone I am now going to name."

Shabby Protopopov caught passing soldiers by their greatcoats and asked in a loud whisper,

"Do you know *where*?"

The small, hunched, almost-dwarfish Minister of War, Belyaev, with his empty eyes, not having caught up with the fleeting Kerensky, stood up straight in front of an ensign:

"I am the most honest of men and I have been defamed. I was only doing my job and never interfered in anything. I am subject to discharge with a pension . . ."

Znamensky answered him and the others in a bass voice:

"Get dressed! Quickly collect your things!"

Old Goremykin, having put his blue St. Andrew's chain on his frock coat, unwilling to part with it, now already in his fur coat and hat, was ready before everyone else. He had passed through so many governmental storms safely and knew that without the Lord not a single hair would fall. Long had he lived in this world like a guest detained. He did—and didn't—watch, and he whispered a prayer. He was led away.

Golitsyn passed like a polite shadow.

Dobrovolsky sagged, depressed; what price would he have to pay for his two-month-long ministry?

Protopopov kept collecting his things and just couldn't get ready, although he had nothing to collect.

It had reached gross, bulky Khabalov.

One might have thought that Shcheglovitov would be least prepared of all. After all, when he was arrested they'd brought him to the Tauride Palace without his coat, and he had nothing to wear on top. But he asked for nothing. Round-headed and tall, he bore himself so calmly and knowingly, as if he were the one in charge of the whole ceremony. Or as if by doing so he meant to insult Kerensky's lofty impulse.

One of the officers got concerned and sent for a soldier's greatcoat for Shcheglovitov. They brought one, a bit tight, but they put it on him.

Down the corridor, all the way to the entrance, the back entrance, the entire Preobrazhensky sentry company was lined up, spaced out, and this was menacing, like for an execution, with the dignitaries being led one by one, spaced out—and they encountered no one else in the whole dim corridor.

Everyone was silent, there were no orders shouted, everything had been coordinated. It was frightening.

Maklakov was walking with a bandaged, injured head.

Outside the door there were several Duma deputies or other newly important individuals. They took two prisoners in each of the five closed motorcars that drove up, putting them next to each other in the back seat, and facing backward, looking at them, knees to knees, they put a party representative and a sergeant with a drawn revolver aimed at the prisoners. There was an officer next to each driver.

Znamensky warned each seated pair, savoring this: Don't move, don't look to either side. Any attempt to flee will bring on the use of a weapon.

As if any of them were capable of escaping.

The motorcars' curtains were drawn; they couldn't see where they were going. The big revolver, which boded no good, was aimed in turn at first one, then the other.

Once again, they did not get to speak to their sole neighbor.

Protopopov so wanted to find out, to confer, to conjecture! But fate had brought him together with the somber Belyaev, who even without the convoy would not have spoken with him out of caution. Yes, his soldiers had been correct dubbing him "dead head." After all, Protopopov had himself for some reason nominated him to be Minister of War! And he had gone and ruined everything.

Maklakov ended up next to Makarov, the Minister of the Interior after Stolypin and lately Minister of Justice, dismissed by the Emperor for obstinacy: his refusal to close the case against Sukhomlinov and Manasevich and his unsatisfactory investigation into Rasputin's murder. So that he himself would have actually been useful to the Duma, and only became one of the ten most dangerous and prime culprits on account of Kerensky's revenge.

And so they went. In the weak light of the passing streetlamps, they could see that the sergeant was not lowering his large revolver from their torsos. But the fidgety civilian escorting them suddenly broke the silence and addressed Makarov:

"You don't know me, Your Excellency. Though seven years ago you sent me into Yakutsk exile."

It was obvious the entire escort procedure was affording him satisfaction.

Administrative exile? Possibly. But people ran away from there freely.

"And what's your name?"

"Zenzinov."

No, he didn't remember. And the name was rather clownish.

"I'm a well-known SR. I'm a member of the CC!" he proudly recommended himself.

And these were the terrible revolutionaries? He could picture just how distorted everything governmental must look to them from below. And how everything had been turned around in their minds.

But all kinds of distortion occurred from the ministerial height as well. Makarov had been resting up in the Crimea with a bad heart. Summoned by telegram, he had arrived in Petersburg, where the Duma dais was languishing for answers, and before he could sort things out, he'd gone out and announced that it was the worker crowd itself that had attacked the troops, and the cavalry captain had had no choice but to open fire. Years pass, though, and it's shameful and painful to recall.

In ordinary life, we always blame an external cause. But when misfortune overtakes us, then we rake up the internal, root cause.

At sixty, Makarov had had his day. But he had one son, and that was everything in life. What would happen to him under these villains?

The motorcars weren't going fast. Sometimes, evidently, they were stopped by patrols, and the driver in front would shout:

"Motorcars of the Provisional Government!"

These five dark motorcars must have looked strange, spaced out, curtained, in the middle of the night—and all of them governmental.

They couldn't see where they were going until they went onto a bridge— the rise in the road, the evenly spaced triple streetlamps on both sides, the silhouettes—you could guess it was the Trinity Bridge.

For a while it was lighter in the motorcar.

Maklakov, bandaged up, rode as if made of stone, not letting the SR in front of him suspect his agitation. Anyone who was able to wield power and send people to prison had to be able to be sent there himself all the more.

Over the past few days, he'd had time to contemplate the vicissitudes of individual fate. Russia's vicissitudes still loomed up ahead, undiscernible.

Where in fact were they going? . . .

They'd already guessed from the Trinity Bridge, although the idea seemed outrageous.

But now obviously they'd gone through the deep, desolate gates of the Peter and Paul Fortress.

They'd forgotten about the fortress, which had just stood like a monument. For several years it had gone empty, but now the stony stronghold had been opened for the infirm and dismissed ministers.

All the motorcars stopped. And waited. Interchanges could be heard between the arriving officers and those already there.

More drove up. And an unkindly, harsh command rang out:

"Get out!"

The revolutionary representatives got out. The sergeants with revolvers got out. The dignitaries and generals started getting out one by one, looking around at the dark towers, chilled.

They were between the chief commandant's building and the mint.

A number of armed soldiers formed a wide cordon, as if expecting the dignitaries to try to break out. In addition to the fortress soldiers, a detachment of sailors had also shown up.

They didn't have time to look around but were ordered to walk over, one after another, toward the ribbed stone wall, stopping two feet short (the snow hadn't been cleared away enough there and they got stuck), and stand facing the wall without turning around.

Freezing moisture had seeped into Goremykin's boots, and for him this was the most unbearable of all.

One sensed an unbending confidence in all the commands. These were, of course, the officers of the fortress's corps de garde who had already served here five, ten, or fifteen years under these same ministers, insignificant and unknown then and now so menacingly efficient under the new government, so that it was impossible to remind or ask them about anything.

(Zenzinov recognized the prison colonel, who had once received him right here. Report him to Kerensky right away and we'll put him in jail!)

They took two at a time from the end, not using their names, an arm on the shoulder from behind—and led them away.

Single file.

Skirting the mint.

That meant to the Trubetskoy Bastion.

In one motion they led away three prime ministers. Three ministers of the interior, from different times. Three ministers of justice.

All that constituted governmental power.

Several Tsarist governments in a row were ceasing to exist in a single hour, a single minute.

Right then, the melodic bells of the clock on the Peter and Paul Cathedral began mournfully ringing "How Glorious Is Our Lord in Zion" in the bleak nighttime air.

The very same sad melody heard in their cells, back in their day, by the Decembrists and the People's Will, and . . .

[3 5 1]

A good supper after good successes and at pivotal points in life gives us a more vivid sense of them. And of ourselves in them.

It was just this kind of supper that Ruzsky proposed to the deputy delegates from the Duma or the new government, whatever they were to be considered. The supper, served in the train car by a military chef in the military way, did not hold a candle to the best Petersburg ones—there wasn't even any champagne, so essential for the moment—but the table was spread with an abundance from the Russian provinces in things smoked and pickled and a sufficient choice of beverages.

Only now, having come here and taken their seats, did they all sense that they were experiencing a liberation; it turned out they had all been quite tense.

Revolution is one thing, but the former pleasure of a good supper—that was retained.

Finally, here, without the court's stuffed scarecrows, they could speak candidly.

Yes, they had anticipated resistance from the Tsar, even desperate resistance. But for him to surrender like that? At once? . . .

"He'd already surrendered this afternoon!" Danilov said, wanting to tell them how he, too, had been present at that crucial point of the afternoon abdication. Broad-jawed and sturdy, he was already eating from the rosy ham.

"And how he demanded the telegram back, and I wouldn't give it to him!" Even Ruzsky himself was amazed. "He wanted to wiggle out of it and take the abdication back! And he would have gotten out of it. And he would have left. But I didn't allow that!"

More and more, with each passing minute, Guchkov felt relief and triumph. After all, it might have come about differently: they might have left without an abdication. The Tsar might have dug in his heels—and then what? But now they had unburdened themselves of *that* task! Now they had only to shake off the obstacles in the Tauride Palace and in Luga—and crush Germany with renewed strength!

Ruzsky had also wanted to tell them before the negotiations that the troops sent against Petrograd were a fiction, and Ruzsky had made sure that they got strung out from the start, delayed, and now they were being recalled.

Yes, it had all gone beautifully. Although, no matter his feeling of liberation and intoxication, Guchkov first got down to business:

"We will take one copy of the abdication with us and leave one at your headquarters for safekeeping, Nikolai Vladimirovich. It would be even more proper—the abdication needs to be encoded immediately—to transmit it by telegraph to the General Staff, and they can send it on to our people at the Duma. They are waiting there impatiently."

Only the two of them, he and Shulgin, had seen that Tauride Palace frenzy, and anyone who hadn't could not imagine it. Only they knew what this meant for the people in the Tauride—to find out quickly.

Yes, this was sensible. With the abdication in hand, they must not waste time even on dinner.

But to whom could they entrust the encoding besides Danilov? And oh how he wished he didn't have to tear himself away from this table and conversation with high-ranking guests!

And also, even more swiftly—send a brief telegram to Rodzyanko from the two deputies saying "assent obtained."

There was no avoiding it, so Danilov took the telegram and one abdication and went to town.

Aleksandr Ivanovich's health had long forced him to watch his eating and drinking, and what made the table precious to him was not this vital fleshly delight, or even any dinner table conversation—for example, right now he was not particularly well disposed toward it. Rather it was this feeling of soaring above the tablecloth and glasses.

This achievement! His mission — perhaps his entire life's mission — was complete. No longer did he have to struggle to build a conspiracy and seek out supporters. And nothing threatened him if the conspiracy was revealed.

Liberation!

Indeed! Clear features of his former design showed through, there was even an undoubted insight: between Tsarskoye Selo and GHQ, as planned, almost en route, with just a slight detour to Pskov. And *where* had the meeting with the Tsar taken place? In his train car! The very car they were supposed to seize! There was another idea in the conspiracy as well, that Alekseev submit, not interfere — and indeed he hadn't! There was not simply a resemblance here — this was *precisely the same* intention: seize the bewildered Tsar and wrest an abdication from him. He wouldn't be able to refuse. Such was the prognosis! And after that let him go to England.

"Gentlemen!" Gray-whiskered Ruzsky, with the square crewcut, raised his glass with concentration, and his eyes swiveled behind his glasses, and sitting right there was one other witness to the event, Savich, provisions chief for the front. "We are the first Russians to be able to drink the first toast in Russia not to the future Russia but to the Russia that has already arrived! Everyone will learn this later, but we are the first! An entire era of freedom has begun, not a single century, an entire era of Freedom from which there is no going back, into the darkness!"

But Ruzsky's face, even when he wanted to express joy, still retained something indelibly bleak.

Shulgin was very much created for handsome, lofty moments, though. He perceived them with an inner trembling. He wasn't any kind of political figure at all, this was all a misunderstanding, he was an artist of the gesture and word, and only for that reason did he shine so in his Duma speeches. He was a dramatic artist, a writer, and even a dreamer — flights of fancy made reality sway for him, and this was when his best discoveries were born. But now, utterly inexplicably, a ballad for some reason sounded inside him:

> Recall the waltz's sound, so very splendid,
> that springtime night, the hour so late . . .

But as if for spite, that lofty moment, that keen, unique moment was spoiled for him by a migraine. The corner of his head near his right temple started hurting badly.

And Ruzsky was recounting how the Tsar had been behaving these past few days. But was there a major argument? Oh yes, there was an argument, and what an argument, yesterday, but today he consented more easily.

"Gentlemen" — Guchkov couldn't help but be amazed — "think about it. Why did he have to cling to his prerogatives for decades if he was going to lay them down so lightly in a single day? And this was our opponent? . . . Is that it? . . ."

Our opponent? Shulgin was shaken. No, even in his thoughts he could not apply such a word to the Emperor. He was a beloved interlocutor who had to be convinced to concede in the name of Russia. And now, things would be good and safe for both Russia and the Emperor himself.

"He was incapable of ruling this country, gentlemen!" The slight Ruzsky opined, leaning back. "His is too unstable a character."

It was reported that the royal train was pulling out. Did they need anything? What were their instructions?

Instructions? They exchanged glances. No. They weren't going to go say goodbye. Accounts had been settled, so let him go.

There was one thing which Aleksandr Ivanovich could not help but share, something much too evident:

"But what a wooden character, gentlemen! Such an act! Such a step! Did you see any serious agitation in him? It seems to me he never understood. His entire life he has always slid fatefully on the surface. That was where all our troubles stemmed from."

Did he so fail to understand that maybe he didn't even feel his defeat after his many years of struggling with Guchkov? Not that this diminished the victory. No! A crowning hour. Where did that prophetic presentiment in Guchkov come from, to see so accurately in advance these nocturnal, train-car circumstances in which he would accept the abdication?

And no blood shed. This wasn't the bloody night of Paul's murder, on 23 March. This now would be 15 March. Bloodless. Glorious. The abdication, like a simple piece of paper, lay in his inside jacket pocket, over his heart, in his wallet, so it wouldn't get crushed.

But Shulgin's migraine was raging:

"Ah, Nikolai Vladimirovich, this is insufferably annoying! Might you have any headache tablets here? If you will permit me, I would like to lie down for ten minutes."

Thus the dinner fell apart. Savich departed soon after as well. Ruzsky and Guchkov were left sitting at the table.

Completely alien to each other, never having liked each other. Chance allies at their hour of triumph.

This triumph had been badly spoiled for Ruzsky by a great deal. His role as the one who'd wrested away the abdication had been blurred—as if it wasn't he who had obtained it. Alekseev had usurped his role, had queried the commanders-in-chief and sent the draft Manifesto. And these men had arrived to a done deal, without even knowing the government's laws. Nor did it bring Ruzsky any joy that Nikolai Nikolaevich had been immediately appointed Supreme Commander: the precipitate signature of the Tsar, whom no one had tried to stop. They had taken a picturesque but vapid grand duke without noticing what an injustice they were committing. By virtue of his intellect, and his post, and society's and Rodzyanko's sympathies, as well as his proximity to Petrograd, Ruzsky could well have counted on being appointed Supreme Commander. (That might yet happen; the grand duke might not last.) Yet this was how it had begun. They should be uniting, not settling scores. Here before him sat the new Minister of War.

"Around the throne"—Ruzsky grinned crookedly—"there was always a poor opinion of me. That I hated the Empress. Finally we can live without intrigues with the new government. There won't be these bureaucratic mazes. Or this formality and inaccessibility. Or this venality. The Army Group's warehouse was required to release to the Court 1800 pounds of first-quality meat a day—clearly for the servants, footmen, and stablemen—and this was at the soldiers' expense!"

Basically, a new era had opened in relations between the High Command and the government. The government's help would be very important for keeping up the army's spirit, especially in the coming days. Was it possible to send in some political representatives? A tour by Duma speakers? Look what happened with Nepenin. So that the same doesn't happen in the Northern Army Group.

But Guchkov sat there replete, taciturn, and unresponsive. Seemingly burdened even by the relief of victory.

Only then did Shulgin realize and exclaim from his resting position:

"Gentlemen! We forgot about Aleksei. After all, the troops have sworn an oath to him as Heir, and now they wouldn't have had to repeat that oath!"

Yes, yes. The abdication had been accepted, but what work now faced them with Mikhail! Mikhail wasn't all that clever, either; he was not a majestic figure. Mikhail, too, had to be led, steered, and inspired—and who was going to do that?

"Gentlemen! We left out something else!" These thoughts rolled into Shulgin's aching head, and through the pain he said languidly: "How was it we didn't think of this, eh? What are we going to do about Mikhail's spouse? Can Madam Brasova, thrice-married, really become Empress?"

So true!

So true! How everything was eclipsed when they agreed. But it was because they were unused to these dynastic nuances.

Ultimately, however, this was important only for dynastic fossils. In the revolutionary upheaval that was Russia, who could that offend?

"Nikolai himself ought to have thought of this, not us."

But the new Emperor's inspiration, Madam Brasova, was known for her liberal sympathies. She held a liberal salon attended by leftist Duma deputies.

They needed to unite now, not fracture. However, Ruzsky sat facing Guchkov and thought that Guchkov was taking on too much. What kind of Minister of War was he?

And Guchkov sat facing Ruzsky and noticed more precisely his weasely appearance with his tobacco-stained teeth and scraggy intellectuality, and thought: "No, he's a dawdler, not a real soldier."

While Shulgin let the headache medicine work, he relaxed his gaze and let his eyes lose focus. He barely saw anything right next to him. But he did see Mikhail's face. That ordinary cavalryman with the twisted mustache.

My God, that man was to lead Russia?

Documents – 11

To GHQ, Adjutant General Alekseev

Vyritsa, 16 March, 1:30 a.m.

So far I have no information about the movement of the units assigned to my disposition. I have secret information about the halting of my train's movement. I request urgent measures be taken to restore order in the railroad administration. . . .

Adjutant General Ivanov

[3 5 2]

At twelve-forty that night, Northern Army Group headquarters informed GHQ that the Manifesto proclaiming the Tsar's abdication had at last been signed.

Well, at last! A great tension had been eased.

An unfortunate reign was ending, and Emperor Nikolai II was no more. Nor had Aleksei II ascended, but rather Mikhail II. The names seemed to be pushing back to the dynasty's very roots.

Soon now, soon, the Northern Army Group would transmit the text, too.

The unfortunate reign was ending, and now a calming would ensue. However, as always in life, great moments mix with insignificant ones. Before any manifesto could bring about any calming, GHQ had a roiling mass of urgent concerns. The Polotsk commandant reported that several dozen lower ranks had arrived, armed with revolvers and swords. As they emerged from the train, they demanded the disarming of the station guard. When the commandant asked by whose order they were demanding this, they replied, by the order of an officer who had remained in the train car. The commandant sent a gendarme into the car to verify this—and the soldiers from the "deputation" fell on him and disarmed him. Fortunately, right then a platoon of dragoons showed up at the station, and all the newly arrived soldiers scattered. Turned out there wasn't any officer in the train car.

But now they could once again converge and travel to Vitebsk, or a new self-styled "deputation" might show up, or even ten such. The Hughes telegraphs transmitted the historic royal Manifesto, but they had to send another telegram to irresponsible Rodzyanko, and in patient and respectful expressions, because he now loomed over them somewhat like a new Tsar, and the entire military High Command, even if it was Supreme, had now fallen under him. In modest expressions, Alekseev reminded him that in time of war and in the vicinity of the field army it was utterly impermissible to allow the disarming of a railroad guard. The sternest measures would have to be taken against gangs of soldiers and self-styled deputations in order—Alekseev was indignant and his reproach showed through the text—in order to protect the army in the field from the profound moral degradation that all the Petrograd garrison's units were experiencing.

Unfortunately, no more precise expression could be found for the Petrograd revolution, for the air that it exhaled outside.

That fussy Rodzyanko. For three nights in a row he had been beleaguering all the commanders-in-chief with telegrams and summonses to the telegraph. But one and then a second precise military telegram had been sent to him about an alarming occurrence—and he was behaving as if he hadn't received it.

What Alekseev did have, though, was high-level staff training. The ability to simultaneously consider and rigorously direct many affairs, including the most trifling ones, to which others had not even given thought.

The Tsar's irrevocable Manifesto had barely been received from Pskov and Alekseev was already giving orders to send it immediately by Hughes wires to all army groups simultaneously—and onward to all the armies and heads of all military districts, to be sent without delay to all troop units. It was awaited everywhere!

And they should probably be thinking about a new oath for the troops.

He sent a telegram to this effect to Rodzyanko and Lvov.

Simultaneously, though, Alekseev immediately thought of what had been omitted in the Pskov and Petrograd confusion: What about informing the Allies of the abdication? That couldn't wait either! Most dignified of all would be for the abdicating Emperor himself to do this—and it had to be suggested to the new Petrograd government to prepare such an announcement.

He sent a telegram about this to Lvov and Milyukov.

Before the letter trains left Pskov, the proper thing was to hurry and report through Voeikov to the former Emperor the news received from Tsarskoye Selo that General Groten and other court military leaders had been arrested at the town hall. (Shouldn't he be wary of going there himself?)

And now Pskov had reported the appointment of Grand Duke Nikolai Nikolaevich as Supreme Commander. (As might have been expected, all well and good.) Now Alekseev was obliged to hasten to report there, beyond the Caucasus range. But how? "Your most loyal subject"? Not any more. Find a new term. "Yours most faithfully."

Most faithfully request instructions: when can we expect His Imperial Highness's arrival at GHQ? And temporarily, until his arrival, would His Imperial Highness see fit to grant General Alekseev the rights of Supreme Commander? Or would he prefer to establish a different procedure?

Well, for now apparently . . . for now apparently, that was everything. . . . The old man with the careful, sharp, squinting eye had seen this through.

A mere three days had passed since the moment when, also in the dead of night, the Emperor had left for the train station and Alekseev had also gone off to bed.

In those three days, what a clod they had cast aside, the clod that had been blocking Russia's path!

[3 5 3]

In his petrifaction, in his many years' habit of not expressing himself, Nikolai suffered through a very late tea with his suite, but even that wasn't the end: Voeikov and Nilov addressed him. In the final few minutes, his face was completely drained of life. His eyelids, cheeks, and lips had lost their ability to move.

Finally, though, they left his car—and he stepped into his sleeping compartment—and immediately felt mollified. The light wasn't burning and he didn't have to light it; his valet had had the good idea of lighting the icon lamp. Ordinarily, Nikolai lit it himself when he wanted it, but today the valet had, in advance. Had he sensed? Realized?

Nikolai immediately stepped into this warm little gloom and saw only the bluish edges of the lamp above the oil, the small spear of flame barely flickering—and in a convergence of sternness and kindness, the eternally unknowable face of the Savior, holding in one hand an open Testament for us—open, but we can only read and grasp the first few letters.

Locking the door behind him with a final movement of his fingers, now completely uncoupled from everyone, from all men, alone with Him—to relax and weep—Nikolai felt a blissful grief. He dropped to his hard bed as if cut down, fell forward on one elbow—and wept.

And wept.

Everything he could express to no one, everything he had failed to accomplish, everything he had not managed to correct—everything now broke loose and came out in blows of weeping.

Alix alone on earth could understand him—even if demandingly, even if at times even blaming him. But even more exhaustively, totally embracing him—only the Savior could.

We cannot guess the Savior's ways, but He understands us immediately, every part of us, and in everything we do, contemplate, and omit. This full and instantaneous understanding makes you feel suddenly like a child, weak but defended.

At His hand, he wept, the abdicated Emperor wept, and all the unexpressed insult, all the pain for his incompetent self, all his hopeless longing, and even all the horror came surging out of him, relieving him.

Now much relieved, he got on his knees to pray.

The floor under his knees was rattling. He hadn't noticed the train start to move.

He was weeping more weakly now, but suddenly there began to swirl—outside his car? inside his chest?—something like feverish whirlwinds. They struck the walls—were they the whirlwinds of Judgment Day? The end of the world? Nikolai shuddered from their burning cold blows. Then they passed. That happened several times.

Had the Evil One been trying to burst in? And been repelled by prayer?

Nikolai knew many prayers, a great many, both of petition and of gratitude, by heart. He now whispered many. And in this work, in this steady repetition, in his penetration of different phrases (while others were spoken without attention), he became more and more at peace, more and more consoled, understanding that what will be will be, it was all God's will, the Divine plan, and he should not struggle against it.

A moment of balance arrived and then a tipping point, when he was sated with prayer and nonprayer thoughts began to push in more and more. This was the sign that he should end his praying.

Nikolai got up and sat on the bed. And surrendered to the train's even knocking. However much he had traveled the railroads, however often he had read to this noble knocking of the train, however many times he had awoken, looked out the window, and written in his diary to it, he had never envisioned that it would be on a train, on his beloved train, that the end of his reign would come to pass—but not by death. It was odd. His life should have ended first. But now his reign had ended and he remained.

For what purpose?

He sat without lying down or undressing, without sensing the late hour. He sat sideways to the lamp, under the spell of the rocking and knocking.

All kinds of different things crowded chaotically in his mind.

He could hear his bitter foe say with malicious glee:

"Any struggle is pointless for you, Sire."

Yes, for some reason, this was how it had come to pass. Struggle had been impossible even before it began. Everything was so tightly bound that you couldn't change or reconfigure anything. At forty-nine years of age, Nikolai, full of health and, apparently, full of strength—felt no strength whatsoever to fight for the throne.

One cannot fight for everything, everywhere, always. It was much more precious to let universal domestic peace and good will establish itself in Russia. He had been in the way. It was because of him that there was still no peace. Well, he was removing himself. He had agreed to all repudiations just so discord would not be brought to his country.

Just so Russia would be saved.

We would see how all of *them* . . . How it would go for them . . . May God help them. Although Nikolai did not see among them, truly, well truly, such remarkable workers any better than his own unsuccessful ministers.

After all, of all the Duma presidents there had been—well, other than Khomyakov—Guchkov had at one time been the closest to his heart: He loved Russia, no doubt about that, and he was intelligent, and vibrant.

The first time Guchkov presented himself, during the Japanese war, Nikolai and Alix had liked him. They had received him so warmly and for so long and had had such good conversations. There had been no presentiment that he would become such a fierce enemy.

But he was a base man, it turned out. Today he had been anticipating signs of the Tsar's humiliation and had wanted to take pleasure in them.

And how he had descended into a lecturing and condescending tone: Go pray!

From someone who himself had forgotten how to pray. And an Old Believer, too. . . .

All these years, the Emperor had had so many opportunities to take revenge—and hadn't.

But thanks to him for allowing the return to GHQ. Nikolai was in such a hurry to get to Tsarskoye Selo, so sought Alix's support! But something still had to be decided, strength and courage were still needed. As soon as the abdication had been accomplished—suddenly he had no more struggle or missions (his shoulders were unused to this lightness, they still couldn't believe it). And suddenly inside him the arrows of the compass switched. To his family, the deputies had promised safety. And until his dying day Nikolai would be with his family, with whom or what else? But GHQ—he would never see his GHQ again. To say goodbye to GHQ, to spend a few final days in this courageous and extended family—he could only do that now, before Nikolasha's arrival.

There was fate for you! One sole destiny to dream of, to love—not of an emperor at all, but of a commander, an army leader, the father of all soldiers—but he hadn't gone to the Japanese war (if he had, everything might have gone differently!), then he hadn't ventured in when the German war broke out—and with this extraordinary effort finally wrested the Supreme Command from Nikolasha—only to hand it back to Nikolasha now. Fate.

How Nikolai loved the soldiers! What a soldier he felt himself to be! How he did—amid these courageous, simple, and intelligible people. There was no greater family man than he! But if God placed before him two destinies for his life and one excluded the other—either to marry Alix and have his present family, and Aleksei, but to never put on a military uniform, or else to be a soldier his whole life, a general, or just a colonel, as now, but never to marry—he might well have chosen the latter.

Manly will and freedom from the fear of death, the victory over death that streamed in the spirit of the army, was the highest spirit, a spirit Nikolai admired. This spirit imparted an unearthly ease even to a mortal.

Yes, he needed GHQ now like he needed to breathe. So he wouldn't die this minute.

How many of these courageous, brilliant officers had he known in the twenty-two years of his reign, seen, rewarded, listened to, and observed in parades, inspections, maneuvers, and banquets—they in their totality were that very nation for whom it was worth reigning.

Where had they all been today? Where were their ecstatic hurrahs? Where were their sword-oaths lifted to the sky? Why had their host not come to his support? Why had it not defended the throne?

Many were dead, many were no more, take them, Lord, but how many still lived—and where were they? Everyone had scattered, hidden, they were sitting in their dugouts, looking through stereotelescopes, lying in infirmaries. Everyone had hidden and in their place the five commanders-in-chief had poked their heads out—and not one had offered a hand of support. Rather, all five had given him a good push: abdicate!

For the first time today it occurred to him that he had chosen the wrong officers as commanders-in-chief. In any event, he had not chosen the best.

It was a long time since Nikolai had been bitter about being hated by the revolutionaries, Kadets, Zemgor, and high society—because he had not set a high value on them in return.

But that the closest, highest officers, the very ones who were supposed to have defended him . . . this was the blow that had felled him.

And once again his throat was squeezed by tears. And they welled up in his eyes.

He remembered about his diary. No matter what happened, even on the day of Tsushima, he couldn't deviate, couldn't fail to record the day.

That afternoon he had already begun his entry, still Emperor, still not knowing his evening future. Now he had to finish it.

The leather diary lay in its place, in the drawer of his little table. He found it easily by feel. He needed to light a small bulb, if only a night light, but right now his eyes couldn't withstand even that blow.

But right then there was a stop. The curtained train stood still in the deep silence and as if in darkness.

Nikolai opened to the silk bookmark and brought the notebook as close to the flickering icon lamp as he could. He made out the end of his entry and the sense of his last daytime words: that he had **assented.** And GHQ had sent a draft manifesto.

And so, standing under the icon lamp, holding the open notebook in his spread left palm, he wrote the letter loops with an automatic pen, more by heart, but seeing the evenness of the line with his eyes:

"This evening, Guchkov and Shulgin arrived from Petrograd. I spoke with them and handed them my signed and redone Manifesto. At one in the morning I left Pskov with a heavy sense of what I had been through."

That was all. He could not entrust to paper his sobbing or his prayers. He closed it.

But he felt once again this sponge full of gall from the commanders-in-chief—so unexpected and so unmerited!—and once again he opened the notebook and added one more line:

"Surrounded by treason and cowardice."

And again he finished. But he hadn't finished. The most important thing:
". . . and deceit!"

You can't sit up all night long. He began undressing. And only while un-dressing did he recall Misha—only then, for the first time! Everything that evening had been so much, too much for his head that there had been no room for Misha; everything had fit except for Misha.

He was probably at the Winter Palace now. And it was to the Winter Palace, by the finger of God, that the crown of Russian emperors raced through the dark air—and it would have been odd not to explain anything to him, not to speak for himself.

Evidently, he needed to send a telegram from some station.

Misha! His dear, glorious, previously so obedient brother, and such a desperate warrior, he had mangled everything with that marriage—and what kind of Empress was this to be now?

There had been many disagreements, but it could all be forgotten. But now he had to apologize: he had handed over the crown without warning, without asking.

Send him a telegram tomorrow.

Once he had decided, this was pushed out of his head. And a cherished search blossomed inside him: for his dear mother. Who else is over us, who else is with us when we are in powerless misfortune?

Perhaps there was one last hope of meeting before their long separation. Send her a telegram tomorrow, too: ". . . come see your lonely son, whom all have abandoned . . ."

And once again he felt like a small, weak boy who hadn't found his feet. He lay there.

But maybe there would be some miracle. Would God send a Miracle rescuing everyone?

The train rocked, knocked.

Gradually all the burning thoughts that had passed through him and been overcome by thinking and submission, submission to the Divine will, receded.

They receded and somehow everything in the world went back into balance. In this world, where tomorrow he had to begin to live anew.

*   *   *

THE TSAR AND THE PEOPLE—ALL RETURNS TO DUST

*   *   *

Maps

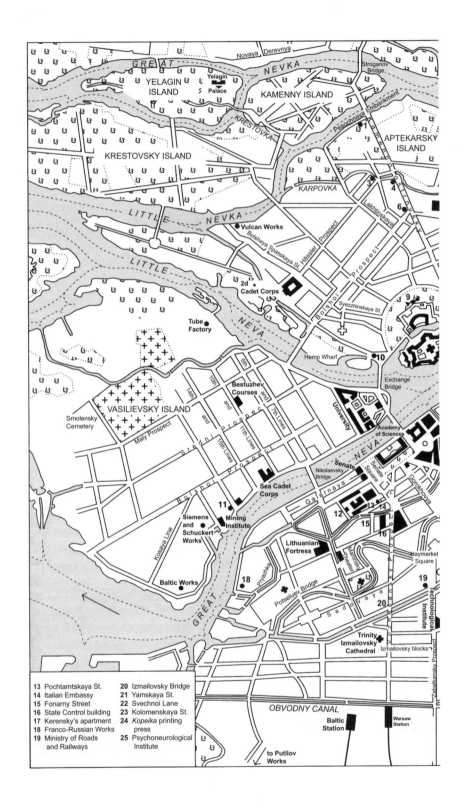

GREAT NEVKA

Novaya Derevnya

Stroganov Bridge

YELAGIN ISLAND

Yelagin Palace

KAMENNY ISLAND

Peschnaya Embankment

1

APTEKARSKY ISLAND

KRESTOVKA

KRESTOVSKY ISLAND

KARPOVKA

3

4

Lakhtinskaya

6

LITTLE NEVKA

Vulcan Works

Bolshaya Spasskaya St.

Hässler

Prospect

LITTLE

Bolshoi Prospect

Syezzhinskaya St.

9

2d Cadet Corps

NEVA

Tube Factory

Hemp Wharf

10

Exchange Bridge

6th and 7th Lines

Bestuzhev Courses

14th and 13th Lines

10th and 11th Lines

Sredni Prospect

University

Academy of Sciences

VASILIEVSKY ISLAND

Smolensky Cemetery

Maly Prospect

NEVA

Senate

Senate Square

Nikolaevsky Bridge

Bolshoi Prospect

Sea Cadet Corps

Gagernaya

Galernaya

Gorokhovaya

11

12

13

14

Kosaya Line

Siemens and Schuckert Works

Mining Institute

15

16

Lithuanian Fortress

Mariinsky Theater

Haymarket Square

19

Baltic Works

18

Pryazhka

Potseluev Bridge

Sadovaya

20

Technological Institute

GREAT

Trinity Izmailovsky Cathedral

Izmailovsky blocks

13 Pochtamtskaya St.
14 Italian Embassy
15 Fonarny Street
16 State Control building
17 Kerensky's apartment
18 Franco-Russian Works
19 Ministry of Roads
   and Railways

20 Izmailovsky Bridge
21 Yamskaya St.
22 Svechnoi Lane
23 Kolomenskaya St.
24 *Kopeika* printing
   press
25 Psychoneurological
   Institute

OBVODNY CANAL

Baltic Station

Warsaw Station

Zabalkansky Prospect

to Putilov Works

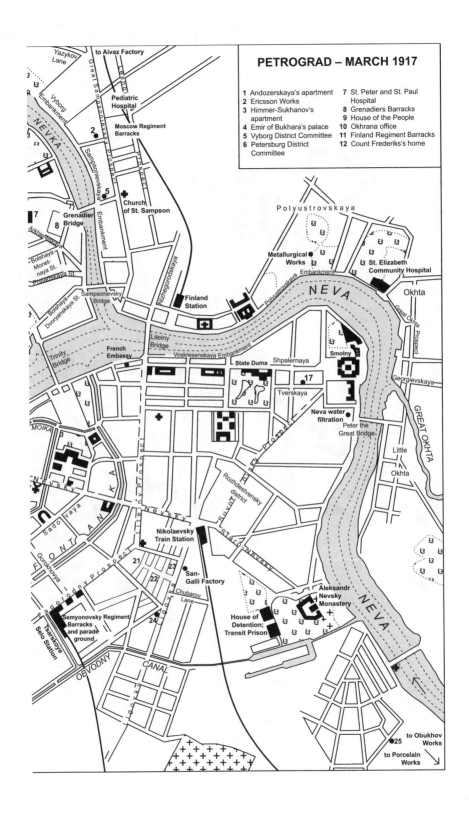

PETROGRAD – MARCH 1917

1 Andozerskaya's apartment
2 Ericsson Works
3 Himmer-Sukhanov's apartment
4 Emir of Bukhara's palace
5 Vyborg District Committee
6 Petersburg District Committee

7 St. Peter and St. Paul Hospital
8 Grenadiers Barracks
9 House of the People
10 Okhrana office
11 Finland Regiment Barracks
12 Count Frederiks's home

Yazykov Lane
to Aivaz Factory
Vyborg Embankment
Great Sampsonievsky Prospect
NEVKA
Pediatric Hospital
Moscow Regiment Barracks
Sampsonievskaya
Embankment
Church of St. Sampson
Grenadier Bridge
Arkhierereiskaya
Bolshaya Monetnaya St.
Prosarskaya St.
Bolshaya Dvoryanskaya st.
Sampsonievsky Bridge
Nizhegorodskaya
Finland Station
Polyustrovskaya
Metallurgical Works
St. Elizabeth Community Hospital
Embankment
Polyustrovskaya
NEVA
Okhta
Great Okhta Prospect
Liteiny Bridge
Voskresenskaya Embankment
Trinity Bridge
French Embassy
State Duma
Shpalernaya
Smolny
Georgievskaya
17
Tverskaya
GREAT OKHTA
MOIKA
Prospect
Nevsky
Sadovaya
FONTANKA
Neva water filtration
Peter the Great Bridge
Little Okhta
Rozhdestvensky district
Staro Nevsky
Nevsky
Gorokhovaya
Zagorodny Prospect
Tsarskoye Selo Station
Nikolaevsky Train Station
21
23
22
San-Galli Factory
Chubarov Lane
24
Semyonovsky Regiment Barracks and parade ground
House of Detention; Transit Prison
Aleksandr Nevsky Monastery
NEVA
OBVODNY CANAL
25
to Obukhov Works
to Porcelain Works

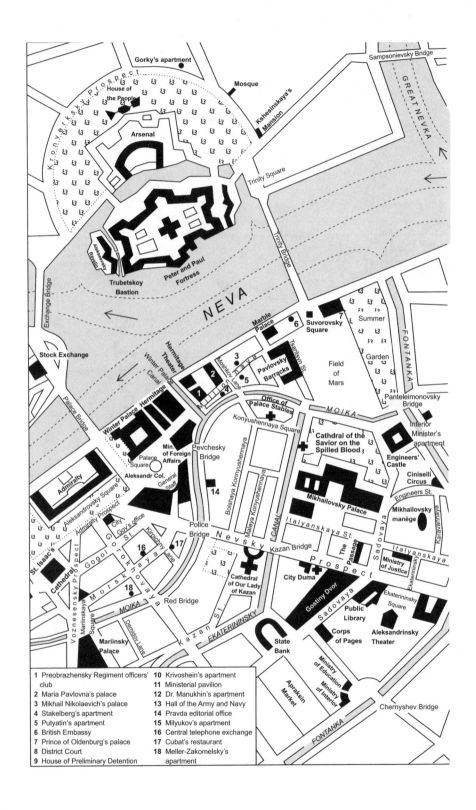

Gorky's apartment

House of the People

Mosque

Kshesinskaya's Mansion

Arsenal

Trinity Square

GREAT NEVKA

Sampsonievsky Bridge

Kronverksky Prospect

Aleksevsky Ravelin

Trubetskoy Bastion

Peter and Paul Fortress

Exchange Bridge

Trinity Bridge

Stock Exchange

NEVA

Marble Palace

6

7 Summer

Suvorovsky Square

Tsaritsyn St.

Field of Mars

Garden

FONTANKA

Palace Bridge

Winter Palace Canal

Hermitage Theater

Millionaya

Moshkov Lane

3

2

1

5

Pavlovsky Barracks

Office of Palace Stables

MOIKA

Panteleimonovsky Bridge

Winter Palace

Hermitage

Palace Square

Min. of Foreign Affairs

Pevchesky Bridge

Konyushennaya Square

Cathdral of the Savior on the Spilled Blood

Interior Minister's apartment

Engineers' Castle

Ciniselli Circus

Admiralty

Aleksandr Col.

General Staff

14

Police Bridge

Bolshaya Konyushennaya

Malaya Konyushennaya

CANAL

Mikhailovsky Palace

Italyanskaya St.

Engineers St.

Mikhailovsky manège

Karavannaya

Aleksandrovsky Square

Admiralty Prospect

City Gov's office

Kirpichny Lane

Nevsky

Kazan Bridge

The Passage

Italyanskaya

Sadovaya

Ministry of Justice

Ekaterininsky

St. Isaac's Cathedral

Gogol

Gorokhovaya

Morskaya

16

17

18

Red Bridge

MOIKA

Demidov Lane

Kazan St.

Cathedral of Our Lady of Kazan

Prospect

City Duma

Gostiny Dvor

Sadovaya

Public Library

Corps of Pages

Ekaterininsky Square

Aleksandrinsky Theater

Voznesensky Prospect

Mariinsky Square

Mariinsky Palace

EKATERININSKY

State Bank

Ministry of Education

Ministry of Interior

Apraksin Market

FONTANKA

Chernyshev Bridge

1 Preobrazhensky Regiment officers' club
2 Maria Pavlovna's palace
3 Mikhail Nikolaevich's palace
4 Stakelberg's apartment
5 Putyatin's apartment
6 British Embassy
7 Prince of Oldenburg's palace
8 District Court
9 House of Preliminary Detention

10 Krivoshein's apartment
11 Ministerial pavilion
12 Dr. Manukhin's apartment
13 Hall of the Army and Navy
14 Pravda editorial office
15 Milyukov's apartment
16 Central telephone exchange
17 Cubat's restaurant
18 Meller-Zakomelsky's apartment

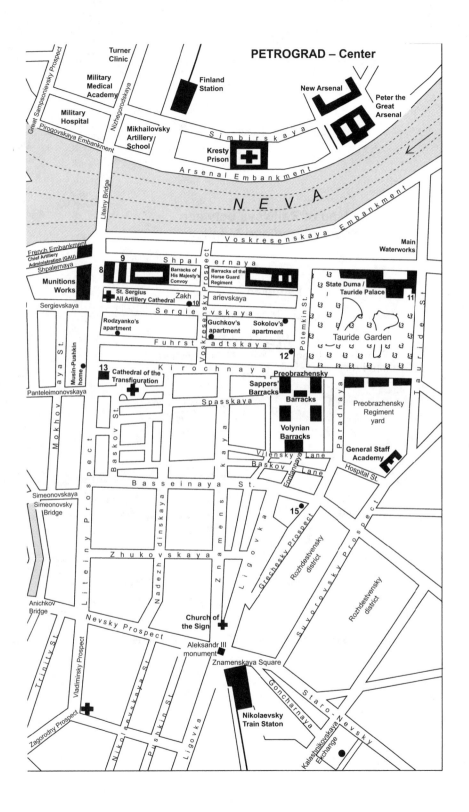

PETROGRAD – Center

Turner Clinic

Military Medical Academy

Great Sampsonievsky Prospect

Military Hospital

Pirogovskaya Embankment

Nizhegorodskaya

Mikhailovsky Artillery School

Finland Station

New Arsenal

Peter the Great Arsenal

S i m b i r s k a y a

Kresty Prison

A r s e n a l   E m b a n k m e n t

Liteiny Bridge

N E V A

V o s k r e s e n s k a y a   Embankment

Main Waterworks

French Embankment
Chief Artillery Administration (GAU)
Shpalernaya

Munitions Works

9

8

S h p a l e r n a y a

Barracks of His Majesty's Convoy

Barracks of the Horse Guard Regiment

State Duma / Tauride Palace

11

St. Sergius All Artillery Cathedral

Zakh   10   arievskaya

Sergievskaya

S e r g i e v s k a y a

Voskresensky Prospect

Rodzyanko's apartment

Guchkov's apartment

Sokolov's apartment

Tauride Garden

Tauride St.

Mokhovaya St.

Musin-Pushkin home

F u h r s t   a d t s k a y a

12

Potemkin St.

Panteleimonovskaya

13

Cathedral of the Transfiguration

K i r o c h n a y a

Preobrazhensky

Sappers' Barracks

Baskov St.

S p a s s k a y a

Barracks

Volynian Barracks

Paradnaya

Preobrazhensky Regiment yard

V i l e n s k y   Lane

B a s k o v   Lane

Fontannaya Lane

Hospital St.

General Staff Academy

Simeonovskaya

Simeonovsky Bridge

B a s s e i n a y a   St.

Liteiny Prospect

dinskaya

Znamenskaya

Ligovka

15

Grechesky Prospect

Rozhdestvensky district

Suvorovsky Prospect

Rozhdestvensky district

Anichkov Bridge

Z h u k o v s k a y a

Nadezhdinskaya

N e v s k y   P r o s p e c t

Church of the Sign

Trinity St.

Vladimirsky Prospect

Nikolaevskaya St.

Pushkin St.

Ligovka

Aleksandr III monument

Znamenskaya Square

Zagorodny Prospect

Nikolaevsky Train Staton

Goncharnaya

Staro - Nevsky

Kalashnikovskaya

Exchange

Map of Railways between Petrograd and Mogilev

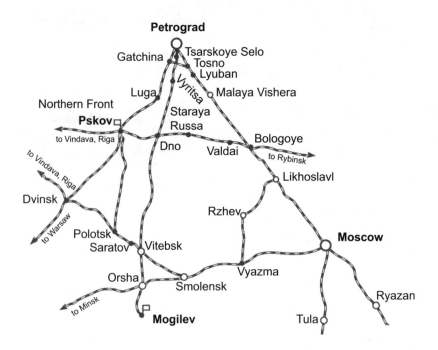

Petrograd

Gatchina   Tsarskoye Selo
            Tosno
            Lyuban
       Luga Vyritsa Malaya Vishera
Northern Front   Staraya
Pskov   Russa
to Vindava, Riga   Dno   Valdai   Bologoye
                                to Rybinsk
to Vindava, Riga   Likhoslavl

Dvinsk   Rzhev
to Warsaw
     Polotsk
     Saratov   Vitebsk
Orsha   Vyazma   Moscow
       Smolensk
to Minsk   Ryazan
   Mogilev   Tula

Petrograd to Moscow = 400 miles, or 603 versts

Map of Railways between Petrograd, Tsarkoye Selo, Gatchina, and Vyritsa

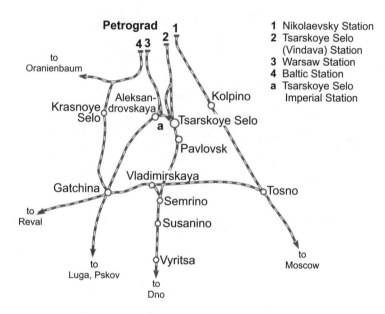

Petrograd

1 Nikolaevsky Station
2 Tsarskoye Selo (Vindava) Station
3 Warsaw Station
4 Baltic Station
a Tsarskoye Selo Imperial Station

to Oranienbaum

Krasnoye Selo

Aleksan-drovskaya

Kolpino

Tsarskoye Selo

Pavlovsk

Vladimirskaya

Gatchina

Semrino

Tosno

to Reval

Susanino

Vyritsa

to Luga, Pskov

to Dno

to Moscow

Petrograd to Tsarskoye Selo = 14 miles, or 22 versts

Index of Names

Adrian: First name of Admiral Nepenin and his nickname among the "Decembrists of the Fleet."

Adzhemov, Moisei Sergeevich (1878–1953, USA): Deputy in Second, Third, and Fourth Dumas. Prominent member of the Kadet Party.

Aleksan Nikolaich, Aleksandr Nikolaevich. *See* von Fergen.

Aleksan Palych. *See* Kutepov, Aleksandr Pavlovich.

Aleksandr I (Aleksandr Pavlovich) (1777–1825): Tsar in 1801 following the assassination of his father; defeated Napoleon in 1812, entered Paris in triumph; his reign is known for promises of reforms that continuously went unfulfilled.

Aleksandr II (1818–1881): The "Tsar Liberator," presided over the emancipation of the serfs, the introduction of the zemstvo system of local government, modernization of the judicial system, easing of the burden of military service. Assassinated 13 March 1881 by members of the Narodnaya Volya (People's Will) organization.

Aleksandr III (1845–1894): Became emperor following the assassination of his father, Aleksandr II. Discontinued and in part reversed his father's program of reform. Father of the Franco-Russian Alliance.

Aleksandr (Aleksan) **Aleksandrovich** (Aleksanych, Sanych). *See* Rittikh.

Aleksandr Dmitrievich (Dmitrich). *See* Protopopov.

Aleksandr Fyodorovich (Fyodorych). *See* Kerensky.

Aleksandr Gavrilovich (Gavrilych). *See* Shlyapnikov.

Aleksandr Ivanovich (Ivanych). *See* Guchkov.

Aleksandr Mikhailovich ("Sandro"), Grand Duke (1866–1933, France): Grandson of Nikolai I, friend of Nikolai II in his youth. Married Nikolai's sister Ksenia.

Aleksandr Sergeich. *See* Lukomsky.

Aleksandr (Aleksan) **Vasilievich** (Vasilich). *See* Krivoshein.

Aleksandra Fyodorovna ("Alix"), Empress (1872–1918): Born Princess Alix of Hesse and by Rhine. Married the future Nikolai II in 1894. Nickname "Sunny" in letters with her husband. Murdered together with her husband and children by the Bolsheviks.

Aleksandrovich, Vyacheslav. *See* Dmitrievsky.

Alekseev, Mikhail Vasilievich (1857–1918): Infantry general, chief of staff, first on the Southwestern, then on the Northwestern Front. From September 1915, chief of General Staff. On sick leave 21 November 1916 to 7 March 1917. Advised the Tsar to abdicate in March 1917. Supreme Commander until 3 June 1917. After the October Revolution organized the first White Army on the Don.

Aleksei ("Baby," "Sunshine") (1904–1918): Son and youngest child of Nikolai II and Aleksandra Fyodorovna, hemophiliac. Murdered together with his parents and sisters by the Bolsheviks.

Aleksei Maksimovich (Maksimych). *See* Gorky.

Aleksei Vasilich, Aleksei Vasilievich. *See* Peshekhonov.

Aleksei Yermolaich, Aleksei Yermolaevich. *See* Evert.

Alix. *See* Aleksandra Fyodorovna ("Alix"), Empress.

Anastasia (1901–1918): Youngest daughter of Nikolai II and Aleksandra Fyodorovna, murdered with her whole family by the Bolsheviks.

Andrei Ivanovich (Ivanych). *See* Shingarev.

Andrew, Saint: This apostle is known in the Orthodox Church as "the First-Called" (cf. Matthew 4:18–20; John 1:35–40); patron saint of Russia, which he evangelized according to legend.

Andronikov, Mikhail Mikhailovich, Prince (1875–1919): Political adventurer, friend of Rasputin, numerous connections among the ministers, executed by Bolsheviks.

Andrusov, Vadim Nikolaevich (1895–1975, Paris): Sculptor, grandson of Heinrich Schliemann. After the Revolution fought on the side of the Whites in the Civil War, evacuated via Finland and settled in France.

Anna Sergeevna: Refers to **Milyukova** (née Smirnova), **Anna Sergeevna** (1861–1935, France), wife of Pavel Milyukov.

Anya. *See* Vyrubova.

Apraksin, Pyotr Nikolaevich, Count (1876–1962, Belgium): Master of the Court, chief of the private secretariat of the Empress, member of the ecclesiastic council of 1917; last mayor of Yalta, evacuated with Wrangel.

Apukhtin, Sergei Aleksandrovich (1893–1969, USA): Captain in the Russian army, decorated veteran, fought in the White forces in the Civil War until late 1920.

Argutinsky-Dolgorukov, Konstantin Sergeevich (1876–1920): Veteran of the Russo-Japanese War and the First World War. Joined the Guards in 1905, made colonel in Preobrazhensky Regiment in 1915. Executed by the Bolsheviks in Tiflis (Tbilisi).

Armand, Inessa (née Steffen) (1874–1920): Bolshevik. French wife of the industrialist Armand and subsequently of his brother. Close friend and ally of Lenin from 1909. Buried in Red Square.

Baby. *See* Aleksei ("Baby," "Sunshine").

Balk, Aleksandr Pavlovich (1866–1957, Brazil): Major general, Petrograd city governor from November 1916 until March 1917.

Bark, Pyotr Lvovich (1869–1937, France): Russian Minister of Finance February 1914–March 1917. Subsequently a banker in the UK, where he had a successful career and was knighted Sir Peter Bark.

Bazarov (pseud. of Rudnev), **Vladimir Aleksandrovich** (1874–1939): Social Democrat from 1896, first a Bolshevik but in 1917 a Menshevik Internationalist, like Himmer; perished in the purges.

Bazhenov, Vasili Ivanovich (1737 or 1738–1799): Russian architect; many of his projects never came to fruition.

Bazili, Nikolai Aleksandrovich (**Nicolas de Basily**, 1883–1963, USA): Russian diplomat, drafted the abdication manifesto of Nikolai II, emigrated, author of books about the Soviet economy and posthumous memoirs, *Diplomat of Imperial Russia: 1903–1917*.

served in government in the Russian south under the White forces, then emigrated and was a noted publicist in Yugoslavia.

Bublikov, Aleksandr Aleksandrovich (1875–1941, USA): Deputy of the province of Perm, progressivist. Last name refers to a bagel (*bublik*). In March 1917 summarily took control of the railways and telegraph and thus ensured the revolution would spread from Petrograd.

Buchanan, Sir George William (1854–1924): British ambassador in Russia 1910–1918. Close to the leaders of the Kadet Party.

Büchner, Georg (1813–1837): German poet, participated in subversive movements and fled to Switzerland, author of the dramatic poem *The Death of Danton*.

Butakov, Aleksandr Grigorievich (1861–1917): Rear admiral, chief of staff at the Kronstadt harbor, murdered by sailors.

von Buxhoeveden, Sophia (Sophie) Karlovna, ("Isa"), Baroness (1883–1956, England): an honored matron of the Empress, succeeded in rejoining the imperial couple in Siberia.

Catherine II (Ekaterina II) **the Great** (1729–1796): Became Empress in 1762 after a palace revolution deposing her husband, Peter III. Led Russia through a golden era of military might but exacerbated Russia's inequality, granting ever more privileges to the nobility and entrenching serfdom of the peasantry.

Cavos, Yevgeni Tsezarevich (1858–1918): Mining engineer, husband of the artist Ekaterina Cavos (née Zarudnaya); their home was often visited by leading artists and thinkers of the day (Repin, Roerich, Filosofov, and Cavos's cousin, Alexandre Benois). His livelihood destroyed by the revolution and his wife rendered mentally ill and dying in 1917, Yevgeni Cavos died in early 1918.

Chebykin, Aleksandr Nestorovich (1857–1920): General of the Guard, member of the Emperor's suite, in charge of the Petrograd garrison, but was away for rest and recuperation during the February Revolution.

Chelnokov, Mikhail Vasilievich (1863–1935, Yugoslavia): Industrialist from Moscow, one of the founders of the Kadet Party; elected mayor of Moscow (1914–1917), chief representative of the Union of Towns, co-president of the Union of Zemstvos; emigrated after October.

Cherkassky, Mikhail Borisovich (Misha) (1882–1919): Rear Admiral (during March 1917, Captain First Rank). Supported the February Revolution but later joined the White Volunteer Army, was taken prisoner, and shot by the Bolsheviks.

Chernyshevsky, Nikolai Gavrilovich (1828–1889): Philosopher, literary critic, inspirer of populism, educator of several generations of revolutionaries. Arrested in 1862 for having participated in the writing of a revolutionary proclamation, he spent two decades in prison (where he wrote *What Is to Be Done?*), forced labor, or exile.

Chistyakov, Aleksandr Sergeevich (1892–1923, France): Staff captain in the Pavlovsky Regiment, emigrated.

Chkheidze, Nikolai Semyonovich (1864–1926, France): Menshevik leader, deputy at the Third and Fourth Dumas; in February 1917, president of the Petrograd Soviet. After October, president of the Georgian Constituent Assembly. Emigrated in 1921, committed suicide.

Engelhardt, Boris Aleksandrovich (1877–1962): Deputy of the Fourth Duma, military officer who sided with the Revolution but fled Soviet Russia in 1918. Emigrated to Latvia; following its Soviet annexation in 1940, lived in exile in the USSR.

Erlich, Henryk Moiseevich (1882–1942): One of the leaders of the General Jewish Labor Bund. In 1917 a member of the Executive Committee of the Soviet of Workers' Deputies. Lived in Poland, fled to Soviet territory in 1939, where he was sentenced to death for espionage.

Evert, Aleksei Yermolaevich (1857–1918 or 1926?): Infantry general, commanded 46th Army, then Western Front (from 1915). Recalled by the Provisional Government; murdered.

Feodosi (Theodosius) **of Chernigov,** Saint: Superior of the monastery at Kiev and Chernigov from 1664 to 1692, then archbishop of the latter city. Restored monasteries and churches following warfare. Canonized in 1896.

Feodosiev, Sergei Grigorievich (1880–1937, France): Chamberlain, last state comptroller of the Empire.

von Fergen, Aleksandr Nikolaevich (?–1917): Decorated for bravery in the First World War, served as staff captain in the Moscow Regiment when killed by soldiers during February Revolution.

Filippovsky, Vasili Nikolaevich (1882–1940): Navy lieutenant, Socialist Revolutionary. Died in a labor camp.

Fleckel, Boris Osipovich (1891–1918): Socialist Revolutionary, executed by the Bolsheviks during the Civil War.

Frederiks, Vladimir Borisovich, Count (1838–1927, Finland): Vice Minister of the Court 1893–1897, Minister from 1897.

Friend (the, our). *See* Rasputin.

Fyodor Izmailovich. *See* Rodichev.

Fyodorov, Sergei Petrovich (1869–1936): Doctor, surgeon, professor of the Military Medical Academy, who attended to Nikolai II and his son Tsarevich Aleksei. Continued to practice in the USSR.

Gadd, Georgi Ottovich (1873–1952, Denmark): Captain First Rank in the Baltic Fleet; was on the side of the Whites in the Civil War; refused to join newly formed Finnish fleet; emigrated with his Danish wife to Copenhagen, worked in shipbuilding.

Gardenin, Mikhail Fyodorovich (1887–1977, Belgium): Naval engineer, officer, served in the Arctic Ocean; during the Civil War fought for the Whites along the Northern Front, at Arkhangelsk; evacuated.

George, Saint: Martyr executed under Diocletian in 303; became the patron saint of Russia and, more specifically, of Moscow, whose pre-revolutionary and, again, post-Soviet symbol is the image of St. George defeating the dragon.

Georgi Evgenievich. *See* Lvov, Georgi Evgenievich, Prince.

Gerardi, Boris Andreevich (1870–1919): Police official, served in Moscow and Petersburg; was taken hostage and executed in Petrograd.

Gessen (Hessen), **Iosif Vladimirovich** (1865–1943, USA): Lawyer, member of the Second Duma, advocate for Jewish rights. In the 1920s and 1930s, in France, published 22-volume *Archive of the Russian Revolution*.

Military District; soon fell out with the Soviets, joined the Whites, died in the Civil War.

Guchkov, Aleksandr Ivanovich (1862–1936, France): Founder of the Octobrist Party. President of the Third Duma March 1910–March 1911. Chairman of the All-Russian War Industry Committees. Minister of War in the first Provisional Government, February–May 1917. Emigrated in 1918.

Gurko, Vasili Iosifovich (1864–1937, Italy): General. Participant in the Anglo-Boer and Russo-Japanese wars. After two years of fighting in the First World War, served as chief of staff during Alekseev's illness (November 1916–March 1917), returned to command Western Army Group March–May 1917. Dismissed and exiled by the Provisional Government.

Gvozdev, Kozma Antonovich (1883–1956): Worker, Menshevik leader, defensist, president of the central Workers' Group. Member of the Central Committee of Petrograd Soviet, then Minister of Labor under the Fourth Provisional Government. Imprisoned from 1930 on.

Halfter, Viktor Petrovich (1868–1951, England): General, veteran of Russo-Japanese War and First World War, one of the leaders of the Red Cross in Russia; fought on the side of the Whites in the Civil War.

Halperin, Lev Efimovich, pseud. **Barrivé** (1872–1951): Bolshevik and Menshevik publicist, authored historical works, participant in the 1917 revolution in Moscow.

Herzen, Aleksandr Ivanovich (1812–1870): Writer, philosopher, and Russian publicist, first revolutionary to have lived half his life abroad, editor of the journal *The Bell*; emblematic figure of the intelligentsia.

Himmer (Sukhanov), **Nikolai Nikolaevich** (1882–1940): Menshevik theorist, Zimmerwaldist, and important memorialist; shot after many years in prison and exile.

Hughes, David Edward (1831–1900): English-American engineer, inventor of a telegraphic apparatus bearing his name that enabled conversation at a distance.

Igor Konstantinovich. *See* Konstantinovich grand dukes.

Ilya Isakovich: *See* Arkhangorodsky, Ilya Isakovich (under Principal Non-Historical Characters).

Ilyich: Patronymic of Lenin, an informal address.

Inessa. *See* Armand.

Isuv, Iosif Andreevich (1878–1920): Menshevik, supported the war effort; after October, contributor to the Workers' Museum.

Iudovich. *See* Ivanov.

Ivan Fyodorovich: Refers to Ivan Fyodorovich Pavlov, old tailor of Protopopov.

Ivanov, Nikolai Iudovich (1851–1919): Artillery general. Commanded Southwestern Army Group August 1914–March 1916. Charged by Nikolai II in March 1917 to reestablish order in Petrograd but did not even reach the city. Died of typhus during the Civil War.

Kapnist, Aleksei Pavlovich (1871–1918): Navy captain, chief of Naval Staff at GHQ, then aide-de-camp to Guchkov, rear admiral, dismissed after October, murdered by Bolsheviks at Pyatigorsk.

Karakhan, Lev Mikhailovich (1889–1937): Revolutionary, joined Interdistrict group, later Bolshevik; became a high-ranking Soviet diplomat. Executed in the purges.

Krupskaya, Nadezhda Konstantinova (1869–1939): Lenin's wife. Teacher by profession. Active as educationalist after the 1917 Revolution. Avoided being noticed under Stalin.

Krym, Solomon Samuilovich (1867–1936, France): Kadet party member, State Duma deputy; prime minister of a short-lived White government in Crimea, evacuated in April 1919.

Kshesinskaya, Maria Feliksovna (Mathilde Kszesinska, "Malechka," 1872–1971, France): Ballerina of Polish origin. Girlfriend of Tsarevich Nikolai Aleksandrovich before his marriage and ascent to the throne as Nikolai II; then of Grand Duke Sergei Mikhailovich; then wife of Grand Duke Andrei Vladimirovich. Her private mansion in Petrograd, of refined and modern architecture, was requisitioned by the Bolsheviks, who made it their first headquarters.

Kulchitsky, Nikolai Konstantinovich (1856–1925, England): Professor of anatomy and the last Minister of Education of the Russian Empire.

Kulyabko, Nikolai Nikolaevich (1873–1920): Head of the Kiev division of the Okhrana from 1907 to 1911; Prime Minister Stolypin was assassinated on his watch; was dismissed but escaped further punishment.

Kurlov, Pavel Grigorievich (1860–1923, Germany): Director of the Police Department; in 1911 headed the Okhrana; the Stolypin assassination occurred on his watch. Arrested and released after the Revolution, emigrated.

Kutepov, Aleksandr Pavlovich (1882–1930): Colonel (as of 1917), later General. Fought in Russo-Japanese War and First World War. One of the few officers who tried to lead organized resistance to the February Revolution; then fought in the Civil War on the side of the Whites, being one of the last to evacuate from Crimea in November 1920. In emigration, led the Russian All-Military Union, an anti-Soviet veterans' organization; was kidnapped by Soviet agents and killed.

Kvashnin-Samarin, Nikolai Nikolaevich (1883–1920): Captain, later colonel of the Preobrazhensky Regiment; decorated for valor; joined White forces in the Russian south and died in the Civil War.

Kvetsinsky, Mikhail Fyodorovich (1866–1923, Norway): Served much of his career in the Far East; then in the First World War at the Southwestern and Western Fronts; in 1917 took a soft line on military discipline and was dismissed; later briefly led White forces in the Russian north, evacuated in 1920.

Lebedev, Dmitri Kapitonovich (1872–1935, Estonia): Colonel of the General Staff; joined the Red Army in 1918, emigrated and served in Estonian army.

Lebedev, Yuri Mikhailovich (1874–after 1917): Deputy to the Fourth Duma, representing the Don Cossack region, member of the Kadet party and the Progressive Bloc. Fate after 1917 unknown.

Lenin (Ulyanov), Vladimir Ilyich (1870–1924): Bolshevik revolutionary and Marxist theorist; was caught by surprise by the February Revolution but took advantage of it, famously making his way to Russia in a sealed train to Finland Station; led multiple efforts to overthrow the Provisional Government and ultimately succeeded; announced the Red Terror, War Communism, backtracked by creating the New Economic Policy; was the founder of the USSR.

Malakhov, Nikolai Nikolaevich (1827–1908): General, participant in all of Russia's wars of the second half of the nineteenth century; as head of the Moscow Military District in 1905 stood firm against the revolutionary street.

Manasevich-Manuilov, Ivan Fyodorovich (1869–1918): Jew converted to Protestantism, civil servant in the Ministry of the Interior (until 1906), journalist, reintegrated in 1913, head of Stürmer's chancery, arrested in September 1916, liberated, then arrested again by the Provisional Government; killed in February 1918.

Mannerheim, Carl Gustav Emil, Baron (1867–1951): General in the Russian Imperial Army, then became the dominant military and political figure of Finland, commander of the Finnish army in the wars of 1918, 1939–1940, 1941–1944; president of Finland (resigned 1946).

Manuilov, Aleksandr Apollonovich (1861–1929): Economist, professor, rector of Moscow University; entered politics as a member of the Kadet party, was briefly Minister of Education under the Provisional Government. Under Bolshevik rule, participated in language reform and was an administrator of the State Bank.

Manukhin, Ivan Ivanovich (1882–1958, France): Doctor noted for his innovative methods in treating tuberculosis and pneumonia, friend of Gorky; investigated tsarist officials after the revolution, left Soviet Russia in 1921.

Marat, Jean-Paul (1743–1793): French revolutionary, born in Switzerland.

Maria Fyodorovna (1847–1928, Denmark): The dowager Empress, widow of Aleksandr III, born Princess Dagmar of Denmark, daughter of King Christian IX. Returned to her native country after the revolution.

Maria Georgievna *See* Pavlova.

Maria Ilyinichna. *See* Ziloti.

Maria Nikolaevna ("Marie") (1899–1918): Third daughter of Nikolai II and Aleksandra Fyodorovna, murdered with her whole family by the Bolsheviks.

Maria Pavlovna the elder ("Aunt Miechen") (née Marie Alexandrine Elisabeth Eleonore von Mecklenburg-Schwerin) (1854–1920, France): Wife of Grand Duke Vladimir Aleksandrovich, held high influence at court.

Markov, Nikolai Evgenievich (1866–1945, Germany): Deputy in Third and Fourth Dumas, leader of the far right; one of the leaders of the Union of the Russian People. Called Markov the 2nd, as the younger of two Markovs in the Duma.

Maslovsky (Mstislavsky), **Sergei Dmitrievich** (1876–1943): Socialist Revolutionary who became, after the Civil War, a Soviet writer.

Mayakovsky, Vladimir Vladimirovich (1893–1930): Famous Russian poet, singer, and speaker of the Russian revolution and of the Soviet regime. Futurist. Was formally listed as in service at the military's automobile training school in Petrograd, simultaneously wrote antiwar poems.

Meller-Zakomelsky, Aleksandr Nikolaevich, Baron (1844–1928, France): Member of the State Council, known for his active role in suppressing the 1905 revolution.

Mengden, Georgi Georgievich (1861–1917): Major general of the suite, commander of the Guard cavalry in Luga, murdered by the Luga garrison in March 1917.

Meyer, Pyotr Petrovich (1860–1925, Yugoslavia): Military, police, and civilian official; headed the police departments of Vilna and Warsaw before becoming the last pre-revolutionary mayor of Rostov-on-Don; was then mayor of Sevastopol during the Civil War; evacuated.

Mikhail Aleksandrovich, Grand Duke ("Misha") (1878–1918): Younger brother of Nikolai II, refused the crown in March 1917 after Nikolai's abdication. Murdered by the Bolsheviks.

Mikhail Fyodorovich (1596–1645): The first Romanov Tsar, elected in 1613.

Mikhail Vasilievich. *See* Alekseev.

Mikhail Vladimirovich. *See* Rodzyanko.

Mikhailichenko, Aleksei Yakovlevich (1867–1924, Belgium): Career military officer, served in the Moscow Regiment from 1890, promoted to colonel in 1913. After the Revolution joined the White forces opposed to Bolshevism; evacuated in 1920 from Batum.

Milyukov, Pavel Nikolaevich (1859–1943, France): Politician and historian, professor at the University of Moscow, dismissed in 1895; emigrated (1895–1905); main founder of the Kadet Party (1905) and its recognized leader; editor-in-chief of *Rech* ("Speech"); leader of the Progressive Bloc and its spokesman in the Duma; Minister of Foreign Affairs in the first Provisional Government; emigrated in 1920.

Minin, Kuzma (died around 1616): Butcher from Nizhny Novgorod who organized the militia that, led by Prince Pozharsky, expelled the Poles from Moscow in 1612.

Misha. *See* Mikhail Aleksandrovich.

Molotov (real name Skryabin), **Vyacheslav Mikhailovich** (1890–1986): Bolshevik since 1906; for a long time Stalin's right-hand man; untouched in all the purges. Foreign minister before and during World War II.

Mordukhai-Boltovskoi, Dmitri Dmitrievich (1876–1952): Mathematician, teacher, professor at Warsaw University, then Rostov University; among his students there was Aleksandr Solzhenitsyn.

Mordvinov, Anatoli Aleksandrovich (1870–1940, Germany): Colonel, member of the Emperor's suite, chamberlain; emigrated after Revolution; wrote memoirs.

Motya: diminutive for Matvei Ryss.

Mrozovsky, Iosif Ivanovich (1857–1934, France): General, head of Moscow Military District, was arrested following the revolution; emigrated.

Muromtsev, Sergei Andreevich (1850–1910): Professor of law at Moscow University. One of the founders of the Kadet party. President of the First Duma, signatory of the Vyborg appeal in 1907.

Myasoedov, Sergei Nikolaevich (1865–1915): Military intelligence officer, accused by Guchkov of espionage in favor of Germany, convicted (by most accounts, wrongly) and hanged. The "Myasoedov Affair" is described in *November 1916*.

Nabokov, Vladimir Dmitrievich (1869–1922, Germany): Lawyer. Active participant in Zemstvo congress 1904–1905; one of the founders of the Kadet Party. Signer of the Vyborg Appeal. Secretary general of the Provisional Government. Emigrated, assassinated by a Russian right-wing extremist. Father of the writer Vladimir Nabokov.

Nadya. *See* Krupskaya.

Nikolasha: *See* Nikolai Nikolaevich.

Nilov, Konstantin Dmitrievich (1856–1919): Admiral, adjutant general in the Emperor's suite. Executed by the Bolsheviks.

Novikov, Nikolai Ivanovich (1744–1818): Famous writer, publicist, and Russian editor; published satiric journals, scholarly works. Leased the printing company of the University of Moscow in 1779, then became the greatest propagator of the Enlightenment in Russia.

Orlov-Davydov, Aleksei Anatolievich, Count (1871–1935, France): Deputy of Fourth Duma, held interests in beet sugar industry; assisted Kerensky; emigrated.

Paléologue, Maurice (1859–1944): French ambassador to Russia 1914–1917.

Paley, Princess Olga Valerianovna (née Karnovich, divorced Pistohlkors, 1865–1929, France): Married Grand Duke Pavel Aleksandrovich in 1902, made Countess von Hohenfelsen in 1904, became Princess Paley through a 1915 decree; emigrated.

Paramonov, Nikolai Ellidiforovich (1878–1951, West Germany): Industrialist, hailing from local Cossack family, built coal mines; sympathized with revolutionaries, but after the revolution supported the White cause; emigrated to Germany.

Parvus, Aleksandr Lvovich (nom de guerre of Israel Lazarevich Helfand) (1867–1924, Germany): Played prominent part in 1905 Revolution. Invented theory of "permanent revolution." Successful businessman; funded revolutionaries (especially Bolsheviks).

Paul I (Pavel I Petrovich) (1754–1801): Son of Peter III and Catherine the Great, emperor from 1796. Tried to undo his mother's policies elevating the position of the nobility. Murdered by a palace conspiracy in March 1801. The Pavlovsky regiment and military school were named after him.

Pavel Aleksandrovich, Grand Duke (1860–1919): Son of Aleksandr II, uncle of Nikolai II. Cavalry general. Shot by the Bolsheviks without trial at the Peter and Paul Fortress.

Pavel Nikolaevich. *See* Milyukov.

Pavlov, Dmitri (Mitya, Mitka) Aleksandrovich (1879–1920): Worker from Sormovo, member of Social Democrat party from 1899; a leader of the 1905 Moscow armed uprising. After Revolution fought on the side of the Red Army, died of typhus. Gorky memorialized him in a short sketch, *Mitya Pavlov*.

Pavlova (née Klimanova), Maria Georgievna (1887-after 1967): Wife of the laborer Dmitri Pavlov who secretly sheltered Shlyapnikov.

Peretz, Grigori Grigorievich (1870–?): Journalist, briefly became commandant of the revolutionary Tauride Palace; already in 1917 wrote a memoir entitled "In the Citadel of the Russian Revolution."

Perrin, Charles Louis (Perin, Carl Louis): Palm reader, astrologist, occultist, author of *Perin's Science of Palmistry* (1902).

Peshekhonov, Aleksei Vasilievich (1867–1933, Latvia): Social populist, banished in 1922, buried in Leningrad.

Peter III (Karl Peter Ulrich von Schleswig-Holstein-Gottorf, 1728–1762): grandson of Peter the Great, married to Sophie d'Anhalt-Zerbst, the future Catherine II. Reigned for seven months in 1762, giving away Russia's victories in the Seven

Years' War and adopting a pro-Prussian policy. Was deposed by a palace coup led by Catherine's supporters, then assassinated.

Petrunkevich, Ivan Ilyich (1843–1928, Czechoslovakia): Lawyer. One of the organizers of Zemstvo congresses. Prominent member of the Kadet party. In 1904–1905, president of the "Union for Liberation"; deputy in the First Duma, signer of the Vyborg Appeal, editor-in-chief of *Rech* ("Speech"). Emigrated in 1920.

Pitirim, Metropolitan (Oknov Pavel Vasilievich, 1858–1921): Metropolitan of Petrograd; arrested in March 1917, resigned his Metropolitan position and finished his days in a monastery.

Platten, Fritz (1883–1942): Locksmith, then designer, secretary of the Swiss Social Democrat Party; at the Zimmerwald and Kienthal conferences; organizer of and companion in Lenin's return to Russia. Founded the Swiss Communist Party in 1918; from 1923 lived in the USSR, where he died in exile.

Plekhanov, Georgi Valentinovich (1856–1918): Major figure of Russian social democracy, first Russian Marxist, sometimes for and sometimes against Lenin; during the war, a defensist; unitarist; played only a symbolic role after his return to Russia in 1917.

Poiret, Maria Yakovlevna (1863–1933): Actress, singer, songwriter; after an early arranged marriage and forced institutionalization, escaped to the theater and became a leading star; bore the child of her admirer, Prince Pavel Dolgoruky; was the subject of a scandal and trial involving Orlov-Davydov; died in poverty in the USSR.

Pokrovsky, Nikolai Nikolaevich (1865–1930, Lithuania): Last Foreign Minister of the Russian Empire. Banker. Emigrated, taught finance at Kaunas University.

Polivanov, Aleksei Andreevich (1855–1920): Infantry general, close to Guchkov, dismissed by General Sukhomlinov; Minister of War 1915–1916, overcame the munition crisis, offered his services to the Red Army, died of typhus.

Polovtsov, Pyotr Aleksandrovich (1874–1964, Monaco): Lieutenant General, commander of troops in the Petrograd Military District in the summer of 1917. Escaped Russia in 1918; later lived in London and was a director of the Monte Carlo casino.

Potemkin, Grigory Aleksandrovich, Prince (1739–1791): Field marshal and Russian politician, favorite of Catherine II, who named him the Prince Tauride for his conquest of Crimea and Tauride Province and offered him a palace by the same name. Unoccupied after his death, the palace was refurbished in 1906 to house the State Duma of the Russian Empire.

Pozharsky, Dmitri, Prince (1578–ca. 1642): Leader of the popular militia that dislodged foreign invaders and marauding armies during the Time of Troubles and cleared the way for establishing the Romanov dynasty.

Pozhoga, Aleksandr Fyodorovich (1874–1919?): Cavalry captain; served in the White forces, fate unknown.

Priklonsky, Aleksandr Petrovich (1882–1936): Served in the Preobrazhensky Regiment with Kutepov; stayed in Soviet Russia, arrested, served sentence in Solovki; arrested again in 1936 and executed.

Shmuskes, Eduard: A revolutionary student.

Shulgin, Vasili Vitalievich (1878–1976): Duma deputy, leader of the right. Member of the Progressive Bloc. With Guchkov, received Nikolai II's abdication. Emigrated, made a clandestine trip to the USSR. Captured in Yugoslavia in 1944, spent twelve years in a prison camp, welcomed by Khrushchev, lived out his days in the USSR.

Shutko, Kirill Ivanovich (1884–1941?): Bolshevik from 1902, active in October Revolution; held posts overseeing cinema, culture. Friend of the painter Kazimir Malevich. Arrested in 1938, executed.

Skobelev, Matvei Ivanovich (1885–1939): Social Democrat from 1903; Menshevik, deputy in the Fourth Duma. Patriot during the war. Minister in Second Provisional Government July 1917. Joined Bolshevik Party in 1922. Worked in foreign trade organization. Expelled from the Party in 1937; died in the purges.

Skripitsyn, Boris Vladimirovich (?–1923): Preobrazhensky Regiment officer; shot by the Bolsheviks.

Smirnov, Vladimir Vasilievich (1849–1918): Infantry general, Commander of the First Army. Killed while held hostage by the Bolsheviks at Pyatigorsk.

Sokolov, Nikolai Dmitrievich (1870–1928): Lawyer, Bolshevik sympathizer. Drafted Order No. 1, which in effect destroyed discipline in the Russian army in March 1917. After the Revolution worked as a lawyer in various Soviet agencies.

Somov, Viktor Viktorovich (1881–1938): Member of Social Revolutionary party; helped shelter his friend Kerensky's family before their escape from Soviet Russia. Worked as a dentist in the USSR. Was arrested and executed during the purges for alleged secret ties to Kerensky.

Sosnovsky, Captain (pseud. of Iosif Rogalsky): Convict who in February 1917 fled prison, committed murder, dressed up in military uniform, led street action against the government, joined the Ministry of Roads and Railways under the Provisional Government.

Stakelberg, Gustav Ernestovich (1853–1917): Lieutenant general; equerry; murdered in March 1917 by revolutionary soldiers.

Stankevich, Vladimir Bogdanovich (Vlada Stankevicius, Vladas Stanka) (1884–1968, USA): Lawyer, philosopher, military engineer, publisher of a textbook on fortifications; one of the leaders of Russian military efforts during 1917; arrested by Bolsheviks, emigrated; settled in Berlin, then Kaunas; after World War II worked in Berlin helping displaced persons; then left for USA in 1949.

Steklov. *See* Nakhamkes.

Stepanov, Vsevolod Nikolaevich (?–1918): Captain in Moscow Regiment; killed by Bolsheviks in Bukhara, Central Asia.

Stishinsky, Aleksandr Semyonovich (1851–1921, Turkey): Member of the State Council, right-winger, in charge of "de-Germanification" of Russian society during the First World War. Died destitute in Constantinople following evacuation of White forces.

Stolypin, Pyotr Arkadievich (1862–1911): Minister of the Interior and Prime Minister, 1906–1911. Initiator of important land reforms aimed at a stepwise elimination of the oppressive rural commune and fostering individual initiative among

Trepov, Fyodor (the younger, 1854–1938, France): Cavalry general, general aide-de-camp; General Governor of Kiev, Podolia, and Volynia from 1908 to 1914, then from 1914 to 1917 of the Southwest Territories. Died in emigration.

Trepov, Vladimir (1860–1918): Court squire, senator, member of the State Council. Murdered in Petrograd.

Trotsky (pseud. of Bronstein), **Lev Davidovich** (1879–1940, Mexico): Revolutionary Social Democrat from 1897. Chairman of the Petersburg Soviet during the 1905 Revolution. Returned to Russia after February and engineered the Bolshevik seizure of power in October 1917. Founded Red Army and led it through the Civil War. Lost struggle for power and expelled from USSR in 1929; murdered by a Soviet agent.

Trubetskoy, Sergei Nikolaevich, Prince (1862–1905): Philosopher, zemstvo activist. In June 1905, at the head of a delegation, he gave a speech on a program of moderate reforms in front of Nikolai II. Died of heart attack in the office of the Minister of the Interior. Father of the well-known linguist Nikolai Trubetskoy.

Tugan-Baranovsky, David Ivanovich (1881–1941, Poland): General staff colonel during the revolution, then fought for the Whites in the Civil War, emigrated first to France, then Poland.

Tumanov (Tumanishvili), Georgi Nikolaevich (1880–1917): Actively supported the revolution and served in the Provisional Government under Kerensky; saw the oncoming demise of the Provisional Government but was powerless to stop it; was beaten to death by a mob during the Bolshevik coup.

Tyazhelnikov, Mikhail Ivanovich (1866–1933, France): Led the HQ of the Petrograd Military District. After the Revolution, fought for the Whites, then emigrated.

Ulyanov, Aleksandr Ilyich (1866–1887): Older brother of Lenin, member of the People's Will organization, hanged 8 May 1887 for preparing an attempt on the life of Aleksandr III.

Ustrugov, Leonid Aleksandrovich (1877–1938): Railway engineer, continued to serve as deputy minister for roads and railways under the Provisional Government; during the Civil War served as Admiral Kolchak's chief officer for railways; retreated to Harbin, taught at Harbin Polytechnical University; returned to the USSR in 1935, arrested in the purges and executed.

Valberg, Ivan Ivanovich (1859–1918): General, head of Pavlovsky Military School, which throughout 1917 was known for its counterrevolutionary sentiments; was deposed in October 1917, died shortly thereafter.

Valuyev, Fyodor Mikhailovich (1858–1917): Railway engineer, served for over three decades in railroad operations, in 1908 appointed head of the Northwestern railroads, killed by revolutionary mob in March 1917.

Vanya: diminutive for Ivan.

Vasilchikov, Illarion Sergeevich (1881–1969, Germany): Prince, deputy of Fourth Duma, served in 1917 in the Duma's provisional committee, then in the Red Cross. Emigrated to Europe with his wife Lidia, née Vyazemskaya.

Vasilchikova (née **Vyazemskaya**), **Lidia Leonidovna**, nickname "**Dilka**" (1886–1948, France): Worked in the Red Cross in the Russo-Japanese War and First

World War; two of her older brothers, Dmitri and Boris Vyazemsky, were killed in 1917; emigrated in 1919, lived in Paris, then Lithuania, Italy, Germany, Bohemia, and again France. Died tragically, run over by an automobile.

Vasili Alekseevich (Alekseich). *See* Maklakov, Vasili.

Vasili Vitalievich (Vitalich). *See* Shulgin.

Veinshtein, Grigori Emmanuilovich (1860–1929, France): Industrialist, flour-milling magnate, was elected to the State Council, entered the Progressive Bloc; emigrated after the revolution and worked in Paris.

Vekhov, Sergei Ivanovich (1857–1919): Librarian who over four decades amassed one of the empire's leading collections, at Warsaw University, where he was also rector; led the university's evacuation to Rostov; shaken by revolutionary events, succumbed to typhus.

Velyaminov (Voronotsov-Velyaminov), **Vasili Konstantinovich** (?–1919): Volynian Regiment lieutenant; after the Revolution joined the White cause in the Civil War; killed in Chernigov province.

Viktoria Fyodorovna (née Victoria-Melita de Saxe-Coburg-Gotha) (1876–1936, Germany): Wife at first of Ernst, older brother of Aleksandra Fyodorovna; then divorced; then married Grand Duke Kirill Vladimirovich against the wishes of Nikolai II.

Vinaver (Winawer), **Maksim Moiseevich** (1863–1926, France): Lawyer born in Warsaw, founder of the Kadet Party, deputy in the First Duma, signer of the Vyborg Appeal; in 1919, member of a White government in Crimea; emigrated to France that same year.

Viren, Robert Nikolaevich (von Wirén, Robert Reinhold) (1856–1917): Admiral, the military governor of Kronstadt from 1909; assassinated by soldiers and sailors of the garrison.

Vladimir Dmitrich. *See* Bonch-Bruevich, Vladimir Dmitrievich.

Voeikov, Vladimir Nikolaevich (1868–1947, Sweden): Palace Commandant, General of the Emperor's suite, son-in-law of Count Frederiks, chairman of the first Russian Olympic committee. Had the reputation of a capable but self-serving organizer. After the Revolution lived in Finland.

Voronovich, Nikolai Vladimirovich (1887–1967, USA): Cavalry captain who held Socialist Revolutionary views, disarmed regiment sent to quell the revolution; after the revolution settled near Sochi, fought against the Whites, emigrated via Georgia; in emigration worked as a journalist.

Voskresensky, Boris Dmitrievich: Railway engineer, state councilor, operated the Southern railroads, later the Moscow-Kazan railway; during the First World War devised methods to increase railway throughput.

Vyacheslav. *See* Molotov.

Vyazemsky, Boris Leonidovich, Prince (1883–1917): Personal secretary of Stolypin, heir and owner of the exemplary Lotaryovo estate, which was destroyed in September 1917 by revolutionary mobs, who beat Prince Boris to death.

Vyazemsky, Dmitri Leonidovich, Prince (1884–1917): Younger brother of Boris Vyazemsky. Organized a field hospital and treated wounded during the First World War. Was killed in Petrograd in March 1917 by a stray bullet.

Vyrubova (Taneeva), **Anya** (1884–1964, Finland): Lady-in-waiting to the Empress. For some years her closest friend and intermediary between the imperial couple and Rasputin. Victim of a railroad accident in 1915, arrested in 1917, liberated, rearrested, emigrated.

Weiss, Vladimir (1864–?): Actual State Councilor, senior official for the Ministry of Agriculture, entrusted with securing provisions in the capital during the first months of 1917.

Wilhelm: Wilhelm II (1859–1941), the Kaiser, emperor of Germany, king of Prussia (1888–1918).

Witte, Sergei Yulievich (1849–1915): Minister of Finance 1892–1903. Urged civil reforms and modernization. Prime Minister October 1905–April 1906, when he resigned (replaced by Goremykin). Author of an important memoir.

Wrangel, Pyotr Nikolaevich (1878–1928, Belgium): Cavalry captain in 1914; by 1917 he was a general and St. George medalist, division commander. Participated in the White movement beginning in August 1918; had serious disagreements with Anton Denikin, whom he ended up replacing after the defeat of the White forces in the Russian South. For most of 1920, Wrangel not only held on to the Crimean peninsula but also sought to create there a viable economy based on private land ownership by the peasantry. Wrangel's Crimea was recognized by France as the de facto Russian government but was overrun by the Red Army in November 1920. Led the orderly evacuation of 120,000 people from Crimea to Constantinople. While he was an emigrant, he created the Russian All-Military Union. Died in Brussels, buried in Belgrade.

Yakovlev, Pyotr Mikhailovich (1878–1931): Captain. Entered service in the Moscow Regiment in 1896. After the Revolution, retired, then joined the Red Army, taught military courses, held low-level jobs; arrested, charged with helping old regimental church to hide its silverware from government expropriation; executed.

Yakubovich, Konstantin Antonovich (1881–1931?): Captain, then colonel in Moscow Regiment. Stayed in Petrograd after the revolution, taught at a technical school; was arrested in 1931, presumably executed.

Yanushkevich, Nikolai Nikolaevich (1868–1918): Infantry general; in 1914, Chief of Staff to the grand duke Nikolai Nikolaevich, who he accompanied to the Caucasus; retired after March 1917; arrested in 1918 and assassinated by the convoy that brought him to Petrograd.

Yatsimirsky, Aleksandr Ivanovich (1871–1925): Russian Slavist, professor at Warsaw University (relocated during wartime to Rostov), major connoisseur of ancient Slavic manuscripts and Slavic apocrypha, historian of contemporary Polish literature.

Yermansky-Kogan, Osip Arkadievich (1867–1941): Menshevik; after the Revolution, professor of political economy, arrested in 1937, again in 1940, died in the Soviet penal system.

Yurevich, Vadim Aleksandrovich (1872–1963, USA): Doctor, professor at Military Medical Academy, held leftist views and joined the revolution, was briefly commandant of Tauride Palace and "social governor" of Petrograd; later joined White forces and emigrated.

Yuri Nikiforovich. *See* Danilov.

Yuri Vladimirovich. *See* Lomonosov.

Zamyslovsky, Georgi Georgievich (1872–1920): Representative of Vilna Province in the Third and Fourth Dumas, a right-winger.

Zankevich, Mikhail Ippolitovich (1872–1945, France): General, fought in the First World War; in 1917 was chief of the General Staff in Petrograd. Fought against the Bolsheviks in the Civil War.

Zashchuk, Iosif Iosifovich (the younger, 1882–1924 or later): Colonel who sided with the revolution, joined the Red Army; nevertheless was arrested as a former officer and exiled to Siberia.

Zaslavsky, David Iosifovich (1880–1965): Menshevik Bundist (since 1903), defensist, fought the Bolsheviks from 1917 to 1918, but soon joined to become one of the leading propagandists of the Soviet regime and its policies on literature.

Zasulich, Vera Ivanovna (1849–1919): Populist terrorist, tried in 1873 for an attempt on the life of the governor of St. Petersburg, acquitted, fled abroad, became one of the Menshevik leaders, opponent of the Bolshevik regime.

Zeeler, Vladimir Feofilovich (1874–1954): Governor of Rostov-on-Don in 1917; during the Civil War, served as president of the Committee of the Don and Minister of Foreign Affairs of the Government of Southern Russia. Had sympathies for the Kadets, emigrated to France, one of the founders in Paris of the newspaper *Russian Thought.*

Zeidler, Hermann Fyodorovich, Doctor (1861–1940, Finland): One of the leading physicians of his day, surgeon, unsuccessfully tried to save the wounded Stolypin; ran the military hospital organized inside the Winter Palace during the First World War; organized humanitarian aid, saving lives during the Civil War; then lived in Finland.

Zeitlin-Batursky, Boris Solomonovich (1879–1920): Menshevik (worked in 1917 for *The Workers' Gazette*). After October, adversary of the Bolsheviks; arrested; imprisoned in Vitebsk, where he died during a prison epidemic of typhus.

Zenzinov, Vladimir Mikhailovich (1880–1953, USA): Hailed from a family of wealthy merchants. Member of Social Revolutionary party, active in 1905 Revolution. Elected to Constituent Assembly, opposed Bolshevism, emigrated. Worked as a correspondent.

Zhilinsky, Yakov Grigorievich (1853–1918): Cavalry general, commander of the Northwestern Front in August 1914, relieved of his duties following the disasters suffered in East Prussia, representative of Russian GHQ at the French military headquarters.

Zhuk, Iustin Petrovich (1887–1919): Revolutionary, chemist, arrested in 1909 and held at Schlüsselburg Fortress until freed in March 1917; sided with Lenin, was one of the leaders of the storming of the Winter Palace during the Bolshevik coup; died in combat in the Civil War near Petrograd.

Ziloti, Maria Ilyinichna (Masha) (1871–1938): Sister of Sergei and Aleksandr Ziloti, wife of Aleksandr Guchkov.

Zinaida Aleksandrovna: Wife of General Ruzsky.

Znamensky, Sergei Filimonovich (1878–1929 or later): Associate of Kerensky, a leader of the Trudovik party; as an ensign in reserve supervised the detention of tsarists at the Tauride Palace; arrested and imprisoned in the 1920s; was sent to exile; further fate unknown.

Zoya Lvovna: *See* Arkhangorodskaya, Zoya Lvovna (under Principal Non-Historical Characters).

Principal Non-Historical Characters

Andozerskaya, Olda Orestovna: She was said to be the most intelligent woman in Petersburg. Professor of world history, she nonetheless supported the monarchy, a rare case in learned circles. In November 1916 she met Colonel Vorotyntsev, who was passing through Petrograd. They began a passionate affair, which continued through correspondence during the winter of 1916–1917.

Arkhangorodskaya, Sonya: Daughter of the engineer Arkhangorodsky. Studied at Kharitonova's high school in Rostov-on-Don, at the same time as Ksenia Tomchak.

Arkhangorodskaya, Zoya Lvovna: Wife of the engineer Arkhangorodsky, failed theater actress, exuberant and friendly character.

Arkhangorodsky, Ilya Isakovich (he and his family are drawn by the author from life and under their real names): Engineer specializing in mills. Although he had "progressivist" ideas, he considered the building and prosperity of Russia to be of primary importance, instead of destroying it through the revolution.

Diomidovich, Agafangel: Peasant turned city worker who gives shelter to Captain Nelidov. His first and last names are reminiscent of the Russian countryside, its heartland.

Greve, Pavel: A young, newly trained midshipman of the Cadet Corps. In the Moscow Regiment, resisted the revolutionary disturbances in Petrograd along with the Nekrasov brothers, Sergei and Vsevolod.

Koronatova, Kalisa Petrovna: Daughter of the landowner of the house where the Vorotyntsev family rented an apartment, at the time when the colonel was a child. Although she was younger than him, Kalisa still shared in his games. Married almost forcibly to a merchant of respectable age, when she was barely nineteen years old. Widowed without children at age thirty, she lived in her deceased husband's townhouse.

Korzner, David: Well-known Moscow lawyer, progressive, member of the municipal duma. When disorder began to capture Moscow, Korzner decided to propose the creation of the Moscow Provisional Revolutionary Committee.

Lenartovich, Aleksandr ("Sasha"): Student, enrolled in the army at the beginning of the hostilities. Raised by his aunts in the revolutionary tradition of the intelligentsia and in respect for his uncle Anton's memory, he militated against the aristocracy and was opposed to war. In August 1914 he met Colonel Vorotyntsev at the front, where he did not display courage or military valor.

Lenartovich, Veronika (Veronya): Sister of Sasha Lenartovich. Although brought up in the family revolutionary tradition, she escaped its influence and showed no interest in politics. Eventually, however, she became a fierce militant, to the great satisfaction of her aunts and her brother, which led her to drift away from her school friend Likonya.

Likonya (Yelenka, Yolochka): School friend of Veronika Lenartovich, although their friendship was broken. A devotee of the arts, she is the opposite of the ideal of revolutionary militancy. Nonetheless, Sasha Lenartovich was charmed by her.

Obodovsky, Pyotor Akimovich (modeled closely on the historical character Pyotr Akimovich Palchinsky): Mining engineer, charged by the All-Russian Union of Engineers to form a committee of military technical assistance in the central War Industry Committees. A revolutionary, prosecuted twice, he was imprisoned, exiled, and even managed an escape abroad, always faithfully supported by his spouse, Nusya (Nina). Although he did not give up on his ideas, Obodovsky did not believe the revolution should take place before the end of the war.

Olda Orestovna. *See* Andozerskaya.

Raitsev-Yartsev: Captain portrayed in *August 1914*, chapter 18, as the prototype of a true combat officer; now a lieutenant colonel, he finds the reserve regiments of Petrograd laughable and the revolution a sordid affair.

Tomchak, Ksenia Zakharovna: Daughter of self-made landowner Zakhar Tomchak. Completed her secondary studies in Rostov-on-Don at Kharitonova's high school, where she discovered a thriving intellectual environment. Ksenia Tomchak is the prototype of the author's mother, Taisia Shcherbak.

Vera (Vorotyntseva, Vera Mikhailovna): Sister of Colonel Vorotyntsev. Lived in Petersburg with their old nurse. Worked at the Public Library. Fourteen years younger than her brother, she spent her childhood without him and was very influenced by the traditional peasant world of her nurse. In love with the engineer Dmitriev, she led a solitary life, while he was embroiled in a complicated love affair.

Vorotyntseva, née Siyalskaya, **Alina**: Wife of Colonel Vorotyntsev. Trained as a pianist, she devoted herself entirely to her husband's career during the eight years of her marriage preceding the 1914 World War. When he was sent to the front, Alina, who had no children, was left alone in Moscow and became extremely active, organizing concerts for the troops. During the war, she felt she had come alive again as a person, until she learned that her husband was having an affair with a famous woman from Petrograd.

Vorotyntsev, Georgi Mikhailovich: Graduated at the top of his class from the military academy. Colonel. After his studies in Petersburg, he and his wife Alina lived in garrisons in the Vyatka region until he was sent to Moscow. After a brief rise that took him to GHQ (General Headquarters), he was sent on a mission in East Prussia. He escaped the encirclement of the Samsonov army at Tannenberg in August 1914. Eventually he was "exiled" to a regiment because of his positions on war strategy. In early November 1916, on a mission in Petrograd, he met Professor Andozerskaya and they began a passionate affair.

ABOUT THE AUTHOR

Aleksandr Solzhenitsyn (1918–2008) is widely acknowledged as one of
the most important figures—and perhaps the most important writer—
of the last century. His story *One Day in the Life of Ivan Denisovich*
(1962) made him famous, and *The Gulag Archipelago*, published to
worldwide acclaim in 1973, further unmasked communism and played
a critical role in its eventual defeat. Solzhenitsyn won the Nobel Prize
in 1970 and was exiled to the West in 1974. He ultimately published
dozens of plays, poems, novels, and works of history, nonfiction, and
memoir, including *Cancer Ward*, *In the First Circle*, *The Oak and the
Calf*, and *Between Two Millstones, Book 1: Sketches of Exile, 1974–1978*
(University of Notre Dame Press, 2018).